PENELOPE

DAPHNE LEIGH

MARBLE CITY PRESS, LLC

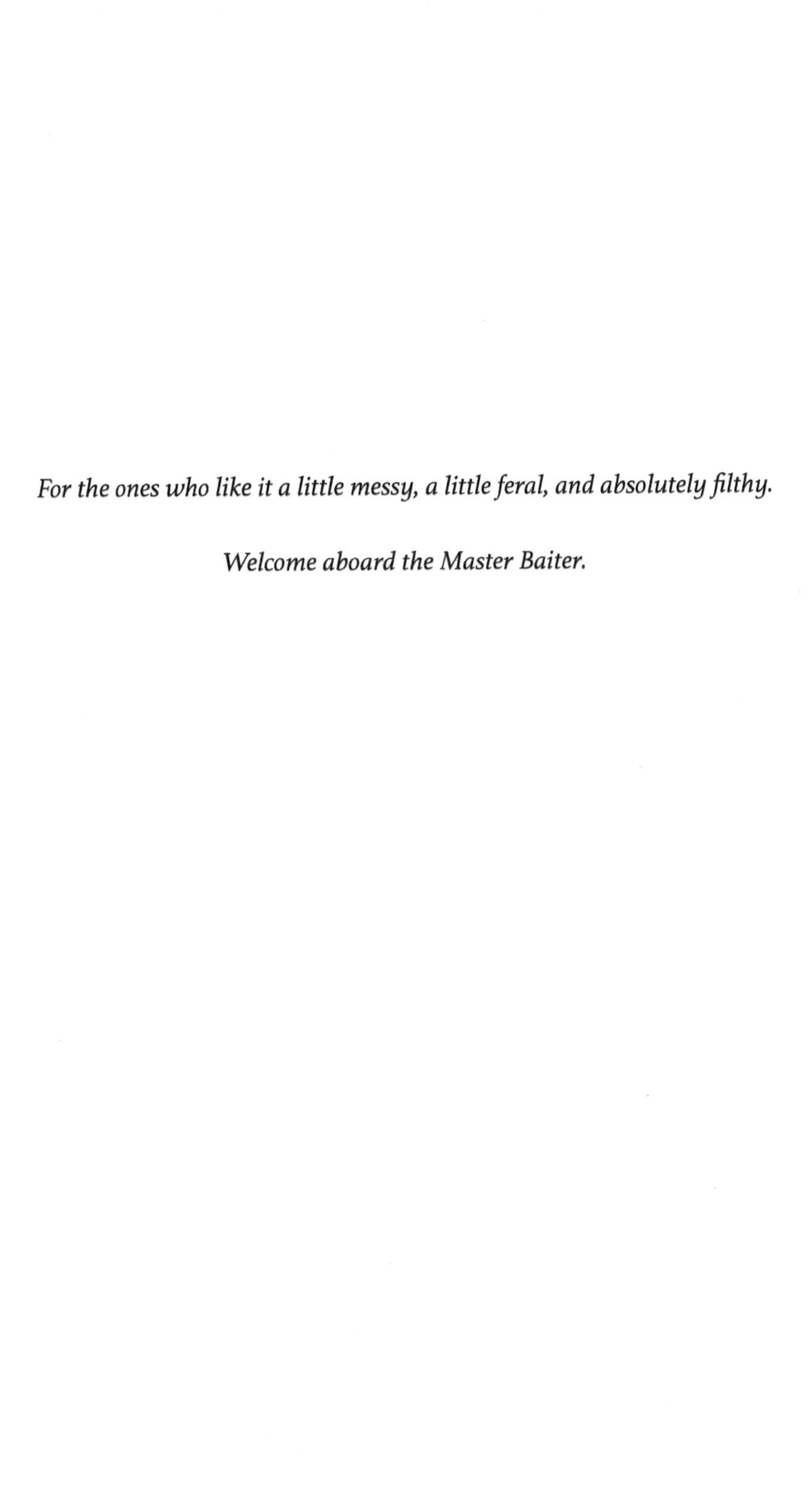

For the ones who like it a little messy, a little feral, and absolutely filthy.

Welcome aboard the Master Baiter.

1

———————

There's a certain moment, suspended between denial and reality, when you realize everything you've built is about to disappear. For me, it comes as I tie a kitchen towel around my face and pull the pin on the fourth—and last—fire extinguisher, my hands trembling so violently I almost drop it. The flames are everywhere now, racing up the wooden walls like they've been waiting years for this exact moment. Hungry. Wild. Personal.

The restaurant smells like burning dreams and heartbreak, but under that, under the smoke and char, there's still the faintest trace of pine and lemon oil, and something softer. Home.

The heat slams into my skin, blistering from six feet back, a living, breathing monster sucking the oxygen out of the room. Every breath I take feels like punishment. Every blink stings like regret. Deep down, I know it's a lost cause, but if this ship is going down, I'm going down with it.

My heart shatters as the fire extinguisher sputters pathetically, then dies. That sound—that hollow, wheezing gasp—is the soundtrack to my world collapsing. I take a couple of steps back, the ceiling above me groaning like a dying animal before a chunk crashes down exactly where I'd been standing moments before. I don't even flinch. What's death when everything that matters is already burning?

"FUCK!" I scream, the word tearing from my throat raw and primal. Not a word but a howl of pure, undiluted rage against the universe. I want God, or fate, or whatever cosmic asshole is in charge to hear me —to feel the white-hot fury coursing through my veins. As if cursing loud enough might create a forcefield around the last ten years of my fucking life. Around the restaurant that isn't just my business but my heartbeat, my sanctuary, my redemption story.

I sprint to the sink, cranking the water on full blast, and grab the hose attachment. I spray the water wildly, knowing somewhere in the rational corner of my mind that it's like fighting a wildfire with a water gun. The fire department is twenty minutes out. Twenty minutes might as well be twenty years. These walls have stood for a century, weathered wars and storms and neglect, only to meet their end because I wanted a midnight snack.

"PENELOPE!"

Sammy's voice cuts through the inferno, my name on his lips a desperate prayer. I know that voice—have heard it tell jokes as we're pulling in fish and tell stories over late-night drinks—but I've never heard it fracture with raw terror like this. The sound slices straight through my heart.

"GET THE HELL OUT OF HERE, SAMMY!" I scream back, tears carving clean tracks through the soot coating my face. My eyes sting, my lungs burn, but it's the fear for him that truly hurts—a pain so sharp it cuts between my ribs and nestles against my spine.

"Pen! You stubborn, beautiful idiot!" Sammy materializes in the doorway, his silhouette appearing through the smoke like an apparition. Flames lick around him, casting his dark ebony skin in amber light, transforming him into something otherworldly, half man, half fury, entirely terrified.

"Go make sure the fire department is coming," I yell, squeezing my eyes shut as I blindly aim the water stream.

"Not without you," he roars, the words scraping out of his throat like they've been dragged over broken glass. He navigates the kitchen with the grace of someone who's spent thousands of hours in this space, who knows every tile, every corner. A support beam groans, then crashes behind him, a geyser of orange sparks erupting, backlighting him like some tragic hero in a renaissance painting.

"I'm not leaving, Sammy," I sob, my fingers cramping into claws around the sprayer. The smoke has thickened to the consistency of wet wool, making each breath an act of pure will.

"Then let me take your place. There are too many people who love you for you to go out like this. Nobody would even notice I'm gone." The words fall between us like stones, heavy with a lifetime of feeling invisible. Of being overlooked. Of being the one who holds everyone else together while quietly falling apart himself. His eyes meet mine through the haze—devastatingly sincere, heartbreakingly brave—and in that moment, I understand what it means to love someone enough to die for them. What I can't understand is why he thinks I deserve that sacrifice.

Fury explodes inside me like a grenade. "Don't you fucking dare say that again! I would care, Sammy. I would fucking care!" My words are punctuated by a section of ceiling collapsing over the stove, sending in a fresh burst of air that the flames gobble up like they're starving. The fire roars in triumph, a living, breathing monster celebrating another victory.

Sammy yanks the sprayer from my hands and douses me with water before turning it on himself. "You may hate me forever, but I'm not going to let you do this, Pen." He scoops me into his arms, gripping tight as I twist and thrash. His muscles lock around me like steel cables, unyielding against my rage. The water drips down my face, mixing with tears and soot into a toxic cocktail that stings my eyes and blurs my vision.

"You're going to kill us both. Is that what you want?" I shriek, going limp in his arms, trying to loosen his hold. I'll sacrifice myself to this goddamned restaurant, but I'm not taking him with me.

A familiar figure materializes through the smoke.

"Take her out of here," Sammy yells, his voice harsh as he hands me over to Spencer.

"No. No!" I flail in Spencer's arms, but he only holds me tighter as he carries me through the dining room and outside. "We have to go get him, Spence. Please!" I'm practically hyperventilating, my lungs burning from smoke and panic. I claw at Spencer's arms, leaving angry red trails across his skin that I'll feel guilty about tomorrow, if there is a tomorrow.

"He'll come out before he gets hurt, Sugar," his soothing southern drawl wraps around me like warm honey, but does jack shit to calm my rising panic. Like trying to fix a shattered heart with a Band-Aid.

"He said nobody would care if he died, Spence." The words feel like razor blades in my throat. How could he not know? How could he think for one second that his absence wouldn't tear a hole in my world?

"Fuck that!" He sets me on my feet, gripping my hand like he knows I'm about to bolt straight back into the inferno. He yells for Liam. "Don't let her back inside," he instructs, making sure Liam has me before heading in to help Sammy. My wrist aches where Spencer's fingers dug in, his desperation leaving marks on my skin.

"What's happening?" Jamie asks, skidding to a stop next to us, Archer on his heels. They're both in pajama bottoms, having clearly come straight from their beds.

"We came as soon as we saw the smoke," Archer gasps, chest heaving. His hair stands up in wild tufts, face pale with shock, two huge duffel bags balanced on each shoulder, like he grabbed everything he could before leaving the bunkhouse.

"Sam and Spencer are in there," Liam says, fear etched into every line of his face. "Looks like it's just the kitchen so far." He swallows hard, fighting back his own terror.

Both Archer and Jamie run inside without hesitation, and I feel like someone's crushing my chest in a vise. They're my best friends, my family, my everything. I can't let them risk their lives for a pile of wood and stone and metal. For my mistakes.

"It should be me in there," I whisper, watching as my entire life goes up in smoke.

"The kitchen can be rebuilt, Penelope. We can't bring you back to life," Liam says, his voice cracking. His grip on my shoulders is the only thing keeping me upright.

"But it's my fault," I wail, furiously wiping at the tears streaming down my face, smearing dark streaks of soot everywhere. "I just wanted some damn fish and chips. Who burns down a restaurant trying to make fish and chips?"

"We'll get you your fish and chips, Darlin', don't you worry," Liam murmurs, smoothing his hand over my hair like I'm a kid who dropped her ice cream cone. His callused fingers catch on the knots in my hair.

"Do you really think that's what I'm worried about now, you fucking idiot?" I try to squirm from his grasp, but he holds tight, his sea-chiseled body pressed hard against my back like a human straightjacket. His heartbeat hammers against my spine, too fast, too hard.

"I'm not going to let you go, so you may as well quit rubbing your body all over mine," he says stiffly.

"I don't want them to die in there!" My voice breaks on the last word, terror stealing the air from my lungs.

"They're all trained in fire safety, Pen. They'll be fine." He doesn't sound convinced.

"Yeah, so am I! It's my restaurant. I'm the one responsible. They don't need to be in there fighting for something that means nothing to them!" My fingernails dig crescents into my palms, drawing blood.

"You mean something to them! They don't want to see you die in there, either, Penelope! Did that ever occur to you?" His Australian accent thickens with emotion, making his words sound like both a prayer and a curse.

We both jump as glass shatters, dark smoke billowing into the air. The sound is like a gunshot, making my heart stutter.

"They need to get out of there, Liam. I could never live with myself if something happened because of me." My voice is raw, scraped hollow by smoke and fear.

He turns me toward him, pushing his ever-present leather hat higher on his forehead before looking down at me. "Darlin', even if something did happen, they'd tell you it was worth it." His dark eyes reflect the flames, turning them to citrines rimmed with fire.

The faint wail of the fire truck rises over the roaring of the flames, and I sag against Liam in relief. He hikes me over his shoulder and walks toward the front of the restaurant to meet them.

The blood rushes to my head, making my vision swim with dark spots.

"You can put me down. I won't go anywhere," I protest, kicking my legs, knocking his hat off. I feel like a sack of potatoes. A very angry, very sooty sack of potatoes.

His chuckle vibrates through me, his hand tightening on the back of my thigh. "You think I believe that? I'm not letting go of you until that fire is out, and I know you're not going to go and get yourself killed."

The firefighters move fast, blasting what's left of the kitchen with water until the last flames sputter into steam. As soon as they wave me in, I sprint through the door, and stop cold.

The kitchen is gone. Everything's black and melted and twisted, the air still heavy with smoke and scorched metal. This used to be my heartbeat. My future. Now it's just ash.

But the dining room's still standing. Smoke-stained and dripping, yeah, but it's there. Salvageable. The bunkhouse is a different story— just a smoldering skeleton now, collapsed into itself.

And then I see them.

The guys—my guys—covered in soot, shirts clinging to sweat-soaked bodies, still throwing buckets of water on the hot spots. The wall between the kitchen and dining room is dripping wet, and it hits me, they were the ones who kept the fire from spreading. They didn't wait. Didn't hesitate. They stood between the flames and what little I had left.

They risked everything for *me*.

"Thank you," I croak, trying to hold back my sobs.

Sammy comes to my side, crouching down. "I'm sorry we couldn't save the kitchen, boss," he says softly. Steam rises from the charred remains, creating a hellish fog around us.

"I don't care about the kitchen," I hiccup, throwing my arms around his neck, nearly knocking him over. "I'm just glad you guys are safe. You could have died in there." I trace his features with my fingertips, needing to confirm he's really okay.

"You were ready to die for this kitchen, Penelope," he reminds me, his voice hoarse from the smoke. His eyes search mine, looking for answers I don't have.

"That doesn't mean I wanted you to die! You don't owe me that kind of loyalty." I taste salt and ash as tears run into the corner of my mouth.

"Yes we fucking do, Pen. You gave us a home. A life. We owe you the world." He wraps his arms around me and rises to his full height, my toes dangling in the air. "Let's get you home before you collapse. You look like you're about to pass out." He's right—the adrenaline is crashing, my entire body trembling as the weight of what just happened slams into me like a freight train.

As he carries me away from the smoking ruins, I catch Liam watching us, his expression unreadable. Something passes between us—something that feels dangerously like understanding. Like maybe this fire burned away more than just my restaurant. Maybe it burned away pretenses too.

What I don't know yet is that losing everything is only the beginning of my story.

I wake up the next morning to sunlight stabbing through my eyelids. I groan, stretching as I slowly become aware of my surroundings. I prop myself up on my elbow and look down at the sooty towel twisted beneath me.

The memory of last night comes roaring back.

The fire.

Tears start immediately, hot and relentless. I sag against the headboard, dropping my head to my knees as sobs wrack my body. I don't even know where to start to fix this. The restaurant is my primary source of income, and now that the kitchen is gone, so is my summer season. I'll have to call the seasonal hires today and tell them to look for something else. Fuck my life sideways.

"Hey."

Archer is standing at my bedroom door, leaning against the door jamb, sweatpants slung low on his hips, his hair wet like he just stepped out of the shower. I swallow hard, averting my eyes before I can start cataloging every inch of exposed skin like some sort of deranged cartographer. Jesus, I need to get it together.

"Good morning," I croak, wiping at my cheeks, my fingers coming away with black smudges.

"How ya feeling?" he asks, studying my face.

"Not great," I admit. "I can't believe I passed out like that. I don't even remember you guys bringing me back home."

"Stress can do that," he says, his gaze traveling over my body like he needs to be sure I'm still in one piece.

I nod, sniffling. "Why are you here?"

"With the bunkhouse gone, we weren't sure where to go, so we stayed here."

Oh my God. The bunkhouse. Their home. Their belongings. Their lives. "What about all of your stuff?"

"I was able to go in and grab some of our belongings, but I don't know how much will be salvageable."

Goddamnit. "Where did you guys sleep last night?" Where will they sleep tomorrow? Will they leave now that they don't have anywhere to call home? The thought makes my heart squeeze painfully.

"In the living room," he says sheepishly. "I hope you don't mind."

"No. I'm glad you stayed here," I murmur, my gaze wandering to the tattoo on his chest, tracing the outline of the coast of Maine down to his— Nope. Not going there.

"No rush, but breakfast will be ready in twenty minutes. I thought you may want to shower first."

I squeeze my eyes closed, my cheeks burning. I nod, embarrassed, broken. Devastation consumes me without warning, a tsunami of grief tossing me around, battering me against the rocks. I bury my face in my hands, my body shaking. The bed dips, and then Archer's arms are wrapping around me, pulling me onto his lap.

"It's okay, Nel. I promise we'll figure something out." He rubs his hand in small circles over my lower back, soothing me. The gesture is so tender it makes my chest ache.

"Don't say 'we,'" I sob. "You guys will have to find a new job. I won't even have any money coming in this summer. I can't pay you. I can't house you. I can't do shit."

"We still have the *Master Baiter*," he objects.

"That doesn't bring in nearly enough, Archer. Most of what you catch is to supply the restaurant, and the restaurant writes your paycheck. And in case you haven't noticed, the restaurant is currently missing several key components—like, you know, a kitchen and a roof."

"We're not leaving, Nel. The five of us have already talked. We're not going anywhere."

"But—"

"No buts. We'll figure it out together once you've had a shower and something to eat." He stands, carrying me into the bathroom. My feet hit the cold tile, and then he's turning on the shower spigot, waiting for it to get hot before releasing me completely. "You'll feel better after. I promise." He kisses my head, my hair so dirty it leaves a black smudge on his lips.

He was right. I do feel better after showering. I towel dry my hair and pull on a tank top and shorts before padding to the kitchen. The scene that greets me stops me dead in my tracks.

Five sleep-mussed, warm-bodied, heavily muscled men in various states of undress are in my kitchen cooking and lounging at my dining table. I haven't had a single man in this house since I bought it, except for my brother, so this is an incredible shock to the system. Jamie's greeting dies on his lips as his gaze slides down my body, snagging on my nipples, which have decided to come out and play. Great. This may be the second or third time they've seen me dressed in something other than coveralls, and they sure as hell have never seen me in a tank top and shorts.

"I—I'll be right back," I stammer, running down the hallway back to the safety of my bedroom. I tear through my dressers until I find my baggiest pair of sweatpants I own and one of my brother's old sweatshirts. No more nipple shows for these guys.

I try to walk back into the kitchen without being noticed, but all the guys look at me the second my foot crosses the threshold. Sammy turns away from the stove, lifting an eyebrow as if to say, 'We already saw what's underneath that, darling, and we're not going to forget any time soon.'

"Good morning," I murmur, twisting the sleeve of the sweatshirt in my hands. I get an immediate response from all five, varying nicknames cascading over me like a verbal waterfall. "I've been thinking about everything, and we need—"

"Not yet. We can talk after we eat," Sammy says, cutting me off. He shoves a big bowl of scrambled eggs into my hands and gestures for me to take it to the dining table.

I set the bowl on the table, and Spencer walks up behind me, pulling a chair out and gently pressing on my shoulders until I sit down. He scooches me in, and Liam places a steaming cup of tea in front of me.

"I could get used to this," I murmur, wrapping my hands around the mug, inhaling the comforting aroma of Earl Grey. Five gorgeous men cooking me breakfast, making sure I eat, making me tea? There are worse ways to start your day after a catastrophe.

"You may have to," Liam says, chuckling as he sits beside me, that megawatt smile making my insides flip.

Does that mean what I think it means? Have they talked about possibly staying here? In my two-bedroom, one bathroom, postage-stamp size house? With me? The woman who just lost her restaurant in the world's most spectacular culinary failure?

Would I even be okay with that?

Dumb question. I'm pretty much okay with anything when it comes to them. I've been harboring some serious crushes that have only gotten worse over the last two years. I've been trying to get a handle on it, but my heart refuses to cooperate with my head. It's like trying to herd cats—impossible and slightly painful. So, until today, I've been giving them room. Staying scarce. Trying to put some distance between us so I have time to get over them. But being in a tiny island town on the west coast of Scotland doesn't exactly give me a lot of options for meeting anyone who would help me get over said crushes. Five of them. Because apparently I'm an overachiever when it comes to hopeless romantic entanglements.

Jamie sits on my other side and loads my plate with food before serving himself, giving me a wink that sends heat rushing to my cheeks.

After two minutes of silence, I can't take it anymore. "You guys have obviously talked already. Let's hear what sort of plans you came up with."

"We'd rather hear your thoughts first," Archer says, pushing his glasses up his nose, those serious brown eyes pinning me in place.

"I don't have any thoughts other than panic at the moment, so, please, go ahead. My brain is currently a dumpster fire. Much like the restaurant."

Sammy clears his throat when nobody starts talking, taking one for the team. "We know you're going to tell us to leave, but we're not going to, just to make that clear from the start."

I take a bite of eggs, trying to hide my trembling chin.

"We think you should take the summer to do what you've been saying you wanted to do for the last two years. Rehab the restaurant. With the kitchen gone, and with our help, we can start from scratch and build a state-of-the-art professional kitchen. We can strip down the dining area and revamp that as well. Most of it will need to go due to the smoke, anyway."

"But what about money?" I ask, my voice cracking, hopelessness trying to worm its way into my heart.

"We'll take turns fishing and we can use that money plus whatever insurance gives you for the restaurant. It'll be tight, but we're used to that."

"No, you guys are used to soft beds and two restaurant meals a day," I protest, pursing my lips. "Not living like sardines and surviving on whatever we can scrape together."

"We had lives before we came here, Sugar. We can handle it," Spencer reminds me, his deep voice making my toes curl. I've heard his stories about growing up in Appalachia, so I know he's telling the truth.

"That still doesn't solve where the five of you are going to sleep. With the bunkhouse gone, we're five beds short."

"We measured, and we can fit two sets of bunk beds in your guest room," Liam says, leaning back in his chair, the small gold hoop in his ear catching the morning sun.

"And the fifth?"

"Don't you have a king bed?" Sammy asks, his eyes dancing wickedly.

I choke on my food. "You can't—" My face feels like it's on fire. The thought of sharing my bed with any of them sends my mind straight to the gutter, where it does a cannonball into the dirtiest part.

"I'm kidding, Pen! We'll take turns sleeping on the couch." He winks at me, and I swear my heart does a somersault.

Fucking hell. So my options are firing them, having no income, and having nobody to help me fix the restaurant. Or letting them live in my house and help me rebuild. I know my brother would help me in a heartbeat, but I'm too proud for my own good. I don't want to take his money when I know I can do it myself. Well, by myself with the help of five ridiculously hot men. Who I may or may not be in love with.

"Okay," I whisper, massaging my forehead, trying to ease the ache between my eyes.

"Okay to what part?" Jamie asks, his Irish lilt more pronounced as his soft green eyes come alive with hope.

"You can stay and help me." I hold up my hand to keep them from talking. "Thank you for being here for me and offering to help. I appreciate it more than you'll ever know."

"Thank you for allowing us to stay in your home, Sugar," Spencer says, that deep southern twang sending goosebumps skittering over my arms and making my stomach clench.

"So, where do we start?"

2

———————

CHAPTER 2

The crisp morning air carries the scent of salt from the harbor as sunlight streams through the kitchen window, illuminating the dust motes dancing in the air like tiny, glittering performers. A seagull's cry punctuates the quiet before Millie's voice rings out, loud as a fucking foghorn:

"Penny! Where are you? I brought coffee!"

She comes barging into the kitchen with a drink carrier in one hand and a half-eaten scone in the other, her long brunette hair bouncing with each determined step like she's filming a damn shampoo commercial. She stops dead in her tracks when she sees the guys, her mouth falling open, utterly oblivious to the crumbs falling out and sticking to her pink lip gloss like sprinkles on a cupcake.

"Morning, Millie," the guys call out, smirking.

"Thank you, Millie." I take the drink carrier from her and wave my hand in front of her face, trying to snap her out of it.

"What?" She blinks at me dazedly, then abruptly goes into a tirade, her entire demeanor shifting from shocked to fiercely protective in an instant, like she's about to throw down at a bar fight. "Why didn't you call me last night? I had to hear it from my neighbor! I'm supposed to be your best friend, Penny Lou. I would've been here in a heartbeat!"

"I know, I'm sorry." I wrap my arms around her, hugging her tight, inhaling the cloud of sweet perfume that always surrounds her. "You are my best friend. It was late, and I passed out the second I got home."

"I'm the one that should be sorry," she says, switching up in the blink of an eye. "I drove by the restaurant on my way here and saw the damage." She grabs my shoulders, her eyes scanning me from head to toe as if checking for injuries. "What happened?"

"I wanted a snack."

"You wanted a snack," she repeats dumbly, her eyebrows lifting toward her hairline like they're trying to make a break for it.

"I don't know what happened. I was using the fryer for fish and chips, and then the wall was on fire. Just your average Thursday night kitchen apocalypse. No biggie."

"Holy shite. I'm so glad you're okay. At least it wasn't the entire restaurant, right?" She takes another bite of her scone, her eyes narrowing as she looks between me and the guys with all the subtlety of a neon sign at a strip club. "If any of you lot had let anything happen to my girl, there'd be hell to pay," she says, making a quick throat-slitting gesture when she thinks I'm not looking. "Okay, well, I'm off to work. I'll stop by later and see what you need help with. Love you, Penny." She blows me a kiss and then bounds back out the door, the sound of her car peeling out of the driveway following seconds later.

"Penny Lou?" Archer asks, looking at me over the top of his glasses, his dark gaze shooting straight through me.

"Long story," I say, waving my hand in dismissal.

"Any relation to Cindy Lou Who?" Sammy asks, his voice warm as melted chocolate. "You have a nose just like hers." He swipes one long finger down my upturned nose.

"Screw off and leave me and my Whoville nose alone," I grumble, stomping out of the kitchen to go change into my work clothes. If the last twenty-four hours have taught me anything, it's that five gorgeous men and my self-esteem cannot peacefully coexist in the same zip code, let alone the same house.

. . .

By the time I'm dressed and outside, the humor's gone, stripped away by wind and reality. A brisk sea breeze whips across the island, carrying the acrid smell of burnt wood and melted plastic that makes my nose wrinkle in disgust.

I'm standing in front of the still-smoldering ruins of the kitchen and bunkhouse, trying not to cry—a battle I've been fighting and losing since I woke up this morning. Two of the kitchen walls are entirely gone, the roof caved in, and not a single scrap of the bunkhouse is left standing. Gray clouds hang low in the sky, threatening rain—because of course they are—a fitting backdrop to match my mood, like Mother Nature herself is setting the scene for my personal tragedy. In the distance, waves crash against the rocky shore, their steady rhythm a stark contrast to the chaos before me.

One of my neighbors was nice enough to drop off a dumpster early this morning, and we've been filling it ever since—one charred dream at a time.

Three hours later, we're covered in soot, sweat, and varying levels of emotional instability. I sink down onto a warped hunk of metal that probably used to be the prep table, my limbs aching, my lungs full of ash, and my usefulness ranking somewhere between a chocolate teapot and a wet matchstick.

"Hey, we've got this, boss," Sammy says, sitting beside me, his shoulder bumping mine companionably. "Tell you what. I'll go to the store right now and get what I need to make a delicious lunch. You'll feel better after you eat my food. I promise." He pats me on the head awkwardly, and a minute later, I hear the rumble of the work truck, and he's pulling out onto the road, kicking up gravel in his wake.

Two hours later, the kitchen is cleared of debris, the dumpster is almost full, and somehow I feel even more hopeless than I did before we started. There's nothing left of the kitchen. Not even a spatula survived the inferno.

"It'll be okay, Sugar," Spencer says, walking up behind me, warm hands squeezing my shoulders, his drawl wrapping around me like a weighted blanket.

When I don't respond, he moves to stand in front of me, pulling me to my feet before wrapping his arms around me. I haven't been hugged by anyone other than Millie in so long that I don't know what to do, so I stand there, stiff as a board in his arms, like someone replaced my skeleton with a broomstick.

"Sweet Jesus, relax." He pushes on the back of my head until I rest it in the crook of his shoulder. I turn my face into his neck, his skin warm against my forehead, the scent of sweat and smoke and him filling my nose, and I break. He gathers me close as sobs rack my body, making soothing shushing sounds, his lips pressed to my hair like I'm something precious and not a walking disaster who managed to set fire to her own life.

"We need to go meet Sammy at the house before the food gets cold," I mumble, hiccupping, still clinging to him like he's the last lifeboat on the Titanic.

"We will."

I pull back a little, wiping my sooty hands over my sooty face. "You give good hugs," I sniffle.

"It's because I'm short, Sugar. But thank you all the same," he says, his voice like warm bourbon on a cold night.

"You're not short," I protest, craning my neck to look into his steel-blue eyes with those distinctive flecks of gold.

"Maybe not to someone that's five-foot-nothing, but I don't know many people that consider five-foot-eleven to be tall. I make up for it in other ways, though, don't you worry." He winks, and his meaning hits me a second later like I just chugged a shot of tequila.

I pull away from him, my cheeks on fire, probably creating actual steam where they meet my tear-dampened face. "I—I'm not worried," I stammer. "Why would I be worried?" My voice cracks, and I'm suddenly wishing a hole would open up beneath my feet and swallow me whole. Or that I could rewind the last ten seconds of my life and just respond with literally anything other than what just came out of my mouth. "Cool" would have worked. Even "neat" would have been better.

He looks at me, tilting his head, awareness flashing in his eyes.

"I was teasing. Sorry if that made you uncomfortable," he says gruffly, his gaze sliding down to my lips.

"So you don't make up for it in other ways?" I ask, my mouth working faster than my brain. Fuck. I tilt my head toward the sky, closing my eyes. Breathe, Penelope. Fucking breathe. Whatever voodoo curse has taken over my verbal filter needs to GO. "Will you round up the guys so we can go back to the house for lunch?" I ask him, not daring to look him in the face in case I accidentally proposition him or ask him to father my children.

"Sure thing, Sugar, but for the record, I wasn't lying."

I mumble something incoherent and flee toward the truck, my dignity trailing behind me like toilet paper stuck to a shoe. The ride back is mercifully short, with me pressed against the window trying to look fascinated by the passing scenery while actively avoiding eye contact with anyone who might have heard my verbal self-immolation. By the time we pull into the driveway, my cheeks have downgraded from "surface of the sun" to merely "bad sunburn," and I've almost convinced myself I can face everyone without spontaneously combusting from embarrassment.

The house smells incredible, like someone figured out how to bottle comfort and set it free in my kitchen. "What are you making?" I ask as we walk into the kitchen, trying and failing not to ogle a shirtless Sammy as he stirs something in a pot on the stove. But honestly, asking me not to look at him is like asking someone not to notice the Northern Lights—it's a natural phenomenon that demands attention.

"Oxtail stew." He turns toward me, full lips pulling into a grin. "You'll love it."

"I'm sure I will. It smells amazing." I squeeze my hands into fists to prevent myself from doing something stupid like reaching out and running my hands over his skin. He looks so soft. And warm. Like a sexy, human-shaped electric blanket. I clear my throat, reeling myself in. "I didn't know you could cook."

He shrugs. "I haven't needed to since coming to work for you, but I'm glad to have the chance now. I don't want to forget everything my mother taught me."

The timer on the oven dings, and he takes out a tray of freshly baked, yeasty rolls, the aroma of warm bread filling the kitchen like heaven itself decided to stop by for lunch.

"I didn't make these, they were frozen," he says apologetically.

"I think we'll survive," I tease, grabbing what I need to set the table.

Jamie walks into the kitchen, looking over Sammy's shoulder to see what he's making, his curly brown hair still damp from washing up, clinging to his forehead like he's auditioning for a bodice-ripper cover.

"Jesus, that smells amazing," he says, inhaling deeply. "Almost as good as what I'd like to be eating later, if you catch my drift," he adds with a playful wink, those dimples making an appearance like they're getting paid overtime.

He runs his hand up Sammy's arm, squeezing his bicep gently before sitting at the table.

I look at the spot on Sammy's arm for a little too long, trying to puzzle out what I just saw. The casual touch, the lingering fingertips, the way Sammy's mouth quirks up slightly at the corners—there's an easy intimacy there I hadn't noticed before, like they're speaking a silent language I don't understand. Sammy catches me watching and hands me a trivet to set on the table, interrupting my thoughts before I can follow them down the rabbit hole of speculation. The six of us dodge and swerve around each other as we grab drinks, and then we're all sitting down, talking over each other as we serve ourselves. The table quickly descends into silence as we start eating, all of us appreciating an incredible meal after hours of hard work.

Once finished, I sit back, watching as the guys clean their plates. The silence eventually turns into them making jabs at each other and then sharing stories back and forth, laughter filling the tiny space.

I like this—a lot. More than I should, probably. I didn't realize how lonely I was living here by myself. How much I missed the sound of multiple voices filling up the empty spaces in my house and my heart.

"We need to talk about meals," Archer says, rapping his knuckles on the table to get everyone's attention. "I assume all of us at least know how to make one meal?" We all nod. "Perfect, what do we think about taking turns making dinners? Lunches can be leftovers or easy things we can grab on the go. Sandwiches, cheese and crackers, stuff like that."

"I'll take the extra day every week," I offer, liking the idea of being able to cook for them.

"Perfect. Is that settled, then? Anything else we need to discuss before we get back to work?"

"How are we going to handle grocery shopping?" I'd love to be able to say I could handle it myself, but just thinking about shopping for six people gives me hives.

"We can make a weekly list and go shopping together every Sunday," Spencer suggests, tipping back in his chair and locking his hands behind his head.

"We should be able to get most of the fresh stuff out of the garden at the restaurant." I stand and walk over to the kettle to make myself another cup of tea. "I just realized it's my responsibility now since the kitchen staff won't be around to take care of it."

"No," Liam says, "Our responsibility. If we're all eating from it, we can all help take care of it."

"Let me know if anyone thinks of something else we need to discuss. Should we draw names to see who cooks tonight?" Archer asks, looking around at us.

"Let's start tomorrow night. I want to take you guys out to the pub as a thank you." I push my hand through my hair, tucking it behind my ear. "And because I need a drink strong enough to make me forget that I burned my restaurant down. Or possibly two drinks. Or twelve."

"Thank you for what, Penella? It's our job." Jamie says, squeezing my shoulder.

"A thank you for sticking around, because fixing my screw-ups isn't what I hired you for," I say softly, the words trying to stick in my throat like they don't want to be said out loud.

I know he's just trying to help me feel better about everything, but am I really just a job to them? Their boss? Are they hanging around because they're still getting paid, have somewhere to sleep, and have a full belly? Or are they staying because they care and want to help? I'm too much of a chicken shit to ask, so I'll probably spend the next two months overthinking it, creating elaborate scenarios in my head where they all secretly resent me, and then crying myself to sleep. Fuck me.

"Don't do that," Archer says, nudging my chin up with his knuckle so I'm looking him in the eye, his gaze so intense I can practically feel it burning through my skull. "We're not going anywhere, Nel, and it's not because you're paying us. It's because you've been there for all of us the last few years, and now it's our turn to be there for you."

His words settle over me like rain on a scorching summer day, and for the first time since the fire, I feel something resembling hope.

We spend the rest of the afternoon clearing more debris, salvaging what little we can, and making lists of what we'll need to rebuild. The work is exhausting but oddly satisfying—each charred piece we remove feels like letting go of something I was never meant to hold onto. By the time we finish for the day, my muscles are screaming and my lungs still burn from the smoke, but there's a lightness in my chest that wasn't there this morning. Maybe Archer is right. Maybe we really can do this together.

The late afternoon sun bathes the island in golden light, while storm clouds gather on the horizon over the sea, like the weather is as indecisive as my heart. After a day of clearing up debris, I should be showering, but I'm watching the guys hose off in my backyard instead, because apparently I have the self-control of a toddler in a candy store. Being the tallest, Sammy is the one holding the hose. The guys strip down to their skivvies, yelling as they step under the cold water, goosebumps immediately breaking out over their bodies.

"Why is it so fucking cold? My bits are about to fall off!" Jamie calls out with his infectious laugh, water droplets catching in his hair like tiny diamonds.

Spencer must make a crude remark because Sammy sticks his thumb over the end of the hose and directs the spray at his face. "You better watch your back tonight," Spencer warns in response, shaking water from his hair.

I can't tear my eyes away as Sammy tips his head back and laughs, his teeth blinding white against his dark skin. Water cascades down the defined muscles of his chest, highlighting every ridge and valley. He's so beautiful it almost hurts to look at him. All that taut, smooth skin painted over thick muscles—it's like watching living art come to life.

"Darlin', if you're going to stand there watching them, do you mind if I use the shower?" Liam asks, poking his head through the crack in the bathroom door, catching me red-handed.

I startle, pressing my hand against my heart as I turn toward him, cheeks flaming hotter than the kitchen fire. I peek at him through my eyelashes, then squeeze my eyes closed when my gaze catches on a bead of water sliding down his chest like it's on a mission to reach places I definitely shouldn't be thinking about.

"Sorry. They just look like they're having so much fun. Give me five minutes, and the bathroom will be all yours." Yeah, that's it. I was watching them because of the FUN they were having. Not because of all the miles of skin on display. Nope.

"Fun, hey?" he asks, biting his lip and winking before pulling the door closed, leaving me to wallow in embarrassment and the knowledge that I'm the world's worst liar.

I take the quickest shower of my life, towel off, pull on my robe, and call out to Liam before crossing the hallway to my bedroom. The bed creaks as I sit down and towel-dry my hair before raking through an air-dry serum. I get lost in thought, and the next thing I know, Liam is opening the bathroom door, clenching a towel around his hips, steam clinging to his sun-bronzed skin. He looks up and sees me sitting right there, in full view of the bathroom door, as if I was waiting for him like some peeping Tom.

"Sorry," I croak, ducking my head, but not before I get a good eyeful. My mouth dries up like the Sahara Desert. If I had a glass of water right now, you could hear it sizzle as it hit my tongue.

"Sorry for what?" he asks, shaking the water from his shaggy brown hair, droplets raining down over his chest.

"I wasn't planning on sitting here like a creep when you walked out of the bathroom. You deserve privacy." I clutch my robe tighter, suddenly aware of how little I'm wearing, which would be less of an issue if he wasn't also mostly naked.

"I don't even know what the word privacy means anymore," he chuckles. "Thank you for letting me use your shower."

"You're welcome," I whisper as he turns to walk down the hallway, trying not to notice the way his muscles taper down his back or the gnarly mark on his shoulder blade. But I'm only human, and that back deserves its own Instagram account.

"What is that?" I ask, walking over to him without realizing what I'm doing, tracing my finger over the bumpy skin.

He shivers under my touch, going preternaturally still, like a statue carved from veined golden marble. "It's my family's ranch brand," he says softly. "Everyone in my family has one. It's the mark we give the cattle on our ranch."

"Did it hurt?" I ask, running my finger over it again, fascinated.

"Yes," he says, his voice hoarse.

Liam's POV

I swallow hard, refusing to say what's on the tip of my tongue—that I would gladly re-live the pain every single day if it meant she would be standing close to me like this, running her fingers over my skin. My breath catches as her touch sends lightning through my veins, like a wild stallion finally feeling a gentle hand.

I've made it three years. Three years of pretending not to notice the glances she casts my way. Three years of pretending not to return them. Three years of flushing cheeks. Three years of wondering what other places might flush. Three years of torture disguised as self-control.

This is going to be the year that fucking breaks me.

When I opened the bathroom door and saw her sitting on her bed, practically drowning in that fluffy white robe, those wide hazel doe eyes drawing me in, I almost fell to my knees and confessed right there. I don't move a single muscle while she examines my shoulder, terrified I won't be able to control myself if I turn and meet her gaze, that I won't be able to resist those rosebud lips for one single second longer.

As badly as I want her, I know I can't ruin this—whatever this is. I can't risk losing her. Yes, she's my boss, but she's become so much more than that. I would sell my soul for this woman without a second thought. She's my sun, my moon, and every damn star in the sky.

"Did you use my body wash?" she asks, leaning closer, her nose skimming my neck. "You smell good."

Crikey. I take a deep breath, then curse myself when it's only her I can smell—like vanilla and honey and sin. "Yeah," I say roughly, "We'll have to grab some regular soap when we go grocery shopping."

"You don't like the smell?" she asks, a pout in her voice.

I steel my shoulders, clenching my fists before I turn and plow my hand between her legs to find out what she really smells like. I bet it's cotton candy. Or peaches.

The second she lifts her hand from my shoulder, I stalk down the hallway without looking back. I know without a shadow of a doubt that if she sees my face right now, she would know exactly what I'm thinking. She'd see it in my eyes...and other places. My towel isn't exactly concealing the situation that's developing.

Once I'm out of view, I press my back against the wall, taking deep, shuddering breaths as I try to wrangle my body under control. There's no room for mistakes in this house, no way to hide the effect she has on me. At least in the bunkhouse, there were multiple showers, so I had plenty of time to tug one out when I needed to. That's not going to be so easy here. We're packed in like sardines—very frustrated, very horny sardines.

Sam passes me on his way to the bathroom, flashing a sympathetic smile. "It isn't going to be easy, mate."

He can say that again. Pen's tinkling laugh floats down the hallway, and jealousy pricks at my heart. I immediately slam the door closed on that emotion. There's no place for jealousy in this house. Groaning, I scrub my hands over my face. I'm so damn screwed. Figuratively speaking, unfortunately.

Twenty minutes later, I'm sitting on the couch dressed in the only clean clothes I have. I hear Pen's faltering step on the stairs, and when she starts talking to herself, I get up to see if she needs help. My heart stops in my chest. Gone is the woman that wears gaudy coveralls and chicken print wellies.

"Is this too much?" she asks, smoothing her hands over a cream-colored dress with tiny yellow flowers, billowy sleeves extending just past her elbow. The material clings to her curves in all the right places, making my mouth go dry.

When I just stare at her, she lowers her gaze and starts fiddling nervously with the charms on her necklace like she's trying to decode a secret message. I clear my throat and try to talk, but nothing comes out. I try again, feeling like a teenager asking his crush to prom.

"You look—absolutely stunning." My voice cracks, and I drag my hand over my face, mortified. Smooth, Liam. Real smooth.

Her eyebrows almost hit her hairline and she giggles, her eyes sparkling as she pads down the stairs on bare feet, her cute little toes painted a peachy pink that matches the rising blush on her cheeks.

"You forgot to put your earrings back in." She holds out her hand, three earrings nestled in her palm. "Want me to help?"

"Yes, please," I croak, nearly choking as she stops on the last stair, a cloud of her scent wrapping around my cock and tugging hard. I try to hold my breath while she puts my earrings in, but instead, I find myself inhaling deeply through my nose, trying to breathe in as much of her as possible. I'm like an addict getting his fix.

"You look nice," she murmurs, her gaze sliding down over my crisp white t-shirt and jeans.

"I'm glad you think so because this is all I have." I grab my leather outback hat from the table by the stairs, worrying the brim, keeping my hands busy so I don't do something stupid like touch her. Like pull her close and see if she tastes as good as she smells.

"We'll have to fix that. I can take you guys shopping this weekend— it'll be like a reverse Pretty Woman!" She jumps up and down excitedly, her hair bouncing just above her shoulders, and I have to force myself not to stare at other things that are bouncing.

"You need to save your money, Darlin'."

"Insurance will pay me something eventually, and you guys need to replace the stuff you lost. I know the living situation sucks, but you at least need some autonomy." She tucks her knuckle under my chin, lifting it, running her fingertips over my two-day-old stubble. "Maybe some razors, too? God knows I could use one, too. I don't know the last time I shaved." She pats my cheek, smiling at me before heading into the kitchen.

I sag against the wall, letting my head thump against it as I close my eyes and will my heartbeat to calm the hell down. All because she mentioned shaving. Shaving.

And now? Now my brain has gone completely rogue. I'm picturing her standing in the bathroom—dewy skin, bare legs, lathering up with shaving cream—and nope. Nope. We are *not* going there. She could turn into a werewolf by moonlight and I'd still be a goner. But right now? I'm about three seconds away from offering to help. With the shaving. And maybe also the rinsing.

Jesus.

I cram my hat on like it might somehow cage the chaos going on in my head and shove open the front door. I need air. Cold, brain-clearing, hormone-diffusing air. Preferably with a side of reality check.

Outside, the evening sky's painted in those watercolor streaks of orange and pink that make people pull over just to take pictures. I drag in a breath—crisp, cool—and try to focus on literally *anything* other than her laugh.

Which, of course, floats through the open window like a damn siren song. Jamie's booming laugh. Spencer's low rumble. And then hers—Pen's giggle, light and impossible to ignore. Like bells. Or the first pop of champagne.

We've worked together for three years. But lately, something's shifted. Or maybe it's just me. I feel like I'm straddling this weird line between feeling completely at home and totally unmoored.

And tonight—tonight—we're going out. All of us. Drinks and music and probably way too much eye contact if I don't pull myself together.

I exhale and tip my face toward the sky.

This summer is going to wreck me.

And the worst part?

I can't fucking wait.

3

The air is thick with salt and fresh seafood as we step into the pub. Golden sunlight spills through the old windows, catching on glassware and dancing across the warm wooden floors. Outside, the harbor glows amber, boats bobbing gently like they're raising a glass to our night out. Our local pub is part of a gorgeous hotel and restaurant here on North Uist. It's my favorite seafood restaurant in Scotland. We supply them with the bulk of their seafood, so I know what we eat tonight will be fresh. Should I be splurging like this when I have a kitchen to rebuild? Probably not. Are the guys and their loyalty worth it? One thousand percent, yes. My bank account might be sobbing, but my heart is doing cartwheels.

As the hostess seats us, the warmth from the hearth fire washing over my chilled skin like a cozy blanket, I look around at the guys, wondering what I did to deserve them. Why are they still here? They could've walked away. They had every reason to. No house, no jobs, no clear plan. But here they are. Choosing to stay. Choosing me.

I haven't even thought about what it will be like having all five of them living in my house long-term. If I'm being honest, I'm not upset about having the opportunity to find out. And if I'm being honest—which, apparently, we are now—I'm not exactly dreading it.

I've spent three years choking on feelings I never said out loud. Swallowing glances. Biting back confessions I was too afraid would blow everything up. I buried so much, I half expected it to fossilize. But after yesterday? After the way Liam looked at me like I was something he'd lost and just found again? I think I'm not the only one with a little emotional excavation to do.

So maybe this is our chance. To finally say the things we didn't say. To throw it all on the table, even if some of it's jagged and raw and terrifying.

Of course, five ridiculously attractive men sharing my home is probably going to be catastrophic for my mental health. And my laundry situation. Mostly my underwear drawer, which frankly deserves hazard pay at this point.

"Are you doing okay?" Spencer asks, reaching under the table and squeezing my leg, his calloused fingers brushing against the inside of my knee.

I want to cover his hand with mine and drag it between my legs. I want to see if those calloused fingers feel as good as they look. I clear my throat, ignoring my sky-rocketing pulse and the sudden heat between my thighs.

"Yeah. I'm good." I glance over at him, and the second our eyes meet, I can't fucking look away. A lock of dirty blonde hair has fallen over his forehead, partially obstructing his earth-shatteringly blue eyes. The two-day-old scruff on his cheeks adds a mysterious edge to the smile pulling at his lips. "Thanks for asking," I say breathlessly, looking away. I pick up a langoustine and de-shell it, terrified that if I meet his gaze, he'll be able to see what I'm thinking.

"So, what's the plan, boss?" Sammy asks, taking a bite of butter-drenched shrimp.

I'm like a deer in headlights as I watch him lick the butter from his lips, his gaze burrowing into my soul like he knows exactly what's going through my head. Like he can hear the chorus of "Love on the Brain" by Rihanna playing on repeat in my brain. His smirk all but confirms it.

I don't answer right away. I take my time dipping my langoustine in butter, meeting his gaze as I take a bite.

"I'll have to go into town and get a permit tomorrow," I say, watching his eyes darken as I lick the butter from my fingers. "Do any of you happen to have building experience?"

Sammy and Jamie raise their hands.

"Perfect. Can the two of you make some sketches so I can turn them into the building inspector? Once they're approved, we can get a supply list going and order everything."

"No problem," Jamie murmurs, his gaze glued to my lips, making me self-conscious.

"Do I have something on my face?" I ask him, wiping my mouth with my napkin.

"No. Fuck me, but I'm just not used to seeing you like this, Penella. You clean up real nice." He smiles, his dimples appearing as his eyes crinkle, not embarrassed in the least.

A flush creeps up my neck like wildfire in dry grass as Spencer clears his throat, shooting Jamie a look I can't quite decipher.

I clear my throat. "Okay, well, once the supplies are delivered, I'm going to order new appliances, which hopefully will arrive as we finish getting everything rebuilt."

"What about the bunkhouse?" Liam asks, tipping his chair back onto two legs, his hat pushed high on his forehead.

"If all of you are okay with it, the bunkhouse will be the last thing we rebuild. I want to get the restaurant back up and running as soon as possible so we have some money coming in. Does anyone have any objections?" I look around the table at them, biting my lip to hold in my smile. If they shook their heads any harder, they'd need neck braces. "Okay. Good. That's our plan, then. Sammy and Jamie, you guys will stay with me tomorrow. The rest of you can go out on the boat."

"Wouldn't it be better to hire a contractor?" Archer asks, taking on the role of the sole voice of reason at the table.

"It would, but that's not exactly in the budget."

"What about your brother?" he asks, pushing his glasses up his nose.

My temper flares. "What about him, Archer?"

"You know Lach would have a crew down here tomorrow if you told him what happened."

"I'm not asking him for money." I refuse to ask for help when I know I'm perfectly capable of figuring it out on my own.

"It's okay to ask for help, Nel."

"If you don't want to help rebuild, just say so." I snap my mouth closed before I say something I'll regret.

Archer throws his hands up in a sign of surrender. "God, you're frustrating. He'll be upset when he finds out what happened."

"That's for me to worry about."

"You're right, it is." He clenches his jaw, jerking off his glasses and scrubbing his hands over his face before downing his beer in several large gulps, frustration rolling off him in waves.

I pull my credit card out of my pocket and slap it on the table. "You guys finish up. I'm going for a walk on the beach to clear my head." I stand up and walk away before they can protest.

This isn't the first time Archer and I have butted heads, and it definitely won't be the last. It's hard to stay mad for long when I know he's only looking out for me.

The wind whips around me as I make my way down the path to the beach, my dress fluttering around my thighs like butterfly wings. I smooth my hair out of my face, wondering for the hundredth time what I was thinking when I cut it all off a month ago. It's not even to my shoulders now, and I still can't pull it into a ponytail. It's the absolute bane of my existence.

"Hey! Wait up!" Liam's voice carries on the wind, that Australian accent bringing a smile to my lips.

I stop, waiting for him to catch up. The beach stretches before us, a ribbon of pale sand against the dark, churning waters of the Atlantic. Seabirds wheel overhead, their cries mingling with the rhythmic crash of waves against the shore.

"You didn't need to follow me, Liam. I wanted you guys to finish eating."

"I wasn't hungry anymore, Darlin'."

Well, that's a damn lie. He's always hungry. The man could eat a horse and still ask what there is for dessert.

"How are you really feeling?" he asks softly, walking beside me.

"Devastated," I answer honestly, too exhausted to come up with a better answer.

He grabs my wrist, pulling me toward him and wrapping his arms around me, squeezing tight. "I'm so sorry."

I squeeze him back, my cheek against his chest, breathing in leather and sandalwood.

"We'll build it back better than it was," he promises, his lips moving against my hair.

"I know," I whisper, my voice breaking, tears leaking from my eyes. I'm stronger than this, dammit.

He leans back, cupping my face in his hands and wiping away my tears with his thumbs. "Chin up, Buttercup."

I give him a watery smile, my eyes drifting down to his lips before I pull away and continue walking to the beach. He grabs my hand, threading his fingers through mine.

That simple touch has my entire body lighting up like a goddamn Christmas tree. I glance over at him, his hat casting half of his face in shadow, his bottom lip caught in those straight white teeth.

God, the man is fine.

He turns toward me suddenly, his gaze roaming over my face. "Darlin', I—"

"Incoming!"

That's the only warning we get before Sammy barrels into me like a freight train, scooping me into his arms and running toward the water.

"Let me go!" I shriek, pounding on his back with my fists.

"Not until you're smiling again, boss."

I bare my teeth at him like a maniac.

"Jesus, Penelope. A real smile, not whatever the bloody hell that is," he says, widening his eyes in mock horror.

"Put me down!"

"No," he growls, water splashing up as he runs along the shoreline.

A series of deep barks stops him in his tracks, his body tensing. I twist in his arms, trying to see where it's coming from.

"There!" I point to where the biggest dog I've ever seen is tucked between two rocks farther up on the beach. "We need to go see if it's okay," I beg, struggling in his arms.

He sighs, sets me down on my feet, and follows me into the soft sand. The closer we get, the bigger the dog becomes. A wolfhound, maybe?

"I think she's a girl," I whisper, crouching about two meters away, not wanting to scare her. She's too skinny. She smells like she rolled in something that's been dead for a week. In July. "Hi, doggy," I croon, gazing into her warm brown eyes. "You look hungry."

The dog barks, startling me, and I fall backward on my ass. She eyes Sammy and must decide he's safe enough because she bounds toward me, pushing me flat on my back, huge paws pinning my shoulders to the sand as she tries to suffocate me with her tongue.

"Hey, girl," I laugh, trying to shield my face. "She doesn't have a collar on. Do you think she was abandoned?" I ask, looking up at Sammy.

"We know nearly everyone on this island. I don't know anyone with a dog like that. Someone probably dumped her."

"Oh, you poor baby," I murmur, scratching behind her ears.

"Who's this?" Liam asks, finally catching up with us.

"This is Pearl. She's coming home with us." I stand, brushing the sand from my butt. She's exactly what I need—another female to balance out all that masculine energy before I drown in it.

"Are you sure?" he asks, holding his hand out to Pearl tentatively. "She's awfully big."

"Yes, I'm sure. Haven't you ever had a dog?" I ask, belatedly realizing he seems nervous.

"No."

"Oh. Well, this will be new for all of us then."

"She's dirty, Penelope," Sammy says, his nose wrinkling in distaste.

"Then we'll wash her, Samuel."

He shakes his head but squats down anyway, patting the top of her head when she gets close enough.

"Have we added a new member to the family?" Jamie calls out. I look up to see the other three guys walking toward us. Spencer is already patting his thighs to try to get Pearl to leave my side. She doesn't. What a good girl.

"This is Pearl. We think she was dumped," I explain, tickling her chin.

"Pearl? Does she have a collar on?" Archer asks, his forehead wrinkling.

"No collar."

"Then how do you know her name?"

"I just named her." I scowl up at him. "Don't you dare ruin this for me."

"I'm not trying to ruin anything, Nel. It was just a question." He tries to sound grumpy but I can see the way his eyes soften when he looks at both of us, and it's impossible to miss the smile tugging at the corner of his lips.

"Come on, let's get her home," he says, holding out his hand to help me up.

Pearl rides in the front seat on the way home, which means Spencer and Sammy are in the truck bed, looking like they're being punished for stealing cookies. The dog is the size of a small pony and somehow manages to take up the entire bench seat, leaving me practically sitting in Liam's lap. We stop at the grocery store to grab some shampoo and dog food, then head back to the house just as the sun dips below the horizon. It takes Archer, Spencer, Jamie and me to get her washed and towel dried.

"Hold still, ye great beast," Jamie laughs as Pearl tries to escape the suds.

The scent of wet dog fills the yard as Pearl shakes her burnished gold fur, droplets of water catching the last of the sunset like tiny prisms, creating a personal rainbow around her. The second we let her go, she sidles up to Sammy and shakes, covering him in water like she's getting revenge for all dogs everywhere. Sammy's shriek has us all descending into a fit of laughter.

"You think that's funny, Penelope?" He captures me with one arm, digging his fingers into my ribs with his other hand.

I twist away from his grip, laughing so hard that tears stream down my eyes, my stomach muscles clenching like I'm in an ab workout from hell. "I thought you wanted to see me smile again!"

"I didn't know it would involve a dog," he grumbles, wrapping his strong arms around my torso, refusing to let me go. The press of his chest against my back sends a wave of heat through my body, his breath warm against my ear.

I shrug. "Beggars can't be choosers." I tip my head back and look up at him, surprised at the heat in his eyes. It's like looking directly into the sun. I drop my gaze before he can see my blush—or before I burst into flames—breaking out of his hold and calling for Pearl. "I'm taking her for a walk, anyone want to come?" I ask casually, hooking my thumbs in the pockets of my neon pink coveralls.

"I will," Liam says immediately, jumping up from the stump he'd been sitting on.

I notice the guys all look at each other and then between me and Liam before they make excuses not to come. They're about as subtle as a marching band in a library.

"You're a good person, Pen," Liam says as we walk side-by-side down the empty one-track road.

"Why? Because I brought her home?"

He nods. "I don't know that many people would have. She's the biggest dog I've ever seen."

"She's beautiful," I coo, cradling Pearl's face between my hands, her soft brown eyes capturing my heart. We walk in comfortable silence, the evening sky painted in strokes of pink and orange, hills of green stretching out in every direction, gravel crunching beneath our feet. A cool breeze carrying the scent of heather and sea salt wraps around us like a gentle embrace. "Thank you for staying," I blurt, the words tumbling from my lips.

"I don't really have a choice," he says, taking off his hat and pushing his hand through his shaggy brown hair.

"What does that mean? Of course you have a choice!" I stop walking, and turn toward him. He meets my gaze, indecision warring in his eyes. Awareness crackles between us like static during a summer thunderstorm. Like if one of us moves too quickly, we might actually see sparks fly.

"I'm a loyal person, Darlin'. I'm not going to leave when you need help," he finally says.

"Say what you really mean," I whisper, stepping forward, the toes of my boots touching his. I hold his gaze and wait. "Scaredy cat."

He clenches his jaw, tips his hat out of the way, and slides his hand around my neck, pulling me close enough that I can count his individual eyelashes. "I didn't have a choice because I couldn't stand the thought of leaving the only place that feels like home," he says, his breath warm against my ear.

He's still not telling me the truth, dammit. I struggle to breathe through the tension, determined to get him to open up. I lean forward, running my nose along his neck, breathing him in while clucking like a chicken. If he wants to chicken out, I'll help him with the sound effects.

He growls, clenching his hand in my hair, tugging my head back to look me in the eyes. "I didn't want to leave you, Darlin'. Is that what you want to hear?"

"Good boy." I can't look away from him. Those perfectly arched brows over warm brown eyes. Full lips—"Are you growing a mustache?" I ask, noticing how his stubble is a little longer over his top lip. I like it—a lot.

"Do you like it?"

I swallow hard, adrenaline burning through my veins like liquid fire as he tightens his fingers in my hair, his gaze dipping to my mouth. "Yes," I breathe, my voice shaking.

"I want to kiss you so badly right now," he says, taking a deep breath and closing his eyes like that will help dissipate what he's feeling. "Tell me it's a horrible idea. Tell me it'll ruin everything. Tell me you don't like me," he begs, opening his eyes and cupping my face with his other hand.

"I can't do that, Liam." My entire body is buzzing with anticipation, desire kicking up a steady beat between my legs.

Something flashes in the depths of his eyes—hunger, need, possession—and then his lips are sliding along my jaw. I moan, my head falling back as I surrender to his touch.

"Do you know how long I've dreamed of touching you like this?" he murmurs, tugging at my bottom lip with his thumb, his breath hitching.

"Three years?" I rasp.

"Did you guys forget about Pearl?"

Liam and I jump away from each other like we've been electrocuted. Jamie is walking toward us with Pearl by his side. It's hard to be frustrated at the interruption when Jamie is the human embodiment of sunshine and rainbows.

"I promise we didn't forget about you," I say, scratching Pearl's head before looking up at Jamie. "Thank you. I didn't realize she had wandered off."

"I bet you didn't," he says, one eyebrow cocking, a ghost of a smile on his lips, his dimples flashing. "Caught in a moment, were we? Don't mind me, just the friendly neighborhood chaperone." He winks playfully, the last of the sunset catching the gold flecks in his green eyes.

"What does that mean?" I ask, my heart in my throat.

He only shakes his head. "She wouldn't have gone far," he says instead of answering my question. "She's already in love with you, just like the rest of us."

Liam looks at Jamie, his eyes wide enough that I'm worried they might fall out of his head.

"What!" Jamie exclaims, looking between us. A moment later, his words register, and he goes white as a sheet. "That–that came out wrong," he stammers.

I push up on my tiptoes and wrap my arms around his neck. "Thank you. I really appreciate it."

Heat slides down my spine as he buries his face in my neck, one large hand cradling the back of my head like I'm something precious. "Anything for you, Penella."

"Enough with that awful nickname!" I laugh, pulling away from him and swatting his shoulder.

With him on my left and Liam on my right, we follow Pearl down the road and into the twilight.

4

———————

I toss and turn for hours that night. The endless list of things I have to do keeps scrolling through my mind. Then I'll think of something else and tell myself not to forget it by morning. Cue the anxiety about forgetting it. It's a loop that never ends. My brain is like a hamster doing lines of coke, racing on its wheel at mach speed. I finally give up at 1 AM and head to the kitchen to make some tea.

I recognize Jamie's bulky shadow immediately, even before turning on the small light. Tension zips through me like I just touched a live wire. I'm not sure if it's the time of night or the soft music he's playing. Or maybe it's the fact that his Godlike torso is on full display, thin joggers hanging dangerously low on those hip bones that could cut glass. Moonlight streaming in the kitchen window traces the contours of his muscles, highlighting the dimples at the small of his back. I turn away from him before he sees me looking at places I shouldn't and grab a mug from the cupboard.

"Can't sleep?" I ask, taking the kettle to the sink and filling it with water.

"Not a bloody chance," he says, his voice husky. "The couch isn't made for big guys like me. It's like trying to sleep on a torture device designed specifically for my spine."

I spin toward him, mortified. "God, I'm so sorry. My bed is plenty big enough if you want to sleep there tonight until we figure something out." The words leave my mouth before my brain can catch up. Did I just invite this mountain of a man into my bed?

"As tempting as that is, Penella," he says, eyes twinkling with mischief, "I couldn't do that."

"Why?" I ask, turning on the kettle, the soft click and burble of heating water filling the silence between us.

"That's your safe space. Your sanctuary."

"And I'm inviting you into it." I tuck my hair behind my ears, looking at him through my eyelashes. Not that I'm trying to be coy or anything. That would be ridiculous. I'm a grown-ass woman who runs a restaurant and a fishing boat for a living. The vision of his massive body in my bed stirs dangerous feelings. Feelings that have no business being stirred at 1 AM in a dark kitchen when I'm wearing practically nothing. "Would you like some bedtime tea?" I ask, rummaging through the cabinet, stretching up on my toes to reach the top shelf.

"Allow me," he says with that delicious Irish lilt, coming up behind me, his chest pressing to my back as he fetches the box of teabags. "It's called Go The Fuck To Sleep Tea?" he asks, laughing, his dimples flashing.

I grip the counter, my knuckles white, trying to resist the urge to lean back into his warmth, to haul his arm around my stomach, and snuggle into his bulk. I'm like a touch-starved cat who's spotted a sunbeam after weeks of rain.

He must feel me stiffen because he backs up quickly, tossing the box on the counter.

"Sorry," he mutters. "I didn't mean to make you uncomfortable."

"You didn't." I turn and meet his gaze head-on so he can see the truth in my eyes.

"Why did you go all stiff like that? You were gripping that counter like it was the edge of a cliff."

Leave it to Jamie to call me out. The man doesn't miss a thing—which makes me wonder what else he's noticed over the years.

"The truth, Penella," he insists, crossing those massive arms over his chest.

"The truth is scary sometimes," I hedge, pulling out two tea bags.

He nods. "You're right, it is."

I swallow hard, my heart beating in my ears like a drum solo. Fuck it. I'm tired of dancing around this. Do I lean into the attraction? Allow myself to be honest? Or do I keep pretending that I don't regularly imagine what those hands would feel like on my skin?

"I was stopping myself from leaning back against you," I say quickly before I lose my nerve. The kettle beeps, saving me from the awkwardness. I turn, grab a second mug, and throw the tea bags in. I feel Jamie's heat closing in on me as I pour the water. He bands his arm around me, pulling me back against his body.

"Like this, then?" he asks softly, the scent of him—something spicy and warm with hints of clove—enveloping me. His body radiates heat like a furnace against the cool night air.

I snuggle my face into the arm that's crossed over me. Holy mother of biceps. I want to inhale him, lick him, bite him. The yearning in my heart for something intimate is paralyzing. I've been alone for so long, I'm practically a virgin again, and now I'm getting a full-course meal of man. He presses his nose against my hair, inhaling deeply.

"You always smell so good."

"What do I smell like?" I ask, smiling against his skin. I haven't worn perfume in ages, and I would have hedged some bets that I smell like fish and body odor.

"Sunshine, lemonade, and orange blossoms," he murmurs, his lips moving against my ear, sending shivers down my spine. His breath is warm, tickling the sensitive skin beneath my earlobe.

There's a delicious tightening low in my belly—the kind that makes you question every life choice that led you to this moment of exquisite torture. I wonder if he's feeling this too—this magnetic pull that's threatening to snap my willpower like a wishbone.

My body is practically humming like it's been mainlining espresso shots, but my brain is flashing warning signs brighter than a Vegas casino.

I grab both mugs with hands that are definitely not trembling and turn to face him, pressing my back against the counter for structural support. I push his mug between us like it's some kind of mystical force field that can protect me from bad decisions.

Spoiler alert: it can't.

"Thank you." He leans against the opposite counter, his golden-brown eyes never leaving mine, emotions flitting across his face like storm clouds.

"What are you thinking?" I ask finally, unable to stand the silence any longer.

"I'm wondering why the hell you've been hiding behind your coveralls for the last three years," he says, his voice rolling over me like thunder, deep and decadent. "Yesterday was the second time I've seen you in regular clothes. And now this."

I look down at what I'm wearing for the first time that night. The tank top and booty shorts reveal an exorbitant amount of skin. I'm practically naked.

"Your brain is just as magnificent as your body, and you don't try to hide that away," he says, tilting his head, studying me like he's trying to figure me out.

"I'm not hiding," I protest, licking my lips.

His eyes darken, his gaze zeroing in on my mouth. "Bullshit."

"What would I be hiding from?"

"You tell me." His accent thickens with each word, rolling my name around in his mouth like it's candy.

Oh fuck me sideways. He knows. I've been trying to play it cool all these years, and he knew exactly what was going through my head the whole time.

"Never," I say, lifting my chin stubbornly. Because I'm nothing if not stubborn, even when I'm caught red-handed.

He throws his head back and laughs. I've never seen anything quite so beautiful in my life. Pure, unfiltered joy personified in six-feet-plus of man. "Bloody helll, Penella! Playing the long game?" he asks, his eyes sparkling.

"I have no idea what you're talking about." My nose grows a good two inches with that lie.

He prowls closer, reaching around me to set his mug on the counter before grabbing mine and doing the same. Leaning close, he plants his hands on either side of me, caging me in with his body. My breathing goes shallow, like my lungs have suddenly forgotten how to function. "Funny thing is," he breathes, his gaze dipping to my lips, "it fucking worked."

Holy shit. I can't breathe. Every cell in my body is focused on the microscopic distance between his mouth and mine. "What worked?" I ask, my voice shaking.

His trademark smile is gone, replaced by something fierce and feral. Something hungry. Something that makes my insides turn to liquid fire. He doesn't answer; instead he slides his hand over my throat, tilting my chin with his thumb, forcing me to look at him. I feel vulnerable and out of control, and I've never been so turned on in my entire life. I tremble as desire shoots through me, making my knees shaky.

He backs up immediately, looking stricken, rubbing his hand over his lips. "Christ almighty. Sorry."

"You didn't do anything wrong," I breathe, clutching the countertop like it's a lifeline. My body is screaming at him to come back, to finish what he started.

I know without a shadow of a doubt that this is the turning point. I can walk away now, and everything will be like it was, or I can fling myself into new territory. I can keep pretending I don't feel what I feel, or I can admit that I've been harboring feelings for not just him, but all five of them, for years. I boost myself onto the counter, putting myself at eye level with him.

"You're right, you know," I say, looking at him over the rim of my mug, the warm steam carrying the scent of chamomile and valerian, the soothing herbs already working their magic on my frazzled nerves.

"How so?"

"I was playing the long game—the game of keeping my personal life separate from my employees. To avoid getting wires crossed. To keep it professional. To stop myself from doing exactly what I want to do right now, which is jump you like a rabid koala."

"And then you burnt down the bloody kitchen," he says with a knowing smirk.

"And then I burnt down the kitchen," I echo.

"Those wires aren't just crossed, love. They're fucked. They're going to be so tangled by the end of this they'll never be able to be fixed."

"That's exactly why I'm drawing a line now," I say, drawing an imaginary line with my finger between us.

"Is that what you want?" he asks, taking a step toward me. His gaze promising me things I've only ever dared to think about in the dead of night with a vibrator between my legs and his name on my lips.

I nod.

"Are you sure about that?" He steps past the line, a predator cornering his prey. His eyes never leaving mine as he closes the distance between us inch by inch.

"No," I whisper, the word barely coming out.

Jamie reaches toward me, his fingers sliding along my jaw, holding tight. "I think what you want," he says, voice dropping an octave, "is someone to be in control for once. To tell you what a good girl you are." His words are like a match to gasoline—I'm instantly aflame.

Jesus motherfucking Christ. My knees fall open, allowing him to come closer, his lips only inches from mine. My heart pounds so loudly I'm certain he can hear it. Every nerve ending in my body is on high alert, anticipating his touch, his taste.

"Would you like that, angel?" The endearment slips off his tongue as if he's been saying it for years.

"Why the hell are you two up?" Spencer mumbles, shuffling into the kitchen, his eyes scrunched closed against the light, his drawl thick with sleep. The moment shatters like glass, reality crashing back in with jarring suddenness.

Jamie gives me a look that tells me we'll finish this discussion later. A look that promises heat and satisfaction and all kinds of delicious things that make me clench my thighs together. "I couldn't sleep," he says casually.

"Did we wake you up?" I ask Spencer.

"No," he says, blinking slowly, giving me a sleepy smile. "Just needed some water, Sugar. Though seeing you like this is even better."

I reach behind me, grab a glass, and hand it to him, watching him fill it from the fridge dispenser. I drink the rest of my tea and jump down from the counter, my jelly-filled knees nearly buckling beneath me. If Spencer had walked in two minutes later, he'd have gotten a free show starring yours truly.

"Goodnight, both of you. Jamie, if you can't sleep, my offer still stands." I walk back to my bedroom with the confidence of someone who definitely has not practiced this exit in the mirror seventeen times. I don't dare look back to see if Jamie is watching me leave, but I can feel his eyes on me like physical touch, burning into my back with every step I take.

Actually, burning into my ass is more like it. The man has never been subtle about his appreciation for what my mama gave me.

If he thinks I'm inviting him into my bed, he's right. Absolutely, one hundred percent right, and we both know it. There's no universe where I'm actually going to sleep tonight, not with him under the same roof and this electricity between us threatening to short-circuit my common sense. The ball is in his court now, and God help me, I hope he decides to play.

5

The soft gray light of dawn filters through my curtains as I wake up slowly, my senses coming back online one at a time. The weak light of early morning glowing through my eyelids. The silence of a house that hasn't quite woken up yet. The distant cry of seagulls outside my window. The warmth of the arm thrown over my stomach.

My heart launches itself into an Olympic-level floor routine. My eyes fly open like a pair of cartoon blinds being yanked by an invisible hand.

Jamie. Jamie is in my bed.

Apparently, he slipped in sometime last night, and now he's cuddling me like I'm a body pillow with a pulse. I need to get out of here before he wakes up and realizes he's committed a felony-level sleep snuggle. Not that I'm complaining. But still—he might be mortified, and that just feels unnecessarily cruel for this hour of the morning.

I inch toward the edge of the bed like I'm defusing a bomb. One toe, then the other. Slow. Steady. Almost there—then just when I think I may be in the clear, he hauls me back against his body, sighing into my hair.

"Where do you think you're going?" he mumbles, his voice hoarse with sleep, his accent stronger than usual, vibrating against my back like a purring cat.

"I was trying to sneak out from under your arm before you woke up. I didn't want to make it awkward." I pull at his hand, trying to ignore the way his cock is digging into my ass.

"You're the one that cuddled into me last night, Penella," he says, the nickname rolling off his tongue like honey. "Who am I to say no when a beautiful woman wraps herself around me? I'm not exactly known for my self-restraint."

"Are you serious?" I whisper, mortified. "I'm sorry."

"I'm not. Not even a little bit," he says, and I can hear the smirk in his voice. "I'm enjoying every second."

"I can tell," I choke out, my heart beating so fast I feel like I'm going to pass out. The "it" in question is pressing against me with what feels like increasing enthusiasm.

"I know I should let you go, but I'm having a hard time. Pun absolutely intended." He nuzzles into the space between my neck and shoulder, inhaling deeply, the scent of his sleep-warm skin making my head spin.

"Jamie!" I gasp, squirming in his grip.

"I wouldn't do that if I were you," he groans, releasing me. "Unless you want to turn this spooning session into something considerably more athletic."

My brain is telling me to move away from him. To get out of bed. To forget this ever happened. But my body is rooted in place, his cock pressed intimately against my ass crack, need pounding through my body like a heartbeat. It's been so long since I've been held like this, and it feels so fucking good. Like chocolate cake after a year of kale salads.

"Penella."

My name is a warning falling from his lips.

"If you're not going to move, do I have permission to touch you?" he asks, his voice strained.

Oh God. This is it. The point of no return. "Yes," I breathe.

He flattens his hand over my stomach, sliding it up my torso as I arch into his touch, my ass pressing into his lap. I assume he's going to stop high on my ribs, but he doesn't. I whimper as he drags his hand up over my breast, my nipple puckering against his palm. One squeeze, one groan of maddening need from deep in his throat, and then he keeps moving, circling my neck with his fingers.

"How long have you wanted this?" he asks. The lilt of his accent, coupled with his sleep-roughed voice, is the spark that starts a wildfire of desire roaring through my body.

"Tell me, Penelope" he says, "Because I've been thinking about this since the moment I met you."

I know he can feel my pulse racing beneath his fingertips, that he knows exactly what he's doing to me. My heartbeat is probably sending Morse code signals straight to his hand: S-E-X P-L-E-A-S-E.

Two quick raps sound on the door before I can answer, and then Archer pokes his head in. "Nel, have you seen Jamie?"

I know we should have jumped apart, that anything else would have been better than Archer finding us cuddled in bed with Jamie's hand wrapped around my throat, but neither of us move a muscle.

Archer sucks in a sharp breath. "Well, shit. Um. Sorry." He closes the door gently, giving us privacy. "I'm taking Pearl for a walk. Breakfast will be ready in ten!" he calls out before his footsteps disappear down the hallway.

"Oh my God." I sit up in bed, drawing my knees to my chest and covering my face with my hands. Humiliation burns through me like acid reflux after too much whisky.

"Relax, sweetheart," Jamie says, rubbing circles on my back. "It's just Archer. Not the Queen of England."

"How can I relax when he's going to think we were fucking in here?"

Something dangerous flashes in Jamie's golden-brown eyes. "I was thinking about fucking in here, among other places. The shower. The kitchen counter. Against the wall in the hallway. On top of the washing machine during the spin cycle..."

"Jamie!"

"Don't tell me you weren't thinking about it, too," he growls, eyes dark, dimples flashing. "Because I've seen the way you look at me when you think I'm not paying attention."

"I—"

"The truth, Penella," he insists, "I want to hear you say it."

"Fine. Yes, it did cross my mind. Several times."

"That's my good girl."

"Don't say that to me!" I jump out of bed, grab a change of clothes, and rush from the bedroom before he sees what those two little words do to me.

I can barely look at Archer as we eat breakfast. I feel ashamed, and I'm angry that I feel that way. I'm an adult. If I want to invite Jamie to sleep in my bed instead of the couch, I should be able to do so without worrying about being judged. But here I am, staring at my scrambled eggs like they hold the secrets of the universe, waiting for his disapproval to crash down on me like a tidal wave.

Archer's gaze burns into the top of my head, and I finally get to the point that I can't take it anymore. I push back from my seat, motioning for him to meet me outside. I stand on the porch, waiting for him to join me, feeling like I'm about to be sick.

The morning air is crisp against my skin, carrying the scent of salt and wet grass. A light drizzle has left everything with a glistening sheen, the kind of Scottish spring morning that can't decide if it wants to rain or shine.

"What?" he asks as he steps outside, closing the door firmly after him.

"Just say whatever you need to say. Let's hash it out now and get it over with," I say, scared to look him in the face.

"What you do is your business, Nel," he says, his voice gruff. "You don't need to explain yourself to me."

"Don't even. I saw the way you were looking at me in there. Like I ripped out your heart and stomped on it."

"I wasn't looking at you like that," he says stubbornly.

"Archer! Enough. Stop fucking pretending."

Anger flashes across his face. "What do you want me to say, Penelope? That I wish it were me in bed with you? That I'm jealous? That I've been trying to keep my hands off you for three fucking years and Jamie gets to sleep in your bed after two nights?"

"Well, are you?"

"Am I what?" he snaps, his eyes flashing.

"Jealous?"

"Don't do this to me," he says, looking up at the sky, his throat bobbing.

"I'm only asking you to be honest," I whisper, my voice thick.

"Yes, I'm fucking jealous, okay?" The words come out like they're being ripped from his chest.

I step backward, pressing my back to the wall, steadying myself before I collapse from nerves. My knees feel like they're made of Jell-O, wobbly and unreliable. "Then do something about it."

"You don't mean that."

"Yes, I fucking do."

He steps closer, reaching out tentatively, his thumb ghosting just under my bottom lip. The touch is so light it's almost not there, but it sends electricity zinging through me like I've stuck my finger in a socket.

I take a stilted breath, butterflies rioting in my stomach, his shrewd gaze pinning me in place as I reach up and slide his glasses off his face.

"Should we do this when you were just in bed with Jamie?" His gaze dips to my lips.

"I didn't sleep with him, Archer."

He raises an eyebrow.

"You know what I mean. We didn't fuck," I say, exasperated. "Though from the look on your face when you opened that door, you'd think you caught us filming amateur porn."

"Would you let me watch if you did?"

His words are a shock to my system. Like being doused with ice water while sunbathing. "What kind of question is that!" I shove at his chest, but he doesn't budge an inch.

"I thought we were being honest with each other."

"Would you want to watch?" I ask, turning the question around on him, anger radiating off me in waves.

"Christ, yes, especially if I could go after." I don't have time to process his words before his lips are crashing against mine. He presses his thumb against my chin, opening my mouth, his tongue sweeping in as he swallows my moan.

Admittedly, it's been a while since I was last kissed. Like, really kissed. But this? This isn't anything like what I remember.

This is full-body, earth-tilting, soul-rearranging.

His lips are firm but gentle, tasting faintly of coffee and something I can't name but instantly know is him. Like rain on warm pavement. Like comfort and chaos all at once. If kissing is a language, he's speaking it fluently—like he was born to do it. Like he's been saving every single word just for me.

He breaks away after a minute or two, breathing hard. "I think all of us need to sit down and have a talk."

"Why?" I ask, trying to drag my gaze away from his swollen lips and failing miserably.

"Because there are four other men in there who have as much right to you as I do."

"I'm not an object to be owned, Archer," I say, my anger already at a simmer. "I'm not the last cupcake at a bake sale you can call dibs on."

"That's not what I'm saying." He catches my wrist before I can walk away. "You want me to be honest? Then I'll be honest, Penelope. I know you're in love with all of us, whether you're willing to admit it to yourself or not. You haven't dated anyone in the three years we've known you. Have you stopped to think why you've never seen us with any women? About what that might mean?"

"Stop." I break away from him, handing him his glasses.

"If you're not ready, that's fine, but it will have to happen sooner or later."

I don't say anything, my head spinning.

"Are you going to tell Jamie that we just kissed?" he asks, dragging a hand through his hair.

My heart lurches painfully. Fucking hell. "I get it, okay? Give me some time to figure this out. I need to call Isla and ask her for advice." And maybe a lobotomy, because my brain is clearly malfunctioning.

He nods his approval. "Let me know what you decide. We've managed to stick together for three years; I don't want this summer to be the one that tears us apart."

I stare at the ground, my heart in my stomach, wondering if this was all a gigantic mistake. If I've just lit a match in a room full of dynamite.

"Hey," he lifts my chin with his finger, forcing me to meet his gaze. "I know I'm hard on you, but it's because I care about you more than I've cared for anyone in my entire life." He brushes his lips over mine, grabs my hand, and pulls me back into the house.

I spend that entire morning thinking about what Archer said. How did I miss that the guys hadn't brought around any women in three years? Looking back, I guess I just thought they were really good at sneaking around. After all, I only went into their bunkhouse if I was invited. It would have been easy for them to have sleepovers and for me to be none the wiser.

But Archer said none of them had.

That doesn't even make sense. Is he lying? Maybe just a little white lie to make me feel better—it has to be, right? Surely, they've slept with multiple people over the last three years. There's no way they've spent all that time tugging one off in the shower. Five gorgeous men living in celibacy? No. Impossible.

I keep myself busy making lists—menu ideas, supply runs, pantry organization—anything that'll keep my hands moving while the guys argue over who's going on the fishing boat and when.

Archer, of course, will be out every day. He's been acting as captain since the old one retired, and apparently, no one's brave—or stupid— enough to challenge him for the role. Which means he'll be gone. All day. Every day.

And I'll barely see him.

Something tightens low in my gut, but I press it down. Smother it with flour measurements and supply delivery dates. I don't have time to dwell on stupid feelings or wonder if he'll miss me too.

I bow my head over my notebook, pretending like the words in front of me aren't starting to blur. Focus, I tell myself. Kitchen first. Feelings... never.

Outside, the soft patter of rain begins against the windows, steady and hypnotic. The sky darkens as thick clouds roll in off the sea, a slow-moving storm wrapping the house in shadows. Inside, the warm glow from the overhead lights and the scent of coffee make everything feel safe. Too safe. Like the world has shrunk down to just me, this kitchen, and the quiet ache I keep refusing to name.

"How's it going, boss?" Sammy asks, sitting down at the kitchen table with me, snagging one of my lists and looking it over.

"As good as it can be. Can you and Jamie put together a supply list in the next couple of days? I want to get them ordered as soon as possible."

He nods, leaning back in his chair. "We could go over there today if you'd like. Once I have measurements, I can plug them into an online program and have that list for you by tomorrow."

"That would be amazing. Do you want to go now? Is Jamie free?"

"You sure you want Jamie to come?" he asks, studying me carefully. "He's been acting weird all day."

"What do you mean by weird?" I ask, my heart dropping. Did he see me and Archer on the porch? Did he witness the kiss that rearranged my molecular structure?

"He's like a giddy bloody teenager. Annoying as hell. I don't know what's gotten into him," Sammy says, his full lips twitching with annoyance.

Relief floods my system, and I can't help the smile that pulls at my lips. "Yes, I want Jamie to come. I'll go get him."

After looking around the house, I head outside to find Jamie working out in the backyard in a patch of sun. The rain has stopped temporarily, leaving the world gleaming and fresh. His caramel skin glows golden in the sunlight, his muscles stretching and bunching as he completes a circuit of bodyweight exercises. Sweat trails down his chest, highlighting the defined ridges of his abdomen, his curly brown hair darkened with moisture at the temples.

"Why don't you take a video? You can watch it later when you're alone," he teases, not even breaking rhythm in his push-ups. "I can do some extra flexing if you want better material. Give you something nice for your spank bank."

Heat blooms in my cheeks, and I step back, hiding from his view, mortification sinking into my bones. Getting caught staring is bad enough—getting caught staring while imagining licking those sweat droplets off his abs is infinitely worse.

"Don't be embarrassed," he says, rounding the corner. "It's flattering. And if we're being honest, I've done plenty of imagining myself."

"I wasn't—"

"Penella, don't lie," he chastises, "your tongue was practically hanging out of your mouth."

Fucking hell. This man. He sees right through me like I'm made of cellophane.

"I like what I see, too, so we're good," he clarifies, his gaze sliding down over my body slowly, straight white teeth sinking into his bottom lip.

"Yeah?" I rasp, looking down at my periwinkle coveralls and sheep-print wellies. "Is this what you find sexy?"

"It's you I like, not your clothes." He says it so simply, like it's the most obvious thing in the world.

"Are you saying you don't like my clothes?" I ask, more offended than I should be. "My sheep wellies are practically couture."

"Stop pouting, angel. You're adorable. Even more adorable when you're wearing your ridiculous outfits."

"I don't want to be adorable." Puppies are adorable. Kittens are adorable. I want to be seductive, alluring, irresistible, not something you'd pat on the head and give a treat.

"Then what do you want to be?" he asks, his gaze dark.

Fuck. I didn't mean to say that out loud. My internal monologue seems to have found the door marked "exit" and waltzed right through it. I hold up my hand, trying to get myself back on track. "I came over here to ask if you wanted to go to the restaurant with Sammy and me."

"Answer my question first."

"What question?" I ask, pretending to have no idea what he's talking about.

"What do you want to be if you don't want to be adorable?" He steps toward me, a lion prowling his domain, and I take a step back, a little lamb scared for her life. A very turned-on little lamb who's secretly hoping to be eaten.

I look at him, debating whether to answer or not. Wondering what he would do if I ran away instead.

Fuck it. I bolt, but my tall wellies are no match for his running shoes, and he catches up within several strides, pulling me down to the ground. He rolls underneath me as we fall, his hand cradling my head.

"Tell me," he demands, looking up at me, dark lashes framing golden-green eyes.

Butterflies explode in my stomach. Not just one or two, but an entire migration of them, swirling and diving and making me dizzy.

His chest expands underneath me, his arm tightening around my middle, trapping me in place.

"I want to be sexy," I whisper, swallowing hard, my heart racing.

"What makes you think you aren't?" he asks, his gaze anchored on my lips.

"Because you just called me adorable."

"You can be adorable and sexy at the same time, Penella. Like how a wolf can be beautiful and still tear your throat out. Different qualities can coexist."

I roll my eyes, trying to ignore the way my nipples are rubbing on his chest every time he takes a breath.

"Trust me, I cuddled you the entire night in the scraps of fabric you call pajamas. You're definitely fucking sexy. I nearly had to take a cold midnight shower because of it. Twice."

"Shhhh!" I look around, making sure nobody else heard him.

"You're worried about that when you're laying on top of me right now, and I'm well on my way to a hard-on?" he asks, chuckling.

"Jamie! You are not!"

"Want to bet?" he growls, sliding his arm over my ass, pressing me down as he lifts his hips, his shaft pressing into my hip. "Bet you five quid I'm as hard as a diamond right now. Care to do a hands-on inspection?"

"Fuck, Jamie," I gasp, wriggling in his grip.

"Jesus, yes, I'd like to," he groans, releasing me, his gaze heavy as I stand and tower over him.

He pushes to his feet, adjusting himself, and I may be imagining things, but I swear I see the head of his cock tucked into his waistband before he pulls his shirt back down. Lust pounds between my legs until I'm delirious with it. I should turn and walk away, but all I can think about is pushing him back down and taking him in my mouth. Finding out if he tastes as good as he smells.

My heart jumps at Pearl's sharp bark, and I turn to find her staring at me, tail wagging like she knows exactly what she's interrupting.

"Hi, girl," I coo, squatting down and patting my leg. She comes to me, licking a long line up my face as I scratch her ears. "Do you want to come with us to the restaurant?"

"Is she taking my place?" Jamie asks, coming over to smooth his hand over her head.

"Maybe. That's what you deserve," I pout.

"For making you tell me the truth?"

"You're a bad man, Jamie O'Connor."

"I am," he agrees, "Do you want to see how bad? I could show you right now. I could take you behind that shed and demonstrate all the bad things I've been thinking about doing to you for the last three years."

"Are you two ready to go?" Sammy asks, poking his head around the side of the house.

Jamie holds his hand out to me. "Let's go, Penella. We can finish this conversation later." His voice is thick with promise, like he's already mentally rescheduling our shed rendezvous.

"There isn't a conversation to finish," I murmur, taking his hand and allowing him to lead me to the truck.

.   .   .

The ride to the restaurant is silent—not awkward, but close to it. Raindrops streak across the windows as we drive through the narrow island roads, the windshield wipers creating a hypnotic rhythm. The ocean appears in glimpses between hills, steel gray under the clouded sky. By the time we pull into the parking lot, I'm nearly vibrating with the need to escape the truck and the crackling tension between the three of us.

My body relaxes as we fall into the familiar rhythm of work, measuring and assessing the damage. But watching Jamie and Sammy move around the charred kitchen—the casual touches, the knowing glances, the silent communication—it becomes increasingly clear that I'm missing something big. Something that's been right in front of me all along.

"Okay, spill," I say when I catch Jamie smacking Sammy on the ass. The slap echoes in the empty kitchen, and I swear I feel it in my own body.

"Spill what?" Jamie asks, winking at Sammy before looking at me, very obviously holding back laughter.

"Are you gay?" I blurt. Filter? What filter? My brain-to-mouth connection is apparently running without supervision today.

He looks at me like I'm nuts.

Oh God. "Of course you aren't, you just—" I gesture vaguely with my hands, realizing too late that I'm basically pantomiming him squeezing my boobs.

"I'm bi, Penelope."

"Oh." That makes sense.

"Same," Sammy offers, smiling apologetically.

"And you two—?" I trail off.

"Fuck?" Jamie supplies.

"Yes, that." I rasp, desperately trying to ignore the vision of them that just popped into my head. Fucking hell. My imagination is suddenly working overtime, providing me with 4K-resolution scenes I did not ask for but am absolutely not rejecting.

"Sometimes." Sammy runs his hand back and forth over his short dreads, looking like he wishes he was anywhere but here having this conversation.

"What does that mean?"

"We like each other. We have fun." Jamie shrugs like it's the most simple thing in the world. Like he's explaining that water is wet or that the sky is blue.

"Friends with benefits?" I ask, looking between them.

"Maybe a little more than that," Sammy says, looking at Jamie for confirmation.

This is a lot. I'm happy for them, but I don't see how I can fit into their equation. Jamie was just acting like he wanted me. Was that just for fun? Was he teasing me? Leading me on? Making me the butt of some joke I don't understand?

"Don't," Jamie says, tipping my chin up and forcing me to look at him. "Don't overthink it. That beautiful brain of yours is going to short-circuit."

"I'm not. It's all good," I lie through my teeth. I'm definitely over-thinking it.

"Sam, come here," Jamie says, his gaze never leaving mine. Sammy approaches us, winding his hands around my stomach, pressing his chest to my back, trapping me between them.

"This is what we prefer," he says, his voice thick. "Having our cake and eating it too."

Fuck. I can't breathe. I feel like I'm caught in a very sexy sandwich, and I am definitely the filling. I turn toward Sammy, looking up into his warm brown eyes. "What about you?" I ask, feeling completely out of my element. Completely turned on.

"You are what I prefer, Penelope," he says softly, those big hands cupping my face. His thumbs brush gently over my cheekbones, the tenderness in his touch making my heart flutter like a caged bird.

"I saw you with Archer earlier," Jamie murmurs, his lips against my ear. His breath is warm, sending goosebumps cascading down my neck. The combined scent of both men—Jamie's spice and Sammy's clean, woody cologne—creates an intoxicating blend that makes my head swim.

"I—" What can I say? How do I explain that I slept in the same bed as him and then ran straight into Archer's arms?

"It's okay," he says, laughing at the look on my face. "All five of us have learned to share over the last three years. I'm sure we can learn to share you, too."

Oh fuck. Five men. Sharing. Sharing me. I need to sit down before my knees give out entirely.

6

SAM'S POV

I don't know what Jamie is playing at, but my heart can't handle this. Pen looks so cute, looking up at me with those wide hazel eyes, her hair curling around her face from the humidity, and wearing that ridiculous outfit. The purple-blue of her coveralls is almost blinding in the morning sun, those sheep-print wellies making her look like she's stepped out of a children's book. Like Little Bo Peep after a highlighter explosion.

This tiny slip of a woman has wormed her way into my heart over the last three years, and now there's no going back. I've been watching her when she thinks nobody is around. I've seen the way she looks at us. The quiet sighs. The rosy cheeks. The way she clenches her fists and turns away every time we get too close.

She's changed since the fire. It's like the second we moved in, her resolve disappeared. Like she couldn't remember why she was avoiding us. As if the walls she built around herself turned to ash along with the kitchen. I can tell by how she reacted to Jamie's comment about sharing that she's thought about it before. That she's open to it. And bloody hell, if that doesn't make me hard enough to cut glass. I can already see her spread out on the bed with Jamie's head between her legs. The image is so vivid it's like a painting in my mind, one I'd hang in a private gallery where only I could appreciate it.

"Sammy?" she asks, narrowing her eyes.

I come back to the present, realizing that Jamie has gone back to measuring, and it's just Pen and me, and her breasts brushing my ribs every time she inhales. Each innocent touch sends a volt of electricity through my body. Her warm summer scent wraps around me like a physical thing, making me light-headed. Like I'm drunk on her very presence.

"Sorry." I step back and close my eyes, scrubbing my hand over my lips, trying to erase the image of her that's now burned into my mind.

"Are you okay?" she asks, peering up at me, concern wrinkling her brow.

"I'm fine, boss," I say easily, smiling down at her. I'm not. I'm definitely not fine. My Oxford education didn't prepare me for this—the feeling of wanting someone so badly that it physically hurts.

"Don't lie."

"You're okay with what Jamie said?" I blurt.

"What part?" she asks, playing coy.

"The sharing part, Penelope."

"Ohhh. That part." She screws up her face, thinking hard before she gives her answer. She's so goddamned cute. Her nose scrunches up like a bunny, those freckles dancing across the bridge.

"Maybe? I haven't even done anything other than flirt with Liam or Spencer. Hell, I've only kissed one of you so far. Why are we even talking about sharing? Isn't that a little premature?"

"I think you know." I take her hands in mine, her skin pale and delicate against the roughness of my palms. Like porcelain against sandpaper. I force myself not to act like a jealous boyfriend and demand she tell me who she kissed. Not knowing makes my stomach twist like a dishrag being wrung out.

"I think I don't," she says stubbornly.

"You can't tell me you haven't thought about it—not with your brother being in a nontraditional relationship. Not with the way you look at all of us when you think we aren't watching."

"Thinking about it and doing it are two different things," she protests.

"So you're saying you have thought about it."

She juts her jaw, spins on her heel, and walks away from me. I catch her by the back of her coveralls, hauling her back to me, banding my arm around her stomach to keep her in place.

"I've thought about it," I confess, dropping my lips to the top of her head and breathing her in. "A lot."

"But we haven't even—"

"Haven't you ever wondered why I'm still here?" I ask, cutting her off. "I was only supposed to stay one summer, then go back to finish my master's. Remember? One summer that somehow stretched into three years."

"You said they kicked you out because of your grades!" she says, turning toward me, her eyes flashing.

"I lied."

"Sammy! Why would you give up your degree to work on a damn fishing boat?"

"I didn't. I gave up my degree because I couldn't bear to leave you. Because the thought of returning to Oxford felt hollow when compared to the possibility of seeing you each morning."

She covers her mouth with her hand, stricken. Like I've just told her I have six months to live. "I don't want to be the reason you gave up on your future."

"You gave me a future, boss."

She meets my gaze, emotions swimming in her eyes—fear, wonder, hope, desire. All of them darting just beneath the surface. "You have to stop calling me that if–if—"

"Okay," I say softly, pulling her into my arms. She's so small against me, I could almost wrap around her twice. The top of her head barely reaches my chest, and it feels like the most natural thing in the world to tuck her under my chin. Like she was designed to fit perfectly against me. "Do you like Pippa? Or Pip?"

She beams up at me. "Yes, I think I do."

"All right then, Pip. The next step is for all of us to get together and talk this through. And by 'talk,' I don't mean the stilted, awkward conversation that happens when everyone's pretending not to want what they want."

"I don't know if Spencer or Liam would be on board." She twists her necklace around her finger until the tip turns purple.

"Don't tell them I told you this, but Liam keeps a picture of you in his wallet, and Spencer has a picture of you as his screensaver on his phone. They're completely besotted with you, just like the rest of us."

"They what?" she whispers, gaping up at me.

I shrug. "We've been waiting a long time for this. If I had known all it would take was burning the kitchen down, I might have done it myself. Committed arson just for the chance to see what you look like first thing in the morning, with sleepy eyes, flushed cheeks and your hair all a mess."

The breeze picks up suddenly, carrying the scent of salt and heather from the nearby hills. Dark clouds gather on the horizon over the ocean—a storm coming in, but not soon enough to dampen my spirits. For now, the sun still warms us, glinting off her hair, turning the lighter strands to gold. She looks like some sort of sea nymph, standing here against the backdrop of the ocean she loves so much.

We both turn toward the sound of a car door slamming to see Millie walking toward us, lifting her sunglasses like she's having difficulty processing what she's seeing. Her timing is about as subtle as her perfume—which is to say, not at all. I release Penelope and go find Jamie, giving them some privacy.

"Hey, so that wasn't on my bingo card for today," I say softly, not wanting the girls to overhear me. I run my hand over my hair, a nervous habit I can't seem to break. "Some warning would have been nice, Jamie. I nearly swallowed my tongue when you mentioned sharing."

"Sorry I sprung that on you," he says, not looking sorry at all, "but this whole thing is coming to a head way faster than I anticipated. If she doesn't think we're interested, it'll be over before it starts. I don't want her to have a single doubt in her mind."

I bite down on a smile, watching him talk about the love of his life like she hung the damn moon. He's completely, irrevocably gone for her.

Truth is, we all are. Have been since the day she gave us that first tour of the boat.

She'd shown up in bubblegum pink coveralls, chicken print wellies, and dangly earrings that swung wildly every time she turned her head. Like she'd stepped straight out of a fever dream. Then there was the boat itself—"Master Baiter" painted in unapologetically bold letters across the hull, like she knew exactly what kind of reaction she'd get and dared us to say something.

She jumped aboard with this radiant kind of confidence, all lit up and grinning like we were the lucky ones. And honestly? We were.

I think I fell for her the second she started explaining how to coil a line with more enthusiasm than I'd ever seen anyone use for... anything. My protective instincts roared to life like they'd just been waiting for her. I've been completely smitten ever since.

Not that it's mattered. Not that I've done a damn thing about it.

Lately, she sees us coming and turns around like the tide's pulling her the other way. Always busy, always out of reach.

But it's the blush that gives her away. That soft, impossible pink that blooms high on her cheeks like a secret she doesn't want anyone to know. The way her breath stutters when I get too close. The way her hands tremble—just for a second—when ours brush.

And I cling to those tiny tells like a fool who hasn't learned better. Because I haven't. Because some part of me still hopes she'll stop running. That one day she'll look at me and stay.

"You're worried," Jamie says, because of course he does. He's always been good at stating the obvious with zero judgment. Like naming it somehow makes it lighter. Easier to carry.

"Yeah," I say, rubbing the back of my neck. "You could say that."

"Want to tell me why?"

I let out a breath that feels like it's been sitting in my chest for hours. "Now that it's out there... she can say no. And honestly? Who could blame her? What woman in her right mind would want this?" I gesture vaguely, like that'll somehow capture the chaos of five men, five different personalities, five different sets of needs.

Jamie just shrugs like I didn't just spiral into a full-blown existential panic. "She would."

I blink. "You're that sure?"

"She would've shut it down the second we brought it up if she didn't want it," he says. "But she didn't. She's scared, yeah. But who wouldn't be? She just needs time, Sam. We have to keep showing her it's worth the leap. That we're worth it. That she's worth it."

And then he grins—that slow, lazy grin that's always gotten me into trouble. The one that somehow makes everything feel less like a disaster and more like a promise.

Heat curls low in my stomach. Not for the first time, I'm reminded of the delicate, impossible balance Jamie and I have built. The quiet tenderness. The shared care. The way we orbit her—always together, always aligned. It shouldn't work.

And yet it does. Like a machine that shouldn't even run, but hums like it was made for this. The question now is whether she can slip into that rhythm with us, or if adding her will shatter the whole thing.

"Hi, boys!" Millie walks over to us, hand-in-hand with Penelope, and pulls off her sunglasses so she can look us in the eye. A cloud of sweet perfume announces her arrival seconds before she does, the scent almost comically at odds with her grease-stained clothes. Like someone sprayed a bouquet of flowers with motor oil.

"Hi, Millie," we say, echoing each other.

"Are you off to work?" I ask, eyeing her holey jeans and stained tank top.

"Yeah, my dad has a new car he's trying to get ready for a show in a month. It's all hands on deck until it's finished."

It still surprises me that Millie's a mechanic. If I had to guess, I would have said she was a hairdresser or maybe a makeup artist—never a mechanic. Never someone who could strip an engine apart and put it back together again with her eyes closed. Just goes to show you can't judge a book by its cover, especially when that cover is doused in enough perfume to asphyxiate a small village.

"Did he ever find the help he needed?" Jamie asks, bending down to tie his shoe.

"He ended up striking a deal with one of the automotive schools. They send over a batch of recent graduates every six months. It works for all of us—we get help, and they get experience. It seems to be working out well so far."

"That's amazing. You'll have to show us the car when it's finished."

"I'll make sure to drive it by before my dad takes it to the show." Her phone rings, and she pulls it from the back pocket of her jeans. "I better go. Take care of my girl." She drags her thumb across her throat, lifting her eyebrows to make sure we get her point.

"We always do," I say, unsure if I should laugh or be scared. The woman is five feet nothing but somehow manages to be more intimidating than a grizzly bear.

"Good." She gives me a look that says 'I know exactly what's going on here,' her eyes narrowing slightly. She turns to Penelope and hugs her tightly. "Have a good day, Penny Lou. Don't do anything I wouldn't do." She flounces to her car and peels out of the parking lot, leaving her perfume and a cloud of dust behind.

"I can't think of a single thing she wouldn't do," Pen says, laughing.

"Maybe that was her point," I suggest, a smile tugging at my lips.

She takes a deep breath. "Maybe it was." She looks between us, hope shining in the depths of her hazel eyes. Like stars peeking through clouds after a storm.

"We should probably talk about what this means—all of us," I say, my voice more serious than I intended. "Before things get complicated." I almost laugh at myself. Things have been complicated since day one.

"Tomorrow night?" she asks, her voice small, uncertain.

"Tomorrow," I confirm, fighting the urge to pull her back into my arms, to reassure her that whatever happens, we'll figure it out together. That five men who've managed to form a bond despite their differences can surely find a way to include her in that circle without it falling apart.

She nods, a blush creeping up her neck, painting her cheeks a pretty pink. There's fear in her eyes, but determination too. That's our girl—terrified but brave. Ready to jump off the cliff even while her knees are shaking. It's one of the countless reasons we all love her.

For the first time in three years, I feel the universe clicking back into place, like that perfect moment when the last puzzle piece slides home.

Penelope's POV

My head is still spinning when we get back to the house. Five guys. Five guys sharing me. It sounds like something out of one of those spicy romance novels, not something that happens in real life. But then again, nothing about my life is exactly conventional.

I ditch my wellies by the door and pad through the house to find Liam in the kitchen, his hands covered in flour as he kneads bread dough with an intensity that suggests it personally offended him.

"You okay there, champ?" I ask from the doorway, arms crossed, one brow arched. "That dough do something to personally offend you?"

Liam looks up, and just like that, bam—megawatt smile, full wattage. "Hey, Darlin'. Just taking my frustrations out on the sourdough. Figured if I've gotta feel this tightly wound, we might as well get something delicious out of it."

I step into the kitchen, letting the warmth and the scent of flour and citrus wrap around me. "And what's got you all wound up today?" I ask, even though I have a pretty good idea.

He gives me that look—you know the one. The you already know, stop making me say it out loud look.

"Archer said he walked in on you and Jamie this morning."

Oh.

Heat climbs up my neck. "It wasn't what it looked like."

"And what did it look like?" His tone is even, casual, but his hands are pounding that dough like it owes him money.

"Like we were... cozy," I say, wincing as the word comes out.

"Cozy," he repeats, flat. "Is that what we're calling it now?"

I roll my eyes and walk over, hopping up onto the counter like I don't have a hundred and ten feelings ping-ponging around inside me. "We didn't sleep together. If that's what you're asking. Not that it's any of your business."

He slams his palm into the dough with a thud. "Wouldn't it be, though?"

My breath catches. "Would it?"

He freezes. And then, slowly, he looks up at me, his face serious and open in a way that guts me a little. "That's what I'm trying to figure out. Because I can't keep pretending it doesn't kill me, watching you fall for everyone but me, when I've been in love with you since the day we met."

My heart drops straight to the floor, then ricochets off the tile like a pinball.

"What did you just say?"

"You heard me," he says, eyes dropping back to the dough like he didn't just detonate my whole morning.

I slide off the counter and step close enough to feel his warmth. "Liam..."

He doesn't look at me.

"God, you are the most ridiculously stubborn man alive," I mutter, grabbing his flour-dusted jaw and turning it toward me.

"That's rich coming from you," he says, but he's smiling now—soft and crooked, with those smile lines I love a little too much.

"I'm going to hold a house meeting tomorrow night. For all of us. We're gonna talk about... this. Whatever this is."

He hesitates. "Am I gonna like what I hear?"

I push up on my tiptoes and press a kiss to his lips. It tastes like salt and flour and hope. "I don't know," I whisper. "But I think you might."

He stares at me like I've just set fire to every plan he's ever had—and he kind of likes it. Then that grin spreads across his face like the sun breaking through the clouds. "If you're messing with me, Darlin', I swear I'll—"

"You'll what?" I tease, my voice light, even though my chest is tight with the weight of what I just admitted.

"I'll think of something," he says, grabbing my waist with those floury hands and pulling me in.

"Oh no. So scared," I deadpan.

"You should be," he says, low and rough, and then he's kissing me like the kitchen's spinning and I'm the only thing holding him upright.

This kiss is different from Archer's. Where Archer kissed like he was claiming territory, Liam kisses like he's discovering it—slow but thorough, taking his time as if we have all the time in the world. His lips are soft, and he tastes like the coffee he must have been drinking earlier. It's sweet and unhurried and perfect.

When he pulls back, his eyes are dark, and there's flour all over both of us.

"Well, shit," comes a deep voice from the doorway.

We both turn to see Spencer standing there looking like he just walked in on someone kicking his puppy.

"Spence—" I start, but he holds up a hand.

"Don't mind me," he drawls. "Just passing through." He turns to leave, his broad shoulders tense.

"Spencer, wait!" I call, breaking away from Liam and hurrying after him. I catch him in the hallway, grabbing his arm. "It's not what you think."

"Pretty sure it's exactly what I think, Darlin'," he says, not unkindly. "I've seen kissing before. Know what it looks like."

"No, I mean—" I struggle to find the words. "We're having a house meeting tomorrow night. All of us. To talk about this... situation."

His eyebrow raises. "Situation? That's what we're calling it?"

"I don't know what to call it," I admit. "But I need you there."

He studies me for a long moment, his dark eyes seeing right through me the way they always do. Finally, he nods. "I'll be there. But Penelope?" His voice drops to that low rumble that always makes my toes curl. "If this is going where I think it's going, you should know I don't share well."

I swallow hard. "Noted."

I watch him walk away then collapse against the wall, suddenly exhausted. Four down, one to go.

7

I toss and turn for two hours before finally giving up on sleep. My brain's stuck on repeat, playing back the day's conversations like I'm binge-watching the most awkward reality show ever. All five of them. Me. Together. Holy mother of Mary. It's like my mind's running a slideshow of R-rated possibilities, and let me tell you, my imagination deserves an Oscar for special effects.

I fumble my way down the hallway in the dark, praying I can flip on the kitchen light without waking whoever drew the short straw for couch duty tonight. The last thing I need is another awkward encounter to add to my growing collection, at this rate, I'll be able to publish an anthology before the end of summer. The floorboards creak softly beneath my feet, the sound amplified in the stillness of the house. The distant crash of waves against the shore filters through the windows, a rhythmic backdrop to the quiet night. A fine mist of rain has started, pattering softly against the window panes, carrying the scent of brine and wet earth.

I'm about to sneak into the kitchen when something moves in my peripheral vision. For a second, I freeze. Maybe it's just shadows? Maybe it's Pearl shifting in her beauty sleep? Then I hear a soft groan from the couch that instantly disproves both theories, and I step back so fast you'd think the floor was lava, heat flooding my cheeks like I've face-planted into the sun. I bump into something hard, a rough hand coming up to clamp over my mouth before I can scream.

"Shh, Nel. You don't want him to know you're watching," Archer rumbles, his voice like gravel wrapped in velvet.

I shake my head, wanting to tell him I wasn't watching, but he keeps his hand firmly in place. My traitorous eyes, however, have other plans. They're drawn back to the rhythmic movement, and now that I know what it is, I can vaguely make out the shape of a hand jerking up and down. The back of the couch is too high for me to see who the hand belongs to, but my imagination fills in the blanks with high-definition clarity. The next moan has desire hitting me like a freight train, need burning through my veins like top-shelf whiskey. After three years of keeping everyone at arm's length—hell, more like football-field length—the sudden proximity is intoxicating. Like I've been surviving on water and someone just handed me champagne.

"You like what you see, don't you?" he whispers, his lips pressed to my ear.

My breath catches in my throat as he drags his free hand up my body, staying just shy of my breasts. His body radiates heat behind me, the scent of his skin making my head swim. The calluses on his hands catch slightly against my thin tank top, rough from years of hauling nets and tying knots that could survive a hurricane.

"Answer me, Penelope," he demands, his hand hovering, telling me exactly what he'll do when I answer him.

I whimper softly, nodding.

"Good girl," he whispers, palming my breast, memorizing the shape and weight before pinching and rolling my nipple between his fingers.

Another groan comes from the couch, creating a shockwave of lust that feels like an electrical current running from my ears straight to my core. My back bows as I push into Archer's hand.

"Want more?" he rasps, pulling me closer, his cock digging into my ass.

I should say no. This is when mature, responsible Penelope should slam on the brakes and retreat to her room for a cold shower and a TED talk on housemate boundaries. But I watch that shadow hand pause, making a slow pass, revealing a cock standing tall and proud in the middle of my living room. The voice in my head that's been chanting "professional distance" for three years suddenly goes radio silent. Like it packed an overnight bag and took off without even leaving a sticky note.

"God, yes," I mumble against Archer's palm.

"Touch yourself," he demands.

Oh my God. He didn't just—

"Touch. Yourself." Each word hits like a hammer on hot metal.

I slide my hand over my stomach and inside my shorts, choking back a moan as I drag my finger along my slit. I'm so wet I could probably solve Spain's drought problem, my fingers dipping inside to tease that spot that makes my toes curl.

"That's my girl," Archer breathes, his cock throbbing with need.

I slide my fingers to my clit, circling it, rocking against my hand. Every nerve ending in my body is firing SOS signals, like they've been hibernating for years and suddenly woke up starving. Archer palms my arm, following it down until he gets to the waistband of my shorts.

"Let me help you, Nel," he begs, uncovering my mouth to allow me to speak.

"Please, Archer," I whimper. For once in my control-freak life, I'm exhausted from calling all the shots. The relief of surrendering hits like a drug, making my head spin and my knees weak.

He has his hand back over my mouth half a second later, his other hand diving between my legs. I gasp as he covers my hand with his, his fingers alongside mine.

"Christ, you're soaked," he growls, his breath hot against my cheek.

I grind against our hands, a moan building in my throat as I get closer, the tension boiling so tight it's almost unbearable. My heart lurches to my throat as the person on the couch shifts, disappearing from view.

"Spence," Archer calls out.

I yank my hand out of my shorts so fast you'd think it caught fire, shrinking back against Archer, completely mortified. Spencer's head pops above the back of the couch, his face covered in shadow.

"Our girl here likes watching," Archer says, throwing me under the bus without a second thought. "Tell him what you want, Penelope." Archer moves his hand to my throat, his other hand still inside my shorts, his fingers brushing lightly over my pussy.

Fuck. I don't know if I can do this.

I take a deep breath. "I want to watch you come," I say, my voice cracking as my libido steamrolls right over my dignity. I can't believe this is happening.

Spencer looks between me and Archer, unsure at first. A flicker of concern crosses his face—the nurturing side that makes him cook enough food to feed an army, the part of him that's always sliding extra food onto my plate when he thinks I'm not looking.

"Please," I rasp, gasping as Archer finally presses his fingers over my clit.

"Sweet Jesus, Sugar," Spencer groans in that same molasses-slow voice he uses every time he talks to me, the kind that makes you want to lick the words right out of his mouth.

He pushes himself to his feet, walking closer, pausing in a shaft of moonlight. He drops his boxers to the floor and then looks back up at me, shaggy hair falling over his eyes. I watch in a daze as he spits on his hand and wraps it around his cock, sliding it back and forth, his abs jumping with every stroke. The moonlight traces his body like a spotlight, highlighting every ridge and valley like he's a freaking Greek statue come to life.

Oh God. I tense in Archer's grip, moaning as he fits three fingers over me, sliding them back and forth, timed perfectly with Spencer's strokes. I clamp my thighs around his hand, watching the head of Spencer's cock disappear inside his fist, then slowly make its way back out, swollen and angry. God, I want him. In my mouth. In me. On me. Sideways, backwards, upside-down—any configuration he's willing to offer. My desire isn't just knocking at the door anymore—it's kicked it down and set up camp.

"Eyes on me, Penelope," Spencer demands, his voice rough.

I meet his gaze, desire sparking along my nerve endings.

"Fuck," he groans, his face crumpling, his hips flexing, cum shooting in ropes, painting the hardwood. It's the most erotic thing I've ever seen.

My core spasms, and I come hard, bucking against Archer's fingers. The orgasm crashes through me like a tidal wave, sweeping away everything in its path—my inhibitions, my boundaries, probably my ability to ever look either of them in the eye again. He slides his other hand back up to my mouth, muffling my cries as I grind on him, which is probably for the best because otherwise I'd be waking up the rest of the house and tomorrow we'd be fielding noise complaints while sitting down to breakfast.

"Good fucking girl," he growls, his cock jumping against my ass as he brings me down slowly. The praise sends another aftershock through me, reminding me of how Jamie's "good girl" in the kitchen earlier had turned my legs to jelly. Apparently those two words are my kryptonite—my own personal self-destruct button.

Spencer approaches us, his gaze dark. He picks up my hand, holding it to his nose. "Were you touching yourself while you were standing in the dark watching me?" He doesn't wait for my answer before taking each of my fingers into his mouth and swirling his tongue over them.

I groan as his eyes roll back like it's the best thing he's ever tasted. My breath catches in my throat as he swipes his thumb over the head of his cock and spreads the drop of cum over my lips.

"If I wasn't dead set on taking this slow with you, I'd be dropping to my knees and eating you out while Archer here keeps you from waking the whole damn island," he says softly, dangerously. His hands tremble slightly as they cup my face, like he's holding onto his control by a thread so thin it might snap if I so much as breathe wrong.

Slow? This is his version of slow? This feels like I'm strapped to a rocket with no hope of return. Three years of tension unraveling in seconds, like a rope pulled too tight finally snapping. Like a dam breaking after years of holding back the water.

And then his lips are on mine, his tongue sliding into my mouth, our tastes blending into our very own vintage. The kiss is hot, demanding, thorough—the kind that ruins you for all other kisses. My knees sag, but Archer only strengthens his grip, holding me up for Spencer to plunder. The taste of him is intoxicating—warm, male, with hints of the whiskey he must have had earlier and something uniquely

Spencer that I'd recognize blindfolded. The contrast between Spencer's soft lips and Archer's rough grip is dizzying, a perfect balance of tenderness and control. Like being caught between a thunderstorm and a soft summer rain. By the time Spencer pulls away, my breathing is ragged, my body thrumming, ready for more.

"You should sleep like a baby now, Nel. Just holler next time you need help," Archer says, his voice hoarse. He presses his hips against me, his cock digging into my ass one last time, before he releases me, slapping my butt as I stumble away down the hallway. If I had an ounce of courage left, I'd grab both of them by their waistbands and drag them into my bedroom. But my bravery meter's running on empty, so I retreat to my room without looking back like the good girl they think I am. A very satisfied, very confused good girl with an identity crisis.

I face-plant onto my bed, my body humming with satisfaction, my mind racing. The dynamic has officially gone nuclear. Tomorrow, I'll have to face them across the breakfast table, pretending this didn't change everything. I'll have to look Spencer in the eye while remembering the taste of him on my tongue. I'll have to stand next to Archer, knowing exactly what he feels like pressed against me. And I'll have to face the others, wondering if they know, if they heard, if they're waiting for their turn. My body throbs at the thought.

What the hell have I started? And more importantly, do I have what it takes to see it through?

8

———————

I wasn't sure what to expect when I tiptoed out of my room that morning. Morning sun filters through the windows, bringing with it the distant cry of seagulls and the scent of salt air.

Archer has positioned himself so that he's first to see me as I amble toward the kitchen, a slow grin spreading across his face, his glasses perched on the end of his nose as he looks up from his clipboard. My stomach flip-flops as I look around for Spencer.

He's at the stove, facing away from me, an apron tied around his bare torso, boxers slung low across his hips. Holy mother of hotness. Desire rips through my body, making my knees wobble. Memories from last night flash through my mind like a spicy movie montage.

Fuck me sideways. I feel like I can't breathe.

A line forms between Archer's eyebrows, but I don't stop to explain. I head straight past the kitchen and out the front door. The door closes softly behind me several moments later, footsteps crunching in the gravel.

"Archer, I—"

"Not Archer," Spencer says, his drawl wrapping around me like a warm blanket on a cold morning. I spin on my heel, looking him in the eye for the first time since he painted my lips with his cum, my heart in my throat, the incessant pounding between my legs hard to ignore.

Christ on a cracker, it should be illegal to look this good before breakfast. Golden scruff glints on his cheeks, his shaggy hair begging me to run my fingers through it, those impossibly blue eyes watching me cautiously. He reaches behind him and unties the apron, pulling it off and then holding it awkwardly in front of him.

"I'm sorry," he says finally, his gaze dropping to the ground.

"Sorry?" I echo, confused.

"Sugar, I don't know what I was thinking last night. It was like some erotic dream that I couldn't wake up from."

"I was the one watching you, Spencer. I'm the one that should be sorry."

"Yeah, but—"

"You didn't do anything wrong. I told you I wanted to watch."

"And then I jizzed all over your floor," he mutters, looking down, a blush blooming over his cheeks.

"And I've never been more turned on in my life," I reply, holding his gaze.

Something changes in him: a slight shift in his shoulders, the angle of his jaw, his eyes darkening. Like watching a switch flip from gentleman to sex God in 0.2 seconds. "Did you like when I painted your lips with my cum, Sugar?"

"Yes," I croak.

"I always thought you were too good for us, but you're not, are you?" he asks, his gaze dropping to my lips.

"Rude."

"You're filthy." He steps closer, and I grab the apron to give my hands something to do. He jerks it toward his body, pulling me against him. "You liked me watching Archer finger you."

"And you liked watching him do it."

"Hell yeah, I sure fucking did." He runs his thumb over my lower lip, gasping as I sink my teeth into his skin. He growls, hooking his thumb on my teeth and pulling my mouth to his. He tugs my jaw down, opening my mouth, allowing his tongue to slide right in. I moan, pushing my hands into his hair and tugging him closer.

"Why do I feel like we all just wasted the last three years?" he asks, pulling back to look me in the eyes. Something close to panic flits over his features.

"Wasted? I wouldn't call it that. I'd like to think we all know what we want now."

"Yeah?" he sweeps my hair away from my face, trailing his fingers over my cheeks. "And what is it you want, Penelope Grace?"

"All five of you," I say clearly, squaring my shoulders, knowing this is my chance, and I'm sure as hell going to take it.

"All five of us?"

"Did I fucking stutter?"

The corner of his mouth kicks up. "And what about Sammy and Jamie? That doesn't scare you?" His voice is concerned but his face says he already knows the answer, like he's asking me if I'm afraid of puppies.

"Should it?"

"No. They both head over heels for you. We all are."

"Good," I say softly, my heart in my throat.

"How is this going to work exactly?" he asks, scratching his jaw.

A snort escapes me. "Fuck if I know. I still haven't talked to Liam and I don't want to just spring it on him when we all talk tonight. I haven't even kissed Jamie or Sammy yet. It feels like everything is incredibly fragile right now. It's scaring the hell out of me."

"Why don't you and Liam do the grocery shopping together? That'll give you the time you need."

"But how do I bring up all of this? What if he misunderstands?"

"Sugar, that man's been looking at you like you're the last biscuit in the basket for years. Have a little faith in yourself. You've managed to get the point across to the rest of us. He probably already has an idea, anyway."

"Fine. I can do this." I bounce up and down on my toes like I'm getting ready to run a marathon, nerves attacking my stomach like a rabid eclipse of moths. "Not like I'm about to ask a hot-as-hell cowboy to join my harem or anything." I turn away to walk back inside, but he grabs my t-shirt and hauls me right back.

"Last night is not how I would have chosen to start things off. I'd like a do-over," he says softly, cradling my face in his hand.

I look into his eyes, at the gold streaking through the blue, the crinkles in the corners.

"Okay," I whisper, my heart pounding.

"Penelope, will you be my girlfriend?"

"Wow, moving fast there, Romeo. Making it official already?" I ask, trying not to act like a giddy teenager.

"Only three years late."

"Yes, I'll be your girlfriend, Spencer."

"Sweet baby Jesus, thank you." He steps back, bending over, his hands on his knees. "God, I feel like I'm either going to puke or pass out." He grabs my hand, holding it to his chest, his heartbeat hammering under my fingers.

"Are you okay?" I ask, biting my lip to keep from grinning like a fool.

"I'm losing my damn mind. I was so fucking nervous you were going to say no. My stomach feels like it's doing the Macarena."

"Why were you nervous?"

"You're the most important thing in my world, Sugar. Promise me that this—all of this—isn't going to change anything."

"I can't do that. This is going to change everything, Spencer."

He groans, staggering away several steps, turning away from me before gagging.

I burst out laughing. Here I am, getting my happy ending, and the man I just agreed to date is about to throw up from anxiety. "It'll be fine, I promise!" I assure him, rubbing his back.

"Will it, though? I'd rather have unrequited love for the rest of my life than lose you."

"But how will we know if we don't try?" I ask, the seriousness of the situation settling over my shoulders.

"We won't," he says simply, looking at me, his gaze tracing my features like he's trying to commit this moment to memory. "What if we're asking too much of you?"

"What if I'm asking too much from you?" I ask, turning his question around. "To share a relationship when there's one of me and five of you? I'm the one being selfish, Spencer."

"Sugar, you're about as selfish as a saint at a soup kitchen."

I chuckle. "I feel so many big emotions when it comes to you guys. It's terrifying. Why do you think I avoided all of you as much as possible? I've been running from this like it's a zombie apocalypse and you're all infected."

"That's why?" he asks, his shoulders relaxing. "I thought you couldn't stand us."

"And the Academy Award goes to me! I'll take my Oscar now, thank you."

"You deserve one after that."

"Just wait till you hear how I burned down the bunkhouse on purpose. I wanted an excuse to get you all in my house. The fish and chips were just a diversion."

His eyes bug out of his head, and I nearly fold in half, suffocating on my laughter, tears streaming down my cheeks.

"Hellfire, you scared me there for a second," he says, looking at me askance like he's still trying to be sure I was kidding.

"All I wanted was some damn fish and chips. And you know what? I still haven't gotten any."

"We'll have to remedy that quickly. I'd hate for you to resort to arson again. The neighbors might start to talk." He pulls me into his arms, looking down at me with his soulful eyes, making me feel all warm and fuzzy. "Thank you for opening your house for us, Sugar. Things wouldn't have come to a head if we had found somewhere else to stay. I'll always be thankful for your late-night cravings." He kisses me softly, his scruff tickling my lips, making me shiver, the lingering taste of coffee on his tongue. "Come on, let's go back inside so you can convince Liam it's worth the risk."

Spencer twines his fingers through mine and pulls me toward the house, stopping short when we see Liam standing ten feet away, his leather outback hat jammed down on his forehead.

"Convince me what's worth the risk?" he asks, his gaze drifting to our hands before looking me in the face. I can see the hurt behind his eyes, and it makes my heart ache. He shifts uncomfortably, his jaw clenching as he waits for my response.

"Do you want to go shopping with me today? I can explain then."

"With you, Darlin'? Always." His voice is tight, but he tries to smile, those dimples I love making a brief appearance despite the tension radiating from him.

"Okay, give me twenty minutes."

I retreat to my room, my heart fluttering with a mixture of excitement and anxiety. Five men. One me. What am I, collecting them like Pokémon? How could this possibly work? And yet the thought of choosing just one makes my chest ache, like being asked to pick a favorite limb to keep. I sink onto my bed, the sheets still rumpled from my restless night, and try to imagine what I'll say to Liam. How do I tell him that I want all of them—that I need all of them—without sounding greedy or uncertain?

I pick up my phone and create a group chat with everyone, fully aware this might be the last moment of peace and quiet I get before the chaos begins.

Me: What does everyone need from the store? I need the ingredients for your weekly meal and anything else I need to replace from the fire

Archer: What was that thing you gave me last night? It tasted like...

Spencer: Jesus fucking Christ

Me: I don't think they sell that at the store, Archer

Liam: What did I miss?

Liam: Hello?

Jamie: Fucking hell, we need stuff for salad, sliced cheese, ground beef and buns.

Sammy: Buns?

Jamie: 🙄

Liam: I definitely missed something. Pen, is this what you wanted to talk to me about?

Me: Something like that.

Archer: I want to make something incredibly juicy. Any ideas?

Archer: Roast chicken with a banana cream pie for dessert?

ARCHER HAS LEFT THE CONVERSATION

Me: Okay, who kicked Archer out?

ARCHER HAS JOINED THE CONVERSATION

Me: Behave, Archer

Archer: Yes, ma'am 😏

Sammy: I'll make bangers and mash

Jamie: Jesus yeah, you will. 😈

Sammy: for fuck's sake, man

Me: Spencer, just waiting on you

Archer: He could make chicken alfredo. He just has to be sure not to spill it on the floor this time

I throw my phone face down on the bed before anyone else responds, the morning light streaming through my bedroom window catching on Pearl's fur as she jumps up to join me. I bury my fingers in her scraggly coat, seeking comfort in her solid warmth. She settles beside me with a contented sigh, her presence steadying my racing thoughts.

My heart is thundering in my chest. My cheeks hurt from grinning. What the actual hell was I so scared of? This is going to be the best year of my life. I just know it. Or possibly the biggest disaster since the Titanic hit that iceberg—but either way, it'll be memorable.

9

___

"**D**arlin', rip the bandaid off. You know you want to." Liam looks over at me from the driver's seat, one hand on the steering wheel, the other on the seat between us, his sun-kissed skin practically glowing.

"What are you talking about?" I ask, playing dumb like the chicken I am and refusing to look at him. My fingers fidget with a loose thread on my coveralls like it's suddenly the most fascinating thing ever created.

"Yes, you do," he says softly.

When he doesn't say anything else, I cave and sneak a glance over at him, immediately regretting it when I'm hit full-force with the whole package—the leather outback hat tilted over his face, the corner of his mouth pulled up into that damn smirk, the light smattering of freckles over the bridge of his nose. The man literally looks like he just walked off the set of an Australian tourism commercial. Like, hey there, mate, come visit the outback and you too could meet a sexy cowboy who'll make your lady parts tingle.

"Liam..." The words catch in my throat, my pulse hammering against my ribs like it's trying to escape.

He reaches over, sliding his hand over my thigh, squeezing gently, the touch sending lightning bolts straight between my legs.

"I..." Fuck. Why is this so impossible? I pinch the bridge of my nose, trying to pull myself together. I've faced down angry customers and kitchen fires, but this? This scares me. Maybe because he's soft and sweet, and I can't bear to see disappointment in those warm brown eyes.

The truck slows as he pulls over onto the side of the road, the tires crunching on gravel. He hops out, walks around to my side, opens the door, and stands there patiently. Like he has all the time in the world. Like we're not literally parked on the edge of a cliff—both figuratively and literally.

"I want to kiss you, Penelope, but I want you to say what you have to say first, on the off chance it has something to do with our walk the other evening."

"I don't want you to kiss me until I've told you, either," I say, my heart practically doing the mambo in my throat.

His face falls, those gorgeous warm brown eyes shielded from view by the brim of his hat as he looks down at his boots.

"It's not what you're thinking, Liam!" I practically shriek, grabbing his chin and yanking it until his gaze meets mine, hurt creasing his face.

"I like you," I blurt. "A lot."

"Thank God," he whispers, looking up at the sky, swallowing hard. "You had me thinking the worst."

"I don't care what it is, then. Please say I can kiss you. We can have this conversation after."

I'm about as strong-willed as a melting popsicle when it comes to this man. "Come here," I murmur, pulling him closer. His gaze dips to my mouth, a small puff of breath grazing my cheek as he exhales, the scent of leather and sandalwood enveloping me.

"Liam..." I groan, impatient.

"I've been waiting three fucking years for this, Darlin'. Don't rush me."

I close my eyes, mentally recording the way the roughness of his palm feels against my cheek, the sweep of calloused fingertips along my eyebrow. He presses between my knees, pulling at my chin with his thumb, his gaze pinned to my mouth like it's the last lifeboat on a sinking ship.

"If you're going to take your time, how about I go ahead and say what I need to say?" I suggest, my nerves getting the best of me.

He nods once. "Okay. Let's go for a walk while you tell me. I think it'll help."

"Good idea." I blow out a slow breath, trying to steady my heart as he helps me out of the truck. He grabs my hand, pushing his fingers between mine before guiding me to a trail on the other side of the road.

We walk side by side for several minutes, the breeze carrying the scent of heather and salt, the distant cry of gulls punctuating our silence. I finally decide there's no pretty way to say this.

"I like you, Liam. A lot," I say, echoing my earlier words. "I also like Spencer. And Sammy. And Archer. And Jamie." I look over at him, and the bastard is just looking at me with a wide-ass smirk on his face.

"I like them, too, Darlin'."

"You know what I mean."

"Sure do," he drawls, grinning, those dimples flashing in the sunlight like they've got their own spotlight.

Silence.

"Well?" I ask.

"Well, what? Did you think I'd be mad? I've lived with them for three years, Pen. They're great guys. I'd have to be an idiot not to see what you see in them."

"But..."

"There are no buts."

Jesus Christ. "How are all of you just okay with this?" I ask, perplexed. I sure as hell wouldn't be okay sharing any of them with another woman. Which is totally unfair and hypocritical, but whatever. My jealous streak runs wider than the Scottish highlands and twice as wild.

"Am I the last to know?" he asks, hooking a finger in my pocket and tugging me closer.

"Yes. It's just the way it worked out. I'm sorry."

"There's nothing to be sorry for. If Jamie hadn't interrupted us on our walk the other night, maybe I would have been the first." He studies my features, his eyes sparkling with pent-up laughter.

"I don't understand," I say, shaking my head.

"Understand what?"

"How can you just be okay with it?"

"How can I not when I see how happy they make you?"

"That doesn't make you jealous?"

He barks out a sharp laugh. "I'm jealous of those coveralls, Darlin', because they get to touch you in ways I never thought I'd get the chance to. And your wellies—even those ridiculous chicken ones—I'm jealous of them too, just for being on your feet. I'm jealous of the air you breathe, the ground you walk on. But that's just how it is for me. If I've managed for three years, I can handle it for a lifetime, as long as I get to be with you."

His words wrap around my chest and squeeze until I can barely breathe. How the hell does he make jealousy sound like the most beautiful thing? Like a poem or a sonnet instead of a bitter pill. The complexity of what we're attempting suddenly hits me—five separate relationships with five distinctly different men, all tangled together like fishing nets. What if I can't balance them all? What if someone always feels left out?

Fuck. I blink back tears, running my fingertip over the shell of his ear, down to his earrings, gently tugging on them, my focus solidly on his mouth. His mustache has grown out a little more and it's the hottest damn thing I've ever seen in my life. How does he have such perfectly full lips? Like they were designed specifically for kissing. And... other things.

"Stop staring and do something about it," he challenges, his voice dropping to a gravelly whisper.

My self-control snaps like a dry twig in a drought. It's like flipping a switch—from hesitant to hungry in 0.2 seconds flat. I attack him like I haven't eaten in days and he's a five-course meal, fitting my mouth over his, angling my head as I sweep my tongue over his lips.

He hauls me into his arms, his groan adding to the wave of desire pulsing through my body. Pulling back suddenly, he cups my face between his hands, looking at me like he's trying to convince himself this isn't some cruel dream before kissing me again. I savor it this time. Savor the tenderness in his touch, the slow brush of his lips, the way they pull back into a disbelieving smile before covering mine again.

His kiss is devastatingly slow, like he has all the time in the world to memorize me. Like he's kissing me with intention, not urgency. With devotion. His lips brush over mine in soft, measured passes, while his hands—rough and sea-worn—frame my jaw as if I'm something breakable.

The contrast nearly undoes me. Calloused fingers. Tender mouth. Gentle and consuming all at once. Time collapses. I don't know if it's been thirty seconds or the entire goddamn day. Just that I could stay here—anchored in him—for however long he'll let me. When I finally break the kiss, my chest is heaving and my heart feels like it's trying to claw its way out of my ribcage.

"Fuck, Liam." The words tumble out, barely more than a breath. A prayer. A warning. A confession.

"I'm not done yet," he practically purrs, his lips ghosting over my cheek, my jaw, my neck. "God, I wish you had told me this at the house. Where there's a bed."

"Moving a little fast, are we?" I try to laugh, but it comes out as a gasp as he drags his tongue over my collarbone.

"Fast?" He chuckles, the sound vibrating through me, making my nipples stand at attention. "This isn't fast, Darlin'."

He's right. It feels like we've been waiting for this forever. Fast would have been falling into bed with him in the first few weeks I knew him. Now, there are three years of conversations. Three years of looks. Three years of yearning to catch up on. Three years of "what ifs" demanding answers.

He grabs my waist, holding me tightly, his hands slowly inching down.

"Do you think we should, uh, get to the store?" I ask, breathless and clinging to the last thread of my self-control. If we don't leave now, we're absolutely going to end up naked and panting in the middle of a farmer's field, with the sea breeze doing nothing to cool the wildfire we just started.

He grins, all heat and cocky promise. "If we're pressing pause, just know this isn't over. Not even close. If I'm the last one to figure it out, that means you've already spent more time with the others. It's my turn now."

His turn. Something about the way he says it—possessive and a little growly—makes my knees feel like boiled spaghetti.

"Y-yes, sir," I whisper, and oh God, who even am I right now? Because part of me wants to drop to my knees in the dirt and beg him not to wait another second.

He grabs my hand instead, lacing our fingers tight, like he's afraid I might disappear. "Hope you're ready for me to have my hands on you every chance I get," he says, dragging me back up the path toward the truck. "Three years, Penelope. That's how long I've been dying to touch you. Torture doesn't even begin to cover it."

"You've really liked me for three years?" I ask as I climb into the truck, trying—and failing—not to inhale like a weirdo when he leans across me to buckle my seatbelt. He smells like soap and leather and something warm I can't quite name. Probably heartbreak. Probably home.

"Yes, Penelope," he says, voice low and sure. "I don't think it's possible not to fall for you. You're the kindest, funniest, most genuine person I've ever met. I knew the second I saw you that I was screwed."

"So what was the plan?" I ask as he slides into the driver's seat. "Just... never act on it? Hope I'd never notice?"

He exhales hard through his nose, hands tightening on the steering wheel. "It was complicated."

"How?"

"We all fell. Hard. And none of us wanted to be the one who tore your life apart just to satisfy our own selfish need to have you."

I blink at him, then deadpan, "So what I'm hearing is, I should've burned the kitchen down a long time ago."

He finally turns to me, eyes crinkling as he reaches for my hand again. His fingers thread through mine like it's the most natural thing in the world. "Something like that."

. . .

I stare out the window at the steel-gray waters of the North Atlantic. Wind slips through the small crack at the top, sharp and briny, cutting straight to the bone. The ocean doesn't waver. Not ever. It just keeps going—steady, relentless, indifferent. The one constant in a life that suddenly feels like it's been thrown in a blender without the lid.

The restaurant, my relationships, my entire concept of what love means—it's all shifting beneath my feet. Transforming. Like a butterfly shedding its cocoon, maybe. But messier. Hornier. And with five potential soulmates instead of one.

By the time we finally pull into the village store, the sky's gone from moody to straight-up dramatic. Of course. Nature's a sucker for a love story too.

The shopping trip takes twice as long as it should, because apparently, we've entered our teenage rom-com era. Lingering touches when we both reach for the oatcakes. Stolen glances that say way more than either of us is ready to admit. Liam keeps brushing past me like the aisles are half the size they actually are, like he needs the excuse to feel my body against his. Spoiler: he doesn't.

When we finally make it to the checkout, the elderly cashier looks between us, then gives me a knowing smile so smug it might as well be winking. And just like that, my face goes full tomato. Pretty sure I could fry an egg on my cheeks. Possibly two. With a side of bacon.

Out at the truck, we tuck the cold groceries into the cooler, and I'm just about to climb into the passenger seat when Liam turns to me. His brow is furrowed, but not in a bad way—in a thinking very serious thoughts about undressing you slowly kind of way.

"I'm not ready to share you yet," he says.

I freeze, one foot on the running board, stomach flipping like a carnival ride. "No?" I manage, my voice suddenly about three octaves too high.

He takes a step closer, the sea breeze tugging at his hair. "What do you think about grabbing some lunch and then parking somewhere a little more private?"

Oh.

Oh God.

"Th-that sounds good," I croak, heart now firmly lodged in my throat, possibly doing somersaults just for fun.

Ten minutes later, we're pulling up to a roadside fish and chips stand, the kind with hand-painted signs and the heavenly smell of hot oil floating in the breeze.

Liam shoots me a grin, the kind that makes my toes curl in my boots. "Ready for that fish and chips, finally?"

I let out a huff of laughter. "I've only burned down a kitchen and a bunkhouse and waited three whole days to get it. No big deal."

We find a spot at a weathered picnic table, its paint sun-bleached and peeling, overlooking the kind of Scottish shoreline that looks like it was painted by a God in a wistful mood. The sea is sparkling. Taunting, really, like it knows something we haven't dared to say out loud yet.

The air is thick with salt, vinegar, and something that might just be hope. Or maybe that's indigestion. Hard to tell when your heart's doing cartwheels and you're two seconds away from making out in public next to a fish stand.

We're quiet for a moment—the kind of quiet that settles deep, like a warm coat around your shoulders. The waves crash against the rocks in a rhythm so steady, it feels like a stand-in for my heartbeat. Except mine's erratic and dramatic and absolutely losing it over the man sitting across from me.

Liam hands me a tray piled high with golden fried bliss. We both go feral on the vinegar like it's a competition, and the first bite? Holy. Hell.

Hot, crisp batter. Flaky white fish. Actual heaven on a paper plate.

"This place is my go-to when I'm craving it and it's not on the restaurant menu," Liam says, tossing a chip to a seagull who snatches it out of midair like it's auditioning for Top Gun. Then his tone shifts, softer. "Have you thought about how this is going to work?"

He pulls off his hat and sets it beside him on the bench. Something about the gesture feels intimate. Real.

"Up until a couple hours ago, I didn't even know there was something to figure out," I admit, sipping my drink like it might drown the nerves churning in my stomach. "Have you guys talked about it?"

"No. That's not something for us to decide." His gaze finds mine. "It has to come from you, Pen."

I break a chip in half, watching the steam curl into the air like it might spell out the answers I don't have. "It should be a decision all of us make together."

"I agree," he says, "but you get the final call. This is your heart. Your body."

I let out a sigh so deep it feels like it drags the entire weight of the earth with it. "I don't even know what the options are. I was scared to imagine it too clearly—like I'd jinx it or wake up and it'd all be gone."

"Well," he says, nudging his tray aside. "There are two options I can think of right now. First? We all date you separately."

"Taking turns?" I ask, instinctively hunching over my tray to shield it from a seagull giving my fish a very predatory look.

He nods. "Yeah. Rotate date nights. Rotate who gets the bed."

His nose wrinkles slightly, like he's just tasted something off. I can tell—he hates that option already.

"The second is we don't rotate. We're all in it. Together. All the time."

I blink. "That doesn't seem fair to you guys. Can't we do... both? I want to have individual relationships, but also... do things together."

"Things?" he asks, one eyebrow lifting in a way that should be illegal with that smirk.

"Dates and..." I pause, my brain slamming into a wall of mortification. "You know."

"Sex?" he supplies, like he's offering me a glass of water.

"Yeah," I mutter, cheeks blazing like I've just french-kissed the sun. "That."

His smile tips sideways. Mischievous. Too-knowing. "Well, that sounds mighty interesting."

I choke on my next bite and pound my chest like I can force dignity back into my body. "That's ridiculous, right? That would never work.

It'd be like a very adult version of Twister. Left foot blue, right hand on... Oh my God, stop thinking about it, Penelope!"

"Why wouldn't it work?"

My eyes dart up to his. "Would you want it to?"

His grin falters, replaced by something quieter. Realer. A blush rises along his cheekbones, and when he speaks, it's like I'm hearing the truth he's been sitting on for years.

"Asking the hard questions, are we?" he says. "I think I'd like it very much. As much as I'd love having you all to myself, I want to see you with all of us. I want to see you taken care of. Blissed out. So wrecked you forget everything but what you're feeling. By me. By them. By all of us."

My breath catches. Because that? That wasn't just a fantasy. That was a promise.

"All of you?" I echo faintly, trying to do the math in my head and failing spectacularly. "I don't think that's possible."

"Anything's possible, Darlin'."

"How?" I ask, my voice cracking as blood rushes between my legs.

He grins, his face red. "Do you want me to explain it to you?"

"Yes, please."

"I'm not doing that here where someone could overhear us. Do you want to take a walk on the beach?"

I practically leap off the bench, already abandoning the remains of my lunch. We kick off our shoes and walk down a narrow sandy path to the beach. The wet sand squishes between my toes, cool and grainy against my overheated skin. Once he's sure the waves will drown out our conversation, he turns to me, biting his lip as he tries to figure out how to explain it to me.

"Just say it," I press, about to die from anticipation.

He takes a deep breath, as if preparing to dive underwater. "You have three holes, Darlin'."

"Yes, I'm aware. But there are five of you." I try to sound cool and collected like this is a completely normal Tuesday conversation, but three holes? I've never...

"Plus one can go here," he whispers, sliding a finger down my cleavage.

"And the fifth?" I rasp, my mouth drier than the Sahara during a drought.

He looks up at the sky like he's praying for divine forgiveness. "There's going to have to be a two-for-one." His words hit me like a truck, leaving me speechless.

"Oh," I breathe, comprehension dawning slowly. "OH." Holy shit. The image forms in my mind with startling clarity, and suddenly I'm lightheaded. Jesus Christ. My nipples pebble against my shirt as blinding need crashes through my body.

He continues, "Or Sammy and Jamie..."

I hold up my hand. "I get the point, Liam. Thank you." I bend over, hands on my knees, sucking air into my lungs like I've just run a marathon.

"What's the problem, Darlin'?" he asks, prowling closer, his gaze narrowing, seeing straight through me. "Is it turning you on?" He pulls me upright, brushing his thumb over my nipple, making me jump.

"No," I choke out, my knees wobbling like a newborn foal.

"No? How wet are you right now, Penelope?"

"Dry as the Sahara," I rasp, backing away from him, recognizing this for what it is—fucking dangerous.

His smirk tells me he doesn't believe me for a second, but he gives me space anyway, sitting on a rock while he waits for me to come to grips with my new reality.

I stare out at the water, watching the surface shift from steel-gray to silver where the sun breaks through the clouds. The vastness of the ocean mirrors the overwhelming possibilities stretching before me. It's intoxicating and terrifying at the same time—like being offered the keys to a Ferrari when you've only ever driven a golf cart with a top speed of 10 mph.

"Do you really think this can work?" I ask, turning toward him.

"You're not responsible for us, Penelope," he says gently, his voice low and steady like the tide. "You're responsible for you. The five of us have managed to live together for three years without killing each other. We'll be okay. I promise."

He holds out his arms, and I step into the space between his legs like it's the most natural thing in the world. His hands curve around my back, pulling me in until there's nothing but warmth and salt air and the sound of my pulse crashing louder than the waves.

"When we get back," he murmurs, "we'll light a bonfire. Talk this whole thing out. I know we can make it work, Nel. We all want the same thing."

"And what's that?" I ask, my voice barely more than a breath.

He smiles, soft and sure. "To make you happy."

I blink. "I thought you were going to say 'to sleep with me.'" My laugh bursts out, surprised and sharp.

His gaze drops to my mouth, and oh hell—there's something behind his eyes now. Something dark and hungry and completely unapologetic.

"That too," he says, dragging his thumb across my bottom lip in a slow, precise pass. Like he's testing it. Like he's imagining exactly what it would feel like to...

Yep. There it is. A bolt of heat spears through me, straight down, and I suddenly wonder if I remembered to charge my vibrator. It's about to get a workout.

"Penny for your thoughts," he murmurs, tucking a strand of hair behind my ear like he knows damn well I'm not thinking about anything appropriate.

I hesitate, torn between the part of me that wants to be coy and the part that has completely given up on shame.

Honesty wins.

"I was just thinking I might need to, uh... pull out my vibrator when we get home," I say, like a fully feral, filterless heathen.

He goes absolutely still. Then bites his lip—hard—and lets out a low laugh that makes my toes curl in my boots.

"I can help you with that," he says, voice a little hoarse.

I grin, because somehow we've crossed a line and I am very much okay with it. "I'm sure you could."

Eyes darkening like storm clouds right before lightning strikes, his eyebrows creep up his forehead as if I've presented a challenge he's all too willing to accept. He grips my hips, pushing his knee between my legs and pulling me closer.

His hat lands beside him as he knocks it off his head, his hand warm on my lower back, anchoring our bodies together. With a firm grip on my chin, he stares at me, savoring the moment before tilting my head and pressing his lips to mine.

Soft and gentle at first, just the lightest brush, the soft slide of his tongue over my bottom lip. I moan, and it's like a switch flips inside him.

He pushes his tongue into my mouth, dragging it over mine, demanding, insistent. I sink my hands into his silky hair, gripping the strands between my fingers as I hang on for dear life.

A low growl creeps up his throat as he drags his hand down my neck, over my collarbone, not stopping until he's cupping one breast.

"Fuck, Sugar," he groans, pulling back to look down at his hand as he squeezes. "They're perfect." One more knead, and then his lips are back on mine, his hand moving down, joining his other one to grip both of my hips. His groan of approval has something sparking through my veins as he drags me up his thigh, my core riding over hard muscle. My breath stutters against his lips. He doesn't let up with the onslaught, pulling me closer and closer to the abyss. I start moving on my own, unashamedly riding his thigh like I'm auditioning for a mechanical bull competition.

"Liam," I gasp, clenching my thighs around his leg.

"Use me, Darlin'." He rocks my hips back and forth, helping me. "I bet that feels good, doesn't it? That's my girl," he murmurs, his gaze dark as he watches my lips fall open. "Look at me."

I look up at him and meeting his hooded gaze is all I need to tip over the edge. The orgasm crashes through me, destroying everything in its path like a category five hurricane. In this moment, I cease to be Penelope Campbell, restaurant owner and professional over-thinker. I'm just sensation and need and release.

"God, you're beautiful." He pushes my hair back from my face as I come down. My limbs feel boneless, like I might melt into a puddle if he weren't holding me up. I don't need to look at the bulge in his pants to know he's in a bad way. He kisses me softly, his lips curving against mine.

"Your turn?" I ask, reaching for his belt.

He grabs my wrist, pulls it up to his chest, and flattens my palm over his racing heart. "Not yet, sweetheart. I want this to be about you for a while. I don't want any doubts in your mind when we're together."

Jesus Christ, he's going to kill me with this gentleman act. "Fair enough." I lick my lips, trying not to think about how he'd feel. How he'd taste. The weight of him on my tongue. The salty-sweet taste of his...

"Don't," he chokes out, his gaze frozen on my lips, like he knows exactly what's going through my mind.

"Are you ready to go back?" I ask, changing the subject before my mind goes even further into the gutter.

"Only if I can help you make dinner tonight," he says, looking down at our hands as he guides his fingers through mine.

"Of course you can."

"Do you think you're ready to talk to the guys tonight? I can text them to get a fire going. We may want to stop at the liquor store on the way home. This is going to be a rough conversation."

God Almighty. "I feel like I need to sit down and write out a speech so I don't miss anything. Maybe create a PowerPoint presentation with bullet points and a Q&A session at the end. Or just drink until I black out and deal with this tomorrow."

He laughs, the sound rich and warm in the salt-laden air. "We're not going anywhere, Pen. If you forget something, there's always tomorrow."

Several hours later, I'm in the kitchen working on dinner prep, my stomach tied in more knots than a sailor's convention. The calm from earlier has evaporated, replaced by mounting tension as the moment of truth approaches.

"Breathe," Liam murmurs, nudging me over and taking my place at the cutting board, carefully extracting the knife from my death grip.

"I don't know if I can do this, Liam. Can't we not talk about it? Just let things happen?" I'm a grade-A chicken and I'm not even trying to hide it.

"If you want this to be a summer thing, maybe. If you want it to last, we need you to lay ground rules, Darlin'. What they are is completely up to you, but talking with all of us is the first step."

"Are you sure?" I ask, gnawing at my lip. I've untied and retied my apron strings at least a dozen times, trying to keep my hands busy so my brain doesn't explode from the pressure.

"Yes, I'm sure. If us guys make the rules, there will be a war within a week. Trust me."

"Why do you say that?"

"You weren't in the bunkhouse that summer we all started. We got in fights over you. Actual fist fights. That's when we decided that none of us would make a move."

Oh. Good Lord in heaven. The image of these five grown men throwing punches over me is both horrifying and oddly flattering. I go to the fridge and pull out another beer, guzzling half of it before Archer ambles into the kitchen and pries it from my fingers.

"Easy there, Nelly," he says, a smile tugging at his lips.

I make a grab for it, but he takes a giant step back and guzzles it down.

"What has you all hot and bothered?" he asks, looking at Liam for answers when I don't say anything.

"The talk is tonight."

"Oh, that," Archer mutters, leaning back against the counter, and crossing his arms over his chest. "And you're not ready?" he asks, his dark gaze pinning me in place like a butterfly in a collection.

"I'll never be ready for that. Especially since you just chugged the rest of my beer. The only thing that could have prepared me for this conversation was at least two more of those and maybe a shot of tequila."

"Alcohol isn't going to make it better, Nel. You need a clear head." He pulls me into his arms, chuckling against my hair when I remain stiff as a board. "Tell you what, why don't you take Pearl for a walk? Some fresh air will help settle your mind. Liam and I can finish up in the kitchen."

"Okay." I nod, my cheek smooshed against his chest. He releases me, gently turning me around and pushing me toward the door, landing a solid smack on my butt that makes me yelp.

Outside, the evening air carries the tang of wood smoke mixed with sea salt. Jamie and Sammy are outside starting a fire. When I step out onto the deck, they look up as one.

"Is everything okay?" Sammy asks, his brow crinkling.

"No. Yes." I sigh, close my eyes, and take a deep breath. "I'm just nervous about talking to all of you tonight. I know it's stupid, but I don't know how to do this."

"It's us, Penelope. It'll be fine. We're the same people we've always been."

Ugh. Not helping. "That doesn't make it any better," I grumble. "That just reminds me I've been harboring totally filthy and completely inappropriate thoughts about my employees for three years." I squat down to scratch Pearl's ears. She leans into my touch, her tail sweeping through the gravel. "Pearl and I are going to take a walk," I tell them, not waiting for a response before I head toward the road.

"Hey! Wait up!" Sammy calls, his footsteps crunching through the gravel. "Is it okay if I walk with you?" he asks, looking down at me, his eyes crinkling at the corners in that way that makes my stomach flip.

"Yeah." The flash of awareness that blooms in my belly is exactly the distraction I need right now.

Unlike Liam's loping, golden-retriever-on-a-mission stride, Sammy moves with this quiet, precise grace. It's the kind of elegance that screams boarding school and bespoke tailoring, but with a looseness in the shoulders that says he's finally unlearning half the rules.

He's like Mr. Darcy if Mr. Darcy had better social skills, access to therapy, and a smartphone with zero unread messages.

We fall into step beside each other, that easy kind of silence settling between us like a worn-in sweater. Pearl trots ahead, nose to the ground like the fate of the universe depends on her sniffing every single blade of grass. When the lane spills out into the dunes, Sammy doesn't hesitate—he takes my hand and scrambles up the sandy rise with the kind of competence that makes my stomach do an annoying little flip.

He helps me down the other side, guiding me onto the beach. The wind catches my hair. Seabirds shriek overhead. Waves crash in their slow, ancient rhythm. And it feels... pivotal. Like I might remember this moment for the rest of my life.

"How will it work," I ask quietly, "with you, Jamie, and me?"

Sammy exhales a breath that feels like he's been holding it since I opened my mouth. "You ask so many questions."

"You say that like it's a bad thing."

"It's not." He runs a hand through his hair, looking beautifully exasperated. "But not everything needs a roadmap before we hit the road, Pip. Sometimes you just get in the car and go. If we crash, we regroup. If the road's closed, we reroute."

"If you think I'm capable of winging it, you clearly haven't seen my Google Calendar. I have color codes. And back-up color codes."

He laughs, tipping his head back in a way that makes my chest ache. "God, I love how direct you are. I don't have all the answers, Pip. I don't know if it'll work. Or if jealousy will get in the way. Or if we'll be jealous of you, or of each other. We won't know until we try."

"That's... kind of terrifying."

"Is it, though?" he asks softly.

He spins me to face him. He's tall enough to block the sun, casting his face in shadow while the light outlines his hair in gold. He looks almost unreal, like something from a fever dream I didn't know I was having.

"Or is this the most exciting, terrifying, incredible time in all of our lives?" he murmurs. "Don't get lost in the details when the joy is going to be in the figuring out."

"I don't know how..."

He gently covers my mouth with his fingers. "Shhh," he says, smiling. Then he slides his hand along my jaw, cradling my cheek. "Can I give you something else to think about for a little while?"

His gaze drops to my mouth. His thumb lingers at the corner like he's already imagining how I taste.

I nod, every word in my head disintegrating into ash.

He kisses me with the kind of focus that makes me feel studied. Like I'm a piece of music and he's memorizing every note. Where Jamie is all wild enthusiasm and Liam is devoted slow-burn, Sammy kisses like he's conducting an orchestra—every movement calculated, precise, devastatingly thorough.

His hand finds the nape of my neck, fingers tangling in my hair as he pulls me closer, deeper. When his tongue brushes mine, I gasp, and he takes full advantage. Sand shifts beneath my feet as I press into him, the waves crashing behind us like applause.

When we finally break apart, both of us panting like we've just sprinted a mile, I rest my forehead against his.

"Well," I whisper, breath shaky, "that's definitely something to think about."

"Just a little distraction," he says, winking.

We head back toward the house, fingers twined, my lips still tingling and my brain blissfully blank for the first time in what feels like days. The sun paints the sky in streaks of pink and gold behind us, and everything feels... right. Not figured out. Not solved. But right.

Dinner is a blur of motion and laughter, like a scene from a movie I didn't realize I was starring in. Liam's at the stove, sleeves rolled up, doing ungodly things to a cast iron skillet. Archer's meticulously placing mismatched dishes on the table like he's arranging a magazine spread. Spencer and Jamie drag chairs out to the firepit, arguing about who always forgets the bottle opener. Sammy keeps catching my eye from across the kitchen, his smile that private, promise-laced one that sends my pulse rocketing every time.

The kitchen smells like heaven—garlic and herbs and roasted meat and decadence—but underneath it all is the woodsmoke, drifting in from the open windows like a memory you can't shake.

By the time we finish eating and step outside, the sun's dipped below the horizon, leaving only that soft, in-between light. Twilight. The kind of glow that makes even bad decisions feel poetic.

We settle around the fire, our stomachs full and beer bottles balanced on knees, the warm orange light throwing flickering shadows across the five faces I can barely look at without forgetting how to breathe. Five sets of eyes. All on me.

Tension hums in the air—not quite dread, not quite desire. Something in between. Like a storm just offshore.

The fire crackles, sending little sparks skyward. The longer the silence stretches, the more it feels like I'm not just sitting in a circle of men I love—but standing on a cliff with no idea how high the drop is.

This is either about to be the most romantic moment of my life or the world's most awkward group intervention. My money's on the latter.

I clear my throat. Open my mouth. And immediately choke on absolutely nothing but air and anxiety.

"Cool," I rasp, blinking tears out of my eyes as I try not to die in front of all of them. "Great start."

I bring my beer to my lips like it's going to save me. My hand's shaking so badly I'm surprised I don't spill it down my front. I take a long sip—okay, chug—because apparently liquid courage is the only kind I have access to right now.

Then Liam's hand finds mine.

He pulls it to his mouth, warm lips brushing the trembling skin of my palm. His eyes are steady when they meet mine. Quiet. Fierce.

"The faster you do it," he says, his mouth moving against my skin, "the quicker it'll be over."

The fire snaps behind him. My heart is doing gymnastics in my chest. Five men. Five hearts on the line. And mine? Mine's been split five ways for years.

I just have to find the words.

I square my shoulders like I'm walking into battle, even though I'm surrounded by five of the most beautiful men I've ever laid eyes on. Which, let's be honest, makes this way more terrifying than a battlefield.

"Okay. Just—give me a second to get all of this out before anyone says anything," I start, voice shaking just a little. My stomach is doing full-on gymnastics, and I'm pretty sure my heart is trying to climb out of my throat for a better view.

They all nod, eyes locked on me, quiet and waiting. The firelight dances across their faces—casting soft shadows, lighting up their cheekbones, turning them into some unfair combination of rugged

Viking and brooding romance novel cover. It's honestly rude how good they look just existing.

"I like all of you," I say, and my voice actually wobbles on the word like. "A lot. I have for a long time."

I take a breath so deep it scrapes the bottom of my lungs.

"I want to explore whatever this is between us—but there have to be some ground rules." I glance around at the circle, every one of them more intense than the last. "I want individual relationships with each of you. But I also want to make sure the group dynamic is strong."

"So..." Archer smirks. "You want your cake and to eat it too."

"I definitely want to eat your cake if you're offering," Jamie cuts in, grinning wide enough to make his dimples dangerous.

God. Dammit, Jamie.

My face ignites, and I thank the night sky for its mercy in hiding the absolute inferno coloring my cheeks. "I—I think we need to focus on strengthening relationships before we focus on sex," I manage, even though my entire body is raising its hand in the back like um, excuse me, sex is a perfectly legitimate relationship-building exercise, thanks.

"That sounds like common sense, not ground rules," Sammy says gently, his voice soothing in the way lavender tea and forehead kisses are. "Keep going, Pip."

"There's too much going on to schedule time together," I continue. "But I want you to promise—if any of you feel left out or hurt, you come talk to me. We have to be honest. We have to communicate. Getting here took three years. I don't want to ruin it in one summer. I'd rather pump the brakes now than crash and burn later."

Spencer leans forward, his elbows on his knees, the fire catching in his scruff. "So what does that mean exactly?"

"It means... we take it slow," I say. "Day by day. Check-ins. Communication."

"That's not what I mean," he says, his voice low and a little rough. "We already do that. I'm talking about sex, Sugar."

My mouth opens. Then closes. Then opens again like I'm a fish gasping for oxygen. My brain short-circuits, my dignity flees the scene, and I let out a noise that can only be described as a squeak.

I'm officially the mayor of Flusteredville.

"Do you want to be with all of us at the same time," Spencer asks, his eyebrow raised, "or are we gonna need a shared Google Calendar for your bed?"

The tension around the fire shifts. Tighter. Heavier. Like someone's turned the dial from flirty to feral.

Testosterone? Meet bonfire.

"No!" I blurt, hands flying up like I'm waving down a plane. "I mean —yes? But no—I don't want it scheduled. What we've been doing? The whole no-plan, just-letting-things-happen thing? That's been working. I think we should keep doing that. As long as we promise to communicate, I think it'll actually work."

"So you do want to be with us all at the same time?" Spencer asks again, tone deceptively casual. But the glint in his eyes says he already knows the answer. He just wants to hear me say it.

I bite my lip. Hard. Then I close my eyes, swallow the last ounce of hesitation, and go full truth bomb.

"Yes, Spencer," I whisper, every nerve in my body lighting up like a Christmas tree. "I desperately want to be with all of you. At the same time."

The silence that follows is thick. Charged. So filthy with promise it might as well be its own character in this story.

It's like someone flipped a switch. One second, I'm staring down five barely restrained storms of testosterone, and the next... it's something else entirely. The competitive edge vanishes, replaced by something collaborative. Cohesive. Like whatever jealousy or hesitation existed moments ago has alchemized into shared anticipation.

Five pairs of eyes darken in unison, like they've all just reached the same very dirty conclusion. And spoiler: it absolutely involves me.

"Come here," Liam says, his voice low and rough, all gravel and hunger. He opens his arms, and I rise on shaky legs like I'm walking straight into the fire.

I melt into his lap, cheek pressed to the warmth of his chest. His arms curl around me, grounding and steady.

"My brave girl," he murmurs, brushing a kiss to the top of my head like it's a vow.

"Nel."

I blink up. Archer's standing over me, backlit by firelight like he just walked off the cover of a fantasy novel titled Lord of the Longing. My throat goes dry.

Liam shifts me gently so I'm facing forward, his hands resting—casually, possessively—on my thighs. I can feel the heat of them through the thin fabric of my pants.

"I'm proud of you," Archer says, dropping to his knees between my legs like it's the most natural thing in the world. "I know that wasn't easy."

He holds my gaze like he's trying to read the thoughts I haven't even had yet. "Do you think we should try to keep things even, before we take the next step?"

My brain short-circuits. "What do you mean?"

"If you're developing something romantic with all of us, I assume you want to wait on group intimacy until you've had time with each of us?" His hands settle on my knees, and it takes everything in me not to whimper and drag them higher.

I lean back into Liam's chest, eyes fluttering closed. "I hadn't even thought about that," I admit, my voice barely a whisper.

"What do you think?" Archer presses gently.

"I think you're right. I don't want anyone's first time to be... overshadowed. It's too important."

"Well," Jamie says, popping to his feet like a golden retriever who just heard the word walk, "since we're being fair and all—Penelope and I haven't kissed yet. So if I may..."

Before anyone can protest, he plucks me out of Liam's lap like I weigh nothing and settles into his chair with me tucked against his chest like I'm something he's claiming.

"Much better," he murmurs, burying his nose in my hair.

"You're trouble," I say, laughing under my breath.

"You're the only one who's slept in my bed," I point out. "Technically, that gives you a head start. Even if you were a perfect gentleman —which, now that I think about it, was a completely wasted opportunity."

"That's not how it works," he grumbles, his voice muffled against my temple. His cologne—spicy, warm, and a little wild—wraps around me like a second skin. His hands are all tease and play, but his confidence is its own form of pressure, low and steady and very, very effective.

"Good talk, everyone," Sammy says, standing and stretching, before gathering plates like we didn't just emotionally detonate in front of a fire. He winks at me and Jamie as he heads for the house.

The others follow, quiet but at ease. Spencer squeezes my shoulder as he passes, warm and solid. Archer's fingers trail lightly against my arm, and it sends goosebumps chasing down my spine.

And just like that—it's over.

All that intense anxiety, all that stomach-twisting dread... for this?

I sit there in Jamie's lap, surrounded by his spicy scent and the smoke of the fire, and laugh to myself—quiet, disbelieving.

I'd been bracing for a roller coaster. And it turns out... I'd boarded the world's sexiest carousel.

"How do you feel after getting that all out in the open?" Jamie asks, his breath warm against my ear as we watch the rest of the guys head back inside to give us our privacy.

"Better. Why are they leaving us out here when they were just acting like jealous teenagers two seconds ago?"

"Because they want me to be on a level playing field with them. The faster that happens, the faster other things happen. They're basically throwing me the ball and trusting I won't fumble it."

"Is that it? They just want to get to having sex faster?" I ask, feeling slightly used.

"You don't?" he asks, his eyebrows nearly hitting his hairline.

Damn. "You have a point."

"You don't have to worry about all the crap you would in other relationships, Penelope. We all like you. We have for three years. We're not going anywhere. Yes, we want relationships with you. Yes, we want to have sex with you. Lots of it. The kind that makes the neighbors consider calling the police because they think someone's being murdered."

A startled laugh escapes me, and I feel some of the tension drain from my shoulders. I let his words marinate, realizing how freeing it is to know that I don't have to pretend to be someone else. They like me despite myself—or maybe because of myself. I don't think I've ever had that before. Five men who've seen me at my absolute worst and still look at me like I'm their entire universe.

"Thank you, Jamie."

"Will you turn around so we can kiss now?" His fingers trace a path from my shoulder to my neck, pulling my hair away and pressing his lips just below my ear. The sound he makes low in his throat is enough to make my core clench with need.

With careful movements, I swing my body around, stretching a leg across his lap until I'm straddling him. "God, Jamie," I breathe, my voice cracking as his hardness settles between my legs.

"Fuck," he groans, his jaw clenching. "I didn't think this through."

I shift, trying to take the pressure off him, but it only makes it worse.

"For the love of everything holy, Penelope. Stop wiggling around." His fingers dig into my hips with almost bruising intensity, at first to hold me still, and then to pull me down as he flexes his hips, grinding himself against me. "God almighty. I shouldn't be allowed within a hundred feet of you." His dark gaze meets mine, a million emotions warring in their depths. "I'd love to say I have the control of a saint, but fuck if you don't bring out the monster in me."

"Stop talking and kiss me, Jamie," I whisper, the words tumbling out in a breathless rush, more plea than command.

He freezes, eyes searching mine like he's waiting for me to take it back—but I don't. I can't. My hands rise to cradle his face, fingers threading through the soft hair at his temples. His stubble scrapes against my palms in the best way—raw and real and just a little bit dirty.

Then he moves.

His mouth crashes into mine like we've been circling this moment for years—and maybe we have. His hand slides up to the back of my head, cradling me there as his tongue pushes past my lips, claiming and desperate and so much more than I was prepared for. It's not a kiss —it's a damn collision.

The fire crackles behind me, warming my back, but all I feel is him —Jamie's heat pressing into every inch of me, his arm hooking around my waist and yanking me closer like he wants to fuse us into one body.

I melt into him, completely lost, like my bones have been replaced with liquid longing.

Lust sparks between us like a live wire, snapping through me in sharp, electric bursts. He kisses like he's starving. Like I'm the last taste of something sweet before a long, dark winter.

And the way our bodies slot together? It's not just chemistry. It's precision. Like the universe carved us to fit—curve into curve, breath to breath, soul to soul.

Jamie tears his mouth from mine, breathing hard. His thumb strokes along my jaw, tilting my face toward the stars as he trails kisses down the column of my neck.

"You're wearing my favorite ones today," he murmurs against my skin, teeth grazing my collarbone.

"Your favorite what?" I gasp, brain still blissed out and barely functional.

"Easy access," he growls, and then I feel the quick pop of the clasps on my coveralls. The fabric slips off my shoulders, pooling at my waist like it's been waiting for this moment. His eyes darken as he brushes his thumbs over the swell of my breasts through the thin cotton of my shirt.

"I knew they'd be waiting for me," he says, the words so deep they vibrate straight through my spine. "Do you have any idea how many times I've dreamed of doing this?"

"Doing what?" I ask, practically panting. My skin tingles with anticipation, my body arching toward his like it already knows what's coming.

"This." He tugs my shirt up, baring me to the cool air and his hot, hungry stare. The groan he lets out hits me straight between the legs, like the sound itself is an aphrodisiac.

"Why aren't you wearing a bra, Penelope?" he rasps, cupping me like I'm the most precious thing he's ever touched.

"I never do with coveralls," I whisper, my voice cracking as electricity sparks under my skin.

His eyes blaze as he dips his head and takes me into his mouth, lips closing over one aching peak in a slow, greedy pull. I suck in a breath, trying to keep the moan locked behind my teeth as I grind against his thigh, utterly lost to the heat between us.

And then—

Creak.

The deck boards groan, and we freeze like guilty teenagers. I crane my neck over my shoulder and catch sight of Sammy settling into a chair across the fire, totally casual. Too casual.

"Can I help you?" Jamie asks, not even bothering to shift, one brow cocked, a smirk curling at the corners of his kiss-swollen lips.

Sammy raises an eyebrow, completely unbothered. "I'm conducting an experiment," Sammy says, cracking open a beer and taking a long swallow. The firelight catches on his cheekbones, making him look like something out of a GQ photoshoot.

"What sort of experiment?" Jamie prods.

"I want to see if I get jealous."

"Are you sure about this, Sammy?" I ask, suddenly panicking that this is happening way too quickly.

"Positive. Better to get this out of the way now."

There's something unbearably hot about the way Sammy watches us. His gaze isn't possessive or sharp with jealousy—it's measured, assessing, curious in a way that sends a fresh rush of heat through me. It feels like a moment suspended in firelight, not just from the flames crackling nearby, but from the tension threading between the three of us. This isn't just attraction anymore. It's a quiet test—of boundaries, of feelings, of whether this impossible, beautiful, chaotic arrangement we're inching toward might actually hold.

Jamie tilts my face back toward him, drawing my attention away from Sammy with a gentle grip under my chin. "Is this okay with you?" he asks, his voice low, the weight of it grounding me.

"Yes," I whisper, the word trembly on my lips, thick with nerves and need.

He doesn't hesitate. With a kind of strength that still startles me, he lifts me, shifting me in his lap until my back is flush against his chest, his thighs framing mine. "Watch him," he murmurs into my ear, and I feel his smirk as much as I hear it. "Make sure he's being a good boy."

My breath catches at the command, my body already thrumming. Jamie's arms wrap securely around my waist, and then his hand slips lower, slow and sure, until he's inside my coveralls. The warmth of his palm finds me instantly, cupping the damp heat between my legs, and the soft sound he makes in response nearly unravels me.

"You've soaked your panties, Penelope."

A whimper claws up my throat as I press into his touch, desperate for more friction, more pressure, more of him.

"Want to know what I really want to do?" he murmurs, dragging a single finger up the center of my underwear, just enough to tease and torture.

"Please," I manage, barely more than a breath.

"I'd strip you completely, sit you just like this, and slide my cock between your thighs. I'd let you rock against me until you were dripping down my length, until you couldn't take it anymore. Until you came all over me."

The image is so vivid, so blindingly erotic, that it hits me like a wave, my body tightening in anticipation. I tilt my head up just as Jamie's fingers find my clit, pressing and circling in a rhythm that makes my hips move of their own accord.

Across the fire, Sammy rises from his chair, slow and sure, and moves toward us with purposeful intent. He doesn't break eye contact. He doesn't ask permission. He just drops to his knees in front of me, settles between my open thighs, and presses forward until the solid heat of his body nudges against Jamie's hand.

Then he kisses me—hard, hungry, devoted.

The climax rips through me like lightning, sharp and overwhelming. I moan into Sammy's mouth, my body bucking as Jamie keeps his hand steady, coaxing every last tremor from me until I collapse, trembling, against his chest.

Sammy eventually pulls back, his lips slick, his expression dazed and dark with want. Behind me, Jamie's breath is hot against my neck, his heartbeat thudding a wild rhythm against my spine. The fire snaps and pops beside us, the scent of smoke and peat mingling with the salty tang of the ocean and something more primal.

The air feels different now. Thicker. Heavier. Like something essential just shifted into place.

Sammy exhales, dragging a hand through his hair. "Well," he says, voice still raw, "I think it's safe to say I'm not jealous. Just... thoroughly turned on."

Jamie's chuckle rumbles through my body. "One down. Four to go."

And if this is any indication of what's to come, I have no idea how I'm going to survive it.

But I already know I won't want to stop.

10

ARCHER'S POV

I wake up in a foul mood, and I won't pretend it's not because I didn't get to spend the night with Penelope. I wanted it to be me by the fire. Me holding her. Me listening to that laugh that always hits me square in the chest and leaves me breathless.

Instead, I was inside watching through the window like some sad, territorial creep while Jamie and Sammy got handsy with what's basically mine.

Well.

Partly mine.

It's complicated.

I've got so much of her in my system after the last three years that she might as well be my blood type. She's in every breath, every dream, every time I so much as blink. She's the high I'll never come down from. And fuck, it hurts to have to share her. The image of Jamie's hands on her, his mouth on her throat, has been stuck on repeat in my head all night—each loop tighter than the last. My jaw clenches so hard it aches. My stomach feels like it's been gutted and stitched back wrong.

I've always been territorial by nature. Chalk it up to how I was raised or just how I'm wired. But this?

This is primal.

I'm dead set on getting her alone today. No interruptions, no fire pit audience, no fucking window between us. I'm on the boat every day this week, and the thought of not touching her before that stretch makes my skin itch. I can't decide whether to offer her a choice or just throw her over my shoulder and deal with the fallout later. Option two is winning.

I haven't been the same since the night the kitchen went up in flames. That fire didn't just torch her restaurant—it lit up something in me. A terror I haven't been able to shake. A picture of her silhouette against the orange glow, hair wild, eyes wide. It hit me like a punch to the chest. Like a premonition I didn't want to survive. The thought of never seeing her again, of never getting the chance to figure out what the hell this thing is between us—it keeps me up at night. Wakes me sweating and gasping, like my heart's trying to claw its way out of my chest.

I take a long sip of coffee, bitter and grounding, the ceramic mug warm between my palms as I sit at the kitchen table. The wood beneath my elbows is worn, full of little nicks and burn marks from years of her life I wasn't part of. There's a familiarity to it that both comforts and stings. The faucet drips—sharp, steady—and I track each fall like it's syncing with my thoughts.

I've fixed that damn thing three times already. Still drips. Still refuses to be tamed.

Just like her.

"Morning."

I look up to see Penelope standing in boxer shorts and a tank top. She stretches her arms over her head, yawning, cheeks flushed, hair wild. Her tank rides up, flashing a strip of skin that damn near stops my heart.

"Good morning, Nel," I whisper, my throat suddenly desert-dry. My gaze drops to her bare legs before I can stop myself. They look a mile long on her tiny frame. "You're up early." My voice comes out like sandpaper.

She shrugs. "I slept better last night than I have in a while." The sleep-rough edge to her voice sends a jolt straight to my dick.

I open my arms wide, silently daring her to resist. I'm not above using guilt as a weapon. When she finally walks closer, I swoop her into my lap, holding her tightly. "Why do you think that is?" I ask, brushing my lips over her temple, breathing her in like she's oxygen. She smells like coconut and wood smoke and everything I've ever wanted.

She flushes bright red up to her hairline. "Probably because we all talked last night and things are more settled."

"Oh, is that why?" I choke out a laugh that sounds more like I'm being strangled. I refuse to admit that I was watching them. It's not like I meant to, but once I started I couldn't look away. She's so fucking beautiful when she comes. The flashback of her head thrown back against Jamie's shoulder gives me the most confusing hard-on of my life. It's like being split in two: half of me wants to put my fist through Jamie's pretty-boy face, while the other half wants to buy him a beer for making her come.

"Shut up, Archer." The floor groans as she stands and walks over to the kettle I already started for her. She tosses a tea bag in her cup and pours the water before looking back at me, suspicion written all over her face like she knows I'm up to something. Smart girl. "Thank you for putting the kettle on," she murmurs begrudgingly. "Why are you up so early?"

"I'm planning out a date." I keep my tone casual, like I haven't been obsessing over this since four freaking AM.

"A date?" she asks, looking at me, confusion flashing across her features.

"With you, Nel. Today, if you'll go with me." I lean forward, trying to look chill even though my heart's going ballistic.

"Should we be taking time off?" she asks, fishing out her teabag with a spoon. The clink of metal on ceramic fills the quiet while earl grey steam rises between us. It smells like her—like home.

"I'll be on the boat for the next five days. We'll barely get to see each other," I remind her, my voice catching because five days might as well be five years. Five days of imagining which of the others might be taking her down to the beach and fucking her brains out while I'm trapped on a fishing boat surrounded by nothing but ocean and the smell of fish guts.

She meets my gaze, her expression softening. "You're right. God, I'm sorry. You're getting the raw end of the deal, aren't you?" She sits in the chair next to me, one foot planted on the seat, her knee to her chest.

"I'm sure we can figure out a way to make up for it." I drag her chair closer, close enough that I can count her freckles.

She raises an eyebrow. "Like what?"

"Maybe I can find my way into your bed a couple of nights a week." I try to sound like I'm joking, but the hungry growl in my voice gives me away. Just the thought of her legs tangled with mine has me shifting in my seat.

"Moving a little fast, are we?" she asks, looking up at me through her eyelashes.

Not nearly fast enough. Three years of waiting has me ready to crawl out of my skin.

"I just want to be close to you, Nel. Even if we're just sleeping."

Her gaze drops to her mug, an emotion I can't place creasing her forehead.

"What's wrong?" I ask, tipping her chin up with my finger.

"We wasted so much time. I spent three years running from this when I could have just embraced it."

"You need to stop looking at it like that, baby. It wouldn't have worked before now. We know each other so well that we'll be able to spot any issues before they blow up. It's perfect timing." I need her to believe this as much as I need air to breathe—that everything that came before was just the universe lining us up for this exact moment.

Her eyes widen at the pet name, her gaze dropping to my lips before flicking back up to my eyes. "You're so smart even though you're annoying," she says, the tip of her tongue peeking out to wet her lips.

I throw my head back and laugh. "Maybe I should be annoying more often, if it gets you to look at me like that." My gaze never leaves her face, drinking in every detail—the little quirk of her mouth, the flush spreading across her skin. I'm memorizing her like I'll be tested on it later.

"What did you have in mind for this date?" she asks, blowing softly across the surface of her tea. The tiny gesture makes everything below my belt tighten, imagining that breath ghosting over my skin.

"I found a restaurant I think you're going to love—the interior is stunning. Thought it might give you some design inspiration." I try to sound casual, but I've already got the whole day mapped out in my head: the furniture place up north first, then the design store, lunch after. I even built in a buffer for when things inevitably go sideways. Because they always do.

"That's a good idea." She grins, a flash of white that nearly knocks me on my ass. She's so beautiful it physically hurts. I rub at my chest, trying to ease the ache.

"What's wrong?" she asks softly, covering my hand with hers. The warmth of her palm seeps through me, chasing away the phantom pain.

"Nothing's wrong, baby."

She abandons her tea without a second thought and climbs into my lap, her eyes scanning my face like she's searching for something only she knows how to find. Her weight settles against me like she was made to fit. Soft curves molding into the sharp lines of my body with devastating precision.

When she moves my hand and presses her cheek to the spot I'd been rubbing, something in me fractures. A strangled sound escapes before I can stop it, raw and helpless.

I'm not religious, but—fuck. This? This is spiritual.

I groan, the sound dragged from somewhere deep in my chest, and wrap my arms around her like I might never get the chance again. One hand cradles the back of her head, fingers threading into her hair as I bury my face in the curve of her neck.

Holding her like this feels like confession and salvation all at once.

"You're so fucking precious to me, Penelope. I hope you know that." My voice cracks like I'm thirteen again.

I startle when I feel a tear slide along my thumb.

"These aren't sad tears," she clarifies, burying her face in my chest in embarrassment.

Fuck. This woman. If she ever figures out how completely she owns me, I'm screwed. She's invaded every part of me, filled up all my empty spaces until I don't know where I end and she begins.

"Will you pick out something for me to wear to the restaurant?" she asks, her voice wobbly.

"Whatever you wear will be fine. It's not fancy," I say, my voice tight as I try to ignore how her thighs are pressing against parts of me that are very, very interested.

"I need some fashion help. I think I'm ready to branch out from the coveralls. I only wore them nonstop for the last three years to try to be inconspicuous."

"You think neon pink overalls and sheep-print wellies are inconspicuous?" I snort. "You might as well have worn a flashing billboard that said 'Please Don't Notice Me' for all the good it did."

She lifts her head to glare at me, all scrunched nose and puffed cheeks. Like a pissed-off kitten that thinks it's a tiger.

I raise my hands in surrender. "Okay, okay. I'll pick out your outfit. I would offer to have you do the same, but I'm still waiting for what I ordered online, so I'll be wearing the same old jeans and t-shirt."

"Don't ever get rid of those jeans and t-shirt," she murmurs, her voice dropping to a whisper that feels like fingers trailing down my spine.

"I won't, baby. Come on." I link my fingers with hers and lead the way to her bedroom, letting her go in first and waiting for her to pull me over the threshold. Her scent wraps around me, and I breathe deep, shivering as it hits my system like a shot of whiskey.

She opens her closet door for me, and I pretend to browse even though I zeroed in on what I want her to wear immediately. I pull out a pair of low-rise baggy jeans, a gray-blue tank top the same color as the blue in her hazel eyes, and white Chuck Taylor high-tops. I throw a hoodie on top of the pile for good measure.

"Really?" she asks, eyebrow raised, nose scrunched in that way that makes her freckles dance.

"Really. Unless you want to go in what you're wearing." I close the gap between us, each step heavy and measured. I'm not hiding the way my gaze slides up her bare legs, over the swell of her hips. I stare at her nipples, smirking when they harden under my gaze, before looking her in the face.

She holds my gaze, that unmistakable spark of challenge flaring behind her eyes as she sinks onto the bed, the mattress dipping beneath her. Her legs part just enough as she leans back, her body stretching out like a fucking invitation—silent, purposeful, and absolutely destroying me.

The sight of her like this—laid out, waiting—nearly brings me to my knees.

"Whose boxers are those, Nel?" I ask, my voice dropping to a low growl that reverberates in my chest.

Her smile curls slow and wicked, all promise and provocation. "Come here, Archer."

God help me.

There's a command in her voice, and it hits me like a punch I didn't see coming. I'm not used to taking orders. But for her? I'd crawl through fire. I'd jump off cliffs. I'd rip the sky down and hand it to her just to see that smile again. I move toward her like I've got no control over my body, like gravity itself has shifted to revolve around her. Each step is heavy with three years of want, boots dragging like they're made of stone.

"Are you sure about this?" I ask, the words barely making it past my clenched jaw. My whole body is screaming at me to shut up and kiss her, but I have to be sure. She's too important not to be sure.

She doesn't answer—not with words.

She just reaches up, slow and certain, and hooks one finger into my belt loop. A gentle tug. Not desperate. Not urgent. Just enough to undo me completely.

I lower myself over her carefully, bracing my weight on my forearms, trying not to crush her, even though the way I feel right now? I'd fuse us together if I could.

She's so small beneath me—soft where I'm all sharp edges, gentle where I've only ever known control. That contrast? It slices through me. Makes my chest ache with something that feels like longing and adoration and everything I've been too afraid to name.

"Hi," she whispers, her breath sweet and warm against my face.

"Hi, yourself," I murmur back, my eyes taking in every detail—the constellation of freckles across her nose, the way gold seeps into the green in her eyes, the rapid flutter of her pulse at her throat. I want to remember her like this, spread out beneath me, eyes dark with desire.

When my mouth finally meets hers, it's like touching a live wire— jolting, electric, impossible to forget. She tastes like Earl Grey and something deeper, something that's only hers. Something that's mine. Her lips are soft, yielding, parting for me like she's been waiting for this just as long as I have.

I keep it gentle at first, devoted. Like I'm kissing something sacred. But then she makes this sound—half-whimper, half-moan—and it destroys me. Something inside me snaps, clean and total.

My tongue slips against hers, claiming, exploring, memorizing. Her hands tangle in my hair, nails scraping over my scalp in a way that drags a groan straight from my chest. I shift, settling more firmly between her thighs, and the heat of her against me nearly short-circuits my entire nervous system.

She gasps into my mouth as she feels how hard I am, her hips lifting to meet mine like her body can't not react. The thin layers of fabric between us feel like a lie—like one more barrier that needs to be torn away.

"Fuck, Nel," I pant against her neck, my teeth grazing the delicate skin just below her ear. "Do you have any idea what you do to me?"

Her laugh is breathy, wicked, intoxicating. "I think I'm getting the picture," she whispers, rolling her hips again—and it's devastating. My vision goes hazy at the edges, my control slipping one second at a time.

I crash back into her mouth, kissing her harder now, deeper, like I'm trying to make up for every moment I didn't get to touch her. My hand slides under her tank top, the soft warmth of her skin meeting my palm like a gift I didn't earn but can't stop taking. Her stomach jumps beneath my fingers as I trail higher, higher—until I'm cupping her breast, my thumb grazing over her nipple.

"Archer," she breathes, and the sound of my name in her mouth— like that—is pure fucking addiction. I'll do anything to hear it again.

Her legs wrap tight around my waist, pulling me down, closer, until there's not a single inch of space between us. I grind against her, and the pressure—God, the pressure—is so perfect it's almost cruel. Every roll of her hips threatens to unravel me, and I know I'm hanging on by a thread, one breath away from losing every ounce of self-control I've ever had.

And still, somehow, I pull back.

Barely.

My forehead rests against hers, both of us breathing hard. My heart is pounding so loud I can barely hear anything else. Every cell in my body is screaming stay, stay, don't stop, not now.

But she's too important to rush. And I want every single second to count.

"We need to stop," I rasp, the words feeling like they're being ripped out of me.

Her eyes widen, hurt flashing across her features before she can mask it. "You don't want—"

"Don't even finish that sentence," I growl, pressing my forehead against hers. "I want you so badly I can barely think straight. But if we don't leave right now, I'm going to lock that door and nobody's seeing you for at least a week."

Her pupils blow wide, nearly swallowing the hazel. "Is that a promise or a threat?"

I groan. "Both. Neither. I don't know." I press a quick, hard kiss to her lips. "I want to do this right, Penelope. Take you on a proper date. Wine and dine you. The works."

"You've known me for three years," she points out, her fingers playing with the hair at the nape of my neck.

"Exactly. I've waited this long—a few more hours won't kill me." I don't tell her that if I start, I won't be able to stop. That I'll consume her whole, like wildfire burning everything it touches. That the need I've been tamping down is a monster inside me, scratching to get free.

"Fine," she sighs, but the smile playing at the corners of her mouth tells me she's not really disappointed. "Help me up?"

I stand, tugging her up with me, but misjudge my strength. She crashes into my chest, all soft curves colliding with hard muscle, and the impact knocks the wind clean out of me.

For a moment, we just stand there, frozen. Her hands splayed across my chest. My arms wrapped tight around her waist. Her body pressed so perfectly against mine it feels like a cosmic punchline—every nerve in my body lit up, screaming more, more, more.

"You should get dressed," I manage, though every cell in my body protests like I've just suggested cutting off my own oxygen supply.

She nods.

But doesn't move.

Neither do I.

Her eyes are locked on my mouth, that bottom lip caught between her teeth like she knows what it does to me. And she does. God help me, she absolutely does.

"Nel," I warn, my voice tight as a drum, tension coiled in every muscle.

"Going," she says, voice breathy and entirely too smug, stepping away with all the grace of a woman who knows she's got me on a leash —and isn't in any rush to unhook it. She snatches up the clothes I laid out for her, casting one last scorching look over her shoulder before disappearing into the bathroom.

The second the door clicks shut, I let out a breath like I've been holding it since the moment her skin touched mine. I adjust myself in jeans that now feel at least two sizes too small and mutter a string of words I probably shouldn't say aloud.

This woman is going to be the death of me.

But what a goddamn way to go.

While I wait, I try reciting boat specs in my head. Hull designs, engine models, anchor weights. Anything to cool the wildfire still burning through me. But it's no use. Every mental detour leads straight back to her: the taste of her mouth, the feel of her hips grinding against mine, the sounds she makes when she loses control.

God help me.

Because I don't think I'm going to survive her.

And I'm not entirely sure I want to.

11

---

s we pull out of the driveway and onto the open road, it feels like the weight of the world slips off my shoulders and rolls into the sea behind us. I lean my head back and stretch my hand out the window, letting the wind curl around my fingers as I close my eyes. Music hums through the truck, low and warm, wrapping around me like a favorite sweater.

For the first time in a long time, it feels like freedom.

Like I've been holding my breath for three years and I'm finally breaking the surface, lungs burning and full again.

The morning air is crisp, threaded with the scent of salt and heather carried in from the hills, the whisper of waves crashing somewhere beyond the rise. The breeze lifts my hair, tugging at the edges of something tender and wild inside me.

Then the truck swerves—just slightly—but enough to jolt me back to reality. My eyes snap open.

"Sorry," Archer says, wincing as he pushes his glasses up his nose with one finger, eyes flicking back to the road.

"What happened?" I ask, heart still kicking up a beat.

"I was looking at you," he says simply, sheepish and sincere.

I don't even try to fight the grin that spreads across my face. It takes root in my chest, blooming slow and sure, like wildflowers after a spring rain.

Holy shit. I love this man.

The thought hits me with the weight of truth and the softness of surprise.

Love.

God, that's a big word. Too big to say out loud. Too big to ignore.

I glance sideways at him—one hand on the wheel, the other riding the wind. His hair is an effortless mix of bedhead and breeze, the sun catching on strands like it knows he's its favorite. He looks like something off the pages of one of those rugged outdoorsy magazines—except the difference is, he really did wake up like this. No pretense. No filter.

I let my gaze follow the line of his arm, from wrist to shoulder, pausing on the veins disappearing beneath his sleeve. Even now—wind-tousled and sleepy-eyed—Archer is all precision and control. Every movement purposeful. Every breath measured. He's the kind of man who always knows where his feet are planted.

And somehow, that careful steadiness makes me want to come undone.

He smirks, biting his bottom lip like he knows exactly what he's doing to me—and he does. The tension between us is so thick it could be spread on toast and served with breakfast.

"Don't look at me like that, Nel." His voice is low, tight. "I'm not a saint. Just a man with a breaking point."

My man.

My gaze drops to his mouth—those sinful lips that should come with a warning label and a liability clause.

His fingers flex against the steering wheel, knuckles whitening, and he drops his head back for a breath, though his eyes never leave the road. "I should've locked us in your bedroom when I had the chance," he mutters, jaw clenching like he's barely holding himself together.

"What would you have done?" I ask, shifting in my seat, my voice already breathy.

"What I want to do? Or what I would have done?" His voice dips into something darker—gravelly, intimate, dangerous.

My mouth goes dry. "Want."

He glances at me from the corner of his eye, and I swear I feel it like a touch. "I want to sink my cock into your tight little cunt and fuck you so hard it makes up for the last three years."

His words hit me like a truck—hot and sudden, stealing the air from my lungs and replacing it with pure, undiluted want.

I stare at him, stunned, lips parting but no sound coming out.

And then he smiles—slow and wicked. The devil in denim and a white T-shirt. Temptation with sexy forearms and a filthy mouth.

"Let me feel what that did to you, baby," he murmurs, eyes flicking back to the road like this is any other conversation. Like he didn't just detonate a bomb between my thighs.

"W-What?" I manage, pulse hammering so loud I can barely hear myself.

"Undo your jeans."

My breath leaves in a shaky exhale. This is insane. We're on an open road. Daylight. Visibility for miles. Every part of my rational brain is screaming what the fuck are you doing?

But my body? My body is already reaching for the button on my waistband.

"Now," he growls, and I whimper as his hand slides over to my thigh, fingers curling tight in a way that says mine without needing to say a word.

My fingers tremble as I unfasten my jeans, dragging the zipper down with a gasp. My skin hums under the pressure of his grip, and every nerve in my body sparks to life, hot and pulsing and desperate.

"Good girl," he murmurs, and I nearly come from just the sound of it.

I clench my jaw, biting down on the moan clawing up my throat as his fingers slip beneath my underwear, cupping me in a way that feels both possessive and devoted.

Good girl.

Two little words—soft, devastating, absolutely lethal. They melt my spine, fog my brain, leave me breathless and aching. My bones dissolve, and I forget how to be anything but his.

"I knew it," he murmurs, voice full of dark satisfaction, as his fingers glide through the slick heat between my legs.

I groan, helpless, legs parting to welcome him in like my body's been waiting years for this moment. Goodbye, dignity. It was a good run. My eyes roll back as his middle finger dips between my folds, not quite inside me, just enough to make my thighs tremble as he slides up to tease my clit with agonizing precision.

"Archer," I gasp, my hand flying to his wrist—maybe to stop him, maybe to ground myself. I tell myself it's resistance, but instead I pull him closer, silently begging for more.

"You like it when I talk about fucking you?" His voice is sin wrapped in silk, low and rough in my ear as he sinks a finger inside me, curling up to stroke exactly where I need it.

"Yes," I breathe, thighs snapping closed around his hand as I grind against the pressure of his palm. The friction is maddening, delicious, not nearly enough and somehow already too much. I'm caught in it, strung so tight I might shatter from a whisper.

Every movement of his hand is fire under my skin. Every filthy word he whispers is a spark I can't put out.

And then—of course—

A siren blares behind us.

My head snaps up, and in the side mirror I spot the only cop car on the entire island flashing its lights. Because of-fucking-course. The universe really has a sick sense of humor.

Archer chuckles—chuckles, the absolute menace—as he pulls over to the side of the road. His hand is still in my pants. I'm so close, it's criminal. Literally. If he keeps going, I might just let us get arrested. I could argue in court that orgasms are a basic human right.

He doesn't stop. Not until the police cruiser door opens and the officer steps out. Only then does he finally withdraw, leaving me half-destroyed and this close to climbing into the driver's seat and flooring it just to get away from my own embarrassment.

I button my jeans with shaking hands, burying my face in my palms. Mortified doesn't even begin to cover it.

"Morning, Pen. Archer."

Oh God.

He knows my name.

I peek through my fingers just in time to see Archer casually sucking his finger clean, grinning like the bastard he is. It's so overtly sexual I'm honestly surprised we're not being cuffed on the spot.

"Good morning, Officer Murray," Archer says smoothly.

"Everything okay? Noticed you were swerving a bit."

"This dirty girl's due for an alignment," Archer replies, patting the dash affectionately.

I gape at him. The truck, he means. I think. Maybe?

"I'd say so," Murray says, tipping his head. "That where you're headed now?"

"We were," Archer says, eyes flicking to me as he winks.

"Good. You two take care."

As Officer Murray drives off, I finally find my voice—and unleash it. "This dirty girl needs an alignment? That's what you came up with? Not 'I hit a pothole,' or 'a bird flew out,' or, I don't know, anything else that didn't sound like foreplay?!"

Archer's only response is to unbuckle my seatbelt and haul me into his lap like I weigh nothing, settling me astride his hips. His hands grip my thighs, firm and unrelenting.

I should protest. I should care that we're still on the side of a public road and that Officer Murray might loop back around at any moment.

But I don't.

Because honestly? Let him watch.

My common sense is currently sunbathing somewhere in Tahiti, sipping something with a mini umbrella, while I'm doing my best to get arrested for public indecency. Which, given our track record, very well may happen.

"Do you know how badly I've wanted to kiss you again?" Archer's voice is rough, full of restraint he's moments away from losing. He brushes my hair back, his thumb sweeping gently over my cheek. He tilts my chin, holding me still as he leans in, dragging his lips over mine in a kiss that's more tease than relief, like he's determined to drive us both insane.

His grip tightens on my hip, pulling me flush against him. I melt into him, soft heat yielding to the hard length of his body, like chocolate on a hot day—sweet, slow, completely undone.

And then he loses it.

He pushes his tongue into my mouth, hips straining up to meet mine as his control crumbles beneath me. My hands slide to his jaw, feeling the scrape of his stubble against my palms as I deepen the kiss, angling my head and grinding down on him. The contrast between the man who lives by structure and spreadsheets and this—all hunger and heat and chaos—makes me dizzy with want.

It's like watching a perfectly folded map get crumpled and tossed out the window.

I only pull back when my lungs threaten mutiny, breathing hard, pulse hammering like I've just swum across the English Channel while being chased by sharks.

"The things I want to do to you, Nel. Fuck." He drags a hand through his hair, wild and destroyed. "Do you know how long I've had to catalog them?" His voice drops, and he bites my bottom lip gently, then sucks on it like he can't help himself. "I want to pull my cock out and watch you wrap those tiny hands around it. Then your lips. Then your pussy."

He kisses me again—hard, devouring—and my knees damn near give out.

"If I weren't planning to spend the rest of my life fucking you," he growls against my mouth, "I'd pull it out right here and make you watch me enter heaven for the first time."

Sweet baby Jesus.

When did Archer learn how to talk like that? And when did I become the kind of woman who spontaneously combusts from words alone?

"Archer," I gasp, gripping his shoulders. "You can't say things like that."

"Why?" He flashes a grin that could bring entire kingdoms to their knees. "Am I making you hot and bothered, baby?"

I whimper as he grips my hips, dragging me over his cock with slow, maddening pressure. The friction is unbearable—not nearly enough, and yet far too much.

"I bet you're so wet I'd slide right in," he murmurs, his tongue tracing the shell of my ear.

"Archer," I rasp, barely hanging on, "I either need you to stop or get me there."

He stills. Waits.

"What do you say?"

"Please," I whisper, already trembling.

"Good girl."

And just like that, anticipation shivers down my spine. My whole body goes liquid as Archer reaches between us, unbuttoning my jeans with slow, practiced hands that tremble ever so slightly. Those two little words—good girl—are still ringing in my ears, turning my insides to melted Sugar.

"I didn't know these had twenty-five fucking buttons when I picked them out," he mutters, working his way down with increasing frustration. For a man who usually moves with precise control, he's clumsy now—drunk on want, tripping over the very thing he's been craving.

When he finally tugs the last one free, he groans like the sound has been caged in his chest for too long. Both hands slide down, rough palms gliding over my hips, cupping the curve of my ass like he's been imagining it for years.

I grind back into his touch, dragging my clit along the thick line of his cock, rubbing against him with wild, frantic rhythm like I'm trying to start a fire. I probably am. I should be embarrassed by how shameless I am right now, but I left embarrassed behind somewhere around the first dirty word and am now deep in the land of don't care, need orgasm.

His fingers slide past the swell of my ass, finding the slick heat at my center with devastating accuracy.

"Fuckkk, Archer," I moan, arching against him as my body clenches tight.

"You're so wet for me, baby," he groans, dragging his lips along the slope of my neck, voice hoarse and destroyed. "God, I knew you'd be hot, but I wasn't prepared for this. For how perfect you feel."

"Please," I gasp, every part of me begging to be filled.

He growls, low and rough, before thrusting two fingers inside me. I cry out, rocking down to meet each stroke, grinding against his cock like my life depends on it. Every movement, every pass of his fingers against that spot inside me sends sparks through my body like he's rewriting my nervous system, tearing out old wires and replacing them with something only he can control.

"Fucking hell, Nel. I can't do this here," he rasps.

And then he moves.

He reaches past me, starts the truck with one hand while the other stays buried inside me. Without warning, he yanks the wheel hard left, driving us straight off the side of the road and down into the grass. The truck bounces over a small embankment and rolls to a stop in a shallow valley, shielded by trees, tucked safely between the road and the wild.

Mr. Safety First just went full caveman.

And I've never been more turned on in my life.

"Take your pants off," he pleads, voice ragged.

I brace on my knees and shift to the middle seat, shimmying out of my jeans with zero grace. The logical part of my brain is whispering something about ticks and poison ivy, but the horny part is screaming WORTH IT like a stadium chant.

"Leave your underwear on," he says as he shoves his jeans down over his hips, like that one thin scrap of fabric is going to somehow save us from crossing the line we've already obliterated.

I try not to look. I do. I fail.

My eyes lock on his cock. Thick, veined, and so hard it looks painful. My mouth waters at the sight of it, and for a second, I wonder if this is what addiction feels like—this desperate, all-consuming ache that coils low in my belly and won't let go.

Archer reaches for me, gripping my hips like he's trying to keep himself grounded, then manhandles me back into position, dragging my body over his. My underwear's the only thing separating us now, and it's doing a terrible job.

"Yes," he breathes, pushing his cock down between my legs, grinding up against me with slow, controlled thrusts. If it weren't for that damn underwear, he'd already be inside me. He flexes his hips again, and I feel the blunt head of his cock press against my entrance, just barely parting me before the fabric halts his progress.

"I wish I deserved you," he groans, voice breaking, fingers tightening on my ass.

"Don't say that," I whisper, cupping his jaw.

"Someone who deserved you wouldn't do this," he says, slumping lower in his seat like the guilt is physically pulling him down. But his hands never leave my body. "Someone who deserved you would wait."

He shifts, dragging his cock up along his stomach, and then hooks a finger in my underwear, pulling it to the side. He nestles my slick heat directly over his shaft, and the contact is electric. I gasp as I settle on top of him, our bodies finally skin-to-skin, heat to heat.

"Fuck, Archer," I whimper, grinding slowly along his length, my arousal slicking his cock. The friction is heaven. Torture. Everything.

This moment, this vulnerability, from the man who's always so composed, so in control, makes something crack open inside me. I want to show him he deserves it. Deserves me. Deserves every kind of love and pleasure and messy, complicated joy we're building together.

"God damn," he chokes out, his gaze fixed between my legs. I glance down and see it too—the flushed, angry head of his cock peeking out from between us, glistening with my need.

"Take your shirt off," I beg, sliding my hands beneath the fabric, palms flattening against his abs. His muscles twitch under my touch, tense and trembling, and I want all of it—every inch, every sound, every secret he's ever kept locked away.

He leans forward, jerking his shirt over his head in one smooth motion before gripping my ass with both hands and slowly pulling me forward. I gasp as my clit catches on the swollen head of his cock, heat flashing through me like lightning.

"Put all of your weight on me, Nel."

I let go, muscles relaxing as my full weight settles onto him. I look down, mesmerized, watching as my slick pussy cradles the length of his shaft. It's the most erotic thing I've ever seen. We fit—like we were made for this.

"That's my girl," he groans, dragging me back and forth with a firm grip on my hips.

"I'm close," I whisper, voice cracking like a prayer.

He holds me still with one hand, the other slipping between my ass cheeks. The unexpected touch makes me jerk, a sharp gasp tearing from my throat as pleasure explodes in a new direction.

"Archer!"

"What?" he chuckles, the picture of wicked innocence. His fingertip glides along the sensitive strip of skin between my pussy and ass. "You don't like it?"

I can't even form words. I just moan, helpless as sensation overloads my system.

"That's what I thought." His hand moves lower, two fingers sliding into my cunt with practiced precision. "I can't wait until I can do this properly and make you squirt," he growls, holding me down as he fucks me with his fingers.

"I don't think I can do that," I pant, clenching around him, drunk on pleasure.

"Then you've never been with someone who knows what they're doing." His voice shifts, sharp and commanding. "Look at me, Nel."

That tone. Captain mode engaged. It cuts straight through the haze and pins me in place.

I meet his eyes, and it starts a chain reaction. He dips his head, captures my mouth in a kiss that's more possession than affection, more promise than apology. His lips claim mine as he drags me along his cock, slow and devastating.

"Come for me, baby."

I tilt my hips just a little too far as he pulls me forward, and the head of his cock presses against his fingers, stretching my entrance. It's the closest we've come to actual penetration, and it's too much. The teasing. The pressure.

"Don't you fucking dare," he growls, lifting me and grinding me along the length of him, the head of his cock now pressing insistently against my clit.

"Archer," I whine, squirming as we both look down and watch—

watch—the red, swollen head of his cock disappear, then slide back into view like some X-rated magic trick. It should be degrading.

It's not. It's holy.

"Fuck, Nel." His hand trembles against my hip before he grips tighter, knuckles white.

I can feel how close he is, and I want it—I want to see him unravel, want to see him fall apart beneath me. I sit up straighter, putting more of my weight on his cock, and pull off my shirt in one smooth motion. I take his hand and press it to my breast, watching his pupils dilate.

"Do you want me to embarrass myself?" he groans, words breaking on a sound that's almost a growl. He hooks a finger into the chain around my neck, dragging me down for another kiss that's all teeth and tongue and desperation.

Then his thumb brushes that sensitive spot near my ass again, and the shock of pleasure that jolts through me is volcanic. I bite his lip as the orgasm hits, my whole body locking up before it detonates outward. I cry out, loud and raw, grinding down as I come apart.

Archer grunts, trying to hold me still—but I don't let him. I ride it out, dragging myself up and down his length, pushing him past the edge.

He groans, shuddering violently, and I pull back just in time to watch it happen—ropes of cum spilling across his abs, thick and hot, evidence of everything we've just done. I stare, heart racing, as the last shiver leaves his body.

I did that.

I made him—the man of endless patience and neat lines and laminated checklists—lose it.

"Jesus Christ, baby," he groans, cock still pulsing beneath me. "I don't know the last time I lost control like that."

Satisfaction rolls through me, deep and sinful.

Then he drags a finger through his cum, lifts it to my chest, and writes one word across my skin.

MINE

I should be offended. I should be scandalized. I'm a strong, independent woman who doesn't need a man. But all I feel is claimed. In the best, most devastating way.

I am so fucked.

I can't concentrate on anything during lunch other than the way my shirt is sticking to the cum on my chest. He didn't let me pull on my shirt until his cum was dry. Who knew Archer had such a kinky side? Not me, but I'm here for it. It's like I'm wearing an invisible badge that says "Property of Archer" and only we know it's there.

The restaurant Archer chose sits perched on a bluff above the sea, its massive windows framing the gray-blue sweep of the North Atlantic like a living painting. Inside, the space strikes this perfect balance between rustic and refined—exposed stone walls, warm wood tables, soft light glinting off sea glass vases.

"Earth to Nel!"

His voice pulls me back, and I turn to find him watching me, one brow raised.

"Hmm?" I murmur, dragging my dreamy gaze from the view back to the man across the table.

"What are you thinking about?"

"Getting a tattoo."

The words just happen—no filter, no logic, just full-blown, post-sex chaos brain.

"A tattoo?" He tilts his head, amused. "Of what?"

And I should stop. I know I should stop. But his face is so open, so damn beautiful with that relaxed smile.

"Do you think they'd tattoo over your cum?" I ask sweetly. "Or would I have to wash it off first? Or maybe—hear me out—they could tattoo with your cum."

A beat of stunned silence. And then—he laughs. A real one. Deep and low and completely unguarded. It's fucking glorious.

Those dimples peek through the scruff on his jaw and I swear my heart skips like a rock across a lake. It's a version of Archer I almost never see—a man stripped of all his rules and protocols, the clipboard shoved aside for the sheer audacity of living in the moment.

It's like finding out your stuffy high school math teacher used to play bass in a punk band.

Unexpected.

Hot.

Infinitely dangerous to your emotional stability.

"What were you saying?" I ask, pursing my lips to keep from laughing.

"I was asking what you thought of the restaurant."

Oh yeah. The restaurant. I should probably pay attention to that since it's supposedly the reason we're here. I look around, taking in the ambiance as a whole and then focusing on the more minor details. "I really like the mix of textures—the wood, the leather, the brass. It makes it feel luxurious. The lighting is great, too." I run my fingers along the edge of the table, feeling the polished wood grain. "I love how they've incorporated maritime elements without being kitschy. The ceiling beams are amazing—reminds me of the hull of a ship."

"I like it, too."

"How'd you find this place?"

"On Yelp. I spent hours looking at pictures to get a feel for the place before I decided on this one." Of course he did. This is Archer we're talking about—the man who probably has a spreadsheet ranking every restaurant within a fifty-mile radius by ambiance, taste, and whether the bathrooms have those fancy hand lotions.

"Hours? You didn't need to do that."

"There's not much I can do to help, Nel. The least I could do was find you some inspiration."

"Oh, you did that, alright." I give him a suggestive look that would make a sailor blush.

"Not spank bank inspiration, you dirty girl."

We both lean back as the waiter arrives with our food. Archer ordered salmon, I went with fish and chips again. It feels right somehow—like honoring the chaos that started this whole beautiful mess. At least this time, I'm not burning anything down in the process.

"Am I crazy?" I ask, the words slipping out before I can stop them.

"In what way?" he says, lifting an eyebrow as he tears into a warm roll.

I roll my eyes. "To try this. With all five of you. It's insane, right?

Like, clinically questionable. The kind of thing that would make my therapist schedule an emergency session—with her therapist."

"Stop," he says, setting down his fork. He reaches across the table, covering my hand with his. "Nothing good comes from overthinking. You need to look at the facts."

He flags down the waiter for a couple of beers, then turns back to me like he's about to present his case in court.

"When it comes down to it," he says, completely deadpan, "the only thing that's changing is us having sex."

I nearly choke on a fry. "You can't just say that like you're reading the weather report."

He shrugs. "Well, it's true."

And it is, isn't it?

I've had relationships with all of them for years—layers of connection, of laughter and fights and quiet moments hauling nets or repairing engines or patching bruises. It's not like I'm diving in with strangers.

But the sex part... that's the deep end. That's the part that sends a shiver of fear straight down my spine.

"I'm going from having no sex at all to sex with all five of you, Archer. That's not just a leap—it's like going from a kiddie pool to the Mariana Trench."

He chuckles, unfazed. "We'll make it work."

"But—"

"You shouldn't be the one stressing about this, baby," he says, voice gentler now. "It's our job to make you feel good."

I hesitate. "But I want you all to feel good, too." I twist my necklace, fingers working the chain like it can hold me together. "What if I can't be enough for everyone? What if someone ends up feeling left out? I've spent three years keeping all of you at arm's length because I was so afraid of ruining what we have—our crew, our friendship. And now we're just diving in, headfirst, and I..." The words catch, soft and scared. It's the first time I've said any of it out loud.

Archer doesn't let go of my hand. Steady as always.

"Listen to me," he says quietly. "What makes you think you haven't already been enough, just as you are, these past three years? The sex is new, but the way we feel isn't. We've all stuck around, haven't we? Through storms. Through bad catches. Through your terrible cooking."

I bark out a laugh, tears stinging at the corners of my eyes.

"You've always been enough," he says, squeezing my hand. "And nothing—not even the Mariana Trench—is going to change that." He laughs, that easy, beautiful laugh I only ever get to see when he lets his guard down. "We're good, trust me," he says, grinning. "Case in point? Me making a complete fool of myself earlier. Pretty sure I'll have cum stuck to my chest hair for days. Not exactly my finest moment."

"You didn't make a fool of yourself."

"I appreciate that," he says. "But I disagree."

I lean in, lowering my voice. "I like knowing I make you lose control." I peek at him from beneath my lashes, my voice soft but teasing. "It's like having a superpower."

He groans, dragging a hand down his face. "That won't be the last time. You're so fucking sexy. I swear, it was like an out-of-body experience. I blacked out somewhere between the button on your jeans and —God." He tilts his head back, throat working as he swallows hard. "We need to talk about something else. Immediately. Before I drag you into the bathroom and finish what we started."

"Like what I need to do to be able to be fucked in the ass?" I say it calmly, like I'm asking about the weather.

His fork clatters to his plate. "Jesus Christ, Nel!"

He glances around wildly, like someone might leap out from behind a fern and arrest us for indecent conversation. His expression is a chaotic cocktail of shock, arousal, and actual fear. "Not that, not here," he hisses. "Not in a public restaurant, for God's sake."

"I'm serious," I say sweetly, keeping my voice low. "I'm curious. I want to be prepared. For... educational purposes. For science."

I bat my lashes at him, and he stares like he's not sure whether to kiss me or throw me over his shoulder and sprint for the truck.

Without a word, he shifts into the seat beside me, and casually reaches under the tablecloth—grabbing my hand and pulling it straight into his lap.

I gasp. Because he is rock hard. Like, smuggling-a-baseball-bat hard.

"See what you do to me?" he growls in my ear, his voice thick with want, rough with restraint. "Still think you're not enough?"

"Do you want to meet me in the bathroom?" I tease, biting my lip because I already know the answer, and the look on his face is worth every second of torture.

"Don't fucking tempt me." He runs a hand through his hair, visibly exasperated. "How did you hide this side of you for so long? I don't get it."

"It was always there," I say innocently, sipping my beer. "I was just saying it in my head instead of out loud. Like a devil on my shoulder who used to whisper—and now she's upgraded to a megaphone."

He drops his head to the table for a beat, groaning. "Okay, listen. I promise we can talk about your ass when we're back in the truck. But for now, can we stick to safe topics so I don't nut in my pants right here in the restaurant?"

I pout, sticking my bottom lip out in mock innocence. "But it's so fun to tease you. You get this little vein in your forehead that pops out."

"You can tease me with your hand down my pants when we're not in public."

"Deal."

"Now, back to business." He pulls out his phone, scrolling with intense focus. "There's an interior decorating place a few blocks from here," he says. "We could stop in, see what they've got."

"That sounds good." Now that I've got some ideas in my head, I'm itching to make choices. The faster I start rebuilding, the faster I start healing.

"There's also... another kind of store about twenty minutes from here," he adds casually.

I pause. "What kind of store?"

He wiggles his eyebrows.

Wiggles. His. Eyebrows.

It's such an un-Archer-like gesture I nearly snort my drink. "What does that mean?"

"A sex store," he whispers, like we're on a spy mission. "We could pick up something that might help with... you know. What you mentioned earlier."

Oh. Oh.

My brain short-circuits, arousal spearing through me so fast it makes me lightheaded.

"Really?"

"Unless you're scared."

"Scared?" I scoff, a little too loud. "Pshh. Never."

I am. I'm terrified. A sex store with Archer sounds like the last place I should be. Or maybe the first. My moral compass is spinning like it just knocked back three tequila shots.

"Good," he says, his voice dropping low again. "Finish up."

My heart's doing a full-on drum solo as Archer eases into the parking lot of Passion Palace—a building that looks like it should come with a complimentary penicillin shot. The neon sign over the door flickers like it's debating whether it wants to be involved in whatever's about to happen. The lettering—a chaotic swirl of hot pink and purple—arches over a silhouette that might've been a woman or maybe just a suggestive blob if you tilted your head and squinted hard enough.

"You good, Nel?" Archer asks, his voice low and steady, threading through my panic like a lifeline.

I nod, way too fast to look convincing. "Just... new territory," I manage, tugging at my seatbelt like it personally wronged me.

Archer squeezes my hand, that simple touch punching a hole right through my nerves. "We don't have to go in. No pressure. I mean, we could just sit here and make out until the windows fog up. Classic."

I laugh, breathless and grateful. "No, I want to," I say, before my coward brain can veto. I pop the seatbelt, heart hammering loud enough I'm sure he can hear it.

The bell over the door chimes, cheerful and cruel, and then—we're inside. And holy sensory overload, Batman.

Shelves stretch to the ceiling, packed with technicolor toys, shelves of silky, strappy lingerie, racks of glittery harnesses that look suspiciously complicated, and about a million bottles of lube in every scent imaginable. I half expect a Yankee Candle display next to the dildos. Autumn Harvest: now available in vibrating.

My face erupts in heat so fast I'm pretty sure I start sweating glitter.

Archer presses his hand to the small of my back, a quiet anchor against the storm brewing in my bloodstream. "We can take our time," he murmurs, voice low and rough enough to snag on every nerve ending I have. "Just say the word."

The way he says it—like there's a whole lot more he's offering than just browsing—makes my stomach do a full gymnastics routine. I glance at him, and the look he gives me is molten. Promise and mischief and hunger, all rolled into one devastating package.

Yeah. I was absolutely not walking out of here the same person I was when I walked in.

As we wander, trying not to make eye contact with the wall of dildos that look like medieval weaponry, a guy from behind the counter approaches. He's wearing a black shirt that reads "I'm here to help" in a font that's absolutely not reassuring. His gaze lands on me, a little too long, a little too knowing.

"Welcome to Passion Palace! First time here?" he asks, zeroing in on me like I'm a sample platter.

"Um, yes," I say, voice cracking like a teenager in health class.

"Well, allow me to give you the grand tour," he says, stepping closer with a slimy smile. "I'd be happy to demonstrate some of our more interactive products."

Before I can so much as blink, Archer steps between us like a storm front rolling in. His body blocks mine completely, every line of him taut and dangerous.

"Back the fuck off," he says, voice low and lethal. Not yelling. Worse. Controlled. Flat.

The guy puts his hands up, backing away slowly. "Hey, just trying to be helpful."

"We don't need your help," Archer snaps, jaw tight. "Move along."

The guy retreats, muttering something about customer service under his breath as he slinks back to the register.

Archer turns to me, that protective fire in his eyes softening into something warm and open. "You alright?"

I nod, a breathless smile tugging at my lips. "My hero," I murmur, half-teasing, half-dead-serious.

Archer's fingers intertwine with mine as he guides me through the dimly lit aisles. We stop in front of a display that makes my cheeks flush. The products are arranged by size, from "beginner" to "expert" to "holy shit, is that even anatomically possible?"

"Butt plugs?" I whisper, my eyes widening.

Archer's low chuckle sends shivers down my spine. "Trust me, Nel. It's best to start small and work your way up. Stretching over time makes everything more pleasurable." He says it with such confidence that I wonder if he's speaking from experience.

His husky tone has me squirming. I bite my lip, scanning the options in front of me. A set of neon pink graduated plugs catches my eye. They're the least intimidating of the bunch, which isn't saying much.

"These," I murmur, reaching for them.

Archer's approving growl has me clenching my thighs together. "Good girl. Those will be perfect." Those two words again—my personal kryptonite.

We continue browsing, the sexual tension between us building by the second. Archer holds up a lacy black teddy, his eyes roaming my body hungrily. If his gaze were actual touch, I'd be naked and begging in aisle three.

"You'd look incredible in this," he says, voice rough with desire.

I can only nod, imagining his reaction to seeing me in it. He adds it to our basket along with a powerful-looking vibrating wand that promises "earth-shattering orgasms." Well, that's a bold claim. Challenge accepted.

My fingers trace over a silky blindfold. "What about this?" I ask, looking up at him. The idea of surrendering control, of not knowing what's coming next, sends a thrill through me.

Archer's eyes darken. "And these," he adds, grabbing a pair of padded handcuffs.

By the time we reach the counter, I'm practically panting with need. Archer's hand feels like a brand on the small of my back, the heat of his palm sinking into me and settling in my core. I take the bag from the cashier, trying to hide my grin. I can't wait to get home and show the rest of the guys. Their faces alone will be worth every penny.

The aroma of yeast and herbs wafts from the kitchen as Archer and I step through the front door. I spot Spencer at the counter, his muscular arms dusted with flour as he kneads a mound of pizza dough. He's wearing a faded blue t-shirt that stretches tight across his shoulders, his shaggy dirty blonde hair falling into his eyes as he works the dough with strong, capable hands.

"Well, look what the cat dragged in," he drawls, flashing a warm smile. His Southern drawl wraps around his words like honey. "Y'all have fun?"

Before I can respond, Archer sweeps past me, a mischievous glint in his eye. "Oh, we had more than fun. Gather 'round, boys! Time for show and tell."

My cheeks flush as I realize what he's about to do. Part of me wants to snatch the bag away, but another part is dying to see their reactions. Archer waits until all the guys are gathered around him before upending the contents of the Passion Palace bag onto the coffee table. The assortment of colorful toys and accessories spills out, and I have to bite my lip to keep from laughing at the guys' expressions. It's like watching five men simultaneously win the lottery and get hit by lightning.

Spencer is frozen in place, eyes wide as saucers—a total deer-in-headlights moment. Liam's face turns beet red, and he tugs the brim of his hat lower. Jamie lets out a string of creative curses that even has Archer looking at him in surprise. But it's Sammy's reaction that nearly sends me into hysterics. He staggers backward, bumping into an end table and almost knocking over a lamp. "Bloody hell," he mutters, scrubbing his hands over his face.

Jamie, ever the brave one, picks up one of the butt plugs, examining it with a critical eye like he's inspecting a piece of fine art. "Well, well, well. What do we have here? Is our girl ready for a little ass play?"

His golden-brown eyes are alive with mischief, his dimples deepening as he grins.

For fuck's sake. If the floor could open up and swallow me whole right now, that would be great. I fan my face with my hands, trying to cool down, wondering what I've gotten myself into. It's like accidentally sending a nude to the family group chat.

"C'mon, Nel," Archer murmurs, a mischievous glint in his eye. "Why don't you give us a little fashion show?"

I roll my eyes, my heart flip-flopping in my chest. "In your dreams, Archie." The nickname slips out before I can stop it, and I'm rewarded with a flash of surprise followed by pleasure in his eyes.

"Come on, Penelope," Sammy chimes in, wiggling his eyebrows. "We want to see."

The teddy looks like a scrap of fabric in his large hands. I glance around at them, my resolve weakening. Being desired by five men is a heady thing—like having all your insecurities simultaneously validated and erased. "Fine," I huff, snatching the lacy garment. "But I'm doing this for me, not you lot. Consider it part of my 'giving fewer fucks' initiative."

I take a moment to assess their reactions, pleased at the flash of surprise on their faces. They're used to me being the cautious one, always overthinking, always putting up barriers. But not anymore. I've spent three years denying myself this connection, and I'm done holding back. Life's too short to not wear sexy lingerie for five gorgeous men who look at you like you're the last slice of pizza.

"But if I hear one wolf whistle, I'm kicking you all out." I say it with enough conviction that they all nod solemnly, though the effect is somewhat ruined by the gleam in their eyes.

In my room, I slip into the teddy, its silky fabric cool against my skin. It's such a stark contrast to my usual attire—the neon coveralls and novelty wellies that have been my armor. Those clothes helped me keep my distance, kept me from being seen as anything more than their captain, their boss. This flimsy scrap of lace shows everything I've been hiding. It makes me feel both vulnerable and powerful, like I'm finally stepping into a version of myself I've always known existed but was too afraid to acknowledge.

I take a deep breath, steeling myself. I can do this. I'm a badass bitch who runs a fishing boat and a restaurant. A little lingerie is nothing. I text Archer to put on some sensual music and throw my phone back on my bed, my hands shaking. Fuck.

As the first notes drift through the air, I strut out, channeling my inner Victoria's Secret model (minus the six-foot height and airbrushed abs). The confidence I'm faking must be convincing because the guys' jaws drop in unison, like they're part of some pervy synchronized swimming team.

"Crikey," Liam breathes, taking off his hat and holding it over his heart. His eyes darken as they travel slowly over my body, lingering in places that make my skin tingle.

I spin, giving them the full effect, and they whoop and holler in response, making my entire body flush pink with embarrassment. But beneath the embarrassment is a growing sense of power. I did this—I made these five men lose their composure with just a scrap of lace and a little confidence.

"You're a fucking vision, Pip," Sammy says, his gaze sweeping down my body. His dark skin glows under the low lights, his full lips parting in a way that has my thighs clenching instinctively. Usually the steadiest of the bunch, now he looks like he's two seconds from forgetting all his manners.

Archer's eyes smolder as he growls, "Damn, Nel. I knew that would look good on you, but sweet Jesus. You look amazing."

The men exchange glances, some primal communication passing between them. It's fascinating to watch—the subtle shifts in their expressions, the nearly imperceptible nods. Despite their different personalities, there's an easy understanding between them that speaks to years of working side by side on the boat. It's like watching a wolf pack decide who gets first bite, except I'm not exactly prey and I'm definitely not running.

They move closer as one—slow, inevitable—like I'm gravity and they never stood a chance. Before I can blink, I'm surrounded—pressed between bodies built for work and war, heat rolling off them in waves so thick I could drown in it.

My heart jackhammers against my ribs. My blood sings. Being the center of this much male attention is dizzying—like being caught in the eye of a very sexy hurricane.

"Easy there, fellas," I manage, my voice huskier than intended. "A girl could get used to this kind of attention."

"I hope so," Liam says, turning my face toward him and brushing his lips over mine. His kiss is gentle but confident, tasting of beer and something earthy and warm like leather and sandalwood. I break away when my knees start wobbling, ducking and weaving between their bodies until I'm safely on the other side of their circle. I suck in a deep breath as I watch them all turn toward me, sex radiating from them in waves.

"Who's staying with you tonight?" Spencer asks, his eyes dark.

"You mean who's stuck with the couch?" I shoot back, flashing him a grin that's way too cocky for how fast my heart is hammering.

I reach up, fingers snagging in the messy waves at my temple. Still not used to how short it is—how different I feel with all that weight gone. The gesture is automatic, a nervous tic I've never been able to break.

The boys catch it immediately. I can practically see the mental neon sign flashing over my head: NERVOUS NELLIE, PARTY OF ONE.

"Don't lie to yourself, Sugar. You want us in that bed," he says, voice low and rough enough to scrape along my skin.

His steel-blue eyes—those ridiculous, unfair eyes shot through with flecks of molten gold—gleam with something that twists low and hot in my stomach. Certainty. Possession. A promise I'm already half a second from begging for.

He reads me too easily, like I'm some worn-out paperback he's memorized cover to cover. No amount of fake nonchalance can hide the way my body leans toward him, traitorous and obvious.

I make a face at him and roll my eyes. The most mature response I can muster when he's absolutely right. Really showing my emotional growth here.

"I have an idea," Liam says, his dimples showing as he smiles. "How about we settle this like gentlemen?"

I arch an eyebrow. "Gentlemen? That'll be the day." My tone is dry enough to cure jerky.

Ignoring my jab, Liam continues, "Rock, paper, scissors. Winner gets to sleep in Darlin's bed tonight."

My heart skips a beat. "Whoa, hold on—"

But they're already forming a circle, hands poised like they're about to summon a demon. I watch, torn between amusement and sheer disbelief, as they start. It's like five kindergarteners fighting over the last Oreo—except the Oreo is me and they're all built like lumberjacks.

"Rock, paper, scissors, shoot!"

The first round takes out Jamie and Liam, leaving Archer and Sammy to face off like gladiators. Tension crackles between them, way too serious for what's basically a game you teach toddlers to decide who goes first.

"Come on, guys," I tease, trying to sound breezy and not like my heart is doing cartwheels inside my chest. "This is ridiculous."

(Ridiculously hot, but I'm not exactly volunteering that bit.)

They square off again. And again. On the third try, Sammy's paper smothers Archer's rock.

"Yes!" Sammy crows, punching the air like he just secured world peace. "Looks like it's you and me, Pip."

I roll my eyes but can't stop the grin tugging at my mouth. The pure joy on his face makes something soft and warm unfurl in my chest.

"Don't get too excited," I blurt, nerves getting the better of me. "I fart in my sleep."

The second the words leave my mouth, I want to grab them out of the air and shove them back down my throat.

Why? Why am I like this? Gorgeous man wins the right to share my bed and my first move is to weaponize gastrointestinal facts?

Smooth, Penelope. Real smooth.

Sammy blinks once. Twice. Then his whole face splits into a slow, wicked smile.

"You do?" he says, voice low and teasing, eyes absolutely dancing.

I groan, covering my face with my hands. "Well, I mean, probably?

I'm asleep. I don't exactly have surveillance footage. But statistically, it's likely. Right? Everyone does it. It's science."

I'm babbling now. Full-on chunky peanut butter levels of smoothness.

Sammy chuckles—this deep, rumbling sound that skates down my spine and makes my toes curl. "Good to know," he says, voice a little rougher now. "Guess I'll just have to hold you extra close. You know. For science."

And just like that, my whole body threatens to combust.

As the guys rib each other, tossing insults like kids on a Sugar high, Archer catches my eye. A small tilt of his head toward the kitchen. Serious face. Different from the teasing.

Curious—and more than a little buzzed on nerves—I follow.

Once we're alone, he turns to me, glasses slipping a little down his nose, those intense brown eyes soft in a way that makes my breath catch.

"Nel... I, uh, wanted to thank you," he says, voice quieter now, tugging a hand through his short hair in that way he does when he's nervous.

"Thank me?" I blink, thrown by how earnest he sounds. Archer never half-asses anything, but vulnerability isn't usually part of the package deal.

He huffs out a breath, almost a laugh. "For today. For... letting me in. It meant a lot."

His voice drops lower at the end, and my heart stumbles over itself trying to catch up. This. This right here—this unguarded version of him—is dangerous. The man beneath the clipboard and the controlled smiles. I'm a goner. Someone get me a headstone.

"I had fun too," I admit, the honesty slipping out before I can over-think it. "Even if you did almost get us arrested for driving like a drunk llama."

He chuckles, low and rough, the sound curling around my ribs like a warm hand.

"I'll work on that," he promises, that tiny, shy smile flickering at the corners of his mouth.

We just... stand there for a second. Suspended. Breathless. The kind of silence that's heavy and sweet and crackling with all the things we're not saying.

I reach up without thinking, my fingers sliding over the stubble along his jaw. I trace his bottom lip with my thumb, light and slow, my brain already ten steps ahead, imagining those lips lower. Hotter. Destroying me.

The thought hits me like a sucker punch. My knees wobble.

And right then, of course, Spencer's voice cuts through like a sledgehammer.

"Didn't the two of you already get enough alone time today?" he drawls, sauntering into the kitchen like he didn't just catch me mentally defiling his friend.

I'm about to sputter something when Archer answers for me, low and possessive:

"Not even close."

Before I can blink, Archer surges forward, capturing my mouth in a kiss that's all hard, fast greed—one hand gripping my hip, the other delivering a firm slap to my ass that makes me gasp against his lips.

Then he pulls back like nothing happened, shooting Spencer a smirk as he disappears into the living room, leaving me a breathless, brain-melted puddle. I stare after him, heart slamming against my ribs like it's trying to break out.

I turn back to Spencer, who's watching me with an expression halfway between amused and interested. Where Archer is sharp lines and control, Spencer is all warmth and gravity. The kind of steady heat that seeps under your skin and stays.

Like comparing espresso to hot chocolate—both capable of destroying you, just in very different ways. And honestly? I want both.

"How can I help?" I ask, watching as Spencer dumps the bowl of dough onto the counter, sleeves pushed up, forearms flexing in a way that makes coherent thought very difficult.

He flashes that slow, devastating grin, eyes twinkling like he's already three moves ahead. "Well, Sugar," he drawls, "you can start by washin' those pretty hands of yours."

I salute him with two fingers and head for the sink, scrubbing up to my elbows like I'm prepping for surgery. When I turn back around, he's already working the dough, his strong hands coaxing it with a gentleness that makes my brain short-circuit.

He glances over when I step up beside him, and the sparkle in his eyes nearly knocks me flat.

"Time to get your hands dirty," he murmurs.

He covers my hands with his, guiding me through the motions—slow, purposeful kneading. His chest brushes against my back, and he's so solid, so there, it feels like being wrapped in a weighted blanket—if that blanket had muscles and a drawl that could melt steel.

"That's it," he murmurs, breath hot against the shell of my ear, his voice a low, slow sin.

"Nice and easy. Gotta treat it gentle-like."

I bite my lip, trying to focus on the task at hand and not the fact that my brain is melting into a very undignified puddle. "Like this?" I ask, my voice so breathy it sounds like I'm leaving a voicemail on one of those late-night 1-900 hotlines.

He chuckles—a deep, dangerous sound. "Mmm. Just like that."

Flour gets everywhere. The counter, the floor, my hair, him. I look like I lost a fight with a cocaine shipment, and Spencer's not far behind.

"You've got some flour on your cheek," I say, pointing to the smudge by his right ear.

He wipes at it half-heartedly, missing by a mile.

"You know," I say, fake-sweet, "I think you missed a spot." Before he can blink, I swipe a floury hand across his face, leaving a perfect white handprint.

His eyes go wide. Then narrow. "Oh, it's on now, Sugar," he growls.

And then it's war.

Flour flies through the air, clinging to every surface like it owns the place. We're laughing, shrieking, slipping on the tile in the middle of a full-blown flour war. By the end, we look like we've been mugged by a bakery. Spencer catches me around the waist, lifting me clean off the ground like it's nothing. His hands leave big, floury prints on my ass through the teddy, which is now more white than black.

"Gotcha," he rumbles against my ear, voice low and destroyed.

The laughter fades into something heavier. Thicker. The air between us sparks like static, too charged, too close.

His hands glide up my sides, slow and precise, leaving warm, floury trails. When he cups my breasts through the thin fabric, I gasp, the sensation sharp and electric.

"You wear me well," he murmurs, his thumbs brushing over my hardened nipples through the lace.

I arch into him instinctively, my whole body straining for more.

"Spencer," I whisper, not even sure if it's a plea or a warning. My mind is pure chaos, but my body knows exactly what it wants: him, him, him.

He leans in, lips brushing mine so lightly it's maddening. "Tell me what you want, Sugar," he whispers, his voice all velvet and danger.

Instead of answering, I grab his shirt and yank him down into a kiss that burns all the oxygen out of the room. He tastes like coffee and whiskey and something inherently him—dark and slow and absolutely addictive.

His hands fist in my hair as he deepens the kiss, tongue sweeping into my mouth, coaxing, exploring, destroying me one careful touch at a time. Where Archer demands, Spencer seduces. Every kiss a pull deeper under, a slow unraveling.

When we finally break apart, we're both panting, foreheads pressed together, grinning like idiots.

"Damn, Sugar," he groans, like he's not sure whether to laugh or drag me straight to the bedroom.

Reluctantly—so reluctantly—I step back, my whole body buzzing.

"We should probably finish the pizzas before the guys riot," I say, my voice so husky I barely recognize it, "and before we do something really inappropriate on this counter."

Spencer's eyes darken, his tongue flicking over his lower lip like he's tasting the possibilities. "Lord have mercy," he drawls, slow and devastating. "Would've been the best thing to come outta this kitchen all night."

He winks before turning back to the counter and grabbing a ball of dough. His movements are easy, almost lazy—but there's nothing lazy about the flex of his forearms, or the way his shirt rides up to reveal a teasing strip of skin just above his waistband.

The man could make watching paint dry look X-rated. Hell, he could make watching grass grow feel like premium cable.

"Like what you see?" Spencer asks, catching me mid-stare.

I feel my cheeks go hot, but I refuse to look away. "Maybe," I say, all fake-casual, even though my pulse is doing backflips. "But I'd be more impressed if you tossed it higher."

Two can play this game.

He grins like I've just thrown down the gauntlet. The dough spins higher into the air, and—show-off that he is—Spencer does a little shimmy before catching it perfectly.

It's stupidly hot. Stupid. Hot.

"Your turn," he says, sliding a pan toward me with a wink.

I start layering toppings, hyper-aware of Spencer moving behind me. Too close. Way too solid. My body practically humming from the proximity.

His hands settle lightly on my hips, steadying me as he leans in to peer over my shoulder. His breath skates across the sensitive shell of my ear, sending shivers rippling down my spine.

"Mmm, looks good," he murmurs, voice all slow, syrupy heat. "But I think it needs a little more... sausage."

I snort, elbowing him in the ribs. "You're terrible." But I'm laughing anyway—because of course he can make a bad sex joke sound charming instead of cringe. If it were anyone else, I'd be rolling my eyes so hard they'd get stuck permanently in the back of my skull.

"Terribly charming, you mean," he says, grabbing another ball of dough and tossing it with ridiculous ease.

We fall into a rhythm—him spinning dough, me layering toppings. It feels comfortable. Domestic, almost. If you ignored the fact that my whole body was buzzing like a live wire just from being near him.

As I spread sauce on the fourth pizza, Spencer's hand brushes against mine. Just a graze.

But it sends a jolt of electricity straight up my arm, and when I glance up, he's already watching me.

His gaze pins me there—heated, intense. Like he's seeing all the things I'm trying not to say out loud.

"You've got a little something..." he murmurs, reaching out to brush his thumb across my cheek.

Instead of pulling away, his hand lingers, cupping my face in a touch that feels devoted.

Time hiccups. The kitchen around us fades into nothing but the thundering of my heartbeat.

Spencer leans in slow, giving me every chance to say no. I don't.

My eyes flutter closed just as his lips meet mine—soft and sweet at first. A careful question.

I answer by fisting my hands into his shirt and yanking him closer. The kiss deepens instantly, heat flaring white-hot between us. Spencer groans low in his chest, backing me against the counter like he can't stand even an inch of space between us.

His hands slide down, gripping my ass, lifting me onto the counter in one fluid, practiced move. I wrap my legs around his waist, anchoring myself to him. It's messy and greedy and so, so overdue.

"Where's our pizza?" Sammy calls from the living room, his voice slicing through the kitchen like a bucket of cold water.

We spring apart like guilty teenagers at a high school dance.

Spencer looks thoroughly debauched—hair tousled, lips swollen, his chest heaving like he just ran a marathon.

I probably look like I got hit by the world's hottest freight train. And yeah, I'd happily step in front of it again.

"We're coming!" I shout, my voice cracking halfway through like an absolute traitor.

Spencer chuckles, low and delicious, pressing one last slow kiss to the corner of my mouth before grabbing an oven mitt.

"To be continued, Sugar," he promises, his voice thick enough to spread like honey, as he pulls the last pizza from the oven.

I plop down on the couch between Sammy and Liam, grabbing a slice of pizza like it's the last life raft off a sinking ship. "God, I'm starving," I groan, taking a giant bite. The marinara explodes across my tongue—spicy, rich, life-changing.

I moan. Loudly. Shamelessly.

And immediately realize: they're all just sitting there, staring at me. Watching me moan over my food. Watching me lick grease off my lips like a damn heathen. I freeze mid-chew, cheeks burning. "Eat!" I yell, flailing the slice at them like a weapon.

The guys snap out of it like someone just rang a dinner bell.

"Can't blame us for being distracted, Darlin'," Liam says, shooting me a wink as he grabs a slice.

"Especially when the view is better than the food," Sammy adds, grinning as he loads up his plate.

Jamie laughs, running a hand through his curly brown hair, eyes sparkling. "Sweet mother of God, she's got us all wrapped around her little finger, doesn't she?"

And just like that, the tension melts into laughter, easy and loud.

The conversation flows around me—messy, ridiculous, and perfect. We swap our most embarrassing boat stories, each one more disastrous than the last. I laugh so hard my ribs ache, the knot of nerves inside me unwinding for the first time all day.

This. This feels right.

"Remember when Nel tried to catch that massive haddock with her bare hands?" Archer says, nudging his glasses up his nose.

"And ended up going overboard?" Spencer adds, cracking up. "Never seen someone so small make such a big splash."

"Hey, what about the time Jamie got his pants caught in the winch?" Sammy chimes in, leaning forward like he's sharing classified intel.

Jamie groans, covering his face. "Jesus, are we really bringing that up again?" But his grin gives him away.

As they heckle and rib each other, I sit back and soak it in. The way they move around each other—so effortless, so familiar—like a dance they've been doing for years.

Only this dance involves dick jokes, flying pizza toppings, and the kind of love that sneaks up on you when you aren't looking.

They're chaos and comfort wrapped up together, and somehow, miraculously, mine. It hits me like a punch to the chest: This beautiful mess? This ridiculous, loud, gloriously complicated life? It's exactly where I'm meant to be.

I spent so long being terrified—terrified that wanting more would break everything. But maybe this was always where we were headed. Not the wreckage. The rebuild. The messy, wonderful, terrifying truth of choosing each other out loud.

The restaurant burned. And somehow, from those ashes, something better is rising—like a sexy, feral phoenix with five heads and really good hands.

Despite the chaos, despite the risk, despite everything... I wouldn't trade this life. Not for all the fish and chips in Scotland. Not even for Henry Cavill hand-feeding me chocolate while shirtless.

And that's saying something.

12

———————

I'm in the kitchen making tea when Sammy and Jamie saunter in, matching grins on their faces. I'm immediately suspicious. Those matching expressions scream trouble louder than a car alarm at 3 AM. Outside the window, rain patters gently against the glass, and the distant crash of waves against the shore creates a soothing backdrop to the cozy warmth of the kitchen. The old copper kettle whistles sharply, its high-pitched cry competing with the rhythmic tapping of raindrops against the windowpane.

"Pip, love," Sammy begins, making sure I'm looking at him before continuing. "We have a proposition for you."

My eyebrow quirks up. "Oh? This ought to be good." I set down the kettle, giving them my full attention. The word "proposition" coming from these two could mean anything from "let's organize the pantry alphabetically" to "let's steal a yacht and flee to Mexico."

Jamie steps forward, taking my hand and fiddling with the rings on my fingers. "Sammy and I are wondering if you'd like to spend the night with both of us," he says, a glimmer of hope in his eyes.

My heart skips a beat. Actually, it doesn't just skip, it full-on cartwheels, then backflips, then does that thing Olympic gymnasts do where they twist in the air and somehow land on their feet. "Both of you?" I repeat, swallowing hard.

Sammy nods, his dimples deepening. "Only if you're comfortable with it. No pressure." His voice drops an octave, taking on that velvety quality that always makes my toes curl.

"You don't have to decide right now," Jamie adds quickly. "We can just cuddle or watch that baking show where everyone's nice to each other—"

I hold my finger to his lips, stopping whatever else he was about to say. My body's already made the decision, rendering my brain completely irrelevant to the conversation. "Yes. I'd like that."

Their eyes light up, and I barely hold back a giggle, grinning at them like an idiot. I turn back to the kettle, biting my lip, trying to contain my giddiness while I finish making my tea.

"Shall we get ready for bed then?" Sammy suggests, taking the steaming mug from me and intertwining his fingers through mine, tugging me toward the bedroom.

After I finish my tea, we all somehow end up crammed into the tiny bathroom, the air buzzing with awareness like static before a storm. I wash up first, the sink creaking under my elbows as I lean in. When I'm done, I perch on the counter, feet swinging lightly, watching as they take their turns scrubbing their faces and brushing their teeth.

The mirror fogs over from the steam of the hot water, blurring our reflections into something soft and golden and a little unreal. It feels... dreamlike. Suspended. Us. Together. Here.

"Here, let me," I say, reaching for Sammy's toothbrush. I squeeze a dollop of toothpaste onto it before handing it to him.

"Thanks, Pip," he murmurs, our fingers brushing.

Jamie leans casually against the counter, holding out his toothbrush like a peace offering as he watches us with amusement. "Quite domestic, aren't we?" he says, his dimples flashing as his mouth curves into a slow smile. "Three months ago, you wouldn't let us within arm's reach of your personal space, and now you're squeezing our toothpaste like we're some old married throuple."

I huff a laugh, stretching my legs out along the counter. "It's amazing what almost losing everything will do to your priorities," I say, softer than I mean to. The memory flashes unbidden—flames crawling up the kitchen walls, the smell of smoke sinking into my hair, the helpless ache of watching it all burn. "Sometimes you need things to fall apart before they can be rebuilt better."

Jamie grins, clearly not ready to let me get too philosophical. "Don't get used to it, O'Connor," I add, rolling my eyes. "I'm not doing your laundry next."

While they brush their teeth, I rummage through the overstuffed drawer under the sink, knocking over ancient bottles of toner and forgotten lipsticks. When I find what I'm looking for, I hold it up triumphantly, brandishing the tube like a cartoon villain who's finally cornered the hero. "How do you two feel about face masks?"

Jamie's eyes widen like I just suggested we all get matching tattoos. "You're not serious, Penella," he says, voice full of mock horror.

"Oh, I'm deadly serious," I say, grinning as I unscrew the cap and squeeze out a glob of green goop. "Come here, big guy. Think of it as your ticket to paradise."

Jamie groans but steps between my knees anyway, resting his hands lightly on my thighs as I smear the avocado-green mask across his face. The effect is immediate: he looks like Shrek's hotter, slightly panicked cousin.

Sammy chuckles low in his throat as Jamie glances at him, wide-eyed and betrayed.

"I look like I've been sick on my own face," Jamie mutters, wrinkling his nose at his reflection in the fogged-up mirror.

"Beauty requires sacrifice," I tell them solemnly, barely keeping a straight face. "Besides, Spencer does these twice a week. Swears it keeps his skin 'baby soft.' His words, not mine. And you've seen him— he looks photoshopped in real life."

I point the tube at Sammy with a flourish. "You're next, Mr. Oxford."

Sammy doesn't hesitate. "Wouldn't dream of refusing," he says, smoothing a hand over his short dreads and stepping in close, his gaze holding mine as he offers up his face like a knight submitting to his queen. "One must always be properly exfoliated before engaging in... other activities," he adds with a mischievous glint that makes my stomach do something it probably shouldn't in a cramped bathroom.

As I work the mask across his smooth skin, I can't help but marvel at how easy this feels—how right it feels. Normally, my independent streak would've bolted by now, screaming something about personal space and emotional danger. But not here. Not with them. Jamie, with his endless enthusiasm and terrible jokes. Sammy, with his steady hands and slow-burning smile.

Together, they create a space where I feel both anchored and weightless at the same time—a paradox I never even believed existed. Like being securely tethered while learning how to fly.

"There," I announce, rinsing off my fingers. "Now me."

Sammy takes the tube, carefully smearing the mask over my skin, his gaze dropping to my lips more than once.

Standing between them in the tiny bathroom, I catch our reflection in the mirror and can't help but notice the contrasts. My dirty blonde hair looks almost washed out next to Jamie's rich brown curls, my hazel eyes flickering under the harsh bathroom light while his shine steady and golden. The freckles scattered across my nose—the ones I used to loathe—mirror Jamie's, though his dance across sun-warmed skin while mine dust a much paler canvas.

And then there's Sammy—towering over both of us like he belongs on a marble pedestal somewhere. His dark, glowing skin practically absorbs the crappy fluorescent light and throws it right back, making him look luminous and regal while Jamie and I resemble side characters in a skincare ad gone wrong.

I'm the shortest by far, barely reaching their shoulders, and the three of us together look like some strange, unintentional set of mixed-up measuring cups lined up in a row. Light and dark, short and tall, straight hair and curly and dreaded. Different in every way that matters—and somehow perfect because of it.

Later, after the masks are washed away and I've changed into sleep shorts and a tank top, the laughter has quieted to something softer, something slower, the energy between us shifting. The closeness lingers, sticky-sweet and unspoken, like the last warmth of sun on skin. We fall into bed in a tangle of limbs and soft laughter. I nestle between their bodies, their warmth enveloping me like a cocoon.

Outside, the wind has picked up, whistling around the eaves of the house and making the windows rattle slightly. A sudden crack of thunder makes me jump, and I feel Jamie's arm tighten protectively around my waist. The ancient heating system in the house groans and clanks in protest against the dropping temperature, adding its mechanical grumbles to nature's symphony. The storm intensifies the feeling of safety and intimacy in here—our own little world, protected from the elements.

"So, Pip," Sammy says, "what would you normally be doing right about now?"

I bite my lip, suddenly self-conscious. This feels like admitting I secretly collect taxidermied mice dressed as historical figures or something. "Um, well... I usually listen to an audiobook before bed. I'm about halfway through one."

Jamie props himself up on an elbow behind me, his golden-brown eyes sparkling with interest. "What's it about Penella? Wait, don't tell me—one of those murder documentaries where some suburban housewife poisons her husband with antifreeze?"

"It's, uh... a romance novel," I admit, feeling the heat creep up my neck like rising floodwaters. My cheeks are probably the color of a fire truck by now.

Sammy chuckles, the sound vibrating through me like a low hum. "Brilliant," he says, voice smooth as velvet. "I do love a good literary exploration of human passion." He manages to sound like we're about to dissect Shakespearean sonnets instead of listening to some filthy, sweat-slicked smut.

"What?" I squeak, but Jamie's already reaching for my phone. "Come on, Penelope. Sharing is caring."

With trembling fingers, I pull up the audiobook app and hit play, immediately regretting every choice that brought me to this moment. The narrator's sultry voice fills the room, and of course, by some cosmic joke, it lands smack in the middle of a full-blown sex scene.

Perfect. The universe has a sick sense of humor, or impeccable timing, depending on how you look at it.

Moans and breathless declarations of love echo awkwardly into the charged silence around us, the explicit words threading straight into the tension that's been simmering between us since that night by the fire when everything shifted.

"Oh my," Jamie murmurs against my ear, his breath sending shivers down my spine.

"Sounds like someone knows exactly what she wants." His tone is low, hot, and full of the kind of approval that makes my cheeks burn in the best way.

I scramble to pause it, but Sammy catches my wrist, his grip firm but playful. "Ah-ah. No stopping now. We're invested," he teases, voice gone dark and wicked.

Every point of contact between us ignites like sparks on dry tinder. Jamie's chest pressed against my back, the unmistakable hardness nudging my ass. Sammy's fingers tracing slow, lazy patterns along my hip.

I'm a live wire, every nerve ending tuned to them, to the heat pouring off their bodies, to the rough scrape of Jamie's chin against my shoulder.

I swallow hard, vulnerability crashing over me like a wave. "I, um... I can turn it off if—" My voice scrapes out like gravel, raw and uncertain.

"Don't you dare," Jamie growls, pulling me closer, the low rumble of it reverberating through my bones. "We've waited three bloody years to hear what gets you all hot and bothered. Don't deny us now." He presses his face into the curve of my neck, inhaling deeply.

The honesty in his voice breaks something open inside me. Three years of pretending. Three years of walls and distance and tight smiles and pretending I wasn't burning for them. And now here we are, all those walls crumbling under the weight of a single, breathtaking truth: I was never alone. They were always waiting for me to catch up.

I open my mouth—to say something, anything—And then my alarm goes off. The shrill, Godawful beeping slices through the moment like a chainsaw through butter. We all jump and Jamie nearly tumbles off the bed, his long limbs flailing like a startled giraffe.

"Time to wash off the masks," I gasp, bolting upright and scrambling off the bed like it's suddenly on fire. I need a second. A breath. A buffer zone between me and the very real temptation of begging them both to ravish me at once.

We stumble into the bathroom, all elbows and whispered laughter, a flurry of hands reaching for towels and murmured apologies as we crowd the sink. The cool water offers a momentary reprieve—but it barely touches the fire simmering beneath my skin.

I splash one final rinse over my face and reach blindly for a towel when I feel Jamie step in behind me—solid, warm, inescapably present. His hands slide to my hips like he's done it a hundred times before, and his body presses flush against mine. Warm breath ghosts over the back of my neck, sending a shiver down my spine as I go utterly still.

There's no mistaking the hard line of him through the soft cotton of his pajama pants, firm and purposeful, digging into me like a promise—like he wants to brand the shape of his desire into my skin.

"Jamie," I gasp, my heart rate skyrocketing.

Sammy's eyes meet mine in the mirror, dark with desire. "Do you like that, love? Can you feel how hard he is for you?"

God. If I had known he had such a dirty mouth, I may have jumped in the deep end sooner. His accent makes the words twice as dirty, like hearing a Shakespearean actor recite porn.

"Y-yes," I stammer, my cheeks flaming. I'm probably red enough to be seen from space.

Jamie's hands slide under my tank top, his calloused palms rough against my skin in the best way. "Tell us more, Penella," he murmurs, nipping at my earlobe. "Tell us how much you like it."

My heart is pounding so hard I'm sure they can hear it. It's probably visible through my chest, like in cartoons when the character sees someone hot and their heart punches out of their body in slow motion. I've imagined this moment a thousand different ways, but the real thing? It's overwhelming.

Sammy steps in close, his body boxing me in—warm, solid,

inescapable. "Tell us how wet you are for us," he says, voice thick with need.

I whimper, my hips instinctively pressing back against Jamie's cock, hard and hot and impossible to ignore. "I'm soaked," I whisper, barely able to speak.

Jamie groans, grinding into me more insistently, one of his hands sliding up to cup my breast, thumb brushing across my nipple. The touch is electric—like someone flipped a switch inside me and every nerve lit up.

"Fucking hell," he breathes, voice destroyed.

Sammy's hand slides between my legs, cupping me through the thin fabric of my shorts. He presses firmly, expertly, and my knees nearly give.

"Christ, I can feel how wet you are through the fabric," he growls. "What do you want us to do about it, Pip?"

My head is spinning, caught in the gravity of their bodies and their words. I'm trembling with need, my inhibitions melting away under the heat of their touch like ice cream on a sidewalk—sweet, messy, and impossible to contain.

"Touch me," I breathe, desperate. "Please. I need you both to touch me. But first... give me a minute to pee?"

They both laugh, the sound low and fond, and retreat back toward the bedroom, closing the door behind them.

I grip the sink with trembling hands, trying to gather myself. My reflection looks like a stranger—cheeks flushed, pupils blown wide with arousal. I look thoroughly ravished, and we haven't even started.

After a quick freshen-up, I step out of the bathroom, skin still tingling. The moment I enter the bedroom, I freeze, a laugh caught in my throat.

Jamie and Sammy are spooning under the covers—Sammy tucked against Jamie's chest, clearly the little spoon—wearing matching smug expressions. Sammy flashes me a dimpled grin, completely unbothered by the way my jaw practically hits the floor.

It's equal parts adorable and devastatingly sexy. Like a rom-com poster that got an NC-17 rating.

"Well, don't you two look cozy," I tease, climbing onto the bed and settling beside them, turning so I'm face-to-face with Sammy. His dark eyes gleam with mischief, and the little smirk on his lips makes something low in my belly twist deliciously.

Outside, the wind howls, rattling the windowpanes like the storm is knocking to be let in. Thunder rolls in the distance, low and insistent, a heartbeat behind the silence between us. The moment feels suspended—like we've slipped outside of time. Just the three of us, tucked away while the world comes undone.

"Just enough room for one more," Sammy murmurs, reaching out to tuck a damp strand of hair behind my ear.

My breath catches as he leans in, and then his mouth is on mine—hot, soft, and absolutely devastating. The kiss isn't tentative. It's hungry. He kisses like he's starved for it, like he's been waiting for this moment forever and doesn't plan on wasting a second of it.

His hand finds my breast through my thin pajama top, and I arch into his touch with a soft moan, everything inside me unraveling at once.

"Bloody hell, you're delicious," Sammy breathes against my lips, his voice hoarse.

Desire floods my body, making me bold. I slide my hand down, tracing the ridges of his abs, only to pause when I realize Jamie's hand is already there. Already stroking Sammy's cock in long, slow, teasing motions that make my head spin.

A tsunami of lust crashes through me. It's dizzying. Like I've stood up too fast after lying down too long—lightheaded and aching and ravenous.

Jamie's head pops up, grinning, eyes bright with wicked delight. "Want to help, Penelope?" Before I can answer, he takes my hand gently and guides it under his own. And just like that, I'm touching Sammy.

He's big.

Really big.

My fingers close around him, guided by Jamie's firm, steady grip. The feel of him—hot and thick and smooth, like steel wrapped in silk—has me clenching my thighs.

"Christ," Sammy groans, hips jolting upward. "You two are going to be the death of me."

I can't think, can barely breathe. All I can feel is the weight of Sammy's cock in my hand, Jamie's fingers wrapped around mine, the heat of their bodies and the way everything inside me has gone molten.

"Tell us what you want, angel," Jamie rasps. "We'll give you anything."

My mind races with possibilities, each more sinful than the last. I've never felt so turned on, so cherished, so deliciously wanton in my life. The old me seems like a stranger now. In her place is a woman who knows what she wants and isn't afraid to ask for it.

"I want..." I start, my voice breathy and desperate. "God, I want everything." I swallow hard, gathering every ounce of courage I possess. "I want to watch you two together," I whisper, my cheeks burning. "Please?" My request hangs in the air between us, vulnerable and raw. Like offering my heart on a platter and hoping they don't drop it.

Sammy's eyes darken with lust. "Only if you're getting there with us," he murmurs.

Before I can process what's happening, we're all scrambling off the bed. Jamie pulls me close, his lips crashing against mine in an earth-shattering kiss that makes my knees weak. His hands roam my body, leaving trails of fire in their wake. "You're wearing far too many clothes," he growls, tugging at the hem of my top.

I lift my arms, letting the fabric slide away as Jamie peels it off, slow and devoted like he's unwrapping something precious. His eyes rake over my bare skin, dark and hungry, but there's a softness in them too —like awe and lust got tangled up and forgot how to separate.

"Beautiful," he breathes, dropping to his knees like it's instinct. Like worship.

I gasp as his tongue draws a slow, purposeful line up the inside of my thigh, warm and wet and maddeningly controlled. It's not rushed —it's patient, savoring, like he's memorizing the taste of my skin one inch at a time.

And God, the way he looks up at me—his mouth so close, his hair wild from my grip, those mischievous eyes practically glowing with need—it's enough to short out every coherent thought. Like a fantasy I didn't know my brain could build until he breathed it into existence.

"Tell me I can taste you, Penelope," he murmurs, voice hoarse, lips brushing the soft skin just beside where I need him most. "I'm desperate."

I nod, unable to form a single word. My fingers thread deeper into his hair, and then his mouth is on me.

The first swipe of his tongue is a lightning bolt. A jolt that punches straight through my spine and makes my hips buck against him before I can stop myself. He's relentless—but devoted, like he's savoring me, not just tasting. Every flick of his tongue is purposeful, every press slow and devastating. He moves in deep, measured strokes, building pressure with infuriating precision—drawing out sounds I didn't even know I could make, like he's discovering new parts of me with his mouth alone. My thighs tremble, every nerve tuned to him. My hands are buried in his hair, but he's in control. He always was.

From behind me, Sammy's voice rolls over my skin like a second touch—dark and smooth and sinful. "My turn, I think."

Before I can respond, strong arms scoop me up with dizzying ease. I yelp, laughter and heat colliding as he tosses me onto the bed like I weigh nothing. There's something deeply, wildly erotic about being manhandled like this—trusted and claimed in the same motion. I scramble upright, breathless and flushed, watching as Sammy peels off his clothes with purpose, like he's got no shame and nothing to prove. But God, he does. Every inch of him proves it.

"Like what you see?" he asks, voice low, teasing.

"You know I do," I shoot back, trying to sound playful even as my voice shakes.

Sammy crawls up after me, his lips brushing my inner thigh slow and purposeful, drawing out the anticipation. Heat pools low in my belly, my pulse hammering in unmentionable places.

His breath ghosts over the slick, sensitive skin between my legs, making me ache before he's even truly touched me. And then he does —a trail of featherlight kisses, each one a whisper-soft promise, a vow etched in lips and heat and maddening restraint. By the time his tongue finally slides over me, I gasp, sharp and unfiltered, my hips jerking like he's hit a nerve connected to every part of me.

"Easy, Pip," he murmurs, voice thick with need but steady as always. His hands grip my thighs, holding me open, holding me still. "I've got you."

And God, he does.

He eats me out with a kind of slow, devastating intent—like he's reading my body in braille and memorizing every response. He alternates between broad, steady strokes that make me tremble, and teasing, precise flicks that pull gasps from my throat and have my toes curling.

I whimper, my back arching off the mattress as pleasure rolls through me in waves, crashing and receding only to come back stronger. My fingers twist in the sheets until my knuckles ache, desperate for something to anchor me while he pulls me apart.

Sammy hums against me—a deep, pleased sound that vibrates through my core and lights up every nerve ending it touches.

"God, Pip," he groans, lifting his head for a breathless second. His lips and chin are slick with my arousal, and the sight of him like that—destroyed, wild, worshipful—nearly tips me over the edge.

"You taste like fucking heaven."

I blush at the rawness of it, but I can't look away. Can't think. Can't breathe. Because then he dives back in, hungrier now, tongue circling my clit with maddening precision before dipping lower—slow, shallow strokes that tease my entrance until I'm grinding down against his mouth, chasing more.

I arch again, my body pleading without words, and he answers without hesitation. His chuckle vibrates against me, a low, sinful sound. "Bloody hell," he murmurs, the words nearly swallowed by my heat. "I love the way you move when I touch you."

The praise makes a fresh surge of desperate need flood through my body. I reach down, fingers threading through his dreads, tugging him closer—not that he needs encouragement.

Somewhere in the haze, I feel Jamie watching—his gaze heavy, dark with want.

The knowledge that he's witnessing this—that he's seeing me

come undone under Sammy's mouth—only pushes me closer to the edge.

I've never fantasized about being watched before, but now? I can't imagine anything hotter. My body is strung tight, every nerve buzzing, my release coiled low and sharp like a spring pulled to its limit. One more flick of Sammy's tongue and I'll snap.

"Lube?" Jamie asks, his voice strained.

I manage to lift a trembling hand, waving in the general direction of the nightstand.

"Top drawer," I gasp, the words barely holding shape as Sammy's tongue drags another moan from my throat. "Just—fuck—top drawer."

I hear Jamie rummaging around, then a triumphant, "Got it! Oh, and what's this?"

I lift my head to see him holding my favorite dildo, a wicked grin on his face. I'm beyond embarrassment at this point—I've crossed some invisible line where normal social anxiety can't reach me anymore. He tosses it to Sammy, who catches it without missing a beat.

"Well, well," Sammy says, lifting his head to meet my gaze. "Looks like we're in for quite a night, aren't we, Pip?"

I can't formulate a coherent response as Sammy presses the dildo against my entrance, the cool silicone a stark contrast to his warm mouth. My hips buck involuntarily as he slides it in, stretching me wide. The fullness paired with his tongue on my clit is overwhelming, short-circuiting my brain completely.

"God, you're both fucking gorgeous," Jamie murmurs, positioning himself behind Sammy.

I watch, transfixed, as Jamie enters Sammy in one smooth thrust. And fuck if it's not the most erotic thing I've ever seen.

Sammy's face contorts, not in pain, but in the kind of pleasure that looks sacred. His lips part in a silent gasp, and his eyes flutter shut like he's being kissed by something holy.

Long lashes cast shadows across his cheekbones, and the flush that spreads over his skin only sharpens everything—his jaw, the slope of his neck, the quiet vulnerability in the way his mouth trembles. He furrows his brow briefly before his whole body relaxes, softening around the sensation. He looks like something out of a painting, all contrast and grace. Like someone pressed pause on a Renaissance sculpture right before it came to life.

Jamie behind him is a different kind of stunning. Controlled and completely destroyed. His eyes have gone dark with need, cheeks pink with exertion. His bottom lip is caught between his teeth, red and a little swollen, and a bead of sweat slips down his temple and disappears into the curls at his neck.

When he starts to move, everything shifts. The rhythm isn't just learned—it's felt, deep in the bones. Sammy's eyes snap open, and when they meet mine, the breath rushes out of my lungs like I've been punched.

His pupils are blown wide, only a thin ring of warm brown visible. When he smiles, slow and ruined and radiating bliss, it's like watching the sun rise through smoke.

Each thrust draws a sound from him. A gasp, a moan, a whimper too raw to name. He doesn't hold anything back. He wears his pleasure openly, shamelessly, like it was made to be witnessed. And I can't look away.

Jamie finds his rhythm and moves like he was built for this, like every part of him was made to destroy and worship at the same time. His head falls back, throat exposed, and when he groans, it's deep and guttural and everything I didn't know I needed to hear.

Then Sammy's mouth is on me again. He moans as he licks into me, and the vibration alone nearly tips me over. It's not just the pressure or the way he moves his tongue. It's the devotion. Like this—me, undone beneath him—is the holiest thing he knows.

My fingers tangle in his hair as I cry out, hips bucking helplessly. He doesn't stop. He doesn't even pause. If anything, he holds me firmer, pushes deeper, and every single stroke of his tongue sends another jolt of pleasure through my system, setting every nerve in my body on fire.

And right there, in the heat and sweat and tangle of limbs, I finally understand what it means to be worshipped.

When Jamie's hand finally wraps around Sammy's cock, I adjust my angle so I can watch.

His tan fingers look almost delicate against the deep brown of

Sammy's skin, like he's tracing something sacred. There's nothing hurried or clumsy about it. Every stroke is intentional—slow, controlled, devastating.

Sammy's cock is gorgeous. Long, thick, almost too much to take in at once. Veins stand out beneath smooth, velvety skin, the head flushed and glistening with precum. Jamie swipes his thumb through the slick bead at the tip and spreads it down his shaft, dragging a groan from Sammy so low and rough it makes my toes curl.

The sound of it—Jamie's hand working him, the slick, rhythmic slide of skin on skin—is obscene in the best way. It mixes with our breathing, our moans, our gasps, until the air feels thick with it. Like sex itself is hanging between us. Like it's alive.

I'm completely mesmerized.

Jamie's wrist flicks with each upstroke, just enough twist to make Sammy's hips jerk in response. His forearm flexes, tendons taut, like a musician playing a piece he knows by heart. Not rushed. Not showy. Just... intentional. Devastating. Perfect.

Sammy's hips start to move—slow at first, then syncing with Jamie's rhythm, pushing into the tight circle of his fist like he's chasing something just out of reach. More precum leaks from the tip, spilling over Jamie's fingers and coating them in a shine that makes my mouth go dry.

I realize with sudden, breathless clarity that I've never seen anything more erotic. Not in real life. Not in books. Not in any fantasy I've ever dared to have. Watching them together is like discovering a new color. Something I didn't know the world could hold, and now I never want to unsee it.

Jamie starts to move again, slow and purposeful, his hips rolling in time with each stroke of his hand. With every thrust, Sammy's body rocks forward, the motion translating into me—the hand holding the dildo pushing it deeper, the pressure building fast and unrelenting.

It's too much and not enough, my brain trying to hold onto a thousand sensations at once. I blink, desperate to stay present, desperate to watch it all unfold, to feel all of it.

Jamie glances up, eyes heavy-lidded but focused, like he's trying to memorize the way I look right now—destroyed, open, flushed with pleasure.

"Christ, Penella," he breathes, his voice rough with want. "You have no idea how gorgeous you are like this. Watching you fall apart while I've got my hand on him... fuck, it's the hottest thing I've ever seen." His gaze flicks between my parted lips and the way Sammy's mouth is buried between my legs. "You look like a fucking dream—ruined and radiant. Like you were made for this."

Sammy hums in agreement, the vibrations sending shockwaves through my core. His tongue continues its relentless assault on my clit, circling and flicking with expert precision. I can feel the tension building low in my belly, a coiling spring ready to snap. Each lick, each thrust brings me closer to the edge of oblivion.

Jamie's pace quickens, his hips snapping forward with more force now, every thrust punctuated by the rhythmic slap of skin on skin. The sound alone is filthy and perfect and enough to make my toes curl.

His hand stays wrapped around Sammy's cock, matching the rhythm of his movements so precisely it almost doesn't feel real. It's like the three of us are caught in some kind of feedback loop—one shared, messy pulse of pleasure where every sound, every gasp, every thrust feeds the next.

"That's it, love," Jamie pants, his voice cracking, his eyes locked on mine like he needs to see every second of this unraveling. "Fuck, you're taking it so well. Both of you. So goddamn perfect."

That voice—usually light and teasing—is destroyed now. Rough with something primal. Possessive. Like he's not just inside this moment, he's staking a claim to it. To us.

And it obliterates me.

My hips start moving on their own, grinding against Sammy's mouth, desperate for more. Every part of me is pulled taut, every breath clipped short by the sheer intensity of what's building.

I've never heard Jamie like this. Never seen him this gone. And I want to live in that look on his face. That hunger. That heat.

"I can feel how close you are," Sammy murmurs against me, lifting his head just enough for me to see his lips and chin slick with my arousal.

The sight is obscene. Devoted. Gorgeous. It almost knocks the breath out of me.

"Come for us, Pip," he says, gaze steady and sure. "Let us hear you."

Then he dives back in, and everything disappears.

His mouth is relentless—tongue moving with that same maddening, masterful rhythm—pulling me under, drowning me in the moment.

Jamie's thrusts get wilder, messier. His breath is coming in broken little gasps, like his body's trying to keep up with how close he is. I can feel him shaking from across the bed.

"Fuck, fuck, fuck," Jamie growls, the words a desperate chant now. "I'm gonna come."

And then I snap.

It hits me like a bomb—pleasure exploding across my nerve endings, sharp and hot and completely consuming. I arch off the bed with a cry, every inch of me lit up from the inside. Sammy groans against me, the sound muffled by my body, and the vibration makes everything go hazy and bright and endless. My legs shake. My hands scramble for something to hold onto. And still, he doesn't stop.

Jamie's face twists with release—his jaw clenched, mouth parted, eyes shut tight as his body locks up. His hips stutter, slamming deep one last time, and the sound he makes is somewhere between a moan and a broken prayer. He looks ruined—like the pleasure's too much, too full, like it's burning through him from the inside out.

Sammy gasps against me, his whole body tensing. I watch his cock throb in Jamie's fist as he comes, chest heaving, hands gripping the sheets like he needs something to anchor him through it.

For several long moments, the only sound in the room is our heavy breathing, and the gentle tapping of raindrops against the window, a soothing counterpoint to our racing hearts. The storm has gentled, as if mirroring our spent passion, leaving behind only the occasional rumble of distant thunder. Slowly, carefully, we disentangle ourselves, collapsing onto the bed in a sweaty, satisfied heap.

As we lay there, catching our breath, I'm struck by the sheer beauty of the moment. Sammy's skin glistens with a fine sheen of sweat, his chest rising and falling in a steady rhythm. Jamie's curls are wild, sticking up at odd angles, and his freckled cheeks are ruddy. The air is thick with the heady scent of sex and satisfaction.

"That was..." I start, struggling to find words adequate enough to describe what we just shared.

"Bloody life-changing," Sammy finishes for me, his voice hoarse and filled with awe.

"Poetic as always, Professor," Jamie quips, his laughter bubbling up like a spring. "Always finding the perfect words, aren't you? I was thinking more along the lines of 'holy fucking shit, I think my soul left my body for a bit there.'"

I laugh—loud, breathless, completely unfiltered. The sound bounces off the walls like it belongs here. "If I'd known you two were this good," I say, grinning, "I might not have waited so long."

Jamie groans dramatically into the pillow, and Sammy snorts, but I'm already sobering. The words come out before I can stop them.

"But it wouldn't have been right before. We needed the fire. We needed everything to fall apart first. You know, like when a forest burns and clears out all the underbrush so something stronger can grow in its place."

The truth of it settles over us quietly. No one says anything, but I can feel it—that shared understanding, the kind that doesn't need words because it's already been lived.

I drag my fingers gently across Sammy's chest, mapping shapes only I can see. "I spent so long thinking I had to choose," I admit, voice barely above a whisper.

"Like I couldn't be your captain and also... this. Like wanting you would somehow make me weak. Like it meant I wasn't serious enough, or strong enough, or whatever impossible version of perfect I thought I had to be."

I take a breath. The words feel shaky but right.

"But it's not about choosing. It's about having the guts to be all of it. Leader. Lover. Friend. The whole damn mess. And trusting you see me, all of me, not just the parts I polished up and made palatable."

Sammy pulls me in closer, his hand warm at the back of my head, thumb stroking gently through my hair. Jamie's fingers trace slow circles on my hip, lazy and sure, like he's drawing a map back to this exact moment.

We lie there like that for a while, tangled together in a mess of limbs and skin and quiet happiness. And I feel it, that rare kind of peace that doesn't ask questions. Just settles in your bones and says, stay.

Eventually, reality taps on the door.

"We should probably clean up," I mumble into Sammy's chest, though I don't move an inch. Everything's a little too sticky, a little too perfect. Breaking the spell feels like sacrilege.

"Allow me," Sammy says, pressing a kiss to my forehead before carefully peeling himself out of our tangled mess of limbs.

He disappears for barely a minute and returns with a warm, damp washcloth. The floorboards creak under his feet as he moves, the house groaning and settling around us like an old friend who's seen too much and still chooses to stay.

He starts with me, gentle, unhurried, like he's handling something precious and breakable. Then Jamie. I watch through heavy eyes as Sammy kneels and wipes down Jamie's stomach and thighs, then leans in to press a soft kiss to his hip when he's done. It's such a quiet, tender thing, and my chest tightens around it.

This isn't just cleanup. It's care. It's love. It's the part that comes after, when no one's putting on a show.

"Thank you," Jamie murmurs, catching Sammy by the wrist and tugging him down into a slow, sleepy kiss.

I can't help the smile that pulls at my lips. No jealousy. No weirdness. Just something whole and warm settling inside me. Like the last piece of a puzzle I didn't even know I was working on has finally clicked into place.

When they part, Sammy turns to me, brushing a strand of hair off my forehead, his touch impossibly soft.

"How're you feeling? You okay?"

I nod, but there's a knot in my throat now. One of those too-big emotions you can't name, just feel.

"More than okay," I whisper, blinking too fast. "I spent so long trying to be... perfect. The steady one. The boss who keeps everyone at arm's length because crossing lines felt dangerous." I take a breath that shakes on the way out. "But now that the lines are gone, I just feel... right. Like this was always where we were heading. Like I was running from something that's actually been trying to bring me home."

Jamie presses a kiss to my temple, his voice soft and close. "You're still our captain," he says. "Still our boss. Just... more now."

"You were always more," Sammy adds, barely louder than the quiet around us. "We were just waiting for you to be ready for it."

Jamie's arm tightens around me, and Sammy settles in on the other side, tucking us all back into the warmth of the blankets. The bed creaks under our combined weight, one of the pipes in the wall lets out a gurgling sigh, and the house wraps itself around us again like it approves.

We lie there without speaking. Just breathing, slowly syncing up, three separate pulses falling into rhythm.

And I feel... still. Not stuck, but anchored. Safe.

I've always bristled at the idea of commitment. Always thought it meant giving something up—freedom, identity, control. But here, between these two men who see me so completely, I feel freer than I ever have. It's a contradiction I don't have the energy to unravel right now, but I know I will. One day.

The last thing I hear before sleep pulls me under is the soft crash of waves outside the window. The rhythm of it is old and steady, like a heartbeat I've always known but never truly listened to.

The restaurant will rise again. My life will shift and take new shape. But this, these men, this love, this messy, beautiful truth of us, this is my home now.

Not made of brick or mortar. Made of breath and bodies and choosing each other over and over again.

13

———————

The sharp zing of the line cutting through my hands makes me yelp. "Holy crap, got another one!" My muscles burn as the sea trout fights for its life. Archer moves behind me, his chest pressed against my back as his hands cover mine on the line. His body fits against mine perfectly, like we were made to do this together. The weight of him steadies me, makes me feel rooted.

"Easy," he murmurs, his mouth close enough to make my ear feel like a live wire. "Let her tire herself out first. Just like I had to do with you, you stubborn pain in the ass."

The fish breaks the surface in a spray of silver droplets, thrashing around like it's auditioning for a seafood commercial. Spencer's already there with the net, scooping it up in one smooth motion. "That's what, number fifteen?" His grin is infectious as he adds it to our rapidly filling cooler. "Damn, Sugar, you're on fire today."

I sigh in contentment, breathing deep, the scent of salt mingling with the crisp morning air as spray mists my face when another wave hits the bow. A pair of gannets dive into the water nearby, their white bodies like arrows piercing the surface. The distinctive cry of herring gulls echoes overhead, a soundtrack as familiar to me as my own heartbeat. My stomach interrupts with a growl so loud it could register on the Richter scale, making its opinion on lunch known with all the subtlety of a foghorn.

"You thinking what I'm thinking?" Spencer asks, wiping sweat from his forehead. "Because I'm imagining these babies sizzling in butter, maybe some fresh herbs..."

"God, yes," I groan, already tasting it. My stomach growls again, this time loud enough that both guys turn to look at me. "And we're right by the diving grounds. We could get scallops, maybe even lobster... perfect test run for new menu items when we reopen the restaurant."

Archer's hand squeezes my shoulder. "Lunch first. You've been working those arms hard," he says, his voice gruff but warm. His thumb brushes the nape of my neck, sending shivers down my spine despite the heat. It's ridiculous how the smallest touch from him can set my entire body on red alert.

Spencer disappears into the cabin, returning with a beat-up cooler. The scent of sourdough and herbs fills the air as he pulls out carefully wrapped sandwiches. Each one is nestled in brown paper, tied up like a present with twine. The man could make a gas station sandwich look like it belongs in a Michelin star restaurant. My mouth waters as he hands me one. Thick-cut turkey, avocado, and that spicy aioli that he knows drives me crazy.

"Made the bread fresh this morning," he says, settling beside me on the deck, his gold flecks in his eyes catching the sunlight. "Couldn't sleep, so I figured I'd make something to put that gorgeous smile on your face."

The first bite makes me moan—the bread still has that perfect chew, the aioli hits with just the right amount of heat. It's like a flavor explosion in my mouth, and I briefly consider proposing marriage to this sandwich.

"Holy hell, Spencer," I manage between bites. "What other secrets are you hiding from me? Because this is criminal."

He leans toward me, eyes crinkling at the corners as his fingers brush a crumb from my lower lip. "Wouldn't you like to know, Sugar?" The Southern honey of his drawl wraps around each word. "That's for me to know and you to find out. One delicious secret at a time."

"Have you been holding out on us, Spence?" Archer asks around his own mouthful. A drop of aioli clings to his beard, and my fingers itch to wipe it away. Or maybe to lick it off. Both options are equally appealing right now.

I take another bite, licking sauce from my thumb with slow precision. Spencer's eyes track the movement, his own sandwich forgotten halfway to his mouth. Heat blooms in my chest, then sinks lower, settling in my core like a damn furnace. The air between us suddenly feels charged, like the moment before lightning strikes.

The moment lingers—thick with possibility, but the wind picks up, the boat rocks gently beneath us, and the world keeps moving whether we're ready or not. We finish our sandwiches with a few more glances than strictly necessary, our fingers brushing as we reach for the same napkin.

By the time Archer stands, stretching like a man who's about to cause trouble, the spell has shifted—but not disappeared. "Take the wheel," he says, nodding toward the helm. "Show us how it's done, captain."

The wheel fits easily in my hands, smooth from years of use, and I guide us toward the diving grounds like I never stopped doing this. The North Atlantic stretches out in every direction, an endless sweep of steel-gray water. Off in the distance, sea stacks rise from the water like ancient, stubborn Gods—weathered, sharp-edged, and still standing.

I inhale deep, salt and seaweed hitting the back of my throat, making my lungs ache in the best way. The breeze tugs at my hair, whipping it around my face, and behind me I can feel their eyes on me, warm and heavy.

"Just like old times," Spencer says softly. "Remember when we first saw her out here? Standing at the wheel like she owned the whole damn ocean?"

"I can't believe it was three years ago," Archer sighs. "Thought I was hallucinating. This tiny blonde spitfire driving a commercial boat like she was born with a rudder in her hand."

Heat rushes to my cheeks, the memory hitting in surround sound.

Funny how something can feel both distant and brand-new at the same time. "If I remember right," I say, glancing back at them, "you two just stood there like stunned idiots until I asked if you planned to fish or just admire the scenery."

Spencer barks a laugh, one hand already resting on the cooler. "Can you blame us? Still can't take my eyes off you, Sugar. Some things never change."

The water turns glassy as we slow, the sandy bottom visible beneath us like a living postcard. I kill the engine at our usual diving spot, heart racing a little more than I'd like to admit. The kind of nerves you get before doing something you've done a hundred times—but this time, with an audience that makes your skin hum.

Spencer's shirt hits the deck first. Sunlight slides down his back, catching in the beads of sweat like glitter in motion. Archer stretches, and the tattoo of the Maine coastline on his chest shifts with every breath, like it's alive under his skin. I have to look away before I trip over my own jaw.

I strip out of my coveralls, trying to act normal. Cool. Professional. Whatever. But their gazes are heat-seeking and unapologetic, and suddenly the salt breeze against my bare skin feels more like a lover's exhale than the wind. It's like one of those dreams where you show up to school naked—but instead of horror, I feel... wanted. Confident. Powerful.

I dive in before I can overthink it, the cold shocking the breath out of me in one brutal, perfect second. It's like being reset—every nerve zinged awake, every thought cleared. My mask seals, my fins kick, and I sink beneath the surface like I belong there.

Sunlight slants down in shimmering ribbons. Bubbles trail from my mouth as I scan the seafloor, and the world goes quiet in that sacred, underwater way—just heartbeat and breath and the thrill of the hunt. I spot the scallops almost immediately, nestled in the sand like treasure waiting to be found.

When I break the surface, I hold my prize high, water pouring off my arm. "First catch!" I call out, grinning so hard my face aches.

"Show off," Spencer teases, swimming closer. "But can you do this?"

He disappears with a splash and resurfaces seconds later with three scallops and the grin of a man who thinks he's won.

"Amateur," Archer calls from a few yards out, voice dry and surgical. He lifts a full-grown lobster out of the water like he's just summoned it. "This is how it's done."

The next two hours pass in a blur of dives and flirting disguised as competition. My muscles ache in that satisfying way that says I'll feel it tomorrow, and my skin tingles from the salt, the sun, and maybe something more.

Spencer sneaks up behind me more than once, arms looping around my waist as he drags me under with a laugh in his throat and mischief in his eyes. Every time I surface coughing and laughing, he holds me close a little longer—his mouth brushing my shoulder, his breath warm on my neck. Like he can't quite let go yet. Like maybe he doesn't want to.

Then Archer gets in on the game. His hands find my hips underwater, pulling my head beneath the surface. It's otherworldly down there—quiet and bright and strange and intimate, like we've slipped into some alternate universe where time doesn't matter and touches mean everything.

The three of us chase each other through the sea like kids or lovers or something tangled in between. Fingers brushing slick skin. Legs tangling. Gasps of air between dives. Every time one of them touches me—casually, purposefully—it feels like a live wire lighting up my whole body.

By the time we haul ourselves back aboard, I'm shivering, my teeth clacking like castanets despite the heat of the sun. Water streams from my hair and drips down my body in slow, determined rivulets, and then I realize, with horrifying clarity, my underwear is completely see-through.

Not a little see-through. Not "if-you-squint" see-through. I mean full-on might-as-well-be-naked levels of transparency.

Thunder rumbles in the distance, low and ominous, like the sky's got its own opinions about what's coming next. The air shifts, thick and electric, like it's waiting for someone to make the next move. And I swear, every nerve ending in my body stands up and salutes.

Spencer looks at me like he's just taken a punch to the chest. His gaze starts at my feet and drags upward in slow, worshipful agony. When his eyes hit mine, his throat bobs like he's physically swallowing his better judgment.

"Sugar," he says, voice all gravel and hunger. "You're gonna be the death of me. And I'm not even mad about it."

Behind him, I hear a sharp inhale—Archer. I turn just in time to see him adjusting his fogged glasses, eyes blazing behind the lenses like he's about two seconds from combusting.

"Christ, Nel," he mutters, low and rough. "You trying to kill us?"

I open my mouth to say something—anything—but the words don't stand a chance.

Because Spencer is suddenly behind me, his arms sliding around my waist like he's been waiting for this moment all day. He pulls me back against him, firm and sure, until there's not a breath of space between us. I feel everything—the solid press of his chest, the steady pound of his heart, the way his muscles tighten when I gasp.

His skin is still cool from the water, but it's warming fast against mine. The contrast between the chill of his body and the heat blooming beneath my skin sends a ripple through me I can't control.

"Don't move," he murmurs against my ear, low and rough, like he's barely hanging on.

His breath ghosts over my neck and I shiver, but not from the cold. Not even close.

Archer steps in front of me, quiet and focused, his gaze locked on mine like I'm the only thing in his world. There's hunger there, plain as day—not rushed or reckless, but calculated. A kind of need that doesn't ask permission because it already knows the answer.

He lowers himself to his knees in front of me, and I swear the air leaves my lungs. Spencer's arms tighten slightly, anchoring me in place, like he knows I might float right out of my skin if he doesn't hold on.

Archer's hands slide up my calves. Slow, steady, adoring. Mapping every inch of skin like a professional cartographer. His fingers reach the backs of my knees, and I gasp.

Sharp. Surprised. Completely undone.

His smile is a quiet promise, and Spencer's grip around my waist is the exclamation mark. And I'm standing there—barely breathing, barely functioning—suspended between two men who look at me like they want to worship and ruin me all at once.

And God, I want them to.

"You're shivering," he says, his voice low and husky. His hands continue their upward path, warming my thighs. Each inch they climb sends a new wave of heat through my body. "Let's get you dried off."

Spencer's lips brush my ear. "Unless you'd rather we warm you up another way?"

My heart races at the suggestion, desire coiling low in my belly like a snake preparing to strike. I lean back into his solid warmth, tilting my head to meet his gaze. His steel-blue eyes are dark with want, pupils blown wide.

"Yes, please," I manage to whisper.

Archer's fingers flex on my thighs, his breath catching like he's just lost a fight with his self-control. He rises slowly, with intention, eyes never leaving mine. It's not just about the heat—it's a question. A moment. A checkpoint before we jump off the edge.

Once he's standing, he cradles my face in his hands, thumbs brushing softly along my cheekbones like I'm fragile. "You sure about this, Penelope?" His voice is rough—hoarse with want but laced with restraint. "Because if we start, I'm not going to stop. Not until I've had every single inch of you."

I nod, fast. Too fast. Words are completely beyond me, stranded somewhere between yes and please. Spencer's arms cinch tighter around my waist, grounding me against him, and I feel everything— the heat of his skin, the ache in his body pressed right up against my back.

Archer kisses me like he's starving for it. No hesitation. No build-up. Just mouth on mouth, breathless and demanding, like he's waited years for this moment and isn't wasting a second more. His body presses into mine, caging me between them—Spencer behind me,

Archer in front—and I've never felt so thoroughly surrounded. So fucking wanted. The scent of salt and skin, sweat and sun, wraps around us, and I melt into it. Into them.

Archer's tongue sweeps over my bottom lip, coaxing me open. I moan for him, tasting heat and hunger and something else—like trust wrapped in gasoline. His hands tangle in my damp hair as the kiss deepens, messy and intoxicating. Behind me, Spencer trails hot, open-mouthed kisses along my neck, his lips grazing my pulse like he's memorizing it. His hips roll against me—his cock thick and unforgiving through the thin cotton of his shorts—and my whole body leans into the rhythm, breath catching at the friction.

"God, your mouth is amazing," Archer mutters against my mouth, pulling back just enough to breathe me in.

His hands skim down my sides and around my back, measured and slow, until they find the clasp of my bra. One flick, and it's gone. The fabric slips from my shoulders and the sea breeze immediately teases across my nipples, drawing a gasp from my throat. I should be embarrassed, exposed—but instead I feel powerful. Lit from the inside. Worshipped.

Spencer's hands move up to cup my breasts, firm and warm. His thumbs graze the tight peaks, and I arch into him, a soft whimper escaping before I can stop it.

"That's my girl," he whispers, voice low and thick, every syllable dripping heat.

"Those sounds you make—Jesus. I could live off them."

Archer breaks our kiss, his mouth trailing heat down my jaw, across my throat, until he sinks to his knees in front of me. He drags my soaked panties down my thighs with aching slowness, like he's unwrapping a gift he's been waiting to open for far too long. I step out of them, bare and trembling and more turned on than I've ever been in my life.

He looks up at me—eyes gone dark and dangerous. "Fuck, Nel," he breathes. "You're unreal." His palms slide up my thighs, thumbs brushing so close to where I need him it makes me shudder. "I'm gonna make you feel so good," he murmurs, "you'll forget anything else ever existed."

Then his mouth is on me.

His tongue is hot and wet as it slides over my clit—slow and careful at first, like he's learning how I taste. The first flick makes my hips jump, the sensation sharp and immediate. Spencer's arms tighten around my waist, holding me steady as my legs threaten to give out.

Archer licks me again, dragging the flat of his tongue over my clit and then circling it with slow, precise pressure. The wet glide of it is almost unbearable—too much and not enough all at once. He does it again, slower this time, his mouth warm and open, lips brushing sensitive skin as he sucks lightly. My whole body clenches.

His stubble scrapes against the inside of my thighs—coarse, hot, just rough enough to make me twitch. My breath catches, and I feel my thighs starting to shake. The heat from his mouth spreads through me like a fuse being lit, every stroke of his tongue sending a fresh wave of pressure low in my belly.

He keeps going, licking and sucking in a steady rhythm, each pass more confident than the last. It's wet and messy and focused. His tongue presses tight against me, sliding back and forth, my clit throbbing with every stroke. My body reacts before I can think—hips rolling up into his mouth, desperate for more.

"That's it," Spencer growls, voice low in my ear, his breath thick with lust.

"Let him make you come, Sugar. Let us make you feel good."

Archer's tongue moves with more purpose now—slow licks, deep pressure. He moans into me, the vibration sending a bolt of pleasure through my spine. I cry out, high and raw, and he doubles down, locking his arms around my hips and burying his face like he's found religion between my legs.

"Jesus fuck, you taste like heaven," he groans, pulling back for just a breath. "I could eat your pussy for hours and still want more. Might never stop." Then he's back—sucking, licking, teasing—and when two fingers slide inside me, curling perfectly, I nearly come undone on the spot.

I'm so wet it's obscene, and Spencer's hands are everywhere— kneading my breasts, rolling my nipples, his cock grinding against my ass like it's killing him not to be inside me yet.

"You hear that?" he murmurs, pausing so I can hear the sound my pussy's making as Archer finger fucks me. "That's the sound of how bad you needed this. How fucking soaked you are for us."

I can't speak. I can't think. I'm caught in the middle of them—devastated, unraveling, and aching for more. And we've barely even started.

Archer stands slowly, rising like something primal has taken root in him. His lips glisten with my arousal, and there's nothing shy about the hunger in his eyes when he leans in to kiss me.

It's hot and filthy and devoted all at once. When his tongue slides against mine, I taste myself—tangy and wild, and God, it's more erotic than I ever imagined. His hands move over my body like he owns it, and honestly? He might.

Before I can process the rush of it, Spencer growls—a low, possessive sound that cuts through me like lightning. He spins me to face him, his blue eyes stormy with need as he crashes his mouth onto mine. The kiss is rougher, more impatient. He kisses like he's staking a claim. Like I already belong to him, and he's reminding me.

I reach for the waistband of his shorts and shove them down, needing to feel him without anything between us. His cock presses forward, thick and hard, sliding between my thighs with maddening friction. The head catches on my clit and I jolt, a moan spilling from my lips as the shock of pleasure hits me hard and fast.

"Fuck, Sugar," Spencer groans into my mouth, hips rocking against me. "You're drenched."

Archer steps in behind me again, his presence a second wave of heat. He finds that sensitive spot just behind my ear with his mouth, and I swear I forget my own name.

His hands slide around to cup my breasts, thumbs circling my nipples in lazy, devastating strokes as Spencer keeps grinding against me, every pass sending shockwaves through my core.

"Look what you've done to her, Spence," Archer says, voice rough, dark with need. His hand slides lower, over my ass and between my thighs, dipping into the slick heat there.

He groans as his fingers come away wet, then brings them to my lips. "Taste yourself, sweetheart," he whispers, brushing my mouth open. "See how fucking delicious you are."

I part my lips and suck his fingers in, moaning softly around them.

Spencer watches, eyes dark and blown, his hips never stopping. "Christ," he mutters. "That's the hottest fucking thing I've ever seen."

Archer pulls his fingers free with a wet pop and traces them down the line of my throat, over my collarbone, leaving a shimmering trail that catches the sunlight.

"Want to know what else is hot?" he murmurs, voice dropping to something filthy and sacred. "The way your tight little pussy clenches every time Spencer's cock glides past it. The way your nipples get even harder when I do this..."

He pinches one between his fingers, slow and firm, and I cry out, my body arching into the touch. The movement drags Spencer's cock along my slit again, the head catching perfectly on my clit—and I shatter a little more.

"Fuck," I gasp, the word barely more than a breath. "Please, I need—"

"What do you need, sweetheart?" Spencer says, his voice gone full wreckage now. He grips my hips tighter, grounding me, guiding me. "Tell us. Use those pretty lips. We wanna hear it."

Words dissolve on my tongue the second Archer's fingers slip between my thighs. He finds the mess he made there—because let's be honest, this isn't just arousal, it's surrender—and drags it upward in a slow, intentional trail that leaves me trembling. He spreads it along the cleft of my ass like he's marking me. Like he owns every part of me.

My hips twitch as Spencer's cock continues its maddening slide between my thighs, thick and hot and tormenting. Every time the swollen head brushes my clit, my legs threaten to collapse. Pleasure builds low in my belly, molten and mean. Archer wraps one strong arm around my waist, holding me up like he knows I'm seconds from falling apart.

"That's it," he murmurs against my ear, his voice a dangerous kind of gentle. "Let us wreck you, baby."

His fingers find the tight ring of muscle between my cheeks and circle it, slow and teasing. I should be embarrassed by how ready I am for him, how easily I open to the press of his finger. But all I can think about is more. I need more.

The first push burns in the best way—sharp, delicious, a stretch that drags a whimper from my throat.

"Fuck, you're tight," Archer groans, his voice low and worshipful. "I can't wait until the day comes when you're gonna strangle my cock with this tight ass, baby."

That filthy promise hits Spencer like a freight train. His hips jerk forward, his breath catching. "Jesus," he mutters, his grip on my hips turning bruising. "Where the hell did you learn to talk like that?"

The head of his cock bumps my entrance with every maddening thrust. Not inside—just enough to tease, to make me lose what little sanity I'm clinging to.

"You want it, don't you?" Spencer growls, lips brushing my jaw. "You want both of us inside you, fucking you open at the same time?"

I nod—wildly, pathetically. Words are gone, fled. But Archer isn't having that. He scissors two fingers inside me, stretching me wide.

"Use your words, baby," he says, and it's not a request. "Tell us."

"Please," I gasp, the word torn from my throat. "I need you. I need both of you. Please, just—inside me. Now."

Spencer kisses me then, swallowing my moans as Archer fucks my pussy with his fingers. When he pulls back, his eyes are blown wide, pupils swallowing that bright blue.

"Please," I whisper again, destroyed and raw and begging. "Archer, please."

He stills. Just for a beat. Like he needs to hear it twice. Then his free hand ghosts down my side, mapping the curve of my hip, and I shiver.

"God," he breathes, voice thick with hunger. "I'll fuck you but I'm not coming inside you today. Not yet. When I come in that tight little cunt, I want it to be just me. No distractions. Just you and me and that pretty face losing it for me."

The ache he leaves behind when he pulls his fingers free is nearly unbearable. I whimper, pressing back, desperate for anything. For him. His cock replaces his fingers in the next heartbeat—hot, hard, and so perfectly right it feels like salvation.

He nudges at my entrance, the pressure almost enough—

And then he thrusts. All the way in. One long, claiming slide that punches the air from my lungs.

"Fuck," he groans, voice cracking, holding completely still.

I cry out, the stretch a shock of sensation that melts into need. My body clamps down around him, greedy, gasping. Spencer's cock is still trapped between my thighs, pulsing, slick with need, and I feel him lose his rhythm entirely.

"Jesus fucking Christ," Spencer pants, hooking his arm under my knee and leaning back so he can see where Archer is buried inside me. "I wish you could see how your pussy stretches around him. You're perfect. So fucking perfect."

Archer starts to move, each thrust dragging gasps from me, pushing me closer and closer to that edge I can't step back from.

"Just like that," he grits out. "You're taking me so fucking well, baby."

Spencer grinds against me again, his cock sliding between my folds. This time, the head collides with Archer's shaft and nudges higher, pressing at my entrance. My body screams for more—stretched, full, desperate.

"We'll fill you up, baby," Spencer murmurs, one hand cradling my face as he drags his lips across mine. "You just keep falling apart for us. We'll catch you."

"Fuck!" The word rips out of me as Spencer pushes forward—the tip of his cock slipping in beside Archer's.

It's obscene. It's too much. It's everything.

I tremble, muscles going taut from the overwhelming stretch.

"Spencer," Archer growls, his voice a thunderclap against my neck. "I'm not a fucking saint. That feels too goddamn good for you to be teasing."

Spencer groans behind me, pulling back just enough for the head of his cock to drag across my swollen clit, a jolt of pleasure slicing straight through my spine.

"You feel like sin wrapped in velvet, Sugar," he rasps. "And I'm pretty sure this is the express lane to hell." But he thrusts again, sliding his cock along Archer's, stretching me until I'm shaking. "Fuck, I'm gonna come," he grits out. One hand clamps down on my hip, rough and possessive, while the other fists around his cock, pumping with desperate precision.

Archer's rhythm falters, his breath ragged against my ear. "Come for us," he commands, voice shattered. "I want to feel you squeeze my cock. Want to feel you lose it."

Spencer slaps the head of his cock against my clit and that's it—my body lights up, the orgasm crashing into me like a goddamn tidal wave. My knees give out, my scream muffled by the pleasure ripping through me. Everything goes white at the edges. I shake violently, every nerve ending lit up.

"Fuck, fuck, fuck," Spencer chants, stroking himself hard. A moment later, warm spurts of cum hit my thighs and stomach, and the sight of him falling apart stretches my own orgasm into aftershocks that make me whimper.

Archer pulls out slowly, turning me gently. His cock is thick and gleaming, my arousal coating him like honey. One big hand cups my cheek and then his mouth crashes into mine. The kiss is filthy and sacred, his tongue tasting every moan I have left.

"My turn, Pen."

The need in his voice undoes me. I sink to my knees, muscles still trembling, heart still pounding like it's trying to escape my chest. His cock glistens in front of me, flushed and furious, and I wrap my hand around it with shaky fingers. He hisses through his teeth.

"Jesus, Penelope," Archer groans, his voice nothing but gravel and heat. "Need your mouth. Now."

I glance up at him through my lashes, my need for him pounding through my veins like pure grain alcohol. I lean forward, tongue flicking out to taste the bead of pre-cum glistening at his tip. He tastes like sex and salt and the kind of filth I never imagined craving this much.

"That's it," he grunts, hand sinking into my hair. "Take me. Deep as you can. I want to feel your lips stretch around me."

I part my lips and slide him in. Just the head at first, teasing the underside with my tongue. He bucks forward, hips jerking like he can't help it, and I let him. Inch by inch until he hits the back of my throat. My eyes water, but I don't stop.

"Christ," he pants, his grip tightening. "Your mouth is a fucking miracle."

I hollow my cheeks and pull back slowly, only to take him again, deeper this time, my hand twisting along the base, slick and sure. Behind me, Spencer groans, his hands kneading my ass like he owns it.

"Goddamn," he drawls. "The way that pretty little mouth looks stuffed full while your ass bounces like that? It's goddamn art."

He slips his fingers between my thighs again, and I shudder when he finds our slickness and drags it up. He trails it along my ass, his touch featherlight but teasing. He circles my back entrance. I moan around Archer's cock, the vibration making him groan so deep I feel it in my chest.

"That's it," Archer growls, voice cracking. "Take it. Just like that, baby. Your throat's perfect—fuck—"

I lose myself to the rhythm, to the salt and silk of him on my tongue. His hips start to snap harder, rougher. I match his pace with my hand, stroking what I can't swallow. I want him to come undone. I want it all.

His breathing shatters into gasps, every muscle in his body wound tight. "I'm gonna come, baby," he warns, voice raw.

I pull back, his cock slipping from my lips with a filthy little pop that feels far too loud in the charged silence. My hand keeps moving, stroking him slow and slick as I meet his eyes, breathless and shaking. "Do it," I whisper, lips parted. "Come on my face. Mark me."

Something inside him snaps. His grip tightens in my hair, anchoring me in place as his hips thrust forward once—twice—and then he's groaning, broken and beautiful, as the first hot rope lands across my cheek. The next hits my lips, and I don't even hesitate—I taste him, tongue darting out, savoring the bitter, musky salt of him like it's mine to keep.

"Fuck," Archer chokes out, cock still twitching in my fist. "So fucking beautiful."

His thumb grazes my bottom lip, collecting the mess he left behind. He presses it into my mouth, and I suck greedily, never breaking eye contact. Behind me, Spencer groans like he's dying.

"Jesus Christ," he says, voice thick and awed. "That might be the hottest goddamn thing I've ever seen."

His fingers, still teasing my ass, slide deeper, and I moan around Archer's thumb like I've forgotten how to function.

"Still horny, Sugar?" Spencer murmurs, adding a second finger before I can answer. "God, look at you—already begging for more, even when you're destroyed."

I nod, throat too tight for words, everything inside me pulling taut again.

Spencer helps me to my feet, guiding me to the boat's railing, and spreads my hands across the sun-warmed surface. His body slides against mine from behind, his cock nestled between my cheeks.

"Spread those legs for me, Sugar," he says, voice raw and southern and soaked in hunger. "Wanna see how wet you still are."

I widen my stance, the salty air ghosting over my skin, cooling the slick heat between my thighs. Spencer trails his fingers down my spine, and my whole body shivers. When he reaches my ass, he spreads me open, and I can feel the weight of his gaze settle there—hot, possessive.

"Fuck," he breathes. "You're glistening, baby. Pink, swollen, just begging to be filled."

Before I can catch my breath, two thick fingers plunge into me, stretching me wide. My cry echoes across the water, sharp and helpless.

"There she is," he murmurs. His fingers curl just right, finding the spot that makes my vision blur. His other hand cups my ass, thumb circling that tight, aching entrance. When he presses it inside, the burn is sharp and perfect and maddening.

I push back, greedy and breathless.

"Greedy little thing," he growls. "The way your ass clings to me? Goddamn, I'll never get over it."

His fingers in my pussy never stop—pumping, twisting, coaxing me closer to the edge with every calculated move. My thighs tremble, slick and sensitive, as he finds my G-spot again and again.

"There it is," Spencer says softly, his voice a promise. "Found your spot. Gonna make you squirt all over my fucking hand."

He slips a third finger inside me, and I gasp—stretching around him, full and aching and right on the edge of too much. His other hand snakes around my hip, fingers finding my clit and circling it with merciless precision.

"You like this? Like being stuffed full, used, wrung out?" he growls, owning me, owning my body.

All I can do is moan, barely able to hold myself up as he plays my body like a fucking instrument.

"That's it, Sugar. Let me feel you fall apart."

My legs twitch, my body straining against the railing. Spencer's chest presses to my back, his voice like gravel in my ear.

"Let go," he whispers. "Come for me. Drench my fingers. Show me what a desperate, beautiful mess you are."

His rhythm turns relentless. Fingers thrusting deep. Clit rubbed in tight, ruthless circles. The pressure inside me crests—white-hot and blinding.

"Bet you wish it was my cock, don't you?" he growls. "Wish I was splitting you open, fucking you deep, filling that needy little pussy the way you deserve."

I cry out, high and broken, my orgasm slamming into me like a storm surge. My legs give out but he catches me, his arm banding around my waist as he keeps working me through it.

"Fuck, that's it," he pants. "So fucking perfect. So goddamn beautiful when you come. I could watch you fall apart like this forever."

The aftershocks ripple through me like echoes in a cavern—deep and endless and echoing in places I didn't even know could feel. Spencer slowly pulls his fingers from my body, and the emptiness he leaves behind is almost too much. I whimper, shameless and wrung out.

"Hey," he murmurs, turning me carefully. His chest is solid, his heartbeat loud and steady where I press against him. His lips brush mine, soft, slow, and devastatingly tender. Nothing like the filthy things he was whispering seconds ago. The contrast makes me dizzy.

"You okay, sweetheart?" His voice is gentle as he tucks a strand of hair behind my ear. Those blue eyes—God, those eyes—search my face like he's trying to read Morse code in my eyelashes.

I nod, still breathless, still swimming in pleasure that feels like it melted my bones. Words? No. They left two orgasms ago. But I lean into him, legs trembling, and his arms lock around me instantly, holding me up.

Archer appears, quiet and steady, with a damp cloth in his hand and emotion etched into every line of his face. "Here," he says, voice raw like he's been shouting or feeling too much. "Let me take care of you."

The cloth is cool against my overheated skin. Slow swipes. No rush. Just tenderness and whispered praise. When he finishes, he presses a kiss to my forehead that makes my heart feel like it's cracking wide open.

"You were so goddamn amazing," he murmurs, lips brushing against my temple.

Spencer hums in contentment, his chin resting on the top of my head, arms wrapped tight around my waist like I'm something precious. The boat rocks gently beneath us, the rhythm syncing with the slowing beat of our hearts. The afternoon sun paints us in gold, making everything look a little too perfect to be real.

"Let's get you cleaned up properly," Archer says, taking my hand. He leads me toward the tiny shower tucked into the stern, and Spencer follows, his presence a warm shadow at my back. The space is barely big enough for one of us, so of course we all cram in. Archer turns the spigot, and a stream of cool water rains down. I tilt my face up into it, letting it wash away the salt, sweat, and... everything else.

Spencer's hands are slow and sure as they glide over my skin. He works shampoo through my tangled hair, fingertips massaging my scalp gently. The scent of lemon verbena fills the small space, bright and clean. Archer's hands follow, smoothing soap down my shoulders, my arms, everywhere. Careful. Devoted.

"You're shaking," Archer says softly, his voice close to my ear. "Are you cold?"

I shake my head, blinking water from my lashes. "No. Just... overwhelmed." A beat. "But in a good way."

Spencer presses a kiss to the back of my neck. "We've got you, Sugar," he murmurs. "Let us take care of you now."

And they do. Every touch is intentional, unhurried. No rush, no urgency, just this quiet, tender kind of care that makes my throat ache. When the water finally shuts off, I barely have time to shiver before I'm wrapped in a big, fluffy towel that smells like ocean breeze and warm cotton. Someone—Archer, I think—tucks it around me like he's afraid I'll come apart if he's not gentle enough.

Fingers start patting my hair dry, impossibly soft, and when I glance up through heavy lashes, Spencer's focused on the task like he's handling spun glass. He offers a tiny, crooked smile, and I nearly melt all over again.

The heat of Archer's hands returns as he smooths lotion over my skin, slow and warm, his palms moving over every curve with patient devotion. Somewhere in the mix, Spencer produces a bottle of aloe—God knows from where—and his thumbs start working it into my shoulders, easing the sting of the sunburn I didn't realize had settled there. It's cooling and careful, and I lean into it instinctively.

When Archer helps me into one of his flannels, I don't fight it. The fabric is worn soft from a hundred washes, smelling like cedar and soap and him. It swallows me whole, and I let it. Let them.

"There," he says, pressing a kiss to the tip of my nose. "All better."

Spencer and I settle on the deck in a tangle of blankets and cushions and bare skin. The sky is turning watercolor above us, streaked in orange and pink, like it's trying to outdo itself. Archer starts the engine with a low, comforting rumble, and the boat cuts through the water like a sigh.

Salt spray kisses my cheeks, and the wind catches at the damp strands of my hair, whipping them around my face. I don't bother to fix it. Spencer pulls me closer, his arm snug around my waist, his thumb sketching lazy circles on my skin. Goosebumps follow his path like a tide rolling in.

I lean into him, nose tucked against the warm space between his shoulder and neck. His cologne still lingers, mixed with sea salt and sun and something wholly him.

It smells like home.

14

The salty tang of the sea clings to my skin as Archer and Spencer help me unload our catch onto the kitchen counter. Lobsters scuttle in their crates while iridescent fish scales glitter under the overhead light.

"Good work today, Nel," Archer says with a wink that makes my insides flutter. He's definitely not talking about the fishing. "We'll get the rest to the distributor."

I grin, wiping my hands on my coveralls. "Thanks, guys." I'd be drowning in paperwork and fish guts without them, literally and figuratively. "Don't know what I would do without you."

As they head out, I hear footsteps and turn to see Liam sauntering down the hallway, all long limbs and effortless grace, making my heart do a little flip in my chest.

"G'day, Darlin'," he drawls, that megawatt smile lighting up his whole face as he pulls me in for a quick kiss. "How was the fishing?"

"Productive," I reply, gesturing to our catch with what I hope is an innocent smile. "Where's everyone else?"

Liam takes off his hat and runs his hand through his hair, that adorable nervous tic I've come to love. "Sammy and Jamie are at the restaurant dealing with a delivery. Spencer's joined them to start clearing everything with smoke damage."

I wince, feeling guilty for the fun I just had while they were working. "Guess I should head over soon to help."

"Actually," Liam says, his dimples creating those perfect little craters in his cheeks that make my knees weak, "I was thinking we could cook dinner on the beach. It'll be just the two of us for a while. It'd be nice to have some time alone with you."

"Yes," I breathe, already picturing driftwood snapping in the fire pit, smoke curling around skewers of butter-drenched lobster, the two of us wrapped in blankets and something more intangible. "We'll grill the lobster. Maybe do the fish en papillote—lemon, herbs, garlic..."

He leans in, his lips brushing my temple. "You talking dirty to me, or is that just dinner?"

I blush, but only a little. "Can't it be both?"

Liam chuckles, low and rich. "I love how food turns you on."

I sobered a bit, guilt still licking at the edges of my contentment. "I'm sorry I haven't gotten to spend as much time with you."

He silences me with a kiss—gentle, warm, a soft press of forgiveness. "You've been handling everything like a goddamn superhero. Now that my migraine's gone, I'm yours for the evening."

My hand finds his, fingers lacing together. "You up for a beach walk before we start the fire?"

"Sounds perfect." His dimples flash, and I swear they're my favorite punctuation mark.

We gather supplies, brushing hands too often to be accidental. I let my eyes wander—his forearms, flexed and sun-bronzed, the scruff shadowing his jaw, that damnable twinkle in his eye that says he knows exactly what he's doing.

He hoists the cooler. "Allow me, Darlin'."

I grin up at him. "My hero. What would I do without your strong, manly arms?"

"You'd probably get along just fine," he says, grinning. "But where's the fun in that?"

I tug him closer, brushing my lips over his. I intend for the kiss to be light, but the spark between us has me melting into him like I'm made of butter and he's fresh-from-the-oven bread. He reaches up to cradle my face, his thumb caressing my cheek. He tries to pull his fingers away from mine, but I know if that happens, our dinner plans will go out the window faster than my dignity when I'm drunk.

"Beach... dinner," I manage, sucking on his lower lip before I break away for real.

"Fuck, Darlin'," Liam groans. He presses my hand over his crotch. "Look what you do to me."

"You want to see what you do to me?" I ask, before thinking better of it and taking a giant step away from him. My hormones and my brain are currently in an MMA cage match, and my brain is taking a brutal beating. "Jesus. Sorry. I shouldn't have said that. I'll show you later." I wink at him before turning back to the counter, mentally calculating how many Hail Marys I need to say for the thoughts running through my head.

"You fucking better," he murmurs, his teeth sinking into his lower lip in that way that does absolutely nothing to calm my hormones.

I close my eyes, blocking him out, taking a deep, centering breath. I can do this. I can be around him without taking him straight to the bedroom. I think.

Pearl barks, running out the door ahead of us, darting back and forth like she's scouting for enemy forces. Her scraggly fur catches the evening light as she investigates interesting scents, bravely defending us from potentially dangerous pine cones and suspicious-looking shells.

The sidelong glances we exchange do nothing to ease the sexual tension crackling between us as we walk. It's like there's an invisible thread connecting us, pulling tighter with every step.

The narrow path winds through patches of vibrant purple heather, their honey-sweet scent mingling with the salt air. In the distance, a pair of gannets dive into the sea, white streaks against the darkening blue. I breathe in the salty air, relishing the warm breeze on my skin.

. . .

"So," Liam says casually, too casually, "how was your day on the water? The boys treat you right?"

I nod, a blush creeping up my cheeks as memories from earlier flood my mind. Hot, sweaty, explicit memories that would make a romance novelist reach for their smelling salts. How do I say "Spencer and Archer tag-teamed me on the boat" without actually saying the words?

Liam catches the pink tinge spreading across my face and raises an eyebrow, a mischievous glint in his eye. "Well, well," he drawls, leaning in close enough that I can smell his cologne. "What's got you blushing, Darlin'?"

His warm breath tickles my ear, sending a shiver down my spine. I bite my lip, trying to compose myself as vivid flashes play through my mind—Archer's calloused hands sliding up my thighs, Spencer's lips on my neck, the boat rocking with more than just the waves as we...

"Earth to Penelope," Liam teases, nudging me with his elbow. "You've gone awfully quiet. Care to share what's got you so distracted? Your face is the color of a sunburned lobster right now."

I clear my throat, willing the heat in my cheeks to subside. "Just... thinking about how nice it is to have an entire evening with you," I manage, my voice huskier than Morgan Freeman narrating a whiskey commercial.

Liam's eyes darken, his gaze intensifying like I'm a steak and he hasn't eaten in days. "Is that so?" he murmurs, setting down the cooler and stepping closer. "And what exactly did you have in mind for this evening?"

The tension builds as he crowds me against a nearby tree, his body mere inches from mine. I can smell the faint scent of his cologne mingling with sea salt, a combination that should be bottled and sold as an aphrodisiac. My breath catches in my throat as Liam's fingers ghost along my jawline, my spine just turning to jelly.

"I was thinking," I whisper, my voice embarrassingly husky, "that we could start with dinner... and see where the night takes us." Smooth, Penelope. Real smooth.

Liam's eyes darken further, his pupils dilating like a cat spotting a mouse. "I like the sound of that," he murmurs, finally closing the distance between us.

He leans over me, pushing up the brim of his hat before capturing my lips in a mind-melting kiss that makes my toes curl in the sand. I melt against him, my hands sliding up his chest to tangle in the hair at the nape of his neck. Liam groans softly, pressing me more firmly against the tree as his tongue teases the seam of my lips. I part them, drinking in his taste like I'm dying of thirst and he's the last drop of water on earth.

His hands roam my sides, leaving trails of heat in their wake. I arch into his touch, desperate for more. Pearl starts barking at us insistently, then circles back with a stick in her mouth, clearly unimpressed with our detour from the original mission.

"I'm locking her out of your room tonight," Liam says, taking off his hat and running his fingers through his hair with a frustrated huff.

"Oh, so you're sleeping in my room tonight?" I ask, raising an eyebrow. "Do I get any say in that decision?" As if I'd say anything but yes. I'd clear my schedule for the next decade if it meant having him in my bed.

"You get all the say, Darlin', but don't pretend you don't want me between your sheets. Between your legs. We're past that, I hope. Or did I completely misread the whole 'devouring me with your eyes' situation we've had going all day?"

I purse my lips, giving him the side eye as we pick up our gear and continue down the path. I hate when he's right. Especially when he's this right.

"Don't look at me like that," he laughs, shaking his head. "Tell me, Darlin'. Tell me you want me. I want to hear you say it."

"You first," I grumble, my stubborn streak rearing its ugly head. I'd probably argue that water isn't wet just to be contrary.

Pearl drops her stick at my feet, whining for attention. I reach down to scratch behind her ears, grateful for the momentary distraction as I gather my courage. Good dog.

"Darlin'." His voice is low, like he's afraid if he speaks too loudly, I'll bolt. Or vanish. Or maybe he will. "You're..." He exhales, like the words are too big to fit in his chest. "You're the sun that warms my days and the stars that light my nights. Your smile is brighter than the sunrise, and your laughter better than any song I've ever heard." He takes a step closer, gently cupping my face in his hands. "I want you with every fiber of my being, Penelope."

Tears prick at the corners of my eyes as Liam continues, his voice thick with emotion. "You're the most beautiful person I've ever met, inside and out. Your strength, your passion, your fierce independence —they set my soul on fire. I want to lose myself in your eyes, count every freckle on your skin, memorize every curve of your body."

He brushes a thumb across my cheek, catching a tear. "I want to hold you close and never let go. To wake up beside you every morning and fall asleep with you in my arms every night. To build a life with you, to face every challenge and celebrate every win together." Liam takes a deep breath, his brown eyes boring into mine with an intensity that steals my breath away. "I want you, Penelope. All of you. Your mind, your heart, your body, your soul. Now and always."

His words wash over me like a tidal wave, leaving me breathless and trembling. The raw emotion in his voice strips away all my defenses, leaving me bare and exposed.

"Liam," I whisper, my voice cracking. "I..." I move my mouth but nothing comes out. I'm full—overflowing—with too much to say, so instead I crash into him, lips first.

The kiss isn't sweet. It's not careful or soft or neat. It's a goddamn supernova. It's the gasp you take before going under. It's my whole heart in a single, spine-melting press of mouths.

He groans, hands gripping me like he can't stand the idea of letting go. One dives into my hair, the other slides down, bold and familiar, squeezing my ass like it's his full-time job. I moan into his mouth, part of me laughing at how predictably weak I go for him, the rest of me already unraveling.

When we finally come up for air, we're panting. His forehead rests against mine, and the ghost of a smile curves his lips.

"Your turn," he whispers, voice completely wrecked but teasing. "Tell me you want me, Pen."

I laugh, breathless, and nip his bottom lip like I'm making a promise. "I want you," I murmur, dragging my lips down his throat. "I want your hands on me, Liam. Your mouth. Your body pressed to mine, your cock inside me, slow and deep until I forget every name but yours."

He makes a strangled sound, hips twitching like he can't help it.

"I want to learn every inch of you," I whisper into his skin. "I want to watch you fall apart because of me. I want to wreck you, Liam Taylor."

"Jesus Christ, Darlin'," he groans, tightening his grip.

I pull back just enough to meet his eyes, hands sliding under his shirt to the warm skin of his ribs. "I want you, Liam Taylor. In every way possible. I want your laughter, your terrible puns, your gentle heart." My voice softens. "I want your hopes and dreams, your fears and insecurities. I want all of you, always."

His throat bobs. He looks like he's fighting not to fall apart right here in front of me.

"You've got me," he breathes, eyes locked on mine like they're tethered. "All of me. For as long as you want."

He wipes the tears from my face with gentle thumbs, his touch impossibly tender. He molds his lips to mine, pouring everything he has into this single kiss. We don't part until Pearl starts barking at us again, nudging persistently at our legs with her nose. This dog deserves a raise for her commitment to keeping us decent in public spaces. Employee of the month, every month.

"Bloody hell," he mutters, shooting the dog an exasperated look. "Alright, alright, we hear you."

We both crouch down to give her a few more head scratches—because obviously, she deserves a medal for being the Goodest Girl alive—before grabbing our stuff and heading back down the trail.

A few more steps and the trees pull back like a curtain, revealing a view so ridiculously perfect it feels like someone queued up a dream sequence just for us. The beach unfolds in front of us, wild and wide and cinematic, like it's been waiting for us this whole time. The late afternoon sun is in full show-off mode, throwing pinks and oranges across the sky like confetti, while the waves catch the light and shimmer like someone got drunk and dumped a bag of diamonds across the surface.

The sand is soft and pale and stretches for miles, interrupted only by crooked driftwood and boulders that look like they've been here since the last ice age. It's the kind of place that makes you want to kick off your shoes, spin in a circle, and pretend your life is a movie with a killer indie soundtrack.

"I always worry I'm going to take this for granted, but it blows me away every time," I murmur, taking in the distinctive silhouettes of sea stacks rising from the water in the distance. "When we rebuilt the restaurant, I was so focused on what we'd lost that I nearly missed everything we still had."

Liam squeezes my hand. "That's what good friends do, isn't it? Help you see what's still standing when all you can focus on is what burned down. And you've got the five of us plus Millie doing that job, so you're covered from all angles."

I lean against him, suddenly overwhelmed by how much these men have come to mean to me. It hits me like a freight train—this feeling of belonging, of being surrounded by people who care. Me, the girl who once thought relationships were for suckers. "I'm glad you stayed. All of you. I don't think I've said that enough."

"There's nowhere we'd rather be, Darlin'," he says softly, the conviction in his voice leaving no room for doubt.

For a second, neither of us moves. We just stand there, tucked into each other like puzzle pieces that finally found the right fit. My chest tightens with something dangerously close to hope.

But then the wind shifts, rustling the canvas bag slung over my shoulder, and real life tugs us gently back to the moment.

"Okay," I say, clearing my throat like that'll stop the swell of emotion from turning me into a Hallmark movie. "Before I start sobbing and ruin our evening, let's put our stuff down and go on our walk."

I set the cooking gear down on a sun-warmed slab of rock, the metal clinking softly as it settles. Liam crouches beside a weathered boulder, nestling the cooler into the little hollow between stone and sand like he's tucking in a child for bed.

Then, without a word, we head for the water, our hands finding each other like they always do now—effortlessly, like it's muscle memory. He laces our fingers, lifts mine to his lips, and kisses the back of my hand like I'm some Regency heroine instead of a seafood-scented girl in rolled-up overalls.

The water greets us with a chilly lick around our ankles, a teasing little splash that makes me gasp and Liam grin. We walk slowly, bare feet sinking into the packed wet sand, the surf retreating and returning like it's trying to eavesdrop on whatever this is between us.

Behind us, our footprints trail in a lazy, crisscrossed path, uneven and imperfect and so, so us. Romantic clichés? Yeah. Turns out they hit hard when they're real. And this one is steamrolling through every last cynical bone in my body like it knows it's found its mark.

A trio of herring gulls squabble overhead, their distinctive cries echoing across the water. The sky is melting into gold and rose, that magic-hour glow making everything feel soft around the edges—like the world is giving us permission to just be.

The breeze kicks up, tangling our hair and carrying the sharp-sweet scent of blooming gorse from the cliffs. I breathe it in, letting the moment settle into my bones—like maybe this is the kind of memory I'll come back to, not because I need it, but because I want to remember what it feels like when everything is exactly right.

We walk in that perfect kind of silence—not awkward, not loaded, just easy. Safe.

Then Liam glances at me, and that mischievous tilt to his mouth tells me peace was always going to be temporary.

"So," he drawls, swinging our joined hands between us like we're starring in a Netflix rom-com, "what exactly went down on that boat today?"

Heat rises to my cheeks at the mention of it. Oh God. Is there a cliff nearby I can throw myself off?

"Oh, you know," I say, aiming for nonchalance and missing by a mile. "Just the usual. Fishing, diving, trying not to fall overboard." Being absolutely demolished by two of his best friends. No big deal. Just a normal day.

Liam chuckles, his thumb tracing circles on the back of my hand. "Uh-huh. And I suppose that's why you went all pink earlier when I asked about it?" He leans in close, his breath tickling my ear. "Come on,

Darlin'. Spill the beans. What naughty adventures did you get up to out there on the high seas?"

"You want to know details?" I ask, my eyes nearly bugging out of my head. Is this a trap? Some sort of test? Because I'm terrible at tests that don't involve navigation skills or menu planning.

He only raises an eyebrow, waiting for me to talk.

"Fuck, Liam." I clear my throat, fanning at my cheeks. My face must be the color of a fire engine at this point.

"That bad?"

"Worse," I choke out. "Uh. Fuck." I swallow hard, dragging in a ragged breath. My brain is frantically searching for euphemisms and coming up empty. "They—uh—kind of trapped me between them. Spencer fucked my thighs while Archer... well... Archer fucked my, my um... my pussy but didn't want to come inside me." Eloquent, Penelope. Really nailed that description.

"Jesus fucking Christ, Darlin'. That's enough." He clenches his jaw, closing his eyes as he tilts his head to the sky, exposing the long, sexy column of his throat.

What is a sane person to do other than lick it? I can't fucking resist. It's like putting a chocolate cake in front of someone on a diet and saying "don't touch." I press my lips to his skin, licking a line up his neck. He pulls me against his body, gripping my jaw, crushing his lips against mine in a punishing kiss. I return the energy, nipping at his lip, then biting. Hard. His groan is nearly my undoing. I would crawl across shattered glass to hear him make that noise again.

"Spend the night with me tonight, Darlin'," he rasps, pressing his forehead to mine.

"In my bed, you mean?" I tease, because I can't help poking the bear.

"I don't care if it's the middle of the fucking street." He pulls back, his gaze glued to my lips, lust swirling in their depths.

"Yes, you can sleep in my bed tonight," I whisper. I pull away from him before I do something stupid, like push him down on the sand and fuck him while the waves crash over us like we're in a goddamned music video.

I take a few steps back, my toes sinking into the wet sand. With a mischievous grin, I kick my foot, sending a spray of freezing cold water arcing towards Liam. He yelps in surprise, jumping back as the droplets splatter across his jeans.

"Oh, you're in for it now, Darlin'," he growls, narrowing his eyes.

Before I can dodge, he retaliates—water flying straight at my chest like he's got a personal vendetta against me. I shriek, bolting away, but he's already on my heels, laughing like a maniac. We sprint through the shallows, each step splashing up salty spray and clumps of wet sand, our laughter tangled in the wind.

Then the ocean gets in on the fun.

A rogue wave slams into us like it has something to prove. My feet fly out from under me, and I go under in a swirl of foam and grit and pure chaos. For a second, it's just water and adrenaline and the muffled sound of my own squeal.

Then—arms. Strong ones. Liam hauls me up like some soggy beachside hero, and we stagger toward shore, soaked and breathless and laughing like idiots. His hair is plastered to his forehead, his hat lying abandoned in the wet sand. I probably look just as tragic— seaweed couture, clothes suctioned to every inch of my body like I'm auditioning for a very salty wet t-shirt contest.

And still, somehow, he's looking at me like I hung the damn moon.

"Well," Liam chuckles, pushing his wet hair back, "that was unexpected."

The breeze, which earlier had been a flirtatious whisper against sun-warmed skin, now turns traitor—cool and cutting against our soaked clothes. I shiver, and Liam immediately threads his fingers through mine, tugging me toward a flat rock nestled in the dunes like it's been waiting for us all day.

The stone is still sun-hot, radiating heat into our chilled limbs as we sink onto it. I stretch out beside him, and he pulls me in without hesitation, my cheek finding its perfect place over his heartbeat— steady, soothing, like it's keeping time just for me.

We lie there in a tangle of limbs and damp cotton, salt drying gritty against our skin, clothes clinging like a second, slightly more uncomfortable, skin. But the sun is low and golden, casting everything in that almost-unreal light that makes you believe in slow afternoons and second chances.

"This is nice," I murmur, tracing lazy patterns on Liam's arm.

"Mmm," he agrees, his fingers combing gently through my damp hair. "I used to dream about moments like this back in Australia."

I prop myself up on an elbow, looking down at him curiously. "What do you mean?"

Liam's eyes are soft as he gazes up at me, a small smile playing on his lips. "I'd be out in the paddocks, surrounded by nothing but dust and cattle for miles. And I'd close my eyes and imagine myself on a beach somewhere, holding a beautiful woman in my arms." He cups my cheek tenderly. "Never thought I'd actually find her, though."

My heart swells with emotion, and I lean down to kiss his lips softly. "I'm glad you did," I whisper against his mouth.

We lay there for a while longer, trading gentle kisses and soft caresses as the sun begins its descent towards the horizon. We lose ourselves in unhurried exploration, the world narrowing to just us, this rock, and the sound of waves lapping at the shore. Liam's fingers trail down my neck, leaving goosebumps in their wake. I lean into his touch, craving more, but he keeps things slow and sweet.

"You're killing me," I groan, only half-joking.

Liam chuckles, the sound vibrating against my skin. "Patience, Darlin'. We've got all the time in the world."

I inhale deeply, savoring the mingled scents of salt air and Liam's sun-warmed skin. His lips trace a path along my jawline, and I shiver at the contrasting sensations—the roughness of his stubble and the silky softness of his mouth.

"You smell like the ocean," I murmur, running my fingers through his damp hair. It's coarser than usual, textured by the salt water.

Liam hums against my neck. "And you taste like sunshine."

A laugh bubbles up from my chest. "That doesn't even make sense."

"Sure it does," he argues, pulling back to meet my eyes. "Warm, sweet, intoxicating..."

I roll my eyes but can't fight my grin. "You're ridiculous."

"Ridiculously charming, you mean?"

Instead of giving him an answer, I kiss him. The kind of kiss where the world contracts to just this: the pressure of his lips against mine, the ancient rock still radiating afternoon warmth beneath my back, and the peculiar magic of twilight wrapping around us.

My arms prickle with goosebumps in the cooling evening air, though there's an equal chance they're responding to the way Liam's palm skims down my side with purposeful slowness, like he's appreciating every inch before coming to rest on my hip. It's ridiculous how much I can feel through the damp fabric of my clothes—ridiculous and wonderful and terrifying all at once. The heat of his touch seems to sink straight through to my bones, igniting something I've spent years pretending didn't exist.

My body curves toward his without my conscious permission, a truth I can't hide behind clever words or careful distance. I'm trembling now, suspended in this moment between who we've been to each other and who we might become if I surrender to this free fall.

"Cold?" Liam murmurs against my lips, and I swear my entire body tingles from the gruff warmth in his voice, like someone just set every nerve ending on fire and then suggested we make s'mores.

I shake my head, my lips curving into what I hope is a sexy smile and not the manic grin of someone who's waited three years, one month, and seventeen days for this moment. "Definitely not cold."

Liam's eyes darken in that way I've only ever seen in movies—the kind of look that makes you understand why people write songs and start wars and make terrible decisions in the name of desire. "God, you're beautiful," he breathes, his fingers finding the hem of my shirt with the care of someone discovering a long-lost treasure map. "May I?"

I nod, my heart racing as he slowly peels the damp fabric over my head. The cool air pebbles my skin, but Liam's heated gaze warms me from the inside out.

"Breathtaking," he murmurs, and the way his fingers trace my collarbone makes me think he actually believes it. "I've dreamed of this moment for so long, Darlin'. Imagined taking off your clothes little by little. Discovering every freckle, every curve."

This is the part where I should say something devastatingly sexy, but my brain has apparently decided to clock out for the evening, leaving only my body's most primal functions operational. Like breathing. And wanting. And the overwhelming urge to touch him everywhere.

His touch ghosts over my breasts with the careful precision of someone defusing a bomb, each brush of his fingers a potential detonation point. When his mouth finds my neck, sucking gently at my pulse, I make a sound that I've definitely never made before.

"That's it, Darlin'," he groans. "Let me hear how good I make you feel."

His hands map the topography of my body like he's planning to write the definitive guidebook. When they reach my jeans, he pauses, meeting my eyes with a question.

"Is this okay?" he asks, so softly I almost can't hear him over the percussion section now performing in my chest.

I nod frantically. "Yes. God, yes. I need to feel your hands on me."

Liam grins, slowly working open the button and zipper. He tugs the damp denim down my legs, peppering kisses along newly exposed skin.

"Gorgeous," he murmurs against my inner thigh. "Every part of you is absolute perfection."

His fingers trail back up my legs, leaving goosebumps in their wake. When they reach the edge of my panties, I can't help the whimper that escapes me.

"Shh, I've got you," Liam soothes, pressing a kiss to my hipbone. "Tell me what you need, Darlin'."

"You," I gasp. "I need you, Liam. Please."

He groans, resting his forehead against my stomach. "Christ, the things you do to me, Pen. The way you say my name... I could listen to it forever." He runs his fingers over my back, finding the clasp of my bra. He unhooks it slowly, his eyes never leaving mine as he slides the straps down my arms.

"Your turn," I breathe, tugging at the hem of his shirt. "Take your shirt off. I need to feel your skin on mine."

Liam obliges, peeling the clinging fabric over his head. My breath catches as I drink in the sight of his toned chest and muscled arms, golden skin glowing in the fading sunlight.

"Like what you see?" he teases, dimples deepening.

"God, yes," I admit, running my hands over his shoulders, mentally cataloging every muscle for future daydreams.

His gaze dips to my lips and he pulls me into his lap. I straddle him, gasping as the hardness of his cock presses between my legs. Liam buries his face between my breasts, his stubble scraping against sensitive skin.

"Jesus," he groans, voice rough and low against my skin. "I've thought about this too many times. The way you feel... your tits in my hands—fuck." His palms mold around me like they've always belonged there, thumbs brushing over my nipples with the kind of focus that makes me forget how to breathe.

I whimper, my spine bowing, like my body is trying to memorize this moment from the inside out.

"Yeah, that's it," Liam murmurs, his lips grazing a path along my collarbone. "Let me hear you. I want to know exactly what I do to you." His mouth moves lower, his tongue flicking, teasing, claiming until my nipple is wrapped in heat and sensation and I'm unraveling, piece by desperate piece.

"Liam," I gasp, hips canting forward against the very obvious, very hard bulge in his jeans. "Please—"

He lifts his head, mouth wet, pupils blown. "Say it," he rasps. "Tell me what you want, Penelope. I want to hear it from you."

"I need your mouth on me," I pant, the words tumbling out on a wave of need. "Your fingers inside me. I need you to make me come, Liam. Please."

He makes this sound, half-growl, half-sigh, and grips my hips like he's holding onto his last thread of restraint. "Christ, you're gonna ruin me. That filthy little mouth and the way you beg so pretty for me."

Then he kisses me like he's drowning and I'm the air. It's messy, hot, a collision of teeth and tongue and all the things we've been pretending not to want.

When he finally pulls back, we're both completely undone and breathless. "Lie back for me," he says, voice hoarse and like I'm something precious. "Let me show you how long I've wanted this."

Liam's breath whispers against my skin as he settles between my legs, and something inside me turns molten. My heart performs an elaborate gymnastics routine against my ribs.

"I'm going to taste every damn inch of you," he murmurs, his voice a rough caress that makes my toes curl.

Here's the thing about wanting someone for so long: when they finally touch you, it's like your body has been rehearsing for this moment without your knowledge. Every nerve ending knows exactly how to sing.

He starts at my ankles, pressing soft kisses there, and I nearly laugh at how such an innocent touch can feel so charged. The contrast between his gentle lips and rough stubble creates a delicious friction that sends shivers racing up my spine.

"Liam," I breathe, my fingers finding purchase on his forearms, muscled from years of—well, whatever it is that gives a man forearms like that. Rock climbing? Arm wrestling bears? I've lost the ability to form coherent thoughts.

He chuckles, the sound vibrating against my calf. "Patience, Darlin'. We've got all night."

All night. The phrase echoes in my head, a promise that makes me dizzy with anticipation. I watch, transfixed, as he lavishes attention on every inch of skin, and I wonder if anyone has ever been worshipped quite like this before. By the time he reaches my inner thighs, I'm practically levitating.

"You're so beautiful," he whispers, looking up at me with those eyes —the ones that have haunted my dreams for longer than I care to admit.

I want to say something clever and quippy, something that shows I'm still in control here, but my brain has apparently taken an early retirement. Instead, I thread my fingers through his hair, tugging gently, hoping the gesture communicates what words can't.

His mouth inches higher, and my breath catches. Time does that thing where it simultaneously stretches and compresses, and I'm acutely aware of the heat of his breath through the thin fabric of my underwear.

"Liam, please," I whimper, abandoning all pretense of composure.

He grins up at me, those dimples appearing like exclamation

points to punctuate his smug satisfaction. "What was that, Pen? Didn't quite catch it."

Before I can formulate a suitably scathing comeback, he runs a single finger over my slit, only the thinnest of fabrics separating me from the heat of his skin. The touch is feather-light, maddening, and absolutely intentional.

"Bloody hell," he groans, his accent thickening the way it does when he's worked up. "You're soaked through, Darlin'. All this for me?"

I nod frantically, beyond verbal communication at this point. His finger traces lazy circles, expertly avoiding the one spot where I need him most.

"Tell me what you want," he urges, his voice low and gravelly in a way that makes my stomach flip. "I want to hear those pretty words."

There's something particularly vulnerable about articulating desire, more intimate somehow than the act itself. But I'm desperate now, past the point of pride. "Your mouth," I gasp out. "I want your mouth on me."

Liam's eyes darken, pupils expanding until there's just a thin ring of color left. "My pleasure, Darlin'."

He lowers his head like he's about to pray. Except instead of a sermon, it's the slow, devastating drag of his tongue over the thin cotton of my underwear. The contact shouldn't be this intense—not through fabric—but my body doesn't seem to care. I arch up involuntarily, chasing the friction like a woman possessed.

"Fuck, Liam," I gasp, my voice all breath and no control, "please... more."

He chuckles, the sound low and smug and entirely too pleased with himself. His breath is hot against me, and the faint vibration of his laugh sends sparks skittering down my spine. "So polite," he murmurs, mouth still maddeningly close. "Even when you're falling apart."

I have a snarky comeback on the tip of my tongue, something about him being a smug bastard, but then he closes his mouth over me —fabric and all—and sucks.

The world tips sideways.

I let out a strangled moan, hips rolling of their own accord, trying to get closer, get more. Logic, dignity, language—they all leave the chat.

"Don't stop," I pant, clutching at the rock like it's the only thing tethering me to the planet.

Liam hums in agreement, which is frankly rude of him, because that sound travels everywhere. His stubble drags over the tender skin of my inner thighs, grounding me in sensation even as I start to come undone.

And then, slowly, like he's unwrapping something precious, he slips his fingers into the waistband of my panties and starts to peel them away.

When he finally sits back, resting on his heels, it's not to dive back in immediately. It's to look at me. Really look. Like I'm a painting he's been aching to touch, or a secret he's finally been allowed to hear. His gaze is hot and heavy and makes my cheeks burn and my chest ache in the same breath.

I should feel exposed. But under Liam's eyes, I feel wanted.

"Christ," Liam says, almost worshipfully, his voice low and awed. His gaze drags over me like it's the first time he's seen me—really seen me—and I swear the air around us changes, charged like we're standing on the edge of a summer storm. "You're a bloody vision, Penelope."

The words hit somewhere deep, unexpected. I feel my skin flush, heat blooming up my chest. But there's nothing performative in the way he's looking at me—just this raw, earnest hunger. Like he's surprised I'm real.

"Don't stop," I whisper, reaching for him, grounding myself with the press of my palm against his chest. His heart is pounding. So is mine.

He meets my gaze, eyes dark and impossibly focused, and starts trailing his fingers over my skin like he's memorizing it, like he wants to write a thesis on every shiver he causes. My body is caught in a frustrating limbo—alive and humming, but aching for more.

"You're so wet for me," he murmurs, tracing lazy circles around my entrance, maddening in its restraint.

I make a noise I don't even recognize—half desperate, half

pleading—and arch my hips into his hand. "Please," I say, my voice cracking like I've been holding back for too long. "Liam, I need—"

The rest is swallowed by the sharp inhale I suck in when he finally pushes one finger inside me. Slow. Purposeful. Devastating. I feel it everywhere.

I let my head fall back, eyes fluttering shut. "Oh, fuck," I breathe.

He's watching me, watching every shift in my expression like it's the most important thing in the world. His gaze flicks between my face and his hand, like he can't decide which part of me is more beautiful like this, undone, open, his.

"More," I beg, hips moving on instinct now. I don't care how desperate I sound. I am desperate. For him. For this. For the way he makes me feel like I'm the only thing that's ever made him lose control.

Liam licks his lips like he's starving, jaw tight as he eases a second finger in beside the first. "Jesus," he groans, the sound thick with need. His gaze flicks up to mine, pupils blown. "You're so tight Darlin'. Fuck, I can't wait to feel you squeezing my cock the way you're clenching around my fingers right now."

The sound I make is somewhere between a moan and a sob. He starts to move, slow and spine-tingling, curling his fingers like he already knows every secret nerve ending inside me. Like he's been waiting years for this exact moment and wants to savor every single second.

"That's it," he murmurs, settling back between my legs, his lips brushing over my pussy with every word. "Let go for me. Let me see you fall apart."

I'm already falling. There's no graceful descent, no composure. Just raw, aching need as his mouth replaces his words, his lips parting around me with one devastating swipe of his tongue.

My whole body jolts. I cry out, loud and shameless, hips lifting off the stone in search of more. Liam moans into me like he's the one being ruined, the vibrations sparking through me in electric waves.

"Fuck," he pants when he pulls back just enough to speak. His mouth is shiny, his voice demolished. "You taste so fucking good, Darlin'. I'm never gonna get enough."

I think I say his name. I think I say please again. Everything blurs except the pull of his mouth and the rhythm of his fingers, working me with maddening precision until the pressure spirals sharp and sweet and impossible.

The orgasm is right there, all coiled tension and electric anticipation, when everything grinds to a maddening, breath-stealing halt.

Liam groans, guttural and destroyed, and drops his forehead to my thigh like he's been physically taken out. His chest rises and falls in frantic bursts. His whole body is trembling, like he's trying to wrestle his own desire back under control and losing badly.

"I'm sorry," he rasps, voice all grit and apology. "Just... give me a second. I've wanted this for so fucking long. I'm about two seconds away from coming in my pants like I'm sixteen and this is my first boob graze."

I blink down at him, stunned, breathless, and somehow even more turned on than before. My body's still screaming for release, but now there's something tender layered underneath it, something vulnerable and real. Because Liam looks like a man coming undone just from being here. From touching me. From wanting me.

And I can't handle the idea of him stopping now. Not when I'm hanging by a thread.

"Please, Liam," I whisper, voice hoarse with need. "Don't stop. I need you."

His eyes lock on mine, pupils blown wide, and something in them snaps. He reaches down, fingers shaking slightly as he unbuttons his jeans. The rasp of the zipper is louder than it has any right to be—like the universe pressing play on a new chapter.

"Anything for you, Penelope," he murmurs, and the way he says it makes it sound like a vow.

He pulls himself free, wrapping my soaked panties around his cock with a low hiss that makes my whole body clench. I catch a glimpse— Jesus Christ—and then he's moving, settling back between my thighs, hooking my legs up and over his arms so I'm open and helpless beneath him. Exposed, yes—but not embarrassed. Not with him. With Liam, I feel... sacred.

His tongue meets me again, and this time there's nothing slow about it. He devours me like I'm his last meal, alternating between long, hungry strokes and sharp, precise flicks that make my entire body vibrate. My hips buck against his face, my fingers scrabbling for something—anything—to hold onto.

"Fuck, your pussy is amazing," he pants into me, voice thick with awe.

And just like that, I'm gone again—drenched in heat, flushed everywhere, skin tight with tension. Every word, every groan, every syllable of that filthy praise sends heat spiraling through me.

"Liam," I gasp, rocking harder, wild now. "I'm close. So—fuck—"

He groans like that's what he's been waiting to hear, and doubles down, his tongue working in perfect tandem with his fingers.

"That's it, Darlin'," he murmurs against me, voice low and utterly ruined. "Let go for me. I want to taste it. Want to feel you come on my tongue."

That's all it takes. The pressure snaps, and I cry out, clenching around him as wave after wave crashes over me. My thighs lock around his head, my nails dig into the rock, and still he doesn't let up —doesn't stop—drawing out every last ripple until I'm trembling, boneless, undone.

I barely notice the change in him until I hear the harsh rhythm of his breath and the broken curse that follows. His hips jerk once, then again, and I realize—oh.

He's coming.

Just from that. From tasting me. Pleasuring me. Watching me fall apart.

And holy hell, if that's not the hottest fucking thing I've ever experienced.

He collapses again, forehead pressed to my thigh like he's trying to gather the shattered pieces of himself.

"Sorry," he pants, eyes closed, still trying to catch his breath. "I— shit—I couldn't help it. I swear it won't always be like this once we've done it a few times. I'll have more self-control. Probably."

I let out a breathless laugh, threading my fingers through his damp hair, stroking gently. "Liam. You literally just made me come so hard I forgot my own name. The fact that you got off just from that?

That's the hottest goddamn thing I've ever heard. Don't you dare apologize."

He lifts his head, sheepish and smug all at once, those Godforsaken dimples flashing. "Yeah?"

"Hell yes," I say, tugging him up and into a kiss. "Though I am looking forward to those 'few times' you mentioned."

His smile curves against my lips as we kiss, slower this time. Sweeter. My body still humming with aftershocks, my skin sticky with sweat and salt, but I don't care. All I can taste is him, and me, and this new, dizzying possibility unfurling between us like wildfire.

Eventually, I pull back, dragging my fingers down his jaw, reluctant but practical. "We should probably get dressed," I murmur, brushing my thumb across his bottom lip. "Dinner's not going to cook itself."

As we gather up the scattered remnants of our clothing, I keep sneaking glances at Liam like I've never seen him half-dressed before. Which, to be fair, I technically haven't, not like this. Not with my thighs still trembling and my heart still trying to recalibrate.

He pulls his shirt over his head, muscles flexing, abs catching the last blush of sunlight like they have a personal vendetta against my self-control. His fingers work the buttons slowly, methodically, and I'm pretty sure he knows what he's doing to me.

"Keep lookin' at me like that, Darlin', and dinner's gonna be delayed," he drawls, catching my gaze with that infuriatingly smug half-smile.

I roll my eyes, heat creeping up my neck. "Can you blame me? That was... a lot. In the best way."

His smile softens, something gentler settling over his features. He steps close—close enough that I can feel the warmth radiating off him —and cups my face in his rough, careful hands. Like I'm breakable. Like I'm a dream he's scared to wake from.

"You're incredible, Penelope," he murmurs, voice low and steady. "Every inch of you."

The words hit me square in the chest, crack something open and aching and real. I lean into him instinctively, burying my face against the curve of his throat, breathing him in—salt and skin and whatever aftershave he uses that makes me weak in the knees. And underneath it all: the unmistakable scent of sex. Of us.

I pull back just enough to smile against his jaw. "Come on," I say, lacing our fingers together. "Let's make dinner before the guys riot."

He groans, resting his forehead against mine. "Fine. But I'm calling dibs on dessert."

I raise an eyebrow. "What dessert?"

His grin is slow and dangerous. "I'll show you later."

And somehow, even fully clothed, I'm still blushing.

15

———————

The flames crackle and spit as Liam throws on a couple more logs, the fire catching fast and licking higher like it's showing off. I try to focus on the fish. The foil. Literally anything other than the way the firelight dances across Liam's jaw, casting warm shadows over the angles of his face. Those full lips. That maddeningly skilled tongue...

Holy hell.

I cross my legs, suddenly aware of how my body's still humming from earlier. Apparently, I have the libido of a teenage boy and the memory span of a goldfish. Because satisfaction? Never met her.

"Earth to Penelope," Liam says, dimples in full effect. He's smiling like he knows exactly what I'm thinking. Which, to be fair, he probably does.

I clear my throat, aiming for dignity and landing somewhere between breathless and flustered. "Just thinking about how talented your mouth is. Uh. For eating. Food. You know. Dinner."

Smooth. Real subtle. Ten points to me for absolutely flinging my brain-to-mouth filter straight into the fire.

Liam's chuckle is low and devastating. "I'd be happy to remind you later, Darlin'. But we should probably feed the rest of the crew before they mutiny."

We fall into an easy rhythm, wrapping fish, scallops, and lobster into foil packets stuffed with lemon slices, herbs, and what can only be described as an irresponsible amount of butter. I bend over the fire to position the grates, and suddenly Liam is behind me, his hands sliding under my shirt and around my waist like it's the most natural thing in the world.

And maybe it is. Maybe we're already us, and we just haven't realized it yet.

"You're incredible, you know that?" he murmurs against my neck, lips brushing skin and scattering goosebumps in their wake. "Smart, sexy, and one hell of a cook."

I lean back into him, letting myself sink into the moment. "Flattery will get you everywhere, cowboy."

The scent of burning driftwood mixes with salt air and Liam's impossible-to-bottle scent, leather and sandalwood with something warm and him. His calloused palms are rough against the bare skin of my waist, the contrast making me want to purr. Even the beach sounds —waves breaking, seabirds calling, the low hiss of fire—feel more vivid when he's holding me like this.

But just as things start tilting toward Rated R again, a loud chorus of laughter cuts through the air.

The guys.

They appear at the edge of the dunes, sun-kissed and flushed. Sammy's the first to reach me, grinning wide as he grabs me by the hips and plants a kiss that could start a religion. His hands cup my ass without preamble, and I feel my toes curl into the sand.

"Missed you today, boss," he growls into my ear, and I absolutely forgive him for using the nickname. Somehow, it's the filthiest, sexiest word in the English language when he says it like that.

Before I can catch my breath, Archer steps in and spins me into him, crashing his mouth to mine. His body is flush against me, glasses pushed haphazardly on top of his head like even he couldn't be bothered to wait.

"Fuck, you taste good," he groans, like it's the first sip of water after a desert crossing.

Then Jamie's there, no warning, no preamble, just a wild grin and a kiss that dares me to take it further. He tangles his fingers in my hair and devours me like he's been waiting all damn day, making a low, satisfied sound like I'm his favorite flavor of chaos.

And then Spencer, ever the opportunist, slips behind me, his chest flush against my back, voice teasing and low. "Miss me, Sugar?"

By the time they've all had a turn, I'm one breath away from combusting, and not even pretending to be embarrassed about it.

Part of me wants to shout *Feminism!* and reclaim my autonomy or whatever. But the much louder, currently dominant part, the one basking in attention and affection and unapologetic pleasure, is purring like a cat who just found a saucer of warm cream and decided to drown in it.

I can't stop smiling. Not that I want to.

We gather around the fire, laughter echoing, the air thick with salt and smoke and possibility. I may be independent as hell. Fierce. Capable. But right now?

I'm exactly where I want to be.

We sprawl out on the sand, passing around foil packets of succulent seafood. The setting sun paints the sky in breathtaking hues of orange and pink, its fading light glinting off the gentle waves. Mother Nature is flexing hard tonight, pulling out all the stops for our impromptu beach feast.

"This is bloody amazing, Darlin'," Liam says around a mouthful of lobster.

I can't help but preen a little at the praise. "Why, thank you." Nothing strokes my ego quite like feeding people food they enjoy. It's my love language—butter and salt with a side of culinary competence.

"Jesus, Mary, and Joseph, Penella," Jamie groans in appreciation. "I think I've died and gone to heaven."

We fall into a comfortable silence, too busy savoring the meal to talk much. I glance around at the guys, my heart swelling. They're all absolute messes—shirtless, covered in sand, butter coating their fingers and lips. It's adorably sexy.

As the last traces of sunlight disappear, Liam stands up, stretching languidly. The firelight dances across his muscled body, and I feel a fresh surge of desire from a seemingly endless well.

"Anyone up for a swim?" he asks, a mischievous glint in his eye.

Sammy groans, patting his stomach. "Bloody hell, mate. Give me a while to digest. I'm stuffed," he says, his accent posh as ever. The man could be in the middle of a tsunami and still sound like he's about to pour tea at Buckingham Palace.

The others nod in agreement. Undeterred, Liam's gaze locks onto mine. He extends a hand, his dimples deepening as he smiles. "What do you say, Darlin'? Care to join me?"

I hesitate for a moment, but who am I kidding? I can't resist him—not when he's looking at me like that, all golden and gorgeous in the firelight.

"Alright, cowboy," I say, taking his hand. "Lead the way."

We move away from the group, and Liam starts stripping off his jeans. My breath catches when I realize what he has in mind.

"Skinny dipping?" I ask, my heart already pounding like it knows exactly where this is going.

Liam just grins—gloriously, unreasonably naked—completely at ease with the wind on his skin and the firelight flickering against the curve of his smirk. "Unless you're chicken," he says, head tilting, earring catching the firelight like a wink I feel everywhere.

And look—I've made a lot of questionable decisions in my life, but backing down from a naked dare given by a man who looks like that? Not one of them.

So I strip, fast and clumsy, skin flushed and buzzing under his gaze. Then we're sprinting toward the waves like we're seventeen and this night belongs to us. The cold hits first—sharp and shocking, like being smacked with a frozen frying pan.

"Holy shit," I yelp, breath catching as water clutches at my legs. And then Liam's arms are around me, warm and strong, hauling me into him like gravity itself bent a little in my favor.

I wrap my legs around his waist, arms around his neck, and we float, half-shivering, half-burning. The contrast is almost unbearable. The Atlantic kisses every inch of skin it can reach while Liam's body radiates heat like he's the center of the sun. I don't know whether to scream or kiss him senseless. Maybe both.

The sea rocks us gently, cool and sacred. Moonlight scatters across the waves, turning the water into a shattered mirror of silver and shadows. And it's quiet except for the rhythm of waves against the shore, the distant cry of a night bird, and the sound of our breaths mingling, shallow and unsteady. It feels sacred, somehow. Like we've stumbled into a moment bigger than both of us.

Like maybe this is the part we'll remember forever.

"Thanks for helping with dinner," I murmur, threading my fingers through his damp hair.

Liam laughs softly, the sound vibrating against my skin as his hands slide down and cup my ass like it's second nature. "The appetizer was incredible," he murmurs, voice low and thick.

It's cheesy. It's filthy. It absolutely works.

We float there for a second, locked in, everything quiet but the push and pull of the tide and the thrumming beat of my heart. I look at him—really look—and it hits me like a gut punch, this feeling of rightness. Like we've been circling this moment for years and just now managed to land. Puzzle pieces finally clicking into place after years of trying to jam them where they didn't belong.

Liam leans in and kisses me, slow at first, like we've got all the time in the world. But the softness doesn't last, it never does with us. It sharpens fast, edges catching fire. There's hunger in it, urgency. Like he's starving and I'm the only thing on the menu.

"I've waited three years for this," he says against my lips, his voice barely more than a whisper, hands shaking as they trace down my sides. "There were days I'd wake up in the bunkhouse and think I made you up. Like I'll open my eyes and you'll be gone."

"I'm real," I whisper, pulling his hand to my chest so he can feel the proof. The steady rhythm of my heart, loud and fast and all for him. "I'm right here."

I kiss him again, deeper this time, grinding against the heat of him.

My fingers slip between our bodies, wrapping around his cock, and God. He's hot and hard against my palm, so perfectly real it makes my head spin.

"Darlin'," he groans, his voice cracking as I line him up. "Are you sure?"

"I've never been more sure of anything in my life," I breathe, nearly trembling with it. "Now. Like, three-years-ago now."

He doesn't waste a second. He thrusts into me in one long, devastating motion, and I break—moaning into his mouth as he fills me. It's not just good. It's soul-splitting. It's stars exploding behind my eyelids. It's him.

"Fuck, you feel unreal," he groans, his grip on me tightening like he's afraid I'll float away.

I gasp, overwhelmed by the fullness, the stretch. "Liam," I breathe, hips rolling, chasing the next wave of sensation. "God, you feel so fucking good."

He finds his rhythm, slow and deep, like he's trying to burn this into memory. His fingers dig into my ass as he pulls me back onto him, steady and sure.

"That's it, Darlin'," he murmurs, breath ragged. "Take it all."

And I am. I feel it, every inch of me tuned to the way he moves. There's something ancient in it, something elemental. Like this is more than sex. Like we're answering a question we didn't know we were asking.

I'm right there, right on the edge, when suddenly—

Laughter. Yelling. The unmistakable sound of several fully grown men cannonballing into the ocean.

You've got to be kidding me. If there were medals for cock-blocking, these guys would've swept the damn podium.

"Shit," Liam mutters, freezing mid-thrust.

I laugh, because what else can I do? I'm still wrapped around him, his cock still buried inside me, the tide sloshing between us and chaos erupting just twenty feet away.

"Later," I promise, brushing a kiss over his lips.

But before I can even think about dismounting, a pair of arms wrap around me from behind, lifting me right off Liam's cock like we're in a relay race and I'm the goddamn baton.

"Miss me?" Archer murmurs against my ear, and I barely have time to register the words before I feel him, his cock already nudging between my thighs, teasing along my still-sensitive skin like he knows exactly what he's doing. Which, of course, he does.

And then he's inside me.

One smooth, sure thrust and I gasp, my whole body clenching in sweet, overstimulated shock. I'm still trembling from Liam, and now Archer's precision is lighting me up all over again, like someone flipping every switch in a dark room at once.

"God, Archer," I breathe, reaching back and wrapping an arm around his neck, trying to stay upright as the pleasure hits like a sucker punch. "How could I not?"

He chuckles against my shoulder, smug and sinful. "Felt empty without me inside you, didn't you?"

It should sound cocky. It is cocky. But the way he says it—like he's already read the results of some deeply scientific, wildly X-rated study on the subject, makes my toes curl in agreement.

Because that's Archer. The man approaches sex the way other people approach a thesis defense: focused, analytical, and with a terrifying understanding of cause and effect. He moves like he's solving me in real time, every thrust perfectly timed, every shift in angle a calculated strike.

It's like being fucked by a genius. A very hot, very dirty genius.

I nod, frantic now, desperate for friction, for release, for the sweet oblivion that keeps dancing just out of reach.

"Please," I whimper, not even sure what I'm begging for. "I need—"

"I know exactly what you need," he says, and starts to move.

His thrusts are sharp, precise, merciless in the best way. The water slaps rhythmically around us, a cool contrast to the heat building between our bodies. I throw my head back, eyes fluttering shut, so close I can taste it.

"Fuck, you feel incredible," Archer groans into my ear. "Tell me you missed my cock. I want to hear it."

"Yes," I gasp, body tightening, my voice raw. "God, yes. I missed you. Missed your cock." And then—again—I'm being pulled away.

It's like someone turned my orgasm into a game of musical chairs, and now we're down to the final round.

I blink, breath catching as I'm lifted like I weigh nothing, my legs automatically wrapping around a new waist. Warm hands grip my hips with something gentler, grounding me, and when I open my eyes, I find Sammy watching me with that devastatingly soft, hungry look.

"Hey, beautiful," Sammy says, voice low and rough around the edges. "Missed you today."

I groan, not because I don't love his sweetness. I do. I just also happen to be completely undone, soaked, and desperate in a way that sweet can't quite touch.

"Sammy," I pant, already reaching for him. I wrap my hand around his cock—God, he's hard, hot, and huge—and stroke him firmly. "Please. Please fuck me. Now."

His eyes go wide, the heat behind them intensifying as I guide his thick length along my slit, still swollen and needy from Liam and Archer. And then—

"Hey, sweetheart," Jamie murmurs behind me, pressing a kiss to the top of my head like I'm the prize in some filthy carnival game. He wraps his hand around mine, guiding Sam's cock to my entrance, and then—oh my God—he pushes, impaling me.

I gasp, nails digging into Sammy's shoulders as he stretches me wide in one smooth, glorious thrust. He's massive. The kind of size that borders on outrageous. I cry out, half in shock, half in relief, because this is exactly what my body was begging for.

"Holy fuck," Sam grits out, voice tight as he bottoms out. "You feel... Jesus, Penelope."

I don't respond. I can't. My whole body is buzzing. My brain short-circuits as Jamie presses in behind me, his cock between my cheeks, dragging the head of his cock over sensitive skin.

And then I'm coming, loud and sudden and raw. My body shudders violently, caught in the crossfire between them. The pleasure is too much. Too good.

Sam pulls out quickly, the head of his cock just above the surface as he comes, thick pulses of cum streaking across my skin.

"Fuck that's hot," Jamie groans, kneading my ass cheeks before pressing them together, his hips spasming as he thrusts between them, coming with a soft grunt, his forehead falling to rest at the base of my neck.

Before I can even think, Spencer's behind me, pulling me into him with a slow, practiced confidence that says he's been counting down the seconds. His touch is all flirt and fire, teasing on the outside, desperate underneath.

"You liked that, didn't you, Sugar?" he murmurs, voice rough with restraint. "Being taken by all of us." His gaze meets mine, dark and scorching.

I grin, batting my eyelashes at him. "I haven't been fucked by you yet."

"Not yet," he rasps. "When I push my cock into that tight pussy for the first time, you're going to be begging for it, Sugar. It's only going to be my name on your lips. Understood?"

"Yes, sir," I whisper, my voice a thread of air.

He's hard and ready, cock pressing hot and heavy against my thigh. I slide up his chest, hungry for him, and kiss him—deep and filthy and claiming. My clit catches against the underside of his length as I grind against him, wringing every ounce of friction I can get.

Spencer groans as I catch his bottom lip with my teeth, biting down before pushing my tongue past his lips, fucking his mouth the way I wish he were fucking me. I rock my hips against him as we make out, sliding my clit up and down his length, taking pleasure where it's offered.

And then he uses me. Hands gripping my ass, lifting and dragging me over his cock, sliding between my folds, not inside, not yet, but devastating all the same. It's raw and desperate and a little unhinged.

I whimper at the brutal rhythm, my core clenching as another orgasm looms. We stop kissing as we near the edge, our mouths falling open, breathing each other's air. He walks us into shallower water, keeping the same unrelenting pace.

"Watch, Sugar," he breathes, looking down between our bodies. "I want you to see what you do to me."

There's just enough light to see the way his cock is sliding along my slit. His swollen head dragging over my clit with every thrust. He makes a noise somewhere between a grunt and a whimper, and that sound alone is enough to send me careening over the edge. I watch the first pulse of cum shoot from him, and when he makes that noise again, I'm done.

"Fuck, Spence," I whimper, grinding my clit on his cock, my hips stuttering as my orgasm grips me by the throat, pleasure obliterating everything but the way his cock feels pulsing against me.

"Jesus fucking Christ, Pen," he breathes, kissing me again like it's the only way he knows how to thank me.

A shiver rolls through me, bone-deep, this time. Not from pleasure. From cold.

Spencer stills. "You're freezing. Let's get you dried off and in front of the fire, Sugar."

We stumble out of the water, wrapped around each other, teeth chattering. The fire's glow beckons like a promise.

Liam tosses me a towel with a wink. "Here, Darlin'. You've earned this."

I catch it with numb fingers, laughing breathlessly. The guys gather around, drying off in a lazy circle. It's absurd—five gorgeous, naked men glowing gold in the firelight—five men who just absolutely destroyed my pussy.

And still, somehow, not done.

"You know what's missing?" Liam says, plucking his phone from the pile of clothes. "A little music." He taps his screen, and a sultry melody wraps around us like another layer of heat. He extends his hand toward me, grinning. "Care for a dance, Darlin'?"

I raise an eyebrow. "Naked?"

"Is there a better way?"

I laugh, stepping into him. Our bare skin meets, and everything else fades.

"This is nice," I murmur, cheek pressed to his chest, lulled by his heartbeat and the low thrum of the song.

Liam's arms tighten around me. "Nice? No, Pen. This is bloody perfect."

And in that moment, swaying under the stars, surrounded by heat and salt and laughter and them—I believe him.

I believe in us.

Even if the rest of the world is just waiting to prove me wrong.

16

LIAM'S POV

I've barely got the door closed behind us before Penelope's in my arms, her laughter spilling down the hallway like sunshine I can't help but chase. She's drenched in sea salt and warm skin and the smell of sex—and Christ, it's completely undoing me.

"Oi, fellas!" I call out over my shoulder, my accent purposefully thick. "My turn with the sheila tonight!"

She swats at me, eyes dancing like she's already drunk on the possibilities between us. "Liam! They're going to think—"

"That we're about to do exactly what we're about to do?" I shoot her a grin that feels dangerous even on my own face. Her answering giggle vibrates against my collarbone, and God, I feel it straight down my spine like a struck match.

She's weightless in my arms but heavy in my chest, feather-light against my skin but pressing down somewhere deeper, somewhere under my ribs, somewhere I've never been able to reach before her. I kick open the bathroom door and set her down gently, my hands lingering on her hips as I drink in the sight of her. She's flushed rose-gold, sea-slick, moon-drenched. My fingers trail up her sides, catching on the hem of her shirt. I pull it over her head slowly, savoring each inch of skin revealed.

"Jesus, you're fucking breathtaking," I murmur, my mouth tracing the line of her neck, tasting salt and summer.

She arches into me, chasing the heat. Her bra slips off in my hands, barely a sound, and then she's bare against me, warm, soft skin and nipples already hard under my palms. I cup her breasts, brush my thumbs over the peaks, then lower my mouth to one and suck until she gasps my name.

Her fingers dive into my hair, nails scraping my scalp. It hurts, but the kind of hurt that makes my cock throb. I groan and press in closer, burying my face between her breasts. She smells like coconut and sea air and sex—familiar and fucking addictive. I mouth along her chest, drag my tongue down her stomach, over the sharp dip of her navel.

She's already trembling when I drop to my knees. I undo her jeans, slow enough to watch her squirm, and drag them down her legs. My mouth follows, kissing the curve of her hip, the inside of her thigh. Her skin's hot under my lips, muscles twitching when I nip gently at the tender spot just above her knee.

And then she's tugging me back up, her eyes blown dark with want, pupils swallowing the hazel until just a thin ring remains. Her fingers work my buttons like they're solving a puzzle she's desperate to complete. Shirt off. Belt. Zip. The cool air hits my skin, and her knees hit the tile before I can draw breath.

"Fuck—" The word tears from my throat as her mouth wraps around me.

Warm, wet, wicked. Her tongue traces patterns that make stars burst behind my eyelids. My hips stutter forward, muscles trembling with the effort to stay still. She takes me deeper, eyes locked on mine like she's trying to suck my soul through my body.

I pull her up before I lose myself completely. "Up. Now."

She's smiling when I kiss her, messy and perfect, tasting of me and the sea and something sweeter. I fumble for the shower, steam billowing around us as we stumble inside. Water cascades over us, turning her skin to liquid silk beneath my hands. Our bodies collide, slipping, sliding, finding purchase in each other.

I work the soap between my hands, then slide the lather over sun-kissed shoulders. Her breath catches as I follow the suds down her arms, along the curve of her waist. "Feel good?" I ask, already knowing the answer by the flutter of her eyelashes.

"So good," she sighs, melting into me.

I soap down her belly, over the jut of her hipbones, and then she's grabbing my wrist, holding my hand under the water before guiding me lower with impatient fingers. I groan at the slick heat waiting for me, hotter than the water streaming between us. "Please," she whispers, the word catching on a gasp as she grinds against my palm.

I kiss her hard enough to bruise, slide two fingers inside where she's tight and throbbing and perfect. She clenches around me, her mouth falling open in a silent cry that I can feel vibrating through her chest.

"Christ, you're soaked," I growl, curling my fingers until she's clawing at my shoulders, leaving half-moon imprints I'll wear like medals tomorrow.

She wraps her hand around me, stroking in sync with my fingers inside her, and then—God almighty—she pushes my hand away and lines me up at her entrance.

"Not yet," I grit out, trying to breathe through the need clawing up my throat.

She doesn't listen. Her hips roll forward, and I'm inside her, just barely, just enough to make my knees buckle. I lose the thread, lose my mind. With a sound that's barely human, I drive all the way in, pinning her against the slick tile wall.

She cries my name like it's been torn from her, legs wrapping around my waist. "Fuck, Liam!"

I don't hold back. I can't. I move in her like she's salvation and damnation in one body. The water makes everything slicker, every connection more electric, turning the air to liquid fire in my lungs.

"You're fucking perfect," I growl against the shell of her ear, words punched out with each thrust. "Gripping my cock so tight, like you were made for me, like I was made for you."

"Harder," she begs, breath hitching. "I want to feel it tomorrow."

The challenge sparks through me like lightning. I hitch her legs higher, drive into her deeper. Her cries echo off the tile, bouncing back to me like prayers. She's close. I can feel it in the way she tightens around me, in the flush spreading down her chest, in the wild rhythm of her heartbeat against mine.

But I pull out, lungs burning for air, every muscle screaming.

"Not yet," I say, kissing the salt from her collarbone, tasting the ocean we left hours ago still lingering on her skin. "We've got all night."

I drop to my knees. She braces against the wall, one trembling leg over my shoulder. Water streams down her body like she's a statue come to life, marble turned to flesh under my hands. I press my lips to her inner thigh, following the water's path upward.

The first taste makes me groan like I've been punched. "You taste like fucking heaven."

My tongue starts slow, worshipful, tracing circles that make her hips jerk toward my mouth. She whimpers my name, over and over, like it's the only word she remembers, grinding against my face, desperate for more, like she needs me deeper, harder, everywhere at once. I slide two fingers back inside her, my tongue pressing harder, faster.

Penelope's walls clench around my fingers as I speak. Her head falls back against the tiles, chest heaving. "Please," she begs, voice cracking. "I'll do anything, just let me come."

I groan at her words, my cock throbbing almost painfully. "Anything?" I ask, quirking an eyebrow. "In that case..." I slide my hand down the curve of her ass, fingers dipping between her cheeks. She shudders as I circle her tight hole, teasing the sensitive nerves.

"Relax for me, Pen," I murmur against her thigh. "Let me in."

Slowly, I press the tip of my finger against her entrance. Penelope's breath catches as I breach her, pushing past the tight ring of muscle.

"That's it," I encourage, kissing her hip. "You're doing so well."

I work my finger deeper, my cock throbbing, precum beading at the tip. I've never been so turned on in my life.

"Fuck, you're tight," I groan. "Can't wait to feel you strangling my cock with that tight little ass."

She whimpers as I start to thrust my finger, gently fucking her. I return my mouth to her pussy, shoving my tongue inside her.

"Oh God," she gasps.

My finger moves faster as I seal my lips over her clit, sucking hard. She whimpers, rocking her hips against my face, chasing her release.

"Please, Liam," she begs. "I'm so close. I need to come."

I shove two fingers inside her cunt and fuck her deep, curling just right as I press my tongue flat to her clit. Her whole body locks up. Then she breaks. Lets go with a sharp, desperate cry, thighs clamped tight around my head. She grinds against my mouth, slick and shaking, and I don't stop. I keep licking, groaning as I taste every drop she gives me.

I pull back after I've worked her through the aftershocks, panting heavily as I gaze up at her flushed face. Her eyes are glazed with pleasure, chest heaving as she tries to catch her breath.

"Fuck, I need to get you to bed right now," I growl, rising to my feet. I lift her, still trembling, still gasping my name like a chant—and step out of the shower without bothering to turn it off. Water splashes across the tile, puddles forming at our feet, but I couldn't care less. She's all I see, all I feel, all I want.

And then we're in the hallway—

"Jesus," someone whistles, low and appreciative.

All four of the guys are there, eyes catching on her glistening skin, the marks my mouth has left on her neck, her breasts. I should care. I don't.

"Enjoy the show, boys?" I flash a grin, feeling her heartbeat quicken against my chest. "She's mine tonight."

I carry her past their hungry stares, cock-sure and electric with possession. She buries her face in my neck, laughing, but I feel the heat in her cheeks, the way her breath comes faster. I shoulder open her bedroom door and kick it shut behind us. Before she can take a breath, I've got her pinned. Her back hits the wood, and my mouth is on hers—hungry, messy, claiming.

"You liked that?" I breathe against her lips. "Knowing they all want you, but I'm the one who gets you?"

She moans, rubbing against the hard length of me, soaking wet and eager. "Yes," she gasps. "God, it was so fucking hot."

I grab her thighs, lift her easily, and feel her wrap around me without hesitation. My cock lines up at her entrance, slick and ready.

"Filthy little tease," I growl. "Getting off on them watching. Next time I'll fuck you right there in the hallway. Let them see how good you take me."

Then I drive into her in one hard thrust.

She cries out, head falling back against the door, nails digging into my shoulders as I start to move—fast, relentless, my cock punching deep inside her.

"Fuck, you feel good," I groan, already close. "Is this what you needed? Me stretching you open like this?"

"Yes," she pants, destroyed. "Yes, don't stop. Please."

I slam into her harder, the door shaking with every thrust. The sound of us—skin, breath, soaked heat—fills the room.

"You're gonna come on my cock," I growl in her ear. "And they're all gonna hear you scream my fucking name."

~

PENELOPE'S POV

Pleasure prickles across every inch of my skin, sharp and electric, each thrust from Liam rocking me harder against the bedroom door. The cool wood presses into my back, a stark contrast to the fever in my blood. His fingers dig into my thighs, strong and unrelenting, holding me wide open for him like he's afraid I'll slip away. Like he needs me exactly like this.

"Fuck, you feel incredible," he groans, his voice thick, his accent even heavier when he's like this. Undone and filthy and mine. "Your tight little pussy's got a death grip on my cock."

I don't have the strength to reply. I just moan, loud and shameless, my whole body shaking as he hits that same spot inside me over and over again. My breasts bounce with every thrust, the scrape of my nipples against his chest sending sharp jolts down my spine. Everything is too much and not enough. I can't think. I can't breathe. All I can do is fall apart all over again.

"That's it, Darlin'," Liam pants, and then he shifts—just a little, just enough—and I see stars. My nails dig into his shoulders as my legs tremble. I'm already too close. Too sensitive. Too far gone.

"Oh God—Liam—" My orgasm crashes into me like I never stopped coming in the first place, my body convulsing around him. The world blurs around the edges, sound warping until all I can hear is the pounding of blood in my ears and the filthy sounds of skin on skin.

Liam fucks me through it, his thrusts slowing only when I'm a limp mess in his arms. He stays deep, forehead resting against mine, both of us panting, our bodies slick with sweat.

"Such a good girl," he whispers, brushing my hair back from my face with a tenderness that makes my chest ache. "You're so fucking beautiful when you come."

I hide my face in his neck, but I'm smiling. I can't help it. And when I hear the distant whooping and laughter from the hallway, a shiver of something wicked slides down my spine. They heard us. Of course they did. But instead of shrinking from it, the thought sends a thrill racing through me. I don't feel embarrassed. I feel powerful.

I can't stop thinking about it—what it'll be like when it's all of them. Ten hands. Five mouths. Five cocks. Every inch of me touched, licked, filled. My whole body clenches at the thought.

"You're incredible," Liam says, kissing me like he means it, like he's not even a little bit done with me.

I cradle his face, dragging my thumbs across his cheeks, pulling him back down for another kiss, deeper this time. My body feels heavy and melted, but I still want him. I don't think I'll ever stop.

Liam carries me to the bed like I weigh nothing, lays me out gently like he's preparing to worship me. His gaze drags down my body, slow and hungry, and I can already see it building again.

"Now that you're good and satisfied," he says with a grin that's pure sin, "what do you say we try one of those pretty little plugs you picked out?"

He pulls open the drawer, grabs the smallest one along with the lube. "On your hands and knees, Darlin'. Show me that gorgeous ass."

A shiver rolls through me, sharp and delicious. I shift onto my knees, arching my back, the air kissing the slick heat between my thighs. Liam kneels behind me, warm hands gripping my ass, spreading me open.

"Goddamn," he murmurs. "You're perfect."

Then his mouth is on me, and I jolt forward, gasping. His tongue traces circles around my tight hole, licking and sucking with slow, filthy precision. I rock back against him instinctively, chasing his mouth.

"That's it," he says, voice low. "Push back on my tongue. Show me how much you want it."

I can't answer—I'm too busy moaning, trembling, coming apart again as he spears his tongue inside me. My thighs are shaking. My arms can barely hold me up. Everything is slick and hot and so fucking sensitive.

"Please," I whisper, not even sure what I'm begging for.

Liam laughs softly, like I amuse him, like I delight him. "So greedy."

I hear the cap of the lube pop. A second later, the cool, slick glide of his finger circles my entrance. He presses in slowly, the stretch making me gasp.

"Breathe, baby," he soothes. "Let me in."

I exhale, hips rocking as he works me open, one finger, then two. He's slow but firm, curling and scissoring until the burn fades and I'm pushing back on him, desperate for more.

"You'd come just from this, wouldn't you?" he murmurs. "Just my fingers in your ass."

The hum of my vibrator fills the room a second later. Liam guides my hand between my thighs, pressing the toy to my clit.

"Keep it there," he says.

I can't speak. I just do what he says, body already teetering on the edge. He stretches me wider, thrusting and curling while the vibrator sends sharp pulses through my core.

"Look at you," Liam rasps. "Dripping wet, stuffed full. You like that? Want me to fuck you like this?"

"Yes," I manage to choke out, my voice high and broken. "God —yes."

He leans in, tongue flicking over my clit as his fingers drive deeper, his other hand slipping between my legs to thrust two fingers into my pussy.

The pressure is unbearable. Perfect. Everything.

"Come for me," Liam says, and that's all it takes.

I break with a scream, body clenching around his fingers, hips jerking as wave after wave crashes over me. It doesn't stop—it just keeps rolling through me, sharp and dizzying, my vision gone, my thoughts scattered. He keeps his fingers moving, drawing every last tremor from my body.

And then I feel it, the cool press of the butt plug against my ass.

"Relax," he says, voice soft now.

I take a breath, then another, and as he eases it in, the stretch flares and fades until it's in place, snug and perfect. My whole body feels full, sensitive, alive.

"Fuck, that's so sexy," Liam says, dragging his mouth up my spine.

He flips me onto my back, kisses me deep and slow, tongue tangling with mine. I taste myself on his lips. I don't care. I want more. Always more. He moves down my body, tongue tracing fire across my skin. When he reaches my breasts, he sucks one nipple into his mouth, flicking it, biting it just enough to make me gasp.

"You're gonna come again," he says, lips trailing lower. "And again. Until you're begging me to stop." My stomach growls and he pauses, sitting back on his heels. "But first, we're getting a snack. And some water. Don't move."

He returns a few seconds later with one of his t-shirts, helping me into it, brushing kisses over my cheeks as he tugs it down. Then he steps back, towel slung low on his hips, his cock a thick outline beneath it.

"Turn around," he murmurs.

I do. Slowly. Bending a little, tugging the hem of his shirt higher to give him a view.

Liam growls.

In a flash, he's on me again, towel gone, hands gripping my hips, cock pressing against the plug. My breath catches. "Do you have any idea how fucking sexy you are?" he asks, his mouth at my ear.

I don't answer. I don't have to.

He grabs the towel from the floor, wraps it around himself again, but it does nothing to hide how hard he is. I'm just about to drop to my knees when he catches my wrist.

"Hold that thought, beautiful."

He tugs me toward the door. My heart is still hammering. My thighs are shaking.

"If I go out there like this..." I hesitate, glancing around for something to cover myself with.

"I'm not a jealous man, Darlin'," he says, voice low and certain. "They'll look. Maybe kiss you. Touch you. Then I'm going to bring you right back in here and fuck you senseless."

His eyes lock on mine. "Unless that's not what you want."

Fuck. It's like he can see right through me to the truth of what I need. "I'll go with you," I whisper, slipping past him and out into the hallway, my heart pounding in my ears. I feel like I'm walking a tightrope without a net, terrified but exhilarated.

The air outside the bedroom hits me like a shock—cool and biting against skin that's still fever-warm. Liam's shirt clings to me in places, loose in others, brushing the tops of my thighs with every step. I can feel the plug with every shift of my hips. Every movement is a pulse of sensation, a flicker of overstimulated nerves.

He rests his hand on my lower back, casual but heavy. Anchoring. Possessive. I swear I can feel the heat of it all the way through to my chest. I don't have to look at him to know he's watching me walk—shirt riding up, legs bare, face probably still dazed from everything he just did to me. I feel like I'm floating and buzzing and too full to think.

We round the corner and nearly crash into Archer. His eyebrows jump, and for a second, he doesn't move. Just stares. His eyes drag slowly down my body—the shirt, my bare legs, the flush in my cheeks —and then they snap back up to my face like he's trying to pretend he's not affected by the sight.

Liam grins, lazy and cocky, and gives my ass a light smack. "We're just taking a snack break," he says like we're discussing granola bars. "Need to refuel."

Archer swallows. "Can I—?"

Liam shrugs. "Do whatever you want. I'll be in the kitchen."

And then Archer is on me.

He's in front of me so fast I don't have time to flinch. His hands find my hips and press me against the wall, the impact knocking a soft breath out of me. He presses into me, thigh slotted between mine, hard muscle against the throb still echoing through my center. I moan, embarrassingly loud, and immediately rock against him, desperate for more friction.

His mouth crashes into mine. Messy, demanding, all tongue and teeth and hunger. One of his hands fists in my hair while the other slides over my side, grazing the edge of my breast through the thin cotton. My whole body clenches, aching for him. My brain isn't even functioning—just a flickering mess of yes and please and oh God, more.

His hand disappears beneath the hem of the shirt, knuckles grazing my belly before slipping lower.

"Jesus, Pen," he murmurs, his breath hot against my lips. "You're soaked."

I don't respond. Can't. I'm panting too hard, already falling apart under his fingers.

He dips between my folds and teases me, just enough to make my legs start to shake.

"God, Archer, please," I manage to whisper, head falling back against the wall. "I can't—"

"You can," he mutters. "And you will."

He pushes one finger inside me, slow and deep. I gasp. My whole body clamps down around him like it's been waiting just for this. He curls his finger and I whimper, thighs trembling.

"Is this what you need, sweetheart?" he murmurs, eyes locked on mine as he adds a second finger. "My fingers inside your tight little cunt while Liam watches?"

I don't even realize Liam's still there until I look up. He's across the hall, leaned casually against the opposite wall, towel slung low on his hips, one hand stroking himself through the terrycloth. His eyes are fixed on me—heavy-lidded, dark with need.

The pressure builds again. Fast. Too fast. My whole body pulls tight, chasing another orgasm like it's oxygen.

And then, suddenly, Archer is pulled away.

"Don't hog her," Spencer says, his voice low and amused. His hand slides across my waist like he owns me, and then he's kneeling in front of me.

"Hi, Sugar," he says, looking up through thick lashes. "You still with us?"

I nod because I can't do anything else. My brain is mush. My body is on fire. And then he lifts my leg over his shoulder and kisses the inside of my thigh.

My knee nearly buckles.

"You're so pretty like this," he murmurs, his mouth dragging along my skin. "Destroyed and spread out and waiting."

The first swipe of his tongue is almost too much. I gasp, head thumping back against the wall again.

He hums like he's savoring dessert. "You taste like sin, Pen."

He sucks my clit between his lips and I nearly scream. My hands fly to his hair, fingers tightening in the soft strands as he works me with maddening precision. His tongue moves in slow, firm strokes, then faster flicks, alternating until I'm climbing the edge again.

He groans against me—deep and desperate—and the vibration sends another jolt through my core.

"Fuck, Spencer—" My voice breaks on the second word.

I hear footsteps and then Jamie and Sammy appear at the end of the hall.

"Bloody hell," Sammy says, stunned.

Jamie doesn't say a word, but his eyes are glued to me. His jaw tight. His hands clench and unclench at his sides.

Spencer pulls back just enough to speak. "Come on, boys. She's all warmed up."

They move like they're in a trance. Like they've been waiting for this moment just as long as I have.

Suddenly, it's all hands and mouths and heat. Jamie's lips graze my shoulder. Sammy's mouth wraps around one nipple through the fabric. Archer finds my mouth again, biting gently at my bottom lip. Fingers trace up my inner thighs. One hand cups my ass and squeezes. Someone pushes two fingers inside me again, slow and firm—Jamie, I think—and Spencer doesn't stop. His tongue is merciless.

I can't keep up. The pleasure is too much. It's everywhere. My body feels like it's splitting apart in the best way.

Then Liam speaks, and the room freezes.

"That's enough."

His voice is low. Calm. But final.

The others pull back, reluctantly. Jamie's fingers slip from me. Spencer licks his lips, eyes still on me. Archer brushes his thumb across my jaw once before stepping away.

Liam stands there, somehow composed, holding a tray—two glasses of water, a pile of grapes, some crackers, a wedge of cheese. Like this is just a regular Tuesday and not the hottest thing I've ever experienced.

"Thanks for the help, boys," he says. "But I'm the only one making her come tonight."

There's a ripple of groans and curses behind me, but no one argues. Liam walks up to me, eyes sweeping over my body, and tips his head toward the bedroom.

I follow.

My legs barely work. The hallway feels too long. When we pass the others, I lift the hem of his shirt just enough to show them the plug still snug inside me. Just because I can. Just because it makes their eyes go dark and their mouths fall open.

Liam smirks beside me. "Tease," he whispers.

He's right. And I don't even care. I'm drunk on all of it—on them, on this. And I know, without a doubt, that this is just the beginning.

The second Liam sets the tray down, I'm on him, pressing against him, mouth finding his like I've been starved for days instead of minutes. My hands bury themselves in his hair, and his growl rumbles straight into my chest.

"Fuck, you're insatiable," he says into my mouth, hands catching on my waist like he's trying to hold on. Like I might slip through his fingers if he doesn't. "Did you like that, Darlin'? Having them all watching? All those hands on you?"

"Yes," I breathe, nipping at his jaw, hips rolling into his. "God, yes. I wanted them to fuck me right there in the hallway."

His whole body stiffens. A heartbeat later, he spins me around and shoves me gently, but firmly, against the wall. I brace myself on the cool plaster, breath catching as his cock presses between my cheeks. Hard. Hot. Ready.

"You're a fucking menace," he says, voice low and gritty at my ear. "Letting them get you all worked up. I bet you're dripping wet for me now, aren't you?"

I nod, moaning as he grinds into me. The plug shifts inside me with the movement, and I bite my bottom lip to hold in a desperate sound. Every nerve ending is lit up.

"Please," I whisper, already halfway gone. "Please, Liam."

He slips a hand between my legs, and when his fingers meet slick heat, he groans.

"Christ, you weren't kidding." His touch is featherlight, teasing me, drawing wetness across my folds. "All this for me? Or are you still thinking about them?"

"Both," I admit, voice hoarse. "All of it. The way they looked at me, touched me—I've never been this turned on in my life."

He lifts me into his arms and drops me onto the bed like I weigh nothing. The mattress catches me with a bounce, and before I can blink, he's crawling over me like he's the predator and I'm the prey.

"Tell me," he says, hovering over me, eyes dark. "Tell me what you wanted them to do to you."

I moan when his mouth finds my neck, his teeth grazing skin as he sucks a mark into the sensitive spot beneath my ear. The sting is delicious.

"I want... I want all of them," I pant, my hands clinging to his shoulders. "I want... fuck, I want them all at once," I gasp out. "I want to be filled in every hole, surrounded by cock, drowning in pleasure."

He groans and with barely a warning, he flips me onto all fours, palms gripping my hips. His cock presses against me, slick with precum and heat, sliding through my folds as he lines himself up.

"You want to be stuffed full of cock?" he asks, dragging the tip along my entrance. "We'll start with mine."

He slams into me in one hard thrust. I cry out—loud, raw—my body stretching to take him. There's no easing into it, no gentle warm-up. Just the sharp snap of his hips, the brutal rhythm of his body taking mine. It's perfect. It's everything.

His grip bruises, but I don't care. I need the weight of it, the roughness. Each thrust drives me forward, my breath catching with every movement. The plug adds pressure, rubbing from inside with every shift of his angle.

"Fuck, Liam," I moan, barely coherent.

"That's it," he growls. "Let them hear how good I fuck you. Let them know who makes you scream."

The thought of them hearing us, touching themselves, wanting to be where he is sends a fresh bolt of heat through my blood. He snakes a hand around to my clit, rubbing hard, fast circles that tear another cry from my throat.

"Come for me," he commands. "I want to feel that pretty little cunt squeezing my cock."

It doesn't take long. I break apart like my body's been waiting for his permission. My pussy clenches around him, waves crashing over me so fast I forget how to breathe. My hands claw at the sheets, my head dropping forward as I sob through the orgasm.

He doesn't stop. He fucks me through every aftershock, every tremble, until I'm boneless and spent and limp beneath him. Then, just when I think I can't take any more, he pulls out.

I whimper, thighs shaking.

"We're not done," he says, voice rough with need. "I want to see your face when I come."

He flips me onto my back, pushes my knees up, and fills me again in one smooth thrust. This angle hits somewhere deep, and I arch off the bed, gasping.

He captures my lips with his, swallowing my moans as he rocks into me. "You're so beautiful like this," he murmurs. "All flushed and needy, taking my cock like such a good fucking girl."

I wrap my legs around him, pulling him deeper. He groans, forehead dropping to my shoulder.

"I'm close," he pants. "Come with me again. I need to feel it."

His fingers find my clit again and the pressure coils tight. Too tight.

"I'm—Liam—" I gasp, barely getting the words out before I splinter apart. The orgasm tears through me, white-hot and endless, blinding. My whole body seizes up beneath him, thighs trembling, breath vanishing as everything inside me tightens and then releases all at once.

Liam holds me through it, buried deep, his thrusts faltering. I feel the exact moment it hits him—his whole body goes rigid, his breath hitching as his forehead drops to mine. His hands clutch at my hips like he's anchoring himself.

"Fuck, Penelope," he chokes out, the words ragged and low. He drives in one last time, deep and hard, and then stills.

A shudder runs through him, and then he's coming—hot and heavy inside me. His mouth drops open, his jaw slack with the force of it. A groan rips out of his throat, low and guttural, like it's being torn from somewhere deep. He clings to me through it, muscles locked tight, body shaking with every pulse. I can feel every twitch, every throb, the way his cock kicks deep inside me as he spills everything he has.

We stay like that, bodies fused, breath mingling, hearts pounding against each other's skin.

His breath fans across my collarbone in shallow bursts. Damp skin on damp skin. His arms slowly loosen their grip but never leave me. We're tangled, flushed, and too spent to care that we're both trembling.

I don't want to move.

I want to stay right here, feeling every beat of his heart as it slowly starts to calm against mine.

"You alright, Darlin'?" he asks softly, brushing his lips against my hairline.

"More than alright," I whisper. "You absolutely destroyed me."

He laughs, the sound low and warm. "Could say the same about you."

Eventually, he pulls away just enough to reach for the tray. I sit up slowly, muscles trembling, and take the glass of water he offers me.

"We need to get some food in you," he says, breaking a cracker in half like he's my personal caretaker-slash-sex-God.

I take a bite, letting him feed me piece by piece, his fingers brushing my lips every time. The intimacy of it is disarming. Domestic. Safe.

"This reminds me of when I was a kid," I say between sips of water. "When I was sick, my mom used to bring me snacks in bed."

Liam grins. "Yeah, well, I don't think she had this in mind."

I snort, swat at his arm. "Gross."

He pops a grape into his mouth and shrugs. "Just sayin'."

After we finish, he sets the tray aside and lifts me again—like I weigh nothing—and carries me to the bathroom. The steam from the shower fogs the mirror, warmth curling into the air.

He helps me step under the spray, hands gentle. Caring. Like I'm something fragile now, after everything. I lean into him, resting against his chest, letting the water soothe sore muscles and flushed skin.

"I could get used to this," I murmur.

His hand strokes down my back. "You better, because I won't stop until I'm satisfied."

We take our time, washing each other with quiet touches and unhurried movements. It's not about sex now. It's comfort. Connection. Real in a way I didn't expect.

Later, with his oversized t-shirt swallowing me and nothing else beneath it, and Liam in just a pair of soft, low-slung boxers, we crawl beneath the covers. He pulls me in without a word, tucking me against his chest, his fingers immediately finding my damp hair and combing through it like he's memorizing the texture.

"Promise you'll be here when I wake up?" I whisper.

"Wild horses couldn't drag me away," he assures me, tightening his grip on my body.

My heart flutters, light and full, like it's trying to break into a smile. I don't fight the pull of sleep this time. I let it take me, sinking into the warmth of Liam's chest and the steady rhythm of his breathing. Just as I'm slipping under, the door creaks open. I crack one eye open and see them—Archer, Spencer, Jamie, Sammy—all standing there in the soft glow of the hallway, quiet as shadows.

"Shh," Liam murmurs, voice low and full of something I don't have words for. "Our girl's exhausted. Let her rest."

Our girl. The words settle over me like another layer of warmth, soft and right and anchoring. I let go. Let sleep claim me, wrapped in this impossible, perfect feeling. I've never been so sure I belonged.

This is where I'm meant to be. This is home.

17

———————

The sun is barely up, dragging soft gold across the surface of the water like someone's just spilled light at the edge of the world. I walk the dock slowly, the boards creaking under my boots in that familiar, steady rhythm that always makes me feel a little more like myself. Pearl darts ahead, nose down, tail up, moving in sharp zigzags as if she's on a mission only she understands.

The harbor sounds like it's stretching awake around me. Water slaps gently at the posts. A gull screams overhead, cutting clean through the stillness. Somewhere across the marina, an engine turns over. Ropes creak. Chains clink. All of it folds into the quiet symphony of early morning—the kind of hush that makes you feel like you're borrowing time, tucked inside a moment no one else knows exists.

There's a storm coming. I can taste it in the air, briny and cool, with that electric edge that makes your skin tighten. The clouds to the west are thick and dark, but not close enough to worry us yet. Just enough to make everything feel charged.

The guys are already there when I reach the boat. Always early. Always steady. They move with the ease of people who've been doing this side by side for years, every motion shaped by trust and time. My chest pulls tight when I spot them.

Archer's near the bow, clipboard in hand, jaw set like he's planning to win a war with it. He's ticking off boxes, murmuring something to himself. Spencer's by the crates, stacking them with calm, practiced ease. His sleeves are already rolled up, his arms flexing with each lift. Then there's Liam—just emerging from below deck, hair still damp, T-shirt clinging to his chest in the morning breeze. Our eyes meet, and his expression shifts to something hungry, something possessive, and heat flares low in my belly like a switch flipping.

"You didn't have to come down," Archer says as I step up, but there's no sting in it. His voice is soft. Familiar. His hand finds my waist like it always does, like it belongs there. "I'm glad you did," he adds, quieter this time. Then his lips are on mine, warm, purposeful, claiming. He pulls back just enough to murmur, "I've got plans for you later."

The memory of the last time he had plans for me hits hard and fast. My knees wobble a little.

"Is that a promise, Captain?" I ask, biting my bottom lip when his fingers tighten at my waist.

He growls, low and rough, and for a second, I forget we're not alone.

"Morning, Sugar!" Spencer's voice breaks the spell. He passes by with a crate on his shoulder, grinning like the sun's come up just for him. He plants a kiss on my cheek before I grab his wrist and tug him in for a real one. It knocks the breath out of both of us. His laugh is soft, a little dazed.

Then Liam steps in behind me, and it's like last night slams into my skin again. The stretch of him inside me, the way he whispered my name like a prayer right before he came, it's all there, pulsing at the surface. I turn, and he's already smiling like he knows.

"Good morning, beautiful," he says, voice thick with heat and that accent that ruins me every single time. He kisses my temple and stays close. Too close. Not close enough.

Archer clears his throat like he hasn't just watched all that happen and spreads a chart out over one of the crates. "New grounds are here," he says, finger dragging across a penciled route. I force myself to focus, even as Liam's warmth lingers along my spine.

"We'll work this line first," Archer says, "then move along the channel if the current holds."

"We're tight on cod," Spencer adds without missing a beat. "Focus on haddock. Storage is ready."

I nod, barely catching up. "Don't forget the Inverness delivery. They doubled their order. And Ullapool wants weekly shipments now."

Archer's hand returns to my back, grounding. "We'll handle it. We always do." He kisses me again—slower this time, and longer, like he's reminding me, and then steps back.

"Don't get into too much trouble while we're gone."

I watch them go, the boat easing out past the headland as the sun stretches higher, painting the water in soft hues of gold and pink. Pearl pads up beside me, tail wagging, and leans into my leg like she knows I need it. I reach down and scratch behind her ears.

"Come on, girl," I say, turning toward the shore. "Let's see what today looks like."

～

The restaurant smells like sawdust and sea air and something just shy of hope. Morning light spills through the windows, catching the floating dust in warm halos. Pearl trots ahead, tail swishing, before settling into a sunbeam on the floor.

Jamie glances up from where he's hammering something near the pass-through window. His shirt is already clinging to him with sweat, and when he straightens, wiping his brow, I nearly forget why I walked in here.

"There she is," he calls, beaming at me like I've just made his whole day. "Come see what we've got so far."

Sammy pops his head around a beam, hair sticking up like he's been through a wind tunnel. There's plaster dust in his curls, smudged across his cheek. "Perfect timing," he says, his eyes lighting up. "You've got to see this."

I step carefully through piles of tools and raw lumber while Pearl stretches into a lazy sprawl near the door. Sammy leads me to a half-installed panel of wires and taps the wall beside it.

"Smart controls," he says. "Every room gets its own climate zone. Cooler kitchen, warmer dining. Plus backup shutdowns if anything gets too hot."

He doesn't say fire. He doesn't need to. I feel the unspoken weight of it settle between us.

"Sammy," I whisper, voice catching. "Thank you."

He takes my hand gently, rubbing slow circles into my palm with his thumb. "Of course," he says, his voice quiet. "Anything for you, love."

Jamie sidles in on my other side and wraps an arm around my waist, warm and steady. "Come on," he murmurs. "Let me show you the framing."

I follow him through the shell of what will become my kitchen. I can see it now—the counters, the prep space, the oven where a dozen new dishes will burn the first time I test them. My throat gets tight.

"Hey," Jamie says softly, pulling me into his chest. My cheek rests against him, and his heartbeat thumps slow and steady under my ear. Sam's hand is still on my back, a constant, wordless promise.

"We've got you," Jamie says, his voice a low murmur in my hair.

I don't say anything. I don't need to. They already know.

"Let me walk you through the equipment setup," Sammy says, gently pulling me toward the back wall. He traces a line with his finger. "Power runs through here. Dual backups. No more outages."

I blink against the tears that are still threatening. "You really thought of everything."

Sam nods. "That's the idea."

"That's Sammy for you," Jamie adds with a grin, tapping his pencil against a beam. "Always ten steps ahead."

We spend the next hour deep in the plans, going over every corner of the space. Jamie marks beams while Sammy explains outlet place-ment and fire safety like he's building a fortress. I catch myself staring —at the flex of Jamie's forearms, the focus in Sammy's eyes. Every little thing feels like falling harder.

"It's all happening so fast," I say, dragging my fingers along the new frame.

"That's 'cause you've got the best damn crew in Scotland," Sammy says.

My chest swells with so much emotion it's hard to hold it all in. "I still can't believe you're doing this for me."

Jamie's arm loops around my shoulders. "Believe it," he says. "You earned this. Every bit."

Sammy touches the small of my back, barely there, but I feel it all the way through. "We're in it with you," he says.

Pearl's bark breaks the moment. She's by the door again, tail wagging like a drumbeat.

"Better feed her," Jamie says with a grin, grabbing his hammer. "Before she eats the wiring."

Sammy laughs, holding my gaze. "Are you up for a supply run later?"

The look in his eyes leaves no room for misinterpretation.

"I'd like that," I say, probably too fast. He nods and grins, his eyes dragging over my body before he turns back to the control panel.

I step back outside with Pearl trotting beside me, glancing over my shoulder one last time at the framed-in walls and sawdust-covered floor.

It's not just a restaurant.

It's a new beginning. A rebuild. A love story I never expected—with all of them, and with myself.

And for the first time in a long time, the future doesn't scare me. It lights me up.

The hardware store parking is hot I'm sure the tires are melting. Sunlight bounces off the hood of the truck, heat radiating through the windshield and sticking to the back of my thighs like glue. He pulls into a space near the front, shifts the gear into park with a flick of his wrist, and doesn't move. No music. No small talk. Just the tick of the cooling engine and the high-pitched scream of cicadas in the trees.

His hands stay glued to the steering wheel. Not in a relaxed way. Not in a I'm-just-sitting-here way. His fingers drum against the leather in this uneven rhythm that sounds more like a warning than a habit. His shoulders are locked, jaw tight. He's staring through the windshield like he's trying to see something beyond it.

It's not the Sam I'm used to, the one who's easy and affectionate, quick to laugh, softer around the edges when Jamie's around. This version of him is all tension, like he's coiled too tightly and one wrong move might snap something.

"You okay?" I ask, quiet. Like if I talk too loud, it might break the spell or push him deeper into whatever's got him spiraling.

The truck smells like sun-warmed leather and whatever cologne he always wears, something sharp and earthy and male. I turn toward him, shifting in my seat. My knee brushes his thigh. He doesn't flinch.

His exhale is slow. Measured. Like he's buying time.

Then finally, he turns to look at me. And his gaze? It knocks the wind out of me. All dark and intense, like he's standing on the edge of something and doesn't know how to jump.

"I've been thinking about this," he says. "About us."

I swallow. The air inside the cab thickens. He's not looking away now, and there's nothing in his expression I can soften or reinterpret.

"Okay," I say, my voice barely above a whisper. "Tell me."

His hands tighten on the wheel, skin stretching tight over his knuckles.

"With Jamie," he starts, each word careful. "I'm... submissive. That's how it works between us. It always has. That's what feels right."

I nod once. I knew that. Or at least suspected it.

"But with you," he says, voice getting lower, rougher. "I want something else. Something I haven't done before."

The words hit low and deep. There's heat pooling in my stomach before I can even process why. I feel it in the way my pulse stutters and the way my legs shift restlessly against the seat.

"I want control," he says. "With you. I don't know what I'm doing yet. But I want to try."

The silence stretches long enough that he shifts like he's ready to backpedal. But I lean in, voice steady even though everything inside me is electric.

"Show me."

He's out of the truck so fast it makes the whole thing rock slightly. I scramble for the door handle, but he beats me to it, yanking the door open and offering me his hand.

And just like that, the switch flips.

His grip is firm as he helps me down, but the way he presses me up against the side of the truck isn't soft or sweet—it's confident. Possessive. His body brackets mine, one hand on the metal beside my head, the other curling around my hip, pulling me tight against him. I can feel the heat of him everywhere.

"Is this okay?" he asks, voice low, lips near my ear.

I nod, breathing hard. "Yes."

He makes a sound, somewhere between a groan and a growl, and then his mouth is on my neck, kissing me just under my jaw, his breath warm against my skin. My knees threaten to give out. His fingers tangle in my hair, the other hand still anchored on my hip, keeping me in place like he owns me.

"The things I want to do to you..." he murmurs, voice trailing off as his hand slips lower, brushing the side of my waist like he's trying to memorize the shape of it.

A car door slams in the distance and we both jolt. I blink, reality crashing in hard and uninvited.

"We should probably get what we came for," I say, breathless, even as I press into him.

"Probably," he echoes, and then he kisses me.

Not a tease. Not exploratory. This one is deep and thorough and destroys every nerve ending I have. It leaves me dizzy.

By the time we walk into the hardware store, I'm already a mess.

I don't remember what we pick up. Couldn't tell you if we got rope or paint or fertilizer. His hand stays on the small of my back the whole time, dipping lower than it should, thumb brushing the top of my jeans. Each touch is a promise. A warning.

The drive back is mostly silence, but it's the kind of silence you can't breathe in. His hand settles on my thigh halfway through and never moves. His thumb traces lazy circles into my skin like he's claiming me with the smallest motions possible.

We pull into the gravel driveway and my breath catches. I know what's coming. My body is buzzing with it. Before I can open the door, he's already out and around to my side. He helps me down again, but this time, the second my feet touch ground, he's kissing me. Hard. Hungry. His hands are on my thighs again, lifting me up like I weigh nothing, like carrying me inside is the only thing he's thought about all day.

"The supplies—" I gasp, but he shakes his head.

"Later."

He fumbles the front door open with one hand, the other locked around me, then kicks it shut without breaking stride. Doesn't pause. Doesn't speak. Just carries me through the house like it's instinct, like this is exactly where I'm meant to be, and lays me down on the bed. Then he's on top of me, all heat and solid weight, anchoring me like he never plans to let go.

"Sammy," I whisper, my hands sliding up his arms.

His eyes meet mine, that same intensity from the truck now burning bright. "Tell me what you want."

There's something vulnerable in his voice, like he needs to hear it out loud even though he already knows.

"You," I say, fingers digging into his shoulders. "Any way you'll have me."

He groans, burying his face in my neck.

"I want to take my time," he says, each word a kiss against my skin. "I want to know everything. Every sound you make. Every way your body moves under mine. I want to make you forget anyone else ever touched you."

His hands slip under my shirt. His palms are rough but gentle, dragging across my stomach, up over my ribs, like he's charting me. I arch into him without thinking. His mouth follows his hands, lips brushing against my collarbone, down the curve of one breast.

He strips me slowly, piece by piece, pausing to press a kiss to every inch he uncovers. There's nothing rushed about the way he undresses me. Like he's been imagining this for a long time and wants to savor every second now that it's real.

By the time I'm naked beneath him, I'm shaking.

He sits back, peels off his shirt, and undresses with that same steady focus, like he's not in a rush, like he wants me to look. And I do. The light from the window slices across his chest, down the sharp line of his abs, catching on the edges of his hips in a way that makes my breath hitch.

"Come here," I whisper, reaching for him.

But he catches my wrists gently, presses them into the mattress above my head. "Not yet," he says, voice like smoke. "Let me touch you."

His free hand glides down, slow and sure—over my ribs, across my stomach, between my legs. When he feels how wet I am, he lets out a low, strained curse.

"So fucking ready for me."

I gasp, biting my lip as his fingers find my clit and start to circle, just enough to make me squirm, not enough to give me what I need. My hips rise instinctively, chasing him, but he presses down on them, keeping me right where he wants me. His gaze stays locked on mine, dark and unblinking, like he's watching every second of me coming undone.

"Sammy, please..." It comes out raw. Bare. Need, steady and pulsing through every inch of my body.

His fingers are still moving between my legs—slow, focused, maddening. His eyes don't leave mine. They're dark and full of something almost worshipful.

"What do you need?" he asks. His voice ruined and tender.

"You," I breathe. My whole body arches toward him. "I need you inside me."

There's no hesitation. He releases my wrists and leans in to kiss me, open-mouthed and hungry, like he's breathing me in. But instead of moving straight to what I asked for, he shifts lower. His mouth trails down my neck, past my collarbone, across the curve of my breast.

I shudder.

Then he keeps going.

"Sam—" I gasp as his hands slide beneath my thighs, spreading them wide.

He looks up from between my legs, eyes smoldering. "Let me taste you first."

His voice is low, hushed, like he's telling me a secret. Then his mouth is on me.

The first stroke of his tongue makes me cry out, high and involuntary. He licks slowly, like he's trying to memorize the shape of me. His hands keep me open, his thumbs pressing gently into my inner thighs, keeping me steady while he works. And fuck, he works. Every pass of his tongue, every gentle suck, every teasing pause when I squirm, it's like he's learning me one second at a time.

"Sam," I gasp, my fingers tangling in his hair, gripping hard. "Oh my God—"

He groans against me, the sound sending vibrations straight through my core.

I lose track of time. He doesn't rush. He builds it slow and steady, lets the tension coil tighter and tighter until I'm writhing under his mouth, thighs trembling.

"I can't—I'm gonna—"

"Let go," he says, and then he sucks my clit again, just right, and I shatter.

My orgasm crashes over me, sharp and blinding. I arch off the bed, sobbing out his name, the pleasure ripping through me like a live wire.

He doesn't stop until I'm twitching with oversensitivity, pushing weakly at his shoulders.

When he finally pulls back, he kisses the inside of my thigh, then my hip, then drags his mouth back up my body, leaving heat in his wake. He kisses me, slow and deep, and I taste myself on his tongue.

"You okay?" he murmurs against my mouth.

I nod, dazed. "Yeah. Better than okay."

He smiles and starts to move like he's going to line himself up, but I stop him with a hand on his chest.

"My turn."

His eyes flare, and I nudge him gently until he lies back. He watches me, completely still, as I crawl down his body, fingers dragging along his skin. He's warm and solid, the kind of strength that settles deep.

I press my mouth to his chest, kissing the curve of his pec, then lower, following the line of muscle down his stomach. His abs tighten when I trace my tongue along the edge of his hipbone.

"Jesus, Penelope," he rasps.

I glance up at him and smile, then wrap my hand around his cock. He's hot and heavy in my palm, and when I take him into my mouth, his whole body tenses.

"Fuck," he grits out, hand flying to my hair.

I move slow, teasing, letting my tongue swirl around the head, taking more of him inch by inch. His grip tightens, not forcing, just grounding. His hips shift up, just slightly, like he can't help it.

"God, you look so fucking good like this."

I hum around him, taking him deeper, and he lets out a broken groan.

I stay there a while, enjoying the way he falls apart for me—the way his voice gets rougher, his breath shallower. His thighs flex beneath my hands, and he finally pulls back, panting.

"If you don't stop," he says, eyes wild, "I'm going to come in your mouth."

I lick the tip one last time and crawl back up his body.

"Not yet," I murmur. "I want you inside me when you do."

His eyes burn as he flips me gently beneath him again, settling between my thighs. His forehead presses to mine. The moment stills, heavy and sweet.

"Ready?" he asks, voice shaking with restraint.

I nod. "Yes."

He lines himself up and pushes in slowly. Inch by inch. My breath catches, mouth open on a moan as he stretches me wide, fills me completely. My hands grip his biceps, holding on like I might float away.

He stills once he's fully inside me, just breathing hard against my cheek.

"Fuck, you feel incredible," he groans, his voice ragged.

I wrap my legs around his waist, locking him in. "Then move."

He does. Slow at first, rolling his hips with long, deep thrusts that make my toes curl. He kisses me through it, mouth soft and open against mine, hands cradling my face like he needs every part of me in reach.

His rhythm builds—harder, deeper. My body adjusts to the stretch, to the weight of him, to the constant, relentless pressure. Every stroke hits that spot inside me that makes my stomach tighten.

"God, Sam..."

He buries his face in my neck, groaning as he drives into me again, again. His control is slipping, I can feel it in the way his rhythm falters, in the broken sounds leaving his mouth.

His hand slides between us, fingers finding my clit and rubbing tight, perfect circles.

My body coils again, tighter than before. Pleasure building in my spine, in my thighs, everywhere.

"I want you to come," he pants. "Please, I need to feel you fall apart around me."

That's all it takes. My climax tears through me, loud and shaking, my back arching off the bed. I gasp his name, sobbing through the waves of release as he fucks me through it.

"Jesus, Penelope—" His hips stutter, and then he's coming too, a raw groan against my throat as he pushes deep and stills. I feel the heat of it, the way his body tenses above me before finally sagging, spent.

We don't talk. For a while, we just breathe.

His weight settles over me, solid and warm and anchoring in a way I didn't know I needed. There's nothing performative about it. No pressure to move or fix or say the right thing. Just his skin against mine and the slow, steady thud of his heartbeat syncing with mine like we've done this a hundred times before.

Eventually, he shifts off me, just far enough to pull me with him. We stay tangled, legs twisted, bodies still sticky with sweat. One arm hooks tight around my waist. The other slides up to tuck a piece of hair behind my ear, his knuckles brushing my cheek on the way.

His touch is careful. Like I might break. Or like he might.

I look up at him. His eyes are softer than I've ever seen them. Not just tender, unguarded. There's something raw in them. Something that makes my chest go tight.

"I hope that was good for you," he says quietly, the corner of his mouth twitching up, "because you just ruined me for anyone else."

It should be a line. It almost is. But it lands like a confession. Like he means every syllable and doesn't know what I'll do with them.

I lean in and kiss the corner of his smile. "It was perfect."

He exhales, like maybe he's been holding that breath the whole time. Then he pulls me in closer, his arms wrapping around me like he's bracing himself for something. Or maybe like he's letting something go.

His chin rests on the top of my head. "We should probably get those supplies back before Jamie starts texting you in all caps."

I laugh, low and tired and happy. "He already does that."

"Fair."

I nestle into the curve of his chest, letting my fingers trace the line of his ribs. "Five more minutes."

He hums. Doesn't even hesitate. "Take all the minutes you want."

So I do.

Because the world can wait. The restaurant can wait. Even Jamie and his all-caps texts can wait. Right now, it's just Sam. And the way his arms make everything feel a little less impossible.

18

———————

The morning air has that early warning kind of chill—the kind that doesn't belong in summer and makes your skin pull tight, like your body knows something's coming before the sky does. A storm, probably. Or some other kind of trouble.

I grunt as I hoist another box of ice onto the boat. My back protests. My arms hate me. My soul is still in bed. Nothing like lugging frozen water before caffeine to make you question your life choices.

When Archer knocked on my bedroom door before sunrise, asking for an extra hand, I said yes before I'd even opened both eyes. Because I'm a people pleaser. Or maybe just an Archer pleaser. Either way, here I am. Bleary-eyed. Freezing. Definitely uncaffeinated.

Across the dock, Pearl is living her best life. She's stretched across a patch of sun like it personally invited her, tail thumping every time someone walks by. Zero shame. Maximum comfort.

A few feet away, Archer and Spencer are hunched over a crate, heads tilted together like they're planning a bank heist. Spencer's finger trails along a nautical chart, voice low and syrupy with that Southern drawl of his, smooth enough to butter toast.

"If the weather holds," he says, "that spot off the western channel might be worth a try. Sonar was decent last time."

Archer pushes his glasses higher on his nose, eyes flicking toward the sky where the clouds are already starting to gather into something dark and mean.

"That storm's moving fast," he says, brow furrowing. "We should stay close today. I'm not risking the boat—or us."

I heft another box and turn to hand it off to Liam, who's supposed to be helping me. Except he's not paying attention. At all. His eyes are somewhere else entirely, trained on something over my shoulder, his mouth slightly open like he's forgotten he has one.

I follow his gaze across to the end of the dock.

Jamie and Sammy are unloading supplies in front of the restaurant, all ease and familiarity. Sammy reaches to adjust a beam on Jamie's shoulder, his hand resting there just a moment too long to be nothing. It's subtle. Quiet. But there's something soft in it, something that feels private. Jamie laughs at something Sammy says, his voice light and unguarded. It lands somewhere in my chest and settles there, warm and tender and a little too much to look at for long.

I glance back at Liam. He's still staring. And now the box in his hands is starting to tip.

"Careful," I murmur, nudging his shoulder.

He jerks like I slapped him, cheeks going pink as he sets the box down and straightens. "Sorry, Darlin'."

He drags a hand through his hair, looking everywhere but at me. "I keep noticing things I didn't before," he says. Voice low. A little shattered.

It hits different than his usual flirty quips. There's something in it that sounds brand new. I don't push. Just lean back against the rail, close but not crowding. Letting him fill the silence if he wants to.

He doesn't. Not right away.

But I can see it. Whatever it is, it's working through him slowly. His shoulders tight. Eyes lingering on the parking lot even though the moment's already passed. There's a shift happening inside him—a small one, but it's real.

And I know that look.

It's the same one I had right before everything changed. Before I realized what I felt wasn't just complicated—it was impossible, wonderful, reckless love. For all of them.

That breathless, slow-burning oh-no that hits right before you fall.

So I wait.

Because some truths aren't meant to be yanked out before they're ready. Some things—like feelings, and storms—need time to roll in on their own.

"The way they move together," he says finally, almost to himself. "It's—God, it's beautiful, isn't it?"

Before I can reply, Archer's bark breaks through the moment. "Storm's coming fast. Let's move!"

Liam straightens, lifting the box to his shoulder like it weighs nothing. Show-off. But I see the way his gaze flicks one last time to the parking lot, where Sammy and Jamie work in easy harmony, passing tools back and forth like they've done it a thousand times. There's longing in Liam's eyes, raw and unguarded. Like a kid with his nose pressed against a candy store window, except the candy is two gorgeous men who can't keep their hands off each other.

The storm gathers over the island like the doubts gathering in Liam's eyes, dark, turbulent, impossible to ignore. Mother Nature and human emotions always did have a lot in common. Neither one gives a damn about your plans.

As we push off from the dock, I catch a glimpse of the restaurant's sturdy walls, built from logs and the distinctive gray-blue Lewisian gneiss that's weathered centuries of Highland tempests. The ancient stone seems to whisper that some things can endure any storm, if their foundation is strong enough. God, I hope we're one of those things.

The storm arrives several hours later, slamming into us with gale-force winds and waves that make the boat groan. It's like being inside a washing machine set to "destroy."

Archer's hands grip the wheel, steady as always, but his jaw is set tight. Spencer lashes down the last of the loose gear while barking orders.

"Get below!" he yells to Liam and me as the boat lurches, spray drenching us before we can scramble below deck.

We scramble into the cabin, dripping and shivering. The roar of the storm is muffled now, but it's still loud enough to make conversation feel like shouting. Like trying to talk at a rock concert next to the speakers while drunk and wearing earplugs.

The briny scent of seawater clings to our clothes, mingling with the sharp tang of fear and adrenaline.

"You okay?" I ask Liam, eyeing the tremor in his hands as he brushes water off his face.

"Not really." He laughs, a nervous, broken sound. "But not because of the storm." His voice has that edge that tells me we're about to have a Conversation, capital C intentional. The kind that changes things.

I gesture to the bench, and he collapses onto it, head in his hands. After a long pause, he says, "Jamie and Sammy are just... so in sync, you know? Like they've always been part of each other's lives. I can't stop thinking about it." He sounds equal parts confused and fascinated, like someone who's just discovered that chocolate and peanut butter taste good together and now can't stop eating Reese's.

"Liam," I start, keeping my voice soft, trying not to sound like I'm talking to a spooked animal, "what are you trying to say?"

He looks up, something fragile and uncertain flickering in his expression, his warm brown eyes searching mine. "What if it's not just about watching them? What if it's about... wanting that with someone?"

The boat pitches again, and I grab the edge of the bench to steady myself. Perfect timing for an existential crisis – trapped in a rocking boat during a storm. Because the universe has a sick sense of humor like that.

"Then maybe it's time to figure out what you want instead of what you think you're supposed to want," I say, like I'm some kind of relationship guru and not someone who stumbled ass-backwards into a relationship with five men.

He doesn't answer, but the tension in his shoulders eases just a little. Above us, Archer's voice booms through the storm, pulling us back to the present. The boat pitches violently, tossing us against the slick walls of the cabin.

Liam's hand grips the seat edge so tightly his knuckles are white. His voice is low, barely audible over the pounding storm outside. "I think I might be bisexual."

The words hang in the air, stark and trembling. I see the way his chest heaves, the way his breath hitches like he's just pulled something jagged and sharp out of his own soul. Like he's been carrying this secret around for so long it's grown barbs and teeth.

I reach for his hand, steadying it with mine. "Thank you for trusting me enough to tell me."

His grip tightens, rough and desperate. "What about the others?" he asks, his voice cracking slightly. "Archer's so traditional sometimes. And Spencer—" He breaks off, swallowing hard. "I don't want them looking at me differently. I can't lose what we have as a crew, as friends."

The fear in his voice makes my heart ache. It's one thing to worry about my reaction—I'm practically the poster child for sexual flexibility at this point, but I can see now how much deeper his concerns run. Five men with different backgrounds, values, and experiences— our little family is more complex than I sometimes remember.

His grip tightens, rough and desperate. "I don't want to mess anything up," he says, his voice raw. "I love what I have with you. With the guys, our friendships—it all works so well. But these feelings won't fucking go away." His free hand gestures helplessly, words failing him. "It's like trying to ignore a splinter under your skin – the more you pretend it's not there, the more it hurts."

"Having feelings doesn't mess anything up," I say, keeping my tone firm but warm. Like I'm channeling Sammy's steadiness. "It's what we do with them that matters. And FYI, anyone who has a problem with who you are will have to deal with me. And I fight dirty."

Above us, Archer's voice slices through the chaos, shouting something about the harbor being close. The motion of the boat evens out, but the tension in the air remains electric. Like the calm in the middle of a hurricane, equal parts terrifying and exciting.

Liam's gaze flickers toward me, his expression tortured. "How do you do it?" he asks suddenly. "Balance everything—everyone's feelings?" He looks at me like I'm some kind of relationship guru, which is hilarious considering I fell into this arrangement completely by accident. Like tripping and landing face-first in a pile of hot fishermen.

I consider his question carefully. It's something I've been figuring out myself, day by day, mostly through trial and a whole lot of error. The boat rocks beneath us, a physical reminder of the tenuous balance we're all trying to maintain.

I think of the intricate dance that is my life with all five of them, how love and trust weave their way through every moment, even the messy ones. Especially the messy ones. It's like juggling chainsaws while riding a unicycle, terrifying but exhilarating. "With honesty," I answer softly. "And trust. And a lot of communication."

"Sammy and Jamie make it look so simple," Liam murmurs. "Just being who they are. Loving who they love."

"And you can be who you are, too," I tell him, hoping he can hear the sincerity in my voice. "Whatever that looks like, whoever it's with. You're allowed to want that, Liam. Hell, I'd encourage it. The more love in this weird little family of ours, the better."

His eyes search mine, looking for any sign of doubt or discomfort. "You're really okay with this? With me maybe wanting... something with one of them if they want it, too?"

The vulnerability in his question stuns me. He truly believes I might reject him for this. As if I have any room to judge anyone else's relationship choices. My chest tightens with unexpected emotion. Had I ever given him reason to doubt my acceptance? The thought that he's been carrying this fear makes me want to pull him close and shield him from his own self-doubt. Or smack him upside the head for being an idiot. Maybe both.

"Love isn't finite, Liam. Just because we have something amazing doesn't mean you can't want more. Hearts aren't like pie. Giving a slice to someone doesn't mean there's less for others."

"But—"

"There's no 'but,'" I squeeze his hand gently. "I'm with five of you. How could I possibly expect any of you to only be with me? That would be the gold medal in hypocrisy Olympics. And I don't look good in gold."

He groans, raking a hand through his hair. "God, I hate this. It's like puberty all over again, but with better vocabulary and worse timing. And thankfully less acne."

A laugh escapes me before I can stop it. "That might be the most accurate description of adult sexual awakening I've ever heard," I tell him, relieved to see a small smile tugging at his lips. "But seriously, think about what might happen with the others. Spencer practically radiates Southern hospitality—I can't imagine him having anything but acceptance. And Archer may be traditional in some ways, but as long as you're not hogging me, he's not going to care."

I cradle his face between my hands, making him look me in the eyes. "Embrace it," I whisper, meaning every word. "We've got one shot at this life. Why waste it pretending we don't want the things we do? Denying yourself doesn't make you special; it just makes you miserable. And nobody wants to sleep with miserable."

Liam pulls me into a fierce hug. His damp skin presses against mine, his heartbeat wild and unsteady, the scent of leather and sandalwood enveloping. Even soaked with seawater, this man somehow manages to smell amazing. "Thank you," he murmurs, his breath warm against my ear. "For listening. For understanding. For making me feel like this isn't going to break everything."

"Nothing's breaking, Liam," I promise, my fingers brushing the back of his neck. "You're just learning who you are. That's a gift, not a curse."

The corner of his mouth lifts in a small, hesitant smile, his dimples making a brief appearance. Damn those dimples. "It's still terrifying."

"Good." I pull back enough to meet his eyes. "That means it's worth it."

By the time we reach shore, the rain has softened to a mist, the air thick with the smell of wet wood and salt. Liam and I wave Archer and Spencer off, trudging side by side toward the restaurant to see if

Sammy and Jamie need help. The glow of the kitchen windows cuts through the haze, promising warmth.

We stop just outside, peering through the rain-streaked glass. Sammy and Jamie are inside, working on the wiring, or at least that's what it looks like at first. Sam is standing behind Jamie, his hands guiding Jamie's on the wire strippers, their bodies pressed together.

"Christ," Liam whispers, his breath hot against the back of my neck.

Jamie turns slowly in Sammy's arms, their lips barely brushing as his hands drift up to cradle Sam's face. The kiss that follows is slow, passionate, and all-consuming. Their tools clatter to the floor, forgotten as Jamie's fingers work the buttons of Sammy's shirt, peeling it away to reveal chiseled muscles that glow in the overhead light.

"They're beautiful," I murmur, leaning back into Liam without thinking. His chest is solid and warm, his breaths shallow and uneven against my hair.

"We shouldn't..." he whispers, but his hand slides to my hip, fingers hesitant before pulling me in closer.

I press my ass back against him, need already coiling tight in my belly.

We watch as Jamie trails kisses down Sammy's throat, his touch worshipful, his fingers tracing a path down Sam's side. Liam's fingers echo the movements beneath my shirt, his touch featherlight, teasing. I groan as Sammy turns Jamie around, his hands roaming over Jamie's back with aching tenderness before helping Jamie out of his shirt and pants. The air feels heavy, charged, every inch of my skin alive with desire.

Liam's grip tightens on my hip, his body pressing closer. "Is it wrong to watch?" he asks, his voice carrying more hunger than hesitation.

"If it's wrong, I don't want to be right," I whisper, my voice cracking.

And for a moment, it's as if the storm outside, the tension inside, and everything we've been holding back dissolves, leaving nothing but us, raw and unguarded, standing in the drizzle.

Sammy leans in close to Jamie, his lips brushing the shell of his ear, murmuring something too low for me to hear. Whatever it is, it slides under Jamie's skin, leaving him visibly undone. His head drops forward, a tremor running through his body, as if Sammy's words alone have left him boneless.

And then Sammy turns Jamie around and lowers himself to his knees. The movement is unhurried, purposeful, as if time itself bends to accommodate him. His hands glide up the back of Jamie's thighs, spreading him apart with a care that borders on worship. My breath catches as Sam's tongue darts out, flicking over Jamie's entrance.

Jamie's head snaps back, his lips falling open in a soundless moan. The muscles of his chest ripple as his breath stutters, his body trembling with restraint. The overhead light casts him in a golden glow, sweat slicking his skin until he looks like some pagan God carved from bronze.

Behind me, Liam's breath is hot and ragged against the back of my neck. His hands fumble with the clasps of my overalls, his fingers shaking just enough to make it take longer than it should. When the metal fastenings finally give way, the heavy fabric slips from my shoulders and pools around my ankles with a dull thud. The night air is sharp against my bare skin, raising goosebumps along my arms and thighs.

Inside, Sammy rises to his feet, moving like a predator who knows his prey won't run. He jerks open his pants and spits on his cock. I can't breathe as I watch him align their bodies, his grip on Jamie's hips tightening as he slowly, achingly, begins to push forward. Jamie's fingers curl around the edge of the workbench, his knuckles white, his body bowing as Sammy fills him. There's something unfiltered about Jamie's expression—pure, aching pleasure with no walls up, and it knocks the air right out of me.

Liam's fingers trail over my bare skin, hesitant at first, then bolder. His touch is both electric and grounding, and I press back into his chest, needing the solid weight of him to steady myself. His free hand snakes around my waist, holding me close as his other hand dips lower, his fingers slipping beneath my underwear and stroking in time with Sam's movements inside Jamie.

Every part of me is alive, hypersensitive, caught between Liam's touch and the sight of Sam and Jamie lost in each other's bodies. The sharp crack of the workbench shifting under their weight, the low, guttural sounds spilling from Jamie's lips, the controlled rhythm of Sam's hips—it's all too much and not enough.

Liam's breath catches behind me, his fingers stilling just as I feel myself tipping closer to the edge. "Don't stop," I whisper, my voice raw and broken.

Instead of replying, I hear the low rasp of a zipper being drawn down. My heart lurches in anticipation, heat pooling low in my belly as I feel Liam's cock press against me, hot and insistent. I lean over slightly, my hand bracing against the cold glass of the window, the other gripping Liam's forearm for support as he guides himself inside me.

The stretch is exquisite, slow and careful. Every nerve ending fires as he fills me, inch by inch, until there's no space left between us.

"Jesus, Pen," Liam groans, his voice thick with arousal, his accent slipping into something rougher, more primal. "You're perfect."

He starts to move, slow at first, then falling into rhythm—one that matches Sammy's with almost impossible precision, like they're two halves of the same breathless song. Each thrust from Liam sends pleasure rippling through me, sharp and electric, amplified by the sight in front of us.

Inside, Sam's hand wraps around Jamie's cock, stroking him in time with the push of his hips. Jamie gasps and bucks into the touch, his whole body caught in a rhythm that's desperate and beautiful, like he's chasing something just out of reach.

Behind me, Liam tightens his grip around my waist, pulling me in until there's not a breath of space between us. His thrusts grow deeper, rougher, and his free hand slips under my shirt, cupping my breast. His fingers brush my nipple, teasing it in sync with every drive of his hips, and I bite down on my lip to keep from crying out, my moans caught against the cold glass.

Sam's head falls back, sweat sliding down his temple as his pace quickens. Jamie clutches the workbench like it's the only thing anchoring him, his expression pure and devastated and radiant with pleasure.

"They're beautiful," Liam whispers against my ear, his voice rough and unsteady.

I nod, unable to speak, my eyes locked on them. And then, as if they can hear him, Sammy's gaze lifts, locking with Liam's through the window. There's no shock in his expression, only heat and understanding. Jamie's eyes follow, his lips curling into a wicked, knowing smile.

"They knew," Liam murmurs, his thrusts faltering for half a heartbeat.

The realization hits like a surge of electricity, lighting up every nerve in my body. I come hard, clenching around Liam as the pleasure breaks open inside me, sharp and all-consuming. He groans against my neck, his body seizing with his own release, holding me so tight it feels like we might collapse into one body if he lets go.

Inside, Sam's head snaps back, a broken sound tearing from his throat as he grips Jamie harder, both of them unraveling in real time.

Everything stills. For just a beat, it's like the world forgets how to move. Like the four of us are suspended together, caught in the same electric charge, nothing but breath and heat and something we don't have a name for yet.

Then the air slips cool against my skin again, damp and grounding. My body is shaking, boneless. Liam doesn't let go. His arms stay locked around me, steady as stone, his breath soft and steady where it ghosts across my shoulder.

"They've known all along," Liam says quietly, like he's still trying to catch up to the truth of it.

I don't look away from the window. Sam is brushing a kiss against Jamie's temple, slow and soft, like they've got nowhere else to be. "Sometimes people see us clearer than we're ready to see ourselves," I say.

Liam doesn't respond right away. He just breathes, steadying. We start to pull ourselves together, giving them their moment, and maybe giving ourselves one too. His fingers find mine again as we walk toward the house.

"Everything's changing," he says, not as a question this time, just a quiet fact he's still learning how to carry.

I glance back. The glow from the restaurant windows is fading into the mist, soft and far away now. "Change isn't always bad," I tell him, squeezing his hand. "Sometimes it's the thing that finally sets you free."

The door creaks open with that familiar sound, the air inside warm and humming with life we haven't stepped into yet. As it closes behind us, I feel it—the line we've crossed, the before and after of it all.

And I don't feel scared.

Maybe this is the part where everything begins. Not with certainty, but with hope. The kind that sneaks up on you when you least expect it. The kind that feels like a yes.

19

The scent of sawdust hits me first—sharp, clean, a little overwhelming—and underneath it, the chemical tang of fresh paint. The restaurant is still a skeleton, lit by the harsh glow of work lights that cast long, angular shadows across the plywood and half-finished walls. It smells like effort. Like change. Like possibility.

Sammy and Jamie are bent over a blueprint that nearly swallows the table. Their heads are close, too close for it to be casual, Jamie's fingers resting on top of Sammy's hand like he forgot to let go. His thumb moves in slow, absent circles across Sammy's knuckles. It's so gentle, so deeply familiar, it makes something twist low in my chest.

Outside the windows, the harbor glitters under the moonlight, water reflecting the broken light of the marina like it's breathing.

"Hey," I say softly, setting the cooler down by the door. My voice slices through the quiet hum of concentration, and they both look up. The shift is instant, shoulders softening, lips quirking. Jamie lingers for a breath longer, his hand still on Sammy's, before stepping away.

"Penella," Jamie grins, his voice warm and teasing in that way that always feels like an inside joke. "You're a bloody miracle. Someone's been obsessing over circuits for three straight hours." He nods toward Sammy, who rolls his eyes without argument.

"Some of us would prefer the building not go up in flames," Sammy mutters, his accent more clipped when he's annoyed, which just makes Jamie's grin widen.

Before I can answer, the back door creaks open. We all turn. Liam stands there, framed in the doorway, backlit by moonlight and hesitation. His face is shadowed, unreadable, and for a moment, I think he might just turn around and walk back into the dark.

But Jamie steps forward, easy and open, voice lowered but warm. "Liam," he says, drawing his name out like it belongs here. "Perfect timing. Sam was just about to show us how not to electrocute ourselves. We could use your hands."

Liam hesitates, his eyes flicking toward Sammy and Jamie like he's walking into a memory instead of a room. But then he nods, stepping fully inside. The door swings shut behind him with a soft click, sealing us all into this little world we've built from plywood and tension.

"Here," Sammy says, holding out a pair of wire strippers, his voice calm, like he already knows how this will end. "Firm but gentle. Like this."

He doesn't wait, just steps in and covers Liam's hands with his own. It's not overtly intimate, not at first, but I see the way Liam's shoulders go stiff. The breath he tries to steady. His fingers tremble under Sammy's.

Jamie leans against the wall now, arms folded, watching them with a look I can only describe as knowing. "Reminds me of when you taught me," he says, voice pitched low. "Though I was a complete disaster with tools."

Sammy's mouth twitches like he's fighting a smile. "You were," he agrees. "But you made up for it." His thumb slides along the inside of Liam's wrist, barely a touch, but Liam jumps anyway.

The air shifts. Like a current flickers to life, humming beneath our skin.

Jamie pushes off the wall, his steps slow, purposeful. He stops behind Sammy and rests a hand on the small of his back, fingers splaying wide like he's grounding him.

"It's all about rhythm," Jamie says, voice rough at the edges now. "The right pressure. The right pace."

His hand trails down Sammy's arm, until it's covering both their hands—Liam's and Sammy's—like he's closing the circuit.

I squeeze my thighs together instinctively. The tension is thick enough to breathe in.

Liam's chest rises and falls too fast. His mouth opens like he's going to speak, but nothing comes out. Only a breath, shaky and uncertain.

Sammy's hand slides from Liam's to his waist, fingers curling at his hip. His voice lowers. "Relax." A word meant for calming, but it only seems to make everything more charged. "We've seen the way you look at us. And last night... it wasn't hard to figure the rest out."

He rubs slow circles into Liam's hipbone.

"This is what you want, isn't it?"

Liam swallows, throat bobbing. His voice catches. "I think so," he says, quiet and unsure.

Sammy doesn't look away. He raises an eyebrow.

"Yes," Liam says again, louder this time, like he's saying it for himself as much as for us.

Jamie steps in close, brushing against Liam's other side now, and gently plucks the hat off his head. He tosses it onto the table without looking, his focus all on Liam.

"Then trust us," he murmurs, dragging his hand along Liam's jaw, slow and tender. He tilts Liam's face up with a fingertip under his chin. "Let us show you."

The first brush of Jamie's lips against Liam's is hesitant, questioning, but when Liam doesn't pull away, Jamie deepens the kiss, his hand sliding into Liam's hair. Sam watches them with dark, hungry eyes, his hand still on Liam's hip, steadying him.

When Jamie finally breaks the kiss, Liam's eyes are wide, his lips flushed and swollen. "I've never..." he starts, his voice trembling with vulnerability.

"We know," Sam says softly, his hand sliding up Liam's back. His lips find Liam's neck, pressing a kiss to the sensitive skin there, and Liam shudders, his hands clutching at Jamie's shoulders.

Jamie's eyes meet mine over Liam's shoulder, and there's a question in them, an invitation. I step closer, my heart pounding in my chest, and Jamie reaches for me, pulling me into their orbit. His hand finds my waist, anchoring me to him as Sammy's lips trail up Liam's neck.

The four of us move together, a tangle of hands and lips and whispered words. The air is thick with desire, with the weight of something new and fragile taking shape. Liam's breath comes in shaky gasps, his body trembling between Sam and Jamie, but he doesn't pull away. Instead, he leans into their touch, his hands finding their way to my hips, pulling me closer.

"That's it," Jamie murmurs against Liam's lips, his voice rough with need. "You're doing so well." His hand slides up my back, his fingers tangling in my hair, breaking his kiss with Liam so he can pull me into a kiss that's all heat and hunger.

Sammy's lips find my neck, his hands sliding under my shirt, mapping my skin with a touch that's both possessive and worshipful. Liam's hands tremble as they explore, his touch hesitant but growing more confident with each passing moment.

The room feels like it's spinning, the world narrowing down to the four of us, to the heat of their bodies against mine, to the way their hands and lips make me feel like I'm coming alive. Jamie's kiss is fierce, demanding, while Sam's is slow and careful, each touch a promise of more to come.

"Tell us what you want, Liam," Jamie murmurs, cupping Liam's face.

"Fuck," Liam groans, taking a steadying breath. "What are my options?" he asks, looking between us, his eyelids heavy with desire.

"Suck a cock or get your cock sucked," Jamie says bluntly, laughing at the shock on Liam's face.

"Jesus fucking Christ," Liam chokes out, looking up at the ceiling.

"You're awful," I scold Jamie, glaring at him.

"Then punish me," he says, holding my gaze, challenging me.

A million ideas come to me at once, but only one has me making a mess of my panties. "On your knees," I tell him before turning to Liam. I trail my fingers over his cheek, feeling the slight stubble there. "Is this okay?" I whisper, searching his face for any hesitation.

Liam nods, swallowing hard. "Yes," he breathes, his voice cracking.

I lean in, brushing my mouth over his. Just a taste at first—barely there—but it hits like a jolt, a spark straight down my spine that lands low and heavy between my legs.

Liam groans and pulls me closer, our bodies locking into place like they've been waiting for this alignment their entire lives. The kiss deepens, slow and hungry, his tongue teasing mine until my breath catches.

I slide one hand into his hair, tangling in the soft, overgrown curls at the nape of his neck, tugging just hard enough to make him gasp. His hands find my waist, fingers digging in as he grinds against me, his cock already hard, pressing hot through his jeans. The friction is maddening. Perfect.

My other hand travels down his chest, slow enough to feel every shiver beneath his shirt, the frantic rhythm of his heart beating right into my palm. When I reach his waistband, I pause. Just long enough to feel his breath hitch. The button pops open with a tiny snick that feels loud in the quiet, electric space between us. I drag the zipper down slowly, intentionally, and then pull back just enough to meet his eyes.

Liam is destroyed already, pupils blown, lips parted, chest rising fast like he's trying to keep himself grounded.

I sink to my knees.

He doesn't speak. Doesn't have to.

I tug his boxers down just enough to free him, and he springs forward, flushed and thick, a drop of pre-cum glistening at the tip like a promise. Somewhere behind us, Jamie groans, low and pained, and it only makes the moment feel more charged, like we're on the edge of something we can't take back.

I keep my eyes locked on Liam's as I lean in, tongue flicking out to circle the head. His hips stutter, a strangled sound ripping from his throat. The taste, salty and warm, floods my mouth, and I hum, savoring the way he trembles under the sound.

I take my time, sucking him slowly, letting him feel every inch as I slide deeper. My tongue finds the thick vein along the underside, tracing it with the kind of focus that leaves him gasping. Each time I pull back, his cock is slick and glistening, every muscle in his body tight with restraint. Then I release him with a soft pop and stand, glancing over my shoulder.

"Your turn," I say, voice low and full of heat, crooking a finger at Sammy.

He doesn't hesitate.

Sammy closes the space between us in three slow, intentional steps, his eyes dark, his expression unreadable except for the desire written all over his face.

He cups my face like I'm something he can't believe he gets to touch, then leans down and kisses me—deep and searing, his mouth hot and hungry against mine. I melt into him, my hands sliding up the firm planes of his chest, catching in his dreads, holding him there.

His palms move to my breasts, thumbs dragging over my nipples through my shirt, and I swear I see stars. I arch into him, the contact sparking through my nerves like someone flipped a switch.

Without breaking the kiss, Sammy nudges me back until I hit the wall. The cold surface against my back makes me gasp, but then he presses in, his thigh sliding between mine, solid and perfectly placed. I move instinctively, grinding down against him, chasing the heat building between my legs with shameless urgency. His mouth leaves mine only to find my neck, lips dragging along my jaw before he sucks at the skin just below my ear. I tilt my head, offering more. And when his hand wraps around my waist and he presses his thigh up just a little harder I forget how to breathe entirely.

"That's it, love," Sammy murmurs against my throat, his breath hot, accent roughened with need. "Take what you need."

And I do. My hips grind down harder, chasing friction like it's the only thing anchoring me to my body. His hands settle firm on my waist, guiding me in a rhythm that feels almost too good, like he already knows how I fall apart.

The denim of his jeans rubs against my clit through the thin cotton of my underwear, rough and perfect and absolutely maddening. Pressure coils low in my belly, fast and tight, but not enough. Not yet. I groan, frustrated, restless, and push him back just enough to create space between us. His eyes flick up, confusion flashing first, but then something darker settles in. Understanding.

I drop to my knees.

There's no ceremony in it. No seduction. Just a hunger so sharp it's already scraped the inside of my throat raw. My fingers fumble at his belt, too impatient for finesse. Sammy helps, pushing his jeans down his hips. His cock springs free—thick, flushed, already leaking. My mouth waters.

I look up at him as I lean in, tongue flicking out to gather the bead of precum. He groans, low and devastated, and the sound punches straight through me. I swirl my tongue around the head, slow, focused, then hollow my cheeks and take him deeper.

His hips twitch, his hand curling into my hair as he breathes out something that might be my name.

Behind me, I can feel Jamie watching, like a second layer of heat crawling up my spine. His breath is ragged, uneven, and I don't have to look to know he's hard, pressed tight against his zipper, desperate and held in place by his own rules.

I pull back, letting Sammy's cock slip from my mouth with a slick, obscene sound. It bobs in front of me, glistening with spit and flushed dark at the tip. I press kisses along the thick vein, my hand stroking what my mouth can't reach, slow and deliberate.

"Fuck, Penelope," Sammy growls, and the next second, I'm on my feet again, pulled up before I can finish him off.

I strip quickly, letting my pants and underwear fall to the floor in one fluid motion. The air is cool against my skin, a sharp contrast to the fire burning low in my belly.

The edge of the table digs into the backs of my thighs as I climb onto it, legs spread wide without hesitation. I can feel my heartbeat in every inch of me, throbbing, insistent.

"Liam. Sammy," I breathe, my voice gone hoarse with want. "Come here."

They move toward me without a word, their cocks hard, their bodies tense with anticipation. Each step closer feels like gravity shifting, like the whole room tilting around what's about to happen. I pull them in, one on each side, close enough that I can feel their heat, smell the salt and sweat clinging to their skin. And then I turn my gaze to Jamie. Still kneeling, eyes burning, jaw tight.

"Jamie," I say, voice low but clear. "Your punishment is to get us all there. With your mouth."

A slow, wicked grin spreads across his face. "That's not punishment, Penella. That's paradise." He crawls forward on his knees, eyes dark with lust. For a moment, he seems to consider his options before turning to Sammy.

Jamie's tongue darts out, licking a long stripe up the underside of Sammy's cock. Sammy hisses, his hand flying to Jamie's hair. Jamie takes his time, alternating between soft licks and long, slow strokes. He swirls the tip of his tongue around the head, dipping into the slit to taste the precum beading there. Sammy's breathing grows ragged as Jamie works him over. His hips start to twitch, seeking more.

I watch, mesmerized, as Jamie takes him deeper. His lips stretch obscenely around Sammy's girth, saliva glistening on his chin. Wet sounds fill the air, punctuated by Sammy's low moans. I desperately want to slip my hand between my legs, but I know it'll be worth it if I wait. Jamie cups Sammy's balls, tugging and rolling them gently. His other hand wraps around the base of Sammy's cock, working what his mouth can't reach. Sammy's thighs tremble, his grip on Jamie's hair tightening.

"Fuck, Jamie," Sammy gasps. "Your mouth... Christ."

Jamie hums in response, the vibrations drawing another moan from Sammy. Jamie pulls back, his lips glistening. With a wicked grin, he locks eyes with Sammy and slowly, purposefully, takes him back into his mouth. Sammy's cock disappears inch by inch into Jamie's willing throat until his nose is buried in the coarse hair at the base. Sammy lets out a strangled groan, his hands fisting in Jamie's hair. Jamie's throat works around him, swallowing reflexively. Tears spring to Jamie's eyes as he fights his gag reflex, but he doesn't pull back. Instead, he hollows his cheeks, sucking hard.

The sight is mesmerizing—Jamie's lips stretched obscenely wide, Sammy's cock bulging in his throat. I can see Jamie's pulse racing in his neck, feel the tension radiating from Sammy's trembling body beside me.

Jamie starts to bob his head, taking Sammy deep with each pass. Wet, choking sounds fill the air as Jamie gags slightly, saliva dripping down his chin. But he doesn't stop, driven by some primal need to please, to prove himself.

Sammy's hips start to twitch, little aborted thrusts he can't seem to control. "Fuck, Jamie," he gasps. "I'm gonna—"

Jamie pulls back just enough to catch a breath, his hand wrapping tight around the base of Sammy's cock, pumping him fast and hard. His tongue flicks over the head and Sammy unravels.

His hips jerk forward, his hands fisting at Jamie's curls as his body locks up. "Fuck—Jamie," he chokes out, his voice shattered, right before he comes.

He buries himself in Jamie's throat with a desperate thrust, and Jamie takes it all, eyes fluttering shut, throat working around him as he swallows every last drop.

Sammy groans, low and broken, his whole body trembling with the aftershock. Jamie doesn't flinch. Doesn't pull away. Just stays there, mouth still wrapped around him, like he was made for this.

When he finally pulls off, his lips are swollen and red, his eyes watery. He turns to Liam, who's been watching with wide eyes and parted lips. "Enjoy the show?" Jamie asks, voice rough and raspy.

Jamie turns to me, his eyes glinting with mischief. "Don't worry, Penella, I'm saving you for last. Gonna make you beg for my cock."

I arch an eyebrow, a smirk playing at my lips. "Bold of you to assume I'd beg for anything."

Jamie lets out a low, dark laugh that slides straight down my spine, leaving goosebumps in its wake. Then he shifts his focus to Liam—who's watching him like he's not sure whether to lean in or run.

Jamie moves toward him slowly, every motion careful, like a big cat closing in on its prey. His body rolls forward with that same dangerous grace, knees dragging across the floor, shoulders loose but eyes locked in.

And those eyes—God—they never leave Liam's face. He's watching everything: the flicker of breath, the tiny hitch in Liam's chest, the nervous swallow that betrays how close he is to unraveling.

When Jamie reaches him, he doesn't dive in. Doesn't even touch. He just lingers there, so close the heat of his breath ghosts over Liam's skin, raising the hairs on his neck.

Liam goes still, caught in the pull of it, like he knows the next touch is going to undo him, and he's already bracing for the fall.

"First time with a man?" Jamie asks, voice low, rough-edged with desire.

Liam nods. Just once. His Adam's apple bobs as he swallows hard, eyes fixed somewhere between Jamie's mouth and the floor. "Yeah," he whispers. It's not shy, exactly. Just raw. Open in a way that feels private. "Yeah."

Jamie smiles, slow and wicked, like he's just been handed his favorite thing on a silver platter. "Don't worry," he murmurs, leaning in, voice soft enough to feel like a secret. "I'll take good care of you."

He starts low, pressing warm, open-mouthed kisses to the inside of Liam's thighs. Each one lingers a little too long, lips dragging, stubble scraping lightly over sensitive skin. Liam flinches, not away, but toward. A shaky gasp breaks from him, and Jamie smiles against his skin. His hands slide up Liam's legs, broad palms kneading the tense muscle there, slow and tender like he's easing tension out of something sacred. Jamie moves higher, but not fast. Never fast. He kisses along the crease of Liam's hip, tongue flicking close enough to make Liam's whole body jerk in response. So close. Not close enough.

Liam's hips twitch, instinct chasing friction. But Jamie pulls back with a quiet laugh, breath ghosting hot over Liam's skin.

"Patience," he says, voice pitched like a prayer and a promise all at once.

And then Jamie licks him. One long, intentional drag of his tongue up the underside of Liam's cock.

Liam makes a sound like he's been punched in the gut, loud and broken and impossibly real.

Jamie does it again, slower this time, savoring the taste like it's something to memorize.

"Christ," Liam groans, and the sound of it destroys me. His accent's heavier now, like he's barely hanging on. His hands hover awkwardly at his sides, unsure where to go.

Jamie looks up, eyes dark and steady. "You can touch," he says, voice gone gentle. "Pull if you want. I like it."

Liam doesn't need to be told twice. His fingers tangle in Jamie's curls, tugging just enough to draw a low, satisfied moan from Jamie's chest. The vibration of it echoes through Liam's cock, and his hips jerk, completely involuntary. Jamie doesn't even flinch. Just lets Liam sink deeper, swallowing around him like he was made to.

Liam gasps again, the kind of sound you only make when you're not thinking, when your body takes over and language fails. "Fuck... that's..." His head tips back. "Christ, Jamie."

Jamie looks up at him again, eyes heavy-lidded and focused, his mouth stretched wide and wet around Liam's cock. The image alone nearly shatters him.

Jamie starts to move, head bobbing in a rhythm that builds fast and steady, his mouth working Liam like he already knows every pressure point. One of his hands slips lower, cupping Liam's balls, rolling them slowly. Liam's thighs tremble under the weight of it all—too much, too good, too close.

His breath comes ragged now, his body caught in that helpless stutter of nearing the edge. His hips jerk in short, desperate thrusts, chasing the heat of Jamie's mouth like it's the only solid thing left in the world.

Jamie takes him deeper. All the way. His throat relaxes, letting Liam fuck into him with uneven, frantic strokes.

"Jamie," Liam gasps, a warning wrapped in desperation. "I'm gonna—"

Jamie just moans around him, sucking harder, tongue dragging along the most sensitive part of him with deadly precision.

Liam shatters.

His whole body arches, a guttural cry torn from deep in his chest as he comes hard, hips stuttering forward. Jamie doesn't pull away. He stays right there, swallowing every last drop, his throat working around Liam's release until Liam's legs start to give.

Only then—only when Liam's trembling and glassy-eyed—does Jamie slowly ease off, lips soft and swollen, breath coming fast.

He rises in one smooth, practiced motion, like he never doubted how this would end.

Then he cups Liam's face, so gentle it makes my throat ache, and kisses him. Deep and slow and full of something that feels a lot like worship. Liam lets out a low sound, a whimper more than a moan. The kiss lingers. A soft landing after the high.

And then Jamie turns to me.

His gaze is molten. Dark with intent. Every inch of his body screams predator, coiled and ready.

He walks toward me, slow and calculated. My pulse thunders in my throat.

God help me, I'm already soaked.

Jamie crowds into my space like he's always belonged there, like we were just waiting for this moment to snap into place. The heat radiating off him is immediate, consuming. He cups my jaw in one hand, tilting my face up until his gaze finds mine.

"I've been waiting for this," he says, voice thick and raspy, like the words have been sitting in his mouth for hours. His tongue flicks out to wet his bottom lip, and then he's on me.

His mouth crashes into mine, all hunger and pressure and nothing soft about it. The taste of him hits me hard—salt and sweat and something richer underneath. But threaded through it are Liam's earthy musk and Sammy's sweetness, faint but undeniable, and the combination is dizzying. Intoxicating.

My whole body tightens in response.

Jamie kisses like he's starving and I'm the only thing on the menu. His hands roam over me with purpose, calloused palms dragging over fabric, finding heat and exposed skin with maddening precision. He nips at my bottom lip, then mouths a trail along my jaw, sucking gently before moving lower.

When he reaches my ear, his breath hits warm and wet against the skin there. I shiver, completely at his mercy.

"You like that, don't you?" he murmurs, voice a rough purr. "Tasting them on me."

All I can manage is a whimper, my hips rolling, chasing friction like it's the only thing I've ever needed.

He laughs, low and wicked, and it vibrates against my skin. His hands settle at my waist, thumbs pressing slow, teasing circles into my hipbones. I feel like I might unravel just from that.

"Patience, love," he says, voice featherlight now, brushing the shell of my ear.

He takes his time. His mouth trails a path over my collarbone, down to the curve of my breast. He doesn't just touch—he devours. Sucking, licking, scraping his teeth lightly until my back arches and I cry out, shameless and desperate.

He gives both breasts attention, then kisses his way lower, across my stomach, dipping his tongue into my navel, dragging the tension out just when I think I can't take anymore.

When he reaches the apex of my thighs, I'm shaking. Trembling with need. But he doesn't go where I need him. Not yet. Instead, he presses open-mouthed kisses along my inner thighs, sucking marks into my skin that I know will bloom purple-blue by morning. His tongue moves slow, wicked. I can feel wetness slick between my legs, dripping down onto the table beneath me. The air feels impossibly cold against it.

"Jamie," I gasp, my fingers diving into his hair. "Please."

He looks up, eyes molten with lust. "Please what?"

"Touch me," I choke out. I don't care how I sound. "I need you."

A smirk curves across his lips, slow and sinful. "How do you want me, Penella?" His mouth hovers just above the place I need him most. "You want my mouth?" He kisses the inside of my thigh, maddeningly close. "Or my cock?"

The image flashes through my mind, his body pressing into mine, stretching me open, filling me.

"Your cock," I moan, shattered. "Jamie, please. I need you inside me."

He stands, positioning himself between my legs. The head of his cock nudges against me, hot and hard, and I gasp as it slides along my slit. He doesn't push in. Just teases. Up and down. Slow circles around my clit that have my legs trembling and my fingernails digging into his back.

"Fuck," I pant, unable to stop my hips from bucking. "Jamie—please."

"So impatient," he murmurs, amused, voice thick with his brogue. He dips his head to my neck, kissing the sensitive spot beneath my ear, sucking gently.

"I want to savor this," he adds, voice low, like he's making me a promise I'll feel for days.

He keeps up the torture, rubbing the head of his cock against my clit in slow, perfect strokes. Each pass sends sparks dancing across my skin. The tension builds sharp and tight inside me, coiling and knotting like it's about to snap.

"You're soaked," Jamie growls, his voice lower now, rougher. "Dripping for me." He grazes the shell of my ear again. "So fucking beautiful like this."

Then he presses the tip of his cock inside, just barely breaching me, before pulling out again. I whimper at the loss. He does it again. A little deeper. Then retreats. I'm unraveling. The world narrows to the burn, the stretch, the ache. To where our bodies almost, almost connect.

"Jamie," I whisper, voice breaking. "I need you."

He meets my eyes, gaze molten. "Beg for it," he says, low and steady.

"Please," I breathe, everything inside me unraveling at once. "Please, I need you. I need you to fuck me. Right now."

A groan rumbles out of him, deep and guttural.

"My pleasure," he says, voice nothing but gravel and want.

With one smooth, calculated thrust, Jamie pushes all the way in, buries himself to the hilt, and the world goes quiet. Just for a second.

Then everything breaks wide open.

Pleasure rips through me like a flash fire, white-hot and all-consuming. My breath catches, my fingers scrabble for something to hold onto, and I find him—his shoulders, his arms, his back—solid and shaking and real.

For one suspended moment, we're still. Just breathing. His forehead rests against mine, our lips almost brushing, and I can feel the frantic thud of his heart syncing up with mine like a drumline inside my chest.

Then he moves. And the world tips sideways.

He finds a rhythm quickly, deep, careful thrusts that drag his cock along every inch of me. The friction is exquisite, the pressure unbearable in the best way. Each stroke leaves my nerves raw, stripped down to sensation and nothing else.

Jamie presses me flat against the table, my back arching off the surface. He leans in for a kiss, tongue sweeping into my mouth like he's claiming me from the inside out. I gasp against his lips as he adjusts his angle, hips tilting just enough to hit my G-spot. My body bows toward him instinctively, chasing it.

He starts to fuck me harder, rougher, his thrusts growing more urgent, more desperate, the table creaking under us. I hook my legs around his waist, pulling him deeper, grounding myself against the relentless pleasure.

His mouth finds my neck, sucking, biting, dragging his teeth over that sensitive spot beneath my ear that makes me whimper. Then he moves lower, his tongue circling my nipple before he sucks it deep into his mouth, and I cry out, the combination of stretch and sting and heat almost unbearable.

My hands clutch at his back, fingers digging into slick skin and flexing muscle. He groans against my breast, the sound low and guttural, before releasing it with a wet pop and panting against my skin.

"Fuck, Penelope," he grits out, voice destroyed. "You feel so fucking good. Like your cunt was made for my cock."

His hand snakes between us, fingers finding my clit with unerring accuracy. He rubs tight, brutal circles, synced to the rhythm of his thrusts, and my body locks up.

I'm right there.

"That's it," Jamie growls, his voice breaking apart with exertion. "Come for me, my love. Let me feel you squeeze the cum right out of my cock."

The words hit as hard as his thrusts, and then I'm gone.

My orgasm detonates inside me, sharp, fast, and so intense I forget how to breathe. My body arches off the table, everything clenching tight as I cry out, fingers slipping across his back as I come hard around him.

Jamie doesn't stop. He fucks me through it, eyes locked on mine like he's drinking in every flicker of devastated bliss on my face.

Only when I start to tremble, my body overstimulated and raw, does he let himself go.

His hips stutter, his mouth falling open against my shoulder. "Fuck—fuck, I'm gonna—"

And then he makes a sound so filthy it makes my toes curl, his whole body shaking as he drives into me one last time and stays there, buried deep.

"Take it," he gasps, breath hot in my ear. "Take every fucking drop. That sweet pussy milking my cock—fuck."

I feel it, the thick pulse of him spilling inside me, the twitch of his cock as he empties himself in hot, staggering waves. His body presses down against mine, trembling, hips rocking just enough to ride it out.

We stay like that for a long moment. Bodies locked. Breathing hard.

His forehead drops to my shoulder, lips brushing my skin as he whispers something I can't quite make out. Maybe my name. Maybe something darker.

And I let myself lie there, stretched open and full of him, heart still racing, knowing this was more than just release.

It was surrender.

As the haze begins to lift, the world starts creeping back in—the chill of the air, the rough edge of the table pressing into my back, the dull ache between my legs that means I was just thoroughly fucked. Jamie's still draped over me, all heat and sweat and slow, open-mouthed kisses along my collarbone.

His breath fans against my skin, warm and lazy, like he has no plans to move anytime soon. I can feel his heartbeat still hammering in his chest, pressed flush to mine.

Then the sound of zippers cuts through the quiet.

I tilt my head just enough to catch Sammy and Liam, both moving in the soft light, buttoning jeans, smoothing hair. Watching them snaps me back into my body all at once, what we did, what they saw, how far we let ourselves go. A flush blooms hot across my cheeks.

Jamie shifts, and the sudden slip of him pulling out leaves me aching, empty. A soft sound escapes me before I can stop it.

He props himself up on his elbows, grinning down at me like he just won something. "I told you you'd beg for it," he says, his voice low, lips brushing mine.

I huff out a laugh. "Yeah, well... Jokes on me because I wasn't thinking about the fact that there's no running water here. I can't even clean up."

His grin sharpens into something wicked. "Good." He leans in, his voice rough and satisfied. "I like the idea of you walking around with me dripping out of you."

The words hit me like a jolt, sharp, filthy, and utterly possessive. My inner walls flutter in response, like my body hasn't quite decided it's done yet. Jamie sees it. Of course he does. His smirk widens as he slowly peels himself off me, leaving my skin cold in his absence.

He offers me a hand, and I take it, sliding carefully off the table. The air is cool, sticky, damp with sweat and sex. I shift on my feet and feel it—him—slipping down my inner thighs. I bite back a groan.

"Shit," I mutter, glancing around. "We don't even have paper towels."

Jamie catches my wrist. "Leave it," he says, the softness gone from his voice. There's still heat in his eyes, smoldering under the surface. "I meant what I said."

The flush rises higher, but I nod. Not out of submission—out of thrill. Because I want to carry this with me. This reminder of what we did. Jamie helps me dress slowly, carefully. Fingers skimming my skin, tucking my shirt back into place. When he presses a kiss to my forehead, it feels unexpectedly tender.

Sammy and Liam drift closer, and something in the air shifts again —like we're all remembering this isn't just sex, that we've stepped over some invisible line together. Sammy reaches out and gently tucks a strand of hair behind my ear.

"You okay, love?" he asks, eyes warm and searching.

I lean into his hand, smiling. "More than okay."

Jamie turns toward Liam, who's hovering just behind Sammy, still a little wide-eyed. "So, cowboy," he drawls, trying on an Australian accent so bad it's criminal. "How was your first blowjob from a bloke? Live up to the hype?"

Liam turns the color of a ripe tomato, but there's a smile tugging at the corners of his mouth. He runs a hand through his hair before jamming his hat back onto his head like armor.

"It was..." He clears his throat. "Christ, it was incredible."

Sammy steps closer, resting a hand on Liam's shoulder. "Did it help? With figuring things out?" His tone is gentle, open.

Liam's gaze bounces between us. "I think... I've known. For a while." He shrugs. "But I was scared. My family's not exactly—" He trails off.

"We get it," I say, reaching for his hand, squeezing tight.

Jamie pulls him into a hug without warning, arms wrapping around him like it's the easiest thing in the world. "Takes guts," he says. "Letting yourself be seen. Exploring that part of you? That's real courage."

"We're proud of you," Sammy adds, voice steady. "For showing up. For trusting us."

Liam's eyes glisten, and when he speaks, it's barely a whisper. "I've never felt this accepted before."

I step forward, looping my arms around them both. Sammy joins in, and suddenly we're all tangled together, holding each other in a circle of sweat, warmth, and something that feels dangerously close to love. The room is quiet, humming with something deeper than just sex —acceptance, maybe. Relief. Possibility.

When we finally break apart, Liam wipes at his eyes, laughing softly. He looks lighter. More comfortable in his skin.

But then his brow furrows, and his fingers tug absently at the brim of his hat. "So... what does this mean?" he asks, voice small. "For us? Are we... something now?"

The question hangs there. Not scary exactly, but loaded.

Sammy is the first to speak. "It means whatever we want it to mean," he says simply. "No playbook. No labels. Just us."

Jamie nods. "We take it as it comes." Then he winks. "Pun absolutely intended."

Everyone groans. Even Liam. Especially Liam.

"You're awful," I mutter, smiling despite myself.

"You love it," Jamie says, eyes gleaming.

"No pressure," Sammy says. "No timelines. Just know you belong here. If you want to."

Liam looks at each of us, his eyes glassy, but his smile is real. Soft. Hopeful. "I'd like that," he says. "I'd like that a lot."

20

———

ARCHER'S POV

The harbor is still wrapped in darkness when I check the latest weather reports, my thumb smudging the screen as I scroll through data I already don't like. A fast-moving low-pressure system, creeping up the coast quicker than expected. Southeast winds gusting to thirty knots by afternoon. Not ideal. Not a deal-breaker either.

The cabin smells like salt and diesel, sharp and familiar. I spread the charts out again, even though I've already plotted the route in my head. I'm not second-guessing. I'm grounding myself.

Pearl's nails click softly across the deck as she follows me up. The pre-dawn air bites, thick with that static tension that raises the hair on the back of my neck. It's too still, too quiet. That breathless moment before a storm breaks. I look up. The sky's clear. For now.

My phone buzzes in my pocket. Spencer.

"Dude, I'm out," he says without preamble. He sounds like he gargled gravel. "That curry last night..."

"Food poisoning?" I ask, but we both know it's not the curry.

He doesn't answer. Doesn't need to. Spencer's never said it out loud, but rough water makes him green before we even leave the dock. I heard it in his voice the second the forecast changed.

"Something like that," he says. "Sorry to leave you short-handed."

I grunt, glancing up as headlights wash across the parking lot.

Penelope's truck. Right on time.

The knot in my chest loosens, just slightly, at the sight of her. She's been slipping into my mornings so seamlessly I hardly noticed when her presence stopped feeling optional. I try not to think too hard about that.

She steps out, purposeful and sure, wearing those absurd yellow rain boots she swears by, her backpack slung over one shoulder. Her hair's clipped back, a few strands already pulling loose in the breeze. And my sweater. My old, beat-up fisherman's sweater that hangs just a little too long on her, sleeves shoved up to her elbows. I should've known she'd kept it, but seeing her in it does something painful and unnameable to my chest.

Pearl trots off to greet her, tail wagging like a banner of betrayal.

"No boat rides today, girl," I call, but she's already at Penelope's feet, full of hope and puppy dog eyes.

Penelope leans down and scratches behind her ears, her touch gentle. "You'd hate it anyway," she croons. Then she looks up at me. "Southeast winds, building by mid-morning. Thunderstorms this afternoon."

I raise an eyebrow. "Been reading the forecast?"

"Yeah. Spencer told me he wasn't feeling well, so I figured I'd come out and see if you need help." She hefts her backpack, fixing me with that determined look that never fails to make my pulse quicken. "Southeast winds increasing throughout the day, possible thunderstorms by evening. Want to tell me why we're still going out?"

A dozen answers crowd my throat: Because I've never backed down from weather. Because having you aboard makes me feel invincible. Because watching you handle the boat with those capable hands makes me want to see them on my skin instead. I don't say any of that.

Instead: "We leave now, we'll be in protected water before the worst hits."

She studies me with those hazel eyes that seem to see straight through to my soul, then nods. The trust in that simple gesture hits harder than it should. "Where do you want the supplies?"

We fall into sync without speaking. Loading coolers, checking lines, making adjustments. She moves through the space like she was born to it. She knows this like the back of her hand, knows which straps are finicky, which tie-downs need a second glance. Her motions are confident, practiced. It's dangerous how much I like watching her in my space—how much it feels like our space.

She leans over to secure the forward lines, and I have to drag my eyes away from the sway of her hips, the way her body tilts into the roll of the boat without conscious effort. There's something about her ease here that guts me.

Pearl makes a valiant attempt to sneak aboard, one paw on the ladder like she's just stretching.

"Nice try." I scoop her up, pressing my face into her fur. She smells like wind and sun and dog shampoo. It steadies me. "Jamie and Sam'll be here in an hour. Guilt them into slipping some extra food."

The VHF crackles. Another update—small craft advisory bumped up to a full warning. Penelope's hand pauses mid-checklist. She doesn't look at me, but she's listening. I can see the tension in her jaw, the faint crease between her brows. The part of her that's worried.

"You still sure about this?"

She's not just talking about the weather.

And yeah, the right move—the smart move—is to stay in port. But there's a recklessness in me today. Something restless and raw. And there's her—standing there in my sweater, looking at me like I'm someone she believes in.

"We've handled worse." I lean past her to test a line, letting my arm graze her side. She doesn't move. Doesn't flinch.

We're close now. Her scent is sea air and coffee and shampoo that smells like coconut and sunshine. It's burned into me. I've been trying not to memorize it for weeks.

She looks up at me, her gaze catching on my mouth before flicking back to my eyes.

"That's not really an answer," she murmurs.

"You nervous?" My voice comes out low. Too low.

She holds my stare. "Not about the weather."

And that—fuck—that softness behind her words nearly unmoors me.

She licks her lips and my gut clenches hard. Every part of me is screaming to close the distance. To do something reckless like fuck her right here on the deck of the boat while the storm rolls in. The radio cuts through the moment again, sharp and unwelcome. I step back before I can forget what the hell we're doing out here.

"Last chance to back out," I say, hoarse.

She rolls her eyes. "Please. Like I'd let you handle this alone."

Goddamn. Of course she wouldn't.

That's the thing about her—she always shows up. When the weather's shit. When I'm not saying the things I should. She still shows up.

She steps in closer, voice quiet now. "Your call. But whatever you decide... I'm with you."

The light's coming up now, thin and pale over the water. The wind cuts sharper. But she's right here, warm and steady beside me, and suddenly, sensible feels overrated.

I check the weather app one last time. The numbers haven't changed. But the math feels different now.

"Plot us a course east of the shoals," I say, voice rough. "We'll hug the lee as long as we can."

She nods. No smile. Just that look again—the one that sees all of me and stays anyway.

The wind tears her hair loose as we push off, and I have to shove my hands in my pockets to keep from tucking the strands behind her ear. Pearl watches us from the dock, tail still, ears perked. Like she knows we're doing something bold. Maybe something stupid.

The wind shifts again as we clear the harbor mouth, stronger than predicted. Penelope adjusts the trim without prompting, her movements fluid and graceful. The sight of her competent hands on the controls does things to me that have nothing to do with seamanship. Of course she knows exactly what to do - she probably knew these waters before she could walk. Sometimes I forget that, caught up in teaching her things she already understands bone-deep.

. . .

The sky looks like it's holding its breath—clouds bruised and swollen, pressing in on the horizon like they're about to split open. The kind of sky that makes every part of you feel watched. Judged. Dared.

The boat shudders beneath us as we cut through the chop, the waves coming in harder now, like they're testing us. Testing me. But Penelope—God, Penelope—she just moves with it. She's standing at the bow in my old sweater, eyes scanning the water like she's listening to it speak. Like it's a language only she knows.

Her knees bend with every roll, her hips shifting with the motion. Fluid. Unshaken. She looks over her shoulder and catches me watching, one brow lifted, that smirk breaking over her face like sunlight through storm clouds.

"Want me to take her while you check radar?" she asks, voice low and full of gravel and heat, like it's dragging across the back of my neck on purpose.

I nod before I can form words. We trade spots, our bodies brushing in the cramped space, heat meeting heat. She steps up to the helm, hands finding the wheel with the kind of easy, practiced confidence that makes my stomach clench. She doesn't just steer the boat—she knows it. Feels it.

The radar screen glows a sick, unfriendly green. The storm system's picked up speed, accelerating fast, the way your gut drops just before a rollercoaster descends. We've got two hours at most before we're in the thick of it. Not four like I'd hoped. Maybe not even that.

"Weather's closing in faster than forecasted," I shout, wind already rising like a chorus in my ears.

She doesn't look at me. Doesn't need to. "I'll cut east through the channel." She's already turning the wheel, adjusting our heading with that slight grin still tugging at the corners of her mouth.

I swallow hard, trying not to think about how she probably sailed this route a hundred times as a kid, learning the currents the same way she learned to read—by heart. I watch her hands work the wheel, and it feels like the universe is pressing a finger against my chest, daring me to keep pretending this is anything but inevitable.

She's radiant like this. Wild. Her cheeks are flushed, eyes fierce, mouth set with purpose. She belongs here in a way that I can only admire, never match.

"Taking her up," she says, loud enough to cut through the wind. She braces her stance and leans into the wheel as the bow angles into the swell. My pulse is an unsteady thing in my throat.

I step in to help, shoulder brushing hers again, and it's like every inch of contact is amplified. She doesn't even flinch. She's focused, locked in. If she notices how close we are, how my hands linger a second too long, she doesn't say a word.

"Shelter?" I ask, trying to sound casual. Failing.

"Mackenzie's Cove." Her voice is quick, sure. "Deep enough. Sheltered from a southeast push. Mooring's probably still good."

Lightning flashes across the sky like a gunshot. I see her profile etched in blue-white light—high cheekbones, hair whipped around her face, strands clinging to her throat. And somehow, impossibly, she's smiling. Not scared. Not reckless. Alive.

I can barely breathe watching her.

"You're thinking too loud again," she murmurs, not looking back. She leans back just enough to press against me and the contact lights up every nerve in my body like an exposed wire. "We've got this."

We do. That's the terrifying part. The way we move together without thinking. The way she fits against me. The way she's already wrapped around every corner of my life like she's always belonged there.

The first raindrops hit hard, like the sky finally gave in. Fat beads of water soak through fabric, turning everything slick and shining. It streaks down the windows, trails in rivulets along the back of her neck, and all I can think about is following that path with my mouth. Her sweater is soaked through now, clinging to the curve of her waist, the swell of her breasts. I try not to stare and fail miserably.

She adjusts the trim and her shoulder grazes my arm again. I bite the inside of my cheek.

"Forty-knot gusts within the hour," she says, voice thinner now. Not with fear. With restraint. Like she's trying to pretend she doesn't feel it too.

"Do you think Mackenzie's will still work?" I say, checking to make sure we're still on course.

She nods, and within minutes the cove appears ahead, a dark slash in the coastline, half-hidden behind the curtain of rain. She guides us in without hesitation, navigating the narrow inlet like she could do it blindfolded.

The anchor drops with a solid clunk, catches, and holds. We're safe. Technically. But my pulse hasn't gotten the message. Everything inside me is still rolling, still bracing for impact.

Penelope moves with the same calm precision she's had since the first gust of wind hit. Fingers sure, motions efficient as she checks our mooring. Her clothes cling to her like second skin, dark and soaked, her hair a tangled halo around her face. She turns toward me, rain-slicked and radiant, and I'm still staring.

"What?" she asks, catching me mid-thought.

I reach for her waist without thinking, my hand finding warm, damp skin beneath the hem of her shirt. Just need to touch her. To make sure she's real, still here, still mine.

"You're good at this," I murmur, my voice rougher than I intended.

Her smile is all teeth and certainty. "I know."

And then she grabs my hand—no hesitation, no second-guessing—and tugs me below deck with a look that makes everything inside me unravel at once.

The storm howls overhead, but in the cabin, everything narrows to the sound of rain on the deck and Penelope's quickened breathing. She's toweling her hair dry, water droplets trailing down her neck in a path my tongue itches to follow. Her coveralls are long gone, leaving her in only one of my spare shirts and her panties. The sight makes my mouth go dry.

Lightning flashes, casting dramatic shadows across the planes of her face. She's watching me with that look that sees right through my carefully constructed walls, the one that makes me feel both exposed and anchored, like she's the only thing keeping me from drowning in want.

I swallow hard.

The tension in the space is thick—humid, electric, pressing in on all sides. I take a step toward her and she doesn't move. Just lets the towel drop and closes the distance.

"You're spiraling," she says, running a hand down my chest. Her fingers skate lower, dragging heat in their wake. "I can feel it."

"I'm thinking," I murmur.

"That's your first problem."

I can't stop looking at her. At the curve of her hips, the line of her thighs, the way my shirt rides up just enough to show the bottom of her perfect ass. I want to touch it. Want to touch everything.

"Penelope." Her name comes out like a prayer, rough with need. She's close enough now that I can see the droplets clinging to her eyelashes, smell the intoxicating mix of rain and salt on her skin, feel the heat radiating from her body. The boat rocks gently in our protected anchorage, but she moves with it instinctively, her hips swaying in a way that makes my mouth go dry.

"I know." Her hand finds my chest, spreading warmth through the damp fabric as she traces patterns over my thundering heart. "I know all the reasons why you think this is complicated. But it's not." Her fingers trail lower, making my muscles jump beneath her touch. "It's actually very simple."

Simple. Nothing about her has ever been simple—she's as complex and intoxicating as a storm at sea. But she's right about this, about us. Strip away all the complications, and what's left is as clear as a compass pointing true north.

I cup her face in my hands, my thumbs tracing the delicate line of her cheekbones as raindrops trail down her skin. "I love you." The words feel like an anchor dropping, like coming home to safe harbor after a lifetime at sea. "Have for a while now."

Her smile blooms slow and sensual, making my cock harden in 2.5 seconds flat. "I know that too." She rises on her toes, her body pressing against mine in all the right places. "I love you back."

When my lips finally meet hers, it feels like gravity gives out.

Not a kiss, but a breaking point. The shattering of every second we spent pretending we didn't want this. Didn't need it. It crashes over us

—hot and heavy and impossibly slow, like the moment before lightning hits. Her fingers slide into my hair just as mine tug at the damp lace clinging to her hips. The air inside the cabin is warm from our bodies, but the second I push her panties aside, cold air licks at her skin and she gasps, jerking under my hands. Her breath is a whimper I feel more than hear, lodged in the space between our mouths.

I don't wait. I can't. The lace tears with a satisfying rip, and she exhales like she's been holding that breath since the first time I looked at her too long. "Christ, you're soaked," I mutter, my voice low against her skin as I trail kisses down her belly, onto her thigh. She tastes like salt and heat and summer storms—her scent thick in the tight cabin, sharp and earthy.

Her knee knocks the bulkhead as the boat pitches, sending me deeper between her legs. It makes her curse, breathless and guttural, her fingers tangling tighter in my hair as my mouth finds her. The storm outside becomes our metronome, every roll of the sea syncing with the movement of my tongue.

"Fuck! Fuck, your mouth—" she gasps, thighs shaking against my shoulders. Her hips roll up and I lock my arms under them, holding her there, taking her apart piece by piece. The cot creaks under her, the boat groans with the storm, and I keep going until she can't.

"I can't—I'm gonna—"

"Good girl," I breathe, pulling back just enough to watch her fall apart. Her eyes wide, mouth open, flushed and raw with pleasure. "That's it. Come on my tongue."

She cries out, loud and unfiltered, as I suck her clit and slide two fingers deep inside her. She clamps down hard around them, her whole body locking up before shattering. I ride the wave of her orgasm, only easing off when her moans dissolve into broken whimpers, when her fingers push weakly at my shoulders.

Her lips find mine before I can even speak, her kiss messy and hungry. "Off," she growls, tugging at my zipper. "I need you inside me. Now."

Her urgency undoes me. I fumble with my jeans, only half-aware of the way my cock springs free, thick and aching. She drops to her knees without hesitation, her mouth wrapping around me with a heat that makes my vision blur. She takes me deep, her gag reflex kicking in fast, her throat fluttering around me as she tries to take more.

"Jesus," I pant, one hand braced against the low ceiling, the other threading into her wet hair. "Easy, baby—"

She glares up at me, eyes watering but dark with determination. She wants this. Wants to give it. And fuck if that doesn't undo me even more.

I haul her up hard, nearly off her feet, kissing her like it's the only thing keeping me anchored to this moment—like if I stop, I'll drift out with the storm and never find my way back. Her mouth is hot, urgent, tasting like rain and salt and everything I've ever fucking wanted.

"I said inside me," she breathes again, voice shattered, shaking with it. Her eyes are wild—fierce and pleading all at once. Like a demand and a prayer, and I've never wanted anything more than to obey.

And that's it. That's the last thread of control, frayed and snapping in an instant.

I shove her down onto the narrow cot, stomach-first, hands gripping at the sheets as she gasps, hair spilling forward like wet silk. The boat rocks beneath us, the storm howling through the cracks in the hull, but all I can focus on is the slick heat of her as I line myself up and thrust into her in one long, brutal motion.

We both groan, low and guttural, her back bowing, my hands gripping her hips so tight I know I'll leave bruises. The sound of skin meeting skin cuts through the wind, through the thunder, sharp and primal. Her name's already in my mouth, bitten off between curses and gasps, a desperate kind of worship.

She pushes back against me like she's chasing the destruction with me, like she wants to be ruined. And I give it to her. I fuck her like I'm trying to drive out every storm I've ever carried inside me.

There's nothing sweet about it. No slow build. No careful edge. Just raw, reckless need.

Her voice breaks over the sound of the rain pounding above us. "Harder." A whimper, almost. Then: "Harder, you fuck—"

I snap.

I yank her up and flip us, not even thinking, just acting on instinct. Her legs lock around my waist the second her back hits the mattress, her ankles digging into my spine like she owns me. And maybe she does. Maybe she always has.

I catch her wrists and pin them above her head, her body arching, flushed and slick and shaking beneath me. Her eyes meet mine, wild, locked in, full of trust and hunger and that delicious kind of recklessness that says yes, more, take everything.

She clenches around me as she comes again, that gorgeous mouth falling open, a moan catching in her throat. Her entire body trembles, tight and pulsing, and I lose it. I slam into her, harder, faster, chasing that feeling like it's the only thing that exists.

Everything inside me coils tight, blinding. Her name tears from my chest, raw and ruined, as I come—violent and all-consuming—burying myself deep, spilling into her as the world fractures around us.

I collapse on top of her, our chests heaving, breaths ragged. The storm rages outside, but in here, all I can hear is the echo of our bodies, our gasps, the sound of her heartbeat thudding against mine.

I press my forehead to hers. The sweat, the heat, the salt between us—it's holy. It's hell. It's everything I didn't know I needed.

And I'm not letting her go.

"I've been wanting this," she whispers, lips brushing my neck. "Out here. In the middle of a storm. Like one of those dirty books I pretend not to read."

Her laugh is soft, sleepy. My arms tighten around her like instinct.

"So romance isn't dead," I murmur, tracing lazy patterns along her spine.

"Never was," she says, chin resting on my chest. Her eyes shine in the dim light. "Just hiding."

I brush a damp strand of hair from her face, something aching and tender in my chest. "I shouldn't say it, but thank God you burned that kitchen. I've been waiting my whole damn life for this."

Her hand cups my cheek, her touch caring. "I feel the same. Can you imagine if that hadn't happened? If you were still sleeping in the bunkhouse and I was still pretending to want nothing to do with you?"

"Don't even joke," I growl, burying my face in her neck. She smells like rain and sex and salt, and I want to live in that scent forever.

The storm still rages outside, but here, inside this boat, we've carved out something real. Something solid.

She touches the scar on my shoulder, a question in her fingertips.

"Fishing injury," I say. "Back before I had a clue. Back when I thought I had something to prove."

"And now?"

"Now I know who I want to prove it to."

She hums, shifting closer. "I used to watch you," she murmurs. "Working the lines, guiding the crew. You always knew what to do. It made me fall for you before I even realized it."

The words hit like a sucker punch. I pull her closer.

"You can't just say things like that," I whisper.

"Why not?"

"Because I'll never recover."

She laughs, but there's a softness to it. She kisses me slow this time, unhurried. Outside, the rain begins to ease. But we stay tangled together, wrapped in heat and quiet and everything we haven't said yet. Everything we will.

"We should check the anchor," I say eventually, but I don't move.

"We're good here," she murmurs. "I used to anchor in this spot with my grandfather. We'd wait out storms and he'd tell me stories about how he met my grandmother on these waters."

Something heavy and sweet settles in my chest. "And now here we are."

She smiles, kisses my chest. "Making our own stories."

I cradle her face like she's the only real thing left in a world that keeps spinning too fast. Her cheeks are damp—maybe from sweat, maybe the storm, maybe both—but her eyes, God, her eyes are steady. And destroying me.

"I love you," I say again, because now that the words are out, they won't stop. I don't want them to. I want to say them until they're ordinary, until they're the first thing she hears every morning and the last thing before she falls asleep. "Even when the skies are clear and boring and everything's fine."

She huffs a laugh against my mouth, soft and golden and so her. "I love you too. Especially when everything's not."

Outside, the storm slips into something gentler—rain tapping against the deck like it's remembering how to be kind. But we don't move. We stay wrapped in each other, legs tangled, hearts stupidly full, exchanging slow kisses and quieter confessions. Like the whole world just caught its breath so we could figure out how to take the next one together.

There's time now. For all the words we haven't said. For all the nights like this one, and all the ones that'll be harder. I'll take them all, as long as she's beside me.

Because this—her, us—it's the only kind of weather I ever want to be caught in.

21

SPENCER'S POV

Penelope walks in like she owns the fucking air.

Towel clutched to her chest, wet hair clinging to her neck, bare legs damp and gleaming. One droplet slides over her collarbone and disappears into the hollow between her breasts, and I swear to God, I nearly lose it.

My fingers curl tight at my sides, nails biting into my palms. She's not trying to be seductive. That's the worst part. She's just here, wet and flushed from the shower, smelling like coconut shampoo and warm skin, and it's undoing me.

"Oh," she says, like she didn't know I'd be standing here, like she's surprised to find me watching her like she's the last glass of water on Earth. "Didn't realize you'd be lurking."

I manage a half-smile that probably looks more like a grimace. "Didn't mean to lurk." My voice comes out rough, uneven. Like gravel. I clear my throat. "Figured I'd ask if you wanted to come to Glasgow with me today."

She grabs an extra towel from the bed and squeezes the water from her hair. The towel wrapped around her body pulls tight, and I have to look away for half a second before I do something I can't walk back.

"Glasgow?" Her brow quirks, amused. She reaches up to ruffle her hands through her hair and that movement, the stretch of her arms, the curve of her waist, everything about her, is made of heat and electricity and bad decisions. "What's in Glasgow?"

"Vendor meeting," I say, staring hard at the window behind her. "And a restaurant supply store. Thought maybe you'd want to tag along. Help pick stuff out for the remodel."

Her lips curve like she knows exactly what she's doing to me. "Is this your version of a date, Spencer?"

I meet her gaze. It's a mistake. Those hazel eyes catch me in the ribs like a sucker punch.

"Depends," I say. "You saying yes?"

She shrugs, casual, but the challenge in her eyes is molten. "Sure. Why not?"

"Good." My jaw tightens as I bite back the thousand things I want to say, most of them inappropriate. "Pack an overnight bag."

She tilts her head, her smile sharpening. "Overnight?"

"Just in case," I say, letting the words hang.

"Mmm." Her fingers curl around the doorframe, slow and calculated. "You planning to wine and dine me, Tennessee?"

"Something like that." My voice drops, low and destroyed.

She just looks at me. Doesn't move. Doesn't speak. Just stares, eyes sparkling, mouth twitching in the corner like she's daring me.

And I snap.

I close the space between us in two steps and press her back against the wall. My mouth finds hers, urgent and uncoordinated, like I've been waiting years to kiss her and I still don't know if it'll be enough.

She gasps into me, her mouth hot and open, and I swallow the sound like it belongs to me. My hands grip her waist, fingertips sliding over her damp skin, her towel a useless barrier between us.

"Jesus," I breathe into her mouth. "You're gonna ruin me."

Her laugh is a gasp, breathy and electric. "Not if I get to you first."

Her fingers wind into my hair, tugging just enough to make my spine straighten. My hands slide down her sides, rough and greedy, and the towel slips. One hard tug and it falls to the floor, soft cotton puddled at her feet.

I look. I have to.

Every inch of her is flushed and wet and perfect, and the sound I make isn't human. My hands move on their own, over her ribs, up to cup her breasts, thumbs brushing across her nipples. She shudders under my touch, like I've reached some live wire inside her.

I drop my head and kiss a path down her neck, over her collarbone, to the slope of her breast. My mouth closes over one nipple, and she arches with a sharp sound that shoots straight to my groin.

"Spencer," she breathes, my name a whisper, a moan, a command.

I sink to my knees like a man who's finally found religion. Her thighs tremble as I spread them, my hands anchoring her hips.

"You're already so wet for me," I rasp, looking up. Her lips part, her cheeks flushed, and she doesn't look away. That's what gets me. She never looks away.

I press a slow kiss to her inner thigh, then drag my tongue along her slit. She cries out, one hand flying to the wall, the other buried in my hair, pulling.

She tastes like heaven. Like salt and heat and something wholly hers.

My fingers slide inside her, curling just enough to make her hips buck. Her head falls back against the wall with a soft thud.

"God—Spencer," she chokes, thighs tightening around me. Her body shakes under the weight of what I'm doing to her, and I don't stop. I want every last sound. Every twitch and gasp and moan.

"That's it," I murmur, my voice thick and broken. "Let me feel you come."

And she does. Hard. Fast. Her whole body arches, her voice raw as it spills out into the room. My name. Her breath. That soft, stuttering sound that's going to live in my bloodstream forever.

I kiss my way up her stomach, over her chest, tasting her sweat and her release and her skin. Her mouth meets mine again, slower now, and she melts into me like she belongs there.

"Pack your bag," I whisper against her lips.

She lets out a breathy laugh, still shaky. "Bossy."

"Don't pretend you don't like it."

She doesn't argue. Just tilts her head back and looks at me like she's seeing something she didn't expect. Like maybe she wasn't ready for this to feel like more.

I step away, forcing air into my lungs. I kiss her once more, her forehead this time, soft and caring, and head for the door.

"Don't keep me waiting, Pen."

By the time she meets me at the front door, dressed and ready, I've managed to stitch together some semblance of self-control. Barely. The kind that frays every time she gets too close. Which is always.

She tosses me her keys with a lazy arc as we walk outside. "Think you can handle driving my truck, Tennessee?"

"Sweetheart," I drawl, opening the passenger door and gesturing for her to climb in, "I can handle you and your truck. Question is, can you handle me?"

Her laugh is low and warm as I buckle her in, but the challenge in her eyes says everything. God help me, this woman is gonna ruin me, and I'm gonna let her.

The truck rumbles beneath us, the hum of the tires on the road a steady rhythm, but it's Penelope's laugh that keeps pulling my attention. Warm and throaty, it dances through the cab like sunlight breaking through clouds, and I can't stop myself from stealing quick glances at her. She's tucked against the door, one bare foot propped up on the dash despite my earlier mock protest, her hair still slightly damp as it falls in messy waves around her face.

"Okay," she says, twisting toward me, lips quirking with mischief. "Your turn. Worst date you've ever been on."

"That's easy," I reply, gripping the steering wheel tighter to keep my hands busy because God knows if they weren't, they'd be tracing the curve of her thigh right now. "Met this girl once who only talked about her ex the entire time. Not just mentioned him, mind you, full-on compared every single thing I did to him. Like I was some kind of contestant in the 'Not-Her-Ex Olympics.'"

She lets out a sharp bark of laughter, her head tipping back, and I'm struck dumb for a second.

"Please tell me you ditched her halfway through," she teases, leaning closer, her knee brushing against my arm as I shift.

"Course not," I shoot back, feigning insult. "I'm a gentleman, Sugar. Suffered through the whole miserable ordeal, even paid for dessert. Though I might've been imagining it was poison by that point, just so I could escape."

"Poor thing," she coos, fake pity dripping from her voice. "You want me to buy you coffee so you can recover?"

"Don't tempt me," I mutter, though I'm already scanning the roadside for somewhere to stop. Anything to stretch this drive out longer, keep her here with me like this, relaxed, playful, utterly irresistible.

We stumble on a café just off the highway, the kind with peeling paint and a chalkboard menu out front, and something about it feels right. Like a pause button. She orders something long and frothy and drizzled with caramel, and I go with black coffee, predictable, apparently, because she lifts one perfectly unimpressed eyebrow at me like I just failed a personality test.

We take our drinks outside and settle into a pair of lopsided wooden chairs. The table between us wobbles every time we move, and our knees keep brushing under it. Neither of us says anything about it. We just talk about everything and nothing. Her laugh bubbles up easily, filling the space between us like it belongs there, and the more I listen, the more I forget what time it is. Or where we were headed. I only know that I want this part to stretch out longer.

Lunch sneaks up on us. A crooked pub down the street, mismatched chairs and a bar that smells like fried potatoes and malt vinegar. The menu's scrawled on the wall in chalk and questionable handwriting. She doesn't even ask before snagging fries from my plate, stealing one with a look that dares me to stop her. I don't. I just keep pushing the plate closer to her, grinning like an idiot.

If she asked, I'd feed her the whole damn basket, one fry at a time, just to keep her smiling like that.

By the time we hit the city limits, Glasgow's dipped into golden hour. The sky's soft and amber, buildings edged in light. I pull up in front of the restaurant supply store, and she's already halfway out of her seat before I've even cut the engine, practically buzzing, that kind of focused, joyful energy she doesn't even realize she's radiating.

"I'll drop you here," I say, catching her wrist for a second before she slips out completely. "I've got to swing by and talk to a chef, but I'll come back after. Don't buy out the whole damn store before I get back."

She smirks, the challenge already flickering behind her eyes. "Try not to miss me too much," she tosses over her shoulder as she climbs out, hips swaying like she choreographed it just to torture me.

"Not likely, sweetheart," I mutter under my breath, watching her disappear through the glass, already plotting how fast I can wrap up my meeting and get back to her.

I make my delivery stop quick, just enough time to talk seafood orders and pretend my mind isn't constantly drifting to her. By the time I make it back to the store, I'm restless, impatient. I step inside, scanning the aisles until I spot her.

And there she is.

In her element. Brows furrowed, lips pursed, her fingers trailing over stainless steel appliances, her lips pursed in concentration. There's a confidence to her, a quiet intensity that draws me in like gravity. She picks up a set of knives, testing their weight, her movements precise and practiced. The sight of her like this, focused, capable, stunning, hits me square in the chest.

She doesn't see me at first. She's in an aisle at the back of the store now, tapping something into her phone. The moment she's close to the shadowy corner near the stockroom, I move. Quick strides bring me to her, and before she can react, I've got her pinned against the wall, my hands bracketing her waist.

She gasps. "Spencer—!"

Her breath stutters, but her body doesn't tense. If anything, she leans in.

"Couldn't help myself," I murmur, brushing my mouth against hers before she can protest. It's not soft. Not careful. It's all heat and pressure and the desperate promise of everything I'm dying to do with her.

"We're in public," she whispers against my lips, even as her hands fist in my shirt.

"Then you'll need to stay real quiet," I breathe, pressing a kiss to the corner of her mouth, then lower, to the place just beneath her jaw that makes her gasp again. "Unless you want everyone in this store to know how good I'm making you feel."

"You're filthy," she mutters, but her nails are digging into my shoulder now, her leg hitching up against mine, her whole body saying more.

I nuzzle against her throat, breathing her in, lips brushing skin that's flushed and warm. "Only for you, Penelope," I whisper, one hand skimming down, slow and possessive, fingers pressing into her hip like I need proof she's real. "Always for you."

I stay there for a breath, just holding her, letting the thrum of her pulse slow beneath my lips. The world narrows to the heat of her skin, the weight of her against me, the unspoken things crackling in the air between us. But eventually, reality creeps back in: the hum of overhead lights, the sound of a stock cart squeaking down a nearby aisle, the buzz of her phone vibrating against the clipboard.

Reluctantly, I ease back.

She shifts too, smoothing her clothes with one hand and snatching up her phone with the other, already typing something out like we didn't just nearly combust in a storage hallway. Still catching her breath, lips kiss-bruised, cheeks flushed.

That smirk she's wearing? It's practically a dare.

"Got everything you need?" My voice comes out lower than I mean for it to, rough around the edges.

She hums, not quite looking at me. "Unless you've got more hallway surprises planned."

I lean in, the distance between us a thread I can't help tugging. "Not at the moment." I let the words hang there for a second. "But I've got something else. A surprise."

That gets her attention. Her eyes flick up to mine, sharp and curious. "What kind of surprise?"

"Come with me and find out," I say, threading my fingers through hers. Her hand fits in mine so easily, like we've been doing this forever, and despite all her sass, she comes without question. We settle the order with the clerk, stepping back into the crisp bite of evening air, and for once, she doesn't fill the silence with teasing.

The truck ride is quiet, not tense, but charged. That crackling kind of quiet, the kind that fills all the space between glances and makes everything else feel too loud. The city slips away behind us, and I catch her watching the road, then me, then back again.

Eventually, headlights catch the sign on the hill. The hotel rises out of the dark like something out of a dream: massive windows glowing gold against stone walls, the cliffside disappearing into a swath of sea below. Even I'm a little impressed.

She sits up straighter. "Spencer... where the hell are we?"

"Exactly where we're supposed to be," I say, easing the truck into the lot. I kill the engine, heart kicking a little harder as I climb out and circle to her door. She doesn't move until I open it.

"Seriously," she says, her voice low and skeptical. "What is this?"

"Patience, Sugar," I say, grabbing our bags from the back.

She rolls her eyes, but I catch the corner of her mouth lifting before she turns away.

Inside, the lobby is warm and softly lit, all rich wood and smooth marble. Her eyes are moving constantly, taking it all in without saying a word. When I check us in, she hovers beside me with arms crossed, mouth twitching with the effort not to comment.

"Trust me," I murmur, leaning in to press a kiss to her temple as I slide the room key into my pocket. Her skin's still cool from the night air.

"This better not be some elaborate kidnapping attempt," she mutters, but her fingers brush mine as we walk to the elevator, and it feels like a win.

The suite is jaw-dropping: floor-to-ceiling windows overlooking the jagged cliffs and endless ocean, a king-sized bed piled high with plush pillows, and, most importantly, a private balcony with a jacuzzi tub already steaming away.

Penelope steps inside and freezes mid-step, her breath catching audibly.

"Spencer..." Her voice is softer now. Not guarded. Not teasing.

I drop the bags near the bed, watching her take it all in. "Figured you deserved a little spoiling after the way your summer started."

She turns, expression unreadable. "What's the catch?"

I smile and walk over to the dresser, where the hotel staff left the package earlier. I pull out the black dress, sleek, low-backed, sexy as hell, and the matching heels and lay them on the bed.

"You've got options," I say, keeping my voice light even though my pulse is anything but. "Cozy pub downstairs or a trendy downtown restaurant-slash-nightclub. No pressure."

She stares at the dress for a long moment. "You bought this for me?"

I nod once. "Wanted to see you in it." I don't tell her that what I really want is her coming out of it.

"Jesus, Spencer," she murmurs, her voice thick. Then, before I can say another word, she closes the distance between us and grabs my face, dragging me into a hard, searing kiss. "Restaurant," she says against my lips, her breath warm and unsteady. "Definitely the restaurant."

"Good choice," I manage, dazed, just barely remembering where I am. But before I can pull her back in, she snatches the dress off the bed and disappears into the bathroom with a sharp click of the door.

"Give me ten minutes!" she calls.

I fall onto the edge of the bed with a groan and scrub a hand through my hair. Ten minutes feels like a lifetime.

I change into my suit, pace for a bit, sit again, try not to imagine what she looks like behind that door. I fail spectacularly.

When the bathroom opens, I'm mid-thought, not prepared, and then I see her.

Everything in me stops.

The dress fits like it was made for her, skimming her curves and leaving just enough to the imagination. Her hair's pinned up, exposing the soft curve of her neck and the freckles I've kissed a dozen times but suddenly want to map like constellations. The heels make her legs look longer, her posture just a little more dangerous.

"Spencer?" she says, and I realize I haven't moved. Or blinked.

"Fuck me," I whisper. It's not even dramatic, it's the only thing my brain has left.

Her lips part, a flush blooming high on her cheeks, but she holds her ground, eyes locked on mine. "That good?"

"Better," I say, stepping toward her slowly, like she might vanish if I move too fast. I reach up, cup her face in both hands, my thumb brushing along her jaw. Her skin's soft, warm from the shower. She smells like citrus and heat and Penelope.

"You're beautiful," I tell her, and this time there's no teasing in it. Just truth.

"Spencer..." she murmurs, voice all breath and nerves.

"Shh," I say, leaning in to kiss her, slow and caring. She leans into me like she's been waiting for it all day.

"Let me spoil you tonight," I whisper. "Please."

And for once, she doesn't argue.

And I swear, I've never been more gone for anyone in my life.

The restaurant buzzes around us, steeped in the smell of roasted garlic and something buttery and expensive. Laughter hums from the tables, wine glasses clink, and somewhere behind us, someone's fork hits the floor with a clatter. I barely register any of it. All I can focus on is her.

Penelope leans back in her chair like she owns the place, like she's the reason this whole building hasn't collapsed under the weight of its own candlelit ambiance. She lifts her spoon, slow and calculated, and drags it across her bottom lip to catch the last trace of chocolate mousse. And God help me, I forget how to breathe.

My hands curl into fists under the table, knuckles pressing against my thighs just to keep them where they are. It feels like the table between us is the only thing keeping me tethered to this side of sanity.

She sets the spoon down, eyes dancing. "Alright, you win," she says, that smirk curling at the edges of her lips, the one that always looks like it knows too much. "This place is incredible."

"Not half as incredible as you look right now," I say, low enough that it's just for her. A quiet confession I shouldn't say out loud but can't keep in.

Color climbs up her cheeks, but she doesn't look away. She never does. She meets everything head-on: my compliments, my desire, my goddamn unraveling. Like she's daring me to fall harder. And I do.

"Careful, Spencer," she murmurs, lifting her wine glass with a tilt of her wrist that's so fluid it makes my throat dry. "Flattery like that might get you in trouble."

I lean forward, forearms on the table, elbows wide, trying to get closer without making a scene. "Trouble's exactly what I'm after."

Her eyes flick down to my mouth, and her breath stutters just enough that I catch it. She lifts her glass again but doesn't sip, just holds it there, fingers wrapped tightly around the stem.

"You think you can handle it?" she whispers, like she already knows the answer. Like she's hoping I'll surprise her.

I don't blink. "Try me."

For a second, the air between us tightens like a string about to snap. Her lashes lower, and her knees shift under the table. Crossed, uncrossed. The tension is a live thing now, thick and buzzing in the space between my skin and hers.

And then, almost like the restaurant itself can't take it, the lights dim.

Music shifts from quiet background piano to something with a beat. Purple and blue lights pulse softly along the walls. The staff pushes a few tables aside near the bar, opening up a small dance floor that wasn't there an hour ago.

Penelope turns toward the movement, eyebrows raised. "Well, look at that," she says, lips quirking. "Perfect timing."

I stand, reaching for her hand. "Dance with me."

She arches a brow, feigning consideration for exactly three seconds before slipping her fingers into mine. Her hand is warm, small but commanding, and the feel of her palm against mine short-circuits my brain in about three different directions.

"Don't step on my toes," she warns as I tug her toward the growing crowd.

"No promises," I murmur, spinning her once just to see her laugh, really laugh. It bursts out of her like a bubble breaking at the surface, unguarded and golden.

We drift to the edge of the dance floor where the lights are a little softer, the music a little louder. I slide my hand to her lower back and pull her in close. Her body settles against mine like it belongs there.

She rests her hands on my shoulders, eyes lifted, breath already a little shallow. Her hips start to sway in time with the music, teasing, drawing out each motion like she's testing how long it'll take to destroy me.

"Relax," she says, close to my ear, fingers threading into my hair. "You're so tense."

"That's because you're driving me out of my fucking mind," I murmur, mouth grazing the shell of her ear.

She shivers, barely, but I feel it. Every response she tries to hide. Every push and pull.

"Good," she says, her voice low and wicked, her nails scraping gently along the back of my neck. "Now shut up and dance."

And we do. We move like no one's watching. Like it's only the two of us in this room. Her laugh is quieter now, almost secret. Her dress clings closer with every song, the heat building around us until I'm sweating and she's glowing. Her hair slips from its pins and starts sticking to her skin, curling at the nape of her neck.

I can't stop touching her. My hand grazes her hip, her back, the soft skin behind her knee when I dip her toward the floor. Her mouth is close. Always close.

And then, somewhere between songs, when the beat slows and the lights shift warmer, I hear her say my name.

"Spencer."

My eyes flick down. Her fingers are gripping the front of my shirt now, clutching like she needs something to hold on to. Her lips hover just shy of mine.

"Let's go."

I blink. "Go where?"

She doesn't answer with words, just bites her bottom lip and tips her head subtly toward the hallway by the restrooms. Then looks back at me like she's already halfway undressed in her mind.

"Jesus, Pen," I mutter, dragging a hand through my hair. My cock aches, has been aching, but now it's unbearable. I'm trying to hold on, I really am, but she's not helping.

She presses her body flush against me, like she's trying to fuse us together, and drags her nails down my chest with all the intention of a woman who knows exactly what she wants.

"You afraid?" she goads, voice like silk over heat.

I don't say anything. I just move.

One arm sweeps under her knees, the other behind her back, and I lift her before she can even gasp. Her arms wrap around my neck on instinct, her mouth finding my throat in a breathless laugh as I carry her toward the door, ignoring the half-dozen stares we pass on the way out.

"Where are we going?" she asks, breath catching against my jaw.

"Back to the hotel," I growl, scanning for the first damn cab I can find. "Because if I stay here another minute, I'll end up fucking you against a bathroom sink, and you deserve better than that."

"Better, huh?" she teases, as I hail the cab and slide her in ahead of me. Her dress rides high on her thighs, those heels digging into my legs as she settles in, right on my lap.

"Way better," I repeat, planting my hands firmly on her hips as the driver pulls away from the curb. My voice is a rasp, barely controlled. My patience is gone.

She's on me before the cab door even clicks shut. No hesitation. No preamble. Just her hands in my hair, mouth on mine, and the quiet, desperate kind of kiss that feels like it's been building all night, maybe longer.

Her dress is already sliding up her thighs, soft fabric bunching around her hips as she shifts in my lap. One roll of her body and I feel the heat of her, barely anything between us now but the thinnest strip of lace. I bite back a groan, fingers digging into her hips like they're the only thing keeping me grounded.

"Jesus, Pen," I rasp, lips dragging against hers, my voice more exhale than sound.

She grins against my mouth, breath hot and smug. "Can't wait, huh?"

I shake my head, barely. "Not when you're like this."

I slide a hand up her thigh, slow and calculated, knuckles brushing just shy of where she wants me. The cab shifts around a corner and the driver clears his throat like we've forgotten he exists. Maybe we have.

I drag in a shaky breath, sit back just enough to get my damn head on straight, and mutter the name of the hotel. My voice is rough, raw, barely passing as language. She just smirks and tucks her face into my neck, her lips brushing over my pulse like she knows exactly what she's doing. Because she does.

The second we step into the lobby, it starts all over again. Her fingers are undoing the buttons of my shirt before the doors even slide shut behind us, tugging me toward the elevator like she's immune to consequences. The click of her heels echoes across the marble floor, the soft, sunshine scent of citrus trailing behind her, making my chest tight.

"Spencer," she breathes, her tone drenched in trouble, like she's about to do something neither of us will recover from. Her hands slip under my jacket, tugging my shirt free, her knuckles brushing over my skin like she's testing how much I can take.

"You're wearing too many clothes," she says, all mock-innocence and fire.

I smirk, but it falters the second her fingers slip beneath my waistband and skim across bare skin. My breath catches hard enough to make my ribs ache.

"That a fact?" I manage, already losing ground.

"Fact," she confirms, unbuckling my belt with slow, surgical precision.

I catch her wrists, spin her gently until her back hits the mirrored wall, and she gasps. Not from shock, Penelope doesn't get surprised. No, this is anticipation. She wants it just as bad.

"Two can play that game, Sugar," I growl, my mouth finding her neck, then lower. I suck at the soft spot just beneath her jaw, and her laughter breaks into a breathy moan as I trail kisses across her collar-bone. Her dress slips a little more with each touch, my hands greedy, mapping the slope of her waist, the curve of her ass.

When the elevator dings open, neither of us moves.

We're a mess of tangled limbs and ragged breaths until someone on the other side clears their throat, and we break apart just long enough to stumble out, laughing like a couple of teenagers.

We barely make it down the hall.

Her hands are all over me again, tugging at my belt, while mine hike up her dress and find every inch of skin I've been dying to touch since this morning. We hit a wall, maybe two, before I finally fumble the keycard into the lock and shove the door open with my shoulder, kicking it shut behind us like we're being chased.

"Jacuzzi," I manage to get out, pointing toward the deck. It's not a suggestion, it's a lifeline. If I don't put some space between us for just a second, I might combust.

"Romantic," she quips, but she follows me outside anyway, leaning against the railing as I fumble with the controls.

The city lights stretch out below us, but I don't give a damn about the view, not when she's standing there, pulling off her dress like it's nothing. She stands there, bare, glowing, completely unapologetic in the moonlight, and I forget how to function.

"Penelope..." Her name scrapes out of me like prayer.

She steps into the bubbling water like she's stepping into fire. Looks back at me, eyes dark and daring. "Get in."

I strip fast, heart thundering, and grab the champagne and two glasses off the minibar. I slide into the water beside her and barely have time to breathe before she's straddling me. Then she sinks down, slow, taking me in inch by inch.

"Fuck," I hiss, head falling back, hands gripping her hips. Her nails dig into my shoulders, and she starts to move, slow at first, the kind of rhythm that makes my vision blur. I can't think, can't speak. Every nerve in my body is tuned to her. To this. The steam around us, the cool night air on our shoulders, the unbearable heat where we're joined.

I don't know how long I let her ride me, minutes, years, something in between. All I know is my hands are sliding up her slick back, my mouth dragging over the curve of her breast, and I'm seconds from losing it when I pull her off me.

"Turn around," I say, voice rough, nearly gone.

She blinks down at me, confused for a second, then I guide her gently, firmly, spinning her until she's facing the edge of the tub, hands bracing on the lip. Her spine arches when I step in behind her, water lapping at her thighs.

I slide back inside her in one long, slow thrust, and she moans, her head tipping forward, hands clawing for grip. I wrap my arms around her, anchoring her against me as I start to move, water splashing with every stroke.

"Spencer," she gasps, voice thin and breaking. "Jesus—"

I keep my mouth on her neck, my fingers splayed over her belly. The world is white-hot and steam-heavy and so fucking good I think I might come undone just from the sound of her breathing.

But I need more.

I pull out, every muscle in my body straining with the effort not to come. I haul her up out of the water in one breathless movement, water streaming off her skin. I mean to take her inside, I do, but the second her feet hit the tile, she stumbles into me and I lose the thread.

Instead, I spin her, pressing her hands flat to the balcony railing. The metal is cool and slick, her palms slipping just enough to make her gasp. Below us, the city stretches wide and glittering, but none of it matters. Not when she's here, bare, soaked, begging beneath my hands.

We don't care who can see. We can't.

I push into her in one brutal thrust, and she cries out, her hands white-knuckling the railing.

We're past modesty. Past restraint. She's open for me, bent over, wild and fucking beautiful, and I'm pounding into her like I need to live inside her. The wind lifts her hair off her neck. Her body jerks against mine with every thrust. She doesn't try to be quiet, and I don't want her to.

I grip her hips harder. She slams back against me, matching my rhythm, her voice breaking into pieces with every thrust.

"Spencer—God—"

"I know," I pant. "I know. You feel so fucking good."

She's right there, right there, her body tightening around me, the telltale hitch in her breath, the tremble in her thighs. But I pull out at the last second, gripping her hips to still her as she lets out a ragged, shattered sob of protest.

"Not yet," I murmur, voice destroyed.

She's shaking when I lift her, her legs barely holding steady, and I carry her back inside like it's the only thing anchoring me. I grab a towel off the stack, spread it on the rug beside the bed, then lower her onto it gently.

She's boneless, dazed, lips kiss-swollen and chest still heaving.

Her hand curls into the fabric beneath her. "What's the towel for?" she murmurs, eyelids heavy.

I kneel between her thighs, already sliding them open wider.

"I'm gonna make you squirt," I say simply.

Her brow arches. "Bet you won't."

I meet her eyes, then dip down.

Challenge accepted.

My fingers move slow at first, easing through the slick heat of her. She's soaked, practically pulsing around nothing, and the second I drag two fingers inside, her whole body jolts. I press in deeper, searching with purpose, curling just slightly until I find it, that soft, spongy patch that makes her gasp like I've stolen the air from her lungs.

"There," I murmur, voice ragged. "Right fucking there."

I stroke it gently at first, almost lazy, watching the way her body reacts in real time. Her back arches off the towel, one hand flying to her mouth like she can't decide whether to scream or sob. My mouth finds her clit and I suck, soft to start, then harder, the flat of my tongue circling until she whimpers, thighs clenching around my head.

But I don't let her close them. I press her legs wider, hold her open with a hand spread firm across her stomach, and pick up the rhythm, fingers massaging that spot harder now, more insistent, a steady pressure she can't run from.

I feel her tighten, her hips starting to rock in time with my strokes, like her body's chasing something her mind hasn't caught up to yet. She's panting, wild-eyed, her hands gripping the towel like she might fall straight through the floor.

"Spence—wait—I can't—" she gasps, shaking her head even as her hips chase every stroke. She's fighting it, but her body is already there, teetering.

"Yes, you can," I growl, licking her again, letting the words melt against her skin. "You're right there, Pen. Let go. I've got you."

My fingers grind into her g-spot now, firmer, faster, not giving her a second to hide. She tries to twist away, some instinct to shield herself from the pleasure building too fast, too strong, but I lock my arm across her hips, holding her down.

Then she breaks.

Her whole body seizes with a sound that's more shock than moan, her thighs snapping tight around me as she gushes, liquid pouring out of her in pulses that drench the towel.

That's it. That's all I can take.

The second she starts to come, slick and gushing, her body seizing around my fingers, her mouth open in that perfect, devastated O, something in me snaps.

I need to feel her. Now.

I yank my fingers free and haul her hips toward me in one desperate, graceless motion, lining up and slamming into her so hard I swear I see stars. She cries out, still mid-orgasm, and I groan, deep and guttural, as her pussy clenches around me like a vice. Hot, soaked, still fucking pulsing.

"Jesus, Pen, fuck," I pant, driving into her again, my grip bruising on her thighs, my rhythm instantly brutal. There's no finesse. No slow. Just raw need. Just the unbearable high of being inside her while her orgasm rolls through her in waves, and her body tries to drag me down with her.

She sobs something I can't make out, too far gone, and arches under me, fingers clawing at my back as I pound into her, over and over, each thrust prolonging the spasms ripping through her.

"God, you're still coming," I groan, barely recognizing my own voice, low, ragged, tender. She clenches around me again, tighter this time, the kind of grip that steals the air from my lungs, and that's it. That's the edge.

My hips jerk once, twice, completely involuntary, and then I break apart inside her.

It hits hard. Too hard. Like something tearing loose deep in my gut, a heat that burns up my spine and hollows me out at the same time. My vision flashes white, stomach locking tight as I spill into her, helpless to stop it. It's overwhelming, violent in its intensity, my body emptying with each pulse, every thrust grounding me deeper, deeper, like she's anchoring me in the storm she created.

And she's still fluttering around me, her walls milking every last drop from me, her body pulling at mine like she's not done taking. Like she needs it all, every ounce of cum, every broken sound I make, every last piece of me.

And fuck, she can have it. She can have everything.

22

____

The whisk clinks against ceramic, rhythmic and soft, like a heartbeat. I tilt the bowl to catch the light, watching the eggs froth into golden swirls, the smell of browned butter and bacon making my mouth water. The windows are streaked with condensation, the sky outside pale and heavy, like it hasn't decided whether it wants to rain or stay soft and gray forever.

Pearl's weight presses against the tops of my feet, her body humming with anticipation. She lets out a whine so quiet I feel it more than hear it, her whole posture vibrating with hope. Her eyes, big, ridiculous, and tragically expressive, stay pinned on the plate of bacon cooling on a paper towel beside the stove.

"You're shameless," I murmur, nudging her with my toes. She huffs and thumps her tail like I'm the one being unreasonable.

Behind me, the old pine floor groans. I don't need to look to know it's Sammy. There's a quiet shift in the air that's unmistakable, like gravity tipping ever so slightly in his direction. Then: the press of lips, low and warm, to the back of my neck. Slow. Intentional. A spark that sinks right to the base of my spine.

"Morning," he murmurs, voice rough and frayed with sleep.

I glance at the clock. "Barely," I say, but I'm smiling. He reaches around me, snagging a piece of bacon with that maddening ease, and I slap at his wrist too late.

"If you're not going to help, get out of my kitchen," I grumble.

"Your kitchen?" He laughs, his breath ghosting against my ear, and suddenly I'm bracketed by his arms, his chest flush against my back. The heat of him soaks into the thin fabric of my shirt, making my skin prickle, traitorous.

He doesn't move. Doesn't need to. He just exists, too close and too comfortable, and I can feel the smirk on his face even without seeing it. "Does that mean you want me to stop cooking for you?"

"Do you want breakfast or not?" My voice should be sharper, but it wobbles at the end, giving me away.

Sammy grins against my neck and retreats with exaggerated slowness. "Fine, fine." He shuffles toward the coffee pot, shirtless and smug, his hair perfect as always, which makes him more infuriating. Or endearing. Or both.

The kitchen settles into a kind of warm quiet, soft footsteps, the sputter and hiss of the coffee maker, Pearl's tiny sounds of canine yearning. I reach for the skillet, ready to pour, when I hear the bedroom door creak.

And then Spencer walks out.

He's half-asleep, wearing nothing but boxers and the kind of lazy confidence that comes from knowing exactly what he does to me. His hair sticks up in every possible direction, like he fought a windstorm in his sleep, and there's a faint crease running down one cheek from the pillow. His eyes are still heavy-lidded, but they land on me with a slow, purposeful kind of focus that makes my breath catch.

"Mornin', Sugar," he drawls, voice rough velvet. He stretches, long and languid, the movement pulling every line of muscle into view like a goddamn Renaissance painting. My mouth goes dry.

I barely register the space between us before it disappears. He closes the distance in three easy strides and then I'm airborne, his arms locked around me, my back dipping in a ridiculous swoop. My yelp turns into a laugh that stutters out halfway when his mouth crashes into mine.

The kiss is reckless. Sleep-warm and desperate in a way that makes the floor feel miles away. I melt against him, fingers tangling in his messy hair, the scent of his skin, clean, warm, familiar, filling my head like a drug.

When we finally surface, our foreheads rest together, his hands still splayed wide on my back.

"That," Spencer says, breathless and grinning, "is how you say good mornin'."

"You're incorrigible," I mutter, still floating.

He kisses the corner of my mouth. "And you love it."

I do. God help me, I do.

He sets me down, finally, but keeps a palm on my lower back like he can't quite let go. Then, predictably: "So... bacon?"

"You're all insufferable," I huff, turning away even as my lips curve. I've barely recovered when the doorway fills again.

Liam.

Just sweatpants and a sleep-rough voice, the sharp lines of his hips disappearing beneath the waistband like a goddamn invitation. His hair's a wreck. His eyes are still half-lidded. And his mouth, his mouth is already smiling like he knows exactly what I'm thinking.

He crosses the kitchen and presses a soft kiss to my temple. "Morning, Darlin'."

I almost drop the whisk.

He doesn't linger. Just grabs a piece of bacon and starts munching, like he hasn't just set my entire nervous system alight.

"You're worse than Sammy," I say, glaring at the eggs like they're to blame.

"Untrue," Liam says around a bite. "I'm objectively more charming."

Pearl whines in agreement, or possibly hunger, and Liam crouches to ruffle her ears.

"Enough," I mutter, laughing despite myself. "If you want breakfast, go sit down before I burn the whole thing."

He straightens up, leans one hip against the counter, eyes glinting. "You love having us underfoot."

I open my mouth. Close it again.

Then Pearl barks, loud and sharp, the kind of bark that means something's coming. She bolts for the front door, claws skittering across wood, tail wagging like a metronome set to chaos.

"Mailman?" I ask no one in particular, wiping my hands on a towel as I follow her. She spins in a frantic little circle, practically vibrating with anticipation.

The brass mail slot flips open and a flutter of paper lands at my feet. Pearl sniffs, snorts, sniffs again.

"Calm down," I mutter, scooping up the envelopes. "It's just bills."

Except it isn't.

Because the second envelope isn't paper-white and soulless. It's thick. Cream-colored. The kind of stationery that screams wealth. There's a faint shimmer to the surface, and at the center, pressed into waxy gold foil: the MacLeod crest.

My stomach flips.

I don't need to open it to know.

The masquerade.

A shriek slips out before I can stop it. I do a ridiculous little hop-dance in place, the excitement spilling out of me before I can contain it. It's always the same, over-the-top, elegant, drama wrapped in silk and champagne. But this time...

My eyes scan the names, written in careful calligraphy: To Penelope, Jamie, Liam, Archer, Sam, and Spencer.

All of us.

Together.

I go still.

The envelope suddenly feels heavier. Like someone just tied a string around my ribs and gave it a tug. I flip it over, trace the seal with my thumb, but don't break it yet.

Behind me, the kitchen hums with life, coffee bubbling, bacon sizzling, low voices I love like background music to a life I never thought I'd get.

Pearl noses my knee impatiently.

"It's okay," I say softly, more to myself than to her.

Because something's shifting. I can feel it in my bones, in the way my heart does a weird, tripping stutter. Like that envelope is more than an invitation. Like it's a door cracking open to a future I'm not ready to name yet.

"Morning, Pen."

Jamie's voice, gritty with sleep and just unfairly intimate, slides across the room and lands squarely on my skin. I don't even have to look up. I feel him before I see him. That particular heat. The quiet confidence. The way the air seems to part for him and then fill with something heavier, something that sticks to your ribs.

But of course I do look. Because I'm weak.

He's barefoot, damp hair tousled in a way that looks accidental but probably isn't, sweatpants hanging low enough on his hips to be classified as a personal attack. His chest is bare, bronzed and muscled and lightly dusted with hair, and the line of it on his abdomen disappears below the waistband like it's inviting me to follow.

"Morning," I manage, but it's not casual. Not even close.

He notices. He always does. His mouth curves into a slow grin, eyes dragging over me like he's reading every thought I've ever had. He crosses the room like the kitchen was built around him, like the rest of us just orbit here.

"What's that?" he asks, nodding toward the envelope in my hand, but he doesn't wait for an answer. Instead, he leans in, brushes his mouth over my temple, soft, lazy, familiar. It's nothing. It's everything. My breath catches, stupid and loud, and I roll my eyes to cover the fact that my knees are close to buckling.

"Just the mail." I back toward the counter before I say something dumb. Something like get on your knees and kiss me again.

Pearl trots over, nails clicking against the hardwood, tail swinging like a banner. She makes a beeline for Jamie and bumps her snout into his thigh. He drops to his haunches to scratch behind her ears and mutters something low I don't catch. She barks once in delighted reply before flopping in a sun patch by the stove.

Jamie straightens and steps in close again, toeing the edge of my space like he's testing boundaries he already knows he'll ignore. His fingers brush mine as he reaches for the envelope, and the contact is nothing more than a whisper, but it sparks anyway. All the way down.

"It's from Lach," I say. "Masquerade party. Two weeks from Saturday."

Jamie tilts his head, amusement dancing in his eyes. "That'll be fun," he says, distracting me while his hand shoots out like a viper, snatching a piece of bacon from the plate on the counter.

"Jamie." I slap his arm, mostly for show.

He grins around a mouthful of bacon, eyes twinkling like he's never been sorry a day in his life. "You should've hidden it better."

I want to be annoyed. I really do. But he's standing there shirtless and smug, licking the bacon grease from his lips like it's foreplay, and I'm just a woman trying to make breakfast while pretending I'm not in love with five men.

Before I can retort, another voice slides through the air, gravelly, low, the kind of voice that always sounds like it just woke up in someone else's bed.

"Already?"

I glance toward the doorway. Archer.

He's leaning against the frame, dripping onto the floor like he means to ruin the hardwood. A few beads of water cling to the edge of his glasses, and he swipes at them lazily with the corner of what may once have been a T-shirt but is now more suggestion than substance.

"Can't believe it's been a year already," he says, straightening, his gaze catching on the envelope, then on me. He doesn't smile, not really, but there's a flicker at the corner of his mouth. Something warm and dangerous and familiar.

His chest is bare, of course. Tattooed. His abs are tight, water running down the defined planes like we're in a cologne ad I didn't sign up for.

"Good swim?" I ask, trying not to stare.

"Cold," he says, stepping forward. "But worth it."

"Dry off before you drip all over breakfast." I point the spatula at him like a weapon, which would work better if I wasn't actively fighting the urge to stare at his V-line.

Archer raises a brow like he's unimpressed with my attempt at authority and yanks a towel off the back of a chair. He scrubs it through his hair, water flying, and somehow ends up looking even more like trouble, rumpled and smug and real.

I grip the counter like it might keep me grounded.

"Breakfast is done. Sit down or starve. Your choice," I bark, louder than necessary.

The invitation still sits on the counter, fat and cream-colored, the gold crest catching the light just so. It looks like it means something, like it's holding its breath. But I shove the thought down and start plating eggs.

They trickle in one by one, like characters assembling in a play I'm somehow both starring in and directing. Archer takes the seat closest to mine, towel draped around his neck like he owns the room, the house, me.

I set the pan down a little too hard.

"All right," I say, hands planted on the edge of the table, pretending I'm not distracted by bare chests and smirking lips. "Let's talk costumes for the masquerade party."

Archer doesn't even look up from his plate. "Pirates."

It's so dry I almost miss it. But then his eyes flick up, brown and sharp and steady, and there's something in them. A dare. A quiet go ahead and argue, see what happens.

"Of course you'd want pirates," Liam says. "What are you going to do, carry around a parrot on your shoulder all night?"

"Better than being trussed up in tights," Archer deadpans, taking a bite of toast. Jamie muffles a laugh behind his coffee mug.

"Hey," Sammy cuts in, perking up now that his second cup of coffee has likely hit his bloodstream. "Don't knock tights. We could do Renaissance. Doublet. Hose. Ruffles. You and Jamie could match."

"Absolutely not," Jamie says without missing a beat. He holds up a hand like a traffic cop. "No tights. Not now. Not ever."

Sammy looks far too pleased with himself. He sips his coffee like he's tasting victory. "Coward," he says cheerfully.

"What about a group theme?" I offer, because if I don't redirect this, we're going to end up arguing about the sex appeal of sword fights for the next hour. "Something bold. Superheroes? Circus performers?"

"Crocodile hunters," Liam says, dimples flaring. "I'll be Dundee."

"Oh my God." I groan, already smiling despite myself. "Do you even own khaki shorts?"

"Don't need 'em," he replies, winking like the devil. "Got the accent already. The rest's just details."

"Details like the fact that no one under forty-five will know who you're supposed to be?" Spencer says dryly, not looking up from his coffee.

"Okay, okay," I say, laughing now. "Let's not descend into chaos before we've even cleared the breakfast dishes. Two weeks. That's how long we've got. Nobody is showing up in tights unless they've got a damn good reason."

My gaze lands on Sammy, who just shrugs, grinning like a fox caught with feathers in his mouth.

"Challenge accepted," he says, and then, with a criminal level of confidence, he leans forward and plucks the last piece of bacon off my plate.

"Sammy."

"You weren't going to eat it," he says, already halfway through the bite, cheek puffed like a squirrel.

"Don't test me," I warn, brandishing my fork like it's a weapon. But my voice cracks; he knows I'm bluffing. Pearl huffs from under the table, clearly unimpressed with all of us, though more likely disappointed there isn't more food hitting the floor.

"Careful, Sam," Jamie drawls from across the table, leaning back in his chair with easy confidence, one hand curled around his coffee mug. "Penelope might actually stab you one of these days."

"Only if I ask nicely," Sam says, eyes twinkling.

"You wish," I mutter, jabbing my fork in his general direction.

"Stop encouraging each other," I say. It comes out more fond than stern, which kind of defeats the purpose. But they're all so unbothered. All bare skin and rumpled hair, grinning and barefoot, like this is a perfectly normal way to exist.

"Encouraging?" Liam says, pouring more tea into my mug without asking, his forearm brushing mine. "That's optimism, Darlin'. This lot thrives on chaos." He nudges my knee under the table, the warm press of his leg against mine sending a ripple of awareness through me.

"Breakfast is too early for chaos," I reply, even though I know I'm lying. I'd let them banter for hours if it meant I could keep this. Keep them.

"Speaking of chaos," Jamie says, pointing his fork at Archer like it's a gavel, "if you bring up pirates again—"

"Leave me and my pirates alone," Archer snaps, mock-offended. "It's a timeless concept. Sexy. Swashbuckling. Classic."

"Sexy for who?" Spencer asks, arching one skeptical brow. "The parrot?"

"Enough," I say, laughing into my tea. "If you start a food fight over fictional birds, I'm not cleaning it up."

"Deal." Archer lifts his coffee in a toast. "To parrots and tights-free costumes."

I groan, but I'm grinning. This moment, this kitchen filled with teasing insults and too much skin for me to not be affected, it's chaos. But it's mine.

When the plates are picked clean and the coffee pot is making its last pathetic sputters, I push to my feet and reach for the dishes. It's automatic. It's what I do.

But Liam stops me. One warm hand on my wrist, firm and gentle at once.

"You cooked." His voice is low, teasing, but there's a current under it. Something resolute. "Sit. Drink your tea. We've got this."

"But—"

He's already sliding the plate from my hands and passing it to Archer, who gives me a mock bow before carrying it to the sink.

Liam nudges me back toward my chair, his palm lingering on the small of my back. "Let us take care of you."

I hesitate. Not because I don't want to. But because I do. And it scares the hell out of me.

Still, I sit. I wrap my hands around the warm ceramic of my mug and try not to fall apart at the feeling of being looked after. They move around me, messy, loud, uncoordinated. Sam knocks over a spoon. Spencer sings off-key into a spatula. Jamie critiques Archer's loading technique like it's a sport. And somehow, between the clatter and the

banter and the warmth radiating off every inch of this kitchen, something inside me settles.

It's imperfect. It's chaotic.

It's home.

The house is still echoing with the aftershocks of breakfast laughter
when I slip outside, leash in hand. Pearl's already tugging with the
kind of righteous determination only a dog can possess, like every
squirrel is a personal affront she's been stewing over all morning.

Liam catches up before I reach the gate, his hand brushing mine as
he opens it for me. He doesn't say anything, he doesn't have to. There's
something about the way he moves beside me, easy and close, like the
heat from earlier hasn't just scorched across my skin in the form of five
gorgeous, ridiculous men arguing about pirate costumes. Like he
didn't just take over the dishes while I sat there pretending my heart
wasn't doing something stupid every time he looked at me.

We need the air. Or at least, I do.

Now, the leash is taut in my hand as Pearl leads us down the gravel
path, nose twitching like she's scanning for woodland friends. Her tail
wags so hard it rattles her entire body, locked in on something invisible
and apparently urgent. The sun slips through scattered clouds, casting
everything in that kind of gold that forgives every flaw, turns weeds
into wildflowers, turns moments into memories. Dew clings to the
grass like sequins, each blade catching the light like it wants to be
noticed.

The air smells like wet earth and green things trying to bloom. It
fills my lungs the way I imagine fresh starts are supposed to feel.

Liam walks beside me, hands shoved deep in the pockets of his
worn-in jeans. The denim's faded in that perfect, unfair way, hugging
his hips like it's proud of the job it's doing. His hat shades his face just
enough that I can't see his eyes, but I feel them on me. That look. That
maddening, spark-eyed glint that means he's either about to say something flirty or dangerous. Or both.

"All right, Crocodile Dundee," I say, breaking the silence as we round the bend. "You really think you can pull that off at the masquerade? You're missing the giant knife. And the... I don't know, the je ne sais quoi." I wave my free hand like that explains anything. Pearl promptly swerves, and I nearly trip over my own feet.

Liam chuckles. It's low and honey-thick, the kind of laugh that slides up your spine and makes a home there. "I could make it work," he says. "But I've been thinking... might be time to go full Highlander instead. Kilt. Sporran. The works."

He tosses me a sidelong glance, and those dimples flash like a weapon. "What do you reckon?"

I falter. It's barely a hiccup in my step, but he catches it, like always. The image flashes through my head before I can stop it: Liam in a kilt, wind teasing the hem, that particular smug glint in his eye. I feel the heat rush up my throat before I can form words.

His smile goes crooked. Predatory. Like he knows exactly what I'm imagining and plans to exploit it.

"Highland regalia?" I say, aiming for indifferent and landing somewhere in the vicinity of breathless. "If you want to attract half the town's grannies, knock yourself out."

I bend to unclip Pearl's leash, desperate to redirect both my words and my bloodstream. He takes the bait, but not entirely.

"Will it attract you?" he murmurs.

He's closer now. So close his voice hums in my ear, his breath warm against my neck. "Admit it, Pen. You're picturing it."

"Absolutely not," I lie. Badly. My face is already betraying me, burning with heat that has nothing to do with the sun. I keep my eyes trained on Pearl, who's barreled into the field, nose to the ground and tail wagging like mad.

"Pearl!" I call, too loudly, but she ignores me, of course.

"She's fine," Liam says, his voice gentling. "Let her run."

And then he turns toward me fully, crowding into my space without ever touching me, and suddenly there's nowhere to go. The rough stone wall at my back is cool and scratchy through my shirt, a stark contrast to the heat radiating off his body as he leans in.

"I miss you," he says, and it's not a joke, not a tease. It lands like a weight in my chest. A soft ache that makes my lungs feel too small.

"You saw me yesterday," I whisper, trying to smile. It comes out shaky.

"Not the same," he says, eyes dropping to my mouth. "I haven't had you to myself in days."

And then he kisses me.

Soft. Barely there. But it strips me clean anyway.

I lean into him, my fingers curling in his shirt, feeling the worn cotton and the steady thrum of heat beneath it. The kiss deepens, like a question turning into a plea, and when his hand slides up to cup my waist, I swear the earth tilts under my boots.

His thumb brushes over the swell of my breast, a teasing stroke that makes my whole body tighten. I gasp against his mouth, and he groans like he's been holding that sound back all morning.

"I've been wanting to do that since breakfast," he rasps.

Then there's no more patience. No more teasing. Just lips and heat and hunger. He kisses me like he's trying to climb inside me, like the air between us is a problem he needs to fix with his hands and mouth and body.

He grips my thigh, hooks it around his waist, presses me into the wall until every inch of him is against every inch of me. I can feel him, hard and urgent, through the denim, and it sends a spark racing through me so fast I forget how to breathe.

"Pen," he whispers, voice ragged. "Be quiet, okay?"

Oh God. I nod, biting my lip.

His hand dips inside my overalls, fingers slipping past the waistband of my panties with terrifying precision. And then,

"Fuck," he breathes, forehead pressed to mine. "You're already soaked."

I let out a sound, something between a whimper and a moan. My head falls back against the stone, eyes fluttering shut as he strokes through my slick folds, lazy and calculated. Like he's in no rush at all to get me off. Like he wants to savor it out here in the open.

"Have you been thinking about this since we left the house?" he murmurs. "Naughty girl."

He slides two fingers inside me and I forget my name. My body bucks against his hand, chasing more, chasing everything.

He works me open, slow and controlled, his thumb circling my clit with maddening focus. I feel like I'm unraveling, pulled taut and trembling, trying to keep my cries contained behind bitten lips.

"Let go," he whispers. "Come for me, Darlin'. Right here."

And I do.

The climax crashes over me like a wave breaking on rock. It splits me open, steals the air from my lungs, and leaves me gasping into his shoulder as he covers my mouth with his hand, muffling my broken sounds. He whispers praise into my ear, a steady stream of "that's it, just like that" and "so fucking beautiful."

By the time I can breathe again, my legs are jelly, my head spinning. He pulls his hand away and I watch, still dazed, as he licks his fingers with a sinful little smirk.

"Sweet as sugar," he says, and that look, that look, makes me want to drag him back in for more.

Pearl barks.

Loud and sharp. A lightning bolt to our system.

Liam startles, then laughs against my cheek, his arms still braced around me.

"Saved by the dog," he mutters. "Again."

I let out a shaky groan, swiping at the damp hair clinging to my forehead. "Perfect timing, really."

Pearl bounds toward us with a giant stick in her mouth, her tail wagging a million miles a minute.

"Don't give me that look," I tell her, trying for stern but failing miserably.

"Do you think she's scandalized?" he asks, brushing a kiss to my temple before letting go of my hip reluctantly.

"Please," I scoff, bending down to hook the leash to Pearl's collar. "She'd probably sell tickets if she could."

"Entrepreneurial spirit," Liam says dryly, slipping his hand into mine as we fall into step again. There's a swagger in his stride now, cocky and self-assured, and I roll my eyes even as I trip over my own feet.

"Easy there, Darlin'," he murmurs when I stumble a bit. "Your legs still working?"

"Barely," I grumble.

"You're so pretty after you come," he says quietly, so matter-of-fact it nearly kills me. "All pink and flushed. Glowy."

I elbow him lightly. "God, you're insufferable."

He laughs again, low and smug, and I can't even pretend to be mad. Not when I'm still reeling. Not when his thumb is still tracing soft circles against my knuckles.

"Thank you," I say, and it comes out too quiet, too raw.

Liam glances down. "For what?"

I look at our hands, the way his grip stays steady and warm. "For this. For being here."

His gaze softens, and when he speaks, it's a murmur. "You're my home, Penelope. There's nowhere else I'd rather be."

I can't speak around the lump in my throat, so I squeeze his hand instead.

He squeezes back.

And we keep walking.

23

____

The sharp crack of wood splitting in the fire pit pierces the night air, sending a flurry of glowing orange sparks dancing upward. They swirl past the strands of twinkling lights strung between the gnarled oak branches overhead, ephemeral fireflies flitting into the darkness. The rich scent of sizzling meat fills my nostrils as fat drips from the sausages on the grill, each drop hissing angrily as it strikes the smoldering coals below. Curling my fingers against the rough denim of my overalls, I inhale deeply, savoring the mingled aroma of woodsmoke and freshly turned earth still clinging to my skin from an afternoon spent in the garden.

Across the flickering flames, Spencer and Jamie stand close together, their faces gilded in the warm firelight as they hover over the grill, lost in quiet conversation. Archer sprawls carelessly on a weathered wooden bench, long legs stretched out before him, his second bottle of beer dangling from his fingertips, its glass slick with condensation in the humid night air. But it's Sammy's eyes I feel the most, his dark gaze tracking my every movement, sending an electric shiver racing down my spine and coiling warmly in my core.

"You're going to burn them." Jamie's tongs click against the grill grate.

Spencer's bottle clinks against Jamie's elbow. "Relax. A little char builds character." That grin, sharp, easy, unfair, flares in the firelight. My thighs press together instinctively. Jesus. I look down, anywhere, pretending I'm not on the verge of combusting.

"Where's Liam?" Sammy's chair groans as he leans forward, his sleeve pushed to his elbows, veins standing out along his forearms. I drop my gaze to the ground, heat crawling up my neck.

Liam chooses that exact moment to join us, two wine bottles in his arms, Pearl panting happily at his heels. Just looking at him brings back the way he made me feel earlier, the way his fingers...

"Penelope." Sammy's voice cuts through the haze. He stands, eyes narrowing at my flushed cheeks. "What's got you so bothered?"

"I think I'm sitting too close to the fire," I lie, standing up and making a show of pushing the bench back a little.

"Mmhmm." He steps closer. I tilt my head back to meet his stare. His hands grip my hips, pulling me to my feet. My breath catches. Before I can sit back down, his mouth claims mine.

The taste of beer floods my tongue. His shirt bunches in my fists as my knees go weak. When he pulls away, his thumb drags across my lower lip, rough skin catching.

"Sammy!"

His lips curve. "Just in case you forgot." He turns back to the group, leaving me swaying, pulse thundering in my ears.

I sit back down, biting back a smile as I watch Jamie attack the vegetable skewers like they've personally offended him, metal scraping metal with each determined flip. A log explodes in the fire with a loud pop, shooting embers skyward. For a second, they light up the whole yard like we're inside a snow globe made of sparks and smoke and heat.

The ancient bench groans beneath Archer's weight as he settles beside me, his thigh pressing against mine in a very intentional way. Spencer sits in front of me, sprawling at my feet like an oversized cat, head tipped back against my leg, beer bottle precariously balanced on his thigh. His shoulder radiates heat, and the familiar cedar-and-smoke scent of him rises up to tangle with the woodsmoke. It's a dangerous combination, that smell, like comfort and temptation wrapped up in one inconvenient package.

"We should put in an outdoor kitchen." Jamie straightens, tongs clicking against the grill edge. "That way, we wouldn't have to haul everything back and forth."

Spencer perks up. "Only if we can put in a pizza oven." His drawl stretches longer with each beer, vowels soft and lazy in the gathering dusk.

"Why couldn't we?" Jamie lifts his chin toward the darkening sky, gazing at the stars piercing through deep blue, scattered like salt across velvet. The first hint of evening chill whispers across my skin, raising goosebumps despite the fire's warmth.

"I'd vote hot tub over pizza oven." My lips twitch. "Priorities." The word comes out breathier than intended. Archer's body pressed against mine making every nerve ending spark and hum. And it's not helping thinking about what we can do in the hot tub.

"You win," Spencer says easily, looking up at me with firelight dancing in his eyes. The top of his shirt is open, revealing the clean dip of his collarbone. I don't trust myself to look any longer than a second.

"Sounds perfect to me." Jamie brandishes the tongs, metal glinting orange in the flames. Grease sizzles as he turns another skewer. The smell of charred peppers and onions makes my stomach growl.

"Sounds like a lot of work." Archer's arm settles along the bench behind my shoulders, fingertips ghosting across my skin. Behind his glasses, his brown eyes hold mine, something molten in their depths. The firelight catches on his lenses, hiding then revealing the intensity of his gaze. "Someone has to keep your ideas in check."

"In check?" My eyebrow lifts. Heat creeps up my neck that has nothing to do with the flames. "Says the man wanting to build an entire fish market?"

"That's just practical." His mouth quirks, but his gaze stays steady.

I should laugh. Tease him. Say something flirty or sarcastic. Instead, I just breathe him in. Leather, pine, sweat. My head feels full of static. My skin prickles where his fingers rest, like they're speaking in Morse code. Like they're asking a question I'm not sure I'm ready to answer.

On the far side of the fire, Liam says something that makes Sam bark out a laugh, their voices clinking together with bottles and easy camaraderie. The spell breaks, but not completely. Archer stays close. His leg presses into mine again, this time firmer. There's a question in the way his body shifts toward mine. A quiet offer. My pulse hammers in my throat.

"I'm gonna get some water," I say, too fast, standing too quickly. My heart is in my mouth, my whole body buzzing. His touch lingers on my skin like a phantom.

As I cross the yard, Spencer's voice follows me.

"Don't get lost."

The gravel path crunches beneath my feet as I weave between the raised garden beds, their wooden borders silvered with age. My skin tingles where Archer's touch lingered, phantom pressure points that make my steps unsteady. Behind me, laughter spills across the yard like wind chimes, punctuated by the sharp crack and pop of burning wood. Liam's voice carries on the breeze, something about a hot tub that draws another round of chuckles from the guys.

The French doors stand open, gauzy curtains dancing in the evening air. I pause at the threshold, caught between worlds, the wild, spark-filled night at my back and the quiet sanctuary of the living room before me. The change in temperature raises goosebumps along my arms, air conditioning battling against the lingering heat radiating from my skin. My heart still thunders in my chest, an echo of earlier tension that refuses to settle.

The kitchen is quiet, almost reverent in its stillness. Late light filters in through the windows, casting long rectangles of gold across the tiled floor. I move on instinct, filling a glass at the sink, the water running sharp and cold over my fingers. Droplets catch the light, clinging to my knuckles, falling in rhythmic plinks against the basin.

Behind me, floorboards creak, and my spine stiffens. Archer's cologne fills my lungs before I see him. My fingers tighten around the glass until my knuckles ache.

"Thought you might need help." Archer's voice scrapes low, rough-edged.

The glass connects with the counter, the sound echoing in my chest like a warning bell. "Help getting a glass of water?" My voice wavers as he steps closer. The air thickens, heavy with woodsmoke that clings to his clothes and something else, something dangerous and electric that makes my skin prickle.

"Penelope." My name drops from his lips like a stone into still water. Every muscle in my body tightens. The kitchen shrinks around us, walls pressing closer with each heartbeat.

"Archer." His name catches in my throat. His presence fills the kitchen, crowds against my skin. The counter edge digs into my lower back as I retreat, but there's nowhere left to go.

"I can't stop thinking about the other day." His breath skims my cheek, beer and smoke curling into my lungs. His hand plants flat against the granite next to my hip, arm bent, boxing me in. "On the boat. The way you felt... the way your pussy was squeezing around my cock." His voice drops into something dangerous, something molten. His eyes flick to my mouth. Back up. "Tell me you've been thinking about it too."

"Archer..." My fingers curl against the cool granite. The room tilts on its axis as he leans closer.

"Just a taste," he murmurs, his lips grazing the shell of my ear. His voice is barely there, but my whole body reacts, goosebumps erupting down my arms, legs going watery. "Please."

"You're out of your mind," I whisper, even as my body betrays me again, leaning toward him like I don't remember how to stand without his weight against me.

"Maybe." Another step. His thigh presses against mine, denim against denim. He holds my gaze, his pupils blown wide.

"We can't." The protest dies as my body sways toward him like a compass finding north. His fingers dig into my hips, branding me through the denim. The counter edge bites deeper into my lower back, a sharp counterpoint to the heat of his hands.

"We shouldn't," he corrects. Each word falls like matches on dry tinder. His thumb traces a dangerous arc along my hipbone. "But we will."

Archer makes quick work of my overalls and a rush of chilly air kisses my skin, raising goosebumps in its wake as he tugs the denim down my thighs. Goosebumps scatter across my skin. My pulse pounds between my legs. And then he's kissing me, mouth hot, insistent, open, and the taste of him floods my tongue. His hands move over me like he owns the map already. I moan, breath catching as I part my legs, my whole body tuning to the frequency of yes.

"You have no fucking idea how badly I've been craving this," he breathes, and I feel it in my chest, in the place just beneath my ribs where nothing feels safe.

His hand slides under the lace of my panties. He parts me, slick and ready, and his breath catches like he's surprised. His gaze flits over the counter and lands on a freshly rinsed cucumber, glistening in the light.

He grins and strips off my underwear and lifts me onto the counter.

"You can't be serious," I whisper, even as my core clenches.

"Oh, I'm very serious." His hand wraps around it, calculated and slow. The cool skin of it glides along my inner thigh. My head tips back, lips parting. He watches every twitch of my expression like it's his job.

"Tell me I can fuck you with this," he says, voice guttural, his lips brushing my neck. "Tell me I can watch your pussy stretch around it."

I should say no. I know that. But I don't.

"Yes," I gasp, a desperate, broken sound.

He spreads me open with careful fingers, the cucumber sliding along my folds. "You're fucking soaked," he groans, circling my entrance before teasing the end just inside. Then he pulls it out and, God, he licks it.

"Jesus, Archer," I breathe, watching helplessly as he presses it in, inch by slow inch. My body stretches around it, heat and pressure singing through me.

"Fucking look at you," he rasps, dipping his head to my stretched lips, to slide his tongue in whatever space is left.

"Archer," I beg, lifting my hips to take more of it, while at the same time tugging on his hair until his lips brush my clit. "Please."

He groans. "Fuck, Penelope," and then he's there, tongue flattening, lips sucking, coaxing every nerve-ending into a tight, shivering coil.

"Touch yourself," he orders, his cock now in his hand, long and hard and already glistening. I obey, fingers finding my clit, rubbing in tight, aching circles.

"That's it." His voice is nothing but wreckage. "Now come for me."

It hits like a landslide. My spine bows, my thighs shake, and my mouth opens in a silent scream as I shatter around the cucumber, every nerve on fire. Archer doesn't let go. He moves with me, drawing it out, milking every last wave until I'm trembling and wrung out and barely upright.

The cucumber clatters into the sink.

"You're bleeding," he murmurs. His thumb brushes my bottom lip. He kisses me, slow and deep, the taste of blood and want and something sharper.

I slide off the counter, my overalls still tangled around one ankle, legs trembling so hard I nearly fall. The tile is cool and unforgiving against my knees as they hit the floor, but I barely feel it. My hands find his waistband, fingers fumbling with urgency as I undo the button, drag the zipper down. His breath hitches above me, sharp and unsteady, like he's holding himself back by a thread.

I push his jeans and boxers just low enough to free him, the fabric catching on the curve of his thighs before falling away. My gaze locks on him, thick, flushed, already dripping with anticipation. He twitches in the air between us, and the sight alone makes my mouth water.

I take a moment. Just one. Let myself look.

Every inch of him is perfect, veins bulging, tip glistening, heavy with need. My chest rises in a shallow breath as I lean in and run my tongue along the underside of his shaft, slow and careful, tracing the ridge with the flat of my tongue like I'm memorizing him. The taste of skin, musk, salt, it fills my mouth, coats my senses. He groans low and deep, his hand diving into my hair, fingers tightening just enough to make me moan.

Then I take him into my mouth, inch by slow inch, the pressure of him stretching my jaw until my lips ache. I suck gently at first, letting him settle against my tongue, letting myself feel the weight of him. He curses under his breath, hips twitching forward, the restraint in him fraying.

I go deeper.

My hands slide to his thighs, holding him steady as I work him farther in, cheeks hollowing, throat relaxing around him. My nose brushes the soft skin of his abdomen, and he groans again, raw and broken this time.

"Fuck, Penelope," he rasps, his voice strangled. His grip in my hair tightens, tugging just enough to light up every nerve in my scalp.

I hum around him, slow and deep, the vibrations making him shudder. His hips jerk forward again, and I take it, adjust, swallow him down greedily. I set a rhythm, firm and steady, tongue swirling with each upward drag, lips sealing tight around him. Every sound he makes only spurs me on, each harsh breath, each groaned curse, each whispered praise falling like embers across my skin.

His abs tense under my hands, and I feel it, the change, that inevitable edge as his whole body draws tight. His thighs quiver. His chest heaves.

I don't pull back. I want all of it.

He comes with a harsh gasp, cock pulsing against my tongue, hot and thick as he spills down my throat in shuddering waves. I take every drop, swallowing around him, not looking away, not blinking, just holding him inside me as he falls apart, letting him see what he does to me.

When I finally pull back, I wipe my mouth with the back of my hand, tasting him on my lips, still dizzy with how fast everything unraveled. He doesn't hesitate. His hands find me, hauling me to my feet like he needs me against him now, like standing apart even one more second is unbearable.

His mouth crashes into mine. There's no finesse left, just hunger. Desperation. His tongue pushes into my mouth, tasting himself on me, the kiss as consuming as it is grounding. His hand cups the back of my head, holding me steady, holding me close.

When we break apart, we're both panting. Foreheads nearly touching. His thumb brushes the corner of my mouth, then my cheek, his gaze softening with something that makes my throat tighten.

"You're incredible," he says, voice hoarse with leftover arousal, tender like a prayer. He tucks a strand of hair behind my ear, lets his fingers trail down the curve of my jaw.

Then, with gentle hands, he pulls up my overalls, fastening them like it's the most natural thing in the world. Like he hasn't just turned me inside out. His touch is warm and sure, smoothing my shirt back into place, fingers lingering for a second too long.

He fixes me.

And somehow, that part undoes me even more than everything that came before.

"There," he whispers, touching beneath my eyes, "all presentable again."

The weight of what just happened simmers between us, but he doesn't smother it, just cups my face one last time, fingers stroking over my jaw.

"Go on," he says with a lazy, devastating smile. "Before they come looking for you."

"And you?" I ask, already breathless again.

"I've got a salad to finish."

24

———————

Sammy drapes the blanket over my shoulders with a care that feels too tender for how casually it's done, like he doesn't realize what his fingers are doing to me. The fabric brushes the side of my neck, warm and scratchy, and then his knuckles follow, rough against skin that suddenly feels sensitive. He tucks it in loosely around me, and I sink deeper into the Adirondack chair, the ancient wood groaning under my weight.

The fire cracks again, sharp, bright, and I watch it claw up the logs like it's trying to rewrite the night. Smoke curls into the air in lazy spirals. A bottle catches the light on the ground near my foot, green glass turned amber by the flicker. Our laughter tangles in the smoke, warm and private and just a little slurred.

"Don't hog it," Spencer mutters, tugging at the corner of the blanket like a petulant child, though the way his head settles against my leg feels anything but juvenile. His shoulder knocks against my calf and stays there, stubborn and hot. The firelight hooks into his eyes, turning the blue nearly black. Dangerous. Beautiful. A slow smile curves his mouth, crooked, arrogant, familiar.

I lift my glass, the wine sloshing against the lip, catching a glint of firelight as it tips toward my mouth. "Can't help it if I'm Sammy's favorite." The words come easy, teasing, but my pulse betrays me, racing ahead like it knows what game we're playing. The wine hits my tongue, dark fruit and oak and something sinful I can't name. It slides down slow, warming me from the inside out.

Spencer's laugh is low and dangerous and right against my thigh, vibrating through me like a tuning fork. He shifts, muscles flexing under his soft, worn shirt as he gets even closer, and suddenly the blanket's not doing anything at all to keep me warm because every part of me is burning.

"Is that right?" he says, voice pitched somewhere between a dare and a promise. "Well, Sugar, I might have to remind you why I'm your favorite."

The nickname wrecks me. It always does. Soft on the outside, all passion and promise underneath. Like him. I turn my head just enough to meet his gaze, and I don't recognize my own voice when it comes out.

"I'd like to see you try."

The fire snaps like it's in on the tension, a crack loud enough to cover the breath I drag in, trying to keep steady. I don't dare move. Not when Spencer's eyes are fixed on me like I'm already unraveling in his hands. We're all pretending this is just any other night. Just a bonfire. Just some drinks.

But my glass is half-empty and my body's too full of want, and Spencer's mouth is still curved in that maddening smile as his fingers start tracing idle shapes into the bare skin of my shin. Not a single part of me believes I'm going to make it through this night untouched.

A cold, wet nose presses insistently into my palm, Pearl, doing her nightly rounds like a security guard with a shift to finish. I don't look down. Just drag my fingers through her fur, her ears twitching under my hand, and for a second, my pulse slows. Then Spencer shifts, and it spikes all over again.

"Have you thought any more about the masquerade party?" His voice is low, lower than necessary, and aimed squarely at me, like it has weight, like it could tip me over. He tilts his head back, exposing the long stretch of his throat, his gaze climbing up my face like it's a story he wants to memorize line by line. Firelight catches the shadowed dip of his collarbone, and suddenly I can't remember how to breathe right.

My hand finds his hair without consulting me, fingers slipping through the soft strands like they're made to. He leans into the touch, just slightly. Just enough.

"It's a lot of pressure," I say, the words sliding out before I can reshape them into something less vulnerable. "This is the first time the six of us are going as an official..." I trail off, cheeks burning. Not because I don't know what we are, but because the word still feels strange in my mouth. Sextuple? Sounds like a medical condition.

"Family?" Jamie offers from across the fire. Metal scrapes against metal as he flips a steak on the grate. The smell hits me seconds later, seared fat and campfire and something primal.

The word family catches in my throat like a swallowed laugh. Or a sob. "At least they've already met all of you. That'll make it... less awkward."

"You're forgetting the part where we caught Lach and Charlie fucking in that fishing shack bathroom," Liam says around the lip of his beer bottle. His eyes glint. "It's always going to be awkward."

"Fuck, I forgot about that." My face flushes all over again. I think back to that day, how it started, how it ended. How completely unprepared I'd been. "We need to do something different this time. Something classic. Venetian masks. Satin gloves."

Spencer's approval lands soft and slow and utterly lethal. "Sexy," he says, like it's a benediction. His eyes sweep down my body, not subtle. Not even pretending.

"Stop picturing it," I say, trying for stern, but it catches somewhere in my throat and comes out all breath and no bite.

"Can't help it," he murmurs, settling deeper against my legs like he owns the space. Like I belong to him. His lashes drop in a lazy arc, a silent rebellion written in the tilt of his grin.

"Unbelievable." The word is useless, a formality. My fingers are already threading through his hair again, betraying me in real time. I scrape my nails lightly against his scalp. The sound he makes is low, pleased, and entirely too satisfying.

"Tell me more about this costume." His voice has changed, gone smoky, like the first sip of something strong and smooth. It curls around me, makes my legs feel like they've forgotten how to function. "I want details."

"Wouldn't you like to know." My brain floods with images, fabric slipping over skin, heels clicking on marble, the exact moment his pupils would go wide the second he saw me.

"Tease," he says, and it's not an insult. It's respectful. It's a smile that curves slow and deep, like he's both warning me and thanking me at the same time. Like he already knows he's going to win.

And maybe he is.

"Alright." Sammy drags his chair in closer, the legs scraping against stone with a wince of protest that cuts through the still night. A blanket hangs off one shoulder like a half-forgotten cape, the ends trailing through leaves and pine needles, gathering proof of where he's been. The firelight catches his face as he surveys the circle like he's about to make a speech, cheekbones golden glowing ebony, eyes a little too bright from the wine.

"So what's next on our list of outdoorsy bullshit? Fire pit's sorted," he says, gesturing lazily toward the glowing heart of our little universe. "But I think it's time to up our game."

"Up our game?" My fingers tighten in Spencer's hair where his head rests heavy against my knee. His hum of approval vibrates through my thigh, low and indulgent, and then his fingers slide higher, slow, teasing, claiming.

Jamie's eyes find mine across the flames. "We need better lighting before we try building that outdoor kitchen. Can't see shit once the sun's down."

The way he holds my gaze makes the heat bloom up my neck, a slow crawl that has nothing to do with the fire. His smile flickers in the shadows, soft and lethal.

"Maybe some romantic mood lighting," I deadpan, twisting the stem of my wineglass between two fingers.

Liam snorts into his beer, eyes gleaming.

"Sure," Jamie murmurs, mouth twitching. "For when we're fucking you out here under the stars."

I choke on a sip of wine, tears streaming down my face.

"Don't forget about the hot tub." Archer's voice rumbles low and calculated. It reaches into my spine and settles there, buzzing beneath my skin. He stares into the fire, flames playing across the sharp lines of his jaw, his cheekbones, the curve of his mouth. His gaze flicks to mine and my stomach drops right to my feet. "Where we can also fu—"

"Alright!" I interrupt, my voice cracking as I attempt to steer the conversation back to a safer topic. "I'm glad someone finally agrees with me about the hot tub."

"Oh, I think we all agree with you, Sugar." Spencer's voice cuts through the haze, his breath warm against the inside of my knee. His fingers trail higher, just shy of indecent. "None of us have stopped thinking about it since you brought it up."

My pulse stumbles. The words are playful, but the heat behind them is anything but. My breath snags, caught somewhere between laughter and a moan.

"God help me." It comes out as more of a sigh than a prayer. I lean back into the chair and watch them, these men I somehow got lucky enough to love. They're ridiculous, all of them, but the warmth blooming in my chest is thick and real and rising fast, like something wild breaking through the surface.

I straighten, lifting Spencer's head from my lap with gentle insistence. He groans like I've just ruined his life, but lets me go.

"If you guys are actually planning on staying, like, permanently, we need to talk about the bedroom and bathroom situation. For real this time."

Jamie grins, all slow drag and honey. "Do you want us to stay, Penella?"

"Pearl will miss you too much if you leave."

"Only Pearl?" Liam quirks an eyebrow as he lifts his beer, firelight reflecting off the glass as he takes a slow sip.

Archer leans in, arms braced on his knees. The light turns his eyes molten, a deep, unreadable gold. "I'll be the first to admit, I don't want to leave. I like what we've built here. With you."

My chest pulls tight.

This isn't banter anymore. This is a moment. A big one.

"It wouldn't be the worst thing in the world, would it?" I whisper. The words wobble at the edges, barely loud enough to be heard over the pop of the fire and the chirp of night insects. "I..." My throat closes for a second. "I want more nights like this. All of us. Together. Forever, hopefully." I look up at them, wearing my heart on my sleeve.

Silence falls, but not the uncomfortable kind. It's a thick, settling hush, like the world has just shifted an inch to the left and is waiting to see what we'll do about it.

"We can make that happen," Jamie says, his voice soft but certain. "Plenty of projects left to keep us here," he adds with a crooked grin, chasing the weight out of the air like a balloon released from a fist.

"Like the hot tub," Archer says, and the smirk is back, slower, more private now.

"Or the pizza oven," Sam offers, eyes twinkling in the dark.

"Or both," Liam says, lifting his glass. "Go big or go home."

"Idiots," I say, but there's no heat behind it. Just something warm and aching. Something that might be love. It swells in my chest like a second heartbeat, too big to hold down.

The fire casts them all in gold and shadow. We're a constellation, drawn in firelight and breath, arranged in a circle around the flame we built together.

I sink deeper into the chair, the wood creaking softly beneath me, familiar now. The kind of comfort you don't notice until you realize you've stopped bracing for the world to fall apart. The fire hisses and spits, chewing through logs like it's starving. Flames curl upward, licking at the dark like they want to hold it off just a little longer. Around us, the air cools, soft and damp and full of cricket-song and far-off waves crashing against shore.

Liam and Archer move about, gathering plates and stray beer bottles. Liam tosses me a wink that settles warm in my belly before vanishing inside, Archer following close behind.

Spencer calls for Pearl as he moves to join Sammy, who is already halfway down the garden path. He ruffles Pearl's fur, then glances at me, flashing a grin. "Don't let Jamie talk your ear off while we're gone."

"Wouldn't dream of it," I answer, watching them walk away, Pearl's tail waving like a beacon of joy as they disappear into the dark.

And then, it's just Jamie and me.

The fire settles into embers, casting a low amber glow over the backyard. The shadows stretch longer, softer, curling around the edges of us. Jamie leans back in his chair like he owns the night, one arm tossed over the armrest, the other holding a half-empty glass that he hasn't touched in a while. His eyes meet mine, dark as sin in the flickering light.

"C'mere," he says, patting his thigh, voice quiet but sure. Like it's not a question.

I stand and cross the short distance between us, my heart in my throat. I sit sideways on his lap, winding my arms around his neck. He's solid and warm beneath me, cedar and smoke wrapping around my senses as I inhale deeply. He wraps his arms around me, one hand splayed across my lower back, the other curled around my hip. His touch is possessive, his fingers flexing against me like he's memorizing my shape. Like he doesn't trust himself to let go.

"This okay?" he murmurs, and the words vibrate through my chest where we're pressed together, like the low rumble of a storm just past the horizon.

Instead of answering, I shift. Slowly. Purposefully. I slide one leg over his lap until I'm straddling him fully, thighs bracketing his hips. We fit together too well. Too easily. My knees press into weathered wood, my chest flush against his, and I feel every single breath he takes like it's mine.

His hands tighten. His eyes darken. He draws in a sharp breath that sounds a lot like surrender.

And I ask, softer this time, barely a whisper, barely brave, "Is this okay?"

Jamie doesn't answer right away. He doesn't need to. His hands slide up my back, slow and worshipful, pulling me in until our mouths are a breath apart.

"God, yes," Jamie groans, catching my mouth in a kiss that starts like a question and ends like a confession. His lips are soft at first, exploratory, then his tongue slides along the seam of mine, coaxing me open, and I do, without hesitation, with a soft, shattered sound that betrays just how far gone I already am.

He tastes like beer and firelight, like summer air thick with heat and promise, and I want to drown in it, in him. The kiss deepens, messy now, all teeth and tongue and low, desperate noises that I barely recognize as mine.

We break apart gasping, noses brushing. Jamie's hands slide over me like he doesn't know where to touch first. He cups my sides, then my back, then finally my breasts, and it's like he's mapping me. Like he's claiming territory. I gasp as his thumbs circle my nipples, teasing them into stiff peaks that ache against the fabric of my shirt.

It's not enough. Not nearly. My body screams for more, for his skin against mine, for the weight of him, for him.

I shift, slipping off his lap. The gravel beneath my knees is sharp, grounding. The fire crackles behind me, its heat kissing my back as I settle between his legs. My fingers find the button of his jeans, clumsy with urgency, and the second it gives, I feel Jamie tense.

The zipper drags down with a rasp that cuts through the thick, weighted silence. He exhales sharply above me, a sound more felt than heard. I tug his jeans and boxers down just enough for his cock to spring free, hard, heavy, flushed, the head already slick with precum.

My mouth floods with saliva.

I take a second, just a second, to look at him, to really look. He's gorgeous like this. Flushed and wild-eyed, chest rising fast, his thighs trembling with the effort of restraint. I run my fingers down the length of him, tracing veins, feeling the pulse that jumps beneath my touch. Admiring the way he twitches in my hand, the way he groans when I squeeze.

His head falls back, exposing the strong line of his throat. "Fuck," he mutters, voice barely holding together. "Penelope..."

There's nothing polite in the way he says my name. It's a plea. A warning. A promise.

I lean in and drag my tongue over the tip, slow, careful. He jerks beneath me like I've electrocuted him, a strangled noise clawing its way out of his chest. I do it again, firmer this time, savoring the salt and heat and the way he falls apart so easily in my mouth.

I take him deeper, lips stretching, jaw aching in the best possible way. The weight of him on my tongue makes my entire body clench in anticipation. I hollow my cheeks, set a rhythm, one hand working the base while the other braces on his thigh. It's wet, filthy, obscene, and he loves it. His hips twitch. His breathing fractures.

"Fuck," he grits out. "You feel... Jesus."

His fingers thread through my hair, gripping just tight enough to make my scalp tingle. Not to control. Just to connect. He's unraveling and needs something to hold onto. I let him. I want him to.

The tension in his thighs ratchets tighter, every muscle in his body wound and trembling. I take him deeper, until my nose brushes his stomach, my throat stretching around him. I hold there, swallowing against him, letting him feel how much I want this, want him.

He's panting now. Ragged. Frantic.

And then, too fast, he's gone.

His hands grab my arms and haul me up with a roughness that takes my breath away. My lips are swollen, my knees scraped raw, and when I look up at him, he looks destroyed, pupils blown wide, lips parted, chest heaving. Like the only thought in his head is me.

His mouth crashes into mine, all heat and hunger and desperation, his hand tangled in my hair like he needs to anchor himself. The other grips my hip, hard enough to bruise, and I grind against him, unable to stop myself.

"Inside," he growls, breaking the kiss just enough to speak. His voice is ragged, almost unfamiliar, gutted. "Now."

And there's no room for teasing. No room for doubt. Because I am already his. And he's about to prove it.

25

JAMIE'S POV

The air in the room is thick. With leftover smoke. With heat. With the kind of tension that feels like it might split the walls apart if we don't do something about it soon. Bonfire still clings to our skin, to our clothes, and there's an electricity between us that crackles like the sky seconds before a summer storm tears it open.

I don't look at her. I can't. My eyes are pinned to the wall just above her head, and if I even glance at her, I'll lose every ounce of control I've got left.

"We should shower," I say to the drywall, voice rough with want and restraint that's fraying at every seam. "Get rid of the smoke."

She snorts, soft but pointed. "Are you saying I smell?"

My mouth twitches. God, don't look, Jamie. Don't you fucking dare. I close my eyes instead, forcing a breath through my clenched teeth. "No. I'm saying I want you to smell like you."

There's a beat. Just one. And I hear it, her breath catching, her throat working around the words she doesn't say. But I know what she's thinking. Because it's the same thing I'm thinking. My face between her thighs. Her fingers gripping my hair, hips rocking, breathless and undone.

"Look at me, Jamie."

My jaw clenches. "No."

"Fucking look at me."

I exhale like I've just been dragged to the surface after holding my breath too long. Slowly, I open my eyes. And there she is.

Arms crossed. Hair a mess. Cheeks pink, skin glowing. She's got this look, defiant and unsure all at once, and it damn near knocks the breath out of my lungs.

I love her so much it hurts. Physically hurts.

"Better?" I ask, raising an eyebrow, pretending like I'm not coming apart just from the sight of her.

And then, of course, she licks her bottom lip. Slow. Like she knows exactly what she's doing. Like she remembers what it felt like when that same mouth was wrapped around me. My hands curl into fists at my sides.

Her smirk spreads. That little tilt of her mouth that shatters all my defenses.

I reach for the hem of her shirt, moving slowly, offering her the space to stop me, to say no. She doesn't. She unfastens her overalls, lifting her arms without a word, and I pull the fabric over her head, dropping it to the floor.

Her nipples tighten in the cool air, and I groan. Jesus Christ. "Why the hell aren't you wearing a bra?"

She shrugs like it's nothing. "They're small. I only wear one to hide my nipples, but you've all seen them at this point, so..." She trails off, unapologetic and casual in the way that only makes her more lethal.

"Good," I murmur, sinking to my knees. My palms find her tits, and I cup them, thumbing the peaks gently. "They're fucking perfect." I don't wait. I lean in, mouth closing around one nipple, then the other, tongue flicking, teasing. She gasps above me, hands sliding into my hair, anchoring.

I kiss down the center of her chest, slow and unhurried, tracing the freckles down her sternum like a man memorizing constellations. I tug her overalls over her hips, knuckles grazing skin that makes my pulse hammer. She holds onto my shoulders for balance, stepping out of them, and now she's just standing there in this ridiculous scrap of black lace that does absolutely nothing to hide what I want most.

"You're killing me, Penella," I mutter, shaking my head. "I don't know if I'll ever be able to control myself around you. You're just... fuck, you're so..."

"So what?" she prompts, her voice soft now, with no trace of sarcasm. I stand and cup her face in my hands, running my thumbs along her cheekbones, looking her straight in the eye this time.

"So goddamn beautiful." Her cheeks flush darker. She looks away, but I'm not having that.

"Don't." I tip her chin up again, forcing her to meet my gaze. "Don't hide from me."

Something cracks open in her expression, something raw and real. Her fingers twist into my shirt, pulling me in like gravity. And then she's kissing me.

Hard.

Fast.

Like it's the only thing that'll keep her tethered to this moment.

I groan into her mouth, wrap my arms around her waist, and lift her clean off the ground like she weighs nothing. Her legs wrap around my hips, and we just stand there, locked together, her lips on mine, her nails digging into my shoulders, her chest pressing against me with every frantic breath.

She lets out a whimper that guts me completely. I grind into her, my cock pressing against the heat of her through that lace, and she gasps against my mouth. I kiss her like I'll never get the chance again, like the world might collapse outside that window and I won't even care because this, this is the center of everything.

I finally pull back, resting my forehead against hers, breathing her in.

"Shower," I whisper, voice shot to hell. "We need to shower."

Even if the last thing I want is for her to stop touching me.

She nods, barely, but I feel it like a lightning strike straight to the spine. Her breath comes fast and shallow, every inhale like she's trying to keep from flying apart. She's still wrapped around me when I carry her into the bathroom, her thighs tight at my waist, her body already trembling with anticipation.

I set her on the counter, and my hands are already on my clothes like they're suffocating me. Shirt yanked over my head. Pants shoved down with no ceremony. The second I turn toward her, her eyes drop.

She's staring straight at my cock, mouth open, lashes low, pupils blown so wide there's almost no color left in her eyes. When I flex, just a little, her lips twitch into something wicked and desperate.

"Like what you see, baby?" My voice is low and rough now. I step closer and grip her jaw, tipping her face up to mine. "You thinking about choking on it?"

She starts to slide down, but I stop her with a sharp squeeze to her hips. "Uh-uh," I murmur, dragging her back into place. "You'll get your turn. But I get to play first."

She nods, pliant. Hungry. Perfect.

I rip her panties off, literally rip, because fuck it, I'll buy her ten new pairs, and drop to my knees like she's holy and I've got a lifetime of sins to confess.

Her thighs are already slick. I spread her wide, pulling her to the edge of the counter, and just stare for a beat. Soaked. Swollen. Pulsing. My favorite place on earth.

I don't lick right away. I breathe her in like I need it to live. She jerks at the contact, just the heat of my breath, and lets out this raw, guttural sound that makes my cock twitch violently.

Then her hands are in my hair, clawing, trying to force my mouth where she wants it. Needy little thing.

"Oh, you think you're in charge?" I growl, glancing up. "You want to tell me how to eat this perfect pussy, is that it?"

She whines. Shakes her head. But she keeps pulling, so I let her think she's won, and then I press my tongue flat against her clit and suck.

She screams. Head thrown back, spine bowing, legs locking around my shoulders.

I clamp a hand over her mouth before the others come banging on the door. "Quiet," I hiss. "Unless you want them to know how fucking filthy you are."

She bites my palm. I groan. Fuck, I love her wild.

I suck harder, dragging my tongue over her slit in punishing strokes, alternating pressure until her whole body trembles like she's unraveling. Her thighs try to snap shut but I hold them open, relentless.

When she's seconds from coming, I pull back.

"No," she gasps. "Jamie—"

I stand and flip her like she weighs nothing, bending her over the counter. One hand grabs both her wrists and pins them hard to the marble. The other curls around her throat, not tight, just enough to remind her who owns her tonight.

I lean in, lips brushing her ear. "You don't come until I say."

She shudders.

I nudge her legs wider with my knee and drag the thick head of my cock through her wetness, barely dipping in.

"What do you want, Penelope?"

She pushes back against me, panting. "Fuck me, Jamie."

I tighten my grip on her wrists. "You know better than that."

"Please," she whimpers.

"Say it like you mean it."

"Please, Sir."

My entire body lights up.

"Good fucking girl." I slam into her in one savage thrust, and she cries out, her body arching as I bottom out. I don't give her time to adjust. I grip her hips and pull out slow, almost all the way, then drive back in with enough force to rattle the counter beneath us.

"God, you're tight. Like your pussy was made for me." My voice is shattered, filthy. I know it. I don't care.

She's gasping, moaning, eyes locked on mine in the mirror like she can't look away.

"Watch us," I say, curling my hand into her hair and yanking her head back. "I want you to see how pretty you look when I'm ruining you."

I fuck her harder, the slap of skin on skin echoing off the tile. She's shaking, her eyes fluttering like she's seconds away from breaking.

I lean in, licking a stripe along her neck, growling against her skin. "You want to come, angel?"

"Yes, please, Sir, I—"

"One circle," I murmur, brushing my thumb over her clit. That's all it takes.

She shatters.

I hold her through it, fingers digging into her hips as she milks my cock with every pulse. When her legs start to give out, I scoop her into my arms and carry her into the shower, water pounding against both of us as I slam her against the tile and drive into her again.

She takes it, God, she wants it, whimpering and writhing as I pound into her, each thrust brutal and deep and meant to remind her who she belongs to.

"I want you so fucked out you can't remember your name," I grit, slamming into her again. "Just 'Sir,' and that aching little pussy begging for more."

I get close. Too close. I pull out, breathing hard, dropping to my knees behind her. I spread her open and watch her pulse, her hole twitching, greedy.

"God, you're perfect." I lick her there, slow and filthy, circling her rim with my tongue. She makes a sound I'll never forget, shattered and raw and desperate.

When I stand, I wrap her up again, gentler now, pressing kisses along her spine like a benediction. She's limp in my hands, pliant and sweet, a stark contrast to the feral thing she was minutes ago.

I wash her slowly, carefully, then wrap her in a towel and set her gently on the toilet seat. She looks like a painting, hair wet, cheeks flushed, eyes wide and soft and so fucking trusting.

I kneel in front of her.

"You okay?" I ask. "We can stop. Or keep going. Whatever you want."

She looks down, cheeks coloring. "I... I liked it. The dominance. The praise. The rules."

Fucking hell.

"Is that what you want tonight?" I ask, brushing my thumb across her lip. She licks it, slow and hot, and my cock hardens all over again.

She nods. "Yes, Sir."

I exhale sharply, grabbing the edge of the counter to stay grounded.

"What's your safe word?"

"Stop," she whispers.

"Perfect." I press a kiss to her forehead. "You say it once, and we stop. No questions. But until then?"

I sit her on the counter, legs open, arms above her head. My hand closes gently but firmly around her throat, and I kiss her like I've been starving for it.

Because I have.

And I'm going to devour her.

The steam clings to us, curling around our bodies like smoke as I whisk her out of the bathroom. Penelope's giggling, that soft, musical sound I'd chase through a war zone. But the second I throw her down onto the bed, it collapses on itself, sharp and sudden, like a heart skipping a beat. She bounces once, her hair fanning around her like a goddamned halo.

I'm on her before she can move.

"Jamie..." It's a gasp, a warning, maybe a plea. I don't let her finish. My mouth is at her throat, tongue dragging over the droplets still clinging to her skin. She tastes like heat and water and her. Addictively familiar.

"You belong to me tonight," I murmur against her pulse. "Every inch of you."

My hands push under the towel, fuck the towel, and she arches into me like I didn't just make her come twenty minutes ago. I palm her breast, drag my thumb across her nipple until she shudders, then lower, tracing the dip of her waist, the curve of her hips.

She's trembling under me. Not scared, never scared. Ready. Wound tight. Breathing fast.

I pull back just enough to look at her. Her hair's stuck to her cheeks, lips wet and parted, eyes so dark I can barely find the hazel in them. "You're the most beautiful thing I've ever seen," I say, and it's not a line, it's the truth. Too true. It burns in my throat.

She kisses me hard, her tongue sweeping against mine, and I let her take what she needs, for a second.

Then I break it.

"Hands above your head." My voice drops an octave. Commanding. She freezes, like her brain is playing catch-up, and then obeys, arms stretched up, wrists resting on the pillow. Vulnerable. Perfect.

I look down at her, completely spread out for me, breathless and wet and mine. "You ready for more, angel?"

She nods. Soft. Nervous, but open.

"You remember what you said in the bathroom?"

Her tongue darts out to wet her lips. "Yes."

"And what's your safe word?"

"Stop."

"Good girl." My chest aches at how fucking right that sounds coming out of her mouth.

I cross to the nightstand and pull the drawer open, finding everything we'll need, lube, her favorite vibrator, a dildo. I toss them all on the bed, and her pupils go wide. Her knees inch apart.

"Stay still," I warn, and she does.

God, I love how she listens.

I grab her ankles and flip her onto her stomach. She lets out a breathy sound, half shock, half arousal, and I haul her hips up, exposing her completely.

The view makes my mouth water.

"Look at you," I murmur, kneeling behind her. "Dripping already. Do you know how hard that makes me?"

She whimpers, burying her face in the mattress.

"Watch me," I growl, grabbing her hair and turning her face toward the side mirror. "I want you to see what I do to you."

And then I dive in. My tongue slides through her folds, slow and filthy. I suck on her clit until her thighs shake, then trail lower. I kiss her everywhere. Her inner thighs. The back of her knee. Her ass.

She jerks when my tongue circles her rim, but doesn't stop me. Doesn't say no. I take that as permission.

"You're going to let me fuck this perfect ass," I whisper, slicking her up with lube, pressing gentle pressure with my thumb. "You're going to open up for me and take every inch like the desperate little thing I know you are."

She moans, long and low, like the thought alone undoes her.

I press my thumb in, slow and careful. She gasps, her body tightening, so I pause, rub her lower back, let her breathe through it.

"That's it. Breathe, Pen. You're doing so fucking good."

Her muscles slowly give, letting me in. And Jesus Christ, she's so tight, I nearly come just from watching her squeeze around my finger.

"Please," she whispers. "Please, Jamie."

I slide my thumb in deeper and fuck her slowly with it, my other hand stroking her slick pussy, teasing her clit. When I pull my thumb out, I lube the dildo and line it up.

"This is what's going to happen," I say, my voice low and steady. "I'm going to fuck you with the dildo while you hold the vibrator on your clit. When I say come, you come. Not a second before."

She nods.

"I want to hear you."

"Yes, Sir," she whispers, voice ragged.

"Good girl."

I push the dildo in a little at a time, watching her body adjust, the tight ring of muscle yielding slowly. She gasps with every inch, panting now, and I pause to stroke her flanks, kissing the sweat slicking her spine.

"You're taking it so well. So proud of you." When it's all the way in, I hand her the vibrator. "Turn it on. Right there. Yes. Hold it just like that."

Her hair's stuck to her damp cheeks, her thighs slick and open beneath me, her eyes glassy and wet. And I know, know, she'll give me anything I ask for.

"You're doing so well," I murmur, nudging her knees wider with mine, straddling her thighs and locking them down. She's pinned, trapped, between my body and the mattress. Her breath hitches.

I splay one hand across the small of her back and press, forcing her to stay exactly where I want her. She gasps as I slide my cock between her thighs, the friction intense, and then, God, I catch the slick heat of her pussy and thrust through it. Her cunt flutters around me like it's grateful, and it sends a shockwave straight through me.

She looks tiny like this. Breakable. And that thought makes something animal rise up in me. I want to shield her. Worship her. But I also want to wreck her. Leave her marked up, crying out my name, so far gone she forgets her own.

I grind deeper, flexing my hips so she feels every inch.

"Fuck," I breathe. "You're perfect like this. Made for me."

I spread her cheeks and watch her asshole twitch. My cock jumps.

Even just thinking about fucking her there nearly unravels me.

I pull out, breathing hard, licking my thumb and dragging it slowly along her crack. My balls draw tight like I haven't fucked this way before. Not like this. Not with her.

The dildo's still buried in her ass, her body wrapped around it like it belongs there, her muscles fluttering with every tiny shift. She's panting into the pillow, body slick with sweat and need.

"Relax for me, Pen," I whisper, circling the tight stretch of muscle where the toy disappears inside her. She listens, God, she listens, and I feel her soften beneath my touch, her whole body yielding.

I drizzle more lube over the toy, watching it glisten as I rock it gently in and out of her, easing her wider, training her for me. My thumb presses just above where it sinks in, teasing the rim, and she moans, deep and broken, hips twitching like she can't decide whether to run or beg for more.

"That's it," I murmur, working her open around the toy, one slow breath at a time. "You're doing so fucking good for me."

She cries out, not from pain, but from the aching edge of too much and not enough. I keep going, fucking her with the dildo in slow, calculated strokes until she's writhing, clawing at the sheets, her entire body strung tight as a bowstring, waiting for me to finally let her break.

"I want to see your face," I rasp. I flip her over carefully, her body pliant, her cheeks flushed, lips kiss-swollen, eyes wild and unfocused. I have to breathe deep just to stop myself from taking her right there.

"You're so goddamned pretty when you're being fucked."

She whimpers. I swipe precum from the head of my cock and

smear it across her lips. She licks it off, and something primal roars inside me.

I press my mouth to hers, swallowing her moans. When I break the kiss, I'm panting.

I pull back slightly, my palm braced against the curve of her thigh, eyes locked on the spot where her body is stretched tight around the dildo still buried in her ass. The silicone base glistens with lube, the muscle fluttering around it with every shaky breath she takes.

No way I'm pulling that out yet.

I glance toward the nightstand, then back to her flushed face. Her legs are still pressed to her chest, hands looped behind her knees, her cunt on display, dripping, needy, untouched.

"You got another dildo?" My voice drops, low and gravel-wrapped. "Something for this greedy little pussy, since this one's busy stretching out your ass?"

She hesitates. Just a flicker, but it's enough to make her blush bloom deep down her neck. Her lashes lower. Her voice comes out small, like a secret she's never said out loud.

"Back of the drawer."

I reach over without breaking eye contact and slide the drawer all the way open, digging past some books and pens. My fingers curl around something big, thick, silicone with a weight to it.

I pull it out slowly, purposefully.

It's shaped like a cock, but with a wide knot at the base, smooth and bulging, meant to lock in deep. The sight of it alone nearly makes me come. It's curved just right. Made to hit every spot inside her. And when I lift it up so she can see?

She goes scarlet.

My grin is slow and dangerous. "You've been fucking yourself with this and didn't think to tell me?"

She shakes her head slightly, lips parted, too stunned to answer.

I crawl back between her legs, drag the toy through her slick folds, then pause and grip her jaw, making her look at me.

"Tell me the truth. You think about me when you shove this inside you?"

She swallows. Nods.

"Say it."

"Yes, Sir," she whispers, eyes glassy with need.

"That's my girl."

I slick the toy generously, coating every ridge, every curve, and especially the knot at the base. Her pussy clenches just from the anticipation. She's still spread open for me, holding her legs back, but trembling now, so fucking ready.

"Keep your eyes on me."

I press the tip of the toy to her entrance. The stretch makes her whole body tense, her fingers curling into the sheets as it sinks deeper, widening her inch by inch. Her mouth falls open. Her thighs tremble. Her hands go white-knuckled behind her knees.

"That's it," I murmur. "Let it fill you."

I move inch by inch, the shaft curving up inside her perfectly, and her walls cling to it like they don't want to let go. She makes a high, choked sound as I work it deeper, just until the thick knot is nudging at her pussy lips.

Her body stiffens. "Jamie—"

"Shhh," I soothe, pushing her thighs wider. "Breathe, Pen. You can take it."

I hold her down with one arm and apply steady pressure. The knot strains against her entrance, slick and swollen, her folds stretched wide, fluttering with resistance.

"Relax. Let it in."

Her eyes flutter shut. I rub her thigh, circle my thumb over her clit just once, just enough, and pop.

The knot slides inside her with a wet, obscene sound, and her whole body arches off the bed. She screams, raw and desperate, as her pussy clamps down tight, locking the toy inside her.

Her legs shake violently.

"Jesus fucking Christ," I groan, watching her cunt throb around it. "Look at you. Stuffed full. And fucking mine."

She sobs into her arm, her hands falling away from her knees. I catch one and press it back into place.

"No," I whisper. "You keep those hands there. Show me how good you can take it."

She obeys, moaning through clenched teeth.

I lean over, press my lips to her ear. "You feel that stretch, baby? That thick knot locked deep inside you?"

She nods, barely coherent.

"Your pussy's holding it so tight. Can't even move it without watching you shake."

I rotate it slowly, watching her body twitch and ripple with every shift of the toy. Her clit's swollen, flushed, begging for attention.

"You want the vibe?" I ask, trailing it across her lower belly. "Want me to make you come while you're full of knot and cock and so fucking desperate you're dripping down your thighs?"

"Yes," she breathes. "Please, Sir."

"Hold this on your clit," I order, handing her the vibrator again. The second it hits, her whole body jolts.

"Fuck, Jamie—"

I grab her wrist and pull the vibe away just before she tips over.

"Not yet," I growl. "You don't come until I say you do. Understand?"

"Yes," she gasps, tears glittering at the corners of her eyes. Her chest heaves, her tits bouncing with every shaky breath.

"Good. Use your safe word if you need to." I lean in and kiss the corner of her mouth, then reach down to grip the base of the dildo still buried in her ass.

"You're ready for me now," I rasp, voice low and possessive, the kind of tone that comes from years of wanting and barely holding back.

I keep my eyes on hers as I pull it out, inch by slick inch. Her breath stutters, body twitching, the stretch dragging over every nerve as her muscles flutter and protest the loss. She gasps, eyes wide, lips parted. I don't rush it. I want her to feel every second of this. I want her to remember it.

"God, look at you," I murmur. "All stretched out for me. Took that dildo like you were made for it."

My hands shake as I slick my cock with lube, slow strokes from root to tip, watching her tremble beneath me. I add more, dripping it over her ass, massaging it in with the flat of my fingers, sliding some inside her too, just enough to make her squirm.

"You want it, don't you?" I ask, dragging the head of my cock along her crack, letting her feel the weight of it. "You want my cock in your tight little ass?"

She moans, destroyed and breathless, and nods, but I want more.

"Use your words, Penelope."

"Yes, Sir," she whispers, cheeks flushed, voice shaking. "I want it so bad."

Fuck.

"You know how many times I've thought about this?" I say, circling her rim with the head of my cock, teasing her open. "How many times I've been buried inside my fist, and all I could picture was this tight fucking hole wrapped around me instead?"

She lets out a strangled moan, hips twitching.

"Three goddamn years," I growl. "Every time you bent over. Every time you laughed. Every time you touched me and looked away like I wasn't the only thing you were thinking about."

I press just the tip inside her, and her mouth drops open. Her body tenses, so I grip her hip and hold her steady.

"Relax for me," I murmur. "Let me in."

She exhales slow, shaky, her muscles unclenching around me as I push deeper. It's tight, so fucking tight, and my vision blurs at the edges from the effort it takes to hold back.

"That's it. You're going to take what I give you, aren't you?"

Her eyes roll back. "Yes, Sir."

I bottom out with a strangled moan. Her ass is so tight, so warm, every inch of me pulsing inside her. I thrust slow, once, twice, her body adjusting. Her head tilts back, lips parted, pleasure chasing pain across her face.

I pull her leg to my shoulder and bite the inside of her knee, sharp enough to make her jolt. She gasps, grounded.

"There you are," I murmur, watching her come back to me. I lean forward and fuck her ass harder, deeper, rocking the dildo inside her at the same time. She's beyond words now, so I grab the vibrator from her shaking hand and press it to her clit.

Her back bows off the bed.

"Come for me, Penelope."

She screams. Her whole body locks up and her ass clenches

around me so tight I almost black out. I keep fucking her, grinding the vibrator against her as her orgasm slams through her. Her nails tear into my back, dragging down hard as she pulls me closer, her mouth desperate and open under mine.

She breaks our kiss with a sob, her head thrown back, neck arched.

I latch onto her throat and suck hard. She trembles all over.

"That's it," I growl. "Take it all. Show me how much you love my cock in your ass."

Her nails rake my shoulders, digging deep, and the sting only drives me harder. I pound into her, thrusting like I want to live inside her.

"Jamie," she whimpers. "I can't, it's too much—"

"You can take it." I bear down with the vibe. "And you're going to come again."

Her body goes rigid, eyes wide, mouth open, and then she shatters again, a second orgasm ripping through her, and this one undoes me.

With a guttural moan, I slam into her one final time, burying myself to the hilt as she breaks underneath me.

Her ass clamps around my cock like a vice, tight, hot, unrelenting, and it nearly folds me in half. My body convulses, hips stuttering, but I don't move. I can't. I'm caught. Locked inside her while her orgasm wrings every last ounce of control from me.

She pulses around me in sharp, rhythmic waves, tightening, relaxing, tightening again, like her body's trying to hold me in place, keep me. And it fucking works. I cry out, low and broken, as my cock jerks deep inside her, every spasm of her around me dragging more out of me than I knew I had to give.

It's not just release. It's surrender. My balls pull up, my vision whites out, and I come hard, pouring into her in long, involuntary surges, each one chased by the way her muscles clamp down like she needs every drop. Like she's claiming it. Claiming me.

I pant her name like a prayer, my forehead pressed to her shoulder, my entire body trembling.

And still, still, she keeps squeezing.

Every time she twitches around me, my cock pulses again, milking the aftershocks from me with cruel, beautiful precision. Like her body doesn't know how to stop taking from me. Like it doesn't want to.

Like it never fucking will.

"Fuck, Penelope," I rasp. "You're fucking unreal."

She whimpers softly, body still twitching with aftershocks.

I press a kiss to her mouth, then her temple, then her cheekbone. "You did so well."

She mumbles something I can't quite catch, so I move gently, slowly withdrawing from her body. We both flinch at the overstimulation. I carefully ease out the dildo next.

"Breathe, angel," I whisper, kissing the corner of her mouth again.

I pull her into my arms and settle us on our sides, her back to my chest, one arm slung under her neck, the other wrapped around her waist. I press kisses into her hair and stroke my hand over her belly, her hips, her thighs, calming her. Holding her together.

"You okay?" I murmur.

Her eyes flutter closed. "That was... intense."

I wrap the blanket around both of us and hold her tighter. "You're safe. I've got you, angel."

"Jamie," she murmurs sleepily.

"Hmm?"

"Thank you."

And fuck if that doesn't wreck me worse than anything else.

26

ARCHER'S POV

The fire snaps and spits like it's trying to get a word in. Sparks rise into the dark like they're escaping something. My fingers tap restlessly on the sun-warmed arm of the Adirondack chair, the wood still holding the heat from earlier even though the air's started to bite. Spencer leans forward and prods at the logs with a stick, his face tightening with concentration as he tries to coax more heat from the already roaring blaze.

"Pass the beer," I say to Liam, who doesn't even glance up from his phone. He just fishes one out of the cooler and lobs it toward me with frightening accuracy. It lands cold in my palm, condensation slick against my skin. I crack it open on the edge of the chair and take a long pull just as Jamie spears a marshmallow like he's prepping for surgery.

"She's really going as Lilith?" Sam asks. It's supposed to sound skeptical, maybe even judgy, but he's already grinning, his eyes giving him away.

I pull out my phone and reread Millie's text, though I've basically memorized it. *Shopping for costumes now. Penelope's giving a Lilith/sexy devil vibe. You guys better not let her down.*

"Yeah," I say, holding up the screen. "That's what Millie says. 'Sexy devil.' She also says we better not let Penelope down."

"God," Spencer groans, collapsing back into his chair like this isn't the best possible development. "Remember what she wore last year?"

Jamie makes a sound like someone kicked him in the chest. "I walked into a fucking wall because I couldn't stop staring."

"And told everyone you were drunk," Liam adds, laughing.

"Worth it," Jamie mutters, rotating the marshmallow with surgeon-level precision. It starts to brown, the Sugary scent catching on the air and tangling with the woodsmoke.

Pearl lets out a muffled bark in her sleep, curled up at Spencer's feet, her tag glinting gold in the firelight. One of her paws twitches, chasing dream-rabbits or ghosts or whatever dogs dream about. Spencer reaches down absently to scratch behind her ears without looking away from the fire.

I drain half the beer, feel it settle in my stomach like courage, and say the thing that's been lodged in the back of my throat for weeks. "I've been thinking about proposing."

Silence.

Like actual, full-on, someone-just-died silence. Even the fire quiets down. Just the occasional pop of sap and shifting of logs.

"To Penelope?" Liam finally asks, and his voice is tight, too tight. He's still holding his beer, but his knuckles are bone-white around it.

I roll my eyes. "No, Liam. To Pearl."

Jamie's marshmallow ignites like a signal flare, and he doesn't even blink. "When?"

"Before the masquerade party," I say, trying and failing to sound casual. My pulse is hammering so hard it feels like it's in my throat. "On the boat. At sunrise. She loves mornings like that."

Sam jolts upright, so fast he sloshes beer onto his jeans and doesn't even seem to notice. "Wait—what? No. You can't. I was going to propose."

"What?" Jamie and Spencer snap at the same time.

Liam sets his beer down. Carefully. Too carefully. The glass makes a dull thunk against the wood. "So was I."

"You're fucking kidding me," Jamie says, throwing his marshmallow stick in the fire and facing us. "I've had a ring for two weeks."

Spencer throws up his hands. "I've been planning for months!"

And then the five of us just sit there. Staring at each other like we're all trapped in a very niche, very chaotic sitcom where the central plot twist is that we've all independently decided to propose to the same woman.

Jamie breaks first, snorting, then full-on laughing. He's doubled over in seconds, gasping for air.

"We're all such idiots," he wheezes, wiping at his eyes. "Five proposals and not one of us thought to compare notes."

"To be fair," Spencer says, recovering enough to skewer a hot dog like nothing's happened, "there isn't a chapter in any relationship book for this."

"Yeah, because they don't write manuals for 'What to do when five guys fall in love with the same woman,'" I mutter, finishing my beer in one long pull.

"The logistics alone are going to be a nightmare," Sam says, but there's a smile playing at the corners of his mouth. "Five proposals in a row?"

"She'd think the first one was a joke," Liam says, rolling his empty bottle between his palms.

"And by the fifth, she'd be gone before the ring hit the floor," I finish.

There's a pause, and then all of us are laughing, too loud and too long, because what else can we do? Of course this is our life. Of course we're all here, falling apart under a sky full of stars and too much love for one girl who somehow makes room for all of us.

"So what now?" Spencer asks, his hot dog already blackening over the flame. "Fight to the death?"

I reach for another beer, the cold glass slick in my hand, and crack it open just to do something with my fingers. There's a flicker of firelight on the label, the quiet hiss of carbonation, the sound of five grown men pretending this isn't the strangest moment of their lives.

"What if we do it together?" I say. "Not at the same time. That would be weird. But, like, one after another."

Spencer's eyebrows shoot up, then drop into a thoughtful furrow. "A proposal pact," he says slowly. "I like it. Give her a week. One proposal a day. A proper romance marathon."

"I'm going first," he adds immediately, hand in the air like we're in fourth grade.

"Of course you are," Sam mutters, but he's already smiling.

"I'll go last," I offer, lifting my bottle in a lazy toast. "After you've all softened her up. Besides, I need time to get the boat ready."

"The boat," Sam repeats. He says it the way someone else might say *cliff ledge*. "You really think doing it out there is a good idea? What if she says no?"

"Then I drown myself," I say. "Kidding." I wipe my hand over my mouth. "Kinda."

Jamie snorts into his beer. "Nothing says 'forever' like your not-fiancé jumping into the lake out of sheer embarrassment."

"I'm sure it's better than your idea," I shoot back. "What was it again? Naked skydiving?"

"Bungee jumping," Jamie corrects, looking vaguely wounded. "And we'd be wearing clothes. Probably. Also that was before I knew I'd be proposing to Penelope."

"You're both insane," Liam says, shaking his head. "At least my idea won't give her a heart attack."

"Let me guess," Spencer says, grinning. "Something involving your hat and that Australian charm?"

Liam goes a little pink. "I was going to take her camping," he says. "Watch the stars. Tell her that's what it feels like when I'm with her."

There's a beat of silence before Jamie groans and looks up at the sky. "That's so good."

"What about you?" I ask Sam, suddenly curious what his introverted, stormy-silent mind has cooked up.

He fingers the chain around his neck, the one he never takes off. "I was thinking I'd recreate our first real conversation. When she asked why I was still here instead of going back to Oxford."

"When she told you you belonged here with us," Spencer says quietly.

Sam nods, gaze flicking toward the fire. "I'd take her to the restaurant, cook for her. Remind her that it's still true. That I belong with her."

For a second, no one says anything. The fire crackles, and Pearl lets out a long, dreamy sigh in her sleep.

"And you?" Liam asks Spencer, nudging him with his boot.

Spencer brightens. "Picnic. All her favorite snacky things. Ring in her wine glass. Simple."

"Classic," Jamie says approvingly.

"She'll love it," Sam adds.

I shift in my chair, the beer cold against my lips. "Don't forget we need to figure out what we're wearing to the masquerade," I remind them. "Since she's going as the devil, maybe we should coordinate?"

Spencer grins, practically vibrating. "Group theme?"

"The seven deadly sins," I say, and the idea clicks into place like a lock turning.

"Dibs on Wrath," Sam says without hesitation.

Jamie barks a laugh. "Obviously."

"Greed," Spencer says, reaching over to high-five Sam.

"That tracks," I say, taking a long pull from my beer.

He flips me off. I smile.

"I'll take Pride," Jamie says, flexing his biceps. "We all know I've got issues. Might as well roll with it."

"Suits you perfectly," Liam says, calmly ducking the marshmallow Jamie flicks at his head. "I suppose I'll take Envy then."

"Which leaves me with—" I start.

"Lust," Spencer says, pointing at me with a hot dog skewer. "It's perfect. Every time Pen is around you it's like all the air is sucked from the room."

"So it's settled," Sam says, raising his bottle. "The proposal plan and the sins."

We clink bottles, the glass ringing like bells in the quiet night. The fire has settled to a steady glow, casting long shadows across the yard. Above us, the first stars pierce the darkening sky, silent witnesses to our plan.

"You realize we're going to need five rings," Liam points out, reality dawning on him. "Five different rings that all suit her."

Spencer sits up straighter. "I've got a vintage emerald. From that antique place in Edinburgh."

"Sapphire," Sam says. "Matches her favorite sweater."

"Diamond," Jamie adds. "Classic."

"Opal," Liam murmurs. "Like her eyes when the sun hits them."

They all look at me.

I finish my beer before I say it. "Pearl."

There's a pause.

"Because of the dog," Jamie says, grinning. "You sentimental bastard."

"She's going to think we've lost our minds," I say, but there's laughter in my voice now.

"She already knows," Jamie replies, raising his bottle to me. "But she loves us anyway."

I look around the fire at these men who are somehow my brothers and my rivals and the only people who understand what it means to be in love with her, and feel something settle in my chest.

Maybe we've lost our minds, but somehow, it feels like we're right where we belong.

And then, like a scene change, the low rumble of Penelope's truck drifts up the gravel driveway.

Five grown men scramble to look casual as headlights sweep across the yard. Jamie shoves a marshmallow in his mouth. Sam suddenly becomes very interested in his phone. Liam pulls his hat lower over his eyes. Spencer tries to look like he's been tending the fire all along. And me? I just smile and wait for the woman we all love to fall into our arms.

27

___

I spot them through the bug-speckled windshield—the fire pit glowing like an altar, the five of them ringed around it in golden silhouettes. Firelight gilds their skin, their laughter still echoing like the last note of a song I've been trying to remember. A flash of scraggly fur bolts from between their chairs, all paws and momentum, barking so loud it cuts through the drone of the engine. Pearl barrels toward us like she's been shot from a cannon, tail a blur, ears flapping wildly with the sheer force of her joy.

Beer bottles glint in their hands, half-forgotten as they look toward the commotion. Toward me. Their profiles are all sharp angles and soft shadows, like they've been painted there by someone who knew what longing felt like.

And yeah—my chest aches.

Not the cute, fluttery kind. It's the deep kind, the full-body, maybe-I'll-cry kind. That warmth that pools just under your ribs and makes your fingers itch to touch something, anything. Someone. Them.

All five of them.

My men.

Millie reaches over and kills the engine just as Pearl slams into my door with a joyful bark that nearly sends her toppling. I don't move. I just sit there a second, letting it hit me, that stupid, overwhelming wave of want. Of belonging.

I haven't even stepped out of the car, and I already feel like I'm home.

I fumble the door open, the vodka sodas from earlier tilting the ground just slightly. My boots scrape the dirt, but my limbs are loose, relaxed, humming. I feel like a warm, woman-shaped cloud. A little slippery around the edges. Millie catches my elbow before I can face-plant into the gravel.

"Jesus, Pen," she mutters, steadying me like this isn't the third time tonight she's had to act as my human seatbelt.

I lean into her, giggling. "The vodka was medicinal."

She huffs a breath that smells like mint gum and judgment and links her arm through mine. "Just remember what we talked about."

I nod solemnly. "I will not spoil the Big Reveal."

"Damn right you won't." Her grin is sharp. "I want to see their faces when you come out in that outfit. If their jaws don't drop, then they better watch out."

"You're a menace," I whisper as we stumble toward the firelight.

She squeezes my hand. "It's why you love me."

By the time we're in range, Millie's voice goes full dramatic stage whisper. "Look what we have here—the brotherhood of the traveling girlfriend."

Spencer practically launches himself upright, nearly kicking over the cooler. Sam drops his phone like it bit him. Liam adjusts his hat so far down his face it's a miracle he can see anything at all. Jamie is clearly mid-chew and trying not to choke. Only Archer stays still, sipping his beer like a smug bastard, eyes locked on mine like he can see straight through the vodka haze and into the soft, needy place inside me.

"What did we interrupt?" I ask, dragging the moment out, watching their panic like a slow-motion replay.

"Nothing," they all say in terrifying unison.

Millie raises a brow. "Wow. That wasn't suspicious at all."

Five grown men try to look innocent. It's almost cute. If I didn't know better, I'd believe them. But I do. Know better. And them.

"Just guy talk," Jamie says, finally swallowing whatever was in his mouth. There's a smear of chocolate at the corner of his lips. I want to lick it off.

Millie hums. "Sure. Super believable."

Jamie catches my eye and smiles, slow and dark. "How was shopping?"

"Dangerous," Millie says with the smugness of someone who knows she's holding the match to a room soaked in gasoline. "Your girlfriend has a costume that's going to cause a riot."

"I'm okay with that," Jamie says, his voice dipping low. His eyes don't leave mine.

Millie flicks his ear. "You're not allowed to see it until the party." She gives my waist a squeeze and turns to go. "Try not to get her completely naked before midnight, gentlemen. She's got a few drinks in her and the decision-making skills of a concussed squirrel."

"You traitor," I hiss, swaying.

She blows me a kiss. "Text me tomorrow. I want every filthy detail."

Pearl barrels into me like a battering ram just as Millie disappears into the night, keys jingling. Her tail is a weapon of joy, her whole body vibrating as she presses her massive head into my stomach. I collapse to my knees, laughing as her tongue tries to claim every inch of exposed skin.

"Hi, baby," I murmur into her fur, soaking in the warmth and scent of her like she's some fuzzy emotional support animal. Which, frankly, she is. "Did you keep them in line?"

"She snored through most of our secrets," Spencer says, scratching under her chin. "Completely useless in a crisis."

Pearl groans like she agrees and flops dramatically at his feet.

I tilt my head back, catching the firelight, the sky above, the five very guilty-looking men circling me like gravity.

"I missed you," I say, the words slipping out before I can stop them. Honest. Raw. My voice catches a little at the end. "All of you."

"It's been six hours," Archer says softly, smiling behind the rim of his bottle.

"Six hours too long," I whisper, rising to my feet with exaggerated care. My body sings with the heat of their attention, every nerve awake, every part of me aware of the weight of their eyes, humming with tension.

I move slowly around the fire, the way you do when you're trying not to spook something—except what I'm circling is five men I'd happily let devour me whole. My body is humming with the electricity of being watched. Touched. Wanted.

Archer's the first.

He's standing completely still. He doesn't move. Doesn't breathe. Just watches me with that unreadable look he wears like armor. His beer's still in his hand, his jaw tight. But when I get close—close enough to feel the heat radiating off his body—his breath catches. Visibly. And that's all the invitation I need. I rise up on my toes and press my mouth to his, slow and sure, tasting beer and smoke and something distinctly him. It's not a greeting. It's a claim. His hand finds the small of my back like instinct, fingers flexing just enough to say he's not ready to let go, even when he does.

Liam is next, already tipping his hat back before I reach him, revealing those whiskey-colored eyes that make me feel hot and wild and soft all at once. He kisses me like he's memorizing me. Like he's afraid he might forget. His hands cradle my face, rough palms and careful thumbs, possessive in a way that turns my bones to jelly.

"Stop hogging her," Spencer groans, already reaching for me like a kid demanding his turn at a carnival ride.

I pull away from Liam with a soft laugh still tangled between our mouths. "Patience, Montgomery." I don't speed up. If anything, I slow down, taking measured, languid steps toward him, enjoying the way his posture shifts. His eyes darken, mouth twitching like he's holding back something feral.

When I finally step into his space, he doesn't waste a second. His kiss is eager and chaotic in the best way, messy and hungry and real. Like he's been holding his breath since I left and now he's inhaling me in greedy mouthfuls. He smells like pine and smoke and summer. His hands settle at my hips like they've been there a thousand times and plan to be a thousand more.

Jamie is already halfway out of his seat when I reach him, smiling like I've just made his entire week. His kiss is warm and sweet, all melted chocolate and marshmallow Sugar and the kind of affection that melts your defenses without asking permission. He pulls me in with one arm like he needs me close just to breathe properly.

"You're missing my peak marshmallow roasting performance," he informs me, totally serious.

"Can't wait to critique," I murmur, brushing a kiss to the corner of his mouth. He beams.

Sammy watches me the whole time. Unmoving. That unreadable, dark-eyed stare he does when he's thinking too much and feeling even more. When I finally turn toward him, his expression shifts—just barely—but I feel the change like a wave. That quiet intensity he wears like a second skin crackles around him.

"You saved me for last," he says softly. "Does that mean I get to keep you for the rest of the night?"

The words wrap around me like a chord drawn tight, humming in the space between us. I perch on his knee, every nerve alert and burning.

Before I can answer, Spencer appears in my periphery, crouching down beside me until we're eye to eye.

"Sugar," Spencer says, his face suddenly serious, tension radiating from him in nearly visible waves.

"Can I ask you something?"

"Of course." I study him, trying to figure out why he's acting weird. His body language has shifted, shoulders tight, jaw clenched in what looks suspiciously like nervousness, an emotion I've rarely seen from him.

"Would you like to go on a picnic with me tomorrow? Just the two of us."

"A picnic? I love picnics," I say, the alcohol making my voice come out breathy and bright.

"Perfect," he says, relief washing over his features, smoothing the worry lines between his brows. "I'll take care of everything. Can you be ready to go around two?"

But something still feels... off. The crease between his brows doesn't smooth as much as it should, and the way his hand drags through his hair screams nerves.

I squint at him. "Spencer Montgomery, are you up to something?"

"Me? No. Just... you know. Quality time. With snacks."

"Real subtle," Archer mutters without looking up, his tone dry enough to start a brushfire.

Spencer's glare snaps to Archer like a rubber band—fast, precise, and aimed to maim. If looks could kill, Archer would already be a pile of ash drifting into the fire pit.

Before I can ask what the hell that was about, Sam shifts beneath me and pulls me in like he's reclaiming territory.

"You looked cold," he murmurs, voice low, smile lazy and just a little wicked. One arm tightens around my waist while the other slides firmly across my thighs, anchoring me.

"I wasn't," I lie, but my body betrays me, curling into him without hesitation, like his heat's the only thing holding me together.

"Liar," he says, smiling into my hair. "Jamie," he calls out, "stop making heart eyes and make her a s'more."

Jamie blinks like he forgot anyone else existed. "Right. S'mores. One gourmet Sugar bomb coming up."

"I want one too," Archer calls, stretching out long-limbed toward the fire. The glow catches the edge of his glasses, the line of his jaw, the curve of his smirk.

"Make your own," Jamie shoots back, already threading marshmallows onto a stick with absurd precision.

"I only perform for the lady."

"Since when?" Liam asks, raising a skeptical eyebrow. His voice carries a teasing lilt that makes the corners of my mouth twitch upward.

Even in the low light, I can see Jamie blush. It starts at his throat and spreads like watercolor on wet paper—slow, unstoppable, beautiful. It climbs his cheeks, stains the tips of his ears, and makes something deep in my chest twist sweetly.

"Since I became a marshmallow artist," he says, holding Liam's gaze just a second too long. "It's a calling."

"It's warming Sugar on a stick," Archer deadpans without looking up.

"Blasphemy," Jamie shoots back, mock-offended but fighting a smile. He rotates the skewers like they're surgical tools, his attention laser-focused. "It's about timing. Temperature. The perfect golden crust—"

"Just admit you like playing with fire," Spencer cuts in, his voice low and suggestive, threading meaning beneath the words like a dare.

"That too," Jamie says with a shrug, too chipper to be innocent. "Pen, how's your costume coming? Millie was acting like it's a state secret."

"That's because it is." I smirk, letting the words hang between us like smoke, watching as five pairs of eyes immediately narrow with intrigue. "You'll see it when I'm making my grand entrance and not a second before."

"Tease," Spencer mutters.

"What about yours?" I ask, leaning into Sammy's chest as I scan the group. "Any hints?"

"Nope," Archer says, popping the p like a bullet casing. The finality in his voice is almost comical.

"Not a chance," Spencer adds, crossing his heart with exaggerated solemnity.

"Locked down," Liam says with a straight face that could bluff through a CIA interrogation.

"You'll just have to wait and see," Sammy murmurs against my ear. His voice is a gravel-soft promise, and I feel it everywhere—my neck, my stomach, between my thighs.

"You're all ridiculous," I say, but there's no real bite in it. Just warmth.

"Perfection!" Jamie announces, lifting his masterpiece for inspection like a prize-winning science fair project. The s'more is gorgeous. Edges sharp, chocolate glossy, marshmallow golden and slowly melting.

I take it reverently and bite. The chocolate and Sugar explode on my tongue, molten and too much in the best way, smearing across my lips and fingers. I let out a half-laugh, half-moan, trying to keep the mess from dripping down my chin.

"Here," Sammy says softly, catching a drip of marshmallow with his thumb. The world tilts slightly as his eyes lock with mine. He doesn't hesitate, just drags his tongue across the pad of his thumb, eyes locked on mine, like this is a game and I just lost the first round.

The heat in his eyes? That's got nothing to do with dessert.

"Good, right?" Jamie says, either oblivious or mercifully pretending to be.

I nod, still chewing, still recovering. "Mmm. It's incredible."

It comes out more sensual than intended, rich and breathy. Sammy's pupils dilate, his hand tightening on my waist.

"Knew it," Jamie says smugly. "Spencer, you're up."

And just like that, it turns into some unspoken war. Each guy tries to outdo the others. Spencer breaks out strawberries like a Food Network contestant. Liam gets creative with peanut butter. Archer presents a minimalist tower of dark chocolate and sea salt that looks like something off a restaurant menu called Fire & Stone.

By the fourth s'more, I'm a sticky mess—Sugar coating my lips, laughter in my chest, and no room left in my stomach, but still saying yes every time someone offers "just one more." They hover around me with gentle competitiveness, their hands brushing mine, eyes warm and fond and hungry all at once. I let myself bask in it. Let myself take.

The fire's gone from leaping to low, the logs collapsing inward with slow, rhythmic sighs. The night stretches around us like a soft exhale, velvet-dark and star-scattered. Fireflies blink at the edge of the trees, tiny pulsing lights like the universe is applauding quietly from the sidelines.

Pearl ambles over and flops across my feet with a groan, her weight anchoring me to this moment. The smell of woodsmoke clings to my skin. My lips are sweet. My whole body feels like it's wrapped in warmth and touch and affection that runs deeper than I know what to do with.

A yawn escapes before I can stop it. Not a dainty one, either. Full-body, jaw-stretching, soul-leaving-my-body kind of yawn.

"Bedtime for Penelope," Archer says, glancing at his watch. "Nearly midnight."

"I'm not tired," I say automatically.

Another yawn ambushes me before I even finish the lie.

"Very convincing," Liam murmurs, his smile soft around the edges.

"I'll walk you up," Sammy says, his voice pitched low enough that it curls right around my spine.

The guys trade glances, the kind that carry whole conversations I'm not invited to hear. Some silent relay of understanding. Sammy's arms tighten just a little, like he's bracing against something or claiming something.

"Hey, Sam," Spencer says slowly, his voice stretched with unspoken layers. "Don't forget about that thing tomorrow."

Sammy just nods. Doesn't speak. Just curls his fingers into my side —subtle, certain. A quiet claim. *She's with me tonight.*

The others don't say anything either. They just move. Bottles get gathered. The fire hisses into silence. Marshmallows are packed away. It's practiced, wordless, like muscle memory. Domestic. Familiar. Weirdly intimate. Five men moving in orbit around me, and suddenly I realize—I'm the thing they're circling. The gravity they're tethered to.

Inside, they say goodnight like a ritual.

Archer presses a kiss to my temple, murmuring something unintelligible. Liam takes my hand and lifts it to his lips, lingering there for a beat. Spencer cradles my face like it's a thing he can't let go of just yet, brushing his mouth over mine before reluctantly releasing me. And Jamie—Jamie hugs me like he means it. Like he always means it. Like he doesn't know how to hold anything back.

And then it's just Sammy, quiet and unreadable, our fingers locked as he walks me toward the bedroom with something coiled and waiting in the space between us.

He closes the door behind us and doesn't say anything at first. Just watches me.

Then, finally: "Let me sleep with you tonight."

I blink. "Sam—"

"I don't care if it's just sleep," he says quickly, words tripping over each other. "I just want to hold you. I need to hold you."

"I was gone for six hours," I remind him, cupping his face between my hands.

He looks at me, raw and sincere. "We haven't been alone in a while."

There's something in his voice, something that slices clean through my buzz. I rise onto my toes, still wobbly, and kiss him. A soft thing. A yes in the shape of my mouth on his.

He smiles, and it's so full of relief it knocks the breath out of me.

"I don't deserve you," I whisper before I can stop myself.

"No," he agrees, grinning. "You deserve better. But you're stuck with us."

He tugs me toward the bed, and I go easily, eagerly, folding into the curve of him, into the quiet, into the steady drum of his heartbeat against my back.

Tomorrow, whatever they're planning will unfold.

But tonight, it's just this.

The echo of laughter still in the walls. The smell of Sugar and smoke in my hair. Five men's fingerprints on my skin in five different ways. And the slow, certain realization that somehow, impossibly, this is home.

28

———————

The kitchen smells like cinnamon and coffee when I stumble in the next morning, hair sticking up in a million different directions, eyes squinting against the bright morning light pouring through the windows.

Spencer's already moving around the small space, an unusual amount of spring in his step for this early in the morning. He moves like he's lived here for years, like the place was built to fit him. His bare feet are silent on the cold tile, his back to me as he stretches toward the upper cabinet. His shirt, a soft gray thing worn thin at the seams, clings to him in all the right places and rides up just enough to reveal a strip of tanned skin and the carved dip of his lower back. For a second, I forget how to breathe.

He hums low under his breath, something soulful and slow, and my body responds before I can name the tune, hips shifting, thighs pressing tighter together. His voice is still rough with sleep when he says, "Morning, Sugar," without turning around.

God, that voice.

"How did you know it was me?" I ask, sinking into one of the mismatched kitchen chairs, the ancient wood groaning beneath me.

My legs are bare, still warm from the blankets I didn't want to leave, and the worn seat chills the backs of my thighs.

Spencer glances over his shoulder, eyes sparkling like a trick of the light, and the grin he gives me hits with the force of a body shot. "I always know when it's you."

That—whatever that is in his voice—blooms in my chest like a sunrise. I duck my head, pretend to scratch Pearl behind the ears as she wanders over, her giant head landing in my lap with a sigh that smells vaguely like kibble and grass.

I finally look up. "What's all this?"

The table is absolute chaos. Flour dusts everything like new snow. Crushed berries leak their color across the cutting board, red and rich and messy. Honey glints gold in its jar. Eggs wait, lined up like little soldiers.

"Breakfast," Spencer says, shrugging like he's not doing anything special. But something shifts. The easy curve of his shoulders stiffens, the way he measures out the flour too exact, too focused. There's a little line between his brows now, his lip caught between his teeth.

"Thought I'd make us breakfast before we go on our picnic," he adds, voice softer. He doesn't look at me.

And now I'm frowning. "Are you okay?"

His eyes flick up. Another smile, but this one doesn't quite make it past his mouth. "Fine. Just thinking about the weather."

I follow his gaze out the window. Blue skies stretch endless, the kind that make you forget storms exist. "Looks clear to me."

He reaches for a whisk, gripping it like it insulted him. "It's supposed to rain this afternoon."

"We could go another day."

"No." He says it too fast. "We need to go today."

The metal clinks too hard against the bowl as he mixes. His knuckles are white.

"I've got a backup plan," he adds quickly. "Don't worry."

"Spencer—"

"Do you want blueberries or strawberries in your pancakes?" he cuts in, desperate for a diversion. "I have both. And maple syrup. The real stuff, not that fake corn syrup garbage."

I study him. His hair is still damp from the shower, curling a little at the ends where it's gotten too long. There's a smudge of flour on his cheek I want to wipe with my thumb, but something about the tightness in his jaw keeps me still.

He doesn't want to talk. Not really. And trying to get Spencer to open up when he's not ready is like trying to pry open a clam with a spoon.

"Strawberries," I say instead, letting him have this small win. "And tea. Strong. Possibly criminally over-steeped."

He exhales, some of the tightness leaving his shoulders. "Kettle's already hot."

I rise to pour myself a mug, adding cream and Sugar until it barely qualifies as tea. When I settle back at the table, Spencer's back in motion—pouring batter onto the griddle, humming again. I can't look away. The careful way he moves, the clean sweep of his arm, the way his forearms flex when he flips the first pancake.

"Where is everyone?" I ask. It's only just hitting me how quiet the house is. No thudding footsteps, no overlapping voices or laughter down the hall.

"Out," he says, too vaguely. "Errands. Stuff."

"Stuff," I echo, raising an eyebrow.

"Just... the usual." His ears go pink.

My suspicion rises, sharp and hot behind my ribs, but before I can say anything else, he sets a plate down in front of me—golden pancakes bleeding red from the strawberries, a pat of butter melting into them like something from a food magazine shoot.

"Eat up, Sugar," he murmurs. His voice is low, steady. But his eyes— his eyes are soft in a way that makes me ache. "We've got a big day ahead of us."

And suddenly, I know whatever's coming... it's not about the rain. It's about something bigger. Something he's been building up to for days—maybe weeks. And I'm not sure if my heart is racing because I'm nervous, or because I'm hoping like hell I'm right.

~

By the time the old pickup jolts over the fourth pothole in under a minute, I've stopped flinching. The suspension makes a sound like it's begging for mercy, and I swear I can feel the metal bones of this thing groaning beneath us, but Spencer just keeps one hand steady on the wheel, the other drumming a rhythm against his thigh that doesn't match the radio or his usual easy calm.

The seat has molded to my body after all these years, cracked leather softened by time, the springs no longer jabbing me like they used to. It's still too hot where my thighs stick to it, and I can't tell if the heat between us is from the sun or from something else entirely, something tighter, more coiled. The kind of tension that feels like a held breath stretched too thin.

Outside the window, the sky's shifted. What was bright blue this morning has deepened to a steely gray, clouds stacking in layers like a storm's gathering an audience.

I shift, tuck a leg under myself, and finally ask, "Are you going to tell me where we're going?"

He doesn't look at me. His jaw ticks as he stares at the winding road ahead, green fields and weather-worn barns flying past. "It's a surprise."

"You know I hate surprises," I say, even though we both know that's only half true. I hate not knowing. I don't hate this—him, driving us toward something he thinks I'll love.

"You'll like this one," he says. His voice is quiet, sure. He glances over and smiles, grabbing my hand. His palm is warm and a little damp, nerves betraying him even though his words don't. He doesn't squeeze, just holds on like the contact is anchoring him.

Then we leave the pavement behind, turning onto a narrow dirt lane where trees arch overhead, their branches laced together like clasped hands. The air shifts, cooler now, tinged with the scent of rain-soaked earth and something green and alive. Spencer eases off the gas. The tires crackle over gravel and fallen twigs, and something in my chest tightens, slow and hot—anticipation blooming low in my belly like it's been waiting for this moment all day.

The trees fall away without warning, and the world opens.

Color explodes across the meadow. Wildflowers in every shade imaginable, tangled and reckless, like nature stopped following rules out here. Deep violet thistles. Yellow so bright it feels electric. Pale blues and soft pinks threaded through knee-high grasses that bend and shimmer with every breath of wind.

The air is thick with scent—sweet clover, something warm and green, the sharp mineral tang of water nearby. My lungs pull it in greedily, like I've never really breathed before.

Then I see the lake.

Wide and still and impossibly clear, it stretches out in front of us, light skating across the surface like molten silver. Ripples shift across the top in slow, hypnotic circles. And at its edge, a willow tree leans out over the bank—massive and draped in long curtains of green that trail into the water like fingertips.

It's quiet here. Not empty, but full, with the rustle of grass, the soft pulse of the breeze, the occasional creak of a branch above, and bird-song that threads through it all like a melody only this place remembers. Every sound lands softly, like it knows how precious the stillness is.

"Spencer..." I don't even know what I'm trying to say.

He cuts the engine, watches my face instead of the view. "I found it a couple weeks ago. Took a wrong turn and ended up here." He shrugs like he didn't just deliver a perfect fairytale. "Thought it'd be perfect for a picnic."

He jumps out of the truck, and before I can even reach for the handle, he's already there, sliding across the hood like he's auditioning for a movie he doesn't know he's already starring in. The first time he opened my door like that, all casual swagger and old-school chivalry, I'd just stared at him, stunned into silence. Now, it feels like second nature. A quiet ritual I never asked for but somehow came to rely on, folded seamlessly into who he is.

He raises an eyebrow, mouth tilting into that crooked half-grin. "What? Can't a guy be a gentleman once in a while?"

"You're always a gentleman," I murmur, sliding my hand into his, the warmth of him grounding me as I hop down from the truck. "Even when you're copping a feel."

His hand drops to my ass with a dramatic flourish. "Especially then," he says, squeezing, flashing me a grin. "It's just good manners."

Laughter bubbles up at the sheer joy of it, of him. The sound echoes across the meadow, free and unbothered.

"Emily Post would disagree," I say, still giggling as I brush a ladybug off my leg.

"Emily Post didn't have an ass like yours," he replies, fingers trailing down with one last squeeze before he forces himself to let go.

He grabs the picnic basket, his shoulder brushing mine, heat flaring again in that small space between skin and cotton. My heart stumbles over itself.

"Come on, Sugar," he says, taking my hand again. "Let's get set up before the sky decides to crash down on us."

The meadow parts around us as we walk, boots sinking into the soft earth. The scent of crushed grass rises with each step, the flowers leaning in as if listening. Wind tugs at my hair. There's a charge in the air now—lightning close but not quite here.

He stops at the edge of the lake, right beneath the weeping willow. Its branches sway like curtains caught in a draft, draping around us like a secret.

"Here," he says, and there's something quiet in it, like he's trying not to make a big deal out of a big deal.

He spreads the blanket with a practiced flick, red and white checkers bright against the green. It looks almost too vivid, too cinematic, but I sit anyway, the fabric soft and cool beneath me.

"It's beautiful," I say, and I mean it. The view. The quiet. The wildness. Him.

He watches me like I'm the thing worth looking at. "Wait till you see what I packed."

The picnic basket is ridiculous in the best possible way. Spencer pulls out one thing after another like he's unveiling a magician's act: freshly baked bread, its golden crust cracking beneath my fingers; creamy cheese that smells a little like feet but melts like butter on my tongue; berries so ripe they burst the second I bite down, staining my fingers and lips. Chocolate truffles nestled in delicate paper wrappers, each one glossy and dark like something from a patisserie in Paris. Everything tastes like indulgence.

Then he pulls out a bottle of champagne. Not grocery store bubbly —champagne, the real deal. The label alone looks expensive. My eyebrows lift before I can stop them.

Spencer doesn't meet my eyes. "Special occasion," he says with a shrug, like he's trying to make it sound casual. He twists the cage off the cork, the bottle cold and sweating in his hand, and pours into two crystal flutes he pulls from the basket. The champagne fizzes wildly at the rim. His hand trembles slightly. A few drops spill over.

I take the one he offers, the stem cool between my fingers. "What's the occasion?"

"Do I need an occasion to spoil my girl?" he asks, but there's something off in his voice, a rough edge that doesn't match the words. His mouth curves into a smile, but it doesn't hold. I can see it in the tension around his eyes, in the way his thumb keeps tapping against his knee.

I don't push. Not yet. I just take a sip. The champagne is dry and sharp, bubbles rushing across my tongue like static.

We eat in easy silence, the kind that only comes from knowing someone too well to need to fill space. The food is obscenely good. Of course it is. Spencer has always had this uncanny instinct for pairing flavors, like his taste buds are better at communicating than most people.

"This is incredible," I say, licking berry juice from the corner of my mouth as I reach for another truffle. Its shell cracks beneath my teeth, releasing something rich and dark and sinful. "Thank you for bringing me here."

His smile flickers again, slower this time, soft around the edges. There's something naked in his eyes that makes my chest ache. Like looking at someone mid-fall, right before they hit the ground. "Anything for you, Sugar."

The breeze shifts. It sneaks through the willow's curtain, brushing against my bare arms and lifting the ends of the blanket beneath us. The surface of the lake ripples, chased by wind, and a sudden gust carries the first faint rumble of thunder. When I look up, the sky beyond the branches has darkened to a heavy, smoky gray.

"We should probably head back," I say, even though I don't want to. "Storm's moving fast."

"Not yet." His voice tightens. It's barely more than a breath. "There's one more thing."

He reaches for my glass. Our fingers touch, and it's not just contact, it's electric. The kind that buzzes in your bones. He sets both flutes aside, his movements careful, like he's afraid if he shifts too quickly, the whole moment might shatter.

"Spencer?" I ask, pulse skipping.

He exhales, rough and shaky, then drags a hand through his hair. It sticks up wildly afterward, and he doesn't bother fixing it. "I've been practicing this speech for weeks," he says. "Wrote it all down. Revised it like a hundred times. Sounded great in my head. But now that you're here, now that we're here, I can't remember a single damn word."

My heart climbs into my throat, pounding like a bass drum.

"I just..." His voice cracks, but he pushes through. "Before you, life was fine. It was routine. Work, sleep, rinse and repeat. I thought I was happy, or close enough to it. But looking back now, it feels like I was just going through the motions. Like everything was muted. Gray. Forgettable."

A raindrop lands on my forearm, cold as glass. I barely notice.

"Then you came along," he continues, his eyes locked on mine like he's afraid I'll disappear if he blinks. "With your coveralls and those ridiculous chicken boots. And suddenly, everything turned up to full volume. Food tasted better. Music made sense. The world felt brighter. Like I'd been asleep and didn't even know it."

The rain comes faster now, soft at first, a scattered rhythm on the blanket, the basket, our skin. But he doesn't seem to notice. Neither do I.

"This isn't exactly traditional," he says. "The five of us and you. I know it doesn't make sense to most people. But it makes sense to me. Because you're the thing that ties us all together. You're what makes it home."

Lightning flares in the distance, white-hot and brief, catching the sharp line of his jaw, the rawness in his expression. Thunder follows close behind, a low boom that vibrates in my chest.

"I had this whole thing planned," he says, raising his voice over the growing storm. "Candlelight, sunset, the works. But I should've known better. Nothing ever goes according to plan with you. And that's what I love about it. About you. You take the mess, the chaos, the things that don't fit—and you make them beautiful."

The rain starts to fall harder, soaking through my jeans, plastering my hair to my temples. Still, I don't move. Neither does he.

There's something in the air now. Thicker than the rain. Heavier than the storm.

And I know, without him saying the words, exactly what he's about to do.

The rain has fully committed now. Not a drizzle, not a romantic little sprinkle. It falls in sheets, steady and cold, soaking straight through our clothes like we're standing beneath a faucet turned all the way up. My hair clings to my face, heavy and wet, and Spencer's shirt is plastered to his chest, outlining every hard line, every breath he takes. Water drips from his jaw, from his lashes, from the tip of his nose. He looks like some half-wild, storm-swept version of himself. And somehow, it's the most him he's ever looked. No pretense. No swagger. Just Spencer. Raw and real and absolutely undone.

"Spencer—" I start, but he cuts me off with a glance. One of those rare, loaded ones that makes everything inside me go quiet.

"Let me finish," he says, his voice low and shaking, his eyes not quite steady. He reaches into his pocket, and something in my chest locks tight.

"Before I lose my nerve," he adds, "and end up just fucking kissing you instead."

My breath catches in a way that feels like it might never start again. Time doesn't slow so much as it narrows—tightens until the only things in the world are Spencer, the rain, and the small velvet box he pulls out, deep blue and already soaked through with water. His hand trembles as he holds it out, the lid still closed. He looks like he's trying not to fall apart.

"Penelope." My name cracks in his throat. "I love you. I love you more than I knew it was possible to love anyone. And I know this... us... it's not exactly in any handbook. But I want it. I want all of it. I want you. I want to be yours in every way a person can belong to another."

He opens the box.

Inside is a ring, an antique emerald ring, oval cut, circled by tiny diamonds that catch the gray light and scatter it like green fire. It's not flashy, not modern, not cookie-cutter. It's perfect. Like he reached into my soul and pulled out the exact thing I would've chosen for myself. Worn and wild and true.

"Will you marry me?" he asks. His voice is barely louder than the rain, but it's all I can hear. "Will you be my wife? Will you let me spend the rest of my life trying to make you as happy as you make me?"

My mouth opens. Closes. Opens again. No words come. I can't speak. I can't breathe. I'm just staring at him, at the man who somehow sees all of me and still wants in.

"Yes," I whisper, but it's not enough. I find my voice and shout over the rain. "Yes. Absolutely fucking yes."

He exhales like he's been holding his breath for hours. His smile splits his face wide open, relief and joy all tangled up. He slides the ring onto my finger, the metal cool against my skin before it warms. It fits perfectly, like it's been waiting for me all this time.

Then his arms are around me, sudden and sure, hauling me against his chest like he can't stand another second of space between us. I barely have time to gasp before his mouth finds mine, and the world just—falls away.

The kiss is everything.

It's rain-slicked and hungry and trembling at the edges. His lips are warm against mine, tasting like champagne and laughter and raindrops. His hands cradle my face like I'm something fragile, but his mouth is anything but gentle, devouring, aching, desperate. Like he's pouring every unspoken word, every year of loneliness, every ounce of love he didn't know what to do with until now, into this kiss.

I melt into him. I drown in him.

My fingers fist in the back of his soaked shirt, clinging like I'm afraid this is a dream that'll vanish when I blink. Water runs down our faces, slides between our mouths, makes everything slippery and impossibly alive. He kisses me like he's making a promise with every press of his lips, like he's writing vows into my skin with the soft scrape of his stubble and the press of his fingertips.

When he lifts me off the ground, I smile against his lips, my feet kicking into empty air, the world spinning as he turns us in a circle, rain washing over us like confetti. I laugh through the kiss, unsteady and lightheaded and wrecked by happiness.

Eventually, he sets me down—slow, careful, like he's afraid I'll float away if he lets go too fast. We're soaked and breathless and tangled in each other's arms, hearts thudding in sync. The rain is still falling, softer now. I pull back just enough to see his face, rain dripping from his lashes, his lips swollen, his eyes full of everything.

I lift my hand between us, blinking water from my eyes to watch the emerald catch the storm light—deep green and flickering.

"It's beautiful," I say, voice catching on the word. "Perfect."

"You're beautiful," he murmurs, brushing wet hair off my cheek. "Even soaking wet and shivering."

I look down at the ring. At him. At the storm crashing around us and the meadow soaking at our feet. And all I feel is right. This is mine. This is us.

"You're turning blue," he says, running his hands over my arms, trying to warm me up. "We should head back."

"Not yet," I say, grinning as a wicked little idea sparks in my chest. "I think we should celebrate first."

"How?" he asks, brows lifting with suspicion just a second before I tug my shirt over my head.

"Swimming," I announce, stepping out of my wet jeans with zero coordination, hopping on one foot, laughing as I almost fall flat on my face. "You coming?"

Spencer just stands there, dripping, open-mouthed, watching me strip like he's seeing sunlight for the first time.

"Fuck," he breathes, barely audible over the rain, like the word is punched straight out of his lungs.

I don't wait. I turn and walk toward the lake, water sheeting off my skin in silvery rivulets. The cold hits like a dare, like the sky challenging me to feel everything all at once. My bare feet sink into the mud, soft and thick, and I keep going, slipping beneath the willow's draping green and stepping into the lake's waiting arms.

The water is brutal—icy and alive, biting at my calves, my thighs, my waist. I gasp as it climbs higher, curling over my ribs, lapping at my chest like a shock to the system. It steals my breath and gives it back in shivers. But I keep moving, heart hammering, lungs burning, skin buzzing.

When I turn around, he's still on the shore, rooted beneath the willow like he's forgotten how his body works.

"Are you coming in or what?" I call, sweeping wet hair from my eyes, my voice rough with adrenaline and dare.

That's all it takes. His paralysis cracks.

He moves fast, stripping with zero finesse. Shirt off in one motion, jeans shoved down, boxers flung into the grass. Every muscle is defined in the gray light, slicked with rain, his chest heaving like he's just sprinted a mile. His body is solid and familiar and still somehow manages to floor me. His desire is blatant, proud, curved against the line of his thigh even in the cold, and the look on his face—half disbelief, half raw hunger—burns hotter than anything.

He wades in, muttering curses with every step, teeth clenched, muscles tensing against the cold like his body can't decide if it wants to fight or flee. But then he reaches me. And wraps himself around me.

His arms slide around my waist, pulling me flush against him. The heat of his skin feels unreal in the freezing water, like he's burning from the inside out just for me.

"I can't believe you talked me into this," he says, voice breathless with laughter. His nose brushes mine, and there's rain on his lips when he kisses me. "You're insane."

"You love it," I murmur, locking my arms around his neck, my legs slipping up around his waist. I'm weightless in the water, in him.

"I love you," he says, no teasing this time. Just truth. Bare and shivering and real. "God, I love you so much it scares the shit out of me."

My throat tightens. I don't have words for what that does to me, how it lands right at the center of my chest like something that belongs there. So I kiss him.

Hard.

His mouth is wet and warm, his tongue sliding against mine like he's trying to carve the memory of this moment into every nerve ending. I move against him without thinking, my body greedy, alive, pressed tight to the solid length of him. He groans into my mouth, deep and guttural, and I feel it everywhere.

"We should go back to shore," I whisper, forehead pressed to his, breath shallow and tangled. "Before we attempt to fuck in this ice bath and I die mid-thrust from exposure."

"Good call," he says, his voice wrecked and full of everything we haven't done yet. "Because I really, really want to make love to my fiancée for the first time, and I'd prefer not to do it while my dick's at risk of frostbite."

I snort, laugh, kiss him again like I can't help myself—which I can't. He tastes like rain and triumph and something new and big and terrifyingly permanent.

"Take me home, Spencer."

He grins, wide and breathless, dimples flashing like floodlights in the rain. It's the kind of look that could knock the wind out of me if he wasn't already holding me upright. He looks so young and so certain at the same time, like he's seeing the rest of his life unfold right in front of him and is stupidly, wildly in love with every second of it.

His arms tighten around me, and he starts toward shore, water dragging at his legs, storm still crackling in the distance like applause that hasn't died down. Rain traces our faces, our shoulders, fills in every space between us. I cling to him with limbs gone boneless, head tucked against his throat, feeling the thrum of his pulse like a promise.

The moment our feet hit the shoreline, we burst into motion.

We stumble into the half-collapsed picnic setup, everything soaked and sagging, the blanket waterlogged and slick. My clothes are a crumpled pile of denim and cotton, half-buried under the willow's swaying branches.

"God, we're going to catch something," I say through laughter, peeling my underwear from a puddle and stepping into them with a wince.

"I'm catching feelings," Spencer deadpans, winking as he drags his boxers up with exaggerated care. "Real terminal stuff."

I bark out a laugh, shivering as I yank my bra on and fumble with the hooks. My teeth chatter. My fingers are useless. "Pretty sure there isn't a cure for that."

"Oh no," he says solemnly, crouching to gather everything—clothes, the champagne flutes, the leftover truffles sliding in their box. "Guess we're doomed."

We shove everything haphazardly into the basket—blanket, food, bottle still half full. It's all dripping. Ruined. Perfect. My shoes squish when I step into them. We're both soaked to the bone, adrenaline crashing hard and fast now that the moment's winding down.

Spencer hands me the basket and before I can roll my eyes, he scoops me up like it's nothing.

"Spencer!" I squeal, clutching the handle with one hand and his shoulders with the other, legs swinging out uselessly.

"What?" he says, already turning. "You said take you home."

Then he takes off running.

Full sprint.

Barefoot.

Through the wet meadow and the slick grass and the pounding rain, me in his arms, basket jostling against my side, my laughter spilling out of me in great, gasping bursts.

The wind lashes at us. My hair flies into my face. The willow fades behind us like the final frame of a fairytale. His feet slap the ground, each step messy and reckless and beautiful.

"God, you're insane!" I shout, grinning so wide my cheeks ache.

We make it to the truck, breathless and soaked, completely out of control and completely in love.

.   .   .

Spencer fumbles with the handle, swearing under his breath before he finally gets the truck door open and practically hauls me inside like a shipwrecked survivor dragging their last lifeline to shore. I clamber across the bench seat, legs slippery, skin icy, leaving behind smears of lake water. Every inch of me shakes. The wind howls outside like we stole something from it.

Spencer dives in behind me and slams the door shut. The storm vanishes like someone pulled a curtain tight. Just us now. Our breaths fog up the windows almost instantly, painting the cab in soft white streaks and turning it into a cocoon of heat and heartbeat.

"Jesus fucking Christ," Spencer gasps, blue-lipped and shivering as he jams the key in and turns the ignition. The engine coughs to life. "That was the dumbest, coldest, most—"

"Most fun," I cut in through chattering teeth. "Admit it."

He turns his head, water dripping from his hair and tracking down his cheekbones. His eyes find mine, and whatever reprimand he had queued up disappears, replaced by something warm. Something soft.

"Yeah," he breathes, and leans in to brush a soaked strand of hair from my face. "Most fun I've ever had risking pneumonia and permanent testicular damage."

I laugh, sharp and bright and utterly uncontained, the sound echoing off the fogged glass. The emerald on my finger flares under the cab light, throwing shards of green into the haze, and joy surges up so fast it almost chokes me.

"Come here," he murmurs, arms opening.

I don't hesitate. I slide back across the seat and fold into him, skin meeting skin with a sharp, startled hiss. We gasp in unison. Every inch of us is freezing, but we cling to each other like body heat alone could rewrite biology. The heater hums to life, slowly filling the space with warmth, pushing the chill back into the corners.

"You okay?" he whispers, lips brushing my temple.

"Getting there," I breathe, pressing closer. His chest is still damp, still cold, but it's him. Solid. Safe. Mine.

I look up and find him already watching me, eyes dark and focused, as if he's memorizing everything—every droplet of rain, every quiver of my mouth. He leans in and kisses me.

It starts gentle, like a question. But my answer is all urgency.

I press forward, parting my lips, and the kiss deepens in a heartbeat. It tastes like rain and champagne and the impossible certainty that he's mine and I'm his and this is happening. Now. Here. On the bench seat of a fogged-up truck after a proposal in the middle of a storm.

His hands find my waist first, anchoring me like he needs to feel something solid. Then they slide upward, slow and careful, fingers skimming over soaked skin and the goosebumps rising beneath it. I'm already leaning into him by the time his thumbs graze the curve of my breasts, and the breath that stutters out of me fogs the window beside us.

The touch turns exploratory—careful but confident, like he knows exactly where he's going and still wants to rediscover every inch. Everything feels heightened, electric. Familiar territory rewritten in a new language. When his palms cup me fully, heat races through my bloodstream and spills outward, and I can't help the small, helpless sound that escapes my mouth.

"Spencer," I whisper, the word coming out rough, barely formed. I reach for him, one hand dragging down his chest, fingers grazing the damp trail of hair that disappears beneath the waistband of his boxers.

He exhales sharply. "Fuck, Sugar." His voice cracks around the nickname, accent thick with want. "Give me one second, or this is gonna be very, very short-lived."

Before I can tease him, he reaches beside the seat, flips a lever, and the whole bench tips backward with a groan that sounds suspiciously like me. Then he's hovering over me, rain-dark hair dripping onto my collarbone, eyes pinned to my lips like he's starving.

"I want my mouth on your pussy," he growls against my throat, his lips trailing heat down the curve of my neck, breath like fire against my rain-chilled skin. "Been hard all fucking day thinking about how you'd taste."

"God—please," I breathe, the word barely formed, my fingers already buried in his hair, tugging him down, my hips lifting like I've been waiting for this exact moment since the second we got in the truck.

He doesn't rush.

He kisses his way down, teeth grazing just enough to send sparks skipping beneath my skin, each one chasing the next. When he reaches the waistband of my soaked underwear, he pauses, eyes flicking up to mine like he wants to see me fall apart from the inside out.

Then he slides them down, slow and careful, the wet fabric clinging to my thighs before surrendering. His knuckles brush my skin, and the whole motion is so unbearably intimate I forget how to breathe.

His hands grip my hips, firm and grounding, before he settles between my thighs and breathes me in like it's his first full breath all day. Then his tongue flicks against me, slow and sure, and my whole body arches off the seat like I've been struck by lightning.

I cry out—his name, I think—and he groans against me, like he needs this as badly as I do.

He takes his time. Alternates teasing and giving. One finger inside me. Then two. Curled just right. His tongue never stops, never lets up. I'm shaking, begging, on fire. My thighs tremble around his head, heels pressed into the seat for leverage.

"That's it," he growls against me, voice thick with hunger, the vibration dragging another cry from my throat. "Come on my tongue, Penelope. I want to feel you fall apart for me."

The way he says my name, low and passionate and wrecked, pushes me right over the edge.

I come hard, every muscle locking, my hands fisting in his hair, my back arching as I fall apart around him. He holds me through it, relentless and soft all at once, coaxing every last ripple from me until I'm gasping and boneless and completely shattered in the best way.

When I open my eyes, he's watching me like I've just rewritten the rules of the universe. His lips are swollen, slick with me, curved in a smile that's too full of awe to be casual, too soft to be cocky.

"You back with me, Sugar?" he asks, voice hoarse, mouth slick as he swipes it with the back of his hand.

"Barely," I manage, my voice ragged and wrecked. "Jesus... where the hell did you learn to do that?"

He starts crawling back up my body, kissing a trail over my stomach, the space between my breasts, the slope of my throat. Each one lands soft and slow, like he's savoring what he just did to me. "That's classified information," he murmurs against my skin, smiling. "But I'd be happy to go over the method again. For peer review."

I laugh, the sound half-broken, half-dazed. My body still hasn't caught up. "Science, huh?"

"Mmhmm." His mouth finds the base of my jaw. "I take my research very seriously."

"I can tell." My hands skate down his back, tracing muscle and damp skin, heat building again in low, lazy waves. "But I think it's time for a new experiment."

His breath catches as my fingers trail over the hard line of his cock, dragging slow, teasing strokes over the wet fabric of his boxers.

"What kind of experiment did you have in mind?" he asks, his voice dropping low.

Rain drums against the roof in a steady rhythm as I push him back and swing a leg over his lap. His pupils blow wide. I feel him twitch beneath me.

"The kind where I'm in charge," I whisper, grinding down just enough to make him curse. "Any objections?"

His hands clamp around my hips, fingers flexing. "Not one," he breathes, staring up at me like I'm both miracle and torment. "The lab is yours, Dr. Penelope."

I kiss him, hard, swallowing the low groan that rumbles from his chest. His mouth is hot, hungry, all tongue and teeth and open want. There's something addictive about the way he gives in, how this man —this gorgeous, insufferable man—surrenders completely, lets me take control and make him unravel.

My hands roam his chest, tracing each muscle, the rise and fall of his breath. I kiss down the line of hair that disappears beneath his waistband, and when I palm him through his boxers, he bucks beneath me, breath hitching like it's being yanked out of him.

"These need to go," I mutter, tugging at the soaked waistband. He lifts his hips without question, and we peel them off together, damp cotton dragging over his thighs.

When he's finally bare, I pause, just for a second. To look. To take him in. Strong thighs, flushed skin, cock heavy and hard and already leaking for me. The sight sucks the air right out of my lungs.

"You're thinking too hard," Spencer pants, watching me stroke him slowly, each movement coaxing another twitch from his hips. "I can practically hear it."

"Just admiring the view." I lean down, press a kiss to his chest, his skin tasting like rain and heat and something entirely his. "And thinking about how goddamn lucky I am."

He cups my face, eyes locked on mine with so much intensity it steals whatever breath I had left. "I'm the lucky one," he says roughly, thumb brushing my bottom lip. "You're everything."

I kiss down his stomach, tongue teasing across the line of his hip, and when I take him in my mouth, he lets out a strangled noise, raw and guttural. His hands find my hair, not to guide, just to hold. Just to feel.

"Fuck, Penelope," he groans, the sound wrecked. The way he says my name, like it's sacred, like it's the only word he still remembers, makes my thighs press together.

I take him deeper, tongue tracing slow, wet circles, feeling him throb against my lips. He's a mess beneath me—tense, panting, muttering half-formed words I can't make out. The rain is louder now, thunder rolling distantly above us like background music for a storm neither of us want to escape.

"Wait," he gasps, pulling me up with both hands on my shoulders. "Not yet."

I blink, flushed and breathless. "Did I do something wrong?"

"No," he laughs, the sound ragged and full of wonder. "You did too much right. But the first time after this—" his hand brushes the ring on my finger, "I want to be inside you. Want to see your face. Feel you fall apart around me."

My heart flutters hard enough to hurt. I let him guide me up and into his lap again, knees braced on either side of him, thighs shaking as I settle over him.

"You're sure?" he asks, searching my face, even now.

I answer without words, just reach down, wrap my fingers around him, and guide him to where I need him. Our eyes stay locked as I sink down, inch by inch, the stretch burning in the most exquisite way. My breath breaks on a moan. His mouth drops open, and a curse slips out, low and guttural.

His hands grip my hips like they're the only things anchoring him to the earth. "Christ," he breathes, forehead pressed to mine. "You feel like heaven."

I can't speak. I just move. Slow at first, careful. His hands roam my body like he's trying to memorize it all over again. My name slips from his mouth again, broken this time.

"You're so fucking beautiful," he whispers. "It's like staring into the sun. I shouldn't be able to take it. But I can't look away."

"Then don't," I whisper, voice shaking. "Keep your eyes on me."

And he does. Even as I ride him. Even as our rhythm builds, bodies colliding in the heat. Even as his fingers slide between us and circle that spot with practiced, perfect pressure.

"Come now, Penelope."

When it hits, it's violent. My body clenches around him, my vision goes white, my fingers claw at his shoulders. He groans my name like a prayer and crushes his mouth to mine, swallowing every sound I make.

He flips me with surprising strength, laying me back along the seat, his cock still buried inside me. His hips grind deeper from this angle, pace hard and frantic now, the storm outside nothing compared to the one we've created.

"Need to be closer," he grits out, thrusting deep.

"Fill me, Spencer," I pant, wrapping my legs around him. "I want every fucking drop."

That's all it takes. He shudders, hips jerking deep as he spills inside me, his whole body seizing with it.

"Fuckkkk," he half-growls, half-whimpers, like the orgasm ripped the air from his lungs. Another curse follows, low and desperate, muttered right against my skin like a confession. "Jesus—Penelope," he groans, voice wrecked, drawn tight with pleasure that borders on pain.

I hold him through it, arms wrapped around his trembling back, my mouth pressed to the curve of his neck. I feel every twitch, every pulse of him inside me. He's gasping now, breath hot and uneven against my collarbone, one hand gripping the seat like it's the only thing tethering him to this earth. The other holds my waist like if he lets go, he'll disappear.

His control shatters in pieces, and I catch each one—his weight slumping into mine, the quiet noises still falling from his mouth, the wet press of his forehead against my shoulder as he rides out the last sharp waves.

Eventually, he lifts his head just enough to look down at me, eyes still a little dazed. His hair sticks to his forehead in damp curls.

"Hey," he says softly, brushing a strand of wet hair from my face, his thumb lingering like he doesn't want to let go of any part of me.

Then, slowly, he shifts, one arm tightening around my back, the other bracing against the seat behind me as he turns us. I go willingly, limbs loose, heart full, letting him guide me until he's the one stretched out across the bench seat, shoulders pressed to the vinyl, and I'm sprawled on top of him, skin to skin, heartbeat to heartbeat.

His arms loop around my back as I settle into his chest, my thigh draped over his, his body warm beneath mine.

"There," he breathes, his voice in my hair, content and wrecked and golden. "Much better."

The storm outside has quieted into a soft, steady drizzle, just enough to blur the windows and wrap the world in mist. Inside, everything is quiet. Gentle. The air smells like rain and sex and the salt of our skin. His fingers trace aimless shapes along my spine, lazy and grounding. I could stay here forever, curled into him with my ear pressed over the steady beat of his heart like it's the soundtrack of something sacred.

He exhales slowly, almost like he doesn't want to break the spell. "I should've waited," he says after a beat. "Should've done it right. After dinner. After we dried off. There was a whole plan."

I tip my face up to his, raising an eyebrow. "Because this went so terribly wrong?"

He chuckles, low and warm. "I mean... maybe not terribly. But I had a whole speech. Candles. A playlist. Champagne that didn't get shaken to hell in a picnic basket."

"Spencer," I say, sliding a hand up to cup his jaw, "in case you missed it, I said yes. Enthusiastically. With tongue. And other stuff."

He laughs again, the sound muffled against my hair as he presses a kiss to the top of my head. "Okay, yeah. That part was great. But the guys and I had a whole plan worked out and I went and ruined it on the first day."

I lift my head, eyes narrowing. "Wait. Is that why they were MIA this morning?"

His grin turns sheepish. Boyish. Guilty. "They might've been in on it. The whole thing's kind of... complicated."

I stare at him, my heart thudding for a whole different reason now. "There's more to this, isn't there?"

He leans in until our foreheads touch, his voice dropping to a warm hush. "I wasn't supposed to say anything. But yeah. Let's just say... I wouldn't be surprised if you're asked the same question a few more times."

For a second, I just blink at him.

Then the laugh bursts out of me, huge and loud and unstoppable. It rolls up from somewhere deep in my chest and fills the steamy, sex-scented cab with something bright and wild. I fall back against his chest like my heart might split from how full it feels. The ring catches the light, throwing off tiny green sparks like it knows something I don't.

He holds me tighter, both of us settling into the silence again—one that hums with the knowledge of what's coming, with the slow, sweet ache of all the futures we haven't lived yet.

"You know what I'm thinking about right now?" he asks eventually, his voice quieter, steadier.

I glance up. "How we're going to explain to the others why the truck smells like sex and champagne?"

He snorts. "No. Though... yeah, that too. But mostly I'm thinking about fifty years from now. When we're old and gray and I've spent half a century loving you. And we're telling our grandkids about the day I proposed—how nothing went right, and it still ended up being the best day of my life. Because you said yes."

My throat tightens. My eyes sting in that traitorous, all-too-familiar way. "Spencer..."

"I know," he says, voice rough. "I'm a fucking sap. Don't tell the guys."

"Wouldn't dream of it," I whisper, pressing my lips to his. It's a soft kiss this time. A sealing one. Full of promises we haven't put words to yet.

When we pull apart, I settle my forehead against his, the air between us hot and close. "So what now?"

He exhales. "Now we put on some clothes before we both freeze our asses off. Then we go home. Tell them. And then..."

His hand slides over mine, thumb brushing the edge of the ring.

"Then we build the rest of this life. One day at a time."

There's no dramatic music, no fireworks, no audience. Just us. And it's more than enough.

"I can't wait," I say, voice breaking around the truth of it. "Really."

Spencer grins, slow and crooked, eyes soft as he lifts my hand and kisses the ring again like he's sealing it in place. "Neither can I, Sugar. Neither can I."

Outside, the last of the storm dissolves into sunlight, soft gold cutting through the clouds and turning every raindrop on the windows into glitter. The engine hums back to life beneath us, and the radio clicks on like it's been waiting for its cue. The first notes of a familiar song drift through the cab, low, aching, familiar in a way that feels impossible.

For us.

Spencer doesn't say anything, just threads his fingers through mine and holds on. And right then, I know—with that bone-deep, whole-body kind of knowing—this is our song. Not because we planned it. But because somehow the universe knew, and this was its way of making sure we'd never forget.

29

The ring on my finger catches the morning light as I pour water into my mug, sending little green sparks dancing across the kitchen wall like tiny wayward stars. It's been two days since Spencer asked me to marry him in that sudden downpour, and I still can't stop staring at it, this tangible proof of a promise I never thought I'd have.

I'm so mesmerized by the kaleidoscope of emerald light that I don't notice Liam until his arms slide around my waist, his solid warmth pressing against my back. My whole body melts into him without hesitation, like it knows the shape of him instinctively. Like we were built to fit this way. His hips cradle my ass, his chest curving into my back, and just like that, the rest of the world falls away.

"Morning, Darlin'," he murmurs against my ear, his voice sleep-rough and honey-thick, accent heavier than usual. The scratch of his stubble against my neck sends a cascade of shivers down my spine, each one sparking like static electricity as he presses a kiss to my skin. "How'd you sleep?"

"Like the dead," I admit, turning in his arms to face him. He looks deliciously rumpled, hair sticking out in wild tufts, eyes still heavy-lidded with sleep, the lines of his pillowcase temporarily etched into one cheek. His hat is missing, probably the only time of day I get to see him without it. Heat pools between my legs at the sight of him like this —raw and unguarded, for my eyes only. "You?"

"Would've been better with you next to me." His dimples flash as he grins, no real accusation in his tone. A statement of fact, nothing more. His hands slide to my hips, thumbs brushing along my hipbones in that way that makes my brain short-circuit.

"I'm all yours today if you want me," I promise, rising onto my tiptoes to press a kiss to his jaw, my breasts brushing against his chest as I stretch up. Something unreadable flickers in his eyes, there and gone like a fish darting beneath dark water. His smile widens, the kind that transforms his whole face, crinkles the corners of his eyes, makes my heart thump painfully with its simple perfection.

"Funny you should say that. I was hoping you might fancy an adventure."

"An adventure?" I raise an eyebrow, suspicious but intrigued. "What kind of adventure?"

"The surprise kind," he says, maddeningly vague. "Pack a bag with clothes for a couple days of warm days and cool nights. And sturdy boots."

"Liam Taylor, what are you planning?" I try to sound stern but fail miserably when his eyes darken, watching me like I'm the only thing worth seeing.

"Nothing too wild," he laughs, his breath warm against my forehead as he presses a soft kiss there. "Trust me?"

"Always." It slips out without hesitation, because it's true. He's the cliff, and I'm already mid-air, no parachute in sight. And God help me, I'd jump again.

"Good. We leave in an hour."

"Wait—Now? I was going to work on the restaurant." I protest, even as my body leans into his.

"The guys have it handled," he assures me, his palm making soothing circles on my lower back, chasing away tension I didn't realize I was carrying. "Archer's got all your lists, and Spencer is working on the floor. Sam and Jamie promised to keep everything on schedule." He presses another kiss to my temple, his lips lingering just long enough to make my heart skip. "They insisted, actually. Said you deserve a break."

"Okay," I say, curiosity tugging harder than my instinct to micro-manage every detail. I want to know what he's planned too badly to point out that I had a break two days ago. "I'll be ready in an hour."

His grin hits me like sunshine after a storm—teeth flashing, dimples popping, eyes crinkling with that unmistakable *I'm about to wreck you* energy. "Better start packin', Darlin'. And leave the pajamas —they're not exactly on the itinerary." He winks and my stomach nearly drops through the floor.

Fifty-eight minutes later, I'm sliding into the passenger seat of the truck after stowing my overnight bag beside a suspiciously large cooler and what looks like camping gear in the truck bed. The cab is already filled with his scent—cedar and leather and something that makes me want to bury my face in his neck and breathe him in.

"Are we sleeping under the stars, cowboy?" I ask, nodding toward the tent I can see peeking out from beneath a tarp, my stomach fluttering with anticipation.

"Among other things," he says cryptically, that secretive smile playing at his lips again. He's freshly showered, hair damp at the temples where water has seeped from beneath his hat, tiny droplets clinging to the dark strands.

I notice for the first time that he's dressed differently than usual— the worn jeans are the same, hugging his thighs in a way that should be illegal, but he's wearing a deep ochre button-down shirt I've never seen before, the fabric crisp and new against his sun-bronzed skin, the sleeves rolled up to reveal his tanned forearms. The color makes his eyes look warmer, molten amber rather than their usual earth-brown, bringing out gold flecks I've never noticed before.

I shift in my seat, suddenly aware of how little I'm wearing—just a butter-yellow tank top and a pair of cutoffs that hug my hips like they were sewn on. I'd picked them for comfort, something easy for the drive and whatever chaos Liam had planned, but the way his gaze keeps snagging on my thighs every time the denim rides up tells me he's appreciating the outfit for very different reasons.

"You look beautiful," he says, his voice dropping an octave, the words catching slightly in his throat like they've snagged on something sharp. "That color suits you. Like sunshine."

Heat blooms across my cheeks, not just from the compliment but from the raw sincerity behind it. "Thanks. You don't look so bad yourself." I reach over to straighten his collar, letting my fingers linger against the warm skin of his neck, his pulse jumping beneath my touch. "This is definitely your color."

He sucks in a breath, and for a moment I think he might forget our adventure altogether, his gaze darkening as it drops to my mouth. But then he shakes his head, like a man coming up for air, and starts the engine.

We pull out of the drive in a silence that feels charged. The kind of quiet that hums under your skin. We snake along the coast, the landscape a moving watercolor—emerald hills, wet stone, the occasional glint of sea through the trees, flashing silver like a coin tossed into sunlight.

Liam drives with one hand on the wheel, the other resting on my bare thigh like it's always belonged there. His thumb traces slow, mindless circles against my skin. It's not overt, not even meant to be sexy, but the effect is instant. My breath stutters. My thighs press together. Every brush of his thumb sends a pulse straight to the ache blooming low in my belly.

"I brought snacks," I say finally, because God help me, I need something to focus on that isn't the trail of fire his hand is leaving on my leg. I lean forward, digging into the bag at my feet like it holds the answer to every unspoken question between us. "In case your mysterious adventure is, like, actually a hostage situation. Or really long."

He laughs, the sound warm and rich, filling the cab of the truck like music. The vibrations travel through his hand directly to my core, and I have to clench my thighs together. "Sorry about that. I promise it'll be worth it. And there will be proper food at the end."

"Vague. But noted." I lift out a couple of apples and a Tupperware full of trail mix—dried cherries, dark chocolate, and the good cashews I only buy for special occasions. I pop it into the cupholder between us like a peace offering. "These'll tide us over."

He hums, a soft, approving sound, and his hand slips a little higher on my thigh.

And just like that, I'm not sure what's going to give out first—my sanity, or the last shred of my self-control.

I don't realize what's happening until we're already queued up behind a line of cars, the distant outline of a ferry pulling into view.

"We're going to the mainland?" I ask, looking over at him.

He just lifts one shoulder, casual and maddening. "Surprise."

And then we're moving again, tires thumping up the metal ramp, the truck swallowed into the belly of the boat. I barely have time to process it before we're parked and stepping out, the sea breeze hitting like a slap—cold, briny, alive. It steals the breath right out of my lungs and tangles my hair into wild golden ribbons that whip around my face.

We climb the narrow stairs to the top deck, shoes ringing against steel, hands brushing once—twice—before he catches mine fully. There's no one else up here. Just us, the wind, and the slow churn of ocean foam trailing in our wake.

We stand at the rail, my fingers curled around the peeling paint, watching the island shrink behind us, shrinking from landmass to memory. Just a green smudge now, swallowed by sky and sea.

Liam wraps around me from behind, arms cinching around my waist, his chest pressed against my back like armor. His chin rests on top of my head, a quiet weight anchoring me to the moment. The wind claws at our clothes, stings our cheeks, but he's warm and safe. And when he breathes, slow and steady, I match it instinctively, grounding myself in the rhythm of him.

"I haven't taken a real trip in years," I say into the wind. My voice feels small against all that open water. "Not one that wasn't about work."

"I know," he says. And I hear the smile in it, feel it in the way his arms tighten around me, like he wants to tuck me even closer. "That's why we're doing this." His lips brush the shell of my ear, and I have to grip the railing tighter.

We stay like that for a while, wrapped in each other and the sting of salt wind, until the ferry begins to slow, the engine humming lower as the dock comes into view, solid ground rising up to catch us, steady and inevitable.

Forty-five minutes later, we're back in the truck, salt still clinging to our skin, my hair tangled from the wind and damp at the ends. The ferry behind us, the open road ahead. We roll inland, the scenery shifting in slow gradients—coastal brush giving way to rolling hills, hills softening into trees, the road narrowing with every turn. Somewhere along the way, lulled by the low murmur of the tires and the heat of Liam's palm curled around my thigh, I drift off.

When I wake, it's to the gentle pressure of his hand on my knee, his voice warm against the shell of sleep.

"We're here, Darlin'."

I blink, eyes heavy, and take in the world outside the window. A weathered wooden gate, its slats soft with age, the kind that's seen years of comings and goings, of people falling in and out of love. Silvercrest Ranch is carved into the sign above it in looping script, each letter worn smooth by time.

Beyond the gate, the land opens up—broad pastures that stretch out toward the horizon, golden in the late afternoon light, scattered with horses that gleam like hammered bronze and burnished copper. The late afternoon sun sits low, casting the whole world in that too-perfect glow that makes everything look a little more like a dream.

"A ranch?" I ask, turning toward him, something in my chest twisting, warm and tight.

His smile is hopeful. Maybe even a little nervous. "I wanted to show you a piece of my world. I know it's not the same as home, but—"

I lean across the console and kiss him. My hands cradle his face, thumbs brushing the stubble along his jaw.

"I love it," I whisper. And I mean it. With every beat of my heart.

He exhales like he's been holding his breath the whole ride.

We drive through the gates slowly, gravel crunching beneath the tires, the dirt road winding between groves of old trees toward a house that looks like it was born from the earth. Two stories of river stone and rough-hewn logs, a wraparound porch dotted with rocking chairs and hanging baskets overflowing with blooms.

As we park, a man steps out from a nearby barn, stocky and sun-browned, his Stetson casting long shadows over sharp blue eyes. A woman follows close behind, dusting her hands on a flour-covered apron. Her gray hair is tucked into a no-nonsense braid, and warmth radiates from the broad smile stretching across her weathered, welcoming face.

"You must be Liam," the man calls as we climb down from the truck.

"G'day," Liam replies, tipping his hat. I swear my heart actually flip-flops in my chest.

"Dave Thompson," the man says, offering his hand. "Welcome to Silvercrest."

Liam shakes it, then gestures to me. "This is my girlfriend, Penelope."

Dave's grin widens. "We've been looking forward to meeting you." But before I can offer my hand, the woman pulls me into a hug that smells like warm bread and lavender soap. It's disarming in the best possible way.

"I'm Moira," she says into my shoulder. "And we're so glad you're here."

I blink fast, emotion catching me off guard.

"Your cabin's ready," she adds, handing Liam a key carved into the shape of a tiny horse, worn smooth from use.

"Third one on the left, just past the big oak," Dave adds. "And we left a basket of snacks for you in case you're peckish."

"Thank you," Liam says, his voice warm with gratitude. "Any chance we can take a ride before the sun goes down?"

"Of course," Dave nods toward the stables. "Head down when you're ready. I'll meet you there and help you saddle up. Everything's set for tonight."

I glance at Liam, eyebrows raised. *Tonight?*

He just smiles.

Moira winks as we climb back into the truck. "Enjoy yourselves," she says, and I get the distinct impression she knows exactly what Liam has planned.

We follow a smaller road that curves behind the main house, weaving through towering oaks that lean toward one another like they've been whispering secrets for centuries. Three cabins appear ahead, nestled into the trees like they were always meant to be there, porches framed by ivy and rocking chairs, each one quietly waiting for someone to fall in love inside it.

The cabin is just one room, but it's cozy and perfect. Warm stone walls, a fireplace already stacked with kindling. A kitchenette hugs the far wall, its counters smooth with years of use, every edge softened by time. No frills. No noise. Just what's needed and nothing more. There's something special about it, like the space was built with hands that understood how to love quietly.

Through the open doorway—just a frame, no actual door—the bed waits. The quilt is handmade, stitched from soft blues and greens, the lines just a little off, not because it was rushed, but because it was real. Someone took their time with it. It's not flawless, but it's perfect. The kind of bed meant for warm skin and tangled limbs.

A basket sits on the table like it's been waiting for us. Inside, a loaf of bread wrapped in linen, still faintly warm. Cheese sharp enough to make my mouth water. Fruit so ripe it's almost obscene. A bottle of red catches the last of the afternoon sun, glowing like something holy.

And I just stand there for a second, anchored and untethered all at once, my pulse ticking too fast for a space this quiet. This still. Because everything here feels a little too perfect, like the universe laid it out just so we'd know exactly what we're walking into.

Liam's quiet behind me, and I know—I know—if I look at him now, everything I'm trying not to feel is going to pour out of me all at once.

So I don't look.

"This is beautiful," I murmur, fingers skimming the back of one of the pine chairs. The wood is warm beneath my touch, worn smooth where countless hands have clutched it, maybe during arguments, maybe breakfasts with sleepy smiles and tangled hair. Maybe moments just like this. "How did you even find this place?"

Liam sets our bags down with a soft thump, then straightens, rubbing the back of his neck like he's suddenly unsure what to do with himself. There's something different in his face—less guarded, almost shy. His eyes don't quite meet mine when I finally look up at him, and that half-smile on his lips is the kind you only catch when someone's hoping you'll love what they've chosen.

"I did some research," he says, a little too casual. "Wanted somewhere special. Somewhere that might feel a little like where I grew up."

And that's it. The shift. The thread in my chest pulling tight and then snapping.

I don't even think. I just move, closing the distance like I was meant to, like he's the answer I've been walking toward without knowing it. My arms slide around his waist, and he comes to me without hesitation, hands settling on my hips like they belong there. Like I belong there.

"Thank you," I whisper, the words clumsy and insufficient, scraping the surface of everything I wish I could say. "For bringing me here. For letting me have this piece of you."

He kisses the top of my head and somehow I feel it in my ribs, in the wobble of my knees. It's not just affection, it's anchoring. A promise. His lips brush my hair as he murmurs, "There's more to see. But maybe throw on something you can ride in first, yeah?"

His gaze drops, and when it lands on the hem of my shorts high on my thighs, it lingers. Something in him shifts again, something darker, hotter. A slow burn behind his eyes that makes my stomach flip.

"Riding?" I echo, my voice a little breathless. "As in horses?"

He smirks, and it's devastating. "That's usually the idea at a ranch, but if you don't want to, I can find something else for you to ride."

I narrow my eyes. "Getting bucked off a horse was not on my list of things to do today."

He steps closer, voice low and teasing, close enough to taste. "Don't tell me you're scared of a little horse?"

"I've never ridden one," I admit, already rummaging through my bag for jeans, suddenly very aware that his eyes are still on me. "Island girl, remember? I know boats, not saddles."

"Well," he says, that crooked smile pulling slow and wicked across his face, "you're about to get real familiar."

Twenty minutes later, I'm standing in front of a horse that could kill me with a sneeze.

Not metaphorically. Like, a full-body twitch and I'd be a pancake.

She's beautiful, deep chestnut coat, long lashes, eyes like polished onyx, and she's staring at me with an expression that suggests she already knows I'm not built for this.

I'm in jeans now, the soft kind that hug just right in all the right places, and I borrowed a flannel from Liam. It's too big and smells faintly like him and the sleeves are rolled up unevenly at my wrists. The boots are mine, at least. The nerves are too.

"This is Cinnamon," Liam says, voice easy, hands moving with the kind of practiced grace that makes it impossible to look away. He runs a palm down her flank, fingers smoothing over her hide like it's second nature. Like he was born to do it.

"She's good for beginners," he adds, glancing over at me with a half-smile that's somehow both reassuring and wildly unfair to my ability to remain upright.

I nod like that means anything. Cinnamon flicks one ear, then the other, assessing me with cool horse skepticism.

And Liam—God, Liam. Hat pulled low, sleeves rolled up, forearms tanned and dusted with fine hair, body moving in sync with the horse like they're sharing a language I don't speak. There's something in his posture, loose but grounded, that does something to me. Something inconvenient. Something hot.

He looks like he belongs here. Not like he's pretending, not like he's stepping into someone else's role. Like this is the original version of him. The one who existed before he came to work on the boat, before the renovations, before me.

And maybe that should make me feel distant. Disconnected. But instead, something in my chest tightens. A low ache, right under the ribs. Because I'm not sure I've ever seen someone look more like themselves than he does right now.

Dave emerges from the barn, adjusting the saddle as he walks. His voice is low and worn, a little gravelly in that cowboy-grandpa way that feels somehow eternal.

"So you grew up on a station?" he asks, working alongside Liam like they've worked together for years.

"Queensland," Liam says, his hands steady as he double-checks the cinch. "Fourth generation. Cattle mostly. But Mum loved horses. Had me riding before I could spell my own name."

Dave lets out a short laugh, clapping Liam on the back. "Shows. You've got the touch."

And okay, yeah, pride isn't supposed to bloom this fast or this hard, but there it is anyway, unfurling warm and wide in my chest. Because I see it now. The ease. The certainty. The version of Liam that doesn't apologize for taking up space. And it's like watching a light click on in a room I didn't realize had been dark.

"She's huge," I mutter, taking an instinctive half-step back as Cinnamon shifts and gives me a slow blink that feels judgmental.

"She's not even that big," Liam says, laughing, and the sound hits me right in the knees, low and rich and golden like warm honey poured straight down my spine.

I shoot him a glare that's only half-serious.

He steps in closer, that smile still playing at the corners of his mouth, and takes my hand. His is rough, sun-warmed, callused in a way that makes me want to trace every inch of it later, slowly. He guides my fingers toward Cinnamon's nose, his palm covering the back of my hand like a steadying force field.

"Easy," he murmurs, so soft it feels like it was meant for more than just the horse. "Let her smell you."

Cinnamon exhales, a warm breath ghosting across my skin. Her whiskers brush my palm, delicate and sudden, and something about it

—this massive creature choosing to trust me with her softness—makes my throat close up.

"There," Liam whispers. "She likes you."

"You really think so?" I breathe, my gaze shifting between him and Cinnamon.

"Yes," Liam says, giving me a crooked grin. "Time to get on."

"Right." I nod, like this is normal. Like I've ever voluntarily hoisted myself onto a thousand-pound animal before.

His hands land on my waist, and suddenly I'm airborne, weightless for a split second before gravity finds me again and plants me firmly in the saddle. The world tilts. I lurch, grabbing for the horn like it's the last stable object in a collapsing universe.

I'm way too high off the ground.

"She's not going to throw you," Liam says, adjusting the stirrups while I try to remember how breathing works. His fingers brush my calf through my jeans, slow and certain, and it sends a shiver straight up my spine. "But she can feel everything you're feeling. So take a breath for both of you."

I do, or I try. The inhale gets caught somewhere in my throat and comes out shaky. My hands are already cramping from how hard I'm gripping the saddle, white-knuckled and undignified.

Then Liam swings up onto his own horse—Shadow, a sleek black stallion who looks like he eats beginners for breakfast—and suddenly the whole thing looks easy. His movements are seamless, all fluid strength and quiet control, like he's part of the animal. Like he belongs up there.

"You ready?" he asks, guiding Shadow up beside me with barely a nudge of his knees.

"Not in the slightest," I mutter, but I nod. Because of course I do. Because I trust him.

He flashes that devastating grin, the one with the eye crinkles and the dimples and the absolute nerve, and clicks his tongue. Shadow steps forward like it's nothing, Cinnamon trailing without so much as a pause, as if I'm merely cargo.

I bounce awkwardly at first, every part of me stiff with anxiety, but the trail is wide and the pace is slow, and little by little, I find a rhythm.

My body loosens, hips starting to sway in time with Cinnamon's gait, my thighs already aware they're going to be furious with me later.

Liam keeps an eye on me, his expression somewhere between amused and impressed. There's pride there, tucked beneath the curve of his mouth, and it makes something flutter low in my belly.

"You're a natural," he says.

I snort. "Liar."

He laughs, a real one, deep and easy, and it startles me, how good it feels to hear that sound. To be the one pulling it from him.

And the thing is... I'm starting to enjoy myself. Against all odds, despite my fear, despite the fact that I'm still certain Cinnamon is plotting my untimely death—I like it. There's something wild and grounding about it at the same time. A different kind of freedom. One that comes with giving up a little control and leaning into the sway of something larger, something living.

The trail winds through open meadows where wildflowers riot in every color imaginable, their petals vivid against the late-summer grass that glows gold in the afternoon light. We crest gentle hills that offer sweeping views of the land beyond, and dip into cool, shaded pockets of pine forest where the air turns sharper, laced with the scent of resin and earth and the quiet hum of bees in the underbrush.

Liam points things out now and then—names of hills, bits of ranch history, some story Dave told him about a cougar sighting that I really didn't need to know—but mostly, we ride in silence. A soft, companionable kind of quiet, like we're soaking it all in together. Like we don't need to fill the space between us with anything but the sounds of hoofbeats and birdsong and the occasional sigh of wind through the trees.

By the time we reach the high meadow, the sun has started its slow descent, painting the sky in watercolors. Rose and apricot and that impossible shade of violet that only shows up when the day is slipping away. At the top of the hill, a single oak stands alone, wide-branched and ancient, like it's been waiting for us.

"Perfect timing," Liam says, swinging off Shadow with that same practiced ease. His boots land in the grass with a soft thud. He ties the reins loosely to one of the oak's low branches, then strides over to help me down.

His hands find my waist again, strong and careful, guiding me as I dismount. He doesn't let go right away. His gaze catches mine, and something flickers there, warm and heavy. Something that lands in my chest and lodges there.

"How're you feeling?" he asks, voice low and gentle. "Sore?" He loops the reins around a nearby tree branch, then turns back to me, all warmth and worry beneath the soft rasp of his words.

"A bit," I admit, wincing as I stretch my legs. "But worth it."

And it is.

The view unfolds around us like a painting. The ranch stretches out below, its buildings small in the distance, pastures glowing under the last light of day. The trees ripple like dark green waves, and beyond them, the mountains loom in silhouette, blue and solemn and steady. Everything's bathed in that golden hour glow, like someone dipped the whole world in honey.

There's a campsite waiting for us beneath the wide, sheltering arms of the oak. A canvas tent, creamy and soft in the low light, sits nestled into the grass like it's always belonged there. The flap is tied back, revealing a nest of thick blankets and overstuffed pillows inside, casual at first glance, but unmistakably intentional. My pulse stumbles.

Beside the tent, a ring of stones cradles a carefully laid fire, the kindling already arranged in that way that promises a perfect flame on the first try. There's a small folding table set with lanterns, a bottle of red catching the sunset like stained glass, and a covered basket that promises something mouth-watering. It's intimate. Like someone pressed pause on the world and made space for only us.

Liam looks over it all, pleased in a way that softens something in me. His cheeks are faintly pink, like he's not used to being the center of something so deliberately romantic.

"Dave works fast," he says, scratching the back of his neck like he's trying not to look too proud. "I asked if we could camp here tonight, but this is—yeah. This is above and beyond."

"We're staying here?" I ask, a breathless kind of thrill catching in my chest. The nerves are quick and fluttering, like birds startled into flight, but beneath them is something warmer. Something that glows. "Out in the open?"

He nods, stepping closer, his voice low and full of something that feels dangerously close to reverence. "That's the plan. Dave's coming back to collect the horses soon. And apparently Moira sent dinner." He nods toward the covered dish I hadn't even seen until now. "She said something about breakfast too. Tomorrow morning."

Before I can respond, the sound of hoofbeats draws our attention. Dave appears through the trees on a dappled gray gelding, moving with the quiet ease of someone who's lived more years in the saddle than out of it. He dismounts with a soft grunt.

"Everything to your liking?" he asks, brushing dust from his pants.

"It's perfect," Liam says, clapping him on the back. "Way more than I expected."

Dave chuckles, shaking his head like he's heard this kind of thank-you before. "That's Moira's doing. Once she found out it was a special occasion, she insisted. Said young love deserves a proper celebration."

I turn slowly to Liam, lifting an eyebrow. He suddenly finds the grass very interesting. A blush creeps up his neck, blooming into his cheeks in a way that makes my heart do this ridiculous, hopeful little flutter.

"What exactly did you tell them?" I whisper, keeping one eye on Dave as he starts untying the reins.

Liam glances at me, sheepish and golden in the dying light. "Just that you're special," he murmurs. "And that I wanted to make this trip something we'd remember."

The way he says it makes my throat go tight.

Dave, mercifully, chooses that exact moment to clear his throat and spare Liam from further confession. "I'll take these two back," he says, climbing back up into his saddle. "There's more firewood under the tarp if you need it. And Moira's beef stew should still be hot."

He pauses, meeting Liam's gaze with the kind of look older men give younger ones when they're both in on the same secret. "Breakfast'll be up at eight. But no rush."

"Thanks, mate," Liam says, his voice thick with something real. "Truly."

Dave just smiles, eyes crinkling at the corners like he knows exactly how this night's going to unfold. Like maybe he's seen this story play out before, and he already loves the ending.

"Enjoy your evening," he says, tipping his hat before turning and riding off into the sunset.

And just like that, we're alone. The sun surrenders to the horizon, spilling amber light across Liam's face, gilding his lashes and softening the angles of his jaw. The air between us holds more possibilities than I know what to do with.

We watch until he disappears from sight, the rhythmic clop of hooves fading into the hush of the meadow until there's only the sound of the breeze stirring the grass, the soft rustle of leaves above us. The silence that follows isn't awkward, it settles over us like a well-worn quilt, weighted with something unspoken. Anticipation. Gratitude. Maybe a little wonder.

"Hungry?" Liam asks, his voice a little rough around the edges, like maybe he feels it too, the hum beneath the quiet.

"Starving," I admit, and it's true. From the ride, sure. But more from this. The way he's looking at me now, like he can read every thought I haven't said out loud.

His eyes drag over me, slow and heated, and for a second I think he has read my mind. The edge of a grin tugs at his mouth as he moves to start the fire.

I turn toward the table, lifting the lid off the dish with cautious hope. The scent hits me first—rich, familiar, comforting. Moira certainly didn't hold back. Beef stew, still warm, is tucked into a thick ceramic container. There's bread wrapped in a linen towel, a tiny crock of butter, and a mason jar full of bright, vinegary pickles that glint like stained glass in the last of the sun. Tucked in the basket beside them is a generous wedge of cheese, a handful of ripe strawberries, and chocolate cookies that smell like the kind your grandma makes when you visit after a long time away.

By the time I've laid everything out, Liam has coaxed the fire to life. It crackles low and steady, casting shadows that dance against the tent canvas and paint his face in flickering amber. We settle onto a thick blanket beside the fire, plates balanced on our knees, the stars beginning to puncture the deepening blue overhead.

"This is incredible," I say after my first bite, nearly moaning as the flavor hits. The meat is tender, the broth rich and peppery, laced with thyme and something deeper—wine, maybe. Comforting and complex. Like someone's grandmother cooked it slow and stirred in every good memory she ever had.

"So good," Liam agrees, tearing off a chunk of bread and dragging it through his stew. The crust shatters beneath his fingers, and I catch myself watching his hands a little too closely.

We eat in that quiet way people do when the food's too good to talk over. The sky above us deepens into indigo, the stars slowly winking to life. The fire cracks and pops, sending tiny sparks upward like they're trying to join the stars themselves.

By the time we've cleaned our bowls with the last of the bread, I feel loose in a way I haven't in weeks. My body aches from the ride, but it's the good kind. Earned. My skin hums from the heat of the fire and the warmth of him sitting close enough that our thighs are touching, solid and steady and quietly electric.

Then Liam reaches into his bag and pulls out a flask and two enamel mugs. He pours the amber liquid slowly, and it catches the light like it knows it's being appreciated.

"Thought we might toast properly," he says, handing me a cup.

I lift it to my nose, breathing in the scent of oak and smoke and vanilla, rich and familiar and a little dangerous.

"To adventure," I say, clinking my cup against his.

"To new experiences," he says, holding my gaze with a look that makes heat bloom low in my belly.

The whiskey burns in the best way—slow and smoky, creating a fire in my chest that spreads out until it settles in my limbs.

"Thank you for bringing me here," I say softly, staring out at the dark silhouette of the land below, edged in silver moonlight.

Liam doesn't answer right away. He's quiet for a long beat, his eyes trained on the horizon.

"It reminds me a little of home," he says finally, and his voice is distant, touched with something weightier than nostalgia. "Not exactly, obviously. Australia's louder. Rougher around the edges. But there's something about wide open spaces under a massive sky that just does something to you."

I nod. "I think I understand. I grew up surrounded by ocean, not land, but it's the same feeling, isn't it? That bigness. That sense that the world was here long before you, and it'll still be here long after."

"Yeah," he says, his smile barely there, like the idea hurts and soothes at the same time.

"Tell me about it," I say, nudging my knee against his. "About where you grew up."

He's quiet again, the firelight catching the slope of his cheekbone, the subtle furrow between his brows. And then he speaks.

"Red earth, hot enough to burn your soles through your boots if you stand still too long. Eucalyptus trees grow everywhere, scraggly and silver. When it rains, it doesn't whisper like it does here. It slams. Turns dry creek beds into rivers in minutes. Fills the air with the smell of wet dirt and hope."

His accent thickens as he talks, vowels stretching, consonants softening, like the rhythm of the outback is still lodged somewhere in his bones. I close my eyes and listen, the sound of his voice anchoring me in some other hemisphere I've never seen but suddenly ache to.

"The stars at night..." He trails off, his voice catching. "You've never seen stars like that, Penelope. It's like someone spilled diamonds across black ink. You swear, if you reached up, you could run your fingers right through them."

He pauses, then adds quietly, "Then there's the Southern Cross. You can only see it in the Southern Hemisphere. Five stars shaped like a cross—it's on the Aussie flag." He lifts a hand, tracing the shape in the air like the stars might appear if he draws them carefully enough. "For Indigenous people, it was part of a giant celestial emu. For sailors, it pointed them home. And for me..." His voice softens, falters. "I don't know. It was just there. Always. Something constant. Something that felt like it belonged to me."

The longing in his voice splits something open in me. It's not just what he's saying—it's what he isn't. The quiet ache of homesickness he rarely gives words to. The weight of missing the soil that made him.

"You miss it," I say, reaching for his thigh, my hand settling just above his knee. His jeans are warm from the fire. Solid. Real.

"Every day," he admits, covering my hand with his own. His palm is rough, and his grip gentle. "But I've found something better."

He looks at me then, and it's not the firelight that makes my breath catch, it's the honesty in his eyes. The quiet certainty.

"Penelope." The sound of my name in his voice feels different this time—rougher, frayed around the edges with something raw and earnest. Like the words are dragging through gravel on their way out of him. "I've been trying to find the right way to say this since the day I met you. Ran through a thousand versions of this in my head. None of them ever felt like enough. Nothing I rehearsed even came close to what I feel when I look at you."

He swallows, like the words are sharp in his throat, then takes both of my hands in his. Everything about this moment narrows. The night, the fire, the world—it all fades, until there's only his eyes and the gravity they carry. Deep brown. Unblinking. Unmistakably mine.

"I left everything I knew behind to chase something I couldn't name," he says, voice low, thumb dragging slow circles over my knuckles like he's memorizing the shape of us. "Crossed oceans, gave up comfort, all for this ache I couldn't explain. And then I saw you, this tiny, fierce little thing with wide hazel eyes and freckles I swear I'd spend a lifetime mapping. The second you looked at me, I knew. It was you. It was always going to be you."

Then, with a breath that trembles just enough to splinter something in me, he lets go of one hand and slips the other into his pocket.

What he pulls out makes the air stutter in my lungs. A small wooden box, hand-carved with delicate, swirling patterns—like waves or wind, like something meant to hold secrets instead of jewelry. It doesn't look new. It looks sacred.

"The box was my grandfather's," he says, voice quiet but sure. "He gave it to my dad. And before I left, my dad gave it to me. Said I'd know when it was time to pass it on. When I found something worth holding onto."

He opens it slowly. Inside, resting against black velvet is an opal ring that catches the firelight and turns it into a storm. Greens and blues, quicksilver flashes of orange and violet—like fire and sky, seafoam and lightning.

"I mined it myself," Liam says, his voice stripped bare now. "Back in Australia. Had it cut, set, made into this ring two months after I met you."

The air feels too big for my lungs. The firelight reflects in the opal and scatters across our faces like stardust. Like some ancient spell just activated.

"I know this isn't conventional," he says, echoing Spencer's words from just days ago. "You, me. Us. All of us. This whole, wild, beautiful mess. But I've never cared about what makes sense on paper. What matters is that I love you."

His voice drops, barely more than a breath between us.

"I love the way you fight. The way you forgive. The way you give more than you ever take. I love that you're soft and sharp at the same time. That you make everyone around you feel like they matter, even when you're hanging on by a thread yourself. You took a bunch of broken men and built something holy from the pieces."

He takes a breath, then another. His hand is still in mine. Steady. Warm.

"I want to be your husband," he says, and my heart full-on stumbles. "I want to build a life with you. Mornings, nights, stupid arguments about the thermostat. I want to kiss you after bad dreams and good sex and every time in between. I want all of it. The ordinary. The breathtaking. The hard days and the soft ones. I want to love you on purpose, for the rest of my life."

He lifts the ring a little higher, the fire painting color across his fingers.

"Penelope," he says, and my name is the softest vow. "Will you marry me?"

Time folds in on itself.

The stars overhead feel closer somehow, like they're leaning in to hear the answer. The sky holds its breath. My throat tightens. There's too much in me—joy and awe and something wild and bone-deep that refuses to be shaken.

"Yes," I whisper, the word trembling on my tongue. "Yes, Liam."

His smile breaks like dawn. Like light after months of cloud. It changes his face in real time, makes him look younger and older all at once, like I'm seeing every version of him stacked together: the boy who left home, the man who found me, the future I just said yes to. He slides the ring onto my finger beside Spencer's emerald. Two promises. Two different versions of forever melding into one.

And then his mouth is on mine.

Warm. Certain. Full of every word he didn't say and every one he did. His hands cradle my face like he's afraid I'll disappear. I kiss him back like I never want to come up for air. My body lights up under his touch, every nerve tuned to him, to this, to the weight of forever settling into my bones.

When we finally part, breathless and tangled in each other, he rests his forehead against mine.

"I don't think I've ever been this nervous," he says, voice quiet, a little shaky like he wasn't sure how I'd answer.

I kiss him before I say anything, because words don't feel like enough. "It was perfect." I slide my arms around his neck and pull him closer, until his chest is pressed to mine and I can feel the hard, frantic beat of his heart against my ribs.

The fire pops beside us, sending a handful of sparks floating up into the night. Above us, the sky stretches out, wide, star-scattered, indifferent in the way only something eternal can be. But right now, it feels like it's holding space just for us.

Liam leans back on his elbows, eyes still on the stars, his voice softer now. "Not the Southern Cross," he says with a half-smile. "But still something."

I lie down beside him, close enough that our shoulders brush, the press of his body grounding me like gravity. We lie there like that for a long time, the fire burning down to glowing embers. Our voices slip into the hush between crackles. We share childhood stories, half-formed dreams, the kinds of thoughts that only spill out when the dark feels safe enough to hold them.

When the fire dies down to a quiet bed of coals and the night air starts to bite at our skin, we slip into the tent. It's perfect in that imperfect, thrown-together way—blankets tangled into a nest that smells like cedar and clean laundry, like home and adventure all at once.

The lantern glows in the corner, its light casting soft, flickering shadows on the canvas walls. The glow makes the whole space feel like a memory I'm already holding onto too tightly, warm, golden, a little unreal. Like we're living inside a painting that's still wet at the edges.

Liam sits cross-legged in the center, the light behind him gilding his body in gold. "Better than the sleeping bags I packed," he says sheepishly, rubbing the back of his neck. "Remind me to send Moira a thank-you gift basket or something."

I sit beside him, suddenly shy. And it's wild, isn't it? That after everything we've said, after every kiss and every ache, I still feel undone by the quiet closeness of this. The simplicity of being here, alone with him, on the edge of something momentous.

He shifts closer, the space between us disappearing. His hand slides up my arm, slow and careful, sparking something beneath my skin. A slow burn. A low hum. The lantern glows across his face, catching in his eyes and turning them molten. Without his hat, a lock of hair falls onto his forehead, softening him, making him look younger, more open. It does something to me.

"I like seeing you without your hat," I say, my voice barely louder than the wind whispering against the tent. I reach up, brushing his hair back, fingertips tracing down along the edge of his jaw. He hasn't shaved. There's a rawness to it, undeniably him, rough and unpolished, and I want to feel it mapped across every inch of me.

His eyes go dark, and the air tilts, suddenly charged, like the second before lightning splits the sky. The shift is instant. Unmistakable.

When he kisses me, it's slower, but there's weight behind it. Like he's holding back a storm. Heat simmers just under his skin, coiled and waiting, and I can feel it in the way his hands come up to frame my face, gentle, but not soft. His thumbs drag across my cheekbones like he's memorizing the shape of me, and it makes something sharp twist low in my stomach.

The kiss deepens, his mouth parting mine with a patience that feels like tension instead of tenderness. My lips open beneath his, and everything inside me stutters—my thoughts, my breath, the whole damn world narrowing down to this single, burning point where we touch. It's not sweet. It's not careful. It's everything we've been holding back, barely restrained, threatening to snap.

He pulls back just enough to breathe. His lips find my jaw, skimming along the edge before drifting lower, down the side of my neck, over the place where my pulse trips beneath skin. I tilt my head without thinking, giving him more. When he finds the spot just beneath my ear, a soft sound escapes me, half gasp, half plea.

"I need to see you," he whispers, his voice low and close and warm against my skin.

His fingers find the buttons of my shirt, his shirt, technically, still faintly carrying his scent. He undoes each button slowly, carefully, until the fabric falls open. The night air slips in, cool against the warmth of my skin, and my breath stutters.

His gaze follows, slow and unflinching, dragging over me like a touch. Dark. Focused. Hungry. My nipples tighten beneath the lace of my bra, and I swear I can feel him everywhere—his eyes, his breath, the heat building between us—just as real as if he'd already laid his hands on me.

"Jesus," he says softly, like the word is caught in his chest. "You're fucking gorgeous."

He runs one callused fingertip along the edge of the lace, the contrast between rough skin and delicate fabric making me shiver. My back arches without permission, my body reaching for more.

I reach for him, breath caught somewhere between my chest and my throat, but he catches my wrists before I make contact. His grip is firm but gentle, like he's holding something breakable. He lifts my hands, one at a time, and brings each to his mouth. His lips press into my palms, hot and slow, then he's guiding them down to the blanket, keeping them there with his own.

"Not yet, Darlin'," he says, his mouth brushing the hollow of my collarbone. His voice is low, uneven, like he's barely hanging on.

"Tonight's for you. Let me love you the way you deserve. Let me show you what that means."

My whole body tightens with need. With the kind of want that feels like it's been simmering for months, just waiting for this moment to be real. I can't speak. I just nod, my eyes locked on his. Heat builds low in my belly, thick and aching, the kind that blooms behind my hips and pulses with every breath. I shift, thighs pressing together instinctively, the friction not nearly enough but better than nothing. Liam's fingers find the collar of my shirt and ease it from my shoulders with the kind of tenderness that makes my pulse stutter.

It falls behind me in a quiet whisper of fabric, and then his hands return, gentle, warm, skilled—sliding up the back of my neck and into the tight line of muscles where stress likes to hide.

"You're tense," he murmurs, thumbs working slow circles into the space where my neck meets my shoulders. "Carrying the weight of the world again?"

I exhale hard, my head dropping forward, tension spilling out of me in waves. "Old habit," I murmur, eyes fluttering shut. His touch turns me liquid. My limbs go slack, body softening beneath his hands like wax held too close to a flame.

"Give it to me," he says, and his voice is rough now, low and close to my ear. The rasp of it skates down my spine and lodges between my legs. "Let me carry it for you. Even if it's only for tonight."

He punctuates each word with a kiss. The slope of my shoulder. The nape of my neck. The maddening spot just behind my ear that makes me shudder hard enough for him to feel it. Every touch is measured, purposeful, like he's mapping fault lines he fully intends to break wide open.

The clasp of my bra gives way beneath his fingers like it's been waiting to fall apart for him. He eases the straps down my arms slowly, watching every inch of skin as it's revealed. When the fabric drags across my nipples, the friction is quick, sharp, electric. I gasp. The sound barely gets out before Liam growls low in his throat, guttural and hungry, the kind of sound that says patience has its limits.

The kind of sound that says he's right on the edge of losing control.

"Perfect," he whispers, cupping my breasts in both hands, his thumbs brushing gentle, circling strokes over my nipples until I'm arching into him, chasing more. "Every inch of you."

His mouth replaces one hand, warm and wet and thorough, his tongue tracing slow, careful patterns that make it hard to think, harder to stay still. My fingers bury themselves in his hair, anchoring myself as the world tilts beneath me, pleasure rising so fast I feel like I'm drowning in it.

When he grazes me with his teeth—just the faintest scrape—I cry out, hips lifting, desperate for contact.

"Liam," I gasp, voice wrecked.

"Patience, Darlin'," he murmurs against my skin, his breath a cool contrast to the heat he's leaving behind. "We've got all night. I want to taste every inch of you."

And then he does exactly that.

He kisses his way down—throat, collarbone, sternum, between my ribs. Every inch of me becomes a point of discovery. My skin hums, sensitive in ways it's never been before, as if his mouth is waking parts of me I didn't know existed.

When his fingers find the button of my jeans, he pauses, his eyes finding mine through the flickering lantern light. His face is golden, every sharp line softened by shadow and warmth. His voice is quiet but clear.

"Still okay?"

I nod. "More than okay." My hips lift in silent invitation, and something raw flashes in his eyes.

He leans in, kisses the curve of my hip, then carefully works the denim down. Boots, socks, jeans, all peeled away one by one until I'm left in just my underwear, skin prickling with anticipation.

I should feel self-conscious, lying half-naked beneath lantern light in a tent on a windswept hill. But the way Liam looks at me? Like I'm the most beautiful thing he's ever seen?

I've never felt more wanted in my life.

"I dreamed of this," he says, voice thick with that gorgeous accent, desire laced through every syllable. "You, under the stars, wearing nothing but moonlight."

His hands trace up my calves, strong thumbs brushing the soft hollows behind my knees. When he presses his mouth to the inside of my thigh, I flinch—not from fear, but from the overwhelming contrast: warm tongue, rough stubble, tender skin. It scrambles my thoughts.

I can feel the heat of his breath against the thin cotton of my panties. Every inch of me clenches.

"You're trembling," he murmurs, looking up through the valley between my breasts, his gaze like a physical touch.

"Cold," I lie, even as sweat slicks the backs of my knees and the fire inside me licks higher with every passing second.

He chuckles, a low, knowing sound that reverberates through my bones. "Liar," he says softly, and presses his mouth to the wet spot between my legs.

The contact is fire and flood. I cry out, hips bucking. His hands catch my thighs, steadying me, keeping me right there as his tongue moves in slow, maddening strokes. He makes another low sound in his throat, part groan, part praise.

"You're already soaked for me," he says, the vibration of it nearly sends me over the edge. He hooks his fingers in my panties and drags them down slowly, torturously, the damp fabric dragging across my skin like silk and static.

"God," he breathes, spreading me open. "Look at you."

The way he looks at me makes my skin flush hot, color rising to my cheeks, my neck, all the way down to my chest. Like I'm something he's waited a long time to see. Like his head between my legs is the only thing that's ever made sense.

"You're still wearing too many clothes," I rasp, needing to see him, all of him.

"Soon," he promises, his mouth already moving again, closer.

He kisses my inner thighs, leaving trails of fire with every touch, alternating soft lips and the sharp tease of teeth. His hands slide beneath me, lifting me just enough to give him everything he wants.

And then he licks.

Just one slow, unhurried sweep of his tongue, and I swear I see stars. My hips jerk. My hands fist the blanket.

"Liam," I breathe, a prayer, a warning, a plea.

"I've got you," he whispers, voice low and rough, and then he really starts.

Tongue and lips and just enough pressure to unravel me. His stubble rasps against tender skin. His hands hold me wide open, fingers digging into the soft places at my hips. His mouth works like he's starving, like he needs this. Me. My taste. My sounds.

He licks, sucks, groans into me like every second is sacred. Like this is how he says I love you when the words aren't enough.

When he finally shifts his focus to that tight bundle of nerves at my center, it's not tentative—it's precise. Devastating. A pressure so perfect my entire world tilts.

Light bursts behind my closed eyes, white-hot and endless, a galaxy blooming beneath my skin. Need hits so fast and hard it knocks the air right out of me.

"That's it," Liam murmurs, his mouth moving against slick skin. "Show me what you need."

I do. My hips roll instinctively, searching for more pressure, more friction. My body finds its own rhythm, deep and unthinking, desperate in a way my mind can't keep up with. I can't form a sentence. I don't want to. I just want this—his mouth, his hands, the slow drag of pleasure climbing higher with every second.

One of his hands slides from beneath me, and then I feel it, the careful press of his finger at my entrance. Not demanding. Not pushing. Just there, asking the question with his body instead of words.

"Yes," I sob, the sound cracking on its way out. He answers without hesitation. One finger slides in, then another, and curls, hitting a place inside me that makes the world fracture. I cry out, back arching off the blankets, body seizing as if the air itself is too much.

And still, he doesn't stop.

He murmurs something against me and the words ripple through me like touch. "That's it," he says again, his lips brushing against soaked skin. "Let go for me, beautiful girl."

His fingers set a rhythm, sure and patient and utterly relentless, and his tongue moves with the kind of precision that feels unfair. Too good. Too much. My body is already strung tight, but he keeps building the pressure, teasing it higher, refusing to let me tip over until I'm so close it hurts.

Everything inside me is electric. Tense. The pleasure curls in on itself, deep in my belly, coiled and sparking. My breathing turns ragged, shallow, frantic, like my body knows what's coming and is already bracing for impact. I grind against his mouth, chasing it—chasing him—like I'm starving for it.

And when it breaks, it shatters.

My orgasm crashes over me like a tidal wave, ripping the breath from my lungs, stealing sound from my throat. I lock up, every muscle gone taut, my fingers gripping the blankets, Liam's hair, anything to anchor me. My body convulses around his fingers, against his mouth, as he keeps going, coaxing every last drop of pleasure from me like it's the elixir of life. He doesn't let up, not completely, just eases the intensity, softening the rhythm until the aftershocks leave me boneless and undone.

I'm gasping. Drenched in sweat. Barely tethered to this body that feels like it's been turned inside out.

"I wish you could see yourself right now," he whispers, kissing the inside of my thigh with the kind of intimacy that makes my chest ache. One, two, three soft presses of his mouth to flushed skin, each one drawing me gently back down to earth. "Absolutely fucking gorgeous."

His chin glistens in the soft glow of the lantern. His eyes are dark, pupils blown wide, but there's something else there too, something softer. Deeper. A kind of reverence that makes me feel seen. Worshipped. Known.

"You're so bloody beautiful when you come apart for me," he says, kissing his way up my body like he's savoring a path he's carved himself. Warm breath skimming across my stomach, the valley between my breasts, the slope of my collarbone. When he reaches my mouth, it's not gentle. It's real. Desperate. I taste myself on his lips. Salt and heat and something darker, deeper, and it hits me like a freight train. My hips buck beneath him, a sound I barely recognize rips from my throat, half moan, half plea.

He kisses me harder. His body covers mine, solid and hot even through the rough scrape of denim and cotton. The friction makes me whimper, skin burning with the need to feel his skin against mine.

"Off," I gasp, tugging at his shirt with clumsy, impatient fingers. Every nerve is still singing, my limbs molten. "I need you naked. Now."

He sits back on his heels, his mouth curving into something dark and wicked. One button at a time, he opens his shirt, moving slow enough to make my whole body ache. Inch by inch, more of him comes into view—broad chest, lean stomach, the trail of dark hair vanishing beneath his waistband. He shrugs the sleeves off his shoulders, and it's almost too much. He's beautiful, rough in all the right ways, the kind of body that makes your mouth go dry.

"Fuck, Liam," I breathe, voice wrecked. "Do you have any idea what you do to me?"

His eyes darken instantly, pupils swallowing the soft brown until only a sliver remains. "Tell me," he says, his voice nothing but gravel and need. "Tell me exactly what I do to you."

My pulse hammers in my throat. "You make me forget how to breathe," I whisper, voice unsteady. "I get wet just from the sound of your voice. You walk into a room and my whole body aches for you."

A sound punches out of him, half growl, half exhale, and then he's leaning over me, arms braced on either side of my head, his body caging mine.

"Good," he says, and the word lands like a promise.

I look up at him, at my fiancé, running my fingers over hard muscle. His body is a map of stories. Pale scars against tanned skin. A faint farmer's tan from years beneath the sun. The kind of calluses you can't get in a gym. I reach up and trace a small mark near his collarbone, the kind of scar that hides in plain sight.

"Fence wire," he murmurs, watching me. "Fourteen. Thought I could jump it."

I lean up and kiss it.

He inhales sharply, his hands tangling in my hair, the grip just tight enough to make me gasp.

My mouth trails down his chest, over the dip between ribs, the rise of muscle, the line of his hip. When I can't go lower, he rolls us, and now I'm straddling him, my thighs framing his hips, his body stretched beneath me like an offering.

I bend over him, tongue tasting the salt of his skin. His scent is all around me—woodsmoke, sweat, something sharper and unnameable that's just him. I can feel the beat of his heart beneath my palm, the tension in his muscles as I kiss lower, tongue tracing the line that disappears beneath his jeans.

He's trembling. Because of me. The power of it surges through me, heady and addictive.

"Jesus," he groans, voice rough and ragged. "Your mouth should be fucking illegal."

I smile against his stomach, teeth grazing the edge of a muscle as I dip my tongue into his navel. He jumps beneath me, eyes fluttering closed, chest rising and falling with shallow, wrecked breaths. I glance up.

He's watching me. And the hunger there? It's feral.

"Penelope," he says, my name broken on his tongue.

I reach for his belt, fingers fumbling. I want him. In my hands. In my mouth. Inside me. Now.

He swears under his breath, big hands coming up to help, desperate and shaking as we work together to undo the buckle and shove his jeans down. They drag over strong thighs, his cock straining against the black fabric of his boxer briefs, the shape of him making my mouth go dry.

"Should I stop?" I tease, fingers slipping under the waistband, voice like sin. "We can wait 'til tomorrow if you're too tired..."

He laughs, the sound breaking somewhere in his chest. "Don't play, Darlin'," he warns, voice dark. "Not unless you're ready to lose."

"But I like playing with you," I pout, and in one swift motion, I tug his boxers down.

His cock springs free, flushed and heavy and perfect. A bead of moisture glistens at the tip, catching the lantern light. He's all golden skin and hard muscle, every inch of him beautiful and mine.

Before I can even take a breath, he flips us again, his body settling between my thighs, his elbows braced to keep his weight off me. He's looking at me like I'm a question he already knows the answer to, but he still wants to ask anyway.

"We can stop," he says, his voice tight with restraint. "If you're tired, or—"

I wrap my legs around his hips and pull him down, cutting him off with my mouth.

The first glide of his cock against me is devastating. A tease of heat and promise, enough to make me gasp into his kiss. My hips arch, desperate, frantic.

"Fuck me," I whisper, dragging my mouth along the edge of his jaw. "I want my fiancé's cock inside me."

The word hits him like a punch to the chest.

Fiancé.

Liam shudders, the tremor running through him like a fault line cracking open.

"Say it again," he demands, voice barely a sound, more breath than speech.

"My fiancé," I repeat, softer now, letting the word hang between us like a vow, letting him feel it.

"Christ, Darlin'," he groans, his cock twitching against me. "You're going to ruin me."

Then his mouth is on mine, hot and wild and all teeth and tongue. Possessive. Hungry. His kiss is a collision, a claiming. His hand slides between us, fingers dipping down to find me slick and ready, his touch a slow, careful circle that makes my hips buck off the blankets.

"Fuck, you're soaked," he groans, pride darkening every syllable, like he's already halfway undone by the proof of how much I want him.

"All for you." I spread my thighs wider, my body already moving in sync with his touch, chasing every flick of his fingers, every breathless drag.

His groan is raw. "I need to be inside you."

He reaches between us, guiding himself with shaking fingers. The blunt head of his cock presses at my entrance, and even that little pressure makes me gasp, my nails digging into his shoulders as he begins to push in.

My body opens for him, slow and steady, every inch a deep, delicious stretch that leaves me breathless. I arch into him, nails scraping down his back as the pressure builds, full and overwhelming.

"Look at me," he says, stopping halfway, voice gentler now. A thread of something tender woven into the wreckage.

I force my eyes open. And fuck if he doesn't take the rest of my breath away. His hair is a mess, his jaw tight with restraint, eyes dark and locked on mine like I'm the only thing holding him together. Sweat beads at his temple, his lips parted, chest rising and falling like he's fighting not to lose himself completely.

"I love you, Penelope."

It lands right in my chest, a clean shot to the heart. I can't breathe. Can't think.

"I love you too," I whisper, reaching up to touch his face, my fingers brushing across his cheekbones. It's too much and still not enough.

"You don't know what that does to me," he murmurs, voice cracking around the edges. "Hearing you say that..." He presses a kiss into my palm, then holds my gaze as he slowly pushes his cock all the way in.

It's too much. It's everything. I gasp as my body adjusts around him, the fullness so intense it steals my thoughts, leaving only heat and pressure and this ache that's lived in my bones since the day we met.

"Jesus, you feel too fucking good," he groans, his jaw flexing as he struggles for control.

"Don't hold back, Liam. Please," I whisper, wrapping my legs around his hips, heels pressing into him to pull him deeper.

"If I don't hold back," he breathes, lips brushing mine, "this might be over before it starts."

But even as he says it, he starts to move.

His rhythm is devastating. Slow, deep strokes that leave me shaking, each one pulling a new sound from my throat. My hands roam his back, fingers tracing sweat-slick skin, feeling the tension coiled in his muscles as he fights to hold on. I press kisses to his shoulder, his throat, every place I can reach. I want to learn him like this. Burn it all into memory.

"God, Liam, right there," I cry out when he shifts slightly and hits that spot and my vision goes white for a second.

He does it again. And again.

"Don't stop," I beg, voice high and breathless. "Please don't stop."

"Wasn't planning on it," he says, and his smile is strained but real, that familiar dimple flashing like muscle memory.

The tent is filled with the sounds of us. Flesh meeting flesh, sharp gasps, whispered names. Outside, the world carries on—crickets, wind, stars—but in here, we've created something that feels separate. Sacred.

He shifts again, angle changing, and holy shit, my world collapses.

A sob rips from me, loud and raw, as he thrusts over and over, unraveling me from the inside out. My hands clutch at him. My body tightens.

"There it is," he murmurs, eyes locked on mine, his voice like sex and midnight. "That's my girl."

"Liam, I'm close," I warn, every muscle in my body locking down, breath catching, pleasure building to an impossible pitch.

"Me too, Darlin'," he says, his voice fraying at the edges, his thrusts losing some of their polish, growing rougher, hungrier.

His hand slips between us, thumb finding my clit, circling with just enough pressure to push me to the edge.

I break. I shatter.

My orgasm rips through me like lightning across a black sky. Bright, all-consuming, terrifying in its intensity. I cry out, body convulsing, hands scrambling for him, nails digging in as I ride the wave.

"Fuck, Penelope," he groans, and then he's gone too.

His rhythm stutters. He drives deep, holds there, and breaks. His body shakes above me, face buried against my neck, voice nothing but a strangled moan as he comes hard, heat flooding inside me. Every muscle in him goes tight, then slack, his entire body surrendering to mine.

Then his forehead finds mine again, breath coming in ragged, gasping pulls. We stay like that for what feels like forever, still joined, still breathing each other in. Neither of us dares to move. As if any shift might undo the spell hanging thick in the air.

This part—the quiet after—is almost better than the rest. The way desperation melts into something softer, something sweeter. The way it leaves room for tenderness.

"You okay?" Liam murmurs, voice low and warm against my temple. He peppers slow kisses along my jaw and down my throat, each one feather-light, unhurried.

"Perfect," I whisper, my fingers drifting over his back. There's no urgency in the way I touch him now, only awe.

He laughs, a soft huff into my neck. "Christ, that felt good." His voice is muffled, still rough around the edges. "I think I've ruined a perfectly decent pair of sheets more than once, thinking about this."

The admission pulls a surprised laugh from me, and he lifts his head to look down at me, his grin crooked and shameless.

"What?" he teases. "You don't believe me?"

"It's not that," I say, smoothing my palms over the wide span of his shoulders. "It's just... I've done the same."

His eyebrows nearly leap off his face. "Yeah?"

I nod, smile curving slow and wicked. "More times than I can count. Shower. Bed. Once in the family room when no one was around."

"Jesus fucking Christ," he groans. "You're trying to kill me."

"You said you wanted honesty."

"Yeah, but I didn't think you'd hand me fantasy fuel like that while I'm still recovering."

I grin and press a kiss to his cheek. "Just giving you something to think about later."

He shifts to the side, rolling us carefully so we stay close, his arm slung heavy across my waist, his face tucked into the crook of my neck like he's never planning to leave. The cool night air brushes over my bare skin, and he reaches down without a word, pulling a blanket over us. Cocooning us in our own little universe, just heat and breath and the soft hush of nighttime wrapped around us.

"Second proposal accepted," he murmurs, voice lazy and sweet, accent deepening as sleep tugs at the edges. "Three more to go."

I laugh quietly. "Is there a schedule I should know about? Should I start blocking off dates in my planner?"

He snorts. "Wouldn't be much of a surprise, then, would it? Besides, I bet the others are scrambling now. Trying to outdo Spencer's spontaneity and my..." He gestures vaguely at our surroundings. "Wilderness seduction."

"It's not a competition," I say, even though the idea of all of them trying to top each other makes me smile. "I'd say yes even if one of you asked while I was brushing my teeth."

"Don't say that too loud," he warns, laughing softly. "Archer will propose while you're chopping vegetables."

"That does sound like him," I admit, though, knowing Archer, he'd find a way to make even that romantic.

Liam pulls me closer, his body curving into mine like we were always meant to fit this way—his chest to my back, his arm across my waist, his breath soft against my neck.

"What about Jamie and Sam?" he asks, fingers trailing idle patterns across my skin, raising goosebumps even now.

"Jamie'll do it during sex," I say without thinking. "And Sam... something quiet. Something gentle."

Liam hums. "And me? Was this what you imagined?"

I shift, just enough to look at him, brushing hair away from his forehead. "This was perfect," I tell him honestly. "The stars. The silence. You. It was exactly how I'd imagine it, if I had ever let myself imagine it."

"You didn't?" he asks, something quiet in his voice.

"I was too scared," I admit. "Of wanting something I thought I could never have."

He pulls me closer. "And now you have all five of us." His fingers never stop moving, slow, lazy lines drawn across my skin. I could fall asleep like this. I want to. But he shifts suddenly, reaching for the small pack tucked near the edge of our makeshift bed.

"We should clean up before we pass out," he says softly, pulling out some wet wipes.

There's a tenderness to the way he wipes me down, every movement slow, careful, like he's handling something fragile. Like I matter.

And maybe that's what catches in my throat—the way he makes even this feel special.

When he finishes, he tucks the bag away, then pulls me back into him, strong arms wrapping around my waist like they belong there. He folds the blankets over us, sealing in the warmth, the quiet, the us. The ring on my finger catches one last flicker of light before he reaches for the lantern—opal flashing once in the dark, a quick burst of color before the night swallows everything but his arms around me.

"I love you, Penelope," Liam whispers into the dark.

I turn in his arms and kiss his jaw, my words barely more than a breath. "I love you too, Liam Taylor."

And I do. I really, truly do.

As sleep begins to pull me under, I think about the strange, messy, beautiful path that brought me here—to a tent in the middle of nowhere, to the quiet weight of this man wrapped around me, to a love so big it's changed the shape of who I am.

It should feel overwhelming.

But instead, it feels like fate.

30

———————

I lean my head against the passenger window as Liam's truck bumps along the last stretch of road leading to my house. The last two days with him at the ranch have left me pleasantly exhausted, muscles aching in that satisfying way that comes from riding horses and intense lovemaking. I'm half-dozing, thoughts drifting like lazy clouds, when we pull into the driveway and everything shifts. A dark figure I'd recognize anywhere is leaning against the side of the house. Watching. Waiting. My heart does a stupid little somersault that I'd never admit to.

Archer.

Even from this distance, I can make out the rigid set of his shoulders, the way he stands with his feet planted firmly apart. The stance of a man who's used to giving orders and having them followed.

"Looks like somebody missed you," Liam teases. He slides a glance my way, his dimples appearing as he smiles. "Should I be jealous?"

"Never," I say, but my eyes are locked on Archer as he walks to meet us, the determined set of his shoulders, the way his glasses catch the last of the day's sunlight. Something about Archer has always hit differently than the others—the rigid self-control, the dominance.

Liam chuckles. "Your face says otherwise." He doesn't seem even a little bothered, and that's part of what makes this whole beautifully messy thing work.

Before I can say a word, Archer stalks to the driver's side and yanks the door open hard enough to make the whole truck shudder. No hello. No smile. Just his eyes—locked on Liam, sharp and hungry, like getting to me is the only thing keeping him upright.

"Out," he says, voice low and frayed with urgency. Not angry. Just desperate.

To his credit, Liam doesn't seem bothered. He unbuckles his seatbelt with an easy grace. "G'day to you too, mate. Been a while."

Archer just stares at him, jaw tight, until Liam slides out of the truck. I can see the muscle in his jaw jump, the visual evidence of a man barely holding his shit together. They stand there for a moment, a silent conversation passing between them that I can't quite decipher, before Liam tips his hat in my direction.

"I'll see you later, Darlin'," he says, and then he's walking toward the house, whistling like this is a completely normal Thursday.

"What the actual fuck was that?" I mutter to the universe, because clearly no one else is going to explain whatever testosterone-fueled standoff just happened.

Before I can wrap my head around it, Archer slides into the driver's seat, slams the door shut, and starts the engine like he's been waiting days to do exactly that. His scent hits me immediately, and it takes everything in me not to lean in and breathe him deep.

"What the hell, Archer?" I finally manage. "You can't just—"

"I can," he says, throwing the truck into reverse with a spray of gravel. "I am." His voice is sharp, purposeful, each word like a compass point, steady, unshakable, like he's already decided exactly where we're going and how we'll get there.

"This is exactly the kind of Neanderthal behavior I'd expect from Jamie, not you," I say, gripping the door handle as we take a turn too fast. "What's next? Dragging me by my hair to your cave?"

Something that might be amusement flickers across his face before it's gone, replaced by that same intense focus. "If that's what it takes."

The truck lurches forward, and I fumble for the seatbelt, snapping it into place. "You know this is basically kidnapping."

With anyone else, I'd be pissed. Fuming. But with Archer? All I feel is heat. Low, coiled, impossible to ignore. It's not outrage burning through me. It's want. Fast and sharp and so much worse than fury.

He glances at me, just once, and the corner of his mouth twitches. "You want me to take you back?"

I should say yes. I should be furious that he's just shown up right after Liam proposed, manhandled my fiancé, and absconded with me in the truck. I should demand explanations and apologies.

Instead, I cross my arms and mutter, "Just drive, Sullivan."

We tear down the country roads, past the fields of heather and gorse that cover the islands this time of year. The distinctive coconut scent of the yellow flowers drifts through the partially open window, mingling with the ever-present salt of the sea air. The evening is settling in, painting everything in shades of purple and blue. In the distance, the jagged silhouettes of sea stacks stand like sentinels against the darkening sky, timeless guardians of the Hebridean coastline. Archer drives with one hand on the wheel, the other out the window, fingers tapping an impatient rhythm. His knuckles are scraped raw, fresh injuries from work, I assume. The silence between us is a living thing, charged with all the words we're not saying.

"Two days," I finally say, unable to stand it anymore. "It's only been two fucking days."

"Five," he corrects, eyes fixed on the road. "You were with Spencer two days before you left with Liam. And I was on the boat the one day you were home."

The fact that he's been counting makes something warm settle in my chest, but I'm not about to let him know that. "What, do we need to have a shared custody calendar stuck to the fridge?"

"If that's what it takes," he says again, and I can't tell if he's joking or dead serious.

"You could have texted."

"I did."

"'Come back' is not a conversation, you emotionally constipated jerk," I snap.

"Never claimed to be good at conversation." His voice is gruff, but there's something underneath it, a tension that tells me he's holding back. His fingers clench on the steering wheel.

"Where are we going?" I ask, softer now.

"Nowhere specific."

"Ah yes, the classic kidnapping destination of 'nowhere specific,'" I mutter. "Very reassuring."

And that's Archer in a nutshell. Direct to the point of curtness, yet somehow managing to say absolutely nothing useful.

I take the opportunity to study him. His hair is shorter than when I last saw him, the sides freshly buzzed. There's a new scratch along his jawline, still pink and healing. His shoulders are set in a rigid line beneath his flannel shirt, and I can see the pulse jumping in his throat. Everything about him screams tension.

"You missed me," I say, not a question. I'm aiming for teasing, but it comes out breathier than intended.

His eyes cut to me, dark and intense. "Yes."

That one word hits me like a physical touch, trailing heat down my spine.

The truck suddenly veers off the main road, bumping down a narrow track I've never noticed before. Branches scrape against the sides as we push deeper into what seems to be an overgrown field. Finally, Archer stops in a small clearing, sheltered by a copse of trees. He kills the engine, and silence engulfs us.

For a long moment, neither of us moves. I'm acutely aware of my breathing, of the small space between us in the cab, of the way the fading light casts shadows across his face.

Then Archer turns to face me fully, and the look in his eyes steals my breath. There's hunger there, raw and unfiltered, but also something that looks dangerously close to vulnerability.

"You're wearing his ring," he says, eyes dropping to my left hand where the opal sits bold and defiant, spitting fire in the low light.

I flex my fingers, suddenly self-conscious. "Yes."

"And Spencer's." His gaze moves to the emerald.

"Yes," I repeat, my voice smaller now. "Is that a problem?" I ask, my voice catching slightly.

"It's not a problem," he says, his jaw working as if the words are being physically ground out. "I just thought I'd be the first."

"The first?" I blink at him, genuinely confused.

"Not the first to fuck you," he clarifies bluntly. "The first to put a ring on your finger."

His hand shoots out, fingers wrapping around my wrist, tugging me across the center seat and into his lap with a strength that makes me gasp. I end up straddling him, my knees on either side of his hips, his face inches from mine.

His hands slide up my sides, leaving trails of fire in their wake, before one settles at the back of my neck, fingers tangling in my hair. The other grips my hip, hard enough that I know I'll find marks tomorrow. I should be annoyed at his presumption, at the way he's manhandling me, but all I can think is *finally*.

"Did you miss me?" he asks, and there it is. That hint of uncertainty that he tries so hard to hide.

I could tease him. Could make him work for it. But the naked need in his eyes undoes me.

"Every minute of every day," I whisper.

His grip tightens, and I see the exact moment something in him snaps. Control, maybe. Restraint. Whatever it is, it's gone now, replaced by a desperate hunger that mirrors the ache building inside me.

"I've spent days imagining what we'd do when we saw each other again. Now be a good girl and let me remind you who you belong to." His mouth crashes into mine, hot and demanding, stealing the breath from my lungs.

Archer kisses like he does everything else, with absolute focus and zero hesitation. His tongue sweeps against mine, claiming, conquering, and I'm dizzy with it, with him.

"Fuck, I missed this," he rumbles against my lips. "Missed the way you taste."

I should tell him this isn't the way to handle things. That kidnapping your girlfriend when she returns from a trip is not healthy relationship behavior. But his mouth is doing sinful things to my neck, and suddenly I can't remember why I should care about relationship etiquette.

My hands find his hair, fingers sliding through the short strands at the back of his head, tugging just hard enough to make him groan. The sound vibrates through me, settling low in my belly, kindling a fire that's been smoldering since I first saw him waiting for me.

His hands are everywhere, sliding under my shirt, tracing the curve of my spine, palming my ass through my jeans. Each touch is possessive, like he's remapping territory he's afraid he's forgotten. His mouth moves to my jaw, teeth scraping against sensitive skin, before trailing hot, open-mouthed kisses down my neck.

"Five days," he murmurs against my collarbone, his breath hot and damp. "Five days thinking about them touching you, tasting you." His teeth sink into the tender spot where my neck meets my shoulder, just hard enough to make me gasp. "Thinking about you coming for them."

I arch against him, shameless in my need. "Archer—"

"Say it again." His voice is ragged, desperate. "Say my name."

"Archer," I breathe, rolling my hips against his, feeling him hard beneath me. "Archer, Archer, Archer."

He makes a sound like I've wounded him, his hands gripping my waist so tightly I can feel each individual finger branding my skin. "You have no idea what you do to me," he says, breathing hard. "No fucking idea."

I roll my hips again, slow this time, and smile when his eyes flutter closed. "I think I have some idea."

His eyes snap open, dark and wild behind those frames. "You think this is funny?" But there's no anger in his voice, just a raw hunger that makes me shiver. "You think I can just watch you with them and not lose my goddamn mind?"

"I thought you were okay with this arrangement," I say, the words soft but edged with worry. "If you're not—"

"I am," he cuts in, his voice steady despite the roughness in his breath. "I'm okay with sharing you. But sometimes, I need you to myself."

It's a small distinction, but it lands hard. He's not throwing down an ultimatum or hiding behind jealousy. He's naming what he needs, and it hits me right in the chest. He knows what we are. What we all agreed to. He doesn't want more than the others. Just his own piece of me, without distraction. Fully present. Fully his, if only for a while.

"Well, here I am," I tell him, cradling his face between my hands.

Before I can say more, he's kissing me again, deeper this time, his tongue stroking against mine in a rhythm that makes me think of other things, dirtier things. I'm dimly aware of the windows fogging up around us, of the truck's cramped quarters, but nothing matters except the feel of his hands on my body, his mouth against mine.

"I thought about you every second you were gone," he confesses between kisses, words tumbling out like he can't hold them back anymore. "Thought about the way you taste, the way you smell." His hand slides up to cup my breast through my shirt, thumb brushing over my nipple. "Thought about the sounds you make when I touch you just right."

I arch into his touch, desperate. The truck suddenly feels too small, too constraining for what I need from him. What I need to give him.

He pulls back just enough to rest his forehead against mine, his breathing ragged and uneven. This close, I can see the faint crow's feet at the corners of his eyes, the stubble that's thicker than usual, evidence of long days and longer nights. He looks exhausted in a way that has nothing to do with physical fatigue. His hand at my hip loosens its grip, thumb now tracing apologetic circles where he'd been holding too tight.

"Five days," he says again, the words more a confession than an accusation this time. "Felt longer."

I reach up, finally giving in to the impulse to straighten his glasses. "You could have called. There's this amazing invention called a telephone. It's been around for a while now. Even comes with this thing called texting."

He makes a sound that's half laugh, half grunt. "I didn't want to ruin it for you, Nel. I just should have thought this whole thing out better. I would have made different decisions."

"Different decisions about what?" I ask, genuinely confused. "About us?"

He shakes his head, a quick, definitive movement. "About the timing. About letting them go first."

My heart does that stupid little flip again. Archer Sullivan is many things—blunt, demanding, sometimes downright rude—but emotionally articulate isn't usually one of them. This halting confession feels significant.

"What do you mean?" I need him to say it.

He sighs, a sound of frustration directed at himself rather than me. "I told them I would propose last, but I should have been first."

"I didn't know it mattered to you," I say carefully. "The order."

"Everything about you matters to me," he says simply, as if he's stating that water is wet or the sky is blue. An undeniable fact that requires no embellishment.

The sheer certainty in his voice steals my breath. While Spencer's love feels like being wrapped in a warm blanket and Liam's like dancing in summer rain, Archer's is like standing on solid ground during an earthquake, the one stable thing in a world of chaos.

"Besides," he says, "you're not exactly subtle when you're happy. I saw your face after Spencer gave you that ring. Then again in the truck with Liam, one more ring on your hand—" He swallows hard. "That should've been me making you look like that."

The words knock the wind out of me. I hadn't considered that Archer—stoic, unreadable Archer—might feel left out.

"Archer," I say gently, "this isn't a competition."

"I know that," he snaps, too fast. Then softer, regret flickering across his face. "I do. But I also know I'm not the easiest of the five. I'm just—"

"The man who kidnapped me because he couldn't stand to be away from me another second?" I offer, a smile tugging at my lips.

He groans. "When you say it like that, it sounds unhinged."

"It is unhinged," I say brightly. "But also kind of romantic. In a caveman-meets-soulmate sort of way."

He gives a helpless little shrug, hands gesturing vaguely at everything. "I'm not good at this. Any of it."

"You're doing just fine," I murmur, pressing a kiss to the corner of his mouth.

But he doesn't smile. Not really. "I'm serious, Nel. I screwed up. Just because I don't talk about it doesn't mean I don't..."

"Don't what?" I ask, already knowing.

"Feel everything," he says, the words rough, like they've clawed their way out of his throat. "So damn much it terrifies me."

I press my palms to his chest, his heart hammering beneath my hands like it's trying to get out. Archer admitting fear feels like watching the moon crack open.

"You know what's funny?" I say, tracing his jaw with my thumb. "Most people think you're cold. But I've always known you feel more than anyone. You just bury it deeper."

Something shifts in his expression. "How'd you know that?"

"Because people don't fight that hard to control their emotions unless they're scared of what happens when they don't," I say simply. "I see you, Archer Sullivan. Even when you're trying not to be seen."

There's a long beat of silence.

"How long were you waiting in the driveway?" I ask.

"Three hours." His hand slips into my hair. "I saw Liam's stupid grin when you pulled in and almost went back inside."

"But you didn't."

"No." His mouth curves, just barely. "By then I was too pissed. Five days of planning what I'd say, and there he was, with that stupid hat and his stupid accent."

I laugh, even though my chest aches a little. "You know Liam can't help his accent."

"He could talk less."

I shake my head, grinning. "You like him."

"Doesn't mean I don't want to punch him sometimes."

"What were you planning to say to me?" I ask, quieter now.

His eyes drop to my mouth. "That I missed you. That I suck at this, but I want you to know that I'm trying. I know it's not perfect, but—"

"It's enough," I say, framing his face in my hands. "You're enough."

"I want more," he says, voice so low it barely makes it between us. "More time. More of you. More..."

"More what?" I whisper.

His grip tightens on my waist. "Everything," he says. "I want everything with you, Nel."

The words land like a strike to the chest, sharp and hot and breathtaking.

"You have me," I say. "You've had me since the night you told me my fish sandwich was 'adequate at best' and then ate the whole thing."

"I was testing the restaurant's credibility."

"By insulting my food?"

"Constructive criticism."

"'Adequate at best' is not constructive. That's just you being an ass."

"And yet," he says, smirking now, "you're still here."

"And yet," I echo, laughing softly. "Apparently, I have a type."

"Let me guess. Brooding, emotionally constipated men with soft hands and sharp tongues?"

I kiss the corner of his mouth again. "No. Just you."

His pupils blow wide, and his hand slips down over my hip, possessive.

"Say it again," he murmurs, voice low and wrecked.

"You're mine," I whisper against his lips. "Ring or no ring."

His hand on my waist slides higher, spanning my ribs, his thumb brushing the underside of my breast through my bra. I inhale sharply, need racing through my system like wildfire.

"God, I love that noise," he says, his voice a low rumble now.

"I can make more noises," I suggest, deliberately pressing against his hand. "If you're interested in hearing them."

"I'm interested in everything about you," he says, his gaze so intense it's almost a physical touch. "Every sound, every expression, every goddamn freckle."

The mood in the truck shifts again, conversation giving way to something darker. The air feels thick, charged with electricity, and I'm suddenly acutely aware of how I'm still straddling him, of how little space separates us.

And then he's pulling me down to him again, his mouth claiming mine with a fierce possession that leaves no room for doubt or questions. I may have two rings on my finger, tangible symbols from the other men in my life, but in this moment, with Archer's hands and mouth on me, they might as well not exist at all.

Archer kisses like he does everything else—directly, thoroughly, with an intensity that consumes. His mouth is hot against mine, not gentle but not punishing either, finding that perfect middle ground where I can feel his hunger without being overwhelmed by it. His hands tangle in my hair, angling my head exactly how he wants it, and I surrender to his guidance without hesitation.

"Fuck, you taste like heaven," he murmurs against my mouth.

I want to say something clever in response, but his tongue slides against mine and coherent thought scatters like marbles. Instead, I press closer, my hands gripping his shoulders, feeling the solid muscle beneath his flannel shirt. The time apart has made us both greedy, hands grasping, mouths seeking, bodies trying to eliminate any space between us despite the obstacles.

And obstacles there are. The truck, while roomy, still wasn't designed for this kind of activity. The steering wheel jabs into my back when I lean too far. The seatbelt buckle digs into Archer's hip. When he shifts beneath me, trying to get better access to my neck, his elbow slams into the door with a dull thud.

"Fuck," he hisses, but doesn't stop, his mouth finding the sensitive spot below my ear that makes my toes curl.

I'm not faring much better. When I try to adjust my position, my knee bangs painfully against the armrest. I suck in a sharp breath, and Archer immediately pulls back.

"Enough," he snaps, voice low and frayed, like it's been scraped raw by restraint. His hand darts past me, fumbling for the door handle. A second later, the truck door swings open, and cold air rushes in, biting against my overheated skin.

"Out."

"What?" I blink at him, brain still lagging behind the shift.

"Out," he repeats, already pushing the driver's side door wider, his body moving with the kind of sharp-edged purpose that leaves no room for confusion. "We need more space."

"It's freezing," I say, a protest that lands soft and useless between us.

He looks at me, really looks, and the expression on his face is pure tension. Exasperation laced with want. "I'll keep you warm."

It's not a promise. It's a fact. And the way he says it—calm, sure, like nothing could possibly matter more—lights something molten and immediate in my chest. My thighs clench, instinctive.

Before I can say anything else, his hands are on my waist, and then

I'm lifted off his lap like I weigh nothing. My feet hit the ground outside the truck, and the wind slices through me, sharp and shocking. I stumble, legs still half-numb from being curled up, but he's already there, one strong arm catching me like he knew I'd falter.

"You okay?" he murmurs, low and rough, a flicker of softness threading through the heat in his eyes.

I nod, breath stolen clean out of me, watching as he unfolds from the truck like he's made of steel and gravity. He kicks the door shut without looking, gaze fixed on mine. Out here, without the cab around us, he feels bigger. Broader. Wilder.

The grass gives under my shoes as he takes my wrist and guides me toward the edge of the field. His grip is firm, unhurried. My pulse pounds in my ears, every step like a countdown I didn't know I'd started.

We reach a small clearing tucked behind a crooked row of oaks, the last of the sunlight threading through bare branches. Archer stops, turns to face me. His eyes are darker now, barely brown, framed by the glint of his glasses. One look and I feel it, a shiver under my skin, a hum low in my belly.

"Here," he says, not asking.

"Here?" I glance around like I might find a reason to say no, even as my body leans toward him. "You're serious?"

He doesn't answer right away. His gaze sweeps the clearing, all sharp calculation and silent control, like he's checking variables I can't see. The wind ruffles his hair, and I want to smooth it down, press my lips to the line of his jaw, beg for what I already know he's going to give me.

"Yes," he says at last, the corner of his mouth tugging up just enough to show me he's enjoying this. "Is that a problem?"

It's not a question. It's a checkpoint. The kind of check-in that doesn't sound like one, but means everything. That's the way Archer is —possessive, yes, but careful with me. Intentional.

I shake my head. "No problem."

"Good." He steps back, voice low. "Stand there."

I do. The air is sharp and damp, the ground soft beneath me, grass already soaking through the thin canvas of my shoes. Archer circles me slowly, his movements quiet, careful, like he's taking inventory—every breath, every shift, every inch of exposed skin.

Each step he takes winds me tighter. Every pass feels like he's pulling a thread taut inside me, like he knows exactly how to unravel me without ever laying a hand.

"Take off your bra. Slowly. I want to see every inch of what's mine."

His voice is calm. Steady. The kind that doesn't need to rise to make you listen. His gaze holds me there, unflinching, as he says, "Ring or no ring, Penelope. Your body. Your pleasure. Your surrender. They belong to me."

I reach behind my back, fingers finding the clasp of the simple cotton bra I didn't think twice about this morning. It slips off my arms and onto the grass with the rest of my clothes, and I have to stop myself from crossing my arms over my chest. I feel exposed, every inch of me on display, but not unsafe.

His eyes roam over me slowly. "You're beautiful." Just that. No flourishes. Just truth.

"Your turn," I say, trying to steady myself, to balance the moment.

He shakes his head. "Not yet. Finish first."

The understanding settles low in my belly. This is part of it—his control, my vulnerability. He's still fully dressed, and I'm already trembling.

"Shoes. Then pants," he says, arms folded now, watching.

I toe off my damp sneakers, then work the button on my jeans. The denim clings to my thighs from the damp, and I have to shimmy out of them. It's not graceful. It's not sexy. But he watches like nothing else exists.

When I'm down to just my underwear, I look up at him. Wait.

He nods.

The last piece comes off. The air is cool against my skin, dew-damp grass tickling my ankles, but it's the heat in Archer's eyes that warms me.

His breath catches, subtle but unmistakable.

"Turn around," he says, voice rougher now.

I turn slowly, pulse hammering in my throat, aware of every inch of skin he can see. When I face him again, the look on his face makes my legs go loose under me.

"Now," he says, hands going to his belt, "you get to see what you do to me."

There's nothing showy about the way Archer undresses. No flourish. No games. It's careful. Controlled. Every movement is a reminder of exactly who's in charge.

I've seen him naked before, but here, like this, bare under the open sky and undressing just for me, it feels different. Like it matters more.

My eyes trace the lines of his body, the definition that comes from years of doing things the hard way. His strength is earned, not sculpted, and it shows in every inch.

"See something you like?" he asks as he pushes his jeans and boxers down in one easy movement.

"Everything," I say, no hesitation.

He steps out of his boots, kicks the rest of his clothes aside, and stands before me completely bare. Unashamed. Gorgeous.

His glasses are slightly crooked, and that tiny imperfection against all that control makes something in my chest tighten.

"Come here," he says, holding out a hand.

I take it.

He pulls me into him until we're chest to chest, bare skin against bare skin, heat radiating off him like a promise. His hand comes up to cup my cheek, thumb brushing along my bottom lip. His eyes are soft but unwavering.

"Tell me if anything becomes too much," he says quietly.

And in those words, I hear everything else: *I'll take care of you. I'll be careful with what's mine.*

"I will," I whisper.

Archer nods once, then lowers his mouth to mine. Our breath mingles in the cool air, and then he kisses me. Soft at first, almost careful, like he's afraid of breaking something we just figured out how to hold. But it deepens fast, hunger slipping beneath the surface. His hands grip my waist, dragging me flush against him until there's not an inch of space left.

We sink to our knees together, the grass damp and cool beneath us. He lowers me slowly to my back, bracing his weight above me. Behind him, the sky glows faintly, the sunset bleeding out at the edges, and we just look at each other for a second. Like we can't believe it's real.

Then he bends and kisses his way across my collarbone, mouth warm and open and unbearably slow. His teeth scrape against my skin and every nerve ending lights up like a switchboard. I squirm beneath him, breath snagging.

"Stay still," he murmurs, one hand tightening at my hip.

I try. I try. But it takes every ounce of willpower not to chase his mouth with my body.

He rewards me with a kiss just beneath my ear, the kind that makes me dissolve. "Good girl," he whispers, and my entire body clenches around the sound.

His tongue traces the shell of my ear before he catches the lobe gently between his teeth. The tug is just sharp enough to send a jolt between my legs. A moan slips out before I can stop it.

"You like that," he says. It isn't a question.

I nod, already breathless.

"Tell me what you want, Penelope."

"I want..." My voice falters as his hand slides from my hip to the inside of my thigh, not quite where I need him, but close enough to make me ache. "I want you to touch me."

His mouth curls against my neck. "I am touching you."

"You know what I mean."

He pulls back just enough to meet my eyes, serious and sharp. "Then say it. All of it."

It's a challenge. A quiet demand to tear down the last wall. I swallow, pulse hammering in my throat.

"I want your mouth," I say, surprised by the steadiness of my voice. "Between my legs."

His gaze goes molten, and something dark flickers behind it. Approval. Possession. Want. "One rule," he says, sliding lower between my legs. "You don't come until I say so."

He settles between my thighs, his shoulders pressing mine open, his mouth hovering just above where I need him most. The air hits me first, cool and sharp. Then his breath follows, warm and steady, and it makes my head spin.

"What are you waiting for?" I ask, voice ragged.

He looks up at me, his gaze moving across the length of my body like a claim. "Tell me what you want again."

"I want your mouth on me," I say, clearer this time.

"Then what?"

"I want your tongue on me. Inside me. Please, Archer."

He tosses his glasses to the side like he's done being careful and lowers his head. The first sweep of his tongue is so sudden, so devastating, I arch off the ground, a guttural cry ripping from my throat. Every stroke is precise. Calculated. Like he's writing his name on my body with his mouth, and doesn't care how long it takes as long as it's done well.

"God, Archer," I gasp, my fingers threading into his hair. It's short, but I find a way to hold on, to anchor myself as he pulls me under.

He hums low in his throat, and the vibration nearly undoes me. The tension coils fast—too fast.

He pulls back just enough, his eyes meeting mine, voice rough. "Don't come yet."

I nod, panting, thighs trembling. He buries his mouth between my legs again, building me up and backing off in turns that feel like exquisite cruelty.

"Archer—I can't—" My voice breaks as he circles a spot that nearly unravels me. "It's too much."

He replaces his mouth with the pad of his thumb, keeping the pressure steady without letting me tip over. "You can," he says, calm and sure. "I know you can. Breathe."

I inhale sharply, lungs full of cold air, trying to calm the storm inside me.

"I don't know how much more I can take," I admit. "You're making it impossible."

He grins, slow and sharp. "Fight it. The longer you hold out, the better it'll feel when I finally let you fall apart. And you will fall apart, Penelope. But only when I say."

Before I can respond, Archer dips his head again, replacing his thumb with his mouth. This time, he teases—his tongue moving in slow, infuriating circles, never where I need it most. It's maddening. Perfect. Not enough. I'm burning alive and freezing cold at the same time.

"Archer," I breathe, though I'm not even sure what I'm asking for. Relief? Ruin?

He hears it anyway. Of course he does.

"We're not done," he murmurs, voice rough against my skin. "Not even close. When I'm finished with you, you won't remember anyone's name but mine. And tomorrow, when you're sore and aching and still feel me inside you, you'll know exactly who you belong to."

Time starts to disintegrate after that. There's only the tight spiral of tension and his mouth working me open. He brings me to the edge and pulls me back like he's tuning an instrument. Building pressure. Drawing out every second until it feels like something inside me might snap from how tightly it's wound.

Just when I start to shake, his pace shifts again. Gentler now, coaxing, soft enough to make me whimper. Then he builds it back up. Slow. Cruel. Precise.

"Please," I whisper, not even sure what I'm pleading for anymore. To come. To keep waiting. To survive it.

He gives me one long, languid lick and pulls away, eyes dark, cheeks ruddy. His lips are wet, his breath hits my skin like steam. Then he's moving up my body, slow and unhurried, until his mouth finds mine. The kiss is wet and messy and absolutely necessary.

"Your turn," he says into my mouth, voice low and jagged.

It takes me a second to understand. My brain is hazy, every nerve misfiring. But then I get it. I press my palms to his shoulders and guide him back until he's lying in the grass and I'm kneeling between his legs.

The cool air hits my skin. The tips of the grass tickle my thighs. But all I can focus on is Archer—naked and flushed and completely still, like he's waiting for me to strike.

His chest rises and falls in shallow breaths. He's so hard it looks painful. And I feel a rush of satisfaction knowing I did that.

I wrap my fingers around the base of him first, just to feel the weight of it, the heat. He jerks slightly at the contact, a strangled sound catching in his throat. I let my thumb brush over the tip, slick already, and his eyes slam shut like the sensation physically short-circuits him.

The second he opens his eyes, I lower my mouth to him slowly, never breaking eye contact. My tongue flicks out first, tasting him. Salt and skin and something that makes my whole body tighten. He groans, one hand flying to my hair like he needs something to anchor him.

Then I take more, inch by inch, letting my lips slide over him as I adjust to the stretch, to the way he fills my mouth. His hips shift upward, a quiet curse leaving his lips.

"Keep going," he grits out, voice strained and cracking at the edges. "Just don't let me come."

I hum around him in acknowledgment, and the sound vibrates against him. He groans, low and helpless.

There's power in this. In having him like this. I work him slowly, hand and mouth together, mirroring the rhythm he used on me. Learning what pulls that sound from his chest. What makes his thighs tense. What makes him shudder.

Then I take him deeper, all the way in, until my nose brushes the skin of his abdomen and my throat stretches around him. His whole body stiffens, his breath leaving him in one sharp, fractured exhale.

"Jesus, Penelope," he hisses, like the words were dragged out of him. "You're gonna ruin me."

I pull back slowly, cheeks hollowed, tongue teasing, and do it again. Because watching him come undone like this is almost better than being touched. Almost.

"Fucking hell." His voice catches. His hand tangles in my hair, not pulling, just resting there. A reminder. A leash he hasn't tugged yet. "Slow down."

I do, pulling back into a slower rhythm that keeps him right on the edge. His taste lingers on my tongue, warm and heady. He's heavy in my mouth, every pulse of him feeding the ache low in my belly. The tension builds again, sharp and electric, reigniting something deep and hungry inside me.

"Look at me," he commands, and I lift my gaze. His eyes pin me in place.

"You're so fucking beautiful like this," he says, voice hoarse. "With your lips stretched around my cock."

It sends a shockwave through me. I suck harder. His hips twitch.

"Stop." The word is choked out, forced through clenched teeth.

I pull back immediately. His head tips back. His chest heaves. He's barely hanging on.

And I love that I did this to him.

He sits up and grabs me, pulling me into a kiss that's more desperation than finesse. We taste like each other. We taste like hunger.

"Do you get it now?" he asks, voice raw against my lips. "Why I make you wait?"

I nod, even though everything in my body is still screaming for release.

"The anticipation makes it better," I whisper.

His lips brush mine. "Exactly."

His hand slips between my legs, fingers sliding through slick heat. I'm soaked, throbbing, and still completely denied.

"Feel that?" he murmurs, brushing just enough to make me whine. "That's what I've done to you. Imagine how it'll feel when I finally let you come."

"Archer," I gasp, hips rocking toward him, chasing more.

But he pulls his hand back. Slowly. Intentionally. Then brings his fingers to his mouth and licks them clean while watching me fall apart all over again.

"Not yet," he says, quiet and calm and maddening. "Tonight's about learning control."

His body presses against mine, hard and solid. We're both shaking with it now—wanting, waiting. There's power in the restraint. In the tension stretched so tight it could snap.

"I want you," I whisper, breath catching on the words.

"You have me," he says, eyes locked to mine. "And I have you. Exactly where I want you."

The sky is still clinging to twilight, the last scraps of gold fading into blue. A few brave stars blink through the haze, quiet and watchful, like they're waiting for the tension to break.

And then Archer moves.

It's not slow. It's not sweet. It's the snap of a rubber band stretched too far. His hands clamp around my waist and haul me into him like he's done pretending. Like he's finally decided to take what he's been holding back all night.

"Fuck," he mutters, his mouth hot against my jaw. "I lied. I need you now."

His voice isn't soft. It's sharp, guttural. A low growl that vibrates through my spine. And the way he says it—like an order, not a request —makes something inside me go tight and molten.

I barely have time to breathe before I'm kissing him. Hard. Messy. All lips and teeth and hands that won't stay still. The contact is instant and scorching, skin to skin, his chest pressed to mine like he's trying to fuse us together.

The grass beneath me is cold and damp, but I don't care. His hands are on me, fingertips skimming down my spine, gripping my hips, dragging his body tighter to mine like he wants to mark every inch of me.

There's no patience in him now. No teasing. No slow build. Just Archer, unbuttoned and undone, and the sound of our breathing getting faster as twilight falls hard around us.

"Turn around," he says, voice low, controlled again—but only barely.

I move onto my hands and knees, heart pounding. The position is open, vulnerable. The air wraps around my bare skin and raises goosebumps across my thighs, my arms, the nape of my neck.

Archer's hand moves down my spine in a slow line, more reverent than sexual. It makes my throat go tight.

"You have no idea how many nights I've thought about you like this," he says, his voice thick. "Spread out. Waiting. Ready for me."

I moan, loud and raw, his words detonating in me like fire—hot, instant, impossible to contain.

"Tell me what you want," he says, voice rough, both hands gripping my hips like he needs them to keep himself from unraveling.

"You. Hard. Now."

I feel him behind me. Thick, burning, and moving way too slow. I try to push back, to take him in, but his grip tightens. Holding me in place. Making me wait.

"Patience," he grits out, though his voice cracks like he's barely hanging on himself.

"I said now," I snap, twisting to meet his gaze over my shoulder. "Or were you lying when you said you cared about what I want?"

He stills. The muscle in his jaw ticks. And then that look flashes across his face, dark and sharp, like lightning about to hit ground.

"I always care," he growls.

And then he slams into me. One deep, unyielding thrust that knocks every ounce of air from my lungs.

I cry out, fingers clawing into the earth. The stretch is intense. Perfect. My whole body folds around the pressure of him, everything else falling away. There's no teasing now. No space. Just him, buried to the hilt, and the kind of silence that only exists when you've finally been filled exactly the way you need.

He stills, chest heaving like he's trying not to come already. His hands flex on my hips. He moves like he's memorizing me from the inside out, every push grounded, certain, unflinching. Hard enough to make my breath stutter every time he sinks back in.

"You feel so fucking good," Archer grits out, one hand sliding up my back and into my hair, not pulling, just holding. His grip makes me arch into him. "Look at you, so wet for me like you've been waiting all day."

Every thrust hits that spot deep inside me like he owns it. Like he's been searching for it all night and now that he's found it, he's not letting up until I'm ruined.

The pressure climbs fast. Too fast. My arms tremble, barely holding me upright.

"Archer—" I pant, already there, teetering. "I'm close."

"Don't," he snaps, breath ragged. "Not yet. You hold it."

I whimper, the sound breaking out of me like it has claws. My whole body tightens around him, slick and pulsing and so fucking needy I could scream.

He folds over me, his chest pinning me down, his mouth hot at my ear. "You're mine, Penelope. Every moan, every spasm. This cunt —mine."

"Yes," I gasp. "Yours. Please."

His hand slides around to my front, and then it's just fingers and heat and cruel precision. Fast, perfect circles over where I'm already throbbing. My hips jerk against him, helpless.

"Archer—fuck—" My voice cracks. "I can't—"

"You can." His thrusts are losing their rhythm now, going sloppy with how close he is. "You're gonna take it. Gonna let me fuck you while you're desperate and aching. You want that, don't you?"

I shake, bite down on my lip, taste blood and still beg. "Please. Archer, please."

He growls behind me, low and feral. "Look at me."

He grabs my face, not gently, turns it until my mouth is open and my eyes are on his. His stare pins me in place, wild and dark and unbearably intimate.

"Fuck," he breathes. "You're so goddamn gorgeous like this. Wrecked. Begging."

And then—he pulls out.

I sob. Actually sob. A ragged, half-broken sound that spills out of me before I can stop it. My pussy clenches around nothing, dripping, empty. Every nerve in my body still screaming for him.

He drags his cock slowly along my folds, not pushing back in, just rubbing, slick and taunting and careful.

"You'll come when I say," he murmurs. "And not one second before."

A broken sound tears out of me, somewhere between a sob and a curse, but he's already flipping me, flat on my back, legs spread, body bare and gasping. He wraps his hand around the base of his cock, and lines it up with the soaked, swollen ache between my thighs.

"I want to see your face when you come," he growls, voice hoarse and guttural, like it's been torn from deep inside him.

Then he drives back into me in one brutal, perfect thrust, so deep I swear the breath leaves my lungs entirely. My head snaps back. My thighs clamp around his hips.

And then he holds my gaze. Locked in. His eyes are feral, unblinking, like he's hanging on by a thread and I'm the only thing tethering him to the ground.

"Now," he commands, voice splintered. "Come for me now."

I don't stand a chance.

My orgasm crashes through me with no warning, no build—just detonation. Like being electrocuted from the inside out. My body seizes, back bowing hard off the grass, every nerve ending lighting up all at once. I scream his name, raw and loud and shameless, my pussy clenching down around his cock in tight, rhythmic pulses that drag the orgasm out past the edge of bearable.

It doesn't stop. It keeps cresting, my body caught in wave after wave of blinding, white-hot pleasure. My thighs shake. My vision whites out. It feels like falling and flying and being shattered and stitched together at the same time.

And then he's gone, too.

Archer's mouth crashes to mine, muffling his moan as his whole body locks above me. I feel the exact second he loses control. His hips jerk, stutter, and then he groans, deep and broken, forehead pressed hard to mine. I feel him throb inside me, heat flooding me in thick, pulsing spurts, like he's giving me everything he has left.

We collapse together, tangled and soaked and undone.

My legs are still trembling, spread open and aching, his cock still hard inside me. I can feel the mess of us dripping out, hot against the cool grass. His chest heaves against mine. My fingers clench around his bicep, like I still need something solid to hold onto.

Above us, the stars blur into each other. Or maybe that's just me, still coming down, still trembling in the aftermath. And for a long, shivering moment, we just lie there, still connected, bodies wrecked, the whole universe narrowing down to this moment.

"Holy shit," I manage, barely.

Archer laughs, soft and winded, brushing damp hair off my forehead. "That's it?"

"You've literally fucked the vocabulary out of me," I say. "Be proud."

He presses a kiss to my hair, still breathing hard. "I am."

We lie there, breathless and still, our limbs tangled like we haven't figured out how to let go yet. The grass is cool under my back, a little damp, a little scratchy, clinging to my skin in places I'll feel later—but right now, I couldn't care less. Above us, the sky fades from lavender to indigo, the last blush of daylight barely clinging to the horizon. It feels like the world has gone quiet with us, like even the stars are pausing to take it all in.

His fingers trace a slow path down my spine, light enough to make me shiver, sure enough to make me melt.

"You okay?" he murmurs.

"More than okay," I breathe, tucking myself closer.

He hums, low and satisfied, his chin resting against the top of my head.

We'll have to move soon. Pull on our clothes. Get in the truck. Slip back into the rhythm of the life we built with the others. And I want that, I do. I want the noise and the teasing and the crowded kitchen and the five sets of eyes that make me feel alive.

But right now, wrapped in Archer's arms, I just want to stay here a little longer. Skin to skin. Breath to breath. Let the night hold us a while before we step back into all the beautiful, complicated chaos we left behind.

His heartbeat thuds steady beneath my ear, anchoring me. And I close my eyes, knowing this moment is going to stay with me forever.

31

———————

I'm yanked from sleep by insistent hands on my shoulders, my eyes flying open in the dim pre-dawn light. For a second, my brain refuses to make sense of the shadows looming over the bed while Archer's arm lies heavy across my waist, his breath warm against my neck. Then my vision clears, and I'm staring up at Jamie and Sammy's grinning faces.

"What the actual fuck—" I start, voice thick with sleep.

"Rise and shine, Penella," Jamie whispers, his eyes sparkling with mischief. "The kidnapping committee has arrived, and we operate on a strict schedule. Though I did bring tea as a peace offering if you promise not to scream." Like a magician presenting his best trick, he produces a thermos from behind his back with a flourish.

A smile tugs at my lips despite the ungodly hour. Jamie leans over me, his curly hair disheveled like he just rolled out of bed himself. The morning stubble darkening his jaw makes him look roguish, dangerous in the most delicious way.

Beside me, Archer stirs, his arm tightening across my waist like muscle memory. The instinctive possessiveness of it sends a complicated rush through me—part thrill, part tension—especially with two other men standing just feet from our bed. His eyes flick open, still heavy with sleep, and the second they land on Sammy and Jamie, they narrow.

"The hell you doing in here?" Archer's voice is a sleep-roughened growl.

Sammy leans against the doorframe, arms crossed over his broad chest, watching the scene with undisguised amusement. His tall frame casts a long shadow across the floor, something predatory in his stillness. Unlike Jamie's barely contained excitement, Sammy radiates calm, unruffled as always.

"Don't look so alarmed, Archer. We're not here to steal your virtue," Sammy says. "Just borrowing our girlfriend for thirty-six hours."

"Our girlfriend?" Archer mutters, fumbling for his glasses. "Try mine."

"Semantics," Jamie says, waving a hand. "We prefer to think of it as a timeshare. You've had your turn."

I push myself up on my elbows, the sheet falling to my waist. "What's happening?" I ask, brain still struggling to catch up. The cool morning air pebbles my skin, my nipples tightening to points against my nightshirt.

Jamie sits on the edge of the bed, completely ignoring Archer's scowl. "Pack a bag, Penella. Essentials only. Whatever you need for an overnight." He pauses, a wicked grin spreading across his face. "Though to be honest, clothing is entirely optional for what we have planned. I'd be perfectly happy to keep you naked the entire time. Less laundry that way."

Archer pushes himself up beside me, his bare chest warm against my arm. "It's five in the fucking morning."

"Hence the 'kidnapping' part," Sammy says with a smirk. "If we asked permission, it wouldn't be nearly as dramatic. And if there's one thing Jamie lives for, it's drama."

My curiosity is fully awake now, even if the rest of me is lagging behind. A delicious tension coils low in my belly, something electric sparking between the three of us that Archer can clearly sense. "Where are we going?"

"It's a surprise," they say in unison, the synchronicity making me laugh. They've been doing that more often lately—speaking in tandem, finishing each other's sentences. It's both thrilling and weirdly sweet, the way they move in sync without even trying. Like they're tuned to the same frequency, orbiting me with quiet purpose. Not predators, not really, just two men who know exactly what they want. And I love that it's me.

I glance at Archer, whose jaw is tight with obvious annoyance. A muscle ticks in his jaw, betraying the jealousy he'd never admit to feeling. His eyes meet mine, softening slightly when I place my hand on his chest, feeling his heartbeat steady beneath my palm.

"You're seriously taking her somewhere without telling me where?" Archer asks them, eyebrow raised.

"Would we let anything happen to her?" Jamie asks with exaggerated innocence, then winks at me. "Well, nothing she doesn't beg for, anyway."

"That's reassuring," Archer mutters, but there's no real heat behind it. I can see him fighting a smile.

"You have fifteen minutes, Pip," Sammy announces, pushing off from the doorframe. "We'll wait downstairs."

When they leave, I throw back the covers and rush to my closet, suddenly frantic. "What do I pack? Where are they taking me? What's appropriate? Do I need a swimsuit? Hiking boots?" My hands tremble with a cocktail of excitement and anxiety, pulse thrumming in my veins like hummingbird wings. "I should bring some paperwork for the restaurant too—we've got that supplier meeting next week, and there are those menu revisions to go over..."

"You're babbling," Archer says, voice still rough with sleep but warm around the edges. "You only do that when you're excited or nervous. Which one is it?"

"Both? Definitely both. Maybe a little terrified. In a good way."

Archer watches me from the bed, his expression caught between amusement and resignation. There's heat there too, the kind that comes from watching someone you love being wanted by others. He gets up, padding across the room in just his boxers, and wraps his arms around me from behind, stilling my frantic movements.

"I'll miss you," he murmurs against my hair. His cock presses against my lower back, making his meaning crystal clear. "Will you miss me?"

I turn in his arms, cradling his face between my hands. "Always," I say softly. The word hangs between us, heavy with meaning—the promise that I'll return to him, that whatever happens with Jamie and Sammy won't change what we have.

I throw things haphazardly into an overnight bag—toiletries, a pair of jeans, a sweater for the evenings, and on second thought, a strappy dress I've never had occasion to wear. Makeup, hairbrush, phone charger. It all feels strangely exciting. "Can you check in with the contractor about those kitchen tiles while I'm gone? And maybe call that seafood supplier about next week's delivery?"

"I've got it handled," Archer says, voice calm and sure. When I hesitate over my underwear options, he glances up. "Take the blue lace."

His tone is casual, but his eyes aren't. They're already dark with want.

"I've always liked you in blue."

I flush, fingers fumbling as I shove the lingerie into my bag. The idea of wearing something Archer picked out while I'm tangled up with Sammy and Jamie later makes my whole body spark. It's messy and hot and taboo in a way that feels way too good.

By the time I've showered and pulled on jeans and a sweater, my hair still damp around my shoulders, Jamie is calling up the stairs.

"Tick tock, Penella! Some of us aren't getting any younger, and I've got plans that require stamina!"

Archer walks me down, his hand steady at the small of my back. It's a quiet touch, but it says everything. A claim and a goodbye all at once.

Outside, dawn is just starting to break over the Hebrides, silver light spilling across the mist-soft hills like the beginning of a dream. The air smells like salt and heather, the way it always does when the island is still waking up. I hear gulls calling over the harbor, sharp and familiar, and it hits me—this place doesn't sound like anywhere else. Doesn't feel like anywhere else. It's wild and quiet and rough around the edges.

"Try not to worry about the restaurant," Archer says, eyes still sleepy but voice smooth as ever. "I promise it won't catch fire again while you're gone."

"Not funny," I mutter, even as my mouth twitches. "The fire jokes are off-limits. At least for another year."

Down by the truck, Jamie swings the passenger door open with a dramatic flourish. "Your carriage, milady," he says, bowing like he thinks this rusty pickup is a pumpkin-turned-carriage and I'm about to lose my glass slipper. It's absurd. It's also ridiculously hot.

"Though I should warn you, the suspension's seen better days. On the plus side, you'll feel every single bump."

"What exactly am I in for?" I ask, my laugh coming out thinner than I mean it to. My skin feels too tight, like I've been stretched to the edge of combustion and it won't take much—just one brush of a hand, one loaded look—to tip me over.

Jamie grins, slow and wicked. "The time of your life, princess."

"She means where we're going, not what depravity you've got planned," Sammy says dryly, though there's something warm beneath the sarcasm. His gaze snags mine, intense enough to steal the air from my lungs. "That said... he's not wrong."

Jamie places a hand to his chest, mock-affronted. "I would never spoil a surprise. Especially not one involving international waters and creative legal interpretations."

"He's joking," Sammy offers, though the corner of his mouth twitches like even he isn't totally sure.

"Probably," Jamie echoes, eyes sparkling with secrets.

And just like that, my heart is sprinting toward whatever comes next.

Archer steps in, catching them both off guard with quick, solid hugs. First Jamie, then Sammy. Not a word wasted, just grip and release like he's making sure they understand exactly what they're carrying.

"Take care of her," he says.

Sammy meets his eyes. "Always."

Archer nods once, then glances at me, something unreadable passing over his face. "And try not to have too much fun without me." He pulls me in for a quick kiss, then hands me over to Jamie.

Jamie helps me climb in the truck, his hand warm and heavy at the small of my back. Not subtle. Not even trying to be. And just like that, we're off. My pulse is already racing, the island slipping by as we pull out of the drive, and all I can think is: God help me, I hope I survive this day.

As we pull onto the road, I twist around in my seat, hand braced on the window frame, needing one last look.

Archer stands in the driveway, arms folded. The morning sun cuts through the trees behind him, catching in his hair, turning him bronze and shadow all at once—like he's been carved from something older than time and left there to weather. He doesn't wave. Doesn't smile. Just watches, jaw tight, chest rising slow like he's trying not to feel it.

Like he already does.

Something sharp lodges beneath my ribs. A tether pulling tight, begging me not to let it stretch too far. Maybe I should've stayed. Maybe—

Jamie's hand lands on my thigh like he owns it—warm, sure, a quiet kind of possession that settles deep in my core. And then there's Sammy. His gaze catches mine in the rearview mirror. Dark, steady, unreadable at first. Then it shifts. Warms. Sharpens. A flicker of something that makes my stomach flip. Like a fuse being lit. Heat. A question. A promise.

"Ready for an adventure?" he asks, his voice low and rough around the edges, like it's been dragged across gravel. Not his usual polished sarcasm—this is something else. Unfiltered. Real.

I nod, swallowing hard. "With you two? Always."

Jamie snorts, turning onto the main road. "You know kidnapping is technically a criminal offense."

"Stop calling it kidnapping," I mutter, rolling my eyes. "You're making it weird."

"He's making it accurate," Sammy adds, deadpan. "We are, in fact, transporting you against your will—"

"I'm here voluntarily."

"—to an undisclosed location," he continues, unfazed. "No paper trail. No alibi. Textbook kidnapping."

"I packed my own damn bag," I point out, grinning despite myself.

"Stockholm syndrome sets in quickly," Jamie says solemnly. "Tragic, really."

"You two are the worst kidnappers in the world."

"We aim to please," Sammy says, not looking away from the road.

The banter fades, dissolving into something quieter. We lapse into a silence that doesn't feel awkward so much as charged—like the hush before a storm breaks open overhead. I glance between them, suddenly too aware of how close we are, how warm it is in here, how every inch of my skin feels keyed up and waiting.

And then, like the universe heard the tension crackling inside the cab, the sky splits open.

Rain hammers the windshield in rhythmic bursts, the wipers struggling to keep up. Each swipe carves out just enough of the world to remind us it's still out there, wild and soaking and blurred at the edges.

Inside the truck, it's a different kind of storm. The air is thick with heat and tension. The scent of leather, clean cologne, and something unmistakably male clings to everything. I'm wedged between them, thigh to thigh, and every bump in the road jostles us closer. Every point of contact is electric. My skin isn't just buzzing, it's sparking. A steady pulse of heat under my skin, lighting up with every accidental brush of thigh, every shift that presses me closer to one of them. It's too much and not enough.

"The weather is giving us a proper sendoff," Jamie says from the driver's seat, glancing over at me. "Typical Scottish foreplay. Getting you nice and wet before we've even started."

I choke on a laugh, heat rushing to my face. "You're terrible."

"That's not what you said last week," he counters, waggling his eyebrows suggestively. "If memory serves, the word you used was 'amazing.' Repeatedly."

I roll my eyes. "Please tell me we're stopping somewhere for breakfast? I'm hungry enough to consider eating one of you."

"Is that a promise or a threat?" Jamie asks, his grin wolfish in the dim light. "Because I'm quite partial to being eaten, ideally after I've showered. Though Sammy here is always pristine enough to be a meal at any time—one of the many benefits of his fastidiousness."

"I prefer to think of it as basic hygiene," Sammy responds dryly, though there's a quirk to his lips that betrays his amusement. "Something you occasionally treat as optional, especially after a day on the boat."

"Would you two like me to leave so you can continue this lovers' quarrel in private?" I ask innocently.

"We're not quarreling," Sammy says with dignity.

"We're flirting," Jamie corrects. "With each other, through you. Very efficient."

"If you say so," I counter, a smile tugging at my lips.

Sammy shifts beside me, his arm stretching across the back of the seat, not quite touching me but close enough that I can feel the heat radiating from his body. The purposefully casual gesture doesn't fool me—every inch of him is attuned to my presence, waiting. "We're going to that place that makes those chocolate croissants you like."

The fact that he knows my breakfast preference makes something warm unfurl in my stomach. It's the little things that undo me—the evidence that they've been paying attention, cataloging my likes and dislikes, planning this kidnapping down to the tiniest of details. I turn to look at him, finding his face closer than I expected. "You remembered that?"

His lips curve in that distinctive smile that always makes my heart stutter. "I remember everything you like, Pip. Every single thing."

There's no mistaking what he means. He's talking about the bedroom, and my body reacts before my mind can catch up. A flash of memory hits me like a jolt: his hands on me last time we were alone, the way he touched with precision, like he'd studied me, mapped me out in secret and was just waiting for permission to use what he'd learned. He hadn't rushed. He'd dismantled me slowly. Thoroughly.

Jamie clears his throat, low and abrupt, slicing through the moment. I turn, catching the quick flicker of heat in his gaze before he yanks it back to the rain-slick road. But it lingers, something taut and unreadable, tucked just behind his eyes. Whatever it is, it sets fire to the already-charged air in the cab. Every breath feels too loud. Every shift of their bodies a brushstroke across my skin.

I force my hands to still in my lap, fingers curling around each other for balance. "So," I say, clearing my throat, trying for breezy and landing somewhere closer to breathless, "this spontaneous kidnapping —any hints about where I'm being whisked off to, or am I supposed to stay in the dark until we cross a border?"

Jamie chuckles, low and smug. "Patience, Penella. All will be revealed... over breakfast." He pauses, then shoots me a look that's pure mischief. "Unless you're feeling especially curious. In which case, I might be convinced to give you a clue. For a price."

His finger taps his cheek, like he's the world's most charming extortionist.

I narrow my eyes. "You're bribing me for kisses now?"

"Bribing," he says, feigning offense. "Such a harsh term. I prefer 'mutually beneficial exchange of services.'"

"You're disgusting," I say, but the laugh bubbles up before I can stop it. "And you're enjoying this way too much."

"The anticipation's half the fun," Sammy murmurs, voice low and gravel-warm and close. So damn close I feel his breath at my temple, stirring the fine hairs there, sending a whole shiver down my spine like he planned it.

Goosebumps rise along my neck. I don't even pretend to resist the pull. I lean into him instinctively, like his presence alone might anchor me to something steady. Something dangerous in all the best ways.

"By the time we get there," he says, his voice a slow slide of heat, "you'll be so worked up that the payoff'll be unforgettable."

"Jesus," I breathe. "You sound like a cartoon villain. Like I'm about to be dragged off to your evil lair."

Sammy grins, sharp and gorgeous. "Who says I don't have one?"

"No evil lair," Jamie cuts in from the driver's seat. "We checked. Budget wouldn't allow it. But we did book a moderately suspicious hotel room."

"Oh, much less impressive," I deadpan.

"Judgment withheld," Sammy says, his voice dipping low again, smooth as sin. "Until you see it for yourself."

The cab shrinks by the second, every inhale thick with heat and teasing. Their voices, their glances, the way they move—it's all too much. Like they're circling, turning the flame up slow just to watch me melt.

The café flickers into view through the misty rain like something out of a storybook—all golden light and foggy windows, glowing with that particular kind of warmth that feels like it might seep into your bones if you just get close enough. Jamie swings the truck into the last available spot, and before I can even fumble for the door, Sammy's already out, moving with the kind of purposeful ease that makes me feel unsteady. He opens mine and holds out a hand.

I take it.

It's still raining, not hard, just that fine, persistent drizzle that sticks to your lashes and softens the edges of the world. Sammy pulls me in under his arm like I belong there, like shielding me from the rain is an instinct he doesn't think twice about. His body fits against mine so easily I almost miss the shift in my own breathing. The thump of my heart quickens from the heat of him, the way his grip lingers, steady and sure.

Jamie follows close behind, the three of us spilling into the café in a messy knot of wet clothes and laughter and something unspoken that's starting to feel dangerous. Or inevitable.

"Table for three, please," Jamie says to the hostess, flashing her a smile so potent she nearly drops her pen. "Somewhere private, if you don't want a scandal. These two can't keep their hands off each other."

"Jamie!" I hiss, cheeks burning.

He shrugs, utterly unapologetic. "What? I was talking about Sammy."

Sammy just smiles, that slow, infuriating smirk that says he's heard worse, and probably done worse. "Window, please," he adds, hand sliding down to the small of my back. His palm is hot against the soaked fabric of my sweater, a brand I feel all the way down my spine.

The café is all worn wood and exposed brick, the kind of cozy that makes you want to write poetry or confess something you shouldn't. String lights cast a soft amber glow overhead, catching the sheen of rain still clinging to our hair and skin. It smells like espresso and warm bread, and I suddenly realize I'm starving.

We settle into a corner table with a view of the street, all puddles and headlights and people with umbrellas tilted against the wind. I sit in the middle. Between them. Held in place by their heat and their proximity and the low thrum of want that's been following me around like a second pulse.

"Order enough to fill you up," Sammy says, voice low and casual—but his eyes linger on my mouth a second too long. There's weight behind the words. Not hunger for food.

My stomach flips.

Jamie's knee bumps mine beneath the table. Then it doesn't move. He shifts slightly, applies pressure, purposeful and steady. My eyes stay on the menu, but the words blur. I can't remember what I was even going to order.

"You're still not telling me where we're going?" I ask, trying for even. Trying not to combust in public.

Jamie leans in, eyes glittering. "How do you feel about London?"

I blink. "London?" My voice goes thin. "Like... actual London?"

Sammy's face cracks open into a smile. The kind I've only seen a few times, when he forgets to hold back. "Unless there's a knockoff version you'd prefer?"

The laugh that escapes me is wild and breathless and a little bit stunned. "We're going to London?"

Jamie nods like this is totally normal. Like this is what people do on rainy days. "Flight's in an hour and a half. Back tomorrow night. Just like we promised Archer."

He leans closer, his voice dipping into that dangerous whisper register. "Unless, of course, you want to stay longer."

The way he says stay makes my skin prickle.

I glance between them—Jamie with his lazy, loaded grin and Sammy with that unreadable look that makes me feel stripped bare. The café is warm and safe and ordinary, and I think that's the only thing keeping me grounded right now, because everything inside me is already on that plane. Already spiraling toward something that tastes like risk and recklessness and the kind of fun that leaves bruises.

"I've never been," I say, my voice light, almost disbelieving. A laugh slips out, high and giddy and a little breathless. "Not once. All those years living just a short flight away, and somehow I never went."

"We know," Sammy says, quiet but certain.

Something about the way he says it makes me still. Makes the air around the table shift, tighten. He doesn't say it like it's a casual fact. He says it like it mattered to him. Like he'd cataloged every thing I'd never done and was determined to experience them with me.

Emotion catches in my throat before I can swallow it down. "I... I can't believe you did this."

Jamie reaches across the table, tucks a damp strand of hair behind my ear. His fingers are warm, a little rough. Familiar in a way that makes my chest ache. "Don't sound so shocked. We pay attention."

"We've been planning this for weeks," he adds, like it's no big deal. Like it didn't just knock the breath out of me.

"Weeks?" My eyes go wide. "How did I not notice?"

Sammy just shrugs, a hint of a smile playing at the edge of his mouth. "You've been a little preoccupied. Spencer and Liam dropping to one knee every other day. Hard to compete with that."

"And Archer brooding in corners like a scorned lover," Jamie throws in, grinning.

"So this trip is...?" I trail off, unsure how much I actually want the answer.

"Just a trip," Sammy says, and it's too smooth, too easy. He says it like he wants me to believe him, but his eyes give him away. They're too intent. Too full of things he's not saying.

I don't believe him. Not even a little. But I appreciate the lie anyway.

The waitress appears just in time to save me from myself. I order on impulse—the most over-the-top breakfast I can find, plus a chocolate croissant, plus a cup of tea so big it might as well come in a bathtub.

Sammy raises an eyebrow.

"What?" I say, sitting up straighter, grinning. I can feel his gaze dip, lingering on my mouth. My skin prickles. "If I'm going to London, I need proper fuel."

Jamie hums low in his throat. "I like a woman with an appetite." The words are playful but loaded. Crackling with a tension that has nothing to do with food. "Especially one who's not afraid to indulge her cravings."

When the waitress leaves, I pounce. "Okay. What are we doing there? Where are we staying? Should I have packed something fancier to wear?" The questions fall out in a rush, tripping over each other in their eagerness.

Jamie hands me the honey, his fingers brushing mine, lingering. The touch is light, but it sends a little shockwave up my arm. He doesn't move away. Just rests his fingers against my wrist like he's mapping my pulse. Like he's memorizing the beat of it. "We've got it covered," he says, eyes locked on mine. "Including what you'll wear."

"Wait—what?" I blink. "You bought me clothes?"

"Just one outfit," Sammy says.

His voice is rougher now, almost gravelly, and when I look at him, he's not pretending anymore. His gaze skims over me, slow, purposeful, and it feels like a touch. Like his hands are already on me. Like he's imagining exactly what I'll look like coming out of whatever they've chosen.

Heat floods my cheeks. My stomach flips. My heart does something I don't have a name for.

"For tonight," he adds. Just that. No explanation. No details.

But I can feel it in the air between us.

Whatever tonight is—it's not just dinner.

Breakfast lands in a chaotic dance of clattering plates and gleaming silver, the smell of butter and coffee and something Sugary cutting straight through the tension. For a moment, the weight of anticipation lifts—replaced by the far more manageable ache of hunger.

I dig in like I've been starved for days.

Because I have been, in a way. Not just for food, but for this—for Jamie's chaos and Sammy's steadiness. This sense of being wanted and looked after and maybe a little ruined in the best way possible.

Jamie watches me tear into my croissant like it's the first good thing that's happened to me all year. His smile is smug, amused, a little dangerous.

"You eat like you've just crawled out of a bunker," he says, sipping his espresso like he's not absolutely fascinated. "Do we need to call Archer? Is he starving you for dominance points?"

I roll my eyes and point a flaky edge of croissant at him. "Says the man who once ate an entire deep-dish pizza and then asked what was for dessert."

Sammy laughs, a low, indulgent sound that feels like it was made just for us. It vibrates through the table, right into my skin, and settles low in my stomach like something molten. "She's got you there."

"Traitor," Jamie mutters, but the grin never leaves his face.

"Tell me the plan," I say between bites, licking salt and sweetness from my lips. I don't mean it to sound seductive, but the look Jamie gives me suggests otherwise.

"Flight," he says, watching me too closely. "Hotel. A few surprises. You'll love it."

I groan. "Surprises. Of course." I pop a bite of sausage into my mouth to keep from smiling too hard. "You two and your secrets."

"You love it," Jamie says, lazy and confident, like he knows exactly what he's doing to me. "Admit it, the not knowing is half the thrill."

He's not wrong. But I'm not giving him the satisfaction. The truth is, being with them feels like being on the edge of something bigger. A cliff I want to jump off. Something wild and indulgent and a little bit dangerous.

"Maybe," I say into my tea, letting the steam hide my grin. "But just for that, I'm eating your bacon."

He arches a brow. "Steal my bacon and there will be consequences."

I freeze mid-bite.

Jamie's voice lowers. "The kind that might make us late to our flight. The kind that involves me pinning you to the wall of our hotel room while Sammy watches, patiently waiting for his turn."

I stop chewing. My fork pauses mid-air. Heat floods my body, low and curling, like an ember just caught flame. I stare at him. Hard.

"Surely," I say, voice too calm for the chaos inside me, "you can think of a better use for Sammy than just watching."

Jamie's smile is pure sin. "Oh, I've got a dozen uses for Sammy. Some of which might even shock you."

"I doubt that," I murmur, meeting his eyes over the rim of my teacup. "I have a very vivid imagination."

Sammy shifts, leaning in, eyes sharper now. "Do tell."

His voice is all velvet and grit, low enough to make my pulse stutter. Then he clears his throat—an obvious tactical retreat—but the smirk tugging at his mouth gives him away. That grin is right there, simmering beneath the surface like he's daring me to call his bluff.

"If you two are finished with the breakfast foreplay," he says, voice steady again but eyes burning, "we should probably think about making our flight."

The word foreplay hits me like a lightning strike. I feel it behind my knees, between my legs, in every place I didn't know could ache.

"Fine," I say, scraping my plate with the last bite of toast. "But I'm holding you both personally responsible if we don't make it through airport security without incident."

Jamie smirks. "Who says we're trying to avoid incident?"

And just like that, I'm practically dragging them toward the exit—pulse racing, nerves buzzing, appetite still far from satisfied.

The airplane seat feels like it was designed for someone half my size. Or maybe it's just the fact that Jamie is on my left and Sammy is on my right, and the space between us seems to shrink by the second. My thighs are pressed between theirs like pages in a book, tight and unavoidable and full of promise. The plastic armrests do nothing to help. Just flimsy little lies pretending they can enforce boundaries that haven't existed since breakfast.

The flight attendant says it'll be just over an hour to London. Sixty-ish minutes of this. Of heat and thigh contact and the hum of something electric just under my skin.

I clutch my crumpled boarding pass like it might save me, the ink smudged and the corners soft. My palms are damp, my pulse fluttering like it's trapped just beneath my collarbone. I try to focus on the safety demonstration, but it's hard when every brush of Jamie's leg feels like an experiment in restraint and every inhale fills my lungs with Sammy's cologne.

"Nervous?" Jamie asks, his voice pitched just low enough to slide straight into my bloodstream. His hand covers mine on the armrest, thumb stroking over my knuckles in slow, grounding circles.

I shake my head. "Excited. I've only flown twice before."

Sammy turns slightly toward me, eyebrow raised—that slow, calculated lift that somehow short-circuits my entire body. It's unfair, the effect he has. "Twice? How's that possible with Lachlan as your brother?"

I shrug, mouth quirking. "The restaurant's clingy. Doesn't like to share me with others."

Jamie's fingers slide to my thigh, easy, casual, terrifyingly not. The warmth of his palm sears through the denim, each pass of his thumb drawing a tighter circle. Higher. Slower. Watching me. Waiting.

"We'll fix that," he says. "You've got five of us now. Time for us to start collecting passport stamps."

I glance at him, try to keep my voice light even though my heart is thundering. "So this is what it's about. You're just using me for my passport."

"Busted," he whispers, leaning in until I can feel his breath against my ear. "Though to be fair, there are about a dozen other parts of you I'm interested in. Want me to list alphabetically? Or in order of preference?" His voice drops another octave. "It's a long list. Starts somewhere around your ankles and ends behind your ear—the spot that makes you shiver when I kiss it."

"You're shameless," I murmur, throat dry, heat crawling up my neck.

"Yes, I am," Jamie says, wicked smile curling.

"Jamie," Sammy warns, sharp but quiet.

Jamie grins. "That's rich coming from you. I saw what you were doing with your hand under the breakfast table."

Sammy doesn't blink. "I dropped my napkin."

"Three times?"

"I'm very clumsy," Sammy says without missing a beat, his voice a shade too innocent.

I snort, covering my mouth to muffle the laugh. "You two are going to kill me."

The plane starts to taxi, and I turn toward the window, needing air, needing distance—but instead, I get Sammy's cologne wrapping around me like a second skin. He leans back just enough to give me the view, and I shift into his space like being near him doesn't absolutely wreck me.

The plane lurches forward, a low growl building beneath us as it accelerates down the runway. I press back into the seat, breath caught somewhere between my lungs and throat. My stomach dips, that too-fast elevator feeling, only sharper, because it mirrors the emotional free fall I've been in since they showed up in my bedroom this morning, grinning like they already knew how this day would end.

My fingers dig into the armrests without thinking.

Jamie laces his hand through mine.

On my other side, Sammy's palm finds my thigh, solid and grounding and completely at odds with the chaos inside my chest. His thumb rests just above my knee, not moving, but far from still. Every nerve in my body tilts toward that one point of contact.

"Takeoff's the best part," Jamie murmurs, voice warm against the shell of my ear. "That second where everything falls away. You're suspended between where you've been and where you're going. Just that breathless stretch of in-between. All tension and promise."

I turn to look at him, startled by the poetry of it. "That was dangerously close to profound," I whisper.

He winks. "Don't tell anyone. It would ruin my whole brand."

But he's not wrong. The wheels lift, and we rise, and something in me rises too, weightless and shivery and untethered. I let out a soft, involuntary sound, half gasp, half laugh, and Jamie's hand tightens around mine, like he hears it for what it is.

Once we level out and the seatbelt sign dings off, Sammy stretches, long legs shifting beside mine, his thigh pressing harder into me. Not a flirtation. Not quite. But it's intentional. I feel it everywhere.

I'm very suddenly, very acutely aware of how little space exists between the three of us.

When the beverage cart rolls into view, Jamie leans in conspiratorially. "Drink? Or shall we skip straight to the champagne? I've always wanted to join the mile-high club."

"Jamie." I hiss his name, glancing toward the aisle, but the flight attendant is still rows away.

"What?" he asks with mock innocence. "It's a very exclusive club. They have jackets and everything. I bet Sammy would look fetching in one. He's all about the proper attire for every occasion."

"Some of us prefer to maintain certain standards," Sammy responds dryly, though I notice he doesn't actually disagree. "Unlike you, who once showed up to a wedding wearing flip-flops."

"It was a beach wedding," Jamie says, scandalized. "And I wore pants, unlike that time in Majorca when you—"

"We agreed not to speak of that," Sammy says, too fast, though there's a smile tugging at the corner of his mouth.

"Champagne," I decide impulsively. The bubbles might calm the flutter in my stomach, give me something to focus on besides the four hands that could be touching me at any moment. "We're celebrating, right?"

Sammy's smile is slow. Measured. The kind that makes my heartbeat thud behind my knees. "Absolutely."

Jamie orders for the three of us. When the flight attendant finally hands over the tiny bottles and plastic cups, we clink them together in the tight, overheated space.

"To London," I say.

"To firsts," Jamie adds, his gaze catching mine and not letting go. There's heat behind it. A promise he's not trying to hide.

Sammy's voice is quieter. Lower. "To the three of us."

And that—that—makes my breath hitch.

The champagne is lukewarm and faintly metallic, but I drink it anyway, grateful for something to focus on. The bubbles pop on my tongue, sharp and playful, and the warmth trickles down through my chest, easing the knot of anticipation that has settled in my stomach.

As if the universe was just waiting for us to have flimsy cups of champagne in our hands, the plane shudders. A ripple of turbulence rocks us side to side. My body tilts with the motion, first bumping into Jamie's shoulder, then pressing into Sammy's arm. The contact is fleeting but electric, like the aircraft is conspiring against my equilibrium for their benefit.

The champagne sloshes dangerously near the rim. My grip tightens, but not fast enough.

Sammy's hand is there in an instant, his fingers sliding over mine, steadying the cup. His touch is gentle but certain, guiding the drink back toward my lips with an ease that feels absurdly tender. It shouldn't feel intimate. But it does. Like he's memorized how I move. Like he knows where I need support before I do.

"Thank you," I whisper as he lets go. My voice comes out soft and breathy, already unmoored.

"Anytime," he murmurs, and there's something in his tone that feels less like reassurance and more like a promise.

The turbulence doesn't quit. It moves through the cabin like a pulse, unpredictable but rhythmic, each dip and sway knocking me into one of them. The captain crackles to life over the intercom, offering a calm reassurance about air pockets and cruising altitudes. He tells us to stay seated. Buckle up. As if that'll help.

Jamie's arm slides around my shoulders, pulling me closer. Protective on the surface. Possessive underneath. His palm is warm against my upper arm, his thumb idly stroking through my sweater like I'm a comfort object he has no intention of letting go.

"Not a fan of turbulence?" he asks, his lips brushing the shell of my ear. His breath is warm and wicked and makes my entire body gooseflesh.

I shake my head. "Just not used to it."

"Focus on something else," Sammy suggests, voice pitched low. He leans in from the other side, his lips almost grazing the sensitive skin just behind my ear. It's a stereo of seduction—Jamie in my left ear, Sammy in my right. I'm caught in the middle, and I think they both know exactly what they're doing.

"Like what?" I ask, turning my head toward him. Our faces are too close. His eyes catch mine, dark and steady, and suddenly I forget we're thousands of feet in the air.

"What we're going to do in London," he says.

The words land low in my stomach, heat unfurling like a struck match. I forget about the seat. The plane. The weather outside. All I can feel is the space between us evaporating, inch by inch.

"Which is?" I ask, and I barely recognize my own voice, it's too soft, too breathless.

"Everything," Jamie cuts in from my other side, his voice a slow pour of honey and intent. "And a few things they don't even have words for in the Queen's English."

I snort, trying to steady myself with humor, but the tension in my chest refuses to break. "I doubt that. You've clearly never been in the dirty corners of a proper British dictionary."

Sammy's tone shifts, just a fraction colder, clipped and precise in a way that makes my spine tingle. "I assure you, the Queen's English covers every depraved act imaginable. You just have to know where to look."

Jamie chuckles. "God, you're such a dork. You make vocabulary sound like foreplay."

Sammy tilts his head slightly, dark eyes locked on mine. "Would you prefer a demonstration?"

My stomach flips so hard it might've staged a rebellion. "Now that's an educational approach I can get behind," I murmur before I can stop myself.

Jamie laughs, the sound low and delighted. Sammy just raises an eyebrow, like he's cataloging my reactions for later.

I close my eyes. It's too much. The closeness. The promise. The impossible knowledge that this isn't just flirting, it's a preview of what's coming later. Behind my eyelids, my mind fills in blanks that haven't even been drawn yet. Bodies tangled together, the heat of skin on skin, hands everywhere at once.

And when I open them, they're both watching me. Dark-eyed and sharp-edged and waiting.

"What are you thinking about?" Sammy asks, voice pitched so low I feel it in my teeth. The vibration seems to travel straight through me, settling in all the places that make my legs tense and my breath catch.

"You don't want to know," I say, then drain the rest of my champagne like it might smother the fire building in my chest.

Jamie leans in, grin lazy and lethal. "Pretty sure we do, actually." His hand finds my knee, squeezing lightly. "Based on how flushed you just got, I'm guessing it wasn't thoughts of the Tower of London that had you biting your lip. Though I wouldn't be opposed to playing prison guard and captive later, if that's what you're into. I bet Sammy has handcuffs somewhere in that bag of his."

"They are handcuffs," Sammy says flatly, not even bothering to deny it this time. "Padded. Adjustable."

That flash of heat ripples through me again, sharp and low and impossible to ignore.

"You're both trouble," I mutter, rolling my eyes. But there's no bite to it. Because I want the trouble. Crave it, even.

The rest of the flight is an exercise in restraint, and I'm failing spectacularly.

Every movement feels calculated—Jamie's fingers brushing mine when we reach for the same armrest, Sammy's thigh pressing against mine in a way that feels less accidental the longer it stays there. Their voices roll over me like a tide, teasing and low, laced with something sharp-edged and unspoken. Every laugh too close. Every glance too long.

By the time the captain announces our descent, I'm practically vibrating in my seat. My skin feels too tight. My breath's coming too shallow. If one of them so much as whispers in my ear, I think I'll combust mid-air and take this entire overpriced tin can down with me.

Outside the window, London spills out below us, huge and jagged and impossibly alive. Nothing like the sleepy, sheep-dotted hills I left behind. This city is steel and story, fast and unapologetically loud, and I want to drink all of it in. I lean forward, pressing both palms to the tiny oval of plexiglass as if I could absorb it through my skin.

Jamie moves in behind me like he's been waiting for an excuse. His chest flush against my back, heat rolling off him in steady waves. His arms bracket mine on either side, not touching but so goddamn close. A human parentheses.

"There's the London Eye," he murmurs, voice pitched low like he's narrating something meant only for me. "And the Shard. See that little cluster of glass teeth? That's Canary Wharf."

His breath catches on the curve of my neck and I forget how to swallow.

Sammy shifts beside me, not away—closer. "Big Ben's just there. Parliament, too. And if we had better seats or, I don't know, telescopic vision, you'd see the National Gallery, Trafalgar Square, the whole mess of tourists milling like ants."

His lips brush my shoulder, and I find myself leaning into him, caught between the two of them like a live wire.

"Boring cultural crap," Jamie teases, chin grazing my temple as he leans to point something else out. "What Sammy's not showing you is Soho. The real stuff. The basement clubs and dirty martinis and very questionable choices."

"Those are drunk university students," Sammy says with a sigh, but there's amusement stitched through the exasperation. "And tourists trying to cosplay as locals."

Jamie grins. "Semantics. What I'm saying is: there's more to this city than royal landmarks and dusty paintings. And I fully intend to show you every improper bit."

"I want both," I say, like it's a challenge. "History and hedonism. The whole experience."

Jamie's eyes spark. "You heard her," he says to Sammy, smirking like he's just won a bet. "She wants the full London."

"I heard," Sammy mutters. "Though I'm not convinced we're working from the same itinerary."

The wheels hit the tarmac with a judder, the cabin tilting forward in a soft lurch. I drop back into my seat, heart skittering, pulse a steady thrum in my throat. A laugh slips out of me, half nerves, half something a lot closer to thrill.

～

The hotel lobby hits me like a punch to the ego—all high ceilings and generational wealth, the kind of place where even the air smells filtered through a trust fund. Marble gleams beneath my feet like it's been buffed by angels. Gold fixtures gleam. The chandeliers sparkle with a smug sort of light, tossing rainbows across the walls like they know they're too expensive for my tax bracket.

Sammy moves toward the reception desk like he was born into this kind of opulence, all easy shoulders and loose confidence. Jamie stays pressed at my side, his hand warm at the base of my spine, anchoring me even as my stomach knots with nerves I pretend I don't feel.

I try not to visibly gape at the massive floral installation exploding out of a vase the size of a bathtub, or at the guests gliding around like catalog models—perfect blowouts, perfect posture, perfect lives. My sneakers squeak faintly against the floor, traitorous and loud, leaving faint ghost-prints like proof that I don't belong here.

"You didn't tell me we were staying at the kind of place that probably charges for the air we're breathing," I whisper to Jamie, tipping my head toward him. "Pretty sure the chandelier is judging my outfit."

"Would you have packed differently?"

I open my mouth, then close it again. "I don't know. I maybe would have done something with my hair. Or summoned a fairy Godmother for a complete transformation. Something Disney-level magical."

His eyes flick to my still-damp curls, rain-kissed and tangled from earlier, like he's memorizing the shape of them. "I like it like this," he says, voice rougher now, the edge of something unspoken creeping in. "It's how you look in the morning. Or right after I've had my hands in it."

The image slams into me with zero warning. His fingers in my hair, my neck arched, his mouth at my throat, breath catching as I whispered his name like a secret. My knees go a little soft. My face goes up in flames.

Before I can come up with something clever, or anything at all, Sammy's back, key cards in hand and smugness practically radiating off him.

"Fifteenth floor. Corner suite," he announces, like he's just secured us a penthouse at the Ritz for free.

"Suite?" I echo, half-dazed. "Not just a room?"

Sammy's smile deepens. "Nothing about this trip is just a room, Pip."

He steps in behind me as we walk, his palm a slow burn against the small of my back, right where Jamie's hand had lingered, but lower now. Possessive. Intentional. His pinky slips beneath the waistband of my jeans, barely there, just enough to make my breath hitch.

We reach the elevators, and the doors slide open with a low chime. Jamie's hand brushes mine as we step inside, and then the doors seal shut behind us, locking us into a mirrored box that instantly feels too small, too quiet, too charged.

No one speaks.

Sammy presses the button for the fifteenth floor, his movements calm, steady. But when he turns back around, his eyes catch mine in the mirrored glass, and something's different. The teasing curve of his mouth is gone. In its place is something darker. Sharper. Like a decision's just been made. Like the game we've been playing has finally crossed a line.

"I've been wanting to do this all day," he murmurs, voice pitched low and rough at the edges, like he's already halfway gone.

And then he's kissing me.

Not soft. Not tentative. A claiming. A collision.

His hand curves around the back of my neck, guiding me with the surety of someone who already knows exactly what I like. His fingers thread into my hair, tightening just enough to make my breath stutter. My mouth opens to him instinctively, and he takes full advantage, kissing me like he's starved. He tastes like champagne and sin. Like dark promises whispered in back corners and secrets you don't tell anyone.

His kiss is methodical, precise, but there's nothing patient about it. He kisses like he wants to memorize me with his mouth. Like he's mapping territory with his tongue. Every swipe, every drag, every greedy inhale feels like he's trying to undo me one sensation at a time.

I gasp against him, my hands fisting in the fabric of his shirt, just trying to hold on. And then—

Behind me, Jamie makes a sound, low and broken and turned on, and it shivers straight down my spine.

"Fuck," he mutters, voice gone hoarse. And then he's there too, his chest flush to my back, hips pressing forward, arms sliding around me like he's staking a claim.

One hand grips my waist; the other travels slowly, purposefully, until it rests low on my stomach, fingers spread possessively. I'm boxed in, Sammy's ruthless mouth at my front, Jamie's cock already hard against my lower back, and it's all I can do not to melt into a puddle between them.

"My turn," Jamie growls, and there's heat behind it. Hunger. A thread of wickedness I feel all the way down to my knees.

Sammy pulls back reluctantly, but keeps his palm on my waist as Jamie gently turns me in the circle of his arms. His hands are gentler but no less sure, sliding up my sides, thumbs grazing just beneath the hem of my sweater before he cups my face, tilting it toward him.

And then he kisses me.

It's different. Playful, coaxing, filled with that infuriating charm that always makes me feel like I'm the only one in the room. His lips brush mine once. Then again. A soft nip to my bottom lip. Then he deepens it, his tongue slipping in, teasing, tasting, claiming.

I melt into him completely, my body pressed between theirs in the most decadent, dizzying way. Sammy's mouth finds the curve where my neck meets my shoulder, lips dragging across the skin there like he's rediscovering it. I shudder. He groans.

My head tips back, baring more of my throat, giving him access to everything he wants. His hands glide up, fingers skimming the under-side of my breasts through my sweater, and I arch instinctively, a gasp slipping out between kisses.

Jamie swallows the sound with a laugh against my lips. "You're unreal," he breathes. "You feel like a fucking dream."

The world narrows to touch and breath and taste. Jamie's mouth moves on mine, wet and urgent. Sammy's tongue teases the soft spot beneath my ear, his fingers exploring with unhurried precision. I don't know who to respond to. I don't want to choose. I want more. More of their hands. Their mouths. The way they make me feel like a live wire caught in a lightning storm.

In the mirrored walls, we're everywhere, a thousand tangled reflections of limbs and lips and want. I catch sight of myself: eyes heavy-lidded, mouth kiss-swollen, body slack with pleasure and pinned between two men who are absolutely ruining me in the best way imaginable.

"Is this what the full London experience includes?" I gasp, voice wrecked.

He grins, still panting, and bites lightly at my bottom lip. "Just the welcome package," he murmurs. "Wait 'til you see what premium membership gets you."

The elevator chimes, a soft mechanical warning that barely cuts through the haze. Sammy lifts his head, lips still grazing my skin. His eyes are blown wide, pupils devouring the warm brown of his irises.

"To be continued," he says, low and sure, like a threat and a promise all at once.

Jamie presses one last kiss to the corner of my mouth and straightens with a quick, discreet adjustment of his pants. "Definitely continued. Preferably somewhere without CCTV."

He glances at the small black dome in the ceiling and smirks. "Though if anyone's watching, you're welcome, mate."

I try to collect myself, to smooth my hair, to force oxygen back into my lungs, but I can't seem to focus. I feel scorched. Branded. My pulse trips over itself, and my skin hums with the echo of their hands.

We step into the hallway, carpeted in burgundy so deep it swallows the sound of our footsteps. It feels like stepping into a secret. Everything is too quiet, too soft, like the air itself is holding its breath, waiting for something to happen. Sammy walks ahead, sliding the key card into the lock at the very end of the corridor, turning to us with a grin that feels equal parts invitation and mischief.

"After you," he says, pushing the door open.

I cross the threshold and stop cold. The suite is breathtaking.

Floor-to-ceiling windows stretch across the far wall, spilling golden light over everything. London unfurls beyond the glass like a painting brought to life—buildings gleaming, the Thames winding through it all like a silver ribbon. The late afternoon glow casts the whole city in soft magic, making it feel otherworldly, like a dream I somehow stepped into without falling asleep.

The room itself is sleek and rich without trying too hard. Clean lines, warm wood, velvet accents in shades of smoke and wine. Artwork that probably costs more than my truck. The furniture is plush, sculptural, perfect for sinking into with a glass of something strong and an even stronger man.

"This is..." I trail off, turning in a slow circle as I try to absorb the scale of it, the beauty. The fact that I'm standing here, in this space, with them.

"Home for the next day and a half," Jamie finishes, already dropping our bags next to a credenza that looks like it belongs in a design museum. "Modest, I know. I wanted to spring for the presidential suite, but Sammy had some strong feelings about fiscal responsibility."

He actually air-quotes the phrase, rolling his eyes.

"The presidential suite comes with a butler," Sammy says, stepping inside and closing the door behind him. "I figured you'd prefer privacy to a stranger knocking every hour asking if we need more towels."

Jamie smirks. "Fair point. Though I plan on needing a lot of towels."

I laugh, still a little dazed. "It's like I walked into a movie set. One of those 'girl-next-door in the big city' stories where you just know a makeover montage is coming." My fingers brush across the back of a velvet chair, half-expecting it to vanish beneath my touch like some kind of mirage.

"You're hardly the girl-next-door," Sammy says from behind me. He says it like it's just a fact. No embellishment. No flattery. And somehow, that makes it land deeper.

My gaze drifts toward a doorway off the main room and catches on the bed. Enormous. Pristine white sheets. A cloud of down and temptation. It's easily big enough for three. That thought drops like a pebble in my stomach, sending ripples of heat out in every direction. I move to the windows to distract myself, pressing my palm against the cool glass. The city stretches out in every direction, alive and endless.

"Look," Sammy says, stepping up beside me, pointing. His arm brushes mine and stays there, just close enough to feel.

I follow his gesture, finding the giant Ferris wheel through the haze of sunlight. It feels surreal. All of it. Being here. With them. At the edge of something that feels bigger than any of us are quite ready to name.

"We're really here," I whisper. "In London." It hits me then. The full weight of it. The moment. The shift. Not just the view, not just the suite, but them. Us. This thing we've stepped into, no longer just flirtation and tension, but something real and terrifying and electrifying.

"I keep thinking I'm going to wake up," I admit. "Like this is some wildly elaborate dream."

Jamie joins us at the window, positioning himself on my other side, effectively caging me in. His reflection finds mine in the glass. He's smiling, just barely. But his eyes are serious. Watchful. Wanting.

I let out a breath that feels like it's been stuck in my lungs for hours. "Is this where you tell me the real plan is to sell me to an international crime ring?"

"No need to sound so eager," Sammy replies without missing a beat. "Though if that's a fantasy of yours, I'm sure we can workshop it."

I glance between them. "I think I'm more into the fantasy where I get ravished by two devastatingly attractive men in a luxury suite with a view like this."

There's a beat of silence.

Then Jamie whistles softly. "Well. Shit."

Sammy's eyebrows lift. His lips part, but nothing comes out at first. And the shock on their faces, that flicker of surprise before the hunger sets in, is almost as satisfying as the kiss that started all this.

Jamie recovers first. "That can definitely be arranged."

Sammy breaks away, crossing to the small bar in the corner with the kind of elegant efficiency that makes my knees feel like they're made of water. "Drink?"

"Please," I say. My voice still feels a little breathless. "Something strong. Something that makes this feel a little more real."

My fingers drift to my lips, still tingling from kisses that feel etched into me now. As if they've left marks only I can feel.

Jamie touches my shoulder, light and brief, but I feel it everywhere.

His hand trails down my arm, slow and casual and completely intentional.

"Explore," he says. "We'll bring the drinks to you. There's more to see."

I take Jamie's suggestion and let myself drift through the suite, each new room more extravagant than the last. I find a sleek dining table that could easily host six, a half bath tucked off the main room, and then—through another wide doorway—I stumble into a bathroom that makes me stop cold.

"Holy shit," I whisper.

It's bigger than my bedroom back home. Maybe bigger than my entire first apartment if you count the hallway. Polished marble stretches across the floor and halfway up the walls. The shower could fit a football team. A soaking tub sits by a window, perfectly positioned to watch the sun sink over the city skyline.

"Found the bathroom?" Jamie calls from the other room, voice lazy, amused. I can hear the grin in it, like he's been waiting for this moment.

"It's massive," I call back. "The bathtub is the size of a small swimming pool. I've lived in places smaller."

I hear his laughter echo faintly from the suite while I trail my fingers across the porcelain. The reflection that stares back at me from the polished surface of the spigot is warped and flushed. I can already see it in my mind—steam curling up the windows, bubbles spilling over the edges, champagne in one hand. And maybe I'm not alone in that tub. Maybe I'm bracketed by bodies, skin slick against mine, mouths exploring forbidden places. Heat coils low in my stomach before I can stop it.

I shake the thought loose and head back out, pulse still thudding as I re-enter the main room.

Sammy is behind the bar now, sleeves pushed to his elbows, glass bottles clinking softly as he mixes drinks like he's done it a thousand times. Jamie's sprawled across the velvet sofa, the kind of man who knows exactly how much space he's taking up and doesn't bother pretending otherwise. One arm slung across the backrest. Legs spread like he owns the room. He looks over and pats the cushion beside him.

"There's a pool on the roof," he says, casual like he's talking about the weather. "Heated, infinity edge, underwater speakers. Want to check it out after drinks?"

Sammy hands me a crystal tumbler filled with something amber and promising. The first sip burns, but in a way that loosens everything inside me.

"There's really a pool on the roof?" I ask as I settle beside Jamie. Our thighs press together and even through the denim, the friction hums.

"Yes," Sammy confirms as he takes the armchair across from us. He crosses one ankle over the other, the picture of effortless elegance. "And the view's even better than this one."

I take another sip letting the warmth spread through me. The day's tension begins to dissolve at the edges. "You two are spoiling me."

"That's the plan," Jamie says, his voice low near my ear. His fingers reach for a strand of my hair, slowly twirling it. The gesture is almost nothing, but it makes my whole body tighten in anticipation.

"What else is part of the plan?" I ask, glancing between them.

Sammy leans forward, resting his forearms on his knees. The movement draws him closer, pulling us into a smaller circle, like the room is folding in around the three of us.

"Dinner. Somewhere quiet. Somewhere you'll remember," he says, his voice steady, like he already knows exactly how tonight is going to end.

Jamie's fingers brush the nape of my neck, featherlight. My breath catches.

"Then we'll show you the city," he adds. "The landmarks first. All the safe, shiny things."

"And after that?" I ask. The words come out hushed. Tense. Like the question has teeth.

Their eyes meet over my head. Something passes between them, silent but loud in its weight.

"After that," Sammy says slowly, voice lower now, every syllable landing with intention, "whatever you want, love."

I feel that word in my spine. It crackles there like static.

"What if what I want is for you to stop being so careful with me?" The question leaves my mouth before I can call it back. Maybe it's the alcohol. Maybe it's them.

Jamie goes still beside me. Sammy's glass pauses halfway to his lips.

The air shifts. Warms. Tightens.

"Penelope," Sammy says, my name like velvet laced with threat, "be careful what you wish for."

"I know what I'm wishing for," I say, and I meet his eyes. My heart is pounding, but I don't look away.

The way he says my name... it sinks beneath my skin. Possessive. Intimate. Like a hand pressing just beneath my breastbone.

I look down at my drink, the glass slick in my fingers. I try to focus on it, but my mind has already gone elsewhere. Tangled sheets. Hands pulling me apart. Mouths. Heat. Their bodies surrounding mine like gravity.

Jamie finishes his drink and stands, brushing imaginary lint from his pants. "Should we check out that pool?"

He extends his hand toward me, palm up, expression unreadable except for the spark behind his eyes.

I nod, grateful for something to focus on besides the way my heart won't stop tripping over itself. My fingers slip into Jamie's, and he pulls me up with a smooth, unhurried strength that lands me briefly against his chest. Just a second. Just long enough for his warmth to settle through my skin before he lets go.

We leave our glasses on the bar, the clink of crystal against wood the last sound before we step back into the elevator. This time, we ride it all the way up.

The doors open onto a glass-encased terrace, the kind that gives you the illusion of floating above the city while still being cradled in safety. The air is humid and sweet, the faint scent of chlorine mingling with something floral. Music hums quietly, bass low and steady, like a heartbeat just beneath the surface.

The pool glows a soft turquoise, steam curling off the surface in lazy ribbons. Beyond the glass, London stretches out in every direction

—silver and gold and soft shadow, buildings catching the light just before the sun begins to drop below the horizon. To the right, the Shard rises sharp and crystalline. The Thames curls through the city like it's always been there, threading everything together.

I step closer to the glass, fingers brushing the cool pane. "It's beautiful," I whisper. The words feel small in my throat, not nearly big enough for what I'm seeing. The sunlight hits the windows just right, turning the skyline into a sea of glittering glass and gold.

"We can come back up tonight if you want," Sammy says. He appears beside me, close but not touching, his reflection layered over mine in the glass. "It's open until midnight."

I nod slowly, already picturing it—floating in warm water with the city laid out beneath us, stars overhead, soft voices echoing in the glass enclosure. My skin slick, their hands on me, laughter slipping into kisses. The image is so clear it makes my stomach flutter and my pulse race.

"I'd like that," I say, quieter now.

Jamie joins us on my other side, close enough that our arms touch. The contact is purposeful. Steady. He doesn't say anything at first, just watches the skyline with me like he's memorizing it.

Then, with a mischievous tilt of his head, "They have robes up here. Plush. Embroidered. The kind of thing you accidentally forget to return."

I laugh, nudging him. "We're not stealing hotel robes."

"Borrowing," he says, eyes shining. "Temporarily liberating. And for the record, they're technically included in the room cost. I checked."

"You've really put thought into this."

He gives a solemn nod. "Hotel robe acquisition is kind of my thing. I used to have a whole collection. I judged them by embroidery quality and font choice. Very important criteria."

"Obviously," I say, playing along. "Can't trust a serif font."

"Exactly. Serif screams desperation."

"You're both ridiculous," Sammy mutters behind us, but there's a softness to his voice that gives him away.

He steps closer, filling the space at my side until I'm cocooned between them again, surrounded by body heat and cologne and something far more dangerous—want. The air thickens. It hums. My breath catches without warning.

I look between them, heart thudding in my chest. "I still can't believe you did all this. The flight. The hotel. Everything. It must've cost a fortune."

Sammy doesn't hesitate. "It was worth it."

The words aren't flashy or romantic. They're just true. Unapologetically simple. And somehow, that hits harder than any grand declaration.

When I meet his gaze, I feel it, the weight of what he's saying. He's looking at me like I'm something rare, something he never expected to find. Like I'm already the best decision he's ever made.

"Every penny," he says, voice low and steady. "Every hour. Every text. Every call. All of it. Worth it to watch your face when you saw the city for the first time."

The words hit me right in the chest, hard enough to leave a mark. I don't know what to say. I don't know if I could speak even if I did.

We linger by the glass a little longer, tracing the skyline with our fingers, naming the buildings we recognize and inventing stories for the ones we don't. The city feels endless from up here. So does the possibility of what comes next.

When the elevator finally carries us back down, the silence between us feels fuller, a quiet hum of shared tension. Of things not said, not yet done.

"I should freshen up," I manage as we step into the suite, though my gaze keeps drifting to the bed. That impossibly big, impossibly white bed. My fingers find the hem of my sweater, tugging without thinking. My skin feels too hot, too aware. Like it's already been touched. Like it's waiting.

Jamie moves toward the bar again, already pulling out bottles. "Take your time," he says without looking up. "Though not too much time. I might die if you're gone too long."

"Drama queen," Sammy mutters, watching him fondly.

"You say that like it's a flaw," Jamie shoots back with a wink.

I hover at the edge of the room, the space between us thick with potential, like one wrong look will melt it all down.

"We'll be ready when you are," Sammy says, quiet and steady, his gaze lingering like a promise.

I slip into the bedroom and close the door behind me, the click of it sealing me into silence. For a moment, I just stand there, listening to the soft murmur of their voices, the faint clink of glass from the bar. The suite feels vast without them beside me. Too still. Too expectant.

I unzip my bag and start to unpack, placing each item carefully on the long marble vanity like it belongs there, even if it doesn't. My toiletries look small and out of place against the luxury of the space, but I line them up anyway, methodical, needing the familiar ritual.

In the walk-in closet, I hang my one dress—simple, soft black fabric with a neckline that dips just low enough to be interesting. It sways slightly on the hanger, catching the golden light from the bedroom.

At the bottom of the bag, I find the blue lace underwear Archer helped me pick out before I left. The color of ocean water just before dusk. The kind of thing chosen with hope, not practicality. I hold it for a moment, fingers brushing the delicate fabric. It feels like a question. Like a dare. Like some part of Archer is here too, tucked between folds of lace and longing, woven into this night whether I want him to be or not.

In the bathroom, I catch my reflection and freeze.

My cheeks are flushed, lips still kiss-swollen. There's a glint in my eyes I almost don't recognize, something raw and breathless, lit up with anticipation. The mirror reflects back a version of me that looks more like a possibility than a person. Someone on the edge of something.

I press my palms to the counter, grounding myself against the cool marble, but it does nothing to settle the hum under my skin. My sweater hangs loose, my heartbeat loud. This moment, this place, these men—it's all too much and not enough at the same time.

I undress slowly, my skin already tingling with the thrill of what's coming next. It isn't nerves, not really. More like a restless kind of excitement I can't seem to shake. The bathroom is warm and quiet, filled with the soft hiss of water and the clean scent of steam and soap.

I step into the shower, and the heat hits instantly, spreading across my body in a rush. It feels good. Cleansing. Consuming.

I wash slowly, methodically, each pass of my hands a rehearsal. I lather shampoo into my hair and wonder if they'll notice the scent. Every inch of skin becomes its own little battleground—cleaned, smoothed, claimed. The ache low in my belly doesn't fade; it deepens. I think about how it would feel if it were their hands instead of mine. Sammy's mouth at my throat. Jamie's fingers in my hair. I tip my head back, eyes fluttering shut as the water slides over my chest, down my thighs, between my legs. The fantasy blooms, urgent and unashamed.

By the time I twist the dial to cold, my skin is flushed, trembling, water dripping down my legs in rivulets. My breath clouds the glass, the mirror no longer showing anything but a haze of heat and anticipation. The shower did nothing to calm me. If anything, I'm more wound up, skin too sensitive, heartbeat too loud.

I wrap myself in one of the hotel's plush robes, the terry cloth warm against freshly scrubbed skin, my hair damp at the ends from a half-hearted blow-dry with the travel-sized dryer I packed without thinking I'd need to impress anyone. The robe smells like lavender and luxury, and I sink into it for a moment, taking a deep, steadying breath before stepping back into the suite.

Jamie stands near the bed, a garment bag laid across the duvet like an offering. His eyes find me instantly, tracking every step as I move toward him, slow and barefoot on the plush carpet. He doesn't smile right away. Just watches me with that particular kind of heat that lights me up from the inside out.

I tighten the belt, fingers clumsy. It's not modesty. It's the way his gaze lands, like it's already undressing me.

"Perfect timing," he says, voice rough around the edges. He nods to the bed. "We were about to show you what you're wearing tonight."

Something tightens in my stomach. "You really bought me something?"

"We did," he says. His smile tugs wider, laced with mischief. "Sammy picked the color. He insisted."

Right on cue, Sammy appears in the doorway, leaning against the frame. His gaze skims over me, slow and unreadable.

Jamie unzips the garment bag with a kind of quiet ceremony, and the moment the fabric comes into view, I stop breathing.

It's a dress. But not just a dress.

It's moss green and fluid, like it was spun from the forest after a rainstorm. The kind of green that shifts depending on how the light hits it, rich and alive. Simple but striking—sleeveless, with a neckline that drapes low in front and a skirt that flares just enough to skim the tops of my thighs. The fabric catches the afternoon light pouring through the windows, turning the whole thing into something almost magical.

"It's..." I reach out, fingers brushing the fabric. It feels like liquid. Like air. "It's beautiful."

"It'll be better once you're in it," Sammy says, stepping into the room, his voice a little softer now. Still sure.

"You didn't have to—" I start, and Jamie cuts me off instantly.

"Don't even finish that sentence."

"But—"

"Nope," Sammy says, moving to stand beside him. "We're not doing that. Just enjoy it."

I nod, throat tight. "Thank you," I say, because it's the only thing that feels true enough.

"You're welcome," Jamie says. His gaze is still on me, unapologetically steady. "Now, are you going to try it on? Or should we leave you alone to pet it all night?"

I pull the robe loose and let it slip from my shoulders, pooling silently at my feet. I'm left in nothing but a black thong, my skin still damp, flushed from the shower. For a beat, there's only silence.

Then the sound of them both inhaling, sharply.

I feel it like a jolt. That sudden, delicious silence as they take me in. My bare back. My thighs. My chest. Their eyes are greedy, stunned, and there's something wild and powerful that rises up in me at the sight of it. I step into the dress slowly, the cool fabric whispering up my legs.

"I need help with the zipper," I say, not looking at either of them, not yet.

Jamie is already moving. He steps behind me, hands finding the tiny zipper at the base of my spine. He pulls it up inch by inch, painfully slow, knuckles brushing against my skin.

His breath ghosts over my shoulder.

"Hold still," he murmurs, voice lower than I've ever heard it.

Sammy watches me like I'm a puzzle he's already solved but still wants to take apart piece by piece. He doesn't miss a thing—the way my breath catches when Jamie's fingers pause too long, the flush creeping up my throat, the subtle shift of my legs as I press my thighs together without meaning to. I'm caught in the push-pull of it. One man touching. One watching. And both of them feeling it just as much as I do.

Jamie reaches the top of the zipper but doesn't move away. Instead, he leans in, lips grazing the back of my neck so lightly I might have doubted it happened at all, except my whole body shivers like I've been dropped into cold water.

"You smell divine," he whispers, his mouth barely brushing my ear. "Good enough to eat. And I plan to. First course in a feast that's going to last all night."

The words hit low and hard. I feel them more than hear them. Heat pulses between my legs, and I have to lock my knees just to stay upright.

"Turn around," Sammy says behind me, voice thick and rough, the edge of control in it fraying.

I turn slowly. The dress moves with me, gliding over my skin like it was poured on. It hugs curves I hadn't noticed before, shifts with the light like something alive. The mossy green makes my eyes look gold in the mirror, like something ancient and otherworldly. Like I've been transformed.

Sammy steps forward, adjusting the cowl neckline with both hands, his fingers skimming the top of my breasts. "Perfect," he says, his gaze holding mine. "But we're not done quite yet."

Jamie crosses the room with a shoebox held reverently, as if it contains something sacred.

"No outfit is complete without the right shoes," he says, placing it carefully on the bed. "As my grandmother always said, you can tell everything about a person from their shoes."

I raise an eyebrow. "Did your grandmother really say that?"

"Absolutely no idea. I never met her. But it sounds grandmotherly, doesn't it?"

"You're impossible," I say, trying not to laugh.

"And yet," he replies, flashing a grin, "you keep indulging me."

Their playfulness takes nothing away from the weight of what they're doing. If anything, it makes it more intense. Because beneath every joke is something steadier. Something that feels like reverence. They're not just dressing me. They're preparing me. Like a ritual. Like worship.

"Sit," Sammy says, patting the edge of the bed. His voice has dropped into that register again, the one that makes something inside me coil tight and say yes without hesitation.

I sit. The mattress dips beneath me, soft and deep. Both of them lower at the same time, kneeling like it's been choreographed.

Jamie takes my right foot in his hands, holding it with surprising gentleness. His thumb presses into the arch just once, and the jolt of sensation makes me twitch. He doesn't apologize. Just smiles slightly and slides the shoe on—sleek bronze, strappy and elegant, the kind of thing I would've been too intimidated to pick for myself. He fastens the buckle, fingers grazing the delicate bones of my ankle.

"These were made for you," he murmurs, brushing his thumb over the top of my foot. "I had to guess your size, but I've always had a knack for measurements."

On my other side, Sammy cradles my left calf in one hand, steady and sure. His palm is large and warm, completely engulfing me. The contrast in our sizes is striking. It makes me feel small in a way I've come to love. His movements are quieter than Jamie's, more efficient, but no less thoughtful. The shoe slips on with a soft sound, and he buckles the strap with a practiced flick of his fingers.

"Beautiful," he says, tightening the cross-straps over my ankle. His thumb slides along the inside of my leg, just enough to brush the place where my pulse races beneath the skin. He lingers there, not pressing hard, just enough for me to feel the echo of my heartbeat against his touch.

Our eyes meet. He smiles, quiet and slow. And just like that, I'm completely undone.

Even after the second shoe is buckled, neither of them moves. They stay where they are, still kneeling, gazes fixed on me like they don't want the moment to end. The afternoon light catches them just right, painting them in gold and shadow, making them look too beautiful to be entirely human.

Jamie's hand rests on my right knee, thumb tracing slow circles into the silk. With each pass, he moves a little higher, a little closer, testing how much space I'll let him take. On the other side, Sammy's hand curves around my calf, warm and steady, grounding me.

"Stand up," Sammy says quietly. There's calm in his tone, but something commanding too. Not a question. A request that feels more like a demand. "Let us see."

They rise together, each offering a hand, and I let them pull me to my feet. The added height of the heels brings me closer to their eye level, not quite even, but enough to shift the balance. Jamie's fingers stay twined with mine. Sammy's hand finds the small of my back, firm and reassuring, guiding me through the wobble of my first step.

"Turn around," Sammy says, making a small circle with his finger. "Slow."

I obey without thinking. There's no teasing in his voice, no mockery. Just focus. I pivot slowly, the hem of the dress brushing against my legs, the fabric cool and smooth over still-sensitive skin.

"I feel like I'm in a romcom montage," I say, trying to keep my breath even. "You know, where the shy girl puts on a dress and suddenly everyone realizes she's been hot this whole time."

"There's never been anything shy or hidden about you," Sammy says, quiet and sure. "You've always been that girl."

Jamie studies me, his expression caught somewhere between wonder and heat. "Feels more like that part in the movie where she walks in and the whole room goes quiet, especially the guy who's supposed to have something smart to say."

"Is that what's happening?" I ask, glancing between them.

Jamie's smile flickers. "It's been happening since the day I met you, Penelope."

"What's the verdict?" I ask, my voice thinner than I expect, breath catching at the edges like it's struggling to push past everything swelling in my chest.

Jamie glances at Sammy, something flickering between them—unspoken, but loud. A shared language I'm only beginning to understand. Whatever it is, it settles over the room like a shift in weather.

Sammy's gaze finds mine. "I think," he says, slow and certain, "you're the most beautiful thing I've ever seen."

"Stunning," Jamie adds, his voice stripped of its usual humor. "The kind of beautiful that makes everything else disappear."

The words hit harder than I expect. Not because I don't believe them, but because I do. They don't sound like compliments.

I feel taller in the dress, steadier in my own skin, but it's not the fabric doing it. It's the way they're looking at me—like I'm rare. Like I'm theirs. My hand rises to my chest, unthinking, like I need to hold something in place.

"I just need five minutes," I manage, voice thick. "Quick makeup and I'll be ready."

They nod, and I retreat to the bathroom, hands shaking slightly as I apply a smoky eye and the faintest shimmer of blush. I swipe gloss across my lips, check the mirror once, and step back out.

For a moment, I think I've walked into an alternate dimension.

Jamie's in a charcoal suit that looks like it was sewn to his body, dark and understated but impossibly sharp. Sammy wears a deep green button-down that matches my dress perfectly, the collar open just enough to show a hint of his collarbone and that dip at the base of his throat that I want to press my lips against.

Their conversation stops mid-sentence when they see me.

"Ready?" Jamie asks, but his voice is rougher now, like the word had to fight its way out of his throat. It doesn't sound casual. It sounds like he's barely holding it together. Like looking at me has knocked the air right out of him.

I nod, too full to speak. Something catches in my chest, a flutter of nerves or excitement or both. Sammy picks up my evening bag, passing it to me with a small smile. Our fingers touch, and that flicker

I've felt all day sparks again. Not static. Something darker. Something alive.

"Then let's show London what they've been missing," Sammy says, pulling the door open.

"And later," Jamie murmurs, his hand warm on my hip, "we'll show you the parts of London they don't put on the postcards."

As we step into the hallway, I feel like I'm stepping into a different version of myself. The lights are soft, noise muffled, and yet everything inside me feels louder. Sharper. I'm walking taller now. Wrapped in green silk and heels that demand attention, I don't feel like the girl who shied away from life for three years. I feel like someone new. Someone who doesn't flinch at wanting. Someone who leans into it.

A version of me who belongs between these two men. Who deserves to be seen this way. Touched this way. Chosen.

"You know," I say, my voice steady despite the butterflies in my stomach, "I have a feeling this is going to be my favorite kidnapping yet."

Jamie flashes a grin just as the elevator doors slide closed, trapping us in the soft glow of golden light and possibility. "Who said anything about it being over? Far as I'm concerned, this is just the beginning."

"Good," I say, meeting their eyes in turn. The butterflies in my stomach rise, weightless and wild, like they finally have room to fly.

32

I can't stop watching Jamie's hands.

Not in the innocent, idle way you admire something beauti-ful. This is darker. This is want. This is need that creeps beneath my skin and settles there, pulsing. The way he folds his napkin with quiet precision. The way his fingers curl around the stem of his wine glass. Like he's seducing the damn table setting. I can't help thinking about how those fingers would feel inside me—how measured they'd be. How unhurried. How devastating.

My thighs clench beneath the linen napkin, and I squeeze them tighter like pressure alone could solve the ache. Like it'll do anything at all.

Across the table, Sammy hasn't stopped looking at me. Not once. He's quiet, but his gaze is a hand wrapped around my throat, a mouth pressed against my pulse. The dress suddenly feels too thin, too obvi-ous, like a silent invitation they've both already accepted.

The restaurant is all low candlelight and quiet luxury, the kind of place where every detail whispers restraint. Glass clinks. Silverware glides. Wine pours like a secret being kept. Around us, conversations murmur and swell, refined and forgettable. But between the three of us, something louder thrums beneath the surface. Hot. Charged. Indecent. The kind of tension that coils low in your belly and makes everything else fade. I feel it in my pulse, in the way my skin prickles, in the way I can't quite catch my breath.

"To being in London together," Jamie says, voice smooth and warm, the edges softened by his accent. He lifts his glass with the kind of elegance that shouldn't be so erotic.

Sammy's smile unfolds like a knife being drawn slowly from its sheath. "To unexpected pleasures," he says, and it's the most dangerous sentence I've ever heard spoken in public.

Our glasses meet with a soft clink, and the sound vibrates straight down my spine. I drain half my wine in one go, hoping for calm. All I get is fire.

Two months ago, I was safe. Structured. Fine. Now I'm seated between two men who have been circling me like wolves, and every cell in my body is begging to be caught.

The first course arrives, scallops arranged like petals on a slate plate, delicate and glistening. We talk, we eat, we pretend it's just dinner. But beneath the surface, something slower burns. A current threading between us with every glance, every brush of a hand. It's soft. It's dangerous.

Jamie leans in as I talk, his focus sharp in that way that makes me feel like the only person in the room. He asks questions that make me feel seen—specific, thoughtful, a little too perceptive. And when I light up about something, his dimples flash like he's memorizing the moment for later. It's almost unfair, how charming he is when he's actually listening.

Sammy, on the other hand, goes straight for the throat—in the nicest possible way. His critiques are clean and cutting, delivered with clinical precision, and every one of them sends a little thrill down my spine. He challenges me like it's foreplay. Like pushing back is the only way he knows how to flirt. I've never felt so simultaneously aroused and intellectually insulted, and I don't know what that says about me, but it's working.

Jamie shifts in his seat, thigh brushing mine under the table. He stays right there, warm and solid and intentional. I press back without thinking. A silent answer to a question we'll both be asking later.

The waiter clears our plates, and the mains appear—Jamie's lamb, Sammy's sea bass, my risotto. Somewhere between a halfhearted conversation about customer parking and a joke about valet services, Jamie casually slides his fork into my plate and lifts a bite to his mouth. No hesitation. No asking.

It should be nothing. But it lands like a spark. Intimate. Familiar. Like we've done this a hundred times before. Like we've been doing this for years.

"You should try Sam's bass," Jamie says, his voice low and smooth, like velvet just starting to burn. "The sauce is exceptional, Penelope."

He says my name like it tastes good. Like he wants to ruin it.

Before I can reach for my fork, Sammy's already holding out the perfect bite. An offering. A challenge. His eyes lock on mine across the table, unreadable but focused.

I lean forward and take it from his fork. His lips part just slightly as I do, like he feels it too.

"Good?" he asks, voice dipping into something darker. Quieter.

I nod, my mouth too full of heat to form a single word.

Jamie reaches out, thumb dragging across the corner of my mouth. "Sauce," he says, but his thumb lingers like he's writing his name there. Like he's marking me.

A tremor moves through me, too visible to hide. Sammy notices.

"You cold?" he asks, all faux concern. "You're shaking, Pippa."

The nickname lands like a hand between my legs. My breath stutters.

"I'm fine," I lie. My voice cracks anyway.

Jamie smiles like he's already undressing me with his teeth. "Sure you are."

Dessert arrives like punctuation at the end of a sentence that no one wants to finish. A glossy wedge of dark chocolate layered with something gold and glinting, catching the candlelight like it knows exactly what it's doing. It shouldn't be this sensual, but it is. Every detail feels purposeful. Decadent. A little obscene.

Sammy reaches for the same bite I do. Our spoons collide with a quiet, metallic sound that hits like a spark. I freeze. So does he. His gaze lifts to mine, slow and steady. He tilts his spoon toward me in a gentleman's gesture, but there's nothing polite about the look in his eyes. It's heat. It's hunger. It's a promise he's not even pretending to hide.

Before I can move, Jamie slips in like he was always going to. He plucks the spoon from my fingers, his touch light but possessive.

"Allow me, Penella," he murmurs, and my name lands low in my belly, thick with velvet and intent.

He brings the bite to my lips, and I let him. I let the chocolate melt slowly on my tongue, let him watch every second of it. His eyes never leave mine.

And then, under the table, Sammy's hand finds my knee. My breath catches in my throat. My spine goes straight. My thighs part without permission, some part of me ready to take anything he'll give me. I hold Jamie's gaze while Sammy's fingers slide higher, slow and certain, until they find bare skin. My dress doesn't offer much resistance. Neither do I.

My pulse pounds. My skin burns. The world narrows to this, his fingers under the table, Jamie's eyes locked on mine, the taste of chocolate still lingering on my tongue.

I'm flushed, trembling, barely breathing. Every nerve is awake and waiting. Wanting. And I don't care that we're in public. I don't care who sees. Because right now, I'm not composed. I'm not in control. I'm unraveling. And they know exactly how to pull me apart.

"Excuse me for a moment," I manage, though my voice isn't fooling anyone. Not them. Not me. I need air. Real air. Something that isn't laced with their cologne and sexual tension so thick it's practically syrup. "I'll be right back."

The hallway off the dining room is dim and quiet, soaked in golden light that blurs the edges of everything. I press my forehead to the cool wall, trying to slow the riot in my chest. Just breathe. One breath. Two.

Then footsteps. Slow. Certain.

Sammy.

His presence arrives before his voice does, filling the narrow space like smoke curling under a door.

"Penelope." He says my name like it costs him something.

"Yes?" I don't turn. I'm already caught. Cornered. And worse—I don't want to run.

He doesn't answer, not with words. His hand rises to my cheek, thumb tracing the curve of my lip, pressing gently at the corner. Testing. Asking.

I could step away. I could remind him this is a public place, that anyone could walk by. I could pretend I'm not aching for it.

Instead, I part my lips and let him in. His thumb presses onto my tongue—slow, deliberate, unshakable. His gaze doesn't move. Just burns. And then he kisses me.

It starts soft, surprisingly so, like he's trying to memorize the shape of it first, but it doesn't stay that way. In a blink, it sharpens into something reckless. Something desperate. His body surges into mine, all heat and need and years of waiting turned to wildfire.

My hands find his shoulders, fingers digging in as he pins me to the wall. His heartbeat slams through my ribcage like it's trying to rewrite my own. His tongue traces my lower lip and I open for him with no hesitation, greedy and grateful.

One hand fists in my hair, the pull just sharp enough to make my knees go weak. I let out a sound I can't take back, small, broken, real. It tears something loose in him.

The kiss fractures. Turns raw. Unruly. His teeth drag across my lip and I gasp, the sting blooming into pleasure so deep it steals the floor from under me.

"I've wanted to do this since the second I saw you in this dress," he breathes against my neck, his lips brushing the skin just above my collarbone. Then his teeth close around it. Gentle. Claiming. I know I'll carry the mark. I want to.

Before I can catch a thought, he's kissing me again, harder this time. His hands grip my hips, my ass, until I'm pressed against him in all the ways that count. His thigh slots between mine and my body answers for me, desperate and shameless. There's no space for thinking anymore. Just this. Just now.

Then, like a match struck in velvet, Jamie's voice curls through the air behind us.

"The check's paid," he says, smooth and low. He doesn't sound surprised. Or even mildly annoyed. He sounds turned on. Dangerous.

His gaze finds us, and it's a full-body thing. Eyes dark, mouth curled in a lazy, wicked smile, arms crossed like he's weighing how fast he can get us both somewhere private.

"If you two are finished with the appetizer," he murmurs, stepping closer, voice heavy with implication, "perhaps it's time we moved on to the main course."

Sammy doesn't pull away. He just rests his forehead against mine, our breaths tangled, his smile a slow, sinful thing full of promises and wreckage.

"What do you say, Pip?" he murmurs, voice low and warm and broken. "You ready for more?"

My body's already answered—my heart pounding, breath stuttering, skin flushed—but when I speak, it comes out calm. Certain.

"Absolutely."

The night stretches around us as we spill out of the restaurant, the air still warm and buzzing with summer and something more. London glows at the edges of my vision, all smeared lights and soft shadows, too bright and too beautiful through the haze of want still clinging to my skin.

I breathe in deep, trying to clear my head, and get exactly the opposite. Jamie's scent hits first—warm and spiced, clove and amber and something darker that always makes my knees a little unreliable. Then Sammy—clean cedar and salt, like someone bottled control and made it a cologne. And under all of it, the scent of them together. Familiar. Addictive. Mine.

"Where to now?" I ask, my voice still unsteady from our encounter in the hallway.

Sammy leans in close, lips brushing the shell of my ear, and I shiver before he even speaks. "Let me show you my London," he murmurs, teeth grazing my earlobe, breath warm enough to melt bone. "Tourist spots hit different at night. They show their real faces after dark."

Jamie's hand curls around my waist, his thumb sliding under the fabric of my dress like he owns the path it takes. "Unless you're tired," he says, and the teasing in his voice can't quite hide the hunger underneath.

I'm not tired. I'm wired. Alive. Strung up with anticipation so sharp it feels like it's humming in my teeth. I've seen the way they've looked at each other tonight. Felt it in the touch that lingered too long, the glance that said more than words could. There's something they're not saying. Something I think I'm about to be part of. My heart stutters in my chest, like it's racing ahead of me to find out what happens next.

"Show me," I say, surprising myself with how steady it comes out. "I want to see everything."

Jamie's smile is slow and wicked, curling at the edges like a promise he fully intends to keep. "That's my girl. Always hungry for the full experience." The praise makes my stomach drop in the best way.

We head toward the Thames, our steps falling into sync like we've done this a thousand times before. There's a rhythm to us now, unspoken and easy. Jamie walks on one side, his hand resting at my hip, claiming. Sammy takes the other, his fingers brushing mine every so often in a touch that feels less accidental every time.

The city unfurls around us in waves. Taxis grumble past, a burst of laughter spills from a nearby pub, neon flickers against wet pavement. The scent of frying oil and vinegar drifts from a chip shop, sharp and nostalgic. Somewhere close, the air tastes like ozone, rain pressing at the edges of the sky.

Everything about London feels louder than our Scottish island. Faster. Hungrier. Like the city itself is daring me to keep up.

"Look at her," Sammy says as the river comes into view, dark and wide and glittering. "The old girl never changes."

We pause on the edge of the bridge, the view opening around us like a stage. Sammy's shoulder brushes mine as he points out landmarks, sliding into tour guide mode with effortless charm. His voice lowers when he speaks again, a thread of memory winding through his words.

"My grandfather helped rebuild this. After the war. He used to tell me the Thames smelled like history back then. Like coal smoke and iron and stories being carried out to sea."

"You never told me that," I say, surprised by the newness of it. The intimacy.

He glances at me, eyes catching in the gold wash of the bridge lights. "Some stories wait for the right time to be told."

Jamie steps in behind me, his chest pressing to my back as his arms bracket me on either side, hands gripping the cold railing. He doesn't say anything right away. Just his lips finding the soft skin below my ear, his breath landing warm on my neck.

Sammy shifts closer on the other side. Our arms brush, his heat sinking into my skin. I'm caged between them, and I don't want to leave. I don't want to move. I just want to exist here, in the stretch of this night that already feels like memory.

"Big Ben next?" Jamie murmurs, his words rumbling into my skin.

"Still half-covered in scaffolding," Sammy replies as we slowly peel away from the railing. "Looks like London's most famous landmark showed up to a black-tie event half naked."

I laugh, unexpected and loud in the stillness of the street. "Only you could make a UNESCO World Heritage Site sound like it forgot its pants."

"It's a gift," he says with a perfectly serious nod. "Did I ever tell you about the ghost tour I did as a kid? Our guide claimed a Victorian MP haunts the tower. Said he nodded off during a vote and now he's cursed to listen to the chimes for eternity."

"That's brutal," I say, looping my arm through his. I pretend it's casual, but I can feel the way his muscles shift under my fingers. Solid. Real. "Parliamentary purgatory."

The Houses of Parliament rise ahead of us, backlit like something from a storybook. Gothic and grand and impossibly old. We stop, all three of us, caught by the view.

But I find myself watching them instead.

Jamie, intense even in stillness, like every emotion he feels runs too close to the surface. Sammy, steady and warm, revealing himself in pieces I hadn't known were still hidden. I don't know when exactly it happened —when they rewrote the way I understand love. Desire. Home.

"You're staring, Penella," Jamie says, turning just enough to meet my gaze. His voice is gentle, but there's something fragile at the edges of it. Something unguarded.

"I know," I say softly. My fingers reach for his jaw before I think better of it. "I still can't believe I get to keep you both."

Sammy's arm curls around my waist, pulling me into the space between them. His body is warm and solid at my back.

"Forever, if you'll have us," Sammy says, quiet but steady, like he's saying it for the first time and a hundred times all at once. Like he means it enough to will it into existence.

The moment holds. Lingers. Then the rhythm of the city nudges us forward again, folding us back into its pulse. We walk in that easy, unconscious synchronicity we've found. Shoulders brushing, fingers grazing, bodies orbiting each other without effort.

Up ahead, the London Eye comes into view, massive and gleaming under the deepening dusk, its steel frame etched against the sky like something out of a sci-fi dream. And just like that, the calm inside me gives out. My stomach does a graceful little somersault. My hands go clammy.

Sammy doesn't even look at me. He just knows.

"Two hundred and thirty-five feet," he says, like he's reading it from my thoughts. His palm settles at the small of my back, warm and solid. "Though it feels higher once you're up there."

"Oh, sweet Jesus," I groan, trying to laugh and failing.

The capsules hang suspended like glass teardrops, too fragile, too high, held up by steel and a prayer.

Jamie watches me, his expression tightening as he catches the cracks in my façade. "We don't have to do this," he says, voice low and careful, just for me. "London has plenty of attractions that don't leave the ground."

"No," I say quickly, too quickly. "It's on my list." I don't mention that it's sandwiched between "survive a haunted house overnight" and "run with the bulls in Pamplona."

Jamie's gaze doesn't waver. "Penelope."

"I'm fine," I insist, with all the convincing tone of someone seconds away from passing out in public.

They exchange a look behind my back—concern, amusement, and something gentler that wraps around my ribs and squeezes. They don't tease. They don't argue. Just let me have the illusion of control.

As if summoned by fate or poor judgment, the sun hits the horizon, turning the Thames into a ribbon of molten gold. We approach the Eye just as a capsule arrives at ground level, releasing a gaggle of cheerful tourists who seem suspiciously un-dead. The attendant scans our tickets and glances up, smile widening.

"VIP capsule," he says, handing back the passes. "All yours tonight."

Of course it is. Jamie's doing, no doubt. And I should be grateful, but all I can think about is being sealed inside a giant snow globe with nothing between me and a sky-high plummet but tempered glass and a few bolts.

The door slides open with a soft hiss, like the start of a horror film. My feet lock to the pavement for a half-beat too long. Jamie brushes his hand along my spine.

"Come on, Penella," he murmurs, guiding me forward.

Inside, the capsule is larger than I expect, but not large enough to escape the fact that it's hanging in midair. The curved glass walls gleam, and the air smells faintly of expensive cologne and just-wiped-clean surfaces. There's a bench in the center, upholstered in deep blue, and a sleek silver handrail that circles the space. I grip it immediately.

The doors close behind us with a soft click.

My lungs go tight.

Jamie's hands find my waist, steady, grounding. "Come here," he says gently, drawing me toward the bench as the capsule begins its climb.

"You don't have to look down," Sammy adds, stepping in front of me like a human shield. "Or out. Pretend it's the world's slowest elevator."

I let out something that might be a laugh, or a sob. "It's just a Ferris wheel," I say, voice wobbling. "A terrifying, overpriced Ferris wheel."

"With excellent safety records," Jamie offers, trying for reassurance, his thumbs stroking slow circles against my hips.

We're barely thirty feet up when my brain starts screaming. My breath stutters, shallow and fast, and the glass walls suddenly feel like too much and not enough. The view is spectacular and also horrific. My body doesn't know which way to go.

"Hey," Sammy says gently, his fingers cupping my cheek and turning my face toward him. "Eyes on me."

I cling to his gaze like it's oxygen. I count the flecks of gold in his irises. Trace the shape of his lashes. Focus on the warmth in his smile. It helps. Until the capsule sways just enough to remind me where I am.

"We're going to die," I blurt out. "In a transparent death bubble. They'll find us on the riverbank, flattened and tragic, like very attractive pancakes."

Jamie's laugh rumbles against my back. "Statistically," he says, mouth close to my ear, "you were in more danger crossing the street to get here."

"My panicked lizard brain doesn't care about your statistics," I snap, fingers tightening on his forearms. I can feel his laughter in his chest, but I'm too busy trying not to pass out to be properly annoyed.

The city stretches below us now, tiny and glittering, a jewelry box tipped sideways. The river glints copper. The people look like ants. And I make the fatal mistake of glancing down.

"I can't—" My breath breaks. Black spots flicker at the edges of my vision. "I thought I could handle this, but—"

"Shhh." Sammy steps in, his hands warm on my shoulders, his voice firm and soothing. "We've got you. You're not going anywhere."

"You're safe," Jamie murmurs, his body pressed tight to mine, arms wrapped around my waist like a lifeline.

My heart is a jackhammer, my breath a stuttered plea. "Distract me," I say. "Please."

The look they exchange is electric. Wordless. Heavy with possibility.

Sammy's hands slide down my arms, warm and sure, like he's

grounding me in this glass capsule suspended above the world. "Distract you," he repeats, his voice dipping low, velvet-wrapped heat pooling beneath every syllable. "Does that mean what I think it means, Penelope?"

Something in me twists. Sharp, sweet, electric. The panic is still there, clinging to the edges, but now it's tangled with something else— hot and liquid and greedy.

"Yes," I breathe. Not just permission. A plea. I want this. I want them. I want to be torn away from the terror and dropped into something I can't escape, something that makes everything else disappear.

Sammy smiles, slow and devastating. Jamie's breath grazes my neck like a promise. His hands rise from my waist, gliding up to my ribs with aching control, fingers spreading wide like he's relearning the shape of me. His mouth is at my ear, breath curling hot over my skin. "Remember, Penella," he says, voice thick with accent and intent, "no one can see us in here. Just the sky above and London far below."

The reminder should send me right back into panic. Glass walls. Hundreds of feet in the air. Nothing beneath us but empty space.

But then Sammy's mouth crashes into mine.

It's not soft. Not gentle. It's consuming. A fire that tears through the fragile scaffolding of fear in a single sweep. His tongue slides over mine with a calculated, filthy confidence, and all I can do is hold on and burn with him.

He pulls back just enough to breathe me in. "Better?" he asks, his eyes blown wide with lust, so dark they swallow the fading light.

"Don't stop," I whisper. The words fall out, shaky and raw.

Jamie's hands continue their slow, torturous climb, finally cupping my breasts with the kind of pressure that makes my breath catch. His thumbs roll over my nipples through the silk of my dress, teasing until the fabric feels too thin, too soft, too much.

"We've got twenty-five minutes," he murmurs, his mouth finding the edge of my jaw, then the sensitive spot beneath my ear, teeth grazing the skin there like he's marking territory. "Plenty of time to make sure you forget everything but us."

His words sink into me like wine—warm and heady and dangerous. Instead of fear, it's hunger that rises. Wild and reckless. The kind that makes me want to tear something apart just to get closer.

Sammy kisses me, deeper this time, slower. His tongue strokes against mine with the kind of rhythm that makes me ache in places that have nothing to do with vertigo and everything to do with how I want him inside me. Jamie's thumbs keep circling, teasing, dragging pleasure out until my nipples are hard and straining against the silk, each flick of his fingers sending sparks low in my belly.

"Look at her, Sam," Jamie says, voice roughened with need. "Already coming apart, and we've barely touched her." His accent curls around the words like smoke.

Being talked about like I'm a body they're learning, a puzzle they're solving with their mouths and hands—it should make me blush. Instead, it makes me throb.

Sammy's gaze drops, trailing over my flushed skin, the tight peaks beneath my dress. "Gorgeous," he murmurs, like he means it with his whole mouth. He cups my breast, thumb brushing over the aching tip with a slow drag that makes me moan against his lips. "God, I can't stop thinking about the way you taste," he whispers, his voice hot against my cheek, "the way you sound when we touch you just right."

I arch into him, desperate for more, the capsule suddenly too small, too tame, for what's building inside me.

He rests his forehead against mine, breath ragged. One of his hands slides down to my hip, where his grip had been firm a moment ago, now softer, his thumb tracing circles in apology.

"Should we be doing this here?" I ask, even though I'm already tilting into Jamie's touch again, already wet for them.

Jamie's laugh is low and sinful, vibrating against my spine. "I know for a fact you've done far more in far less private places, angel." His hand slides up my thigh, under the hem of my dress, fingers splayed like he's claiming every inch. "And the tint on these capsules? One-way. No one can see in."

Something cracks open inside me at that. Permission. Power. The thrill of being hidden in plain sight.

Sammy leans down, brushing his lips along the curve of my neck before scraping his teeth over the spot where it meets my shoulder. I hiss, the bite sharp and bright, but then his tongue is there, soothing the sting like he wants me ruined and comforted all at once.

"You still thinking about how high we are?" he asks, voice silk-wrapped sin, low and near.

And just like that, I'm not.

Not even a little.

The capsule keeps climbing, slow and smooth, but the fear is gone. Or maybe it's just been replaced—by something hotter, heavier. A different kind of vertigo.

My world narrows to sensation. Jamie's hand inching higher beneath my dress, fingers tracing lazy, possessive paths over my thigh. Sammy's mouth pressed to my collarbone, lips dragging, teeth grazing, sucking just hard enough to leave proof. Every place they touch becomes the only place I can feel.

"I can't think," I groan, my head falling back against Jamie's shoulder, dizzy in the best way.

"Perfect," Jamie murmurs, voice like smoke as his fingers reach the edge of my thong, stroking the lace with maddening, surgical precision.

"Let us think for you," Sammy breathes, his grin pressed to my skin, wolfish and warm, still trailing kisses down the slope of my neck.

"I'd like that," I whisper, and I mean it. I glance out for the first time in what feels like forever, expecting panic, but instead, I'm caught breathless for a different reason.

We're nearly at the top. London stretches out in every direction, gilded by the last light of day. The city glows, glass and steel and history layered over cobblestones and time. The Thames winds below us, a molten mirror. From here, it's impossible not to fall in love with all of it.

"Beautiful, isn't it?" Jamie says, following my gaze, but his hands never stop moving.

"Yes," I say, and I'm surprised by how much I mean it. Up here, it doesn't feel dangerous anymore. It feels vast and golden and untouchable. Like standing on the edge of a map no one else has dared to mark.

"You're not afraid anymore," Sammy says, his voice soft as his fingers brush my shoulder, pausing at the strap like a question.

"I was," I admit, my breath catching as he starts to ease it down. "But your distraction technique is alarmingly effective."

"We aim to please," Jamie whispers at my ear—just before his fingers slip beneath the lace. "Christ, Penelope, you're soaked." His voice drops to that broken, reverent pitch that makes my thighs press together on instinct.

The capsule crests its peak, London spilling below us like a dream. I look down, and feel nothing but need.

Sammy's mouth is at the top of my breast now, dragging across sensitive skin, teeth catching and teasing. Marks bloom where his lips travel, and I want them. I want the reminder tomorrow. I want the memory to live on my body.

"Look at that view," Jamie says softly. But his fingers are moving with more urgency now, coaxing slickness from me, drawing tight circles over my clit that make coherent thought impossible.

"London at your feet, Penella."

There's poetry in it, but I can't hold onto the meaning. All I can do is arch into his touch, my dress now gathered at my waist, my breath a string of broken syllables.

"Now?" I gasp as cool air kisses my bare skin. "When we're two hundred and fifty feet in the air?"

"Why not?" Sammy says, his voice thick, his eyes black with desire.

Something primal stirs deep in my chest. A craving to be taken. Marked. Owned.

He kisses me again, swallowing my gasp the moment it leaves my lips. His mouth is hot and unyielding, coaxing me open like I'm made to be devoured. Jamie's fingers keep moving beneath my dress, harder now, tighter circles that zero in on every nerve ending like he's memorized me. I whimper into Sammy's mouth, the sound ragged and involuntary, stripped down to the barest pieces of me—need, instinct, fire.

Jamie's touch is merciless in its precision, like he's reading my body in a language only he speaks, fluent in every stuttered breath, every tremble of my thighs. There's no room for thought anymore, only sensation layered on sensation. Sammy's tongue stroking against mine,

Jamie's fingers pressing deeper, faster, dragging pleasure out in waves that make my vision blur. I'm caught between them, undone by them, every point of contact a fuse burning toward detonation.

The world tilts. Maybe it's the wheel. Maybe it's me.

Sammy's hands frame my face, anchoring me. "That's it," he says, eyes locked on mine, voice molten. "Fall apart for us, love."

That's what undoes me.

Not just the fingers circling tighter. Not just the mouth at my neck. It's the watching. The wanting. The worship.

My head falls back, and the first tremor hits. A sound breaks from my throat, sharp and high, a cracked version of Jamie's name, or maybe Sammy's, or maybe both tangled together. My legs threaten to give out, but Jamie's arm wraps around my waist, holding me upright, holding me together as I come apart.

"Beautiful," Jamie breathes, voice hushed, like he's watching something holy.

Pleasure crashes through me like a storm. Violent, endless, all-consuming. I'm not sure I'm breathing. I'm not sure I need to. My body clenches around nothing, thighs locking around Jamie's hand, trying to either keep him there or push him away from the unbearable intensity.

The glass capsule spins, or maybe it's just my vision, London a blur of color and light and heat. My nails dig into Sammy's shoulders, anchoring me to this moment, to the only solid thing in the world.

"That's it," Sammy whispers, his lips brushing mine, his eyes never leaving my face. "Let it happen. We've got you."

And I do. I let go.

The aftershocks roll through me, smaller waves breaking over the wreckage. I come back to myself slowly, my skin buzzing, my thighs still trembling, my breath hitching in fits.

When I open my eyes, both of them are watching me like I'm something sacred. Something claimed.

The capsule begins its descent, slow and silent. We still have time, but the edge has softened. For now.

"Better than a panic attack?" Jamie asks, pressing a kiss to my temple as he carefully withdraws his hand, dragging it out slow and slick, making me shudder all over again.

"Marginally," I say, teasing, still breathless and barely recovering. Jamie pulls back just enough to catch my mock glare.

"Marginally?" he repeats, sounding properly offended.

I laugh, the sound weak and a little broken. "Well, now I've got two very aroused men and no acceptable place to put them."

Sammy crouches, dragging the hem of my dress back down over my hips slowly, like he's redressing something precious. His hands linger longer than they should, reverent despite the visible strain in his jaw, the way his control feels like it's hanging by a thread.

"Consider it a preview," he murmurs, voice low and hoarse. "A promise."

Jamie steps in next, smoothing the fabric over my stomach, adjusting one strap with maddening precision. "And now," he says, adopting a tone of mock ceremony, "you can admire the view without trying to claw your way through the floor."

I glance out the window again and realize he's right. London stretches beneath us in a shimmer of lights and glass, alive and sprawling and utterly breathtaking. And I'm not afraid.

"Thank you," I say softly, the words catching in my throat. Because it wasn't just about the orgasm. It never was. It was about what they gave me—control when I needed it, surrender when I craved it. Safety. Permission. Power wrapped in something hot and heavy.

Sammy's smile changes his whole face. Soft, open, devastating in its sincerity. "Our pleasure," he says, and the double meaning sinks deep into my bones.

We step off the capsule, the platform solid beneath my feet, but the ground still feels like it's swaying beneath me. Maybe it's the after-shocks. Maybe it's them. Maybe I've just been unmoored by the way they take me apart and put me back together.

The air is cooler now, the evening settling into its softer hours—streetlights flickering to life, the city humming with quiet possibility.

Around us, the world continues like nothing happened. As if I didn't just fall apart in a glass box suspended above London.

Their hands are still in mine. Sammy squeezes gently, his thumb brushing over the backs of my fingers like he's soothing something only he can feel.

Jamie leans in, close enough that I feel his breath before I hear him. His voice curls against my ear like a secret lit on fire.

"We've still got the whole night ahead of us," he murmurs. "And I'd really like the next item to involve you. Naked. With my cock inside you."

A shiver tears through me, visceral and immediate. My breath catches. My thighs press together like my body's trying to answer for me.

He pulls back just enough to look at me, eyes molten and unreadable, like he's waiting for the words that will tip us past this moment. The hunger in him is quiet, patient, but it's there, burning low and steady like coals waiting for kindling.

I hold his gaze, feel the heat bloom deep in my belly, spreading outward like the promise of what's to come. My voice is calmer than it should be, steady despite the stutter of my pulse. "Well then," I murmur, "we should probably find somewhere private before we get arrested."

We melt into the night, swallowed by the city's glow. London hums around us. Slick pavement reflecting neon and streetlight, the scent of vinegar and fried batter drifting from a chip shop nearby. A bus rumbles past, headlights flaring, and the breeze carries the cool, metallic tang of the Thames. Sammy's arm brushes mine; Jamie's thumb strokes the back of my hand. They fall into step like it's the most natural thing in the world, like I was made to fit between them.

The tension hasn't faded, it's just gone quiet, sunk deeper into the spaces between our steps. We don't rush. The city seems to open for us, a pulse of light and shadow and promise. And as we move through it, just the three of us, tucked into its flickering hush, I don't feel small. I feel claimed. Wanted. Like London is holding its breath, waiting to see what we'll do next.

33

____

We move along the South Bank like the city's holding its breath just for us. Like the three of us are our own weather system, dragging a storm of anticipation in our wake. The world around us slips out of focus, blurred lights and muted voices, footsteps on damp pavement echoing like some distant memory. Couples wander past, tipsy and laughing. Tourists consult maps they can't decipher. A cyclist cuts through the dark. But none of it touches us. Every step we take together, the air thickens. The space between our bodies contracts. My skin hums. My pulse is a drumbeat behind my ribcage.

Jamie's voice cuts through the quiet. "Hungry?" He nods toward a dessert cart that smells like caramel and childhood and sin. But his grin doesn't match the look in his eyes. There's nothing sweet about it. There's hunger there, but it's not for food.

I shake my head. "Still full from dinner."

"Do you want to go back to the hotel?" Sammy's voice is lower. Rougher. The kind of voice that feels like a hand around your throat. Possessive and gentle and completely in control. My mouth goes dry. My thighs clench.

I don't get a chance to answer. Because just ahead of us, a woman approaches what looks like a blank concrete wall, no signage, no markings—just a man in a suit standing guard. She leans in, casual as anything, and says, "The queen's nightcap."

The door opens.

The three of us freeze. Jamie and Sammy exchange a glance above my head, conspiratorial and silent, like a secret language I'm only just starting to learn.

"Fancy a drink?" Jamie asks, casual, except his pupils are blown wide and his hand is warm against the small of my back.

"A speakeasy?" I ask, eyeing the door. "Is this part of the plan?"

Sammy smiles, and the heat of it goes straight through me. "Detours make the best stories."

We walk toward the door, and my heart climbs into my throat. I don't know if it's nerves or excitement, but it's sharp and breathless and alive.

"The queen's nightcap," Jamie says, and we step inside.

It's like falling into another world.

Music seeps from the walls, sultry and low, like it's whispering secrets just for us. The bar glows in amber light. Couples lounge in corners, shadows swallowing their intentions. But it's the velvet curtain across the room that steals my focus. People slip behind it like they're crossing some invisible threshold, one I can't stop imagining myself crossing too.

"This isn't just a bar, is it?" I ask, even though I already know. The truth is vibrating in Sammy's posture, coiled tight. It's in the way Jamie's hand curls protectively around my hip, grounding and claiming at once.

"The front room is," Sammy murmurs, his voice so close it's like it's inside my skin. "Behind the curtain's... different."

Jamie leans in, his breath hot against my temple. "Private club. For people who want to let go. Together."

The words drop between us like a match. Another couple disappears behind the curtain. The woman looks back over her shoulder with a flushed, knowing smile, and something primal twists low in my belly.

"Want to see?" Sammy asks. He's still holding my hand, and his thumb starts tracing circles again, small, tender, devastating.

"Yes," I say. My voice doesn't shake, but everything else inside me does. "But I need a drink first."

"One drink," Jamie says, smiling like he already knows exactly how the rest of the night is going to unfold. Like he's already seen it play out in slow motion. My flushed cheeks, our bodies pressed together, the three of us stepping deeper into something we won't be able to walk back from. "Then we follow the detour."

We find a table tucked into a corner lit by a single candle and order cocktails that sound more like spells. Lavender smoke, blood orange, something with absinthe that makes Jamie's eyebrows lift in appreciation. The drinks arrive in delicate glasses that fog at the rim, the colors rich and strange and promising.

We toast. Sammy's glass bumps mine first. "To us."

I meet his gaze and add, "To detours." My voice is steadier than I feel.

Jamie lifts his own, eyes gleaming over the rim. "To dancing."

The glasses clink, and for a second, it's quiet. The kind of quiet that pulses. That breathes.

Then the bass rolls through the room like a tidal wave, subtle at first, more felt than heard. The kind of rhythm that grabs you by the spine and drags you under. It vibrates up through the soles of my shoes, slides along my skin, takes up residence low in my belly. My body responds before my brain can catch up.

And just like that, we're pulled to our feet. The music sinks its teeth into us, demanding surrender, and we give it willingly.

It's been months since I went dancing. Since I let go of everything but the beat and the heat. Since I let my body speak louder than my thoughts. But here, pressed between them, it's not just movement. It's invocation. Worship. A slow, sacred burn.

We weave through the crowd, the press of bodies parting around us like the night is making room. Jamie's hand finds the small of my back, anchoring. Sammy's fingers brush mine, guiding. We carve out a corner of the dance floor like it belongs to us.

And then I freeze—not from fear, but from the sheer uncertainty of logistics. How does this even work with three? Who leads when there's no clear path forward?

Sammy reads my hesitation like a language he's fluent in. He steps into my space, hands firm on my hips, thumbs grazing just beneath the hem of my shirt. His touch is steady, claiming, grounding. "Just feel it," he says, voice a low hum between us. His breath fans across my lips. "Your body knows what to do."

It does.

The bass coils around my spine as I melt into the rhythm. My hips match his, responding instinctively. Slowly, carefully, we start to move—close, then closer. His chest brushes mine with every breath, heat rising between us like steam off asphalt.

Then Jamie presses in behind me, his chest firm against my back, his breath catching in my hair. His arms bracket my waist, one hand resting just above Sammy's, the other sliding up to ghost over my ribcage, fingers spreading like a brand. We move together, three bodies synced in a slow, grinding rhythm, primal and magnetic.

Jamie leans down, his lips grazing the shell of my ear, voice dark and honeyed. "You move like sin."

The words melt down my spine. I shiver so hard it feels like something inside me breaks open—something waiting, wanting.

And I don't think. I don't analyze. I just let it take me. The world narrows. It's bodies and heat and friction. The press of Sammy's hips. The rasp of fabric against fabric. Jamie's fingers tracing up my thigh. And then, when the music slows, turning smoky and dark, Sammy pulls me harder against him, his body a promise pressed into mine.

"I knew it the first day I saw you," Sammy whispers. "That day at the restaurant. When you were ready to destroy that seafood guy over his mushy scallops."

I laugh, breathless. "That's what did it for you?"

"Competence is sexy," he says, teeth flashing. "On you? It's lethal."

Jamie's hands climb my sides with quiet certainty, the pressure just enough to make me lean into him without thinking. Goosebumps rise in his wake. He doesn't stop until he reaches the bend of my elbows, then trails back down, hands mapping the curve of my waist before settling just above my hips, fingers wide, firm, possessive. His grip says mine without needing the word.

"Sammy's always had excellent taste," he murmurs, voice a gravel-drag of heat, low and unhurried. It rolls through me like distant thunder, something old and inevitable.

The music shifts—darker, deeper. The kind of bassline you don't dance to so much as surrender. It crawls inside me, syncs with my pulse, takes over until every sway of my hips feels like an invitation. Jamie's hold tightens, fingertips digging into my curves, pulling me flush against him until there's not a breath of space between us. His chest against my back. My spine aligned with his. And my head tipping instinctively to that spot just beneath his jaw, like we were designed to slot together this way.

I catch flickers of the club through the gaps between their shoulders—strobe lights cutting across bodies, faces turned toward us with curiosity that lingers a little too long.

"They see it, too," Jamie breathes against my ear, his teeth grazing the edge before tugging, just enough to make heat explode in my belly. "How fucking extraordinary you are. How you fit between us like you were made for it."

The words punch something loose inside me. My limbs go soft. Heat licks down my spine and pools low, my nipples tightening so sharply it hurts. The fabric of my dress suddenly feels like sandpaper. Too tight. Too much.

Sammy moves in closer, unhurried but certain, and slides his thigh between mine. The rough drag of his pants against my bare skin sends a jolt straight through me, sharp, electric, obscene. The ache low in my belly deepens, raw and hollow, a throbbing emptiness that demands more.

"They wonder," Sammy says, voice a dark rumble that doesn't feel like sound so much as sensation. "What we do to you. What you sound like when we're inside you. How you fall apart in our hands."

My breath catches. Heat rushes to my face, not from shame but from the sheer, raw power of being seen like this. Desired. Claimed.

The center of their gravity. It's still new, this thing between us. Still electric and dangerous and addictive.

"Maybe we should show them," Jamie says, his hands moving again, dragging slow and sinful over my ribs, rough palms catching on silk. When he reaches the swell of my breasts, he pauses. Teasing. Thumbs brushing the undersides, featherlight and maddening.

The suggestion floods me. My thighs press together instinctively, but it's useless—my underwear is already soaked, the pulsing need between my legs loud enough to drown out reason.

"Here?" I manage to ask, though my voice barely works. My gaze flicks toward the people dancing next to us. Lights. Movement. Strangers.

"Not everything," Sammy says. "Just enough to let them imagine. Enough to make them ache for what they'll never have."

"Because you're ours," Jamie growls, his hands sliding higher, thumbs sweeping across my nipples through the thin fabric. The jolt of pleasure is so sharp, I bite back a moan. They pebble instantly, tender and oversensitive, the pressure of fabric unbearable.

I should stop them. Should say something about decorum, about public places, about boundaries. Instead, I melt back into Jamie, pressing my ass against the unmistakable bulge in his pants—thick and hard and undeniable. His breath catches, and I feel it in the tension of his body.

Sammy notices. Of course he does.

He cups my cheek with one hand, gaze locked to mine, all cool control with a razor-thin edge of hunger. His thumb brushes my bottom lip, then presses in, slipping past until it's in my mouth. I close my lips around it, tasting salt and heat and the soft roughness of his skin. I suck once, slow and deep, and his pupils flare.

"You're incredible," he says. Like it's a fact, not a compliment. Like I'm something sacred he plans to defile.

The music swells, and the tension between us rises with it, tightening like a thread pulled to breaking. Jamie's hands grow rougher, bolder. One slides higher and cups my breast, his palm heavy and warm through the fabric, fingers closing around my nipple with a slow, calculated pinch that rips a gasp straight from my throat. The pressure is perfect. Enough to burn, enough to make my knees threaten collapse. His other hand presses flat to my stomach, holding me in place, anchoring me against the rigid line of his body.

His cock presses hard against my ass, thick and undeniable, the outline searing through layers of clothes like a brand. I can feel him twitch with every breath I take.

"See what you do to me?" he rasps, his voice scraped raw, teeth grazing my neck, breath humid and hot against my skin. "You just exist, and I'm wrecked."

He slides one hand up my thigh, knuckles catching the fabric and pushing it higher. His fingertips land on bare skin—hot, firm, unapologetic. He stays just shy of indecent, but his meaning crackles through every inch of contact. He's asking, without words, if I'll let him go further.

"What do you want tonight, love?" Sammy's voice is low and close, so close I taste the whisky on his breath and the heat of him in the space between our lips. His eyes search mine, hungry and focused, like I'm something he's studied and still hasn't figured out completely. "Tell us."

It should be an easy question. I want them. Both of them. Every version. Every configuration. The way we've already learned each other and the ways we haven't yet. I want the ring I know Jamie's hiding in his jacket. I want a life with them, not just this night. But in this moment, all I can do is feel.

"I want—" I try, but the words don't survive. Because Sammy's mouth covers mine, and then there's nothing left but sensation. His lips are hard and demanding, swallowing every sound I make. He kisses like he's starving, tongue sweeping into my mouth with no preamble, no patience. It's messy and all-consuming, and I give myself over to it with everything I have.

Jamie kisses the spot where my neck meets my shoulder, teeth catching the sensitive skin, biting down just hard enough to make me jerk. Heat explodes through me, my muscles clenching around nothing, thighs quivering where they grip Sammy's leg.

When Sammy finally pulls back, I'm gasping, dizzy, lips swollen and damp, my chest rising too fast. The taste of him still lingers on my tongue, and my voice is hoarse when I manage, "I want more."

Jamie leans in, his mouth grazing my temple, voice a low murmur that sends a shiver straight through me. "More of what, angel?"

His hand stays firm on my stomach, but his fingers begin to drift—lower, slower—until they reach the sensitive crease where thigh meets torso, hovering there like a question he already knows the answer to.

"More of your hands on me," I say, voice trembling but sure. "More of both of you. More of everything."

Sammy smiles—lazy, lethal. "Look around," Sammy says, his voice smooth and dark, the kind of sound that slides under your skin. "They're already imagining what it would be like to be us."

I lift my head, half-lidded, dazed with arousal, and I see it. Subtle glances from nearby dancers, the way people slow when they pass us, the hunger in their eyes. No one's bold enough to stare, but it's there. A woman catches my gaze, her smile flickering with something between envy and awe.

"They see what we see," Jamie says, his lips grazing the mark he just left on my neck. "How you were made for this. For us."

His words set something loose in my chest. A raw, unfiltered need I've been carrying since the first night I let them touch me like this. There's power in it, in being the object of their worship, their focus. After years of holding people at arm's length, of keeping control tight and trust tighter, there's something dangerously freeing in giving it up. In being the center of their universe, just for a little while.

"Maybe they're imagining being us," Sammy says, his gaze cutting toward a man nearby whose attention hasn't wavered. "Getting to touch you." His hand pushes higher, fingers slipping beneath my dress, brushing against the lace. "Taste you."

A noise breaks from my throat, half moan, half warning. It's not subtle. It doesn't need to be.

Jamie chuckles, low and dark. "She's desperate tonight," he says to Sammy, one hand moving lower, rough fingers slipping beneath the elastic of my panties. "Just imagine the sounds she'll make when we finally get her alone. When she's on her knees. Or bent over. Or screaming our names with both our cocks inside her."

The words land hard—sharp and hot. My whole body clenches around nothing, the ache turning molten. I grind against Sammy's thigh without thinking, chasing the pressure I need like it might save me.

Sammy watches, calm and focused. Unmoved, except for the slow burn kindling behind his eyes.

"Will you make the same sounds, Jamie?" And then Sammy is leaning past me, his hand still gripping my hip, his other sliding around Jamie's neck. Their eyes meet, something unspoken passing between them, and then they're kissing.

It's not tender. It's not careful.

Sammy pulls Jamie in hard, mouths colliding, teeth scraping, like they've been waiting years for this. The heat of it rolls through me, every inch of my body caught in the middle—surrounded, claimed, adored.

Jamie chooses that moment to press one thick finger inside me— and the world fractures.

My body seizes around him, greedy and desperate. My knees nearly buckle. I reach behind me, grabbing for anything, his thigh, his hip, but there's no steadying myself. Not from this.

He breaks away from Sammy's mouth with a sound that's pure heat —wet and possessive—and I feel the shift behind me. His breath goes sharp against my neck. His arm tightens around my waist, holding me still as his hand works beneath my dress.

Then he moves.

He drags his hand slowly free, and with it, spins me to face him. One firm grip on my hip, the other rising to cradle my jaw, tilting my head up.

That's when I see it.

His eyes.

Blown wide and black, wild with something unrestrained. He looks at me like I'm the answer to every question he's ever had. Like he wants to burn the world down and rebuild it around my body.

His gaze drops to the wetness slicking his fingers, then climbs back to my face.

"Fuck," he breathes. "You're soaked."

His lips crash into mine, rough and greedy, and when his tongue slips past, hot and insistent, it's not a question. It's a demand. He licks into me like he's starving, like he's waited forever for this exact moment and doesn't care who's watching.

I melt against him, muscles trembling, balance gone. My hands fist in his shirt, pulling him closer even though there's no space left between us. Every part of me is straining toward him, every nerve lit up and screaming yes.

His teeth catch my bottom lip, a sharp sting that makes me gasp, and he swallows the sound like it belongs to him. He tilts his head and deepens the kiss, sucking on my tongue, dragging another moan from my throat. I feel it everywhere. Between my legs. In my chest. In the way my knees threaten to give out if he doesn't keep holding me up.

And then he growls into my mouth, low and raw, a sound that vibrates straight through me, and I swear I nearly come from that alone.

The dance floor doesn't exist anymore. Neither does the music. We're in our own orbit now, wrapped in heat and urgency, balanced on the edge of something dangerous. Every move is a question of how long we can keep pretending this is just a dance. Every breath dares someone to stop us.

Jamie breaks this kiss, his lips hovering over mine when he speaks. "Do you like them watching me finger fuck you, Penelope?" His breath skates across my skin, every syllable a brand. "Do you like them seeing how wet you are? How badly you need us?"

I nod, too far gone for language, my body trembling with tension I can't release. Sweat gathers at the base of my spine, between my breasts. I'm vibrating, alive in a way I've never been before.

Jamie sees all of it. And he smiles. That dangerous glint in his eyes, tempered by those maddening dimples. Like he's both the storm and the calm that follows it.

"Would you let us fuck you right here?" Sammy turns me around, his voice cutting through me like smoke and gravel, and at the same moment, his fingers press between my legs—not directly on my clit, but close enough to send a jolt straight through me. My whole body pulses, slick and frantic.

"Yes." The word escapes before I can stop it, ripped from somewhere raw and aching. "God, yes. Anywhere."

Jamie laughs behind me, low and dark. The sound rumbles through my spine like thunder rolling over open water. "Perfect," he says, voice thick with possession, his gaze catching Sammy's over my shoulder. "She's fucking perfect."

The music shifts again—deeper, heavier. The crowd folds tighter around us, giving us cover without truly offering privacy. But it doesn't matter. There's no one else. Just the three of us. Just this.

Jamie's hands grip my hips and start to move me—grinding me against him, the hard ridge of his cock sliding over my ass. Sammy presses against my front, the planes of his chest aligned with mine, friction building between my sensitive nipples and the fabric between us.

I'm trapped between them, bracketed by muscle and heat, every breath knocked out of me by the way they touch me, guide me, hold me. I feel owned. Worshipped. Consumed.

People are watching now. Not pretending anymore. A couple near us is fully still, the woman whispering something to her partner that makes his mouth go slack and his hand drop to his crotch.

"I need—" I try, but the words get stuck. I can't explain the ache. The pulsing throb between my thighs, so sharp it borders on pain. The desperate emptiness clenching and unclenching deep inside, begging for relief.

Jamie hears what I can't say. "We know," he says, and the way he says it makes me feel seen in a way that's almost unbearable. "You want to finish this somewhere we can actually touch you the way we want to."

He jerks his chin toward the velvet curtain across the room.

"In there."

"Yes," I breathe. Not a question. Not hesitation. The word lands with total, bone-deep certainty.

Sammy pulls back just a fraction. The loss of his body heat is immediate, jarring. Cool air hits my sweat-slicked skin, turning every inch of me hypersensitive. He laces his fingers through mine, grounding me with the weight of his palm, the heat of his skin against mine.

"You're sure?" he asks, his voice softer now, a single note of protectiveness weaving through the need. His thumb strokes circles across my palm, gentle, comforting, unbearably intimate.

"Yes," I say again. I don't even look away from him as Jamie moves behind me, one hand sliding across the small of my back, anchoring me in place like he knows I might float away.

We move toward the velvet curtain, my hand laced in Sammy's, Jamie pressed close behind me. When we reach the entrance, Jamie pulls out his phone and shows the doorman something. No words are exchanged. Just a nod. A knowing look. And then the curtain parts.

The air changes the moment we step through.

The music shifts the second we step inside. It's slower now, heavier. Each beat rolls through the room like smoke, thick and languid, made for grinding hips and mouths too busy to talk. The bass doesn't just vibrate, it sinks into my bloodstream, finding the same tempo as the throb already building between my legs. The lighting softens into a deep amber glow, warm and intimate, painting everything in gold and shadow, like we've stepped inside the pulse of something alive.

But it's not the music that stops me.

It's the room itself. The bodies. The heat. The way inhibition has been stripped away and left in a neat little pile by the door. All around us, bodies are moving. Intertwined on low-slung couches and wide beds. Some clothed. Some half-undressed. A few bold and bare, skin glowing under the soft lights. There's no shame here. No hesitation. Just pleasure—taken, given, offered freely and without apology.

"Oh," I whisper, the sound catching in my throat. My tongue feels dry. My lips part, and I taste adrenaline and desire, the remnants of their kisses still lingering on my mouth.

Jamie's hand finds the base of my spine, grounding me with a firm, possessive touch. His fingers spread wide, his palm hot through the thin fabric of my dress.

"We can go," he murmurs, his voice pitched low enough to belong only to me. He leans in close, and his breath grazes the edge of my temple, warm and steady. "If it's too much, just say the word."

But I don't say anything. I can't.

The heat rising in me isn't fear, it's want. It builds in my chest and pools between my legs, low and liquid and demanding. I know he feels it too, the way my body tips into his instead of away, the way my breath catches every time his fingers tighten on my waist.

I clench around nothing, already slick, already aching. My nipples press hard against the fabric of my dress, the sensation sharp and impossible to ignore. Around us, the room pulses. My gaze drifts over the scenes unfolding like live fantasies: a woman riding a man on a velvet couch, her sequined dress bunched around her waist; two men kissing with slow, bruising hunger while a woman watches, her hand buried beneath her skirt, her breath hitching in time with theirs; a wide bed tangled with limbs and sweat-slicked skin, bodies moving in reverence and rhythm.

I could back away. Could pretend this doesn't undo me.

But instead, I exhale, and find my voice. "No," I say, and the word is clean and sure and rooted. "I want to stay."

We weave through the space slowly, skirting plush furniture and low beds already occupied, passing close enough to feel the heat radiating off tangled bodies. The air smells like sex and perfume—expensive, musky, thick with arousal. No one flinches at our presence. A few heads lift, eyes scanning with detached interest or quiet approval, but most remain lost in the world they're creating with their hands and mouths.

There's an energy here that's hard to describe. Not just lust. Something deeper. Mutual understanding. Consent woven into every movement, every look. Watching is allowed. Participation only comes when asked for and given freely. It feels like walking into a world with its own rules—rules I want to learn.

A man with a shaved head stands behind the bar, bare from the waist up, his chest marked with dense black ink that climbs across muscle like it was carved there instead of drawn. He gives us a slow, assessing once-over—curious, not unkind.

"First timers?" he asks, already reaching for bottles before we can answer.

Jamie smiles. "That obvious?"

The bartender's grin is amused but kind. "Only because I know everyone else in here."

We order—whisky for the guys, gin and tonic for me—and carry our drinks to a high table tucked near the edge of the room. Elevated just enough to give us a view of everything without putting us in the center.

I perch on the stool, legs crossed, glass trembling faintly in my hand. Sammy watches me, eyes trained on my face, even as moans echo softly around us and movement shifts like heat off pavement in every corner of the room.

"What's going on in that head of yours?" he asks, his voice low and careful, like we're in a storm and he's waiting for the lightning strike.

I take a long sip, the gin burning its way down. It doesn't help. "I'm thinking I shouldn't be this turned on."

Jamie chuckles, a sound so rich and dark it slides right down my spine. "Why not?"

I gesture vaguely with my glass. "Because this isn't me. I plate oysters and argue about wine pairings. I worry about the fuel line on a fishing boat. I don't... do this."

Sammy's hand slides onto my knee beneath the table, his palm hot, his fingers strong and slow as they stroke upward. "And yet," he murmurs, "you're here. And very much enjoying yourself."

My eyes catch on a woman across the room. She's arching under her partner's mouth, thighs spread wide, fingers tangled in his hair. Her head tips back, mouth open in a soundless cry of pleasure, and my thighs press together instinctively, helpless against the ache curling hot and low inside me.

"It's the watching," Jamie says against my ear, his breath warm and deliciously sensual. "That's what's getting to you. And knowing you might be watched in return."

I turn to him slowly, my mouth dry, but there's no shame left to hide behind. "Yes," I whisper, and the word feels like a key turning in a lock I didn't know was there.

"There's nothing wrong with that," Sammy says, voice deepening, his hand climbing higher under the hem of my dress. His fingers don't rush. They don't falter. "Some people need to be touched. Others need to be seen. There's a kind of worship in both."

I think of the tight control I keep over my life back home, how precise I have to be to keep everything running. I think of how exhausting it is to always be composed, measured. Maybe this is the other side of that. Letting go completely. Letting them show me what it feels like to be watched, desired, undone.

Jamie leans closer, so near I can feel the hum of tension in his body. "Tell us what you want, Penelope," he murmurs, his finger tracing the rim of his glass. "We can leave. Go back to the hotel. Close the door and keep it just the three of us."

He pauses, letting his words hang between us.

"Or we can stay. Let this place show you what's possible."

I glance out across the room and spot a woman riding her partner on a low chaise, slow and unbothered, as though the world doesn't exist beyond the stretch of his body beneath her. She's naked except for a choker at her throat, her movements pure control and pleasure. People watch, but no one interrupts.

It hits me then—what I want isn't just about sex. It's about freedom. Visibility. Letting these men take me apart in front of people who understand exactly what it means to be consumed.

"I want to stay," I say, the words steady and true.

Sammy's fingers flex on my thigh, and I shift toward him instinctively, opening just a little wider.

"I want to know what it feels like," I continue, the heat rising to my cheeks as I force myself to say it out loud. "To be watched. While you both take me apart."

Sammy's breath leaves him in a tight exhale. His fingers press into my skin, just shy of bruising. "And watching?" he asks. "That does something for you too?"

I nod. Speechless. Ravenous.

Jamie's smile is slow, wicked, delighted. "I was hoping you'd say that."

He stands, offering his hand.

I take it.

Sammy follows behind, warm and solid, his hand a steady weight at the base of my spine. Together, we move toward an unoccupied couch in the corner—just private enough to breathe, just public enough to tempt. We pass a bed where a woman is spread between two men, their mouths and hands focused only on her. One of them looks up, locks eyes with me, and smiles. Not flirtation. Not invitation. Just recognition. Welcome.

"They're all so uninhibited," I murmur as we reach the couch, my pulse hammering in my ears.

"That's the point," Sammy says, settling beside me. "No shame. No pretending. Just pleasure."

Jamie sits on my other side, thigh pressed to mine. "The rules are simple," he says, voice low, intimate. "Consent above everything. You can watch anything. Be watched. If you want to join someone, you ask. They ask. Everyone agrees."

I swallow, heart thudding. "Have you two been here before?"

Jamie's expression is unreadable, but gentle. "Not here. But places like it, yes."

Sammy adds quietly, "Always together."

I hesitate. "With anyone else?"

"Never," Sammy says, his hand sliding into mine, fingers curling tight. "Until you."

The heat that surges through me is instant, molten. My thighs press together. My dress suddenly feels too tight, too warm, too much.

"What happens now?" I ask, not sure what answer I want.

Jamie smiles, and it's pure temptation. "Whatever you want. We can sit. Watch. Let them watch us. Go back to the dance floor. Or leave."

"No pressure," Sammy echoes, but his thumb is tracing circles across my palm again, slow and knowing.

Across the room, a woman with a spill of dark curls lifts her head. She sees us. Sees me. She leans into her partner and whispers something low against his ear, and when he looks up, his gaze drags over me with slow, open appreciation.

Heat prickles across my chest, rising up my throat like a tide I can't fight. That look—hungry, curious, knowing—it does something to me. Like flipping a switch I hadn't realized was there.

"They've noticed us," I murmur, not looking away. I feel something strange pass between the woman and me. Not threat. Not even invitation. Recognition.

"They've noticed you," Jamie says against my temple, his lips brushing against my skin. "Wondering how you'll look when you fall apart. Wondering what sounds you'll make when you're filled by our cocks."

Sammy presses in closer, the weight of his thigh anchoring mine, firm and warm through the fabric. "Wondering if they'll get to see it happen."

Their words should make me blush. Should make me flinch. But instead, something bolder rises inside me, curling around my spine and settling in my gut like a dare.

"Will they?"

Jamie's hand comes to my jaw, fingers steady, tilting my face toward his with gentle command. "That's up to you, Penelope."

And then he kisses me.

It starts soft—like a question, like he's pausing at the threshold, waiting for me to make a decision. I step across it without hesitation.

My hands grip the front of his shirt. I open to him, let him in, and the kiss deepens instantly. It stops being a question. Becomes everything. Heat. Possession. Need.

Around us, the air shifts, thickening with heat and attention. Sammy watches from inches away, his eyes dark and intent, tracking every flicker of my response like he's committing it to memory. All around the room, people glance in our direction. Some pause mid-movement. Others slow just enough to watch without pretending not to.

Their attention doesn't pull me out of the moment. It pulls me deeper. Every breath feels sharper. Every touch lands harder. The awareness makes everything more vivid, like someone turned up the saturation on the world.

When Jamie finally pulls back, my chest is heaving, lips swollen, skin tingling like I've been standing in the sun too long. Before I can recover, Sammy leans in, cupping the back of my neck, threading his fingers into my hair. His kiss is all heat and purpose. Urgent, consuming, more demand than request. He kisses like he's claiming the space Jamie left behind.

Between kisses, I catch glimpses of the room. More people have turned toward us now. Some are still entwined with their lovers, watching between touches. Others have stopped altogether. Their attention hums against my skin, making my whole body buzz like it's being touched everywhere at once.

"Look at them," Jamie murmurs, his breath hot against my ear, his voice a slow thrum that settles deep in my spine. "See how they want you. How they ache to be where we are, knowing they can only watch while we get to touch."

Sammy's mouth is at my neck, dragging fire across my skin. His lips brush, his tongue teases, his teeth graze just enough to make my pulse spike as he trails lower, pausing at the curve of my shoulder, intent on claiming every inch.

Jamie's fingers trail higher, pulling my dress with them, inch by inch until it's no longer covering anything at all. The sudden cool air makes me shiver, but it's not from chill. It's from the awareness that we're fully exposed. That this slow unraveling isn't private anymore.

"You're shaking," Sammy says, drawing back to study my face. "Are you sure you still want to do this?"

I nod, too breathless to explain that the trembling isn't fear. It's need. Arousal pushed to the edge of pain. "Don't stop."

Sammy's mouth curves into a slow, devastating smile. "She likes it, Jamie," he says, his gaze still locked on mine. "Being the center of it all."

Jamie's fingers ghost along the edge of my panties, close enough to make me ache, cruel enough not to touch. "I knew she would," he answers, his voice thick with heat and something darker. "The only question is how far she's ready to take it."

On the other side of the room, the woman with the dark curls lifts her glass in a silent toast. Her smile isn't mocking. It's not flirtation either. It's recognition. And somehow that burns hotter than anything else.

Because in this moment, it stops being about them. It's not about

Jamie's hands or Sammy's mouth or the hungry eyes following every breath I take.

It's about me.

My body. My permission. My power.

"I need..." I start, but the words falter. I can't find language for the hunger pulling at every part of me.

Jamie leans in, his lips brushing my ear. "Tell us."

I turn to Jamie first, meeting that steady, grounding gaze, the one that never rushes me, never wavers. Then I look to Sammy, his fingers still threaded through mine, his eyes soft with knowing. No pressure. No judgment. Just recognition.

They've seen every layer of me, even the ones I tried to hide from myself. Especially those.

"I need you both," I say, my voice steady, sure, the words slicing clean through the thick heat of the room. "Here. Now."

Jamie brushes my hair back, his knuckles grazing the side of my neck. His hand lingers there, steady and grounding.

"Do you want a safe word?" he asks, voice low and even, like he already knows I've thought about this.

Before I can answer, Sammy's thumb strokes over the back of my hand. "We can use the color system instead," he says gently. "If that feels better."

Relief floods through me, sharp and immediate. "Yes," I say, my throat tight with how real this has become. "I'd like that."

Jamie nods once, eyes locked on mine. "Then tell us. What color are you now?"

I glance between them—these men who've seen me, touched me, waited for me—and then to the room watching us. The weight of their gaze settles over my skin like silk and smoke.

I already know the answer. There's no hesitation left.

"Green," I say. "So fucking green."

Jamie's smile sharpens as he sinks onto the couch beside me. "Then let's show them," he says. "Let's show everyone how goddamn beautiful you are when you come undone."

. . .

Sammy moves first, settling into the corner like it's a throne built just for him. One arm draped over the cushion, the other reaching for me. He draws me into his lap, positioning me to face the room, legs spread just enough to tease, my back pressed firmly against his chest. I can feel the press of his cock beneath me, thick and insistent, even through the layers between us. The hem of my dress slides up my thighs, and I don't adjust it. I let it stay.

Let them see.

Jamie kneels in front of us, his hands warm as they land on my knees, grounding me. He holds my gaze as he parts them slowly, confidently. The movement is gentle, but the meaning isn't. He opens me, exposing me not just to himself, but to the room.

I should be afraid of this vulnerability.

Instead, I burn for it.

His voice is low, rough with restraint. "If anything becomes too much, you tell me. One word, and we stop. Understood?"

"Yes." My voice doesn't shake the way I thought it would. It lands husky, sure. "Please, Jamie."

Sammy's arms wrap around me, one hand flat against my stomach, the other sliding higher with infuriating patience to cup my breast through the fabric. He doesn't rush. He knows exactly how this works —how to draw pleasure out slowly, like smoke curling from a match. His mouth finds the side of my neck, lips brushing the sensitive space between pulse and shoulder.

"You're so fucking beautiful when you're needy," he murmurs, and I feel the words more than hear them, vibrating through my spine like distant thunder.

Across the room, the woman from earlier watches, her eyes locked on mine, her partner's hand buried between her legs. There's hunger in their gazes, mirrored across a dozen other faces. That shared pulse of desire ricochets through the room, a current I can feel buzzing against my skin.

Jamie slides his hands up my thighs, pushing the dress higher in slow, teasing increments. Every inch revealed feels like a countdown. His fingers find the edge of my underwear and he strokes me there, featherlight.

"We're going to take our time," he says, voice low but clear, his eyes never leaving mine. "Let them see how you fall. Let them feel it with you."

His touch grazes again, and I bite back a sound that still slips out, soft and broken.

"I love how responsive you are," Sammy breathes against my ear, his thumb circling my nipple, still restrained by my bra. "All it takes is a whisper and you melt."

The words pull another surge of wetness from me, slick and hot against my panties. I've never felt this desired. Never felt so simultaneously sacred and defiled.

Jamie hooks a finger in the waistband of my underwear, and slides them down my legs slowly, keeping my dress gathered around my hips. That decision—leaving part of me dressed, half-wrapped like a secret being offered—makes the act feel even filthier.

Air hits my bare skin, and I tense, hyperaware of how wet I am. Jamie's eyes darken as he sees it.

"Christ, Penelope," he says, voice thick with awe. "You're soaked."

Sammy's fingers tighten on my thigh. "Look at her," he murmurs, letting the words roll through the space between us like worship. "Pink and swollen and dripping. Her pussy's begging for attention."

A hush has fallen over the room. Every eye is on us now.

Jamie leans in, his breath warm against my ear. "They can't look away," he murmurs. "They see how desperate you are for us. And they know they'll never get this close."

I scan the room. Some watch subtly, others openly. A nearby couple has stopped pretending. They're fully engaged now, the man's fingers working his partner with slow, calculated strokes as she watches us with parted lips.

Jamie's breath ghosts over my inner thighs, his mouth so close it makes me twitch. "Wider," he says, low and certain, like he already owns the yes. "Let them see what belongs to us."

I part my legs. Jamie's hands push them wider, exposing the flushed, aching center of me to the room. His eyes don't leave mine. "So pretty," he whispers. "So fucking perfect."

His thumb strokes the soft folds, sending tremors through my hips.

Then, finally, his mouth finds me—hot and devastating, tongue stroking in long, measured licks that make my vision blur.

Sammy's arm keeps me grounded, his hand in my hair now, tugging gently, anchoring me as my body starts to come apart under Jamie's tongue.

"Let them hear you," Sammy says, voice in my ear. "Let them know how good we make you feel."

I can't hold the sound in. A whimper breaks from my lips, shameless and desperate.

Jamie eats me like he knows exactly what I need, tongue flicking over my clit as one thick finger slides inside me, curling just right.

Sammy unzips my dress and eases it down over my shoulders, baring more of me to the room. Then his hand slides up, fingers curling under my chin. He turns my face toward him, slow and calculated, until my eyes meet his. "Green?" he asks, his voice low, his gaze locked on mine.

"Green," I gasp.

Sammy doesn't remove my bra, just tugs the lace aside, exposing one nipple to the cool air and to the eyes drinking me in. He doesn't touch it right away. He lets it be seen. Wanted.

The crowd has grown. Some watch with soft smiles. Others touch themselves openly. A trio nearby, a man and two women, are stroking and kissing as they watch, completely absorbed in the display we're giving them.

"They're getting off on your pleasure," Sammy murmurs, turning my face toward them. "You're the show."

The heat that floods me at his words is indescribable. Every nerve is on fire. I can't look away from the woman across from me, her hand wrapped around the man's cock, stroking slow and steady as she watches Jamie feast on me.

"You taste like heaven," Jamie groans, adding another finger, thrusting slow and deep while his tongue keeps circling that swollen, aching knot of nerves. "So sweet. I could do this all fucking night."

I'm trembling now, thighs quivering, the first wave building fast. My whole body tightens.

Sammy feels it. "Not yet," he commands, and Jamie pulls back, just enough to leave me throbbing.

I cry out, helpless. Empty.

Jamie stands, wiping his mouth with the back of his hand, eyes blazing.

"Stand up," he says softly.

Sammy helps me to my feet. I'm shaking, dazed. Jamie pulls off his shirt, and for a second, I forget how to breathe.

He sits and holds out his hand. "Turn around," he says. "Face Sammy."

I do.

He pulls me into his lap, my back to his chest, my body bare from the waist down.

Sammy has already stripped off his shirt, every line of him relaxed and confident as he works his belt open without urgency. There's tension in the flex of his stomach, the straining zipper barely holding him back, but his hands move like he has all the time in the world. I feel none of that time. Just heat. Need. Hunger curling hot and low in my belly.

Jamie's hands slide up my ribcage, warm and steady, then cup my breasts over my bra. "Tell him," he says, voice like velvet dragged across my nerves. "Tell him what you want."

It should feel too exposed. It should make me falter. But something about the amber light, the soft thrum of music, the heat of a dozen gazes lingering on our bodies—it burns the shame out of me.

I meet Sammy's gaze. "I want to see you," I say. The words tremble at first, but they sharpen as they land. "All of you."

A slow grin curves his mouth. No teasing, no mockery. Just heat. And then he pushes everything down—pants, briefs, everything. His cock springs free, thick and proud, and it takes my breath. Around us, a ripple moves through the room. Low, appreciative sounds. Soft gasps. I feel them like electricity crawling across my skin.

And fuck, the pride that blooms in me—unexpected, wild. That this man is mine. That I get to touch him. Take him. Make him come apart.

Jamie hums low in approval behind me, his thumbs circling my nipples through the lace. Each pass is a jolt, a direct line from breast to core. "And now?" he murmurs.

I don't hesitate. "I need him inside me," I say, and the words land without a waver. "While you watch. While they watch."

Jamie groans, low and guttural. I feel the hard line of him pressed against my ass. "First," he says, voice rough, "we get this off."

He reaches behind me, fingers skilled, unclasping my bra like he's done it a hundred times. It slips down my arms and onto the couch. Cold air skates over my bare chest, and then Jamie's hands are back on me, warm and sure, cupping my breasts like he already knows exactly how I like to be touched. His thumbs drag over the peaks, slow and calculated.

Sammy's watching, jaw tight, eyes full of heat. And the others— silent, transfixed.

I arch into Jamie's hands, spine straight, pulse wild.

"Breathtaking," Sammy says, stepping forward. His palm curves around my cheek as he leans in, lips brushing the side of my throat. "You are absolutely fucking perfect."

Then his hand slides between my legs. Finds me slick. Needy. Ready. One finger eases in, slow and steady. Then another. My body arches like a bowstring pulled too tight. A sob rips from my throat, raw and unfiltered.

"Her pussy's starving for it," Sammy says to Jamie, his voice thick with hunger. "Tight as hell. Wet as sin. She's gripping my fingers like she never wants to let go."

Jamie lets out a harsh breath. His hand hooks around my knee, spreading me wider. "I can see it," he says, eyes dark and wild. "Look at that greedy little cunt. So fucking pretty."

"She's ready," Sammy murmurs, withdrawing his fingers with a slick sound that makes my thighs twitch. "Desperate."

Jamie shifts beneath me, and it jolts through my whole body—hips rocking, spine brushing his chest. I brace instinctively, hands grabbing his knees as I try to stay steady. The low rasp of his zipper cuts through the haze, loud in the charged quiet. I feel the hitch in his breath as he shoves his pants down, rough and impatient, each tug jostling me in his lap. His hips lift beneath mine, grinding up just enough to make me gasp, and his cock presses hard against me, hot, insistent, straining through the thin stretch of his briefs. Then even that last barrier is gone, dragged down and out of the way, and it's just skin. Heat. Pressure. The full, unfiltered weight of him pressed right where I need him most. His hands return to my hips, grounding me, thumbs stroking over bare skin as he eases me forward. He positions me right at the edge of his lap, where I can feel the full press of him against my pussy, nothing left to pretend about.

"Still green?" Sammy asks. His voice is quieter now. Careful. His thumbs rest on my thighs like a question, his eyes locking on mine like he'll accept nothing but the truth.

"Neon fucking green," I breathe. And it's not just permission, it's a plea. "Please don't stop."

He doesn't stop. Just shifts closer, and then the head of his cock is there, nudging against my entrance, hot and unyielding. I open for him without hesitation, ready, aching. The stretch is slow, devastating, perfect. Inch by inch, he pushes deeper, and everything else disappears. The room fades. There's only the pulse between my legs, the breath I can't quite catch, the raw, exquisite pressure of Sammy filling me.

A hush settles around us, tight and reverent. I don't know if it's our breath I'm hearing or theirs, but it's all held. Waiting. Watching.

He sinks all the way in, bottoming out with a final, shuddering push.

"Oh God," I gasp, my body clenching around him, already shaking from the shock of fullness.

Jamie's hands slide up, steady and sure, cupping my breasts like they're something precious. He lifts them, presenting them to Sammy, who leans forward without hesitation. His mouth closes around one nipple, tongue hot and wet and maddeningly precise. The heat of it shoots through me, direct as lightning. Between the stretch of him inside me and the pull of his mouth, I'm spiraling fast.

"I can't—"

"Not yet," Jamie murmurs behind me, voice low and steady, the sound of control. "We're not done with you."

Sammy starts to move—slow at first, calculated. Each thrust

angled just right, dragging across every place inside me that makes me want to scream. Jamie's hands never stop moving, roaming over the parts of me Sammy can't touch—my ribs, my stomach, my throat, the insides of my thighs. Like he's trying to memorize me. Like I'm something they've both been waiting for.

I can feel the eyes on us, the gaze of strangers soaking into my skin, into this moment, and instead of retreating from it, I burn hotter. The fire under my skin fed by every heartbeat, every breath, every pair of eyes locked on the way Sammy moves inside me. The way I fall apart for him. For them.

"Look at you," Jamie murmurs. "Taking him so beautifully. Fuck, you were made for this."

Sammy groans, his voice raw. "God, you feel unreal. So wet. Gripping me so fucking tight."

Jamie shifts behind me again. One hand slides between my legs, thumb circling that bundle of nerves with surgical precision. My back arches, a cry escaping my throat before I can even think to hold it in.

"Both of you," I pant. "Please. Please—"

Jamie stills, then nods. "Okay."

Sammy pulls out, slow, careful. The emptiness is sharp, a contrast that makes me ache. But Jamie moves quickly, turning me in his lap until I'm facing away from the crowd. His cock presses against me, thick and hot. He guides me onto him, his hands on my hips again, steadying me as I sink down.

He's slightly smaller than Sammy, but the way he fits, God, it's perfect. The curve of him presses right against that spot inside me with devastating accuracy, dragging over it again and again as he sinks deeper. I grip his shoulders, eyes wide, my breath catching on a sound I can't hold back. It's not too much. It's exactly right.

"Fuck," I whisper, the word cracking in the middle. "Oh my God."

"You're perfect," he says against my neck. "So fucking perfect."

Sammy's chest presses against my back, his presence anchoring me in place. His hands slide in beside Jamie's on my hips, grounding me between them. "This might be a lot," he murmurs, his voice barely more than gravel. "Tell us if it's too much."

Then Sammy shifts closer, and I feel him, hot and hard, pressing against the tight space Jamie is already filling. My body resists for a heartbeat. And then yields.

Pressure. Fullness. A stretch that shouldn't be possible, and yet my body takes it—shaking, trembling, clinging to the sensation like it's the only thing anchoring me to this world. It's too much. It's perfect. It's a collision of pain and pleasure so sharp it scrapes at the edge of agony.

I can't breathe. Can't speak. My mouth opens but no sound comes out. Just a raw, broken gasp as they both press deeper, locking me in place with the sheer force of them.

"Oh my God," I choke out, voice ragged. "Oh my fucking God."

The world tilts on its axis. My vision whites out at the edges, body thrumming like a live wire pulled too tight. I feel like I'm vibrating apart, like one more second of this and I'll detonate from the inside out. I'm not just full—I'm consumed. Split open and worshiped and utterly claimed.

"Color?" Jamie asks, his voice tight with the effort of holding still. Barely leashed.

"Green," I rasp. It's not a word, it's a plea. A surrender. "Please move."

They do.

One pulls back as the other presses in, and I lose track of everything except the way they feel inside me. I'm split wide open, filled to the point of breaking, their rhythm relentless, perfect. The slick, obscene slide of them, the grind of hips, the burn of skin against skin. Hands are everywhere. Lips. Teeth. I can't tell who's touching what anymore, Jamie's mouth at my neck, Sammy's breath at my shoulder, because it all blends into one unbearable, exquisite force.

I'm gasping, writhing, clutching at anything solid. My body's not mine anymore, it's theirs. Moving to their rhythm. Owned by it.

"So fucking perfect," Sammy growls, voice broken and unraveling. "Your tight little cunt's choking both our cocks like it was made for this. Like it's been waiting to be ruined."

Jamie's mouth is right at my ear, breath scorching, teeth sinking in just enough to make me whimper. "They're all watching. Every single one of them. And they can see how desperate your greedy fucking pussy is. How you're stretching so sweet around us, dripping down our cocks, begging to be split open and filled again and again until there's nothing left but this."

Then his hand finds my clit again.

That's it. That's the breaking point.

"Let go," he murmurs, low and filthy. "Show them how fucking gorgeous you are when we break you. When we fuck you so full you forget your own name."

And I do.

The orgasm detonates inside me—violent, all-consuming, apocalyptic. A scream claws out of my throat as everything snaps tight, then explodes. My body locks down, shuddering around them, muscles convulsing with a rhythm that leaves no space for thought, only sensation. Too much. Too good. It hurts, it heals, it destroys.

And still, they don't stop.

Jamie's fingers keep circling, merciless, drawing every last wave out of me until I'm a mess of sobs and shaking limbs, my voice long gone, my mind somewhere far beyond coherent thought. They hold me through it, every inch of me trembling and undone, kept upright only by their bodies wrapped around mine.

When the aftershocks finally release their grip on me, I collapse against Jamie's chest, dazed and broken. Sammy is still braced behind me, breath hot against my neck, cock still pulsing inside me like he's just barely holding on.

"Jesus," Sammy breathes, awe threaded through the grit.

"That was the most beautiful fucking thing I've ever seen," Jamie says, his voice rough around the edges. His fingers tremble as they brush sweat-slick strands from my face, like he's barely holding himself together, still buried inside me, still hard, still ruined by the way I came for them.

Around us, the room stirs back to life. A haze of sex and heat clings to the air. But it's background noise now. Nothing matters but the thick, aching need still throbbing between us.

Jamie nudges my temple with his nose, voice low and possessive against my skin. "Should we finish this somewhere quieter?"

I nod, breath catching, my body still clenching around them like it doesn't want to let go. "Yes," I whisper, lips grazing his jaw. "Take me back to the hotel and fuck me until I forget my name."

34

The ride to the hotel is a blur of motion and heat, city lights streaking past the tinted windows while the vehicle hums quietly beneath us. We're a tangle in the backseat, Sammy's hand up my dress, Jamie's mouth on my throat, my body already unraveling. The privacy divider is up, thank God, but even without it, I don't think we'd stop. We're past pretending, past restraint. The driver probably knows exactly what's happening behind him, and he deserves a fucking medal for keeping his eyes forward and his mouth shut. I'm moaning into Sammy's palm, grinding helplessly against his thigh, too far gone to care about anything but their hands and mouths and how close I am to coming.

By the time we stumble through the hotel's glass doors, I'm soaked. Skin, thighs, panties—every part of me slick and aching. My dress clings like it's trying to hold me together, silk dragging across my nipples with every breath, every step sending another rush between my legs. I feel strung out, stretched thin, barely stitched together by need. Every glance they throw me winds the coil inside tighter. Jamie's hand is a promise at the small of my back, dipping lower to squeeze my ass. Sammy walks a few steps ahead, all broad shoulders and controlled power, that steady, quiet swagger that makes my stomach drop and my knees threaten to give.

The elevator dings, quiet and polite, like it has no idea what's about to happen. We step inside. The second the doors close, it's chaos.

Sammy is on me before I can breathe. His mouth crashes into mine, messy and hungry. He kisses like he's starving, like he's furious he had to wait, like he's been holding back for too long and finally snapped. I don't even try to hold on to the moment. I just fall.

Jamie presses in behind me, his body a wall of heat, his cock hard against my ass. His hands roam like he can't decide where to grab first. His mouth finds the curve of my neck, teeth scraping hard enough to make me gasp, to mark. The mirrored wall catches us in fragments. Mouths parted. Hands tangled. Me, caught between them, something precious and broken.

"Christ," he mutters, voice wrecked. "I nearly fucking lost it. Watching you take us like that in front of all those people? Fuck, Penelope."

His hands slide up my waist. His grip tightens with possession, and I swear I can feel his smile against my skin before he adds, voice darker now, "You screamed like we split you wide open."

Sammy's hand is already under my skirt, like he never left. His fingers slip between my legs and find me soaked, still shaking. He lets out this low, filthy sound in the back of his throat and pushes two fingers inside me without warning. I gasp, my body folding into the glass, hips jerking, thighs trembling as the pleasure tears through me all over again.

"You're still dripping for us, love," he murmurs, grinning against my mouth. "So fucking greedy."

My moan is all the answer he needs. I'm unraveling again, and they haven't even gotten me out of my clothes.

Something about tonight unspooled me completely. The exhibition. The stretch. The way they touched me like they couldn't get enough, like I was sacred and filthy all at once. It did something to me. Unlocked something. And now I can't cram myself back into the box I came from.

I don't recognize the woman crushed between them now. This version of me is shameless. Soaked. Starving. Nothing like the one who tallies inventory and solves staffing issues before sunrise. That woman wears control like armor. This one is stripped bare beneath her dress, aching and pliant and hungry to be ruined. And it feels like freedom. Like I've been holding my breath for months and finally exhaled.

I arch into Sammy's touch, desperate for more. My head tips back against Jamie's shoulder, my voice already breaking. "Please."

The elevator chimes. Sammy pulls his hand back with clear reluctance, fingers slick as he smooths my dress down like he's just helping straighten a wrinkled hem and not, seconds ago, knuckle-deep inside me. Jamie mutters a tortured "Fuck" under his breath just as the doors slide open and a woman in a tailored pantsuit steps in.

She gives us a pleasant little nod, totally unfazed. Like we're three normal people, not two feral men and one girl seconds away from getting railed against the wall.

"Going up?" she asks, finger hovering over the buttons.

"Yes," Sammy says smoothly, voice calm, expression wiped clean. Not even a hint of the absolute filth he's just committed.

"Perfect," she chirps. "I'm going to sixteen. Don't mind me."

Jamie makes a strangled sound that might actually be a laugh or a sob. His cock is still hard against my ass. His hand clamps on my hip like he's trying not to do something illegal in front of a stranger.

I bite the inside of my cheek to keep from losing it completely. My body's still pulsing, still aching, and the absurdity of standing politely in an elevator with Miss Pantsuit Executive while my thighs are soaked is almost too much.

"Lovely evening, isn't it?" she says, like we're at a dinner party and not teetering on the edge of a full-blown threesome.

Jamie's voice is tight, strangled. "Getting better by the minute." His thumb is moving in slow, devastating circles over my hipbone like he's punishing me for her presence.

Sammy clears his throat, adjusts himself in a way that definitely isn't subtle, and somehow manages a polite, "Indeed."

The elevator moves like it's in on the tension and just wants to draw it out, floor by torturous floor. It stops on eight. Then twelve. I swear it's moving slower on purpose, like the universe is in on the joke. Every floor is agony. My nipples ache. My thighs are shaking. If someone plugged me into the grid, I could power the entire damn building.

"This is us," Sammy says tightly as the doors finally open.

"Enjoy your evening," the woman calls, blissfully unaware.

"Oh, we intend to," Jamie says, flashing a grin that's pure sin and makes me clench all over again.

The doors slide closed and we don't make it two steps before Sammy pins me to the wall of the hallway. His hand closes around my throat with just enough pressure to make my pulse pound in my ears. His mouth crashes against mine, hungry and unrelenting. His other hand cups my breast, rough and perfect.

"Fucking elevator lady," Jamie growls, pulling me back into his chest. He grinds against me through his pants, hard and furious. "Should've bent you over right there. Shown her how perfect your cunt looks stretched around both our cocks."

His words make my whole body shudder. I laugh against Sammy's mouth, breathless, but the sound melts into a moan when his thigh slides between mine and presses exactly where I need it.

"The room is literally thirty feet away," I manage, though I'm already rocking against his leg like I've forgotten how to think. Logic is long gone.

"Thirty feet too fucking far," Sammy snarls. His voice is all teeth and heat and possession. He grips my thighs and lifts me like I weigh nothing. My legs wrap around his waist on instinct, and his cock presses against me through his pants, thick and hot and maddening.

Jamie fumbles with the key card as Sammy walks us toward the room. His mouth stays on mine, relentless, occasionally bumping into the wall when he loses track of where he's going. One of my shoes slips off, hits the floor with a dull thud. The second follows right after.

"Leave them," Jamie says as the door clicks open, his voice low and wrecked, all gravel and heat. "You won't need anything but that dripping cunt and that tight little ass."

His dimples flash like sin, and just like that, I forget how to breathe.

By the time we reach the bedroom, we've left a trail like a storm tore through the place. My dress is split down the front where Sammy couldn't be bothered to wait, fabric hanging off me in tatters. His shirt's half-off, buttons scattered across the floor like shrapnel. Jamie's belt hangs open at his hips, swinging with each step. His hand stays pressed to the front of his pants, rubbing slow and purposeful, like he's been edging himself just to make sure he doesn't blow before he's buried inside me.

"Shower," Sammy bites out. "We need to wash the club off."

Jamie nods, his clothes already in a puddle at his feet. He steps in close, one hand sliding between my legs, fingers finding me slick and trembling. His other hand grips my jaw, tilting my face up until our eyes lock.

"Then we'll fuck every hole you have until you forget who the fuck you are," he says, voice low and dangerous. His thumb drags across my lower lip, slow and possessive. "You'll remember our cocks. Nothing else."

The words land like a spark to dry tinder, and then we're moving. I don't remember walking, only the blur of heat and hands as they guide me toward the bathroom.

The space is sin dressed in marble. White floors warm against my feet. Mirrors that catch every angle. A rainfall shower big enough to drown in. London sprawls beyond the glass like a glowing canvas, but all I see is steam and heat and them.

The second the water hits me, I jolt. Every nerve already raw, lit up like kindling. The spray hammers my skin, turns my nipples to hard, aching peaks. Jamie steps in behind me, cock hot and thick against my ass. Sammy faces me, eyes devouring every wet inch.

"Fucking hell, Pip," Sammy says, his voice low and brutal. "You don't even know how goddamn sexy you are."

His fingers trace the curve of my breast. Not touching my nipple—

teasing just beside it, making me squirm. He drags his thumb over a mark on my collarbone, then lower, to where his teeth marked me earlier. My whole body locks up, strung tight and pulsing beneath his touch.

Jamie's hands come around from behind, palms cupping my tits. He squeezes, then pinches, and my breath shatters as white hot pleasure licks down to my clit. His mouth is on my neck, tongue slick, teeth grazing.

"These tits," he says, breath thick against my skin. "Fucking perfect. You make the sweetest noises when we play with them. Like they were made for our hands."

Sammy sinks to his knees and spreads my thighs with a grip that's firm, rough, possessive. Hot water drums down my back, steam curling around us as he settles between my legs.

"Still wet," he mutters. "Still fucking leaking." His thumb spreads me open. My clit throbs, swollen and begging.

Then he licks.

One long, slow stroke that drags through my folds and stops at the top. I sob. My knees buckle. Jamie holds me up, grinding against my ass while Sammy eats me like a man with nothing to lose. Tongue circling, teasing, then fucking inside me so deep I can't see straight.

"Fuck," Jamie hisses behind me. His hands grip my hips like he's going to lose control. "Look at how he makes you fall apart. Scream for us, angel. Let us hear how good we make you feel."

I do.

I moan. Loud. Shameless. My hips roll against Sammy's mouth, his face slick with me, his tongue relentless, his hands bruising my thighs as he keeps me spread open for him.

Jamie's hand slides between my thighs from behind, his chest pressed to my back, skin slick with steam and heat. His breath skates along my shoulder as one finger sinks into me, slow and unrelenting. My body jerks, hypersensitive and desperate, already toeing the line between too much and not nearly enough. Then he pushes in a second, filling me deeper, curling his fingers just right. I gasp, shuddering, as Sammy's mouth stays locked on my clit, his tongue moving in ruthless, perfect circles like he's studied me, practiced, memorized exactly how to unravel every last piece of me.

I can't think. I can't speak. My mind blanks completely, mouth parted, breath shallow, body blazing from the inside out.

The sounds echo around us, bouncing off the marble like we're inside some cathedral built for worship and ruin. My moans, the obscene slick of Jamie's fingers moving in and out of me, the wet sound of Sammy's mouth—everything folds into the steady rush of water hitting tile. It's chaos. It's music. It's a symphony of heat and filth and need, and I'm the instrument they're both playing like they're masters.

"Please," I gasp, hips bucking, hands in his wet hair, thighs trembling. "Fuck, I'm going to—"

"Not yet," he snaps. The edge in his voice slices clean through the haze. He pulls away and stands, his face slick with me, his eyes dark and dangerous.

Before I can whimper a protest, he spins me around and presses my hands to the wall. My fingers splay against the cold marble as the water pours down my back. I'm shaking, panting, brainless with want.

"Bend over," he says. "Spread your legs."

I hesitate half a second too long, and he kicks my feet wider.

"Wider."

I do as I'm told, folding at the hips. Dripping. Trembling. Every inch of me exposed.

Sammy steps up behind me, cock thick and heavy and hot as it nudges my entrance. He doesn't push in yet. Just presses, teases, lets me feel how ready he is. How good it's going to feel. One hand fists in my soaked hair and yanks my head back.

"Beg," he says. "Tell me how badly you need my cock." His voice is low and clipped, every word wrapped in that perfect British control that somehow makes it filthier.

"Please," I choke out, barely even a whisper. "Fuck, Sammy, please —just fuck me. I need it, I need you so deep I forget how to fucking breathe." My voice breaks, words falling over each other, messy and raw.

"Good girl." He slams into me with one brutal thrust that knocks the air out of my lungs.

It's too much. It's perfect. The stretch, the fullness, the brutal way his cock slams into the spot that makes my vision flicker—it rips a sound from me that's part moan, part sob.

He fucks me like he's trying to etch himself into my bones. Hard. Fast. Unrelenting. Every thrust drives me higher, slamming me into the wall with punishing rhythm. His grip on my hips is iron-tight, fingers digging into flesh, and I hope it bruises. I want the proof tomorrow.

Jamie steps in beside me, cock in his hand. I lift my head, and our eyes lock, his gaze dark, hungry, fixed on my mouth like he already knows how it's going to feel. I can't look away. I don't want to.

"Suck," he says, voice low and dangerous. "Let's see if that mouth's as fucking greedy as your pussy."

I open for him without a second thought, lips parted, tongue ready. Jamie guides his cock past them, thick and hot, the weight of him pressing against my tongue before sliding deeper. My jaw stretches to take him, my throat tightening as he sinks in slow, and I moan around him, the sound vibrating through him, pulling a hiss from his teeth.

Behind me, Sammy groans, still driving into me with that relentless, punishing rhythm. I'm full everywhere—mouth, cunt, soul—and all I can do is give in to it. Be theirs. Be used. Be broken. And love every second of it.

Jamie fucks my mouth slow, unhurried, like he's savoring every inch as he slides in and out. His grip on my jaw is firm, holding me open and guiding me exactly where he wants me. His thumb traces my cheek, not gentle but possessive, a silent reminder that this mouth belongs to him. His hips move with ruthless control, each thrust deeper and more calculated, fucking my throat the same way Sammy is taking my pussy. Completely. Thoroughly. Like neither of them has any intention of letting me forget this night.

"Look at her," Jamie says, voice thick and wrecked. "Taking both of us like she was fucking made for it." His fingers slide into my hair, gripping tight as he tilts my head the way he likes. "Built to be filled. Built to be fucked. Every inch of her made to take our cocks."

Behind me, Sammy lets out a groan that sounds ripped from his chest. His rhythm falters, thrusts turning ragged as his hands clamp down on my hips hard enough to bruise. And I want it. Every mark. Every ache. I want to wear them.

"I'm going to stuff you full, love," Sammy grunts, breath hot against my ear. "Gonna pump this filthy little cunt full of cum until you're leaking down your thighs. I want you filled front to back, stretched wide and dripping, just how we like you."

His hand slips between my legs, and I jolt when his fingers find my clit again—already throbbing, already swollen. He circles it with brutal precision, no mercy, just pure instinct. He knows exactly how to break me. Not gently. Not sweetly. Just enough pressure to set everything inside me on fire.

It's too much, but it's perfect. Jamie fucks my mouth in slow, calculated strokes, hips rolling with that maddening control he wears like armor. But his face gives him away. His eyes stay locked on mine, dark and glassy, his whole body tight with restraint. His jaw flexes every time I swallow around him, like he's hanging on by a thread. Every drag of my tongue, every wet glide over his cock makes him twitch, makes a vein pulse at his temple. He looks wrecked—like he's drowning in it.

His hand cradles my jaw, thumb brushing the edge of my mouth, tracing the stretch of my lips around him like he can't fucking believe it. Like the sight of me like this, lips wide, eyes wet, throat open, is undoing him faster than anything else ever could.

He groans low in his chest, the sound feral and broken. One more second and he'll break. And God, I want to be the one who shatters him.

That tight coil in my belly snaps hard, unraveling fast, pleasure clawing through me like it's trying to tear its way out.

"That's it," Sammy growls. "Come on my cock. I wanna feel this tight little pussy choke me while I fill it. Yes, just like that."

That's all it takes.

The orgasm hits like a fucking detonation. It crashes through me, violent and all-consuming, no build-up, no control, just raw sensation tearing through muscle and bone. I convulse around his cock, scream around Jamie's, body locking down like it's been lit from the inside. My nails dig into tile, into skin, into anything I can hold onto while I shatter.

"Fuck," Sammy snarls, rhythm breaking. He slams into me one last time and spills inside me with a broken groan, cock jerking deep as he fills me. Thick. Hot. Endless.

His hands clamp down on my hips, holding me there. "Take it," he groans, breath ragged and voice gone to pieces. "Take every fucking drop."

Jamie pulls his cock from my mouth, strands of spit connecting us. His hand takes over, stroking himself slowly, eyes fixed on the place where Sammy is still buried inside me.

Sammy pulls out slow, and the slick, obscene sound of it makes me whimper. My pussy clenches around nothing, already aching for more, already desperate. I don't even get the chance to beg. Jamie grabs me, spins me, and presses my back to the wall. His hand catches under my thigh, lifting it high to hook around his waist. His cock presses against my entrance, thick, hot, pulsing, already slick with everything Sammy left inside me.

"My turn, Penella. I'm going to fuck his cum so deep inside you you can taste it." His eyes have gone almost black, rimmed in green and burning with hunger. Not just want. Possession. "Do you still want me after he used you like that?" he asks, pressing in just enough to make my breath hitch.

"Yes," I gasp, so far past shame it's laughable. "God, please. Fuck me, Jamie."

He drives in with a single hard thrust. My back arches, my nails dig into his hips. The slide of him through Sammy's cum makes everything wetter, filthier. He groans, low and broken.

"Fuck, you're soaked. Still dripping from him, and your pussy's already begging for more, isn't it?" He pulls out slow, then slams back in, harder, deeper. "You're just how I like you—wet, stretched, and fucking mine."

He doesn't rush. He fucks me slow and deep, like every inch is his to take and he wants to savor the stretch. His cock drags over every nerve ending, making my breath catch, my body twitch. Each thrust lands exactly where it should, like he's mapping out all the places that make me lose myself. My mouth falls open, gasps stuttering out with no rhythm, no control.

Sammy moves in behind us, silent and watching. Then his hands are on me like he can't stand not being part of this.

"Jesus, look at you. Stuffed full and still aching. This cunt was made to be shared," he murmurs, sliding a hand between us. His fingers find my clit, already swollen, already pulsing. He rubs slow at first, then sharpens the rhythm until it's brutal and perfect, each tight circle punching sparks through my body.

His hand slides between us, fingers working my clit in tight, relentless circles, and I'm already spiraling, hips twitching with every pulse of pressure. Then I feel him move, his other hand sliding lower, collecting the slick mess coating my thighs. He drags his fingers through it, right where Jamie's cock is buried deep, gathering the cum leaking out around the stretch.

He groans low, then pushes a finger in beside Jamie's cock, slow and unrelenting, like he's daring my body to take it. The stretch is brutal, obscene, and he doesn't give me time to adjust, just forces me open, makes me feel every inch of it. A sharp gasp punches out of me as my pussy clenches around both of them. Jamie, thick and pulsing. Sammy's finger, slick and curling just right. My whole body jerks, nerves sparking like he's lit a fuse inside me.

"Had to get it nice and wet," Sammy mutters, voice rough and broken. But he's not looking at me anymore.

He's watching Jamie.

I feel the shift before I register it. Sammy pulls his finger from my pussy, glistening with slick and cum, and drags it lower. Between Jamie's cheeks. Then he pushes—slow, steady, filthy—and sinks that slick finger into him in one smooth stroke.

Jamie breaks.

He lets out a sound that doesn't sound human, ripped straight from his chest. His hips stutter, falter, then slam back into me with a force that knocks the air from my lungs. His breath shudders against my skin. His control shatters right in front of us.

"Fuck," he grits out, voice torn to shreds. His jaw is clenched, his pupils blown wide, his eyes wild. He looks completely broken, caught between the tight heat of my cunt and the invasion of Sammy's thick finger buried in his ass.

The sight of him like that, undone, panting, flushed with it, makes my whole body seize. I whimper, the sound sharp and desperate. I can feel him twitching inside me, Sammy's hand still working my clit like a weapon, both of them touching me, inside me, around me like I'm the axis they orbit.

Jamie chokes on another groan, his rhythm gone ragged. His forehead drops to my shoulder, his whole body drawn tight as a wire. His cock pulses deep inside me like he's right on the edge and trying to hold the line.

That look on his face—stretched thin, trembling from pleasure and need and the weight of being filled—sends a fresh wave of heat surging through me.

"Oh, fuck," I breathe. I don't know if I'm talking to them or the fire building low in my belly, twisting tighter with every breath.

Jamie's thrusts turn feral. His hand fists in my hair, yanking my head back so I have no choice but to look at him.

"Not gonna fucking last," Jamie snarls, breath ragged. "This pussy's so goddamn tight and you're still clenching around me like you need more. Such a greedy girl."

"Do it," Sammy growls, his fingers never letting up. "Come inside her. Fill her up again. I want to see it spill out of her while I keep working this needy little clit. I want her to fall apart all over your cock."

And I do.

The words rip something open in me. My orgasm detonates—no warning, no buildup, just pure combustion. My whole body locks down, muscles clenching around Jamie like I never want to let him go. I scream, arching hard, fingers scrabbling at his shoulders, at the tile, trying to survive the surge ripping through my core.

Jamie follows me into it. He lets out a strangled groan, slams in deep, and comes with a growl that sounds like surrender. His cock jerks inside me, filling me with heat that overflows immediately, mixing with everything Sammy left behind.

He doesn't pull away. He stays tight against me, forehead pressed to my neck, both of us shaking through the aftershocks while Sammy's fingers keep drawing every last spasm out of me.

"Such a good fucking girl," Jamie breathes, voice hollowed out. "Ours."

We stay like that for a long moment, tangled and trembling, water pouring over us like we might never need to leave this space again. Steam clings to our skin, thick with the scent of sex and sweat and something that feels religious.

Jamie slips out of me slowly, and I feel everything—the stretch, the sting, the rush of cum leaking down my thighs. I feel broken and open and more claimed than I've ever been in my life.

Sammy's hand slows, softer now, like he's soothing me down from the high, each stroke a lullaby written in heat. His touch turns reverent. Worshipful. Like I'm something sacred, not just split open and shivering beneath them but holy in the aftermath.

And Jamie, God, Jamie doesn't stop touching me. His fingers trail up the inside of my thigh, dragging through the slick mess they've both made of me. He catches it with his fingertips, spreads it higher, over the curve of my hip, the dip of my waist. I don't realize what he's doing until I feel it—his finger moving across my stomach, calculated and slow.

"What are you..." My voice cracks on the last word, breath catching in my throat.

Sammy's eyes go molten as he watches. Jamie doesn't answer. Doesn't need to.

Because I look down.

And there, scrawled in thick, glistening strokes just above my navel, is one word.

Ours.

It's obscene. It's possessive. It's the dirtiest, most beautiful thing I've ever seen.

My whole body flushes like it's been lit from within, heat blooming in every nerve ending.

Jamie finally meets my eyes, thumb brushing over the final curve of the s before lifting his hand. "So you don't forget," he murmurs, voice rough, chest rising and falling like he's barely holding himself together, "who you belong to."

35

The bathroom is a cloud—steam curling around us, wrapping everything in heat and haze. The shower's finally off, but the air still feels wet, heavy with the scent of skin and sex and the kind of pleasure that leaves you dazed and shaking.

Jamie's fingers brush drops from my collarbone as he reaches for a towel, and I sag against Sammy, boneless. My legs are trembling, water clinging to the curves of my body like it doesn't want to let go. Sammy doesn't move, just holds me steady with that quiet, anchoring strength of his.

"You're going to have to carry me," I murmur, voice hoarse. "I don't think I can feel my legs."

"I've got you," he says, soft as a vow. He presses a kiss into my temple, then lifts me like I weigh nothing. I melt into him, head tucked beneath his jaw as he carries me out of the steam and into the cooler air of the suite.

Jamie follows close behind, towel slung low, droplets sliding down the sharp ridges of his chest. "Room service," he says, already picking up the phone. "We earned it."

Sammy sets me down on the bed like I'm something fragile. His gaze never leaves mine as he unwraps the towel, the soft cotton dragging slowly over my skin. Every pass of the fabric leaves a wake of aftershocks, setting off tiny sparks that light up nerves that haven't quite settled.

"What are you in the mood for?" Jamie asks, already halfway through the hotel's menu, the receiver pressed to his ear.

"Surprise me," I say, stretching out on the bed, limbs loose, skin buzzing. "Something decadent."

Jamie's eyes go molten as he watches Sammy's hands on me. Slow, calculated, more worship than towel-dry. His stare tracks every movement, like he's cataloging sensation secondhand, hoarding it for later.

"Champagne," he says into the phone, voice low and a little rough, like it's costing him not to touch me himself. "Strawberries. Brie. Figs. Prosciutto."

The line clicks dead a second later. His smirk is slow and razor-sharp, heat curling at the edges like smoke.

He doesn't look away. Like he already knows dessert's standing right in front of him.

"Twenty minutes," he says, tossing the phone aside. Then the towel drops. He crawls onto the bed, eyes on mine, skin damp and glowing, and the heat between us reignites like someone threw a match on dry tinder.

His mouth finds mine before I can breathe, tongue sweeping in deep, slow. His weight pins me, familiar and electric.

"What should we do while we wait?" he asks, already trailing kisses along my jaw, down the slope of my neck.

Sammy laughs, low and wicked, as his hand slides up my thigh. "We let our girl rest," he says, though the way he's looking at me says he's thinking the opposite. "She's going to need her strength."

Jamie hums in agreement, but his fingers keep moving. They skate across my collarbone, down between my breasts, circling one nipple until it tightens beneath his touch.

"You're probably right," he whispers to Sammy, brushing his lips just above my heart. "But I just can't seem to stop."

"I don't want you to," I breathe, hips tipping toward him like I'm magnetized.

There's a knock at the door, sharp and sudden, cutting through the haze like a slap of cold air. Jamie groans, dragging himself upright with clear reluctance. He grabs the hotel robe off the chair, muscles shifting as he slides it over his shoulders.

Before he steps away, he looks back at me. Not casual. Not fleeting. His gaze lingers, tracing the outline of my body tangled in the sheets, eyes catching on bare skin and the rise of my chest. Like he's locking the image into place.

The server wheels in a cart covered with silver-domed dishes and a chilled bottle of champagne nestled in a bucket of ice. Jamie thanks him, tips generously, and locks the door behind him.

When he lifts the lids with a dramatic flourish, the smell hits first —sweet fruit, tangy cheese, warm bread.

"Feast for a queen," he says, pouring champagne into three glasses, the bubbles catching the light.

Sammy props me up, slipping pillows behind me with gentle hands, and we gather in the middle of the bed, the food laid out between us like a picnic.

Jamie lifts a slice of pear toward my mouth, the brie soft and slouched on top. I lean in and take it straight from his hand, lips grazing his fingers as I bite. The pear is crisp, the juice bright and cold, but it's his skin I taste first—salt and warmth and something electric that makes my breath hitch.

"Beautiful," he murmurs.

Sammy offers me a strawberry and I bite, the skin splitting beneath my teeth, juice spilling onto my tongue—bright, sweet, a little wild. Before I've even finished chewing, he drags the rest of it down my throat, then lower, the berry's flesh leaving a trail that cools instantly against my heat. He traces between my breasts, the juice slick and sticky.

"Sammy," I whisper, breath stuttering.

"Waste not," he grins, biting into the berry, letting the juice drip purposefully onto my skin. He follows it with his mouth, hot tongue licking a slow path over my belly.

Jamie watches like he's starving. His gaze is all heat, all hunger. He plucks another strawberry, takes a bite, then drags it across my nipple until the juice glistens in the low light. He leans in and licks it off, slow and messy.

"Delicious," he says against my skin, voice a rasp. "But I want something sweeter."

Then Jamie's there, slipping between my thighs like he never left. No hesitation, no pretense, just his mouth on me, tongue parting me with a sound that's more growl than groan. The heat of it hits hard, and I jerk, back arching, but Sammy presses a steady hand to my stomach, holding me down with the kind of gentleness that makes everything worse in the best way.

"Easy," he says, voice low and close to breaking.

Jamie moans against me, the sound sending shockwaves through every nerve. His tongue moves slow, deep, like he's savoring every leftover trace of what they poured into me.

He looks up at Sammy with lips wet and eyes wild. "Come taste her."

Sammy doesn't pause for even a breath. He moves down the bed and slips in beside Jamie, their shoulders pressed close, heads dipping together like they're conspiring. Like my body is the secret they're about to unravel.

"Oh my God," I gasp, voice catching in my throat. The sight alone undoes me—two of them between my legs, eyes dark, mouths hungry. One leans in to lick, slow and filthy, while the other watches, lips parted, breath warm against my thigh. Then they switch, seamless, like they've done this a hundred times. Like they planned it. Like this is worship, and I'm the altar.

Jamie curls his fingers deep, hitting that spot that makes everything go bright and soundless for a second. My body arches off the bed, spine bowing without permission, but Sammy doesn't miss a beat. His mouth stays locked on me, tongue moving in slow, devastating circles around my clit before his lips seal over it, sucking with a singular, ruthless focus that makes my throat tighten, makes tears well behind my eyes.

"Please," I gasp, not even sure what I'm begging for. Relief? Ruin? Everything? "Please, I need—"

"Tell us, Penella," Jamie says, and his voice is all gravel and command. His fingers don't stop moving. "Use your words."

I sob out a breath, hips chasing their mouths. "I need you inside me," I say, the truth of it pouring from my lips like prayer. "Both of you. I need to be filled."

Sammy lifts his head slowly, lips shining, his eyes dark and blown wide. "You heard her," he says, voice barely more than a growl. "She needs to be filled."

Jamie pulls his fingers from me and brings them to his mouth, sucking them clean while moving up the length of my body, his cock thick and heavy against my thigh. I reach for it instinctively, already aching to be split open again.

"How do you want us?" he asks, voice tight with restraint, eyes burning into mine. "Tell us exactly what you want."

"I want you inside me," I whisper, wrapping my hand around his shaft, guiding him to my entrance. "And I want Sammy's cock in my mouth while you fuck me."

Jamie groans like I've punched the air out of his lungs, his body jolting forward. "You filthy little devil," he murmurs with something like awe, pushing into me in one hard, desperate stroke.

I gasp, legs falling wider, hips tilting up to take more, to take all of him. Jamie drives in deep, thick and unrelenting, every inch a stretch that blurs the line between pain and pleasure. It's too much. It's perfect. I can feel him everywhere, molten pressure that punches the air from my lungs.

Sammy kneels beside us, cock in hand, stroking slow and lazy like he has all the time in the world to watch me come apart. His eyes are locked where Jamie is splitting me open, wet and filthy and obscene.

"Fuck, look at her," he murmurs. His other hand palms my breast, thumb flicking my nipple until it's stiff and aching, pulling another moan from my throat. "She takes you so well. Like she was made for this. Our perfect little slut."

The word hits like lightning—shocking, filthy, perfect. My walls clench around Jamie, and he groans, forehead dropping to mine.

"You like that?" he rasps, beginning to thrust slow and deep. "Do you like when he calls you our slut? Because that's what you are, aren't you? Our perfect, insatiable girl who needs both of us to keep her satisfied."

"Yes," I breathe, the word barely sound. "Use me however you want."

Sammy's expression darkens, something wild and possessive flickering behind his eyes. "Hands and knees," he says, voice rough and edged with need. "I want to watch Jamie ruin you while you choke on my cock."

Jamie pulls out just long enough for me to roll over and rise onto all fours. He positions himself behind me, his cock nudging at my entrance before sliding home in one brutal, beautiful thrust. Sammy kneels in front of me, cock level with my lips, his fingers tightening in my hair.

"Open," he commands.

I obey without hesitation, eager and aching, wrapping my lips around him. He tastes like heat, salt, and pure sin, raw and undeniably him. I moan around his length, the sound vibrating through both of us, just as Jamie starts to thrust again, deep and relentless.

"Fuck, Penelope," Sammy groans, his hips stuttering forward, hand tightening in my hair. "Your mouth was fucking made for this."

Behind me, Jamie growls something close to a curse, his pace snapping harder, faster. His grip on my hips is bruising, desperate, like he thinks I might vanish if he lets go.

"Nothing—fuck—nothing feels like her," he pants. "This pussy was made to be fucked."

Their voices drip heat, low and filthy, crawling down my spine and setting every nerve on fire. Jamie reaches around, fingers sliding between my thighs, and starts circling my clit, like he knows exactly how close I am and wants to keep me right there, trembling on the edge.

"That's it," he murmurs, voice tightening. "Squeeze my cock with that tight little cunt. Show me how much you love being filled at both ends."

That's all it takes. My orgasm slams into me like a wave, sharp and fast and endless. I choke on a moan around Sammy's cock as my whole body convulses, clenching hard around Jamie until he groans through gritted teeth.

"Fuck, that's it," he grunts, hips stuttering.

He pulls out with a ragged gasp, hand pumping his cock as he holds off his own release. I moan as Sammy withdraws too, letting me catch my breath, my lips swollen, my jaw loose with need.

"Roll over," Sammy says, voice dark and full of things I want more of. "On your back. I want to see your face when I fuck you."

I do as he says, limbs trembling. He moves between my legs, cock heavy and slick with my arousal, teasing at my entrance with shallow, taunting thrusts.

"Beg for it," he says, eyes locked on mine. "Tell me how bad you need it."

"Please," I beg, shameless. "Please fuck me, Sammy. I need you inside me. Need to be filled, stretched—fucked."

With a sound between a growl and a moan, he thrusts into me, one powerful motion that knocks the air from my lungs. I spread my thighs wider, greedy for every inch. He sets a rhythm, deep and focused, each stroke landing like he's trying to memorize the shape of my body from the inside out.

"Suck Jamie's cock," Sammy says, jerking his chin toward Jamie, who's already kneeling beside my head. "I want to see those pretty lips stretched around him."

I turn toward him, lips parting, breath hitching as Jamie fists the base of his cock and guides it to my mouth. He drags the head across my tongue first, smearing the taste of me along my lips before pushing in. My jaw stretches to take him, the weight of him heavy, velvet over steel, and I moan around him as he sinks deeper, until he's brushing the back of my throat.

His groan is guttural, broken.

Behind me, Sammy thrusts again, and the force of it pushes Jamie deeper into my mouth. The motion isn't planned, but it flows like instinct—like their bodies know exactly how to move together, how to fuck me as one. Every stroke is timed, every shift seamless, and it feels less like chance and more like inevitability. Like it was always meant to be like this.

"Christ," Jamie gasps, one hand cupping my cheek, his thumb brushing over where his cock bulges obscenely in my mouth. "You're so fucking eager. Look at you. Taking us both like it's the only thing you were born to do."

Sammy groans, his rhythm turning brutal, hips slamming into me with punishing precision. "Fuck, you feel good," he growls, voice broken and shaking. "Come for us. I want you screaming around his cock."

His fingers find my clit—fast, relentless—and I shatter. The orgasm rips through me, splintering like glass, long and punishing and perfect. I cry out, the sound muffled around Jamie's cock, a raw, desperate scream that vibrates through him as I choke on the pleasure.

"That's it," Sammy grits out, holding me through it. "Come for us, beautiful. Show us who this pussy belongs to."

My body bucks beneath him, fists tangled in the sheets, legs trembling. The orgasm tears through me, full-body, bone-deep, a mind-bending rush of heat and pleasure and surrender that leaves me gasping. I feel like I'm coming apart at the seams, unraveling just to be remade in their hands.

"I can feel you pulsing," Sammy groans, his voice raw. "So fucking tight. So fucking ours."

He pulls out at the last second, cock twitching, soaked in the slick mix of all of us. Jamie moves behind me in the aftermath, strong arms curling around my waist, his cock still thick and hard against the swell of my ass, like he's nowhere near done. Sammy collapses beside me, then pulls me into a kiss, slow and grounding. Less hunger, more reverence. Lips gentle even as his hands remain firm, possessive.

I'm surrounded. By their heat, their scent, their bodies. Their mouths taste like sex and champagne and me.

"Bath?" Sammy murmurs, his mouth dragging slow, open-mouthed kisses down the curve of my shoulder. His teeth graze the sensitive skin there, not quite biting, just threatening. "Give you a chance to recover before I finally get my turn with that tight little ass I've been dreaming about since the club?"

I let out a shaky laugh, my limbs liquid and useless, brain still syrupy with the afterglow. "There's another round? You two might actually kill me."

"What a way to go," Jamie says from the foot of the bed, grinning like a sinner who's found his favorite indulgence. "But yeah. Bath sounds good. I'll get it started."

Jamie stands, naked and unapologetic, and grabs the entire room service cart like it's just another part of his plan. Plates clink softly as he wheels it toward the bathroom, disappearing through the doorway with a grin that promises trouble. A moment later, the faucet groans to life, and the quiet splash of water begins to fill the suite. The citrus-lavender scent of the hotel's bath oil follows, warm and clean, threading into the air like a slow invitation.

Sammy doesn't move. He stays wrapped around me, skin to skin, fingers tracing lazy shapes on my hip like he's sketching something only he can see. Every now and then, he slides lower, dipping between my thighs to gather the mess we've made, dragging it over my clit in soft, maddening strokes. I twitch beneath him, gasping, still too raw and too full of them to handle even the sweetest kind of torture.

"You were unreal tonight," he murmurs against the shell of my ear. "At the club. In here. Taking both of us like you were made for it."

I turn toward him, still breathless, my hand wrapping around his cock—somehow still hard, still ready. "You were too. Both of you. I never thought I'd want something like this. And now I don't know how to need anything else."

His hips roll into my hand, just a little, and his eyes flick up to mine with something softer than lust. "I'm so fucking in love with you, Penelope," he says, like the words have been waiting on his tongue, desperate to be spoken.

Before I can breathe, Jamie steps back into the room, arm extended and smiling like he didn't just walk in on the edge of something seismic.

"Bath's ready."

The tub is massive, a soaking dream surrounded by marble and soft light, full of steaming, fragrant water and a cloud of delicate bubbles. Sammy scoops me into his arms and steps into the tub, the water lapping gently as he sinks down with me cradled against his chest. I settle between his legs, my back to his torso, his cock heavy and warm along the curve of my spine. Jamie climbs in next, stretching out opposite us, our legs tangling beneath the bubbles.

"This is heaven," I sigh, sinking deeper into the water, letting it soak into my sore muscles. "Can we just live here now?"

"Not forever," Sammy murmurs, voice rough against the curve of my neck. His hand slides underwater, fingers coasting up my calf, the heat of his touch making my skin spark. "Just until you're ready for me to bend you over the edge and make you scream my name."

The words cut clean through the hazy warmth I've been floating in, sharp as a blade and just as effective. My whole body tenses, every nerve lighting back up, already aching for more. He cups my breasts from behind, his grip firmer now—less tease, more claim—thumbs circling my nipples until they tighten against his palms.

"Still sensitive?" he asks, voice low and far too pleased.

"Everything's sensitive," I breathe, shifting slightly. His hands follow without hesitation, and I feel the unmistakable twitch of his cock against the small of my back.

"You've both ruined me," I add, half-laughing. "No one else stands a chance."

"Sustenance," Jamie announces, holding a perfect bite of meat and cheese to my lips. "Can't have you passing out on us before Sammy's had his turn with your sweet ass."

He winks at me as he pops the champagne, not bothering with glasses, instead offering the bottle directly to me. I take a long swallow, the bubbles tickling my nose. I pass the bottle to Sammy, who drinks deeply before handing it back to Jamie.

I reach for a grape, the sweet-tart flavor exploding on my tongue. Sammy's hands slide up my sides to cup my breasts again, his touch lazy and possessive rather than demanding now. The water shifts as he adjusts our position, pulling me more fully into his lap.

"Insatiable," I accuse with a laugh, wiggling my ass against his cock.

"For you, Pip? Always," he confirms, his hand sliding lower, beneath the water to tease between my legs. "I don't think it'll ever be enough."

I shift into his touch, my body responding despite being thoroughly sated. The champagne has left a pleasant buzz humming through my veins, lowering what few inhibitions I have left after the events of the night.

"To us," Jamie says suddenly, raising the bottle in a toast. "And to our future wife."

The words drift through the haze—champagne-soft, pleasure-dazed—and for a second, they don't land. But then they do.

And my breath stutters.

My heart trips over itself.

"What... what did you just say?" I whisper, the words catching on the edge of something that feels a lot like forever.

Jamie reaches for a small velvet box sitting on the edge of the cart, opening it to reveal a stunning ring nestled in satin. A large sapphire gleams in the center, flanked by two trillion-cut diamonds that catch the light like captured stars.

"The sapphire is you," Jamie explains, his usual cocky demeanor replaced by something softer, more vulnerable. "The diamonds are me and Sammy. Three stones, one setting. Separate but inseparable."

"We had it made specially," Sammy adds, his arms tightening around me. "Been carrying it around for weeks, waiting for the perfect moment."

I look between them, tears welling in my eyes. "You're proposing? Now? In a bathtub?" It's perfect.

"Not just any bathtub," Jamie points out with a smile that doesn't quite hide his nervousness. "A very expensive hotel bathtub in London. With champagne and everything."

"While Sammy's cock is literally pressed against my ass," I add, a half-hysterical laugh bubbling up.

Jamie's eyes widen comically. "Is it? I didn't know that part." He glares at Sammy.

"You're both ridiculous," I say, trying for playful, but my voice cracks under the weight of it. "Absolutely ridiculous."

"Is that a yes?" Jamie asks, his usual grin flickering, like hope and nerves are wrestling behind his eyes.

"We haven't actually asked her yet," Sammy cuts in, giving Jamie a look before turning his full attention to me. He shifts me gently in his lap until I'm facing him, his hands steady on my hips, his eyes suddenly steady and serious.

"Penelope," he says, voice low but clear. "We've spent the last three years falling in love with you from afar. And these last few months... we've tried to show you exactly what that love looks like. What it feels like. Will you marry us? Be our wife. Our partner. Our future."

"What he said," Jamie chimes in, the grin on his face crooked and full of feeling. His eyes shine, emotion brimming just beneath the surface. "Except imagine a little more flair. Some Irish poetry, a tragic metaphor or two. I had this whole speech planned out." He shrugs, a little helpless, a little breathless. "But this... this felt right."

"Yes," I whisper, the word trembling out of me like it's been waiting my whole life to be spoken. Tears spill hot down my cheeks, but I barely feel them. "Yes, I'll marry you. Both of you. Of course I will."

The room tilts, the air shifts, everything inside me breaks wide open and rearranges. This isn't just a yes. It's a surrender. A promise. A beginning.

Jamie's face lights up, that radiant, boyish grin breaking wide across his cheeks as he inches closer, the ring cradled carefully just above the water. "Give me your hand."

I lift my right hand, fingers shaking, vision blurred with tears. He slides the ring onto my finger with such reverence it steals the breath from my chest. The sapphire flares in the light, deep and stormy.

"It's beautiful," I whisper, staring at the way it catches the light. "Perfect."

"No," Sammy says softly, pressing a kiss to my temple. "You're perfect. Everything we've ever wanted."

Jamie leans in, his kiss a slow, tender promise that settles deep in my bones. "Everything we'll ever need."

The moment is perfect in its imperfection. Three naked, champagne-buzzed people in a bubble bath, making promises that will reshape our lives. I wouldn't have it any other way.

"I still can't believe you proposed while your cock was literally pressed against my ass," I say to Sammy, shaking my head in disbelief.

"Thanks for stealing my moment with your gigantic cock, you big oaf," Jamie grumbles with mock indignation.

"I'll make it up to you," Sammy promises with a wicked smile.

"Damn right you will," Jamie says, grin turning wicked as he rises from the water. It pours off him in rivulets, catching the light as it traces every hard line of muscle. He reaches for me without hesitation, lifting me from Sammy's lap like I weigh nothing, like I already belong to him. "Starting right now."

He carries me, dripping wet, back to the bedroom, my skin pebbling with goosebumps as the cool air hits my water-slicked body. He tosses me onto the bed with playful roughness, following me down, his mouth finding mine in a kiss that quickly rekindles the desire that's been simmering just beneath the surface. His hand slides between my legs, finding me slick with arousal.

"I'll never get over how fucking ready you always are," he growls, sinking two fingers into me with no resistance. "So eager for us. Dripping and desperate, like your body knows who it belongs to."

Sammy joins us, still damp from the bath, droplets of water clinging to the defined muscles of his chest and abdomen. His eyes are dark with hunger as he watches Jamie's fingers disappear inside me. "What did you have in mind?"

Jamie's smile turns wicked as he slowly withdraws his fingers, slick and glistening. But instead of tasting, he lifts them to Sammy's mouth.

"Here," he says, voice low and dark. "Taste what's yours."

Sammy leans forward without hesitation, wrapping his lips around Jamie's fingers, tongue dragging slow as he sucks them clean.

Jamie's eyes stay locked on mine as his hand trails lower again, fingers teasing between my cheeks until one circles my back entrance—slow, firm, unmistakable.

"God, I can't wait to see the face she makes when you slide your cock into her tight little ass," he growls, voice rough and shaking with restraint. "I'm fucking addicted to every face you make, angel. Every sound. Every time you come for us."

The words crash through me like a tidal wave, heat blooming low and fast, my body clenching around nothing as I arch into his touch, already begging for more without saying a word.

"You think you're ready for me, Penelope?" Sammy asks, voice thick, eyes locked on where Jamie is working me open.

"I'm sure," I breathe, no hesitation, no doubt. "I want everything. With both of you."

Sammy's grin is pure sin as he unzips the suitcase and pulls out a bottle of lube, holding it up like a prize. "On your hands and knees," he says, voice dropping into that dark, commanding tone that makes my whole body melt. "Let me get you ready."

My limbs obey before my mind catches up, trembling as I shift onto all fours. Nerves buzz under my skin, coiling with anticipation so sharp it feels like electricity. I'm exposed, vulnerable, but every inch of me is aching for it—aching for them.

Jamie kneels in front of me, tipping my face up until my gaze meets his. "We'll go slow," he murmurs, thumb brushing the edge of my lip. "And we stop the second you say so. You're in control."

Behind me, the click of the bottle opening echoes louder than it should. Sammy's slick finger circles my entrance, and the cool touch of lube makes me flinch. Then pressure—gentle, steady, impossible to ignore—builds until the tight ring of muscle finally yields.

I gasp. The intrusion burns, a raw stretch that steals the air from my lungs. Not pain, not exactly. Just... different. Overfull. Too much and not enough all at once.

"Breathe," Sammy murmurs, his other hand sliding up my spine, calming and firm. "That's it. Let me in, Penelope. Let me make you feel so fucking good."

I focus on his voice, on Jamie's thumb tracing slow circles over my bottom lip, on the rhythm of my breath as it stutters and evens out again. My muscles unlock one by one, and as they do, that sharp edge of discomfort softens, melting into something deeper, hotter.

Pleasure starts to bloom, low and heady. I rock back, barely aware I'm doing it, chasing more without thinking. Sammy groans behind me, and I feel his finger slide deeper, the motion slow and devastatingly patient.

"There you go," he says, voice thick. "Look at you. Such a fucking good girl for us."

He adds more lube, and then a second finger presses in beside the first. My mouth drops open around a gasp, eyes watering from the stretch. It burns brighter this time, deeper, but it lights something up in me I didn't know was there. Something hungry.

Jamie's fingers slip into my hair and tug gently, tilting my face up to meet his eyes. "Color?" he asks, voice low, his gaze sharp and unwavering.

"Green," I manage, breath catching. "So fucking green. Feels strange, but good."

His grin is all dimple and heat as he guides the tip of his cock to my lips. "Show me how green. Take me while he opens you up."

I moan and open for him, lips stretching around the head of his cock as he slides onto my tongue, thick and heavy. He doesn't push deep, just lets me take what I can, slow and shallow, giving me control as I find my rhythm.

The sensation is mind-breaking. Jamie in my mouth, warm and pulsing, while Sammy's fingers fuck me open from behind—two, then three, slow and steady, filling me until I can't tell where discomfort ends and raw, animalistic pleasure begins. My body trembles, caught in that edge space between pain and surrender, and I give in completely.

"Fuck, baby," Sammy groans, voice hot against my back, breath falling uneven. "You feel what you're doing to us? Mouth so full of Jamie's cock, and still you're opening up for me like you've been waiting your whole life for this."

His fingers push deeper, slow and filthy, and I choke on a moan around Jamie, every nerve lit up and begging.

"Look at you," Sammy keeps going, praise thick and raw. "So damn good for us. Taking it like our perfect little slut, letting me stretch this tight ass while you suck him off."

Jamie groans above me, hand fisting tighter in my hair as he rocks his hips, just enough to nudge deeper onto my tongue. "You do love it, don't you, angel?" he says, voice broken but gentle. "Being full. Being used. You were made for us, weren't you?"

"She was," Sammy answers for me, dragging his fingers back out slowly before pushing them in again, firmer this time.

Jamie's voice dips lower, almost tender. "And you're doing so good, love. So fucking good. Taking everything we give you and begging for more."

Sammy's mouth is close now, his lips brushing my shoulder. "You want more, don't you, Penelope? You want me to fill this pretty ass while you choke on his cock. Say it, sweetheart. Tell us how much you need it."

The words hit me like a lightning strike—hot, electric, impossible to outrun. I'm not just being touched. I'm being used. Owned. Worshipped. And I crave it. Every filthy, consuming second. A fresh wave of arousal crashes through me, sharp and overwhelming, my walls clenching around nothing, aching to be filled.

****

Jamie feels it too. I can tell by the way his breath catches, by the way he pulls out of my mouth like it costs him something, like he's still tethered to me by something more than spit and heat. His cock glistens, flushed and heavy, resting against his stomach as he shifts onto his back. His eyes stay on mine the whole time. No words, not at first. Just that look, burning and steady, like he already knows I'll follow him wherever he wants to take me.

"Ride me," he growls, voice all grit and hunger. "I want to be inside you when Sam fucks your ass."

The words hit like a lightning strike to the base of my spine. Hot, raw, splitting me open from the inside. My body moves before thought has a chance to catch up, already aching, already soaked. I swing my leg over him, knees settling at his hips, and lower myself slowly, achingly, onto his cock.

It's a stretch that steals the air from my lungs. Thick and deep, filling me so completely I swear I feel it everywhere. My moan is involuntary, ragged, torn from my chest as I sink down the last inch, my thighs trembling where they meet his.

Jamie's hands find my legs, fingers digging in like he needs the anchor as badly as I do. His gaze never wavers, not even when I start to move. Slow rolls of my hips that make his breath hitch and his grip tighten.

And behind me, Sam.

He never stopped. His fingers kept working me open while I rode Jamie down, slick and skilled, coaxing my body into readiness like he knew exactly how I'd need it. Even now, while I try to breathe through the intensity of Jamie inside me, Sam's fingers don't relent. They ease in and out, teasing and filthy, stroking me in ways that make my body jolt. I'm already full, already stretched to the edge, but it's not enough.

When I finally settle, grinding down to take Jamie even deeper, Sam pulls his fingers free. One last twist that makes me gasp, my body clenching around Jamie like I might never let him go. And then I feel him.

The blunt head of Sam's cock, hot and thick, nudging against my slick, aching entrance. My whole body clenches with anticipation, my breath coming shallow and fast. Jamie's eyes burn into mine like he can feel it too, like he's daring me to take more.

To let go. To fall apart for them both.

"Ready?" Sam asks, voice rough and strained like he's holding himself together with fraying string.

"Yes," I gasp. It's not just an answer. It's a surrender. The word tumbles out of me, broken and breathless, and I lean forward, pressing both palms to Jamie's chest. His heart thunders against my hands, steady and wild, an anchor in a storm I want to drown in.

"Please, Sam." My voice breaks on his name, caught between pain and need, sharp and unbearably sweet.

This isn't just about the stretch or the slick, aching hunger of being filled. It's the moment I give them everything. No shields, no reservations. Just me—raw, open, entirely theirs.

The pressure comes fast and hot. A sharp sting that steals my breath as Sam starts to push inside. It's nothing like his fingers. This is real. Thicker. Deeper. My body tightens instinctively, then forces itself to yield, every muscle trembling as I fight to stay soft for him.

He goes slow. Patient. Like he knows exactly how much I can take, how long I'll last before I break. Inch by inch, his cock slides into me, every stretch a spark, every movement a flame licking up my spine.

"Fuck, you're tight." His voice is a snarl now, hips grinding forward with a force that makes me shake. His hands clamp down on my hips, hard enough to leave fingerprints. And then he pushes deeper, past the point of no return, until I'm stretched around both of them, impossibly full.

The ring of muscle gives, barely, and I cry out at the burn. Jamie groans under me, his cock twitching inside me from the way I clamp around him. Sam swears, deep and guttural, like he's being dragged under by the heat, the slickness, the way my body pulls him in like it's starving for him.

"I wish you could see this," Sam growls. His thumbs dig into my ass, spreading me wider. "The way your asshole's gripping my cock like it was made for this. Like it's been waiting for me."

And then he's there. Fully inside. Buried so deep I feel it in my throat.

The air rushes out of me in a shattered gasp. My entire body locks around them. And for a breathless second, all three of us freeze.

Held there. Stretched and trembling. Absolutely wrecked by the feeling of being full in every possible way.

The fullness is shattering. Mind-blowing in a way that makes my body feel like it's coming apart and knitting itself back together all at once. I'm stretched to the brink, wrapped around both of them—Jamie buried deep in my pussy, Sam locked inside my ass. There's no room left, no space to think or breathe. Just sensation. Just them.

I can't tell where the ache ends and the pleasure begins. It's sharp and soft, raw and reverent. Arousal woven with pain, each thread feeding the other until I can't untangle one from the next. My body is overwhelmed. My mind is gone.

And still, somehow, I'm safe. Held.

This isn't just fucking. It's surrender. A complete, blinding giving-over of everything I am. My trust. My hunger. My body. It's all theirs, and the way they take it—it wrecks me. They don't just use me. They worship me. Like I'm something precious. Like I matter.

Jamie's hands come up to cradle my face, thumbs brushing my

cheeks like I'm something fragile, even while his cock fills me so deep I can feel it in my spine. Sam's breath stutters against my back, warm and desperate, his hands gripping my hips like he'll never let go. The three of us are locked in stillness, hearts slamming, lungs barely catching breath. Everything quiet except for the thunder in my chest.

"Move," I choke, the word nothing but need. It slips from my throat like a prayer. Like a demand.

They do.

Jamie thrusts up into me, hard and slick, and Sam meets it from behind with a force that knocks the breath out of me. They move in perfect, devastating rhythm—when one pulls back, the other drives in, fucking me in seamless opposition, bodies working like they were built for this. Built for me.

Every stroke feels like too much. Every moment they don't stop makes me crave more. My body is suspended between them, helpless, trembling, stretched to the edge of what I can take. I shouldn't be able to survive this much pleasure. But I do. I want to. I ache for it.

Jamie's chest is damp under my palms, his muscles clenching every time I grind down. His cock grates against every nerve ending inside me, thick and hot and perfect. Behind me, Sam's fingers bite into my skin, dragging me back onto his cock with savage, merciless precision.

"Fuck, Jamie," Sam groans, breath ragged. "You feel how tight she gets when we move together? Like her body's trying to hold us both in. Like she doesn't want to let either of us go."

Jamie's hips jerk up hard, a snarl curling in his throat. "I can feel you," he pants, eyes locked on Sam over my shoulder. "Every time you slam into her ass, your cock presses into mine through her pussy. It's so tight—Jesus, it's like she's trying to fuse us together."

Their words hit me like fire. Not gentle heat—no, this is an inferno. A flash of raw, dirty flame that tears through my nerves and sets everything inside me alight. My body responds before thought can form. I clench down, muscles shaking, every inch of me begging for more. Harder. Deeper. Like they've rewired me with nothing but need.

Jamie's hand slides between us, fingers slick and unrelenting as they find my clit. He rubs fast, brutal, perfectly timed with the rhythm of their cocks moving inside me. My vision whites out at the edges. My legs start to go. I don't know how I'm still upright.

"You gonna come, baby?" Sam grits out behind me, his voice all wreckage and need. "You gonna soak his cock while I stretch this tight little ass wider? Gonna make a mess all over him while we ruin you together?"

Jamie's groan is guttural, low and filthy. "Come on, angel. Let go. Let me feel that pretty cunt strangle me while he's still buried in your ass."

And I do.

My body convulses—sharp, sudden, explosive. I lock up for one suspended second, then break apart completely. The orgasm tears through me like lightning, like collapse, every muscle contracting in a tidal wave of sensation. It's not gentle. It's not sweet. It's ruin. A full-body implosion that leaves me gasping, sobbing, gone.

I scream. Wordless. Wild. My pussy clamps down around Jamie, tight and fluttering, dragging a groan from deep in his chest. Behind me, my ass tightens hard around Sam's cock, pulsing around him like I was made for this. Like this is what my body was built to do—take them, hold them, milk them until they lose control right alongside me.

It's not pleasure anymore. It's devastation. It's surrender. And it's so fucking good I never want it to stop.

Sam's rhythm shatters, hips jerking erratically now, all control gone. He slams deep one last time and stills, cock buried to the hilt as he comes with a choked-off groan.

"Fuck, FUCK," he gasps, voice broken. "That's it, baby. Strangle my cock. Just like that."

I feel every throb. Every pulse. His cum pours into me in hot, heavy waves, the sensation filthy and possessive and perfect. It knocks another tremor loose inside me, smaller but sharp, and I jerk again with the aftershocks, whimpering through them as he holds me there, buried and shaking.

Jamie doesn't stop.

Not even as Sam pulls out, his cum leaking from my ass in slow, hot drips that slide down the curve of my thigh. Not even as my body trembles, still pulsing from the aftershocks. Jamie grabs my thighs and hauls me down harder onto his cock, like he's staking a claim, like he's not done until I'm wrecked all over again.

The sound is obscene—wet, raw, the slap of skin on skin loud in the silence Sam leaves behind. Each thrust punches the breath out of me, my body jolting as he drives up into me with ruthless force. My pussy is soaked, aching, stretched beyond reason, and Jamie just keeps going, fucking through the slick mess they've both made of me like it's his right.

"God, look at you," he grits out, eyes burning into mine like I'm something sacred. "Dripping from your ass, soaked around my cock. Fucked-out and still so fucking greedy."

His thumb slides down and finds my clit again. Tight, ruthless circles that make me jolt. My hips twitch. My mouth drops open around a gasp that gets stuck halfway out. I can't even form words. Just sound. Just sensation. My body's still clenching around him, fluttering and raw, and he feels it all.

"You've got one more in you," he growls, voice low and sure and dangerous. "Give it to me, angel. Let me feel you come again. Let me take it."

And then he moves.

One second I'm on top, trembling and open. The next, the world flips. My back hits the mattress with a gasp, Jamie above me in a blur of motion, his body hot and heavy and locked between my legs. He plunges back inside without hesitation, one hard, deep thrust that knocks the air from my lungs.

His pace is brutal at first. Punishing. His hips slam into mine with a force that makes the bed shudder and the headboard crack against the wall. I cry out, legs wrapping around his waist to anchor him, to hold him in, to beg him not to stop.

But then—he changes.

His rhythm slows. Deepens. Every thrust hits something inside me that makes my toes curl, my breath hitch, my body arch into his. He grinds against me with each movement now, dragging his cock through every swollen, sensitive inch like he's memorizing it. Like he wants to take me apart piece by piece, not just fuck me but ruin me in the softest, hardest way.

"Right there," I whisper, barely audible. "Jamie, right—"

"I know," he breathes, forehead pressed to mine. "I've got you."

He leans down and kisses me like I'm fragile and sacred and his. Like his mouth is memorizing mine. It's soft, almost reverent, but it guts me. Steals the air from my lungs and replaces it with something heavier, something that tastes like forever.

"You're incredible," he murmurs against my lips, voice ruined. "So fucking beautiful like this. I love you so much, Penelope."

The words don't land. They detonate. Right in the center of me. Bigger than any orgasm, louder than any scream. I clutch at him like I'm falling, wrap my arms around his neck and bury my face in his shoulder, holding on while everything in me shakes apart.

He doesn't stop moving. Slow now. Deep. Like he's pulling the words he just gave me down into my bones, anchoring them with every thrust. Not just fucking me, but staying. Stitching himself into the hollow places like he's never leaving.

The pressure builds differently this time. Not like lightning, but like a tide coming in. Sure and unstoppable. His rhythm is measured, intentional. Every roll of his hips deeper than the last, every inch of him saying things his mouth already confessed.

We're not fucking anymore. We're fusing. He moves like he's always known how to fit inside me, like this rhythm was built into us from the beginning and we've only just remembered.

"I can feel how close you are," I whisper, barely managing the words. My voice is torn and trembling, like the rest of me. I can feel him unraveling under my palms, shoulders bunched, spine bowed, breath hitching in his throat.

He looks at me. Looks right into me. "Don't look away," he rasps, eyes wild and shining. "I want you to see what you do to me."

And I do. God, I do. I keep my eyes locked on his and cup his face in both hands, grounding us in this moment where everything's breaking open.

His thrusts lose precision. Still deep, still slow, but ragged now, edges fraying. And still, I rise to meet him. Hips lifting, heart racing, body strung tight as a live wire.

"That's it," I breathe, chasing him into the freefall. "Give it to me, Jamie. It's mine."

He jerks like the words snapped something inside him. Slams into me, cock buried to the hilt, and that's it. That's the moment.

The orgasm hits like a landslide. Hot. Unstoppable. It barrels through me, wracking a sob from my throat as my body locks tight around him, pulsing, pulling him deeper like I could keep him inside forever. Like I need him there to survive.

He groans, broken and raw, and I feel him spill into me, every pulse of his release syncing to mine like we're the same body, the same breath, the same desperate need.

"Fuck, Penelope," he chokes out, forehead pressed to mine, eyes squeezed shut, whole body shivering as he empties into me.

We're still moving. Barely. Just the instinctive roll of hips, the last tremors of something too big for words. Our mouths find each other again, open and gasping, like we're trying to breathe the same air. His cock twitches inside me. My body tightens again, softer now, but still greedy. Still aching.

"You're amazing," Jamie whispers into my skin like it's a secret, like he's afraid if he says it too loud I might vanish. He kisses me everywhere—cheeks, jaw, eyelids, mouth—each one slower than the last, his breath warm and ragged. "So fucking perfect."

We stay like that, suspended. Tangled in breath and heat and the slow, steady rhythm of something that feels like it could last forever. My body's still echoing with aftershocks, every inch of me soft and aching and lit from the inside out. I should be sore. I should be spent. But all I want is to stay exactly where I am, under him, wrapped in this glow, this impossible stillness that feels more like worship than aftermath.

The soft pad of footsteps breaks through the silence, followed by the quiet sound of water dripping onto tile. I turn my head, and there he is. Sam. Barefoot, shirtless, a warm cloth in one hand and something impossibly tender in his eyes. It's not just love. It's reverence, devotion, all braided into something that makes my throat go tight.

Jamie shifts slowly, pressing a final kiss to the inside of my thigh, then moves aside like it's an offering. Like he knows this moment isn't his and he's grateful just to witness it. The way they move around each other, it's seamless. No jealousy. No awkwardness. Just this instinctive understanding that I'm meant to be cared for.

"Let me take care of you, love," Sam says, voice so gentle it barely registers above the sound of my own heartbeat. He kneels between my legs like it's sacred ground. The cloth is warm, and his hands are slow, careful, tender. Not a single rush to the way he touches me. Like I'm something delicate he's afraid to break.

And that's what undoes me. Not the orgasm. Not the fucking. This. The quiet, reverent way he wipes me clean. The way Jamie hovers nearby, still touching my arm, my knee, my shoulder. The way they both hold me without needing to be asked.

Tears prick at the corners of my eyes, hot and stupid and uninvited. But they don't ask. Don't tease. Just love me. In this terrifying, unflinching way I don't know how to brace against.

"You should use the bathroom," Jamie says, brushing a knuckle down my cheek. His voice is low, coaxing. "Especially after all that."

I try to argue. I do. Some mumbled thing about being fine, about walking. But Sam just rolls his eyes like he knows better. And maybe he does.

He scoops me up without ceremony, like it's the most natural thing in the world, like my weight in his arms feels right. My head rests against his shoulder before I can stop it, and his voice drops, teasing and warm.

"Humor me."

He carries me through the soft light of the room, every step easy and grounded. At the bathroom door, he sets me down with impossible care, his hand curling around my lower back like he's reluctant to let go.

"I'll be right outside," he says, thumb brushing over my hip. "If you need anything. Anything at all."

When I emerge a few minutes later, they've transformed the room. When I step out, the world has changed again.

The room is warm and low-lit, quiet in a way that feels sacred. The bed has been stripped and remade, sheets smooth and crisp, pillows fluffed like they've been touched with reverence. Even the corners are tucked with precision, like this space matters. Like I matter. A hotel robe hangs on the back of a chair, waiting for me like it knew I'd need softness.

Sam's there before I can reach for it, holding it open with hands that are all patience and care. He helps me slide my arms in, drawing the plush fabric around me like he's wrapping a gift. His hands linger at my waist for half a second longer than they need to, then he kisses my temple and guides me toward the bed.

"Come here," he says, voice thick with tenderness as he folds back the covers and climbs in beside me. Jamie's already waiting on the other side, his arms opening like a question and an answer all at once. I settle between them and they move in without hesitation, pulling the blankets up, pressing their bodies close, anchoring me in place with warmth and presence.

I'm held. Fully. Completely. Their limbs tangled with mine, their hands finding skin like it's second nature. Like they've always known where I end and they begin.

"How are you feeling?" Jamie asks, his voice barely a thread of sound. His fingers drift into my hair, stroking gently, slowly, like he's etching the shape of me into memory.

I breathe in, deep and steady. Let it all sink in. The scent of them, the heat of their skin, the rhythm of their hearts syncing up with mine. My body is still thrumming, heavy with the ghost of pleasure, but it's my heart that feels stretched and aching in the best possible way. Full. So full it almost hurts.

"I'm good," I whisper, my voice scratchy at the edges. "Better than good. It was everything. You both were..." The words falter in my throat, too big to fit neatly in a sentence. "You were everything."

Jamie exhales hard, like he'd been holding his breath through the silence. He presses his forehead to mine, a soft collision of skin and emotion.

Sam leans in closer, the heat of him radiating against my side. He brushes his lips against my temple and leaves them there, like a promise.

"You were incredible, Penelope," he murmurs, his voice hoarse and frayed in a way that hits somewhere deep. "Our fiancée. Ours."

The word lands like a warm weight on my chest, not heavy, but grounding. The kind of word that builds a home inside you. I glance down and lift my hand between us, the sapphire on my finger catching the low light, glinting like a secret we haven't told the world yet.

"I still can't believe you proposed in the bathtub," I say, smiling against Jamie's shoulder.

He laughs, low and quiet, and the sound vibrates through my spine. "Not exactly how I pictured it, but it felt right."

"It was," I say, pressing a kiss to his jaw. "Untraditional. Messy. Fucking incredible. *Us.*"

Sam tightens his arm around my waist, pulling me even closer. His chest is solid beneath my cheek, his heartbeat steady and sure, like it's been waiting for mine to fall into step.

"Get some rest," he whispers. "We've got forever to plan."

And wrapped in a bed they remade just for me, wearing a ring I never expected and somehow always knew was meant to be mine, I believe him.

36

I hear him before I feel him, those heavy, unhurried footsteps slicing through the stillness like a heartbeat too loud. The sound yanks me out of sleep, abrupt and disorienting. One blink. Then another. The room materializes around me in ghost tones. Archer stands there like he belongs to the dark—carved from it, sent by it, steady and inevitable.

The hallway behind him glows that eerie pre-dawn blue, soft and sourceless, and it silhouettes him perfectly. Shoulders squared, arms loose at his sides, whole body carved in shadow and certainty. He doesn't speak right away, and somehow that says more.

"Time to get up," he says finally, voice low and rough from sleep but already bracing, like black coffee with too much bite. "I need you on the boat."

My brain scrambles. Words fumble somewhere between dream and waking. I manage, "It's the middle of the night."

"It's four-thirty," he says, already moving. No pause. No apology. He crosses the room like it belongs to him. Opens drawers without asking, pulling clothes with easy certainty. A sweater. Thick socks. Leggings. He tosses them onto the bed in a clean, practiced arc. Efficient. Unbothered. Intimate in a way that makes my skin prickle.

"Dress warm," he adds, already halfway to the door. "Tea's waiting downstairs."

The way he moves feels tight and focused, like he's holding something in. His silence isn't just quiet—it means something. Like he already knows what's coming and isn't ready to explain it. And something in me says not to ask. Not now.

So I don't.

I sit up and pull the sweater over my head, and I can feel him watching, not in a creepy way, but the way someone watches the tide roll in, knowing it's going to take something with it.

Pearl waits at the door, tail swishing in slow, sleepy arcs. She's in her best harness, the one she only wears for special occasions. And just like that, the flicker starts. Low in my belly. Anticipation. Wonder. A little bit of fear. Something's coming. I can feel it in his gaze, tucked into the set of his mouth.

"What's going on?" I ask, stepping into the boots by the door.

He hands me a thermos without answering. I unscrew the lid. Tea. Hot. Sweet. Exactly how I like it.

"Tide's perfect," he says finally, his palm settling at the small of my back as he steers me toward the door. His hand is warm through the fabric, so warm it feels like it sinks straight into my skin. I lean into it without thinking, caught in the gravity of him.

The harbor sleeps under a blanket of stars, boats gently rocking with the tide's breath. The boat waits at the end of the dock, already prepped and humming with quiet readiness. He must have been up for hours. Pearl bounds aboard, trotting to the bow and planting herself like she owns the horizon, nose twitching as if the wind is whispering secrets meant only for her.

"Here." Archer drapes a wool blanket over my shoulders, then leans in to tuck it tighter. His fingers linger at my collar, not adjusting, not fixing. Just... touching. The barest graze at the base of my throat. A whisper. A flicker of contact. But I feel it in places I shouldn't. Places that make me ache.

We slip from the harbor without a word, the engine a low, steady murmur beneath us. He stands at the helm like the boat grew around him, like he's stitched into its bones—jaw set, eyes on the horizon, reading some secret language in the shape of the waves. I know better than to fill the silence. Archer speaks when something needs to be said. Not before.

Instead, I settle beside Pearl at the bow, the chill of the deck seeping through the blanket as I tuck my legs beneath me. She rests her chin on my knee, eyes half-lidded but alert, ears twitching with each shift in the breeze. We cut through the still-dark sea like we're part of it, the hull slicing gently through the water, sending ripples trailing out like silk ribbons.

Above us, the sky begins its slow unraveling—black fading to deep indigo, then to that soft, impossible shade of violet-blue that only exists for a heartbeat before dawn. The air smells briny and clean, laced with salt and seaweed and something older, like driftwood and storm.

I draw the blanket tighter, its weight grounding me, the wool catching on the rough edges of my thoughts. Everything feels hushed. Sacred. Like even the world knows not to raise its voice.

Twenty minutes pass before he cuts the engine. The hum fades. We float into a cove I recognize. Calm water, hidden from the wind, the kind of place you bring a rod and a thermos and a long afternoon. But there's no tackle box. No bait.

Just a wicker basket tucked beneath the bench.

I glance at it. Then at him.

"Breakfast," he says. "For after."

After what, he doesn't say.

The sky starts to blush. Not shyly, not soft. It bleeds. Cobalt cracks open into violet, then smears gold across the edge of the world, slow and showy like it knows we're watching. The water catches it all and reflects it back in trembling streaks that look painted by hand.

Archer moves beside me, quiet and unhurried. His hand finds the back of my neck, warm through the blanket, his thumb tracing slow circles. "I've been thinking," he says, voice low, like he doesn't want to scare the moment off.

I tilt my head just enough to look at him, offering a crooked smile to cut the wire-thin tension. "Dangerous."

He doesn't smile back. His fingers tighten—not rough, not possessive. Just enough to anchor me. To make sure I'm still here.

"I've spent most of my life reading tides," he says. "Predicting storms. Navigating by stars that never change." His words are quiet, even, but there's tension coiled around each syllable, like he's trying to keep a secret from spilling out with every breath. "I thought I understood patterns. I thought I understood permanence."

Pearl stirs at my feet, stretches once, then pads to Archer's side, ears forward, waiting. Watching.

"Then you burned down your restaurant," he continues, and now there's a hint of amusement in his tone. "And everything I thought I knew about predictable patterns went up in smoke along with it."

The sun finally breaks the edge of the world, gold pouring over the water like it's been uncorked. The light hits his face and turns his eyes to molten amber, softens his jaw, throws a halo across his hair.

"Pearl," he says, not looking away from me, voice low but certain. "Bring it here."

She moves like she understands, disappearing behind the helm with barely a sound. A beat later, she's back, her paws clicking softly on the deck, something small and silver held delicately in her mouth. She lays it down at his feet with this strange sort of reverence, like she knows exactly what it means. Like she's been waiting for this moment, too.

Archer bends to pick it up. His fingers close around the canister—slow, careful, like it might shatter if he moves too fast. His hands are steady. His breath isn't. His chest rises once, sharp and shallow, like he's bracing for impact. He doesn't open it right away. Just holds it. Turns it once in the light. Lets the silence stretch long enough that my pulse starts to skip.

Then, softly—almost like a confession—"I've never been good with words. I always thought action mattered more. That what I did would always matter more than what I said."

He twists the lid off with careful fingers, and when he opens the container, it's there. A ring. And it wrecks me. Not because it's flashy.

It's not. It's quiet. Intentional. Unmistakably him. A single pearl, creamy and luminous, nestled in a gold band shaped like rising swells. Like the sea is still clinging to it, unwilling to let it go. Like he forged it from instinct and memory and every unspoken thing he's never known how to say.

"I'm not asking you to belong to me," he says, and now his voice is breaking. "You already do. I think you always have."

He lifts one hand to my cheek. His thumb brushes my bottom lip, and the whole world falls away. The cold. The wind. The sway of the boat. All of it disappears except the shape of him, the weight of this, the tremble in my breath.

"I'm asking if I can belong to you," he says. "Forever."

The tears hit before I even know they're coming—hot, sudden, unstoppable. I'm not crying because I'm surprised. I'm crying because this moment feels too big for my body.

"Yes," I say, my voice cracking. No dramatic pause required. No fear. Just that single syllable, yanked straight from the most honest, feral corner of my heart.

And then—God—his face. Relief slams through him like a wave. His expression shatters, not delicately, not quietly, but completely. Like someone finally handed him the key to a room he's been locked outside of for years. He looks broken. He looks complete.

He grabs my hand with that same desperate reverence I feel in my chest—like we've both been holding too much for too long and now there's finally room to let go. He doesn't hesitate. Doesn't ask. Just slides the ring onto my finger like it belongs there. It fits. Of course it fits. It's not just perfect, it's right. Like the final note in a chord that's been building for months.

And in that second, everything clicks. All six of us. The late nights and sharp edges and impossible joy. The fights and the laughter and the way we love like it's survival.

"It's beautiful," I whisper, staring down at the ring, at my hand in his. At this moment that doesn't feel real and somehow feels like the only thing that's ever been real.

He lifts his gaze to mine. His eyes are molten, full of heat and something so tender it makes my chest ache. "So are you," he says.

Then he pulls me in and kisses me like he's staking a claim. Like he knows I'm already his, but he wants the whole world to know it too.

It isn't sweet. It isn't gentle.

It's a promise. A vow. A goddamn forever.

His mouth is hot and consuming, all heat and hunger and no hesitation, tongue sweeping the seam of my lips in a tease that turns into a demand. I give in immediately, open for him like I always do, like my body knows him better than it knows itself. His hand fists in my hair, rough and sure, tilting my head the way he likes. His other arm winds around my waist and pulls me flush against him, hip to hip, chest to chest, the hard ridge of him pressing right where I'm already aching.

I can feel everything.

The solid weight of him. The tension in his grip. The way his breath shudders through his chest like he's barely holding on. And I love it. I love being the thing that undoes him. That turns the careful, controlled Archer into this wild, broken version who kisses like he's starving and I'm his only meal.

I'm breathless by the time his teeth catch my lower lip, dragging a gasp from my mouth. My nails dig into his shoulders, trying to anchor myself as the world tilts sideways.

He pulls back, just barely, and I chase his mouth without meaning to. But then he's moving lower, mouth skimming along my jaw and down the column of my throat. His stubble scrapes my skin and then —fuck—his teeth find the place where my pulse is fluttering like a trapped bird. He bites, just hard enough to leave a mark, and I swear my knees go liquid.

"I've decided," he says against my neck, voice gone hoarse and dangerous, "my favorite place to touch you is right here."

The words hit me low and hard. I feel them in my core. A throb of heat pulses between my legs, sharp and immediate, and my body arches toward him before I can stop it.

His mouth ghosts back up to my ear. "On this boat. With the wind in your hair and no one around to hear how pretty you sound when you come." He grinds against me, slow and careful, like he's proving a point. Like he knows I'm already wet for him.

And he's right.

He's already under my sweater, his hands scorching against my ribs. My breath hitches. "I remember the first time we were alone together on this boat," he says. "You have no idea how badly I wanted to bend you over the console."

My thighs clench. His hands slide up, palms cupping my breasts. Thumbs flicking over nipples already stiff.

"But I planned for today," he adds, stepping back. My body protests the space, but he doesn't let go of me completely. "Wait here."

He moves to the stern, peels back a tarp to reveal a mattress pad, sheets, pillows—everything tied down with sailor's knots. A makeshift love nest.

"Tonight we'll celebrate," he says, eyes locked on mine. "But this morning, you're mine."

His hands find the hem of my sweater, tugging it up with a quiet urgency, like the fabric itself is in the way of something vital. There's no hesitation, no question, just a wordless command I feel deep in my bones. I lift my arms, and he strips it off in one smooth motion, baring my skin to the chill of the morning air.

"You're wearing way too many clothes for what I have planned," he murmurs, voice rough enough to rasp straight down my spine. His fingers move to the button of my jeans. "I want to see every inch of what's mine."

The words land like a spark in my belly, heat curling low and fast. I don't answer. I can't. I just stand there, breathing hard, while he eases my jeans down my hips. His knuckles brush bare skin, dragging lightly along the slope of my thighs, and I can feel the tremble in his fingers, how close his restraint is to unraveling.

When he steps back, I'm left in just my panties, bare from the waist up, the cold licking across my skin like static. His eyes roam, slow, hungry. From my face to my neck, over the curve of my breasts, down to the soft curve of my belly.

"Perfect," he says, and the word isn't perfunctory. It's devotional.

Then he starts to undress, slow like he's savoring it. His fingers work the buttons of his flannel one at a time, fabric falling open to reveal skin I've memorized like scripture.

The smooth column of his neck. The stretch of shoulder I've clung to in the dark. And then his chest. Broad, warm, and marked with that inky map of Maine etched just over his heart. The coastline curls along his ribs in jagged, unapologetic lines, like a place carved into him instead of drawn.

I've mapped it with my mouth—every ridge, every sharp turn, every quiet curve. My tongue has followed the lines like a path home, my fingertips memorizing what the ink only suggests. I've done it a hundred times, maybe more. And still, it unravels me. Every damn time.

He shoves his pants down over his hips, letting them fall, and suddenly he's standing in nothing but his boxers, his arousal thick and unmistakable, pressing hard against the fabric. He steps in close, and the heat of him rolls over me like a tide, sinking into my skin, pulling my breath tight in my chest.

"The water's warmer than the air today," he murmurs against my ear, one hand curving over my backside and squeezing. "Unusual for this time of year."

It takes a second to process what he's saying through the fog in my head. "You want to swim?" I manage. "Now?"

His mouth curves, a half-smile forming like sunrise breaking through storm clouds. "I want to see my fiancée naked in the ocean at sunrise," he says, pressing his thumb into my bottom lip. "Then I want to bring her back on this boat and show her exactly what that ring means."

My whole body throbs at the image his words create, at the weight of his intention.

"What are you waiting for then?" I ask, snapping the waistband on his boxers.

He pushes them down in one clean motion, and then he's just... there. Tall and strong and impossibly bare. All long lines of muscle, sun-dark skin stretched over the kind of body that looks carved by tide and time. Real. Tangible in the way that makes something low in my stomach twist and tighten. I forget how to breathe.

I hook my thumbs in the waistband of my underwear and ease them down, slow and steady, the fabric slipping past my hips, my thighs, until I'm standing completely bare in front of him. The cool air brushes over my skin, but I don't feel it. Not really. All I feel is him—his gaze on me, the charge between us loud and pulsing, sparking in every breathless inch of space.

"Ladies first," he says, voice rough, tipping his chin toward the ladder.

I walk to the railing, not bothering to hide the sway of my hips, and glance back once, just long enough to see the way he's looking at me. Like I'm something he's about to ruin and worship in equal measure.

"Don't keep me waiting."

He makes a sound in response, low and raw, a growl buried deep in his chest.

I climb down the ladder, the metal biting at my palms, slick with sea mist. The water creeps up inch by inch—ankles, then knees, then thighs—until I slip beneath the surface in one clean motion. It's warmer than the air but still cold enough to punch the breath from my lungs. I surface with a gasp, heart hammering, and let myself drift.

On my back, I float, weightless. The sea cradles me in its palm, and above, the sky stretches wide and bruised with color, orange melting into pink, streaks of violet threading through the clouds. Everything glows, soft and surreal, the water catching every hue like a mirror. It feels like floating inside a gemstone.

Then he's there.

No warning, just sudden movement beside me, sleek and sure, like the ocean let him in without resistance. He cuts through the water with quiet precision until he's at my side. His hair is slicked back, dark with seawater, and droplets cling to his lashes. No glasses. Just Archer. Bare-faced, unarmored. And for a second, I see him completely—younger, softer, stripped down to something rare and real.

"So beautiful," he says.

And I don't know if he means me, the morning, or this exact second, but it doesn't matter. Because I'm all in. All his.

He grips my waist and pulls me to him, fitting us together like we've always belonged like this. Chest to chest, heartbeat to heartbeat, surrounded by nothing but open sea and quiet sky.

"I never thought this was a possibility," he says, voice low, words slipping out like secrets he didn't mean to speak aloud. "I never thought you'd actually say yes to all five of us. It only took three years and your restaurant burning to the ground."

Coming from Archer, it's practically a love letter.

I wrap my arms around his neck, legs around his waist, body weightless in the water but tethered to him like gravity itself. I trust him to hold me, to keep us afloat—like he always does. Like he always has.

"I've always been here," I whisper, pressing my forehead to his, our noses brushing. "Since that first day. When you walked in like you owned the place."

He smiles then, really smiles, and it knocks the breath right out of my lungs. It's the kind of smile that feels like something new and rare and quietly spectacular, like the first time the sun breaks through after a week of storms.

"That's called confidence, baby."

"Or ego," I murmur, just before I kiss him.

It starts soft, a meeting of mouths that feels more like a promise than anything else. But it doesn't stay that way. His lips part, and then his tongue is sweeping into my mouth, hot and hungry. His hand finds my backside beneath the surface, gripping hard, hauling me closer until the hard line of him is pressed right against the aching center of me.

"We should get back on the boat," he says into my mouth, voice frayed, breathing sharp. "Before I take you in open water and we both drown."

I roll my hips against him, slow and taunting. "And what if I said I wouldn't mind drowning?"

His hands tighten, fingers digging in with a possessiveness that makes my breath hitch and my toes curl. God, I'll feel that tomorrow. And the day after.

"Then you're playing with fire, Penelope," he growls. My name leaves his lips like a warning and a promise, thick with restraint he's this close to losing. "And you know what happens when you provoke me."

I remember. I remember everything. The way he and Spencer left me trembling and sobbing and thankful for every second of it.

"Maybe I want to burn," I whisper, teeth grazing his earlobe just enough to make him groan.

"Enough," he snaps—low, rough, all control. Then he spins me around in the water, hands firm on my hips, guiding me toward the ladder. "I'm not taking you in the sea," he mutters as he hoists himself out, muscles flexing, water running down his body like it was made to be there. "Not when there's a perfectly good bed waiting."

I start to climb, but his hand wraps around my ankle, stopping me mid-step. A moment later, his chest presses to my back, warm and solid, and his arms slide around my waist, anchoring me there, suspended between water and sky. He holds me like that, saying nothing, and we go still together as the morning unfurls around us. The hush of waves, the blush of sun rising over the sea, everything soft and golden and breathless.

The sunrise is in full bloom now, orange melting into pink, with a soft smear of gold stretching across the sea. For one breathless moment, we just stand there, wrapped in each other and the quiet. His chin settles on my shoulder, his breath warm against my ear, and everything goes still. No teasing. No taunts. Just the low hum of the ocean, the steady rhythm of his heartbeat against my back, and the feeling that the world is unfolding into something entirely new.

Eventually, he shifts, pressing a kiss to the side of my neck before reaching past me to grip the railing.

"Come on," he murmurs, voice still thick around the edges. "Let's get you warm."

I climb first and he follows, legs a little shaky as I step onto the deck. The breeze hits my skin, cooler now that I'm wet and bare, and I wrap my arms around myself instinctively.

"Towels," Archer says, nodding toward a folded stack near the stern.

I grab one and wrap it around myself, the thick terry cloth catching on damp skin, clinging in places as I pat myself dry.

Archer walks across the deck, moving with quiet efficiency, like this is just another morning. His towel hangs low on his hips, water glistening on his skin, catching the early light like he's been dipped in gold. Every muscle shifts under his sun-warmed skin, effortless and obscene. He should not be legal like this. Or real. And yet here he is, half-naked, gleaming, and completely unfazed, while my brain short-circuits over the way his abs flex when he reaches for the champagne.

He returns holding two flutes, champagne bubbling like laughter trapped in crystal. When he passes one to me, our fingers brush, his skin warmer than the glass, and I shiver for an entirely different reason.

"To new beginnings," he says, his voice a little huskier now, a little closer to the edge.

"To us," I reply, lifting my glass to his.

The first sip barely registers—cold and crisp and expensive—but it's drowned out by the press of his fingers against the knot of my towel. One pull, and it slips from my body, pooling at my feet like an offering.

His eyes darken, the brown eclipsed by pupil, his gaze a slow drag from my collarbone to my navel to the place between my thighs.

"I love that you're mine," he murmurs, the words thick with heat and something quieter underneath. "Every inch."

He straightens, eyes flicking toward a length of rope coiled neatly on the deck—one of the soft, double-braided lines used to tie up at dock. It's clean, pale, supple from salt and sun. Without a word, he picks it up, testing the weight in his hand like he's imagining all the ways he could use it.

My breath catches, thighs clenching. My body already knows what's coming.

"On your knees," he says, motioning toward the makeshift bed, his voice low and razor-sharp. Not loud. Not rushed. Just absolute. Like gravity. Like command woven into sound.

I drop instantly, knees pressing into the mattress, hands settling behind my back. The cool air prickles against my skin, but all I feel is him.

Archer moves behind me, the rope slipping through his fingers like silk as he uncoils it, and then he's wrapping it around my wrists, not rough, not hurried, but with the kind of focus that makes my pulse stutter. Every loop is snug but careful, his thumbs brushing against my skin as he adjusts, tightens, ties.

"Does this feel okay?" he asks, voice like warm smoke against my ear.

I nod, throat too tight to speak, and the answering sound he makes is low and dark and deeply satisfied.

"Good," he says, fingers sliding down my arms, "because I'm not rushing a single second of this." His hands skate up my arms, over my shoulders, down the sides of my ribs like he's relearning me. They settle on my hips. "You're so beautiful like this," he says, voice fraying at the edges. "On your knees, hands tied, trusting me to take care of you."

He leans in, the weight of his body ghosting against my back, mouth brushing the line of my neck. I shiver at the contact, squeezing my thighs together. He cups my breasts from behind, thumbs circling my nipples, drawing them to hard peaks that ache under his touch.

"Archer," I gasp, already breathless, my hips tilting instinctively toward more.

"Shhh." His fingers dip lower, finding me wet and throbbing. "I've got you, baby."

He touches me like it's his way of worship, slow and thorough, every stroke hitting with perfect pressure in exactly the right spot. I arch into him, chasing more, already close and desperate to be closer.

"So wet," he mutters, almost to himself, like he's savoring the truth of it. "You love this. Being bound. Spread open. At my mercy."

"Yes," I admit, breath hitching on the word.

He rewards me by sliding a finger inside, curling it just right. I cry out, helpless against the pleasure.

"Wider," he says, voice low and tight.

I obey, parting my knees as wide as I can, the stretch dragging a fresh wave of heat through me, sharp and immediate.

And then he's in front of me. Eyes dark with intent, with hunger. His voice is rough when he speaks.

"I'm going to taste you," he says. "And you're going to watch."

He urges me back until my palms are flat against the mattress. My spine curves with the shift, chest arched, thighs still spread, everything exposed. The position leaves me wide open—on my knees, leaning back, completely at his mercy. But there's no room for shame. Only heat. Only the way he looks at me, like I'm his religion and he's ready to confess his sins.

Archer lowers himself between my legs, his body stretching out along the bed. He doesn't break eye contact, not even as he dips his head.

The first swipe of his tongue is so soft it steals the air from my lungs. My body jolts, hips twitching, a shiver cutting straight through me. The next pass is firmer, more certain, and it rips a moan from my throat so raw it barely sounds human.

He tastes me like it's instinct. Like his mouth was made for this—for me. Every lick is claiming, every flick of his tongue threaded with need. He's not just pleasing me. He's feeding some part of himself that only I seem to touch.

His hands grip my thighs, firm and unrelenting, fingers pressing into the soft give of skin as he holds me wide and helpless beneath his mouth. I try to move. I can't. I try to speak. I don't. There's only the wet drag of his tongue and the slow build of something dark and bright curling low in my belly.

He works me with the kind of focus that feels criminal. Tongue moving slow, then fast, then slow again—reading every breath, every broken sound I make, adjusting like he's memorizing the rhythm of my undoing and setting it to music.

"Archer," I choke out, my voice raw and trembling, torn from somewhere deeper than my throat. It doesn't sound like me—it sounds stripped bare. His name is the only word I can find, and even that barely makes it out before he breaks me all over again.

His mouth closes around my sensitive spot, tongue flicking in tight, ruthless strokes that send my hips jerking off the mattress. I can't think. Can't breathe. The sensation is sharp and perfect and too much, but he doesn't stop. Doesn't even hesitate.

His hand slides up my torso, rough palm skating over my soaked skin until it finds my breast. Fingers close around my nipple and twist. Just enough to send heat flashing down my spine, to punch the air from my lungs. Pleasure laced with pain, tangled so tightly I couldn't separate them if I tried.

"Please," I gasp, not knowing what I'm pleading for. My body feels like it's unraveling, every nerve exposed. I'm shaking. Open. His.

He growls against me, the sound primal and low, and the vibration makes me clench so hard it hurts. Then his fingers are there—thick, sure—sliding inside me. One. Then two. Deep and purposeful. They curl just right, dragging across that spot that sends a shockwave through my core.

His mouth stays locked to me. Relentless. Desperate. It's not slow and sweet. It's feral. Like he's trying to etch himself into the deepest part of me. Like this is the only way he knows how to say I'm his.

And I am. God, I am.

Everything inside me coils tight. I'm trembling, thighs quaking, my vision bleeding at the edges. I don't even realize I'm crying until I taste salt.

Then his voice—low and steady, breaking through the chaos.

"Let go," he says. "Come for me, Penelope. Let me have it."

It shatters me.

I break with a scream, a sob, a sound so raw it could tear skin. My body clamps around his fingers, hips arching, pulse crashing. The climax rips through me like a tidal wave, sharp and consuming, leaving no part of me untouched. I come hard, shaking and crying and barely able to hold myself together as he keeps going, coaxing every last tremor from my body.

He catches me the moment I start to fall, arms wrapping around me with a kind of tender strength that feels like gravity—steady, anchoring, the only thing keeping me from floating out of myself. He eases me onto the mattress, hands already at my wrists, undoing the knot with quiet care.

Once I'm free, he rubs warmth back into my arms, his touch grounding, patient. Then he lifts each wrist to his lips and kisses them —soft, reverent, like they're sacred. Like they've always meant more than just restraint.

But before I can fully melt into the moment, he gathers my wrists again and ties them to the railing above my head. The shift is so fast, so smooth, it takes my breath a second to catch up. My chest tightens, heart pounding hard against my ribs, not with fear, but with the sharp, dizzy rush of wanting. Of trusting him enough to give him everything, all over again.

Because this isn't just control.

It's devotion.

"We're not done," he says, voice roughened and raw. "I need to be inside you when you come again."

He kneels between my thighs, spreads me open, and looks. The hunger on his face makes me ache in places I didn't know I could ache.

"Please, Archer," I whisper.

He grips my jaw, fingers firm, eyes burning into mine. "Look at me," he says, voice low and dangerous. "I want you to see what it means to be mine."

Then he pushes inside me, one slow, brutal thrust that splits me open around him, inch by inch, until there's no space left untouched. I gasp, the air knocked from my lungs, my body stretching to take him. He doesn't move, just stays there, buried deep, locked in place, his eyes never leaving mine.

"Jesus," he groans, the sound raw and splintered. "You feel like heaven."

Then he starts to move. Hard. Unrelenting. Every thrust lands with punishing precision, like he's driving the truth of us deeper with each snap of his hips. The heat of him, the weight, the stretch, it's all-consuming. I can't think. Can't breathe. I can only feel.

His hands grip my thighs, pulling them wider, holding me open like I belong to him. Like he knows I do. His mouth hovers just above mine, close enough that we're breathing the same air, but he doesn't kiss me. He watches instead, his gaze locked to my face like he needs to see every flicker of pleasure as it rips through me.

"You love this," he grits out. "Being stretched around me. Taken like this."

"Yes," I breathe, the word catching on a gasp. "Yes—Archer, please—"

"Look at you," he growls. "Broken on my cock. Dripping. Shaking.

And still begging for more." His voice breaks around the edges, filthy and reverent all at once. "My fiancée is such a perfect girl."

The words hit harder than anything else, slamming through my chest and straight to my core.

His hand slips between us, fingers finding my sensitive spot like he's been aching to touch me there. He starts to circle, steady and firm, keeping pace with the deep, relentless rhythm of his thrusts. I arch under him, thighs trembling, nerves drawn so tight they feel like they might snap.

"Come for me," he says, breath hot against my lips. "Come on my cock. Let me feel it. Let me have it."

And I do. I break open with a cry, back bowing, everything in me seizing as the climax hits. It tears through me, hot and blinding, crashing over every inch of skin. I clamp around him, pulsing, shaking, shattering.

He follows with a broken sound, something between a growl and a prayer, thrusting deep—once, twice—each stroke harder than the last, like his body can't help but chase the end of it. Then he stills, buried to the hilt, every muscle locked tight as he comes, pulsing inside me.

His head drops to my shoulder, breath ragged against my skin, arms wrapped around me like he's trying to hold the moment in place.

"Fuck," he groans, voice rough and splintered, the word ripped straight from his chest. "Mine."

Not a question. Not a plea. A vow.

He unties my wrists like he's undoing something delicate and living. His fingers are warm, steady, moving slowly as he rubs life back into mine, murmuring something low and constant, words I can't quite catch over the riot of my heartbeat in my ears. My hands tingle with sensation, with memory. With him.

"You okay?" he asks, voice low, his thumb brushing across my cheek, then tucking a damp strand of hair behind my ear like it's second nature. Like touching me is something his body does without asking.

I nod. "Better than okay."

And it's true. I feel broken in the best possible way. Scattered. Stretched. Glowing from the inside out.

He brings each wrist to his mouth, presses a kiss to the skin just above the bone—slow, reverent. Like he's thanking them. Then he moves, slipping away from the bed. I miss his heat immediately. But he returns a moment later with a warm cloth, and the way he touches me as he cleans between my legs is so tender, so careful, it makes my chest ache.

He doesn't speak while he does it. Doesn't tease. Doesn't rush. Just moves with quiet devotion, like this—this—is the important part.

When he's done, he tosses the cloth aside and climbs back into bed. I barely have the strength to lift my arms, but I reach for him anyway. He gathers me into his chest without hesitation, wrapping me up in the solid heat of his body, his chin resting lightly on the top of my head. His hand strokes my back in long, slow lines like he's still trying to calm the aftershocks.

"That was—" I start, my voice cracked and worn thin.

"Everything," he finishes, no hesitation. Just certainty. Like he felt it, too. All of it.

I press my face to his chest, into the space just beneath his collarbone, and breathe him in. He smells like salt and sweat and something warmer, something that belongs only to him. I trail my fingers over the tattoo on his chest, tracing the jagged black coastline, the rough lines and angles. The place that made him. The place that brought him to me.

"I love you," I whisper. The words are soft, but they feel enormous. They leave my mouth like a confession and settle between us like truth.

He doesn't say it back.

Instead, he tightens his hold, like he wants to pull me into his skin, and murmurs, "There isn't a word for what I feel for you. But love is a good start."

My throat catches, and I don't try to speak. There's nothing I could say that would touch the way that sentence lands.

So I just hold on.

37

The road to the Castle doesn't just wind, it unspools, slow and sinuous, like a ribbon pulled loose from a story someone's still writing. The countryside stretches out on either side of us, lush and untamed, a patchwork of green that glows under the kind of sun that feels like a secret. It's nearly four, but the light clings to everything like honey, painting the hills gold and the sky a blue so deep it aches a little to look at. Time slows. Or maybe it holds its breath.

Archer's driving, of course. One hand on the wheel, the other curled around the gearshift like it belongs there. I'm in the middle, my thigh flush against his, and I can feel the flex of muscle with every gear change. He smells like soap and sun and something darker, every breath pulling me straight back to last night.

Spencer's on my other side, warm and loose and annoyingly perfect. His arm draped over the back of the bench seat, his knee nudging mine every few seconds like he's keeping time to some internal beat. He's been narrating the drive in a ridiculous half-baked Scottish accent, making up village names and giving them all wildly inaccurate historical facts.

Liam's wedged in the middle seat of the back row, his broad shoulders pressed between Sam and Jamie like someone tried to force three full-grown men into a carry-on suitcase. He's mid-rant—something about personal space being a human right and how this arrangement is clearly a violation of the Geneva Convention, but he's grinning through all of it, the kind of grin that tugs up slow and crooked at the corners, like he's fighting it and losing on purpose.

Sammy's not helping, obviously. He's stretched out dramatically, one leg thrown across Liam's lap like a cat that's claimed its territory. His head lolls back against the seat, eyes closed, a smug little smirk playing at his mouth like he knows exactly how warm and heavy he feels draped over Liam's thighs. Jamie, for his part, is pressed in close on the other side, laughing so hard at Liam's tirade that his whole body's shaking, shoulder bumping Liam's again and again like punctuation.

The sound of it—their laughter, layered and tangled and absolutely them—fills the truck cab and wraps around me like a favorite sweater I didn't know I missed until I put it on again. It's loud and careless and stupidly joyful, and it hits me low and hard in the stomach. That fluttering, too-full feeling that always seems to catch me off guard around them. Like my body knows something my heart's still trying to figure out.

There's this beat, long and tender, where I just watch them in the rearview mirror. The tangle of legs, the way their bodies fall into each other like it's instinct. Like they've always belonged together. Like maybe I belong here too.

I swallow hard and lean back, letting the hum of the engine press in on me. The windows are down just enough to let the breeze snake through, carrying with it the scent of wildflowers and sun-warmed earth.

"Nervous?" Archer glances over, studying my face before looking back at the road.

I let out a laugh that comes out too sharp, too honest to be casual. "I'm only showing up to a masquerade ball with five fiancés. Why would I be nervous?"

He smirks, but there's tenderness under it. "They already know about us."

"Yeah," I murmur, eyes fixed on the castle ahead, rising from the hillside like something out of a fever dream. "But knowing and seeing? Not the same thing."

"They'll be happy for you," Spencer says, squeezing my knee with his hand. His thumb rubs a slow circle, the kind of touch that knows how to steady me without trying to fix anything. "They'd be stupid not to be."

I smile, but it feels forced and too small for the size of everything pressing against my ribs. I want to believe Spencer's right. I want to believe I can walk through those doors and be understood.

The Castle takes up more of the horizon now, ancient walls catching the light like something out of myth. Restored stone, glass windows glowing like fire, and within them, the wild, complicated family Jack, Lach, Cam and Charlie built piece by piece. Tonight, those halls will echo with masked laughter and music and secrets. A masquerade ball. A night to pretend. Or maybe to become.

"I still can't believe none of you will tell me what you're wearing," I say, dragging the words out like an accusation as I twist in my seat to glare toward the back.

"Not a chance," Jamie says, already grinning as he leans forward, chin settling on my shoulder. His breath is warm against my skin, close enough to make my pulse stutter. "You'll see soon enough."

"You're all terrible," I mutter, even as goosebumps break out where his lips almost—almost—brushed my neck. "Suspense is not sexy."

"Speak for yourself," Liam drawls, voice lazy and low. "Anticipation's the best part."

Of course he says it like that—like he knows exactly what kind of anticipation is currently crawling over my skin, sinking deep and setting up camp in places I shouldn't be thinking about right now.

Spencer chuckles from the passenger seat without looking back. "You wanted the fantasy, sweetheart. This is part of it."

I huff, crossing my arms—but the smile's already tugging at my mouth. Damn them. All of them. They know exactly what they're doing.

And it's absolutely working.

. . .

Staff in sleek black suits move toward us the second we pull up, efficient and wordless, like they've been rehearsing this entrance for weeks. Spencer climbs out first, and I follow, legs unsteady the moment my boots hit the gravel. The second I straighten, the castle rises in front of me like it always does. Like it's alive.

It swallows the sky. A jagged silhouette carved from centuries of wind and war and whispered secrets, its gray stone glowing in the late light like it remembers every name ever spoken within its walls. My breath catches. My heart lurches. Even after all this time, it still takes my breath away.

"Penny!"

I turn just as Charlie barrels down the steps, curls bouncing, silk robe flaring behind her like she's the heroine of her own love story.

"I'm so glad you made it!" she cries, wrapping me in a hug that's all warmth and perfume. "Isla and I have champagne and face masks and hair tools and, like, four hours of gossip to unload."

"I missed you," I breathe, hugging her back.

She pulls away, eyes glinting as they flick toward the men gathering behind me. "And look at you, arriving with an entire harem."

Archer rolls his eyes. Spencer kisses her cheek. "A pleasure, as always. Where do we unload?"

"Jack will help you," Charlie says, already looping her arm through mine. "Boys to the west wing. Penny's with us in the east."

"Bring her back in one piece," Sammy warns, grinning.

"No promises," Charlie calls, laughter trailing behind her as she pulls me up the stone steps and across the threshold of something not just old, but timeless. Ancient bones dressed in fresh silk, buzzing with the electricity of what's about to unfold.

The Castle doesn't just welcome us—it announces itself.

Inside, it's nothing short of breathtaking. The grand foyer blooms with candlelight, every flame caught in the gold leaf trim of the vaulted ceiling. Chandeliers drip crystal above us, scattering prisms across the polished floor like scattered stars. It smells like roses and woodsmoke and wax—like opulence and memories. Every inch of stone is polished to a glow, the age of it dressed up in velvet and florals and ceremony.

Charlie tugs me down corridors I thought I knew, corridors I've padded through barefoot and half-asleep—but tonight they feel enchanted. Alive. The walls hum with string music and distant laughter. Garlands of greenery and pale blossoms twist up columns like something out of a fever dream, and the light—God, the light—is golden and thick, catching on sequined fabric and polished marble like it's trying to cling.

I can feel it under my skin—that pulse of something building. Like the castle knows it's the biggest night of the year. Like it's been waiting 365 days to be seen like this.

"Look what I found lurking outside," Charlie announces, voice bright with triumph as she throws open the door and pulls me into a room that looks like it was spun from a dream and then ransacked by a fairy Godmother.

It's technically a bedroom, but you'd never know it. Soft golden light filters through gauzy curtains, catching on clouds of tulle draped across the bed and pooling onto the floor. Silk gowns hang from the canopy like spells mid-cast. The air is thick with perfume, rich and floral, with something smoky underneath that gives a dangerous, heady edge to the atmosphere.

Makeup compacts glint from every surface. Hair tools hum beside half-finished flutes of champagne. There's a sense of movement, of energy crackling in the air, like the room itself is holding its breath in anticipation of the night. The whole space feels like the inside of a jewel box, private, precious, a little chaotic.

Isla turns from the mirror, mascara wand in hand, her red hair pinned halfway into something that already looks unfairly stunning. Glamorous. Alive. Like fire caught mid-movement.

"There she is," she says, crossing the room with her arms already open. "About bloody time. We thought you'd gotten cold feet."

I laugh as she pulls me into a hug, the kind that squeezes out whatever nerves are still hanging around in my chest. "Traffic," I say, though the heat in my cheeks probably says more than anything else.

Isla leans back just enough to study me, eyes narrowed, lips tugging into a knowing smile. "Right. And I'm the Queen of England."

Charlie appears at my side with a grin and a glass of champagne. "Leave her alone. She's glowing. Whatever the reason, I approve."

She hands me the flute, the stem cold against my fingers. I take it, and we raise our glasses, just the three of us, wrapped in candlelight and perfume and the rustle of silk. The room hums around us with something bright and full of promise. The kind of feeling that says you'll remember this forever.

"To wicked women," Charlie says, eyes shining.

"And to the men who adore them," I add, voice soft, but thick with everything I don't quite have the words for yet.

"To masks that show more than they hide," Isla finishes, tapping her glass to mine and then Charlie's.

The champagne is crisp and golden, bubbles darting across my tongue and shooting down my spine like a fuse lit from the inside. It tastes like a beginning. Like the inhale just before the overture starts. Like magic.

"So," I say, cradling the glass in both hands, "what are you two wearing?"

Isla unzips her garment bag with the confidence of someone who knows she's about to drop jaws. "The boys and I are going as the four elements," she says. "I'm fire. Obviously."

And then she parts the bag.

The dress inside is molten. Not red, not exactly. It's copper and gold and every flicker in between, catching the light like it's alive, like it breathes. The fabric moves like flame in a breeze, all shimmer and heat, and I actually gasp, stepping closer like it might disappear if I blink too hard.

"Oh my God, Isla," I breathe. "That doesn't even look real. You're going to set the entire ballroom on fire."

Her mask is just as bold—coiled gold, glittering embers, tiny gems that flicker like sparks when they catch the light. The kind of thing you wear when you want the world to watch you burn.

"Theo's earth, Henry's water, Dylan's air," she adds with the kind of breezy affection that barely hides how much she loves all three of them.

Charlie gestures to her own bag. "We're going Venetian carnival. Jack's idea."

But Isla's already on it, fingers nimble and unapologetic. She unzips the garment bag like she's revealing state secrets, and when the fabric inside catches the light, I swear the entire room exhales.

The gown is midnight incarnate—deep, inky blue that shimmers into silver at the hem, like moonlight being poured down a waterfall. It's the kind of dress that doesn't just look magical, it feels inevitable. Like it was always meant to exist, and it was always meant to be worn by her.

I can't stop staring. "It looks like something you'd wear to dance with a faerie prince," I murmur. "Or walk straight into a dream and never come back."

The mask is just as mesmerizing—delicate filigree and sweeping feathers, haunting and regal. The kind of thing you wear if you want to be remembered forever. If you plan to seduce a prince and kill a king.

Then Isla turns to me, eyes catching the light like twin sparks. "Okay," she says, practically vibrating. "Your turn."

I hesitate, teeth sinking into my bottom lip. Suddenly the room feels too warm, too bright. My pulse is drumming in my throat. "I'm going as Lilith."

Isla stills like someone just spoke sacred words aloud. Her grin turns feral. "Oh, hell yes."

I reach for the zipper with fingers that don't feel entirely like mine and ease it down, slow, the sound loud in the silence. The bag parts, and the room exhales with me.

The dress gleams like a secret finally revealed. Red latex—bold as blood, slick and unapologetic. It clings like sin, dips deep at the front and slices high along one thigh, every inch of it built not for modesty, but for power. For intention.

It doesn't look like something you wear. It looks like something you become.

The boots are just as brutal. Black, glossy, dagger-heeled—and the mask... oh, the mask. Black lace, soft as smoke, with tiny curved horns that crown the temples. It's not subtle.

For one stretched, echoing heartbeat, no one says a word.

Then Isla lets out a breath, slow and sacred. "Holy mother of sin."

Charlie steps closer, like she's been drawn in by gravity. Her voice is a laugh wrapped in awe. "You're going to kill them. Dead. Right there on the ballroom floor."

My fingers twitch at the edge of the garment bag. "Too much?"

They don't even pause.

"It's perfect," they say in unison—like it's not just a response. Like it's a blessing.

"What are the guys wearing?" Charlie asks, already at the vanity, fingers tugging at her curls like she's trying to tame chaos with sheer will.

I groan, flopping back onto the edge of the bed like it might help. "No clue. They're being infuriatingly secretive."

Isla raises a sharp brow. "Even Jamie?"

"Especially Jamie," I say, tipping my head back and staring at the ceiling like it might offer answers.

Charlie laughs softly, lifting her glass like a toast to the drama. "Whatever it is, I'm sure it'll be ridiculously over-the-top and impossible to recover from."

Isla smirks, stepping toward me with a gleam in her eye that feels like the strike of a match. "Let's get you into that dress and see how many hearts we can break before midnight."

And just like that, the air shifts again, charged and humming. Like something big is about to happen. Like we're all about to become someone slightly more dangerous than we were an hour ago.

The next hour unspools in flashes—heat from the curling iron, the hiss of hairspray hanging heavy in the air. Isla leans in close, a blending brush clamped between her teeth like she's gearing up for battle, her elbow jabbing into my ribs as she adjusts her angle. Charlie's fingers work through my hair like she's sculpting something holy, taming the chaos into sleek waves that frame my face like they've always been there.

She pins the final strand into place with quiet triumph, just as Isla tilts my chin and murmurs, "Don't move." Her voice is low, focused.

Hushed. Like this smoky eye she's crafting is less about aesthetics and more about conjuring a version of me I've never dared to be. Her fingers are quick but intentional, painting on danger with every pass of her brush—dark shadow, glinting liner, blood-red lips that match the latex dress hanging ominously on the closet door. I catch a glimpse of myself in the mirror—sharp eyes, flushed cheeks, an edge I didn't know I had—and I almost don't recognize her. But God, I want to.

The dress is its own battle. It takes all three of us, swearing and laughing and sweating, to wrestle the latex over my hips. It squeaks in protest, clings to every curve like it's been waiting just for me. It isn't comfortable. It isn't forgiving. But once it's on, I don't care. I'm not myself anymore—I'm confident, powerful, fucking unstoppable.

Charlie tosses me the black lace gloves from the bottom of the garment bag, her eyes glittering. "Don't forget your rings," she says, motioning to where they sit in a tiny dish on the vanity. I slip them on over the gloves one by one—opal, pearl, emerald, the sapphire haloed in diamonds. Each one settles over the lace like jewels in a crown. I flex my fingers, watching the light catch and scatter. Each ring is a vow. A heart laid bare. A life I've threaded through the fabric of mine and knotted tight.

The last detail clicks into place as Charlie fastens the tail at the base of my spine, her grin one breath away from wicked. It trails behind me like smoke, sleek and sinuous, flicking with every shift of my hips. It's the crowning touch, the exclamation point on my devil's disguise.

When I turn to the mirror, I have to steady myself.

She stares back at me, a creature conjured from myth and midnight, lips painted like sin, curves wrapped in fire. Seductive. Elegant. Just dangerous enough to make people nervous. There's no trace of the woman in muddy wellies and overalls, no hint of the girl who hid for three years.

This version of me doesn't ask permission.

She takes.

"Fuck," Charlie breathes, stepping up beside me. She looks like a Venetian hallucination, elegant and otherworldly in midnight blue and silver, her mask a sweep of filigree and feathers, her hair twisted into something impossibly regal, like she was born under candlelight and velvet.

"We're going to cause a riot," Isla says, joining us in a blur of molten color. Her gown ripples with every step, alive with gold and copper, clinging like heat. Her hair spills around her shoulders like a wildfire in motion, untamed and utterly intentional.

We stand shoulder to shoulder in front of the mirror, a trio conjured from legend and rebellion. Flame, moonlight, and blood-red sin. Each of us a different kind of weapon, wrapped in silk and smoke, dressed not just to be seen but to be etched into memory.

A knock raps at the door. Jack's voice follows, deep, warm, unmistakably amused. "Ladies? The guests are arriving. Time for your grand reveal."

Charlie cracks the door an inch, keeping herself hidden. "We're ready. Are the others in position?"

"They're at the foot of the stairs," Jack answers. His voice lowers to an almost indecipherable murmur. "Can't wait to see you, mo chridhe."

"Five minutes," she says, shutting the door again with a snap of finality.

"Remember," Isla says, handing us our masks, "tonight we're not ourselves. We're whatever the fuck we want to be."

Before we can respond, another knock jolts us. A voice I'd know anywhere calls out, teasing and warm and wonderfully familiar.

"Is it decent to enter?"

"Millie!" I all but squeal, throwing the door wide.

She stands in the doorway like a vision stepped out of a dream, dressed in flowing white and gold, barefoot, radiant, glowing with the kind of light that doesn't come from chandeliers. Wildflowers are threaded through her hair like a crown spun by the wind. She's grinning, wide and unapologetic, the kind of smile that says yes, I'm late, and no, I wouldn't change a damn thing.

Then she drops her bag just inside the door and sweeps me into a hug that lifts me clean off the floor, joy radiating from her like heat from the sun.

"Cutting it a little close, aren't you?"

She pulls back, eyes raking over me. "Holy shit, Pen. You're going to give those men heart attacks. Simultaneously."

I laugh, something unspooling in my chest. "Millie, this is Charlie and Isla. Girls, meet my best friend."

"The famous Millie," Charlie says, extending a hand, warmth pouring from her.

"I heard you're going as Aphrodite," Isla says, eyeing her outfit. "Genius. You're the perfect foil to our devil."

"Well," Millie says with a smirk, already gliding toward the vanity like she was born to hold court in front of a mirror, "if Pen's going full seductress, someone had to embody love. Besides, I'm long overdue for some of the real stuff. Maybe dressing for it will bring me a little luck."

"Single and ready to mingle?" Isla grins.

"Always," Millie replies without missing a beat. "And very ready to watch those five idiots fall at your feet."

My chest swells. She's teasing, sure, but she means it. She's always meant it—every ounce of support, every nudge toward joy. With her here, this night doesn't feel quite as terrifying anymore.

We link arms, the rustle of our gowns brushing together like a secret being passed between us. Step by step, we move down the corridor, toward the grand staircase, past towering portraits and flickering candlelight, through air thick with expectation. The hush is near total, broken only by the soft press of our footsteps and the sound of my heartbeat, loud and wild in my chest.

Every head turns as we pass.

Every breath stalls like the world itself has forgotten how to inhale.

And I don't shrink beneath their stares.

I rise.

The noise hits first—laughter and music rising from the ballroom like champagne bubbles, fizzy and bright and tinged with anticipation. It hits me right in the chest, my heartbeat stuttering to match its rhythm. I'm suddenly sweating beneath the latex, the polished stone under my boots too smooth, too slick. I glance down to steady myself, but it's useless. This moment is a free fall.

The Castle's grand staircase curves out in front of us like something out of a gothic fever dream, all ancient stone and Victorian flourishes. A sweeping descent into decadence. I can't see the ballroom yet, only the glimmering suggestion of movement and masks, gowns like spilled ink and wine, the hush of breathless conversation. The whole thing shimmers like it's breathing. Like it's alive.

We linger just beyond the curve of the wall, tucked in the hush between anticipation and reveal. Jack is waiting. Straight-backed, still, devastating.

He's wearing navy brocade threaded with silver embroidery, the fabric catching the candlelight like starlight stitched into midnight. He looks like he's stepped out of another century—elegant, commanding, timeless.

"They're waiting," he says, voice low and rich, warm even through the mask.

Charlie draws in a single breath, then she slips her arm into his. "See you at the bottom," she says, winking at me. "Make them wait." And then they step into the light.

The moment they appear at the top of the stairs, the hum below stills like someone cut the power. A collective intake of breath. The room's pulse halts, and then starts again, faster, chaotic.

Isla turns to me, her hand finding mine and giving it a squeeze. Her flame-red mask only enhances the wildness in her green eyes. "Count to ten," she murmurs, "then bring them to their knees."

Behind her, Millie adjusts her laurel crown, her gown floating like she's walked out of a Botticelli painting and into this fever-dream of a night. "You've got this," she whispers. "Show them what it means to fall."

I nod, but it feels like standing at the edge of a cliff. I count—one, two, three—and every number is a crackle of adrenaline.

At ten, I step into the light.

And the world stops.

The ballroom stretches out below me in a sweep of velvet and candlelight. Masks and jewels. Gowns like oil spills and wings. But I don't see any of it. Not really.

Because at the base of the stairs, five men stand shoulder to shoulder, unmoving. Unblinking. Watching me like I'm their personal apocalypse.

And I see it immediately.

Their masks. Their costumes. Their fucking audacity.

Five of the deadly sins, each one tailored like a fantasy. They've dressed themselves to match me. The Devil and her court.

My breath goes shallow. My thighs clench. My heart tries to claw its way out of my ribs.

Jamie is Pride, his black suit impossibly crisp, gold woven through his lapels and peacock feathers sweeping up from his mask in a way that should be ridiculous but just... isn't. His fingers glint with gold rings, and I want them on my throat.

Spencer is Greed, in a green velvet jacket with no shirt beneath, his chest adorned with enough chains to make a pirate weep. His mask gleams like treasure, and he watches me like he already owns me.

Archer—fuck—Archer is Lust. Burgundy silk hangs open past his chest, low-slung black pants hugging his thighs like a prayer. His mask is leather, kissed with subtle lip prints, and the cuffs on his wrists are the kind of promise that makes my knees weak.

Liam's Envy is sharp-edged elegance—emerald tailoring, snake-eyed mask, a predatory gleam in his usually gentle gaze. His hair is slicked back and his eyes lock on mine and don't let go.

And Sammy. My proper, composed Sammy has gone full Wrath—blood-red shirt clinging to his chest like a second skin, black leather pants hugging legs carved from something biblical, and a mask that looks like it was forged in fire. He's towering and unapologetically muscular, every inch of him radiating heat and power, like the embodiment of righteous fury barely leashed in silk and smoke.

I take a step. Then another.

The slit in my dress parts with every movement, revealing the length of my thigh like a secret offered piece by piece. The latex clings like a second skin, liquid and merciless, catching the light, sculpting me into something other. Something dangerous. The tail sways behind me with each step, slow and intentional. Like I've become the thing you were warned about in stories whispered too late.

The click of my boots hits the floor like a countdown, echoing through the space like a warning bell in a cathedral. Sharp. Final. Sacred.

No one speaks.

No one can.

The air is thick and aching, like the whole world is holding its breath. Like I've taken the moment in both hands and bent it to my will.

I keep my eyes locked on them—my sins lined up like a reckoning—and I drink in their awe, greedy for it. Five men who've seen every part of me, and still look like I've ripped a hole in their universe and stepped through wearing fire and ruin.

When I reach the last step, they start moving.

Like instinct. Like gravity. Like they were waiting for a signal that only my heels on marble could give.

Archer is the first to break from the line. He steps forward and offers his hand. Simple. Sacred. But the heat in his eyes makes it feel like a vow.

"You knew," I whisper, slipping my fingers into his.

"We planned it," he breathes, voice low enough that it slides across my skin like smoke. "Five deadly sins. For our Devil." He draws me closer, and the air tightens around us, stretched like a bowstring about to snap.

Spencer slides in on my other side, his mouth grazing my ear. "Temptation's never looked so fucking good." His hand settles on the small of my back, warm, steady, possessive, his grin wicked as he adds, "Millie told us the night you picked your costume."

"Traitor," I murmur, breathless, drunk on all of it—lace and leather and the weight of their eyes like worship.

Jamie steps in front of us, his presence slow and intentional, gaze raking over me like I might vanish if he doesn't memorize every detail.

"I knew it would stop my heart," he says quietly, almost to himself. "But this?" He lets out a breath, shaken. "I couldn't have imagined this if I tried."

"You're a vision," comes from Sammy, his voice rough now, stripped of all its usual polish. What's left is raw. Sacred. Ruinous.

Then Liam steps forward to complete the circle, the final lock sliding into place. "Worth every secret meeting," he says, and the grin that follows is bright and unapologetic. "Every hidden fitting. Every lie."

The orchestra swells, strings and brass and something bright and aching beneath it all, and I can't tell if it's the music or my heart about to break open from the inside. They lead me onto the floor, my sins, my saints, my sanctuary, and I follow, the Devil stepping into the light, no longer hiding, no longer afraid.

Finally ready to be seen.

38

The masquerade has come undone at the seams—glittering, glorious, and far past the point of return. The ballroom pulses like a living thing, each beat of the music syncing with the flutter in my chest, the throb between my legs. Light scatters off sequins and crystal, casting little galaxies across bare shoulders and velvet masks.

I've stopped counting glasses of champagne. Not because I'm drunk, but because it's not the alcohol that has me buzzing. It's them. It's tonight.

The thought alone sends a bolt of heat straight through me, sharp and delicious and dizzying. This is it. The night I stop pretending. The night I stop holding back. The night I let go—completely, selfishly, entirely—to all five of them. Every breath feels stretched thin by anticipation. My skin too tight, my body too full of wanting. I shift slightly, thighs pressing together beneath the unforgiving grip of latex, but it only amplifies the ache.

"Penny for your thoughts?" Jamie's voice curls low against my neck, warm and lazy and lethal. His breath ghosts over my skin as one arm slips around my waist, tugging me flush against him. The music swells, something slow and indulgent, but the way he holds me is anything but polite. And neither is the hard length of him pressed against my stomach.

"Trust me," I say, looping my arms around his neck, my lips brushing his jaw, "they're worth way more than a penny. But I'll give you a hint—less clothing, more hands."

He groans like it's been punched out of him. Like he feels it. His fingers tighten at my waist. "You can't say shit like that when we've got hours left to go."

"Hours?" I echo, the word a breathy accusation.

"Dinner. Dancing. Mingling." He ticks them off like curses, every syllable soaked in the same frustration skating under my skin. "If we disappear before midnight, Isla will hunt us down. But after that..." His smile is pure sin behind his mask. Knowing. Hungry. Like he's already imagining me stripped bare and coming apart.

And then—heat at my back. A familiar presence. Sandalwood and leather and something darker.

"Mind if I cut in?" Liam's voice is lower tonight, sensual. The kind of voice that makes my knees forget how to function.

Jamie's smirk deepens. "I think our devil can handle both of us."

And just like that, I'm bracketed—Jamie in front, Liam behind. Their bodies fall into rhythm with mine like we've been rehearsing this for years. I can feel every inch of them through the latex. Heat, muscle, tension. The full-body press of want.

I lean into Liam, my head tipping back against the solid warmth of his shoulder, just as Jamie's mouth finds the tender column of my throat. His teeth drag across my skin—a whisper of threat, a promise of more—and my breath stutters. Liam's hands map me like he's memorizing the terrain, one drifting upward to graze the swell of my breast, the other settling low and sure at my hip, anchoring me in place.

"You have no idea," Liam murmurs, lips brushing the shell of my ear, "how many men in this room want to trade places with us."

I do know. I feel it. The eyes. The whispers. The sharp flare of curiosity behind sequined masks.

Let them look. Let them see. Because this is who I am now—wanted, worshipped, theirs.

"Get a room," Isla sings out as she glides past, her fire-red mask barely hiding the glint in her eyes. Henry trails behind her, smirking.

"We're working on it," Jamie calls back, stepping back just enough to pass for respectable. Barely.

Liam's hands linger for one more heartbeat before retreating, but his presence doesn't fade. "Dinner's starting," he says, tipping his chin toward the massive double doors. "Shall we?"

We're halfway across the ballroom when someone steps into our path. Broad shoulders. Midnight mask. Moonlight haloing the top of his head.

I don't have to see his face to know. I'd know that stance anywhere.

"Lach." My voice catches. My brother. My impossible, steady, infuriating brother.

"Penny," he says, pulling me into a hug that smells like expensive cologne and childhood. I'm ten again for half a second, safe in arms that once lifted me onto boats and out of storms.

"I thought you were avoiding me."

I wince. "Never." A lie.

He pulls back just enough to look at me, eyes sharp and clear. "Liar. Terrace. Five minutes."

Then he's gone, swallowed by velvet and champagne and spinning bodies.

Spencer appears at my elbow. "Everything okay?"

"Family stuff," I say lightly. Too lightly. "Go ahead—I'll catch up."

The air bites at me as I step outside, that particular kind of chill that makes you feel awake and a little too alive. Moonlight skims the terrace, painting everything in soft blues and bruised purples. Lach is already there, elbows on the stone railing like he's trying to hold the whole damn building together. He's always been like that. Solid. Quietly weathering everything, even the things he never says out loud.

"Hey," I say.

He doesn't turn around. "When were you going to tell me about the fire?"

My stomach plummets. "What fire?"

"Penelope Grace." He doesn't yell. Doesn't have to. His voice is all steel.

I close my eyes. "How'd you find out?"

"Angus from the insurance company called. Childhood friend, remember? Asked how you were holding up. And I just stood there, not even knowing what the hell he meant. Do you have any idea what it's like to find out something happened to your sister from a stranger?" He turns now. Arms crossed. Eyes burning. "What I don't get is why you didn't come to me."

And suddenly, the weight I've been dragging behind me snaps its leash.

"Because I didn't want you to worry," I say, small and hoarse. "I wanted to fix it. On my own."

He exhales, long and uneven. "You don't have to do it all alone, Pen. That's what big brothers are for—showing up when everything goes sideways and helping you glue the pieces back together."

"I know," I whisper, but it catches in my throat, tight and traitorous.

"Do you?" he asks, quieter now. Not accusing. Just... tired. Sad.

And something in my chest gives way. "I didn't want to disappoint you."

That breaks him. I see it happen—right there in the way his face folds, like he's just been hit in the gut.

"Oh, Pen." His voice cracks around the edges. "You couldn't disappoint me if you tried. You're my sister. My blood. You've been mine to worry about since the day you were born. I just needed to know you were okay."

He pulls me in, and it's not gentle, it's fierce, desperate, a hug that says don't ever fucking do that again. All muscle and grief and the kind of love that roots itself so deep you forget where it began.

"Don't ever do that again, okay?" he says into my hair.

I nod, tears slipping down my cheeks and disappearing into the fabric of his coat. "I'm sorry."

"No more secrets," he murmurs, holding me tighter. "Swear to me."

"Promise," I breathe.

We stay like that, quiet, unmoving, while the party flickers behind the glass, all golden light and distant laughter. Through the ballroom windows, I catch sight of them—my five—hovering at the edge of the crowd. Watching without watching. Trying not to look like they're waiting for me.

"So," Lach says, finally breaking the silence. "Five guys, huh? That's... ambitious."

I bark a laugh. "One for each weekday."

He raises an eyebrow. "Are they good to you?"

"The best."

"Good." His jaw tightens. "Because if they're not, I'm dragging them out to the loch. One by one."

"God, you're such a romantic."

He ruffles my hair, destroying whatever magic Charlie spun into it earlier. "That's what big brothers are for, Pen-pen."

"Don't call me that."

"Sure thing, Pen-pen." He grins. "Let's go inside before your boyfriends cause a scene."

As we step back into the warmth and light, Spencer meets my eyes across the room. I nod. He smiles, slow, certain, warm enough to melt glaciers.

And just like that, something in me lets go.

The tension, the guilt, the fear I've been dragging around like a shadow, it lifts. For the first time in a long time, everything feels like it's where it's supposed to be. All the broken pieces, finally clicking into place.

The dining room is a fever dream of opulence, like something out of a gothic fairytale—high ceilings carved in hypnotic detail, crystal chandeliers throwing fractured light across ancestral portraits that watch us with eerie solemnity. The table stretches like a spine through the center of the room, set for sixty, each place marked with a perfect little card as though any part of this night is subtle. It's not. Not even close.

I'm seated between Archer and Sam. Across the table—Spencer, Jamie, Liam. And the tension? Palpable. Electrified. Like something's humming beneath the linen tablecloth, waiting to detonate.

The first course arrives, sea-scented and absurdly delicate, more art than food. I barely register it. Wine is poured, glasses topped up the second they dip below the halfway mark. Laughter spills and rises like smoke, conversations bubbling around us like champagne, but I'm not listening.

Because Sam's hand is on my leg.

It starts innocently enough, just resting there. Warm. Steady. But then his thumb starts to move in slow, maddening circles against the skin above my knee. It's such a small touch. Too small. And it's driving me completely out of my goddamn mind.

Across the table, Spencer watches. Not my face, but the shift of my body. The hitch in my breath. He knows. I can see it in the way his pupils darken, even behind the mask.

"Everything okay over there, Penelope?" His voice is velvet and smoke, laced with teasing concern that doesn't fool either of us.

"Fine," I choke out, trying to sound composed, failing spectacularly. "Just... enjoying the food."

He smiles, all teeth. "It is mouthwatering."

I swear he knows exactly where Sam's fingers are—right at the edge of the lace stretched between my thighs. So close to too much. So achingly far from enough.

The meal drags. Endless courses, endless teasing. My skin is too tight. My breath is shallow. By dessert, some decadent gold-leafed chocolate sin, I'm barely holding it together. Sam's fingers have been dancing just out of reach, keeping me tethered to the edge.

"I need some air," I say, my chair scraping back too loudly.

"I'm coming with you," Archer murmurs, already standing, the weight of his gaze enough to make my knees go weak.

The moment we step onto the terrace, the cold air cuts through me, slicing through the heat still clinging to my skin, cool and sharp, perfumed with heather and pine. Above us, the stars are scattered like spilled Sugar across the navy velvet sky, constellations tangled and glowing. Below, the garden stretches out in soft shadow and silver moonlight, every bloom and leaf touched with starlight. Petals catch the glow like glass, and the pathways glimmer faintly, as if the heavens have folded themselves gently into the earth.

"Better?" Archer asks, his voice low.

I nod, exhaling like I've surfaced from deep water. My pulse is still racing. "It was just getting a little intense."

He doesn't smile. Doesn't tease. He steps in closer, slow and intentional, like he's testing how much space I'll let him take.

"Too much?" he asks quietly, the question curling hot at the base of my spine.

"Never," I whisper.

I move to the balustrade, needing something solid beneath my hands. The stone is cool, grounding. I grip it like it can keep me steady. "Just hard to keep up dinner conversation when all I can think about is—"

"This?"

His voice is suddenly right behind me, lower now, almost dark. I don't hear him move, I feel it. Then his hands are on my hips, firm, sure, pulling me back against him. His cock presses against the curve of my spine. He's solid heat against me—thick, hard, undeniable—and the sound I make isn't graceful. It's punched from my lungs, startled and wanting.

My fingers tighten on the stone. My whole body goes still, heat surging through me in one dizzying rush.

He slides one hand up, cupping my breast through the latex, thumb teasing until my nipple peaks painfully. The other dips low, palm flush to my belly, sliding down with infuriating slowness.

"Archer," I hiss, head falling back onto his shoulder.

"Let them see," he rasps, teeth scraping against my neck. "Let them see who you belong to."

My hands grip the stone harder as his fingers press between my thighs, teasing through the dress, not enough and still too much. His hips rock against me, restrained but hungry.

"If I pulled this dress up right now," he whispers, voice rough silk, "would I find you wet for us?"

"Yes." I don't even try to pretend. "God, yes."

The terrace doors swing open behind us with a rush of warm air and laughter.

"There you are," Jamie calls, grinning as he steps outside. "The music's started. Come dance with us, Penella."

I turn, breathless, heart still thudding. "We were just coming in."

"Good." He offers his hand with a little bow, all charm and spark. "I've been waiting."

The door swings shut behind him. Archer doesn't move.

"To be continued," he murmurs, brushing one last kiss along my shoulder before offering his arm, his smirk promising more. "Shall we?"

Inside, the ballroom hums with life. The lighting is golden and a little hazy, like champagne in the bloodstream. Music pulses low and warm through the floor. People move like they've already forgotten the cold night air, all soft smiles and silk and heat.

I spot the others near the staircase.

Sam's eyes meet mine instantly. "You good?"

"Perfect," I say, squeezing his hand.

"Looks like that was quite the conversation," Spencer says dryly, eyes flicking to the mark on my neck.

"We were just—"

"Waiting for the rest of us?" Liam finishes with a grin that suggests he's not even a little mad. "Our bad."

The music shifts suddenly—a low, sultry rhythm you don't just hear but feel in your bones. The lighting softens, casting everything in a golden haze, and the ballroom blurs at the edges. It's too warm inside now, too close, too everything.

One by one, they come for me.

Archer's first. Of course he is. No announcement. No question. Just the heat of him at my side, his hand already there like it belongs to me, like I belong to him. His eyes rake over me, not possessive, not quite, but heavy. Serious. Like I'm gravity and he's finally giving in.

I slide my hand into his and it's not gentle. His fingers close around mine like a vow, his jaw locking tight, the faintest tick in his cheek betraying the effort it takes not to pull me closer, not to crush me against him and let the rest of the world burn.

He does it anyway.

One arm wraps hard around my waist, fitting me to his chest like he's afraid I'll vanish if we don't line up just right. His other hand finds mine again, positioning us with an exactness that feels practiced, disciplined. Like he's choreographed this a thousand times in his head and now finally, finally, gets to feel it for real.

We move.

It's slow. Intentional. A rhythm that's more breath than music, more instinct than choreography. His thigh slides between mine, and I gasp. Not from surprise—because I knew he'd do it—but from the way it lights me up, that pressure, that promise. His forehead dips until it's pressed to mine, and for a moment, there's nothing but his breath on my lips and the beat of his heart under my palm.

Jamie doesn't interrupt, he arrives. A grin, a wink, the quiet confidence of a man who's never been told no, and wouldn't believe it if he was. "May I cut in?" he asks, and it's a joke, a formality, a line in a play he's already rewritten. Because by the time the words hit the air, I'm already spinning, Archer replaced by the warmth and wildness of Jamie.

He catches me like he's done it a hundred times. Maybe he has. Maybe in every version of this moment in his mind, I've always ended up in his arms.

He's all motion and grace and mischief and heat. He twirls me once, then again, faster, lower, dipping me until the blood rushes to my head and I'm laughing, breath hitching, toes barely finding the floor. It's dizzying, delightful, like champagne straight to the veins. His hands sure. His rhythm unpredictable. He dances like he lives—loud, reckless, impossible to look away from.

But beneath the chaos, there's intention. A pause too long when he pulls me against him, chest to chest, heartbeat to heartbeat. His breath brushes my ear, and my laughter dies on a sharp inhale.

Because suddenly it's not just fun.

The song ends, but Jamie's hand doesn't fall away immediately. He lingers, fingers brushing the curve of my waist like he's reluctant to let go, like if he keeps touching me, this moment might stretch longer. But then he releases me with a final, lingering glance, like a promise sealed and pocketed for later, and steps back.

And Spencer steps in.

He doesn't rush. Doesn't need to. Spencer moves like he has all the time in the world and every right to take it. That easy swagger, smooth as bourbon and twice as potent, carries him straight to me.

"Evenin', Darlin'," he murmurs, voice smooth as honey, eyes dipping to my mouth before offering his hand like we're about to make a deal with the devil. I take it, even though we both know he already owns me.

His touch is maddeningly soft. Barely there. Just the brush of his skin against mine, light enough it shouldn't do anything, but it unravels me.

He draws me in with a slow, calculated pull, like gravity's something he controls. His palm settles low at my back, warm and steady, claiming me with a gentleness that feels more dangerous than force. His other hand finds my waist, fingers drifting along the edge of the fabric like he's testing boundaries. Not just mine.

Everyone's.

That's how Spencer touches me. Like he knows every eye is on us and he's making a slow, calculated show of what I do when he gets close. When his lips dip toward mine, they don't land—just hover— his breath skating along my ear like a secret. I don't mean to arch into him, but I do. Like he's strung me up on invisible wire and tugged.

He chuckles, low and knowing, like he felt the tremor run through me. Like maybe he's the one who put it there.

I don't know if we're dancing anymore, or just coming undone in plain sight.

And then Sammy is there.

"May I?" he asks, voice rich and crisp, shaped by an accent that feels borrowed from another era. That voice wraps around the question like silk drawn taut, polite on the surface but humming with intent. I nod before I even realize I'm doing it, already moving toward him, already pulled into the orbit of Sammy in his immaculate black suit.

He steps in like the dance floor was built for him. Like he owns not just the space, but the air between us.

Every movement is intentional. Measured. The angle of his wrist. The precise set of his shoulders. He's elegance distilled, but there's heat beneath it, steady and sharp and impossible to ignore. When his hand closes around my waist, wide and certain, something inside me unravels.

There's no request in his touch. No room for uncertainty. Just the quiet, commanding presence of a man who knows where I belong and intends to keep me there.

Then he adjusts the set of my hips, just slightly, like aligning a painting on the wall. Barely anything. But it echoes everywhere.

"Good girl," he murmurs, almost too low to catch.

Almost.

The words melt into my skin, tracing down my spine and pooling between my legs. I clutch his shoulder, fingers digging into expensive fabric, my breath coming shallow and scattered.

He doesn't grin. Doesn't press his advantage. He just watches me, eyes dark and unreadable, like he's studying the exact moment I fall apart.

One second later, Liam is there, ducking between us with a wicked little smile, wedging himself between our bodies like he belongs there. The warmth of his chest presses against mine, the line of his back brushing Sammy's front, and for a second it's not clear which one of us he's teasing. Sam's hands come to rest on Liam's hips—firmly—and for a breathless beat, none of us move.

"Mind if I steal her for this one?" Liam murmurs, glancing over his shoulder at Sammy, voice low and edged with something that's not quite teasing anymore.

Sammy doesn't move. Doesn't blink. His hands stay firm on Liam's hips, and for one charged second, Liam is caught between us—pressed against Sam's chest, inches from my mouth.

"I didn't hear her say yes," Sam says, quiet and pointed, the words landing like a challenge.

Liam doesn't flinch. Just turns his head, slow and intentional, until his eyes find mine. They're warm, but there's nothing soft about the way he's looking at me now. There's weight in it. Hunger.

"Penelope," he says, voice low and steady, that Australian rasp wrapping around my name like a hand at my throat. "Can I have this dance?"

I glance at Sam, trying for a glare but failing miserably. It comes out more like wrecked and aching than annoyed. Then I turn back to Liam, and the words catch on the way out.

"Yes," I breathe. "Of course."

Sam holds a beat longer than he needs to. His gaze lingers on mine, then flicks to Liam with a look that makes something hot coil low in my belly. He presses one last hand to Liam's back, a slow drag of palm over fabric, before he steps away—fluid and silent, leaving a wake of heat behind him.

And then it's just us.

Liam fills the space Sam left like it was made for him. He catches my hand, fingers threading tight through mine, rough and sure, and my whole body reacts like I've been struck. His other hand slides to the small of my back, wide and hot, settling with a pressure that's not demanding but undeniable.

We start to move, and it's not a dance so much as a pull. A gravity that lives in his chest and draws me in whether I want it or not.

No words. No show. Just the slide of my hips aligning with his, the friction of fabric against fabric, skin remembering skin. My breath catches every time his fingers flex, every time his palm shifts the slightest bit lower, like he's testing how much I'll let him get away with.

The music melts around us. The room doesn't disappear, but it blurs, like we're wading through heat waves, like the world is watching but doesn't matter.

Because all I can feel is him.

The press of his thigh between mine. The way his thumb draws lazy circles at the edge of my spine. The heat blooming low and sharp in my belly as his mouth dips close to my ear, not saying anything yet —just breathing.

And God, even that's almost too much.

Time doesn't just pass. It folds. Blurs. One moment into the next, one body into another, each dance heavier with promise than the last. My skin hums. My mouth is dry. My heart can't decide who it belongs to, so it races for all of them.

By the time the clock edges toward one, I'm loose-limbed and electric—flushed from the heat, wrecked from the wanting, and full of something sharp and sweet that won't let me go.

"We've mingled," Archer says, his breath brushing the shell of my ear, low and rough like gravel in velvet. "I think it's time to get some air."

We slip out like a secret, just the six of us, laughter still warm on our skin, champagne fizz still buzzing on our tongues. Past the clipped hedges and ornamental roses, beyond the places the gardeners manicured into submission. Out where the wild things grow.

The grass thickens, reaching higher, brushing our calves like it remembers us. The flowers abandon neatness entirely—scarlet poppies spilling into spiky thistle, tangled in vines of honeyed jasmine and unruly honeysuckle, blooming like they've never heard the word restraint. It's beautiful in the way chaos always is.

We move deeper. The path vanishes behind us, swallowed by the tangle of undergrowth and shadow. Branches curve overhead, ancient and arthritic, forming a canopy that dims the moonlight and hushes the world. The air shifts too—less floral now, more ancient. Damp earth, moss, the metallic tang of something old and watchful. Like the ground is holding its breath.

A meadow opens in a sudden breath. The grass dips low here, moonlight pooling like spilled milk across stone and shadow. At the center: a ring of standing stones, massive and crumbling, half-buried like the bones of some forgotten giant. Weathered and waiting.

We freeze when we see a flash of movement. A flicker just beyond the tallest stone. A shadow breaking away from darker shadow. My body goes taut, every nerve live-wire sharp. Spencer's hand finds my waist fast, pulling me into him. His body isn't panicked, but it's tense. Ready. Liam takes a half-step in front of me. Archer's already squared his shoulders.

"Who's there?" Sammy calls out, voice cutting clean through the hush.

The answer comes from the dark, familiar and too calm.

"It's just us," the voice says.

And sure enough, a figure steps into the moonlight. Lorna, looking amused and vaguely exasperated, like we've crashed her secret.

"Penelope?" She steps into the moonlight, serene as ever. Her note-book catches the light, silver pen gleaming.

"Studying night bloomers," she says with a knowing smile. "I'd heard the Castle had rare varieties."

Three men step out behind her—one slightly older than her, all calm authority. The other two are around a decade younger. Wild and beautiful.

"Oh," I say, blinking. "I didn't know—"

"Leo," she says, nodding to the oldest. "And Levi and Hudson. My colleagues."

Colleagues, my ass.

There's a charged beat of silence before Spencer steps forward smoothly. "Pleasure," he says. "We were just admiring the gardens ourselves."

"Of course you were," Lorna replies, and Isla's mischief lives in the curve of her smile. Then she leans in, just for me. "The grass is softer on the eastern side of the meadow."

She hugs me quick, no-frills, no judgment, and slips back into the dark like she was never there.

Silence folds in after her.

"That was..." Jamie starts.

"Exactly what it looked like," Sam finishes, dry as bone.

Archer lifts a brow. "The women in this family," he murmurs, eyes flicking to mine, "have exceptional taste."

And now they're all looking at me, and all I can think is RUN.

The pressure snaps like a stretched wire. One second I'm standing there, pulse fluttering, breath caught in my throat, and the next, I'm unzipping my boots and stepping out of them. The wet grass is shock-ingly cold against my bare feet as I gather the slit of my dress in one hand and bolt.

A shout cracks the air behind me, sudden and sharp, jolting through my spine. I whirl around, breath caught somewhere between my ribs and throat. Then the laughter comes, low, masculine, rippling across the field in waves. My lungs sting with the rush of it, adrenaline flooding every vein. My heart pounds so hard it feels like it might split open.

I can't tell if I'm terrified or ecstatic.

Maybe both.

"Can't catch me!" I shout over my shoulder, the words snatched by the wind, thrown into the night like a spark.

"Wanna bet?" Spencer calls, his voice all heat and promise, and then it hits me—the thunder of footsteps, shoes tearing through wet grass, quick and heavy and unrelenting. It's the sound of pursuit, raw and hungry. The kind that sparks something low in your belly. The kind that tells you you're not just being followed.

You're being hunted.

I'm still running, breath sharp in my chest, weaving between the hulking silhouettes of the standing stones. They rise around me like sentinels, ancient and disinterested, as if they've seen centuries of this kind of madness and won't be moved by ours. My feet sink into the earth, slick and soft from the morning rain, and I laugh—wild, breathless, giddy with the thrill of being wanted.

I dart behind the largest stone, back pressed to cold stone, lungs heaving, trying to slow the pounding in my ears. One beat. Two.

"Found you." Liam's voice curls around me, low and thick with heat.

Before I can move, he's there. All of him. His hands bracket my hips, his chest flush with mine, and his mouth finds me like it's a guided missile. The kiss is rough, greedy, a collision more than a connection, and I moan into it, helpless to do anything else. My hands scramble for purchase on his jacket, already trembling with need.

He pulls back just enough to breathe. "Too easy."

"I was catching my breath," I pant, dizzy from more than the sprint. "You cheated."

"There are no rules," he murmurs, fingers already at the back of my dress, tugging at my zipper. "But if you want to play, we can make it interesting. Every time one of us catches you, you lose something."

"And if I catch you?" I ask.

His grin is all slow fire. "Then the same rules apply."

"Deal," I say, glancing down at the skintight latex clinging to me like a second soul. "Although, we've got one small problem. This doesn't come off in pieces."

Liam tugs, frowning. The zipper gives half an inch, then stubbornly stops.

"Jesus Christ," he mutters. "It's like you were poured into this thing."

"Let me try," Spencer says, appearing from the shadows like temptation incarnate, mask still in place but voice unmistakably smug.

What happens next is a symphony of chaos.

Five men. One dress. Zero strategy.

Sam's first suggestion is violence. "Let's just tear it off."

Archer, ever the designated adult, shoots him a look like he's personally offended. "You can't tear latex," he says with the exhausted patience of someone explaining gravity to toddlers. "It resists. It rebounds. It fights back."

Jamie and Liam grab the sides, stretching the fabric like they're about to launch me from a slingshot, while Spencer and Sam do the grunt work—yanking, inching, muttering curses under their breath as they try to coax it past my hips. I'm laughing so hard I can't breathe, equal parts helpless and turned on, caught somewhere between a striptease and an exorcism.

"This doesn't feel sexy," I gasp, nearly choking on my own laughter as they tug and twist.

"It's not," Jamie says brightly. "It's like reverse engineering a sausage casing."

Archer stands off to the side, arms crossed like he's watching a particularly unhinged performance art piece. "Man versus polymer," he deadpans. "The ancient battle."

I'm breathless. Sweaty. Half undressed and laughing so hard my ribs ache.

And still so painfully, achingly turned on I could cry.

Finally, with a sucking sound that defies dignity, the dress peels free. I stand there in nothing but lace panties and gloves, breathless, laughing, skin flushed.

"That was the least seductive striptease of all time," I say, as Liam attempts to fold the dress before setting it gently on the ground.

"But now," Jamie purrs, "you're free. And the game continues. Ten seconds. Run."

He starts counting.

I take off.

The meadow is drenched in silver. The stones stretch like quiet sentinels. I'm barefoot, bare-breasted, wild with the thrill of it. The grass sticks to my legs. The wind teases what little remains of my modesty.

"Ready or not," Spencer's voice drifts in from the left.

They've fanned out, turning the meadow into a minefield of anticipation. I duck behind one of the taller stones, crouching low, heart hammering against my ribs like it wants out. My breath comes fast and shallow, every exhale a giveaway.

A soft rustle to my left—grass shifting. I risk a glance.

Jamie.

He's moving toward me, slow and steady, eyes scanning the dark like a predator who already knows where I'm hiding.

Without thinking, I drop to my hands and knees, the cold shock of dew-soaked grass biting into my palms. My skin prickles, breath tight in my chest, but I keep crawling. Slow. Quiet. Circling until I'm behind him. The earth is wet and unforgiving, my body aching from the cold, but the thrill drowns it all out.

When I'm close enough, I lunge.

We crash to the ground, limbs tangling, breath knocked from both of us in one stunned, laughing grunt.

"Gotcha," I pant, straddling his hips, grinning like a lunatic. "Fair's fair. Shirt off."

He blinks up at me, then laughs. It's low and rich, like I surprised him. "Demanding little devil." But he's already working open the buttons of his shirt, slow and teasing. Each inch of bare skin is a reward. Golden, warm, muscle shifting beneath it. He tosses the shirt aside. "Satisfied?"

I kiss him once, hard and hungry.

"Not even close," I whisper against his lips.

Then I'm gone. On my feet. Running before he can catch me again.

I don't get far.

Sammy catches me next, emerging from the shadows like a storm. His arms wrap around my waist, spinning us to the ground. I land beneath him, grass sticking to my back, his weight solid over me.

"Caught you," he says, eyes dragging down my near-naked body. "Though it looks like you're running out of things to lose."

I lift my chin, eyes sparkling. "The gloves. And my panties. That's two more turns."

"Gloves first," he murmurs, voice gone dark and sacred.

He removes my rings carefully, then slides the lace from my hands one at a time, like unwrapping something precious. When the second glove falls, he lifts my hand to his mouth, kisses my palm, then slips the rings back on.

"Beautiful," he says softly, and releases me.

I scramble away, down to my last layer of modesty. The stakes feel impossibly high, my skin singing with every brush of air. I lose track of time, of who I've caught and what they've taken off. I demand shirts, belts, shoes. Laughter echoes. Breathing turns ragged.

But then Archer catches me. He pins me against one of the taller stones, his breath warm against my cheek.

"Nowhere left to run," he murmurs. His fingers hook into the waistband of my panties. "These are mine."

He slides them down over my hips and just like that, I'm naked. Exposed to the moonlight. To them.

They gather. Slowly. Silently.

"Christ," Spencer says. "You're—"

"A fucking Goddess," Sammy finishes, his fingertips tracing my hip.

Jamie steps in close, his eyes locked on mine like he can already feel what's about to happen. His hands cradle my face, warm and steady, grounding me for the storm he brings with him. Then he kisses me—hard and deep, all tongue and heat and quiet desperation. Like he's not just kissing me but claiming the moment, searing it into both of us.

When he finally pulls back, I'm breathless, swaying. My legs barely remember how to hold me. I'm trembling, wrecked with want, and we haven't even started.

Archer moves in behind me, his chest a wall of heat against my back. His hands slide up, palms flattening against my ribs before rising higher. He cups my breasts, thumbs brushing over my nipples until they tighten beneath his touch. My knees buckle. I barely stay upright.

Sammy drops to his knees like it's instinct. Like the only place he wants to be is beneath me. His hands grip my thighs, thumbs pressing into soft flesh as he parts them. I'm already shaking. Already soaked. And then his mouth is on me, hot, open, relentless. He kisses the inside of my thigh like it's the first course of something he plans to savor. Licks a path up, then bites, just sharp enough to sting.

I gasp, hips jolting. He doesn't stop. Doesn't even slow.

His tongue drags lower, teasing the edge of where I need him most, and then he pulls back, just a fraction, breath ghosting over wet skin. His eyes meet mine, steady and dark and so full of focus it feels like worship and punishment all at once. I can't breathe, can't think. Every nerve in my body lights up, begging for more, for anything.

He leans in again, tongue flicking higher, closer, circling but never landing. It's maddening. Mind-breaking. I clutch at his shoulders, needing him, hating him, unraveling in the space between every almost.

Spencer and Liam are pulling off the last of their clothes, muscles flexing, movements quick and focused. There's no teasing now. No jokes. Just hunger. Just them, all of them, closing in, crowding my senses until I can't tell whose hands are where, only that I'm surrounded.

Warm skin presses against mine. Fingers trail across my waist. A mouth finds the curve of my neck. Breath skims my shoulder. We fall together, tangled and unspoken, into the grass—wet and cool beneath us, sky wide and waiting above.

The meadow breathes around us. Crickets chirp in the grass, rhythmic and unbothered. A breeze sighs through the tall stalks, curling cool fingers over heated skin. The scent of crushed wildflowers hangs thick in the air—sweet and cloying. The stones stand silent around us, ancient and unmoved, as if they've seen this before. As if they remember what it means to worship in the open, beneath the stars.

And in the center of it all—me.

Hands on my body. Lips on my neck. Breath ghosting across my skin like an incantation.

We move without words, without needing them. Every brush of fingers, every stolen kiss, is coordinated chaos. I'm passed between them like something sacred. Like no one wants to let go. Like they all want to be the one who unravels me.

But they don't. Not yet.

Archer lifts me into his lap, my thighs bracketing his hips, and the moment I lower myself onto him, the stretch hits so deep I cry out. He doesn't thrust. Just holds me there. Buried. Trembling. Letting me feel every inch of him, every twitch of restraint in his jaw, every muscle pulled tight from trying not to move.

Jamie's at my side, kissing me slow and filthy. Tongue tasting my whimpers. He holds my jaw like he's steadying something fragile, even as his other hand slides down between my legs to where Archer's cock keeps me full and aching. He doesn't rub. Doesn't even press. Just hovers there. Waiting.

Sam's behind me, his lips finding the curve of my spine, then trailing down the dip of my lower back. His fingers map my ribs like he's charting them. I feel him shift, feel his breath hot against my ass. He spreads me open, mouth grazing sensitive skin, never staying long enough to give relief.

I whimper. Beg. My body is shaking, hips twitching, desperate to move. To do something.

But Spencer's hands are tight around my thighs, holding me in place. Grounding me. His grip bruises. He kisses my knee, the inside of my thigh, my hipbone. Everywhere except where I need him.

"Please," I breathe, head tipping back. "Please, I—"

Liam kneels next to me, one hand stroking my hair back from my face, the other pressed to my chest, right over my heart. "You're beautiful like this," he says, voice rough. "So fucking soft. So desperate."

He leans in and kisses my mouth—gentle, tender, in direct contrast to the feral tension thrumming beneath it all.

They trade positions. Shift around me. Archer slips out and Jamie replaces him, his cock hard and leaking, but he doesn't push in. Just rubs the head against my clit, over and over, until I'm a mess of gasps and pleas. Then he's gone again, and it's Sammy under me this time, fingers holding my hips steady as he grinds up against me once, enough to make me sob, then stops.

They keep me hovering, right on that edge, over and over, like they're sculpting tension into something holy. My skin is flushed, oversensitive, soaked in sweat. My legs tremble with exhaustion. My throat is raw from the sounds they keep dragging out of me.

It's messy. Wild. Perfect.

Sammy lifts me like I weigh nothing, even though my limbs are trembling and my body's gone loose with need. His arms lock around me, firm and sure, and I melt against his chest, breath hitching as the night air brushes over overheated skin.

"We need a bed," he says, voice low and frayed. "Somewhere we can fuck you properly."

My head falls back against his shoulder. "Where are we going?" I ask, barely able to get the words out.

"To our room. We can get in from the terrace."

I blink up at him. "How do you even know where that is?"

"I asked Charlie earlier." He smirks. "Figured we'd be delirious with lust by now and I didn't want to fuck you on the lawn."

A breathy laugh escapes me. "Bit late for that."

He stops walking, just long enough to tilt his mouth to my ear. "We haven't even made you come yet, Penelope." His breath dances across my skin, sending a ripple down my spine. "And we have all night."

Something shifts in me. Not a flutter, not a spark—a detonation. It rolls through my chest, floods my limbs, roots me in the moment with absolute clarity.

This isn't just a surrender. It's a devotion. A holy offering. And for the first time, I don't want to be saved. I want to be ruined beyond redemption.

39

The bedroom door swings open, and we stop short.

It's not just a room. It's a revelation.

The bed dominates the space—massive, four-poster, carved dark wood that looks like it's seen centuries. It's draped in gauzy curtains that shift with the air, half-concealing emerald silk sheets that gleam like wet leaves under golden light. The entire room hums with amber warmth, soft and low, like candlelight pressed into skin. Shadows move along the walls like they've been choreographed, every flicker and curve designed to draw the eye exactly where it wants to go.

It should feel cavernous, all that space. But it doesn't. It feels intimate. Intentional. Like every inch was curated for seduction. For worship. For us.

And yet, it's the bathroom that unravels me.

One whole wall is glass—accordion doors folded back, vanishing into the edges—so the night spills in unfiltered. The courtyard beyond is private, cloaked in shadow, fragrant with dew-soaked stone and the faint, wild sweetness of heather. The tub is sunken, wide enough for all of us, steam rising like breath. Floating petals catch the moonlight, red, lush, obscene in their beauty. Candles glow low around the edges, casting the water in gold and shadow. It smells like sandalwood and smoke and something older than scripture. Something sacred.

Spencer moves first. That lazy, southern cadence curling around something darker as he closes the space between us. "Charlie told us not to spoil the surprise," he says, voice low and smooth like aged bourbon. "Said this was the new honeymoon suite. We're the first ones to break it in."

Archer reaches for me, his fingers barely brushing down the skin of my arm. The heat in his eyes makes my breath catch, even before he speaks. "She asked for feedback," he murmurs, his voice softer now, but no less loaded.

Something shifts low in my belly, tightens and coils and begs.

Jamie steps in close, steady as ever. His hand slips into mine, the pad of his thumb gliding slowly across my knuckles. "You're still covered in grass," he says, voice like quiet thunder. "Let's get you cleaned up."

The tiles are warm beneath my feet, heat rising into my legs like an invitation. I step into the tub, the water curling up around me, higher and higher until it covers my thighs, my hips, my ribs. The scent hits me first—jasmine, maybe, and something deeper I can't name. The petals shift around me, blooming in the water, clinging to my skin as I sink lower, arching back into the curve of the tub.

Liam slides in behind me. His hands settle on my shoulders, wide and sure, his thumbs finding the knots and working them loose until my body goes liquid against him. I tip my head back onto his chest, eyes fluttering shut. A low sound breaks from me without permission.

"You've got leaves in your hair," he murmurs, voice rough against the shell of my ear. His cock nudges against my spine as he plucks them out one by one, fingers gentle, almost sweet.

Sammy kneels in front of me, cloth already in his hand. "Let me," he says, and there's no room for argument in his tone. He drags it over my collarbone, slow and unhurried, his gaze locked on the water beading along my skin before it slips between my breasts. He watches it fall like it's something sacred. Like I am.

Spencer is at my side, kissing the back of my neck, his mouth hot and open, while Archer cups my breasts in both hands, thumbs circling until my nipples tighten under the heat of his touch. I gasp, breath breaking, caught between their hands and mouths and the slow burn building in every inch of me.

Jamie's mouth follows the cloth like a promise, tracing every damp path Sammy leaves behind. His tongue glides over the top of my breast, slow and claiming, before dipping lower. When he closes his lips around my nipple and sucks—firm, focused, like he's been thinking about this for hours—my back arches, spine bowing, breath caught somewhere between a gasp and a moan.

Liam's hand moves lower, between my thighs. His fingers stroke slow, unhurried, and my body jolts, nerves lighting up again like it's the first time. I try to stay still, try to breathe, but I'm already unraveling.

"Spread your legs," Liam whispers at my ear, and I do. Instinctive. Immediate. His fingers slip inside—one, then two—while his thumb finds that aching, swollen place that needs him desperately. My cry is sharp and full and so fucking honest it feels like confession.

"You're soaked," he growls, his fingers curling just right, dragging another moan from deep inside me.

"We're in water," I pant, voice ragged. "You can't even tell—"

Sammy doesn't wait. Doesn't speak. Just lifts me from the water like I weigh nothing, steam trailing off my skin as I rise from the bath, slick and shivering in his arms.

He lowers onto the edge of the tub and draws me into his lap, my back flush to his chest, the strength of his arms anchoring me in place. His cock is already hard, already nudging between my thighs, sliding through the slick heat of me like it knows exactly where I need him most. He grips himself and guides the tip to my entrance, then holds, perfectly still. His mouth is near my ear, breath ragged.

"Take me," he murmurs. "When you're ready."

I lower myself onto him, inch by perfect inch, my breath catching in my throat as my body stretches to take him. The burn is sharp, glorious. I dig my fingers into his thighs, hips rolling to seat him deeper.

The stretch turns to fullness, to pressure, to heat blooming behind my eyes.

"Fuck, yes," I whisper. "Right there."

His hands grip my waist, holding on as I start to move. My pace is slow at first, hips grinding down in slow circles, chasing that pulse of pleasure. Then faster, harder, need surging like a second heartbeat between my legs. Every movement drives him deeper, hitting that spot that makes me see stars.

He groans against my neck. "Use me, Penelope. Take what you need."

I do.

I ride him like I'm burning through time itself, like nothing exists but the feel of him inside me and the edge I'm chasing.

Then movement catches my eye.

Liam steps in front of us, between our spread knees. His eyes lock on mine, then drop to where Sam is already buried inside me. I feel the heat of him before anything else, his cock thick and hard, brushing along my slit, right beside Sam's.

My breath catches hard in my throat. Every muscle locks, clamping down around Sam as Liam steps in close, the heat of him a second pulse between my legs.

The moment his cock starts to push in beside Sam's, my whole body riots.

The stretch is instant and overwhelming, a sharp, dizzying ache that flares through me like a live wire. My cunt pulses, fluttering tight, desperate to make space and failing miserably. I can feel every inch of them—Liam's slow, relentless slide against Sam's thick length already buried inside me—and the pressure is unbearable in the best possible way.

I cry out, high and sharp, the sound torn from somewhere deep in my chest. Wet heat spills down my thighs. I'm shaking, clawing at Sam's legs for something to hold on to as Liam pushes deeper, dragging another pulse of sensation through me that lights up my spine.

They're both inside me now.

Thick. Hard. Grinding together with every shift of my hips.

My pussy clenches down around them, struggling to hold them

both. It's too much. So much. Slick friction and obscene fullness, and the kind of pleasure that makes you forget your own name.

"Fuck," Sam groans beneath me, his voice wrecked. His hands grip my hips, holding me down as Liam inches deeper. "That's—Jesus—Pen, are you okay?"

I nod, wild and breathless, fingers clutching Sammy's forearms. I feel everything. The thick slide of Liam's cock next to Sam's, the way their bodies press together inside me, splitting me open, dragging against every swollen nerve.

Liam grits out a moan as he bottoms out, his forehead resting against mine. "You're taking us so well," he whispers, his voice gone to gravel. "So fucking tight, Darlin'."

"I feel you," I pant. "Both of you. Fuck, I feel everything."

Jamie steps in behind Liam, silent at first. His hands slide over Liam's waist, fingers splaying across the curve of his lower back before gliding down to his ass, firm and sure. The air shifts, tightens. Every breath feels louder.

"Can I?" he asks Liam, voice low and warm.

Liam groans, already moving, already leaning back into Jamie's hands. "Yes," he pants. "Fuck, Jamie. Yes."

Jamie doesn't hesitate, but he doesn't rush, either. He leans in close, lips grazing Liam's shoulder, and slicks his fingers with his own spit, coating them generously. His hand disappears between Liam's cheeks, and I feel the ripple it sends through all three of us.

He starts with one finger, pushing in slow, letting Liam adjust. Liam's breath catches hard, his head bowing, forehead pressing against mine like he needs the contact to stay grounded. Jamie curls his finger just right, and Liam shudders.

Another finger slides in beside the first, and Liam whines, a low, strained sound that seems pulled from somewhere deep. He rocks back instinctively, greedy for more, even as his body trembles from the stretch.

"That's it," Jamie murmurs against his skin. "You take me so fucking well."

A third finger pushes in, slower this time. Jamie works him open carefully, methodically, scissoring his fingers until Liam's panting, sweat beading along his spine, his hips twitching forward with each pass. I can feel it in the way Liam's body shifts against mine, every flick of Jamie's hand translates through Liam's cock, pressed so tight against Sammy's inside me I swear I can feel both of them throbbing in sync.

Liam makes a sound—part moan, part sob—and I'm not sure if it's from need or overwhelm or the sheer depth of what's happening to all of us.

Then Jamie withdraws his fingers, slick and slow, and grips the base of his cock.

I can't look away from Liam's face as Jamie starts to push inside.

The first inch has him gasping, sharp and guttural, his jaw going slack like the breath's been punched out of him. His hands tighten on my thighs, fingers biting into my skin, anchoring himself as his body begins to shake.

Another inch, and his eyes flutter closed, his lips parting around a moan he can't quite release. His whole body is taut, trembling with the effort to take more, to open for Jamie while staying buried in me.

By the time Jamie's halfway in, Liam is wrecked. Utterly undone. His mouth hangs open around a soundless cry, his head dropping forward, forehead nearly touching mine. I feel the tremor in him, the way his thighs quiver and his breath hitches in uneven bursts, like every inch of Jamie is being etched into his body, carved into him with heat and pressure and unbearable pleasure.

He squeezes my thighs again, harder this time, his nails dragging across my skin like he's trying to keep himself grounded—like he needs me to survive the stretch.

And I can feel it too. Every inch Jamie sinks into Liam, I feel echoed in the way Liam grinds deeper into me, their cocks pressed so tight together inside me I can't tell one from the other. It's too much. It's everything.

Liam sobs out a breath, ragged and broken. "F-fuck, Jamie—more. Don't stop. Please."

Jamie groans low in his throat, hands steady at Liam's hips, and keeps going. He doesn't stop until he's buried to the hilt. The moment he bottoms out, Liam jerks forward, helpless, and his cock shifts inside me, grinding against Sammy's, dragging across the sensitive walls of my pussy with devastating consequences.

I cry out, loud and shattered. My whole body clenches, a fresh wave of slick flooding down over both their cocks.

Liam groans, his voice wrecked. "Fuck—Penelope—Sammy—I can't—"

Jamie pulls out and drives back into Liam with a hard thrust, and the force of it pushes Liam forward, his cock slamming deeper into me, right alongside Sammy's. The impact has me crying out, my body jolting. Behind me, Sammy moans, rough and broken, his hands gripping my hips like he's barely holding on. I'm pinned between them, stretched impossibly wide, and every time Jamie thrusts, Liam is driven deeper, grinding Sam against that perfect spot inside me that makes my vision blur.

We're layered. Connected. Built into each other like a structure made of gasping mouths and trembling limbs and pleasure so blinding it borders on spiritual.

This isn't just sex. It's collapse. It's rebirth. And I'm unraveling at the center of it all.

Each thrust pulls me closer to the edge, dragging their cocks against every raw, oversensitized inch inside me. Liam and Sam grinding together, Jamie pounding into Liam from behind—it's a chain reaction of motion and heat and sound. I can't tell where one sensation ends and the next begins. I'm stretched so full I feel like I might shatter, and still, I want more.

It's overwhelming. Addictive. Holy.

And I never want it to stop.

Liam's rhythm starts to break. His breathing's gone ragged, his grip on my thighs bruising. Every muscle in him is pulled tight like a bowstring about to snap.

"Fuck—Penelope—I'm not gonna—" His voice cracks, torn and breathless. "I'm gonna come—Jesus—"

Then he grabs me.

One hand fists in my hair, the other cups my jaw, and he yanks me into a kiss so fierce it feels like drowning. Our mouths crash together, open and gasping, teeth clashing, tongues desperate. He kisses me like he's afraid he'll die if he stops, like this moment is the only thing tethering him to the earth.

And that's when he comes.

I feel the exact second it hits him. His whole body locks up, cock jerking inside me, release spilling hot and thick between me and Sam. A broken sound tears from his throat and into my mouth as he trembles through it, still kissing me like he needs it to survive. Like I'm the only thing holding him together.

Jamie holds him steady from behind, buried deep, his hands splayed over Liam's hips like he's bracing him against the force of it all.

Liam finally breaks the kiss, forehead falling to my shoulder, breath ragged and wet against my neck. His body sags between ours, spent, shaking, overwhelmed. And I can feel his heart, thudding wild against my spine, trying to catch up.

For a breath, the room stills—just the sound of panting, the weight of skin against skin, the lingering echo of what we've just shared. But the hunger hasn't faded. It's only shifted, refocused. I feel it in the way hands start to move again, in the quiet, commanding way they rearrange me like I belong to them.

Sam is the first to lift me, arms strong around my waist as he pulls out with a wet, obscene sound that makes me cry out, the sudden emptiness a sharp ache in its own right. I tremble in his hold, every nerve ending raw and lit up, still pulsing from Liam's release, from the feel of their cocks grinding together inside me.

Jamie steps back, eyes locked on mine, dark, wild, and barely holding the edge of restraint that makes my breath catch. He doesn't touch me. Not yet. Instead, he pumps soap into his palm and wraps his hand around his cock, stroking himself slow and steady, working the suds into every inch. His head tips back slightly, jaw tight, breath sharp through his nose. There's nothing rushed about it.

The muscles in his arm flex as he jerks himself once, twice more, rinses with a handful of hot water, stalks toward me, and his gaze never faltering. It's a promise. A warning.

Jamie steps behind me, heat radiating off his body like a second skin. His hands find my hips, bending me over the side of the tub, steady and possessive.

Then he drops to his knees.

I gasp as he spreads me open, his thumbs digging into the softness of my ass, exposing everything. His mouth is on me before I can even breathe his name, hot, relentless, hungry.

He drops to his knees behind me like he's been starving for this.

His hands spread me open without hesitation, and then his mouth is on me, hot and unrelenting, tongue plunging deep to lap up the mess Liam left inside me. He groans like it's his, like this is the exact meal he's been waiting for, and he's not leaving a single drop behind.

"Fuck," he breathes, mouth slick with it. "You're dripping with him. So fucking messy, Pen."

The flat of his tongue drags through me, slow and filthy, savoring the taste as he tongues my entrance, licking up every trace of cum still leaking out of me. My whole body jolts when he seals his mouth over my pussy and sucks, hard, like he wants it all—wants to taste them, taste me, and claim it with his tongue.

"You taste like all of us," he growls, voice muffled against my cunt. "Sweet, slutty little thing—so full. So fucking perfect."

I sob his name, my thighs shaking, back arching to give him easier access.

He doesn't stop. Doesn't rush. He keeps eating me like I'm the only thing he's ever needed, licking deep, then dragging his tongue up to circle my clit before diving back down to fuck me with it. I'm leaking, trembling, on the edge of coming just from this—and he knows it.

"Gonna fuck it right back into you," he mutters, breath ragged. "You want that? Want me to stuff it deeper?"

I whimper, nodding, too gone for words.

Then he stands, wipes his mouth with the back of his hand, and fists his cock, lining up behind me.

"Now that you're clean," he growls in my ear, "I'm going to fill you until you can't take any more." He grabs my hips, fingers biting deep, and drives into me in one brutal, perfect stroke.

I scream.

The force of his thrust slams me forward, my body jolting, hands splaying against the cold tile as I scramble for something solid to hold onto. He's inside me fully, thick and pulsing, already moving, already taking.

He doesn't ease in. Doesn't ask. He fucks me like he owns me, like every second he waited was agony. Each thrust slams into me with punishing rhythm, splitting me open again and again.

"You take my cock so fucking well," he growls, and he's right—I do. I take it like I was made for it, like his shape is carved into me, his rhythm already coded into my bones.

"Please—" The word cracks in my throat. "Please, Jamie. Please let me come. I need—"

But I don't get to finish the sentence, because Sammy is there again, his hands gripping my waist, pulling me away from Jamie mid-thrust. I scream. Part shock, part rage, part desperation. I'm empty again, clenching around nothing, the ache unbearable.

"Bedroom," Sammy growls, voice feral as he stalks across into the bedroom with me still in his arms. He lays me out in the center of the bed, my limbs trembling, my skin flushed and slick. But he doesn't climb over me. Not yet. Instead, he spreads my legs wide, dragging them open until I'm completely exposed under the amber light.

"Look at you," he says, his voice rough. "Dripping. Fucking soaked for us."

He dips a finger into me, lifts it, lets the slickness catch the light like a jewel. Like something rare.

Jamie joins him, eyes gleaming as he kneels between my legs. "Greedy little cunt," he murmurs, and then his fingers are inside me, two at once, no warning, finding that spot like he's mapped it.

I cry out, back arching off the bed.

"You like this?" he asks, thrusting his fingers deep, slow. "Being opened up. Watched."

"Yes," I breathe, the confession burning my throat. "Yes, I—God, I love it."

"Say why," Archer demands. He's above me now, hand on my chin, thumb brushing my jaw. "Be specific, Penelope. Tell us exactly what it does to you."

My mouth goes dry. But I want to answer—I need to.

"I love being the center of you," I whisper. "I love how you pass me between you, like I belong to all of you. I love being claimed. Used."

Jamie's fingers curl deep, and the sound that tears from me isn't a moan—it's a sob, ripped straight from somewhere buried and aching.

"And what do you want now?" Spencer's voice cuts in, low and hungry, eyes fixed on my body like he can see every little twitch of need.

I don't hesitate.

"I want all of you," I say. "Inside me. Together."

The sound that rises from them is animal, a collective groan of approval that goes straight to my core.

Archer presses his thumb against my lip, and I open for him without hesitation. I suck it greedily, tongue swirling around the pad, wet and slow, never breaking eye contact. His gaze darkens, jaw tightening like he's imagining that mouth somewhere else, and I want him to. I want all of them to.

"Come here," Spencer says, already there, sitting up against the headboard, legs spread, gaze heavy with heat. They lower me into his lap, back to his chest, and the second I settle against him, his arms come around me like instinct. Like gravity. One arm across my ribs, the other sliding low over my stomach, anchoring me.

He's warm. Solid. His heartbeat thuds steady against my spine.

His hands start to move, slow and shameless. Fingers brushing over my breasts, cupping them with a possessive kind of worship. Stroking the curve of my belly. Tracing the inside of my thighs like he's reacquainting himself with territory he already owns.

"I want this perfect ass," he murmurs against the shell of my ear, his voice all gravel and hunger. "It's all I've been able to think about."

I shudder, hips twitching involuntarily.

Archer kneels in front of us, his presence quiet but anchoring. He gently spreads my legs, guiding them outside the width of Spencer's thighs until I'm wide open and completely on display. His hands move over my hips, firm and sure, then slide lower. His thumbs part my ass cheeks, exposing every inch of me without hesitation, without apology.

I feel the first cool trickle of lube, then the press of his fingers.

Confident. Unhurried. He works it in with slow circles, gentle pressure, touching me like he knows exactly how to make my body yield. I breathe through it, chest rising and falling, every muscle trembling as he coaxes me open.

My hand finds Spencer's cock. He's thick and hard in my palm, pulsing against my skin. I guide him to my ass, my grip tightening just enough to steady us both. The head of him presses to my entrance, hot and blunt, and everything inside me clenches. My breath catches, sharp and shallow, the anticipation nearly unbearable.

I'm shaking. Open. Ready.

The pressure is immediate. Hot and sharp, stealing the air from my lungs the second Spencer starts to push inside. My body goes rigid, instinct trying to clamp down against the stretch. I reach out blindly, grabbing his thighs, fingers digging into the muscle as I gasp through the first impossible inch.

"Easy," he whispers, his lips brushing the side of my temple, soft and grounding. "Breathe for me, sweetheart. That's it. Just like that."

I suck in air, slow and ragged, forcing my muscles to release. My head tips forward, jaw slack, the rest of me trembling as I try to melt into him. To open for him. To take him.

He pushes deeper, inch by inch, the intrusion maddening. My body fights it, then surrenders, nerve endings lighting up with every slow, intentional push. The burn is deep, constant, a wildfire that licks up my spine and curls behind my ribs.

And then it changes.

The pain shifts. Softens. Morphs into something thick and pulsing and so exquisitely full I can't think.

It's not just stretch anymore—it's weight. It's heat. It's the overwhelming, consuming sense of being completely filled. Claimed. Stretched around every inch of him with no space left between us.

I arch back into him with a soft, wrecked sound, body shuddering. His arm curls tighter around me, hand sliding up to cup my breast, thumb stroking across my nipple like he needs to touch all of me at once.

"Fuck," Spencer groans, voice breaking apart in my ear. "You feel— Jesus, Penelope. You feel incredible."

I'm trembling, legs splayed wide over his, body stretched around him, aching for more. And the others? They're watching. Drinking in every second like it's the only thing keeping them alive.

Jamie kneels in front of me again, Sammy beside him, both of them hard and ready.

"Fuck," Jamie mutters. "Look at that little cunt—winking at us like she knows we're watching."

Sammy presses my knees to my chest, spreading me wider. "Hold her, Spence."

Spencer's arms lock tight around my thighs, holding me open, holding me still, while Sammy lines himself up. His cock drags through my slick folds, thick and hot, and then he pushes in.

Slow. Deep. Relentless.

And reality ceases to exist.

The world narrows to sensation—two of my favorite cocks stretching me wide, filling every inch. There's no room to breathe, no space to think. Just this—this obscene fullness, this beautiful pressure, this body-breaking pleasure that makes my vision go white at the edges.

I cry out, loud and raw, my core clenching down around both of them, trying to make sense of the impossible. Trying to hold it all.

My body pulses, fluttering tight, struggling to adjust and already desperate for more.

I can't think. I can't speak. I can only feel—wrecked and wide open, ruined and rebuilt, claimed from the inside out.

"It's too much," I sob, my whole body trembling, slick with sweat and sensation. "Too full... too deep... but fuck, please—don't stop."

"You're perfect," Spencer breathes against my skin, voice rough with awe. His arms tighten around me, locking me in place as they start to move, slow at first, building something that feels inevitable.

And then they find it. That rhythm. That unbearable, perfect rhythm.

My body sings. Screams. Every drag of their cocks grinds through me, separated only by the thinnest, most sensitive wall, the friction so sharp and filthy it feels like I'm coming apart at the seams. Every nerve lights up, every breath shatters. I can't hold anything in—not the sounds, not the tears, not the way my hips keep chasing more.

I'm not just fucked—I'm unmade.

Jamie strokes himself as he watches. "I want in."

Sammy adjusts, just enough to give Jamie room, his cock still buried deep. Jamie steps in close, his body flush against mine, radiating heat. I feel the thick head of his cock press against my entrance, already slick, already stretched around Sammy—tight, trembling, barely holding it together.

The pressure is unreal.

My breath catches hard in my throat, and the panic bubbles up before I can stop it. "I can't—" I choke out, voice shaking.

"Yes, you can," Jamie whispers, his lips close to my ear. "You're doing so good for us, angel. Just breathe. Let me in."

His hand curves around my hip, steady and warm, and then he starts to push.

Slow. Controlled. Fucking merciless.

The stretch is fire. White-hot and unrelenting. My body clenches, fights, then trembles. It burns. It steals every thought from my brain, every word from my mouth.

And then—I give.

My pussy gives. My body opens.

Jamie slides in beside Sam, thick and sure, and suddenly I'm filled in every possible way—Spencer still buried in my ass, Sam and Jamie now inside my pussy, their cocks grinding together inside me, every thrust igniting something wild and unbearable.

I sob. Gasp. Shudder. My eyes fly open, vision blurring, the magnitude of it short-circuiting everything I am.

"Fuck," I gasp, voice high and broken, shivering on the edge of panic and ecstasy. "I can't—I can't—Jesus—"

Liam's hand finds my face, gentle amid the chaos, brushing damp hair from my forehead as he leans in. His voice is soft, sure, steadying. "You are, Darlin'. You're taking all three of them. Every inch. You're fucking incredible."

And then the rhythm locks in.

They fall into it without speaking—three bodies, one rhythm, moving inside me like a tide that doesn't pull back. Each thrust lands like a wave, crashing into the next, undoing me over and over. It's unrelenting. Drowning. Divine.

Pleasure and pain blur together, indistinguishable. My cunt aches, stretched and filled and stuffed so completely it feels like I'm being remade from the inside. I cling to Sammy's shoulders, fingers digging into his skin hard enough to bruise. My other hand reaches back blindly for Spencer, needing the feel of him, needing to know I'm still tethered to something even as I come undone.

"Fucking hell," Jamie groans, his voice guttural, ragged. "I can feel Sam's cock against mine. Inside you. Jesus—angel—you're unreal."

"So fucking tight," Sammy grits out, his grip punishing on my thighs as he drives deeper, desperate now. "Like your body was made for this. Like it wants it."

And I do.

I want all of it. Every stretch. Every thrust. Every filthy, unbearable second.

The world around us vanishes. No bed. No room. Just the rhythm. Just the sound of them falling apart inside me. Wet, rhythmic slaps of skin on skin. The scent of sweat and sex and something older than language. Something wild. Something holy.

I grip Sammy's shoulder like it's the only solid thing left in the universe, my nails biting down, anchoring me. Behind me, Spencer's hips slam into mine, his cock grinding deeper into my ass, while my free hand reaches for him blindly, needing the feel of his skin just to remember who I am.

"Jesus fuck," Jamie growls, his voice wrecked, breath hitching as he slams into me again. "I can feel Sam's cock dragging against mine inside you. That slick, tight little cunt—fuck, Pen."

Liam watches from the edge of the bed, one hand stroking his cock slow and steady, eyes burning with need. He takes his time, drinking it all in. Me spread open. Sam and Jamie buried deep. Archer fucking my mouth like it's his right.

Then he moves, kneeling beside the tangle of bodies, his mouth warm and searching as he finds my clit. The second he licks me, I cry out. The sound is swallowed by Archer's cock, my moan vibrating against him. Archer groans, a deep sound that rolls through his chest and into mine.

Liam keeps going, licking deeper, tasting the slick mix of Sam and Jamie where they stretch me full. He groans like he's starving, like he can't get enough, then drags his tongue along the base of Sam's cock where it disappears inside me.

"Fuck," Sam mutters, his rhythm stuttering.

Liam shifts lower, tongue flicking over the underside of Jamie's shaft, wet and slow. Jamie swears under his breath, thrusting harder, deeper, chasing the edge Liam just handed him.

Liam's mouth is everywhere. Hungry. Messy. Devoted to the chaos of us.

And I can't stop shaking. Not with the way they're all inside me. Not with Liam licking every filthy inch of it like it's the only thing he's ever wanted.

"She's close," Spencer says, arms tightening around my waist. "I can feel it. She's clenching down hard."

"Not yet," Archer says, pulling back just enough to meet my eyes, his thumb brushing over my swollen lower lip. "Hold it. Wait."

I whimper, helpless against the tide rising inside me. Everything is too much. Everything is perfect.

"I'm close," Jamie gasps, fingers digging into my hips like he's trying to hang on.

"Same," Sammy bites out, thrusts turning frantic.

"Me too," Spencer says, breath hot against my shoulder. "She feels too fucking good."

"Liam," Archer growls, voice low and ruined. "Get up here. Fuck her tits. She wanted all of us, and she's gonna take every inch we give her."

Liam doesn't hesitate. He climbs up, straddling my chest, his cock already slick and leaking. He presses my breasts together with both hands, groaning as he slots himself between them, dragging the head through the soft, tight valley.

"God, Pen," he pants, hips flexing as he thrusts. "You feel fucking unreal."

I'm so full I can't speak. Spencer still buried in my ass, Sam and

Jamie still grinding into my pussy, their cocks rubbing against each other inside me with every thrust. Liam fucking my tits. Archer feeding me his cock like he owns my throat.

And then Jamie leans in behind Liam. He licks his fingers, slow and filthy, then drags one down between Liam's cheeks. Liam gasps. His hips stutter.

"Let me make it better," Jamie murmurs, voice right against Liam's ear. He presses his finger in, slick and steady, pushing past resistance until it's knuckle-deep.

Liam moans, loud and broken. His thrusts into my cleavage get rougher, messier.

Without warning, Sam's rhythm snaps. His grip tightens on my hips, fingers biting into skin, and he slams up into me, cock buried so deep I can feel it in my ribs. "Fuck—fuck—I'm coming—"

Jamie follows a heartbeat later, his thrusts losing control as he presses deeper into both of us, gasping against my neck. "Jesus, Penelope—you're so tight—I can't—fuck—"

Archer growls above me, voice ragged, breath breaking against his teeth. His hands fist in my hair as he drives into my throat faster, harder, until he's all I can taste. "Take it, baby. Every drop. Swallow it for me."

Spencer's right there, too. I feel the shift in his hips, the way he thrusts up once, twice, deep and brutal. Liam cries out, head thrown back, cock pulsing between my tits as he spills across my chest, Jamie's finger still buried inside him, working him through it. His body shudders above me, muscles locking as he breaks.

And then I fall with them.

My orgasm tears through me like a lightning strike. I seize around them, every muscle snapping tight as white-hot pleasure detonates behind my eyes. My pussy clenches, fluttering violently around the thick stretch of Sam and Jamie. My ass throbs, strangling Spencer's cock. I choke on Archer's length, the scream muffled, swallowed, shaken apart.

My body isn't mine anymore.

It's heat. Static. Stretch and shock and sensation. It belongs to them now.

I'm wrecked. Shaking. Split wide and filled to the edge with everything they've given me. It's not just sensation—it's religion. Like they've worshipped me from the inside out. Like they've rewritten the gospel of my body with their hands.

Every nerve sings like a choir too loud to bear. Every breath is a sob, torn from the altar of my chest. I'm locked in it—this brutal, holy release—so massive it doesn't feel like pleasure anymore. It feels like devotion. Like surrendering to something larger than myself. Something sacred.

The world holds still for one blinding beat of silence.

Then it breaks. Loud and endless.

And I'm nothing but sound and sweat and prayer.

Who I was before this doesn't exist anymore. Whatever name I wore, whatever self I clung to, it's gone. They stripped it from me with their hands, their mouths, their bodies.

They are my ruin and my redemption, and I wouldn't have it any other way.

40

———————

The morning of August 31st slips into the world like it's been hand-picked by the universe. The kind of blue that doesn't just hang overhead, it saturates. It seeps into your bones and makes you believe, just for a minute, that nothing bad has ever happened. The sun warms the house with just enough heat to kiss, not scorch. The breeze carries the sea—salt and heather, the ghost of tide-pools—and I can smell it before I even open the window.

I'm standing there in my robe, bare feet cool on the time-worn wooden floors, staring at the shimmer of light on the loch like it's trying to tell me something. I'm getting married today. To six men. God.

"Stop overthinking," Millie says from behind me, reading my silence like it's a language only she speaks. She's draped across my bed, surrounded by an explosion of hair tools and compacts, perfectly unbothered while I vibrate at a frequency previously unknown to mankind. "Your face is doing the thing. That little scrunch."

"I'm not scrunching," I say, turning away from the window, even though I absolutely am. My feet are doing this nervous shuffle on the floorboards, toes curling and uncurling against the wood like they might dig roots through it.

"You are," she says, lazily flipping her curling iron like it's a baton. "And spiraling."

"I'm not spiraling. I'm—" I exhale, rubbing my hands down my robe, which is suddenly too warm and sitting wrong on my shoulders. "Processing."

Millie sits up, shoving her dark waves behind her ears. "Processing what? Second thoughts?"

The words make my stomach drop like a stone. "God, no." It's out of my mouth before I can think. Automatic. Fierce. "Not even a little."

She eyes me. "Then what's got you pacing like a Victorian ghost?"

I glance down, toes curling against the floor like they're trying to hold me steady. "It just feels... big," I say quietly. "Like everything I've ever done—every mess, every miracle—was pointing to this. And now that I'm standing in it, inside the moment, it's so perfect I don't even know how to exist in it."

She smiles, the corners of her mouth tugging up. "That might be because you're marrying five men today. That's not just big, babe. That's continental drift."

A laugh slips out of me, breathless and a little disbelieving. "It's more than that. It's like... every mistake, every meltdown, every moment I thought I'd completely screwed up. Even burning down the damn restaurant. It all lined up, like coordinates. Like I was being aimed here the whole time."

Before Millie can answer, a knock splits the quiet, followed by Charlie's voice—bright, fizzy with excitement, like she's already halfway through her first glass of champagne. "Hope everyone's decent."

She peeks around the doorframe, auburn curls bouncing, the morning light catching the freckles across her nose like gold dust. Behind her, Isla and Lorna sweep into the room like sunshine through stained glass, gorgeous in oceanic shades of blue and green.

"Three hours to go and our bride hasn't even touched hair or makeup?" Isla scolds, mock-offended, though her grin gives her away. She's already halfway across the room, jasmine perfume trailing behind her, a chilled bottle of champagne dangling from one hand. She glances at me and winks. "Unacceptable."

"We brought reinforcements," Lorna announces, holding up a canvas tote like it contains something sacred. And maybe it does—five glittering champagne flutes and a fresh bottle of Dom, cool and sweating in its nest of ice packs.

"No time to waste," Isla says as she begins pouring, the sound of bubbles fizzing like a promise. "We've got a bride to glam and five absolutely wild grooms pacing the castle like inmates on the verge of a prison riot."

"They're all together?" I ask, taking the glass Lorna hands me. My fingers shake around the stem, either from nerves or the impossible, heady weight of what's coming. I'm not sure which.

Charlie smirks over the rim of her flute, lipstick already stamped across the edge like a kiss. "Yep. We've got them locked up. They keep trying to break out to find you."

"Jamie's making awful puns," Isla says, lounging against the edge of the dresser, one leg crossed, the other swinging lazily. "Spencer's reorganizing furniture that was perfectly fine before. Liam's basically vibrating out of his skin. Sam's pretending to read but hasn't turned a page in, like, thirty minutes."

"And Archer?" I ask, already bracing for impact.

"Archer," she says, her eyes lighting with mischief, "is cleaning his guns."

I nearly spit my champagne. "He is not."

"Okay," Isla concedes, totally unbothered, "technically he's just been standing at the window for twenty minutes like he's trying to summon the old Gods. Dylan went to check on them and said, and I quote, 'the tension is spreadable.'"

The image hits so hard I forget how to breathe. Each of them coming apart in their own ridiculous, beautiful way. Pacing, stalling, cracking under the weight of this day. Because they want it. Want me. Want this—as much as I do.

Something loosens in my chest. That tight, fluttery knot of too-much finally letting go.

"To the bride," Lorna says, raising her glass with the kind of steady warmth that anchors you. The light catches in her eyes, blue and unwavering, soft where Isla is blade-sharp.

"To love that doesn't give a damn about societal norms," Charlie adds, clinking her glass against Lorna's with a grin that dares the universe to object.

"To the woman who walked through hell and somehow made it look easy," Millie says, her voice going soft at the edges. "You've earned this."

"To chosen family," Isla finishes, her voice almost a whisper now, both hands wrapped around her glass like it might float away otherwise. "The real kind."

My throat tightens, but I lift my glass anyway, anchoring myself in their eyes, their steadiness.

"To all of you," I say, the words catching before they fall. "For being the first ones to show me this kind of love was possible."

I glance toward the window, where the loch glitters and the wind carries the scent of salt and blooming heather. My voice softens, but it doesn't shake.

"For every late-night pep talk, every brutal truth delivered with kindness, every time you looked me in the eye and reminded me I was allowed to want more."

I pause, because the next part matters most.

"For helping me see this for what it is—not a fantasy. Not a fluke. But something I chose. And something they chose. On purpose. With eyes wide open." I tap my glass gently to theirs, the sound bright and sure. "Thank you. For helping me find the way here."

For a heartbeat, no one moves. Just breath and sunlight and the echo of words that feel like they peeled straight from my ribcage.

Then Isla leans in, glass raised. "To Penelope. To love."

The others follow, our glasses meeting in the middle. The sound is bright, grounding. A note struck just right.

We drink, and the bubbles fizz like happiness rising too fast to contain—effervescent and impossible to ignore.

"Okay!" Charlie claps, her excitement back in full force. "Let's go! We've got a schedule to stick to."

. . .

The next two hours unravel in a kind of enchanted chaos—controlled, intimate, golden-lit. Everything feels close and fragrant and soft at the edges. Isla starts with my hair, fingers deft and careful as she coaxes it into something that feels like it belongs in a painting. Loose waves pinned just so, tendrils falling like whispers against my neck. She weaves in sprigs of wildflower, their scent blooming every time she adjusts them.

Millie's quiet when she works, her brow furrowing just slightly as she angles my chin toward the light, assessing. Rosy cheeks, warm brown liner, lips just a little deeper than my natural color. I look like me, but steadier. More sure of myself than I feel. The smell of foundation and setting spray blends with the lingering fizz of champagne. My skin's a little clammy from nerves, and when she brushes highlighter along my cheekbone, I flinch.

"Sorry," I mutter.

She just gives a soft snort. "Don't apologize for having nerve endings."

Lorna takes over at my hands, filing my nails with the same focus she probably uses to inspect her dahlias for pests. Her touch is light, but her hands are worn—cool from the water she must've used to wash up, scarred in places, her nails short and clean. She doesn't make small talk. Just paints with slow, even strokes, the polish a soft, pearly white that makes my fingers look elegant.

Charlie's the one darting around the room, organizing everything else—my dress hung carefully over the back of the door, hairpins lined up like soldiers, a little spread of crackers and cheese on the vanity. She doesn't ask if I'm hungry; she just hands me a cracker, already stacked with brie and a sliver of fig jam, and says, "Eat this. Or I'm calling Spencer."

That gets me to chew.

She smooths out the straps of the dress, refills the champagne, and tosses a makeup wipe to Isla without breaking stride. Efficient, brisk, bossy in a way that settles me.

And somehow, between the three of them, I stop feeling like someone waiting to be turned into a bride, and start feeling like one.

Millie catches my eye, her voice gentle but steady. "Alright, Penny

Lou," she says, lifting the dress so the hem stays off the rug. "Let's get you dressed."

I push up off the stool with hands that are a little too clammy and legs that don't feel like they belong to me. The dress, simple ivory silk, slips over my head, cool at first, like a sheet of water against overheated skin. Then it warms, molding to me in that way only expensive fabric does. Millie tugs it down gently, smoothing it into place. I shift my weight from foot to foot, bare toes sinking into the rug. The dress moves with me, light and easy. No risk of tripping on the dock or needing anyone to carry a ten-foot train.

When I look in the mirror, it takes me a second. Not because I don't recognize myself, but because... I do. Fully. Completely. I look like me, if I had slept well, fallen in love, and was standing at the edge of something life-changing. My cheeks are pink. My lips are pulled into a smile I can't seem to give up.

Charlie leans in behind me, adjusting a curl near my temple. "Perfect," she says, quiet and soft, like anything louder might knock the air out of the room.

"They're going to lose their minds," Isla adds. She looks proud. A little misty. Like she's already picturing the moment I walk out there.

"One more thing," Lorna says from across the room, pulling something small and silver from her bag. "Your rings."

I look down at my hands—crowded with stones, all of them different, all of them meaningful. Archer's pearl. Spencer's emerald. Jamie and Sam's shared sapphire and diamonds. Liam's opal. It's a mess, really, a beautiful one. The thought of taking them off makes my chest tighten.

"You'll want your finger free for the bands," Lorna explains gently, holding up a delicate chain. "We'll thread them onto this. You can wear them on your neck during the ceremony."

I hesitate for a second. Then nod.

One by one, I slide the rings off. It feels a little like peeling off armor. Lorna threads them onto the chain, then fastens it around my neck. The metal is cool against my skin, the weight unfamiliar but comforting. I touch them instinctively, fingers brushing the little cluster right above my heart.

"Perfect," she says, stepping back to look.

A knock at the door cuts through the quiet, and we all freeze for a beat before turning. Lach stands there in a tailored suit. The shirt is crisp. His hair's actually combed. His eyes find me, and they go wide. He blinks once. Twice.

"Wow," he says, breath catching like he's forgotten how to speak. "You look—"

"Too much?" I offer, half-laughing, half-already spiraling. My hand flies to the flowers in my hair, suddenly convinced they're off-center or wilting or just plain wrong.

"No." He shakes his head, quick and a little stunned. "You look perfect. Mum and Dad would've been really proud."

The words hit harder than I expect. All the air rushes out of me in one breathless, silent whoosh. My throat tightens. My eyes blur. But I nod, because it's all I can manage, because I need to hold on to that moment without falling apart inside it.

Lach crosses the room and offers me his arm. "Ready?"

Before I can answer, Millie slides in on my other side. "Like hell I'm letting her walk out there with just you," she says lightly, linking her arm through mine and giving it a quick squeeze. "You've got both of us, babe."

Then Millie hands me the bouquet. It's small, a little wild. Bluebells, sea lavender, tiny white garlic blossoms, soft pink dog roses. It smells like the hillside we've walked a hundred times. Like morning sun and clean wind and the sea. Like home.

I hold it tighter than I need to, fingers curling around the stems like they might steady me. Then Lach shifts beside me, and Millie squeezes my arm, and together, we start to move.

We walk down the narrow road from my house to the restaurant. It's quiet, except for the crunch of pebbles underfoot and the soft rustle of my dress around my ankles. I'm barefoot, and the gravel bites at the soles of my feet in little sharp bursts. It should hurt more than it does, but honestly, it helps. It keeps me in my body, keeps me from drifting too far into my head where everything is spinning too fast. I welcome the discomfort. It's real.

As we round the final bend, the restaurant comes into view. The walls are new, the paint fresh, the doors thrown open in welcome. It catches the late afternoon light, all clean lines and warm wood, completely rebuilt. Seeing it standing there, solid and whole after everything, hits harder than I expected. It's proof that things can come back. Not the same, but stronger. Better.

People are already gathered, scattered in small, familiar groups near the dock. Our guest list is tight on purpose, friends who've seen every messy chapter, neighbors who stepped in when we needed them, the kind of people who don't flinch at what we've built. No second cousins whispering judgments. No one looking sideways at our choices. Just people who get it. Who love us.

We stop at the edge of the dock. My breath catches as I take it all in. The weathered planks stretching toward the water, the five men waiting at the end, and the way the setting sun turns the ocean into turquoise and gold. Gulls cry somewhere behind us. The breeze lifts the hem of my dress and flutters it around my calves like it's part of the ceremony.

"Ready?" Lach asks from my right, voice low.

Millie's grip tightens slightly on my left. She doesn't say anything, but the squeeze says enough.

I nod, because words are too much right now. My throat's thick and my chest is full. We start forward, slow and steady. Every board beneath my feet registers—each groove and rough patch, every small imperfection worn into the dock by years of tides and time. It makes me feel rooted, like this isn't some dream I'll blink out of. This is happening. Right here. Right now.

Halfway down the dock, I stop. I don't mean to. My feet just... freeze. Like my body knew before my brain did that I needed a second. My heart slams against my ribs, loud enough I'm sure they can hear it. My eyes find them and everything else blurs.

Archer. Spencer. Sam. Jamie. Liam.

They're standing in a line at the end of the dock, five men who've seen every version of me, looking at me like I'm their whole damn universe. And something in me just breaks open.

I can't breathe. Not from panic, but from the sheer magnitude of it. The weight of being seen like that. Known. Loved. It hits in the chest, not like pain exactly, but like something collapsing inward and then expanding, too big to hold, too true to deny. My knees go soft. The world tilts. For a second I'm not sure which way is up.

"Breathe, Penelope," Millie whispers, leaning in, her hand warm on my arm.

"They're waiting for you," Lach says, his voice low and rough, like he's holding something back.

I drag in a breath—sharp, unsteady—and finally let myself look. Really look.

Archer stands slightly apart from the others, like he always does in a crowd. His charcoal suit is simple but razor-sharp, every line exact. His shirt is unbuttoned at the collar, no tie, of course, but even that hint of casual doesn't take the edge off him. Nothing ever does. His gaze is locked on mine, unreadable to anyone else, but I know what I'm looking at. I see the tight set of his shoulders, the flicker in his jaw, the way his hands are curled into fists like he's holding something in. Or holding something back. Maybe both.

Next to him, Spencer is calm in a soft gray that makes the blue in his eyes glow. His smile is gentle, steady. His fingers twitch at his sides, and I know without even thinking that if I faltered right now, he'd be the first to move. He always is.

Sammy stands like a statue in deep navy, the gold of his cufflinks catching the sun when he shifts. His posture is straight, jaw locked. Controlled. But his eyes give him away. Glassy with emotion, unguarded in a way that makes my chest tighten. He's beautiful.

Then there's Jamie, doing his best to look relaxed, like this isn't the biggest moment of his life. His sleeves are rolled to his elbows, the top buttons of his shirt undone—not out of carelessness, but because he's never been one for formality when things get real. And this? This is as real as it gets. His foot taps lightly against the dock, a barely-there rhythm that betrays everything he's holding inside.

And then there's Liam.

God, Liam.

He's in pale linen, the soft beige of sun-bleached sand, and it suits him in that effortless, quietly confident way. When our eyes meet, something in him shifts, subtle, but sure. His spine straightens, shoulders lift, like seeing me sets him right. He doesn't grin the way he does for everyone else. This smile is gentler, deeper. Like it's just for me. Like he's been waiting for this moment and now that it's here, he wants to memorize every second of it. I hold his gaze for a beat longer, my heart thudding in time with the waves against the dock. Then, slowly, I shift my attention forward to the man waiting to guide us into this next chapter.

Father Calum stands at the very end of the dock, prayer book in hand, the breeze tugging at his dark hair. He smooths it back absently, a small, human gesture that somehow settles the flutter in my stomach. His face is young, but there's a depth in his eyes that feels older—steadier. This isn't his first ceremony like this. He married Lach to his three, then Isla to hers. Our arrangement doesn't even make him blink.

As we reach the end of the dock, Lach and Millie move to either side of me, standing like bookends to the story that brought me here. One is my brother. The other, my best friend. Together, they've walked beside me through every heartbreak, every high, every messy, beautiful middle. And now they're here, standing beside me as I step into something I never thought would be mine.

Father Calum clears his throat, his gentle Scottish brogue carrying over the water, momentarily competing with the rhythmic splash of waves against the dock pilings.

"Dearly beloved," he begins, his voice steady and warm, "we are gathered here today to witness the union of Penelope Grace with the five men who stand before you. Love comes in many forms, and when it's given freely and received with joy, who are we to question its shape —or its number?"

A soft ripple of laughter moves through the small crowd. On the shore, I spot Isla, grinning wide and completely at ease. Lorna stands nearby with a quiet smile, one of Levi's hands resting gently on her back while Hudson holds hers, his thumb brushing across her knuckles like he's steadying both of them. Not far from them,

Charlie cradles little Summer on her hip, gently swaying as she watches, her expression soft and full of something that feels like knowing. A little farther down the shoreline, Leo keeps an eye on Daniel and Lorelai, who are happily skipping stones into the loch. The soft plunk of rock meeting water echoes across the surface, threading through the moment and grounding everything in its quiet, familiar rhythm.

Father Calum continues. "Over the past few years, I've had the honor of joining several remarkable unions, each one teaching me something new about the heart's ability to stretch wider than we ever thought possible. Today, we celebrate another such miracle."

He glances down, smiling. "This dock," he says, gesturing beneath our feet, "has seen its share of hellos and goodbyes. Departures. Home-comings. It feels only right that it now bears witness to something new. A journey not away, but toward—a merging of lives, a beginning."

The symbolism is not lost on me. The wood beneath my bare feet is worn and imperfect. Solid. Honest. I think about that first day, three years ago, when five strangers stood on this very dock and rerouted the entire course of my life. And now, here we are. Back where it all started.

"Marriage," Father Calum says, his tone deepening slightly, "is not entered into lightly. It's a vow made with intention, built on trust, nurtured with care. It asks everything of us—our honesty, our loyalty, our willingness to show up, even when it's hard. Especially then."

He looks to each of the guys in turn, then back to me. His dark eyes catch the light, reflecting the gold of the sky, steady and kind. "What you're choosing today is both deeply traditional and entirely your own. The heart of it remains unchanged: the commitment to build a life. A family. One not bound by convention, but by choice."

The words hit harder than I expect. My throat tightens. Heat stings behind my eyes, pressure building behind my sinuses before I can blink it back. Jamie catches my eye and offers the smallest wink, like he knows I'm about to cry and is trying to head it off with charm. It works—just barely. His left dimple deepens, that familiar flicker of mischief still able to knock the wind out of me.

"Who presents this woman to be married to these men?" Father

Calum asks, his voice steady and warm, shaped by tradition and softened by understanding.

"We do," Lach and Millie say together, their voices clear and certain, no hesitation.

They each take one of my hands. Lach's grip is solid, grounding. Millie's is warm, her thumb brushing over my knuckles once before she lets go. They pass my hands into Archer's outstretched palms like something sacred. And maybe it is. Maybe this is the moment everything shifts.

The lump in my throat swells instantly, sharp and full, pressing hard against the back of my tongue. I don't cry, but it's close. Too close. Because it's not just a handoff. It's a tether being passed from one version of my life to the next. Lach catches each of my men's eyes, one by one, and something unspoken travels between them. A warning. A blessing. A promise.

Millie gives me one last look, and it breaks me. Her smile is radiant, proud, full of everything we've survived together. Then she steps back, fingers brushing my arm one final time, and they both return to the circle of people who know us best.

Father Calum turns the page of his prayer book, the rustle barely audible over the hush that has settled around us. "Before these witnesses, I ask each of you to speak your vows," he says. "Archer, please begin."

Archer's fingers are still wrapped around mine. He steps closer, quiet but sure, and draws a breath deep enough that I can see the rise of his chest beneath the crisp white of his shirt. His thumb presses lightly against the inside of my wrist, steadying me, or maybe himself. When he speaks, his voice is low and even, but not without weight. Every word is placed like it matters. Like it costs him something to say it out loud.

"I've navigated by stars most of my life," he says, eyes never leaving mine, "but none has ever guided me as clearly as you, Penelope. I vow to be your shelter in every storm. Your constant in every changing tide." He pauses, barely, like he's making sure I'm still with him. "My love for you doesn't live in flowery words. It lives in what I do. In every choice I make. In the way I'll always come back to you."

He swallows. My grip tightens on his hands, and he tightens his in return.

"You are my true north, Penelope. And I'm anchored to you. For life."

My heart doesn't just squeeze. It clenches, tight and sudden, like it's bracing for impact. Tears press hard behind my eyes, sharp and insistent, but I blink fast, refusing to let them fall. Not yet. His words are so unmistakably him. Plainspoken. Exact. And somehow still gut-deep. No flourishes. No performance. Just love, laid out bare and steady, like a lighthouse cutting through fog.

He steps back, giving Spencer room to move in. Spencer's eyes crinkle at the corners as he steps forward, taking both of my hands in his. His thumbs start tracing slow, easy circles against my palms, his touch soft and familiar. Where Archer anchored me, Spencer lifts me. His presence doesn't press—it soothes, like light filtering through trees on a quiet afternoon.

"From the first moment I met you," he begins, that familiar spark already forming in his eyes, "I knew two things with absolute certainty. One, you were the most remarkable woman I'd ever met. And two, I was one hundred percent destined to be the bane of your existence."

A ripple of laughter moves through the crowd. Mine bubbles up right along with it.

"I vow to be your steady hand," he says, his voice softening, "and your biggest cheerleader when you chase ideas that make no sense to anyone but you. I promise to be your voice of reason, except when being unreasonable sounds like more fun. And I'll love you with the same bold, messy, unapologetic heart that brought us to this moment."

Before I can fully absorb it, he leans in and kisses me—quick, unexpected, and so completely Spencer that it steals the breath from my lungs and draws gasps and laughter from the crowd.

"Just a preview," he whispers against my lips, his mouth still close enough to steal another. Then he straightens, eyes lit up with both amusement and something deeper, something that feels like awe.

He brushes a kiss against my knuckles before releasing my hands and stepping back, the faintest scent of his cologne lingering in the air between us. Jamie practically bounds forward, green eyes bright and burning with barely contained emotion. His presence fills the space instantly, like stepping into sunlight after standing in shadow.

He doesn't reach for my hands. Instead, he cups my face, his palms warm and a little rough, thumbs grazing my cheekbones with a gentleness that doesn't match his usual chaos. The calluses on his hands catch slightly against my skin, grounding me in the moment.

"I'm not exactly known for my patience," he says, his grin tugging at one corner of his mouth, "but I waited three years, two months, and eleven days for you. And I'd wait three lifetimes more."

My breath catches.

"You've seen every side of me," he goes on, quieter now. "The stupid jokes. The too-loud energy. The dark days I don't always talk about. And you still chose me. All of me."

I blink hard against the sting behind my eyes.

"I promise to keep laughter in our house, adventure in our days, and to love you with the same wild abandon you've shown in loving us."

There's no mask, no act. Just Jamie. All in.

He leans forward and presses a kiss to my forehead, soft and lingering, his lips warm against my skin like he's trying to leave a piece of himself with me. When he finally pulls back, he gives me a wink that sends a ripple of laughter through our witnesses. The sun hits his hair just right, catching on the gold, and he grins like he's lit from within. This is Jamie—messy and bright and impossibly full of heart. And he's mine.

As he steps back, the energy shifts again, softer now, almost solemn. Liam steps into the space Jamie just left, his smile bright enough to rival the sunset behind him. It reaches his eyes, crinkling the corners, lighting up his whole face like it's not just joy, but wonder.

"My heart," he begins, voice roughened by feeling, "has crossed oceans and continents, deserts and mountains... just to find home. And it's here. With you." His accent sounds thicker than usual, like the emotion has stripped it bare.

His eyes are wet now, shining with tears he doesn't bother to blink away. "I vow to cherish every sunrise we get," he says, steadier now. "To hold your hand through every storm. To be your warmth when the world turns cold. I promise to love you with every breath in my lungs, every beat of my heart, every single day we're given. You're the journey and the destination, Penelope."

The sincerity in his voice hits me like a wave—heavy and full and completely unguarded. My throat tightens. My eyes burn. His hands reach for mine, steady and sure, fingers curling around mine with the kind of grip that says I'm here. One firm squeeze, and then he steps back, a flush climbing his neck as he lets go. But his eyes stay locked on mine. And in them is everything—joy, awe, love. All of it. Raw and real.

Finally, Sam steps forward. His usual composure is still there—straight posture, steady gaze—but there's a crack in the surface now, just enough to let the feeling show. Of all my men, Sam is the one who holds himself most tightly. Precise. Measured. Always in control. But when he takes my hands, there's the slightest tremble in his fingers, and I can see the rapid flutter of his pulse at the base of his throat. It tells me everything I need to know.

"I've built my life on plans and precision," he begins, voice low but clear. "On knowing what comes next. Then you burned down your restaurant, and every expectation I thought I had."

A startled laugh escapes me, quick and unfiltered. Of course he'd go there. Of course he'd name the moment that changed everything, wrap his vow in something real, something ours.

"I vow to embrace the beautiful chaos you bring into my life," he says, his grip tightening just slightly. "To protect the family we've made together. And to love you with everything I am. Today, and every day that follows."

My throat tightens. A single tear slips down my cheek, hot against my skin until the breeze cools it. Sammy wipes it away with the lightest touch, all the feeling he didn't say out loud poured into that single gesture. He doesn't say anything else. He doesn't need to. His eyes are brighter than usual, that buttoned-up reserve worn thinner than I've ever seen it.

He releases my hands slowly, like he's reluctant to let go, then steps back into the line of men, holding my gaze for a moment longer, something soft and sweet passing between us.

Father Calum turns to me with the kind of gentle expression that says he knows I'm one breath away from breaking, and that it's okay if I do. "Penelope," he says, "please share your vows with these men."

I nod and draw in a deep breath. The salt-heavy air fills my lungs, settles my nerves. My bouquet trembles slightly in my hands, the stems shifting with a whisper of perfume—wildflowers, earth, something green and alive. I grip them tighter and meet each of their eyes in turn, grounding myself in the faces I love. When I speak, my voice comes out stronger than I expected—steady, clear. Like the words have been waiting for this moment, rehearsed and lived-in, but somehow still brand new.

"In a world full of either-or, where love is expected to fit into neat little boxes, we found something bigger. Something more. A love that doesn't need to fit anyone else's idea of what's normal. A love that makes space for all of us, exactly as we are." I pause, scanning their faces. "People call this impossible. But standing here with all five of you, I've never believed in anything more."

I turn slightly, facing each of them in turn. I need them to understand that these words aren't just being spoken out loud. They're meant for each of them, individually and with intention.

First, to Archer. His eyes are locked on mine, unwavering.

"To Archer. You are my quiet strength. My compass when I've lost the map. The steady presence I've leaned on more times than I can count. You don't need to say much for me to feel how deeply you love me. You show it in every action, every choice. I vow to be your harbor, your peace, your constant. The place you can always come back to, no matter how rough the waters get."

He doesn't move. Doesn't blink. But I see it—the slight clench of his jaw, the barely-there twitch at the corner of his mouth. The kind of thing most people would miss. But not me. I know him too well. I feel it like a current between us.

I turn to Spencer. His eyes meet mine with warmth, a familiar spark of heat flickering just beneath the surface. A soft flush blooms across his cheekbones.

"To Spencer. The whisper in my ear. The calm when everything in me feels like noise. I vow to meet you at the edge of every challenge. To keep choosing you, even when it's hard. To laugh with you, lean on you, and let you lean on me. You bring balance when I tip too far, and lightness when the weight gets too heavy. I'm better with you. And I'm so damn lucky I get to walk through this life beside you."

His smile grows, bright and open. His entire face softens. A breeze lifts a lock of hair across his forehead, and he doesn't bother to push it away. His eyes are shining now, completely unguarded, and his shoulders rise slightly, like the weight of my words has landed in the exact place he needed them to. Spencer lets go of my hands slowly, like he's reluctant to break the moment. I hold his gaze for one more beat, my chest full to bursting, then shift to the man beside him.

Next is Jamie. His usual spark is still there, but it's quieter now, burning lower, steadier. His eyes shine with unshed tears, and for once, he's completely still—no twitching, no bouncing on the balls of his feet. Just all of him, focused entirely on me.

"To Jamie," I begin, my lips already tipping up. "My fire. My joy. The spark I never saw coming but can't live without."

His mouth curves like he knows what's coming but doesn't want to miss a word.

"You make everything brighter. Louder. Better. I vow to laugh at your terrible jokes and throw mine right back. To dance in the kitchen, to kiss you in the rain, to follow wherever your wild heart wants to go next."

A laugh bursts from him, wet-eyed and crooked-mouthed, and it hits me square in the chest.

"I vow to never take your energy for granted. To be your quiet when the world gets too loud. And to keep giving you reasons to make me laugh, every day, for the rest of our lives."

He grins through the tears, that devastatingly charming smile crinkling the corners of his eyes. His fingers twitch at his sides like he's one second from grabbing me and crushing his mouth to mine, ceremony be damned. He's holding back—barely—and it's the most tender kind of restraint I've ever seen.

And now, Liam. He doesn't speak, doesn't move, just watches me with that quiet intensity that never asks for attention but holds it all the same. Warmth rolls off him like heat from sun-warmed stone. Even the way he stands—tilted slightly forward, hat casting a shadow across his brow—feels like gravity leaning toward me.

"To Liam," I say, my voice softer now. "My light. My joy. The man who crossed oceans with his heart wide open. I vow to build a home with you that holds everything we've carried and everything we're still becoming."

His eyes are locked on mine, completely still.

"I promise to listen when it would be easier to run. To love you with the same quiet devotion you show every single day. You make me feel safe without ever making me small, and I vow to never take that for granted."

He smiles then, slow and radiant, like sunrise over water. A single tear slips down his cheek, catching the last of the sunset before dripping off his chin. But he doesn't break. He doesn't look away. He just glows. And in that light, I swear I can see our whole life waiting.

And finally, Sam.

Always composed. Always precise. But now, that composure looks delicate—like something fine and glass-thin, light catching in every fracture. The pulse at his throat flutters just under the skin, visible in a way I don't think he realizes. His hands are still, but I can feel the tension radiating off him like a held breath.

"To Sam," I begin, my voice low, my heart aching in the best way. "The one who sees ten steps ahead while the rest of us are still spinning in circles. My order in the chaos. My sharpest thought."

His lips press together, and I see the faintest tremble along his jawline.

"I vow to trust the strength behind your restraint. To lean into the steadiness you offer, and to never mistake your silence for distance. You are my elegance. Command. Hunger disguised as restraint. I see everything you hold back—and everything you give."

I shift, drawing in a breath that feels different—fuller, heavier, like it has to move through every version of who I've been to reach the surface. This part isn't about any one of them. It's about all of them. My gaze trails across their faces, not as separate people but as one whole, impossibly complex and deeply right. What we have isn't just random connections, it's a constellation. Something vast and intentional, each piece holding the others in place.

"To all of you," I say, the words anchoring themselves in the quiet. "I vow to love without fear. To remember every day that what we have is rare and extraordinary. And to protect it. To fight for our joy, even when it's hard. I choose each of you fully, without hesitation, and I choose the us we've built—imperfect, beautiful, real. The world might call it complicated, but we know better. This isn't a compromise. This is love. Multiplied, not divided."

A hush settles over everything. Even the sea goes still, waves softening against the pilings beneath our feet, as if the earth itself is leaning in to listen. The only sounds are breath—mine, theirs, the gathered few who've stood witness to every step of this story. Father Calum clears his throat, but not before swallowing hard, like he's trying to steady his emotions before they spill over. His composure wavers, just briefly, a crack in the polished surface. His eyes glint with unshed tears, his expression open and faithful, like he knows he's not just witnessing a union, but something sacred. Something that rewrites what love can look like.

"The rings, please," Father Calum says, his voice rougher than before, thick with feeling he doesn't bother to hide.

Millie steps forward, drawing five simple platinum bands from a hidden pocket in her dress. The metal catches the golden light, flaring like small stars in her open palm. The symbolism hits hard—my best friend, the one who's held my hand through every heartbreak, every leap, now literally holding the symbols of this wildly untraditional, deeply intentional love. She passes them to Father Calum, who cups them in both hands, murmuring a quiet blessing over the circles of metal before offering them to the men standing beside me.

One by one, they step forward.

Archer is first. His hands are sure, careful, the roughness of his fingertips unmistakable as he slides the first ring onto my finger. It rests at the base, snug and certain, the warmth of his skin a reminder of every steady thing he's ever given me.

Spencer follows. His touch is softer, but no less sure. He brushes my knuckle with his thumb in a gesture so fleeting I nearly miss it—but it lingers. Like him.

Jamie's hands tremble slightly as he adds the third ring, his confidence cracking open beneath the weight of the moment. His fingers graze my palm as he places it, a soft, slow drag that sends a current of heat racing up my arm. His voice catches on the vow, and I feel it in my chest.

Liam's warmth comes next. He cups my hand as he slides the fourth band into place, his thumb sweeping across the back of my hand as if he can smooth the pulse jumping beneath my skin. He doesn't let go right away. Just holds on. Like always.

Then Sam steps forward. Composed, as always. Precise, polished, unshakably sure. He takes my hand with a confidence that doesn't waver, doesn't ask—it simply is. The ring slips onto my finger in one smooth, practiced motion, like he's done it a thousand times in his mind. His fingers are cool against my skin, steady as stone, and though his expression gives nothing away, I feel him. In the weight of his gaze. In the certainty of his touch. Quiet, but absolute.

Then Lach steps forward. From his jacket pocket, he draws a small wooden box, the mahogany polished to a soft sheen, a tiny compass rose carved into the lid. He opens it slowly, revealing five matching bands—subtle variations in tone and texture, but clearly part of the same story.

I take them one by one.

Archer's is first. Hammered metal, imperfect on purpose, rugged like the coastline inked into his skin. It warms quickly in my fingers, like it knows where it belongs.

Spencer's comes next. Polished in the center, brushed along the edges—refined, balanced, exactly him. I slide it into place, his fingers steady beneath mine even as his eyes glisten.

Jamie's ring is next. It's simple at first glance, but there's a single groove etched around the middle—barely noticeable unless you're looking. A quiet, intentional break in the pattern. Just like him. Classic on the outside, but always holding something unexpected beneath the surface. He grins the moment the ring is in place, turning his hand slightly like he's already imagining how it will look when he's touching my body.

Liam's has the faintest hint of rose gold, a soft warmth that glows against his sun-kissed skin. It slips into place as easily as he came into my life. He takes my hand after, pressing it between both of his, his smile tender and unguarded.

Sam's is last. Classic. Clean. Understated in a way that speaks of confidence rather than simplicity. The metal shines as I guide it over his knuckle. He doesn't look at it—just at me.

And then it's done. Five rings on my finger. Five rings now on theirs.

When the last one is in place, Father Calum smiles wide, the kind of smile that crinkles the corners of his eyes and shines with a kind of joy that can't be faked. But instead of offering the final words, he lifts his hand gently, holding the moment in the palm of it. Not yet. There is one more piece. One final promise.

"And now," Father Calum says, "we seal these vows and rings with the ancient Celtic tradition of handfasting."

Lach steps forward, holding a coiled length of rope I recognize immediately. It's from the Master Baiter, weathered and thick, its braided strands still carrying the salt of past storms. Faint streaks of blue paint cling to the fibers, a history embedded deep in the cord. Years of hauling, of anchoring, of holding steady through wind and wave. This rope has seen it all.

"This rope," Father Calum explains, "symbolizes the bond that will unite your six lives through whatever weather may come."

I swallow hard. The significance is almost too much. That rope has held my boat through more storms than I can count. It's been a tether between survival and surrender. And now, it will bind us together. A piece of my past becoming the knot at the center of our future.

"In the Celtic tradition," Father Calum continues, "handfasting marks the symbolic binding of lives. Today, with six hearts joining as one, we adapt this ritual to reflect the shape of your union. Something ancient, made new."

We form a circle, facing inward, each of us extending our left hands into the center, hands that now bear the rings we just exchanged. There's a beat of hesitation as we figure out how to make the shape work. A ripple of laughter escapes, light and genuine, breaking the tension in exactly the way we need. Jamie lifts his eyebrows at me, his green eyes full of mischief, while Sam's mouth twitches with restrained amusement.

"Be still," Archer murmurs, but there's a curve at the corner of his mouth that gives him away.

Father Calum begins wrapping the rope, one loop at a time around our six wrists. The fibers drag gently across my skin, rough and familiar. The rope smells like salt and tar and years at sea—scents that shaped my childhood and carved themselves into my memory. But now, wound around all of us, it carries new meaning. It doesn't feel binding. It feels grounding.

"With this cord," Father Calum intones, "I bind these six souls into one shared life. May your hands be blessed. May they always find each other in darkness and in light. May they hold fast through tempests, and rest gently in peace. Let them lift, steady, and carry when the weight is too much alone. May these hands never let go, no matter the storm."

He makes the final loop, securing the knot.

"These are the hands," he continues, looking at each of us in turn, "that will wipe tears from your eyes—tears of sorrow and of joy. The hands that will soothe in sickness, hold fast in hardship, and guide each other toward your shared dreams."

The wind picks up, just a little. The scent of heather drifts through the salt air. My hair shifts across my shoulders, and I feel the rope pull slightly as we all adjust to the movement, already adapting to the change, just as we'll need to.

"Look at your hands," Father Calum says. "Joined now by this rope. Remember this moment, when six separate paths became one shared destination."

We stand in stillness. Just breathing. I memorize everything—the coarse texture of the rope against my skin. Archer's fingers brushing mine, steady and firm. Spencer's hand trembling just slightly, his thumb grazing the edge of my palm. Jamie's restless energy held in check, buzzing through his touch like electricity. Liam's warmth, grounding and constant. Sam's fingers interlaced with mine, elegant and strong, holding steady like a vow of their own.

"As you are bound by this cord," Father Calum says, "so may your lives be bound in love."

He gently slides the rope free, leaving the final loop intact, and places it in my hand.

"Keep this as a reminder that what has been bound here today is not easily undone."

It sits in my palm, heavy with both history and hope. I curl my fingers around it, grounding myself in its roughness, its realness.

Father Calum smiles, this time with no restraint, joy radiating from every line on his face. "By the power vested in me, I now pronounce you husbands and wife." He pauses, eyes bright. "You may seal your vows with a kiss."

They move together, no hesitation, no doubt, surrounding me like I'm the center of their solar system, every point of light drawn into perfect orbit.

Archer's lips find mine first. Steady. Certain. The way he always is. His kiss is firm, anchoring, the press of his mouth a vow he doesn't need words to make. One hand cradles the back of my neck, fingers sliding into my hair, and the rasp of his stubble against my skin sends shivers down my spine. It's not showy. It's not loud. It's him, and it's everything.

Spencer is next. He leans in with a glint in his eye, nipping play-fully at my bottom lip before kissing me deep, slow, sure. His hands bracket my waist, grounding me as if to say, I've got you. Always. There's heat in it, but more than that, there's trust. Promise. A spark that never stops catching.

Jamie's kiss is pure motion. He all but sweeps me off my feet, laughing through the contact like the joy is too big for his body. His mouth captures mine with wild, unfiltered affection, his tongue tracing the seam of my lips in a way that's cocky, sweet, and utterly Jamie. I smile against him, breathless and dazed.

Then Liam. He kisses me like a prayer. His lips are warm, unhurried, full of reverence. His hands cradle my face like he's holding something holy. The kiss deepens, just a little, just enough to steal my breath and hand it back to me reshaped. I feel sunlight pour through me.

And finally, Sam. He's last, but nothing about him is an afterthought. His kiss is refined heat, controlled, devastating, intentional. One hand curves around my hip, the other cradling the back of my skull as he pulls me in, slow and certain, every movement controlled. There's elegance in it. Strength. A kind of focus that makes the world fall away.

A cheer erupts, rising like music behind us. Jamie's laugh breaks through first, wild and bright, followed by Isla's joyful whoop. Millie's dabbing her eyes, trying and failing to hold it together. And Lach, still the least sentimental man I know, is somehow both laughing and crying. Charlie stands beside him, beaming as she gently dabs at his face with a tissue.

Then Liam lifts me off the dock with a joyful shout, spinning me in a full circle, my dress flaring out around us like a burst of light. The world blurs—sea, sky, guests—all of it streaking past in a dizzying flash of movement and color. I laugh, head thrown back as I lose myself in his arms.

Then I'm passed to each of the others for another round of embraces—Spencer's arms encircling me with enthusiastic tenderness, his scent wrapping around me like a familiar blanket; Jamie's exuberant hug lifting me clear off the dock, his laughter vibrating through both our bodies; Sam's more reserved but no less emotional embrace, his arms strong despite their elegance, fingers splayed wide against my back; and finally Archer's solid warmth, his arms creating a sanctuary that feels like home, his heart thundering against mine through the layers of fabric separating us.

My hair has come loose, wildflowers scattering around my shoulders. I've never felt more content than I do in this moment. Salt air fills my lungs, mingling with the familiar scent of five men who now belong to me as completely as I belong to them. Tears blur my vision, but I don't try to stop them—they're as much a part of this perfect moment as the laughter bubbling up from somewhere deep inside me. For the first time in my life, I feel utterly complete, as if every broken piece of me has finally found its home in the shelter of these five extraordinary men.

EPILOGUE
THE HONEYMOON

The airport is laughably small—less a transportation hub and more a glorified waiting room with delusions of grandeur. One door, one counter, one security line with a guard who looks like he was supposed to retire in the 90s. I've flown out of here before. But never like this. Never with five husbands, twelve over-stuffed suitcases, and no idea where we're going.

"You're seriously not telling me until we're boarding?" I huff, narrowing my eyes at Spencer, who's casually looping our baggage tags like we're just popping down to Glasgow and not potentially flying halfway across the world.

"That's literally the definition of a surprise honeymoon, Sugar." His eyes crinkle at the corners when he smiles, fingers grazing mine as he flips the final tag. The touch is fleeting, but it sparks through me like it always does—unignorable, precise, addictive.

I roll my eyes, mostly for the performance. "Would've been good to know what climate I was packing for."

"Oh, come on." Archer's voice cuts clean and direct as he hands over our boarding passes to the wide-eyed check-in attendant. "We made sure you packed what you would need."

Because of course they did. All week, they'd been stealthily guiding my wardrobe choices with the subtlety of overgrown toddlers trying to keep a secret. Jamie "accidentally" laid out a stack of swimsuits. Liam told me to bring "something slinky." Sammy requested I pack "whatever makes you feel powerful and devastatingly difficult to resist." Now, with all five of them looking way too pleased with themselves, it all makes too much sense.

The attendant stares at the six of us like we've walked straight out of an adult movie. "So... you're all traveling together?"

"Honeymoon," Jamie chirps, tossing an arm around my shoulders. His dimples are criminal, his grin wide enough to swallow the moment whole.

"All of you?" she breathes, professionalism cracking like a dropped champagne glass.

"All of us," he says, the corners of his mouth tugging up like he's hoping charm will outrun the awkward.

Her eyes flit to my left hand. Five matching bands. Five promises made. My single finger weighted with all of them. "Well... congratulations." It sounds like a question, but she stamps our tickets anyway, smile just this side of stunned. "Your flight to London departs in forty minutes. From there, you'll connect to—"

"Don't spoil it," Liam cuts in smoothly, charm turned up to eleven. "It's a surprise for the bride."

She blinks once, then nods. "Of course. Enjoy your, um... journey."

Security is basically one guy and a metal detector with trust issues. Sammy dips beside me, his voice a quiet grin against my neck. "She'll be telling this story until she dies."

"Then maybe we should give her something worth talking about," I say, and then I kiss him.

And I do mean kiss him.

His lips are soft. His hand is steady on my back. He leans into the kiss like he's done it a thousand times and plans to do it a thousand more. When I pull away, his eyes are glazed and a little stunned. It makes me bite down a grin.

I keep going. Liam. Spencer. Archer. Each kiss is fast and warm and full of something that makes my chest ache. Not to be outdone, Jamie grabs me with a grin and dips me low, like we're starring in a two-person musical. Somewhere to our left, a retired couple claps like we've just made their whole day.

We settle into a corner of the waiting room, where the light slants soft through tall windows and everything feels a little too quiet. The chairs are clean but stiff, the vending machine hums like it's trying to fill the silence. Our flight's delayed. My nerves are stretched thin, and the not-knowing is starting to itch under my skin.

"Just one hint," I plead, aiming my poutiest pout at Archer. He's always been the weakest link when it comes to denying me things. I rest a palm flat against his chest, right over his heart, and feel it speed up beneath my touch. His eyes dip to my lips, flicker with heat, then pull back to cool detachment like he's completely unaffected.

"Soon," he says softly. "You'll know soon enough, Nel."

"I'm going to combust," I tell them all, flopping dramatically into a hard chair between Liam and Spencer. "My tombstone's going to read, 'Died of unanswered questions and poor impulse control.'"

Liam's arm slides around my shoulders, pulling me in until our hips are pressed together. "I promise it'll be worth the wait, Darlin'," he says, his voice all warm Southern honey, like he's trying to melt me straight into the floor.

I rest my head against his shoulder for a beat, letting myself breathe, letting the rhythm of all of them—close, steady, real—settle into my bones. There's laughter. Jamie steals half my snack. Spencer starts a heated debate about how middle seats are human rights violations. Archer pretends not to listen, but he's definitely cataloging every word. And Sammy watches me like he's already fast-forwarded to the part of the honeymoon where the clothes are optional.

Time slips. The announcement crackles. Boarding begins.

I'm wedged between Jamie and Archer—chaos and control, mischief and stoicism. It takes three minutes post-takeoff for Jamie's hand to find my thigh. His fingers trail lazy, sinfully light patterns, creeping higher with every pass.

"Behave," I whisper, not moving a muscle to stop him.

"We're married," he murmurs, his dimples making an appearance.

His breath is hot against my ear. "This is perfectly respectable now, Penella."

Archer notices. Of course he does. His gaze flicks down, tracks Jamie's hand. And then, God help me, he shifts in his seat, blocking the view from the aisle like he's giving Jamie permission to keep going.

And that? That's what ruins me.

Because I know Archer. I know the restraint he wears like a second skin. And seeing him choose this, choose to let someone else tease me while he watches, while he controls what everyone else sees, it sets something low in me humming, hungry.

A throat clears beside us.

"Can I get you anything?" the flight attendant asks, smiling like she definitely saw Jamie's hand.

Jamie shifts, barely. His palm lifts from my thigh, but not by much. Archer adjusts in his seat like nothing's happened, like his pupils aren't blown wide and his knee isn't still pressed into mine.

"Water," I say, voice rough, mouth dry. I can't look at either of them.

She gives me the water and moves on, eyes flicking once between the three of us before pretending none of it happened.

Jamie lets out a quiet breath. Archer's fingers drift along the inside of my arm, slow and certain, like he's staking a quiet claim. I take a sip and set the cup down with a hand that doesn't feel entirely steady.

The cabin lights dim. The air is too warm, too still. My body can't decide whether it's buzzing or burning out. I can still feel Jamie's touch, like it left something behind—heat or static or a fingerprint pressed into my skin.

Archer leans back, eyes closed like he's done playing. But I know better. The game doesn't end when he goes quiet. That's when it starts.

Jamie shifts closer, his thigh pressed against mine, heat bleeding through my leggings. Archer's arm slides behind me, his knuckles grazing the side of my neck—light enough to pretend it's nothing. But it isn't. It never is.

I close my eyes, leaning into Archer's shoulder. Just for a second.

And then I'm gone. Not gently. Not gracefully. Just out—head tipped, lips parted, body slack between them.

The next thing I know, we're on the ground, taxiing to the gate.

I blink awake to harsh overhead lights and that sterile blast of recycled air—too cold, too bright. The smell of jet fuel and burnt coffee hits me before the captain's voice does, welcoming us to London.

And then, we're off the plane. Moving fast.

I'm not sure who grabbed my bag or how we got to the terminal, only that the floor is unforgiving under my feet and the world feels one step ahead of me.

We skid to a stop beneath the departures board just as Spencer throws an arm out in front of me like I'm about to wander into oncoming traffic.

"Don't look," he says, which of course means I immediately crane around him.

"Nairobi?" The word punches out of me, jagged and breathless, as I catch a flash of it over Liam's shoulder before he grips my elbow and starts dragging me toward our gate.

"So much for the surprise," Sammy says, not even pretending to look sorry. There's a grin pulling at his mouth. Crooked, smug, entirely unrepentant.

"Wait—Africa?" I gasp. "You're taking me to Africa?"

"Kenya. Tanzania. Maybe a little Rwanda," he says, casual as hell, but his eyes are lit up like Christmas.

"We're going on safari, Nel," Archer says quietly, his voice low and sure like he's been saving those words for the perfect moment. "Two full weeks."

I stop walking. Just freeze in the middle of Heathrow like the floor might give way beneath me. A safari. It's been at the top of my impossible list for years. The kind of thing I whispered about once, maybe twice, in the kind of voice people use for childhood dreams they never expect to come true.

"How did you—"

"You said it that night we got tipsy by the bonfire," Spencer cuts in, stepping close, his hand sliding over my lower back. His fingers are wide and warm, grounding. "Said you wanted to see elephants. In the wild."

"We started planning the next morning," Liam says, his voice all sunshine and mischief, like he still can't believe they pulled it off. "Been saving for months, Darlin'."

And that's what gets me.

Not the destination. Not the secrecy. Not even the fact that they managed to keep it quiet this long.

It's the image of them sneaking around behind my back in the most ridiculous, tender way. Whispering in corners. Pooling their money. Arguing over logistics. Probably building a spreadsheet with color-coded tabs and a Google Doc titled something like "Penelope's Safari of Love (Do Not Let Her See This)."

My throat tightens before I can stop it. The kind of pressure that rises too fast to hide. I blink hard, try to laugh it off, but the tears come anyway, silent and sudden, like they've been waiting in the wings.

Liam doesn't say a word. Just pulls me in, one strong arm around my waist, the other cradling the back of my head like he's shielding something fragile.

"You okay, Darlin'?" he murmurs, lips brushing the top of my hair.

I nod against his chest, even though I'm not. Not really. Because how do you explain the feeling of being loved so thoroughly, so completely, it knocks the breath out of you?

"We're going to have the best time," he says quietly. Like he already knows every perfect moment waiting for us on another continent, and he can't wait for me to see them too.

And I believe him. Even through the mess of nerves and jet lag and snotty tears. I believe him.

Because if there's one thing these men have taught me, it's that the best times don't always start pretty. Sometimes they start like this—on shaky legs, in the middle of a crowded terminal, with your heart cracked wide open and someone you love holding the pieces like they were always meant to.

The flight to Nairobi is eleven hours of sardine-can suffering. Economy class. No upgrades. Just elbows and thighs and regret. I'm wedged between Archer and Liam, limbs tangled, tray tables mocking us with their uselessness, while the other three sprawl behind us—knees in our backs, commentary in our ears.

Everyone copes differently.

Archer whips out a topographical map of East Africa like we're prepping for a summit climb instead of a honeymoon. His brow furrows, fingers tracing imagined paths through mountains and valleys like he's got to memorize the terrain before we land. But when our knees bump, he doesn't pull away. He leans in—quiet, warm, steady. His skin brushes mine in the exact kind of way that makes promises without saying a word.

Liam can't sit still. He's vibrating with barely contained excitement, asking rapid-fire questions about lions and leopards and whether we'll get to hold a baby cheetah. "It's gotta be different from Australia, yeah?" he says, adjusting his seat again. "They both have deadly stuff, but this is, like... romantic deadly."

Behind us, Spencer produces an alarming number of snack containers from his carry-on like a culinary magician. "Just a few things I threw together," he says when I thank him, like he didn't clearly spend an entire evening roasting nuts and wrapping short-bread in parchment paper. He feeds me a piece and watches the way I chew like he's studying a rare species in the wild. I'm pretty sure I am his in-flight entertainment.

Jamie's already best friends with the flight attendants. We've been handed glasses of complimentary champagne and a bottle "just in case," because apparently someone told them we're celebrating a very special honeymoon. I don't ask who. His hands find my shoulders, kneading the tension out in slow, practiced circles while whispering things at my ear that make vowels suddenly feel like a foreign concept.

And then there's Sammy. He's taken over his entire tray table with guidebooks, folded maps, and laminated checklists. "I've categorized everything by habitat and likelihood of sighting," he says, poking his head through the gap between our seats. "There's also a spreadsheet with timestamps and behavioral annotations."

"You made a wildlife spreadsheet?" I ask, fighting a smile.

He lifts his chin, utterly unbothered. "Obviously."

Somewhere over the Mediterranean, my head tips onto Archer's shoulder. He doesn't move, just lets me rest, his lips brushing my temple so softly I almost convince myself I imagined it. Liam's hand finds mine when the plane jolts, fingers lacing tight, anchoring me until my pulse settles. Spencer leans forward without a word and trades his dessert for mine, like he's been keeping track of what I love even when I forget.

Even here—cramped, sleep-deprived, shoulder-to-shoulder with strangers—we move as one. Tethered. A constellation strung together by touch and instinct. Every one of them in orbit around me, and me around them.

When the plane begins to descend, I lift my head from Archer's shoulder, my cheek creased and warm where I'd been resting. He glances down, eyes soft, then leans back just enough so I can twist in my seat and peer past him.

It's not a perfect view—just a slice of sky and a blur of land beyond the smudged plastic—but it's enough.

My breath catches.

The earth below glows red and gold, vast and untamed. It feels ancient. Alive. Like it's been waiting. Like it's been mine, somehow, all along.

And then we're on the ground.

The moment we step outside, the air hits me like a wave, thick, spiced, sun-warmed. Alive in a way that makes everything inside me sit up and listen. The scent of dust and diesel clings to the breeze, layered with something sweet and unfamiliar blooming just out of reach.

It wraps around me, settles into my pores. My skin drinks it in like it's been waiting for this exact heat, this exact moment.

We move through the airport in a quiet daze—sleep-hazed, sun-drenched, sticky with travel.

Immigration is a blur of stamps, scanned faces, and politely arched eyebrows at our embarrassingly tall stack of passports. And then—

"Honeymoon Party of Six," reads a cardboard sign, held aloft by a man standing beside a safari vehicle that looks like it could crush a Jeep just for fun.

"I am Joseph," he says, smiling like the sun's a little jealous of him. "Welcome to Kenya. I'll be taking you to Giraffe Manor for the night."

"Giraffe Manor?" I echo, whipping around to face the guys, who are, quite suddenly, all deeply fascinated by their shoelaces.

"Saved the best for... first," Spencer says with a wink, his voice low and amused as he steps in without hesitation. He lifts me into the car like it's instinct—like his hands belong at my waist. Strong. Certain. Careful in that way that still manages to make me feel a little breathless.

My inhale stutters before I can catch it.

"A little bit of luxury," he murmurs, leaning in just enough for his lips to brush my ear, "to start the trip off right, Sugar."

The drive through Nairobi is a heady collision of sound, scent, and color, this living, breathing organism that doesn't seem to sleep, even long past midnight. Motorbikes slice through traffic like sparks from a flint, their headlights darting and swerving, their riders balancing passengers, parcels, and even the occasional chicken. Street vendors shout their wares under bare bulbs that flicker in the heat, the stalls riotous with color. Bright fabrics, glossy fruit, baskets, bottles. The air is dense with spice, exhaust, and music that thrums low and deep from passing cars.

Then, slowly, the chaos falls behind us. We turn onto a road that narrows and curves beneath a canopy of trees. Headlights sweep over darting shapes—a flash of a mongoose, the thump-thump of a startled hare's escape. The city slips away like a coat shrugged from tired shoulders.

And then, like something summoned from a dream, the manor appears.

It rises from the dark like the final page of a storybook: ivy-clad stone, arched windows glowing gold, all quiet elegance and old-world grace. A 1930s mansion folded into the wild, like it's always belonged there. Colonial architecture meets African night.

"This is where we're staying?" My voice comes out thinner than I mean it to, stretched by awe as Joseph parks and starts unloading our bags.

"Just for tonight," Sammy says, his fingers sliding into mine like second nature. His voice is soft, a little breathless. "We wanted to start the trip with something unforgettable."

They guide me up the steps, past the check-in desk gleaming with polished wood and overflowing flowers, down a hallway that smells like citrus peel and old stone.

Our suite is breathtaking. Tall ceilings and wide-planked floors. Worn leather armchairs circle a stone fireplace, the kind that probably crackles to life the second the temperature drops. French doors swing open onto a shadowed balcony, the curtains caught in a slow, lazy dance. Two king beds pushed together under one impossibly soft-looking duvet, like they already knew we'd need all the space and none of the distance.

I want to explore. To run my fingers along the carved trim, open every drawer, find out what kind of soap they've left tucked beside the basin. I want to soak it all in, to remember every scent, every texture.

But the tiredness settles in my bones, quiet and insistent.

I shower on autopilot, steam and lavender clinging to my skin. One of them, Sammy, I think, pulls me gently toward the bed, and I let go. Sink into the warmth and the weight and the steady rhythm of breath around me.

Five bodies pressed in around me. Too warm. Too close. Exactly right. Someone's breath against the back of my neck. A hand curled loosely around my hip. Fingers still threaded with mine.

I shift once, barely. Sink into the mattress. Into them. Into sleep.

No thoughts. No words.

Just this.

I wake to Archer's voice, low but urgent. "Nel. You need to see this."

I blink against the light, the haze of sleep heavy behind my eyes. He's at the French doors, open now, bathed in the soft spill of early morning. The others are already out there, gathered in a hush that hums with wonder.

"What?" I croak, dragging a sheet around me and padding to join them.

And then I see.

Giraffes.

Dozens of them.

They move across the dew-slick lawn like they've stepped out of a dream. Graceful and surreal, each step impossibly quiet. Their legs stretch impossibly long, necks moving in slow, careful arcs as they wander through the grass. They're close enough that I can see their lashes. Close enough that I could count the spots on their hides, each one sunlit gold edged in shadow.

One stops. Turns her head. Looks right at us. Her eyes—dark and endless—hold mine with a calm so complete it steals the air from my lungs. Like she knows something I don't. Like she's always known.

"Oh my God," I whisper, gripping the balcony railing.

"Joseph said they come every morning," Spencer says, slipping behind me, his hand firm on my waist. His palm spreads over the thin cotton of my nightshirt, the heat of him bleeding into my spine. "The manor's been feeding them for generations."

"We'll eat with them in an hour," Liam adds, his grin stretching wide. "Like, with them, Darlin'. Heads-through-the-windows kind of breakfast."

I watch as more giraffes emerge from the line of acacia trees, graceful and unhurried. One stretches high, plucking leaves from a tree with casual precision. Two of them nuzzle, their necks twining for a moment before they part.

I lean back against Spencer's chest, his arm curling around me, and exhale slowly. "This is already the best honeymoon in history. And we've been here, what—eight hours?"

He laughs against my hair, and somewhere behind us, someone mutters about needing ten more minutes of sleep and stronger coffee.

We rally. Barely. And make our way downstairs, still sleep-soft and rumpled, following the smell of toast and something sweet.

. . .

Breakfast feels like something out of a fever dream. We're seated at a long table beneath tall windows thrown wide to the garden. Sunlight streams in, warm and soft and golden. We've just taken our first sips of coffee when a giraffe appears, its enormous head sliding through the window like it owns the place.

A staff member hands me a small bowl of pellets and gestures toward my palm. "Flat," she says gently.

I offer a few, fingers trembling slightly. The giraffe's lips are velvet and surprisingly deft as it gathers the food. Its eyes hold mine, huge and amber and impossibly gentle, and in that moment, everything else falls away. The hum of conversation, the clink of china, the sense of being on Earth at all.

Spencer steps up beside me slowly. "You're a beautiful beast," he murmurs to the animal, offering pellets with steady hands.

Jamie bursts into laughter when a bold one snatches a piece of toast right off his plate. The sound cracks through the air, bright and buoyant, and somehow makes the whole room feel warmer. He strokes the giraffe's neck with both hands, grinning like they've been best friends since childhood.

Liam leans into the moment, chatting to them in that soft, melodic way of his, full of easy charm and wonder. It's like he was born knowing how to talk to something three times his size.

Sammy, naturally, is already taking mental notes. "That one's reticulated. See how tight the pattern is?" he says, nodding toward the window, eyes flicking between spots. "Definitely female. Look at the ossicone spacing."

And Archer, my quiet, controlled Archer, just stands there with a pellet in his open palm. Still. Breath held. Eyes wide like he's trying to memorize every second. When a younger giraffe leans in to take it, he exhales, slow and soft, a smile tugging at the corner of his mouth.

"They're like something from another world," he murmurs, voice rough with awe.

And all I can think is, so is this.

· · ·

After breakfast, we wander the grounds with a guide who introduces herself as Elizabeth. She walks barefoot and speaks like someone who's known this land her whole life. Warthogs trot past with their tails held high like antennae, absurdly proud of how ugly they are. Dik-diks blink at us from the brush like wide-eyed woodland sprites. Brightly plumed birds dart through the trees, flitting flashes of color I can't name. Everything feels enchanted, like we've stepped sideways into a version of the world where wonder is the default setting.

The air is cooler than I expected, laced with the scent of blooming trees and something earthier beneath it—dust, bark, the hush of heat still waiting to rise.

"I can't believe this is real," I whisper as we pause beneath the shade of an ancient acacia. In the distance, a giraffe strips leaves from the topmost branches like it's harvesting stars.

"As real as it gets, Sugar." Spencer's hand finds mine, warm and sure. His thumb starts tracing circles in my palm, lazy and familiar.

We have lunch out on the terrace, a table set with pressed linens and fresh flowers, the kind of meal that feels too beautiful to eat. Grilled fish, stewed lentils, something with mango that makes me groan out loud and earns me five very different looks from across the table. Someone feeds me a bite with their fingers. Someone else wipes juice from my lip with their thumb. It's intimate and sun-soaked and a little unreal.

Afterward, we're told to rest. "Nap before dinner," Elizabeth says with a wink, like she already knows we won't.

She's right.

The moment our suite door clicks shut behind us, something shifts. The air goes still, heavier somehow. The golden afternoon light slants across the floor, catching motes in the air like suspended fireflies. Five pairs of eyes lock onto me. Five bodies humming with need, strung tight from days of waiting.

"It's been too long," Archer says, voice rough and low. There's no patience left in him, just hunger, bare and unfiltered. He takes a slow step forward, then another.

"It's been two days," I manage, but my voice wavers. Because I'm already soaked. Already aching. Already theirs.

"I haven't thought of anything else," Spencer mutters, jaw tight. He crowds in close, his breath hot at my ear. "All day I've wanted to pin you down and taste you until you scream."

"Those pants," Liam groans, voice thick with heat. "They've been driving me insane. That ass, Darlin'—you have no idea."

"Too much talking," Jamie cuts in, desire sharpening his words. "I need you. Now."

Sammy's eyes trail over me, slow and assessing. "Bed," he says, already pulling his shirt over his head. "Now."

They close in. Archer reaches me first, his hands sliding under my top, dragging it up and over my head with a sound that's part growl, part groan. The shirt hits the floor. Cool air meets overheated skin. My nipples strain against the lace of my bra, hard and aching.

"Fuck," Liam breathes. "Look at you."

Spencer's grip tightens on my hips just as Archer drops to his knees, working my jeans open with jerky movements. The button pops. The zipper slides. His fingers graze my thighs, rough and tender, dragging my soaked panties down with a low sound that curls heat through my core.

"Sugar," Spencer says, his mouth brushing the curve of my neck. "Let me taste you."

Jamie's already on the floor, hands sliding up my legs, eyes blown wide. "I'm going to absolutely wreck you," he promises, voice barely more than a growl. And I believe him.

Behind me, Sammy unhooks my bra with one smooth flick. It falls away, and his hands are on me, palms full, thumbs teasing until my knees threaten to give.

"Mine," he says, voice a low scrape against my ear.

We tumble toward the bed, all mouths and hands and clothes torn off in a frenzy. Archer's tattoo flashes. Liam's thighs flex as denim falls. Spencer's chest rises, slick with sweat. Jamie stumbles trying to undress, swearing. Sammy's already naked—dark skin flushed with heat, every inch of him hard and stunning.

Archer props himself against the headboard, his arousal already slick and waiting.

"I need to be inside you," he says, voice rough. "Need you around me. I've been thinking about it since we boarded the plane."

I straddle him backward, my thighs trembling as I sink down slowly, guided by his hands. He spreads me open, fingers rough where I want them to be, gentle where I need it most. The cool slide of preparation makes me jolt, breath catching in my throat.

Then he pushes in.

The stretch burns—sharp, breathless, perfect. My body fights it for half a second, then gives, greedy and aching. He's thick, and I feel every inch as he fills me, slow and steady, like he knows exactly how to break me open.

"That's it," he groans, voice gone gravel-deep. "Open for me. Let me in."

Spencer kneels in front of me, heat radiating off his skin. He grips my thighs, forcing them wider, until I'm bared completely.

"God, look at you," he growls, staring between my legs like he's starving. "We're going to ruin you, Sugar. You won't remember anything but the way we touch you."

Liam shuffles to my side, hand wrapped around the base of his arousal. "Open up, Darlin'," he says, and there's something tight and trembling behind the steady fire in his eyes. I part my lips. He pushes in slowly, groaning as my mouth closes around him.

"Fuck," he breathes, low and filthy. "That mouth. That tongue. So perfect."

Sammy is beside me, pressed close at my hip, his skin slick with sweat and heat. His arousal is heavy in my hand, and I stroke him in slow, firm pulls that make his breath stutter. He moans low, hips jerking into my fist like he can't help it.

Jamie leans in from behind, kissing Sammy hard—hot and messy and hungry. His hand slides down the long line of Sammy's spine, fingers already slick. He finds the spot he wants, and Sammy groans into Jamie's mouth, the sound ragged and raw.

"You like this?" Jamie murmurs against his jaw, voice dark. "You want to be touched just like our little wife?"

Then he's behind him, lining up and pushing in with a force that knocks all the air out of the room. Sammy bucks forward with a choked moan, thrusting into my fist as Jamie drives into him from behind. The force of it ripples through all of us. I jolt with the motion, grinding harder onto Archer beneath me, Liam thick and steady between my lips, the weight of him against my tongue anchoring me in the chaos.

Spencer sheds his restraint and thrusts into me from the front, thick and relentless, splitting me wide until I'm gasping around Liam. The stretch is brutal—obscene—and I take it anyway, greedy for the burn, for the fullness. My cry dies against Liam's skin, muffled and desperate. Archer is buried deep, Spencer pounding into me, Liam filling my throat. Sammy jerks in my fist, leaking and twitching, and Jamie is taking him from behind, each slam sending a fresh jolt through all of us.

I'm being used. Claimed. Filled to the brim.

And I never want it to stop.

It's not just intimacy, it's sensation stacked and tangled until I can't tell where one of us ends and the next begins. My body isn't mine anymore.

It's all theirs.

"Jesus," Sammy groans, moving into my fist, hips snapping forward as Jamie slams into him from behind. His arousal throbs in my grip, slick and twitching, every thrust making him jerk harder into my hand.

Jamie's breath breaks hot against Sammy's neck, his voice low and broken. "You feel so good wrapped around me. You take me like you were made for it." He thrusts harder, groaning as Sammy jerks into my hand.

Spencer leans in, wrapping his lips around one aching nipple, sucking hard enough to make my vision white out. "You want it all, don't you?" he growls against my skin. "Every inch of you claimed."

I can't answer. Can't move. I'm gone.

Jamie groans, thrusting hard into Sammy. "Touch her," he growls against his ear. "Make her come while I take you. Show her how good you are with your hands."

Sammy's fingers slide between my legs, finding my sensitive spot like he owns it. He rubs fast and rough, no teasing. "You like feeling me fall apart while I play with you?" he pants, grinding back against Jamie. "Bet you're dripping just from watching him take me."

My climax builds with terrifying speed—tight, furious, impossible. Every thrust, every stroke, every sound shoves me closer to the edge I've been holding off since the second Archer touched me.

"Come for us, baby," Archer commands, his voice a snarl under me.

Spencer groans, his pace faltering for just a second as he watches me unravel. "That's our girl," he pants, still thrusting deep. "Let us have it, Sugar."

I shatter.

Spencer groans, his rhythm stuttering as he watches me come apart. "That's our girl," he growls, moving deep. "Let it happen. Let us have it."

My climax slams through me like a live wire. I scream around Liam, every muscle locking, my body convulsing as I come—tight, messy, uncontrollable. My fist clenches around Sammy just as he shouts, spilling hot and fast across my belly and thighs. He doesn't stop touching me, even as his hand shakes and his breath stutters against my skin.

Liam moans above me, his arousal jerking in my mouth as he comes, thick and salty down my throat. I swallow everything, body still trembling, stretched around Spencer and Archer and the brutal rhythm of it all.

Spencer curses, low and raw, thrusts turning frantic. "Fuck, I'm coming," he growls, and then he's emptying inside me, hips pressed flush to mine as he spills deep, twitching as I clench around him.

Archer growls behind me, buried to the hilt, his grip bruising my hips as he slams in one final time. "Fuck," he snarls, jerking as he spills deep, hot and thick. His breath punches out of him, ragged and feral.

"This," he pants, voice shredded. "This is my favorite version of you. Dripping with us. Every inch stretched. Every inch used."

We don't speak for a long time. Just breathe. Just feel.

Eventually, it's Sammy who breaks the silence, his voice low and thoughtful. "We're like a pride," he murmurs, fingers tracing slow, absent circles on my hip. "Lions. Multiple males. A whole social structure built around her."

I blink, heavy-limbed and blissed out. "Really?"

He shifts beside me, the barest curve of a smirk at the corner of his mouth. "Except lions don't work this hard," he says. "We have to earn it."

Jamie groans behind me. "I definitely worked hardest."

That sets them off—another ridiculous, half-hearted argument about who makes me come the hardest, who I beg for the most, who gets to go first in round two. Archer recounts my climax with the conviction of a man delivering a sermon. Liam flicks my nipple until I moan. Spencer strokes between my legs just to make me jerk, laughing when I slap at his hand and beg him to stop.

Sammy doesn't join in.

He just watches me—quiet, calm, certain. "Why are we arguing when she already knows who belongs to? Tell us, love," he says, gaze steady. "Tell us who you belong to."

Bathed in gold light, skin still sticky, heart too full to hold it all, I answer without hesitation.

"All of you. Always and forever."

Want more? Join me on **Ream**, where I post every chapter as I write it —including the next book in this series.

Dying to know what happens during the rest of Penelope's honeymoon? You can read the full extended epilogue by subscribing to my free **Substack**.

PREVIEW OF LORNA
CHAPTER 1

"Cheese and fudging rice!"

The curse stumbles from my frozen lips as headlights slice through the pitch-black night, sweeping across my frost-covered field like I've been caught red-handed. My heart hammers against my ribs, adrenaline surging through my already drained body. It's 3:17 AM, I'm knee-deep in frozen mud, and a massive pickup truck is barreling up my gravel driveway. Just perfect.

I've been out here over an hour, fingers so numb they're useless little sticks, fighting a losing battle against an April frost that's determined to destroy everything I've built. Each crystal forming on my dahlia beds is taking a direct shot at the only thing that's truly mine—not just to my income, but to what these flower represent. Something I created. Something my children can inherit. Something my bastard of an ex can't touch.

The truck engine cuts out, but the headlights stay on, illuminating the pathetic sight of me—a thirty-four-year-old single mom in whatever winter clothes I could grab in the dark—surrounded by inadequate frost blankets and pure desperation.

Leo Robinson unfolds his massive frame from the driver's side, and sweet Jesus, the man is built like a redwood, tall and solid and immovable. Steam actually rises from his broad shoulders as he yanks open the truck bed. Six-foot-four of pure controlled power moving like a man who knows exactly how much space he takes up in the world and doesn't apologize for a damn inch of it.

Levi Walker slips out from the passenger side, his slender figure bundled in approximately seventeen layers. His dark curls escape from beneath a knitted beanie, catching the light as he rubs his gloved hands together, breath clouding around that face that's too pretty for a farmer.

And then there's Hudson—Levi's twin in DNA only—bouncing from the back seat with the barely contained energy of a man who could probably go ten hours in bed and still be up for more. He practically vibrates as he circles to the truck bed, all coiled readiness and restless movement.

For two years, I've kept these men at a distance that would make the health department proud. The first year, I let myself get too close— friendly smiles, shared tools, late-night chats that felt like maybe. Then I caught feelings. Stupid, inconvenient, impossible feelings.

So I spent the next two years doing everything I could to avoid them. Polite waves across the fence line. Quick nods in the village shop. Strategic errands to avoid passing their truck on narrow island roads.

Two years pretending I don't feel it every time Leo's quiet authority makes my stomach flip, or the way Levi watches me when he thinks I'm not paying attention, or how Hudson's laugh hits low and warm like it's wired straight between my thighs.

Two years of protecting my carefully built life from complications I absolutely, positively do not need.

And now here they are, trampling across my frozen field at three in the morning, carrying armloads of frost blankets and heaters like some kind of rescue squad I never called but desperately need.

"Northeast corner's showing the worst frost," Leo's voice rumbles through the darkness, deep and certain, the bass vibration cutting straight through the howling wind to settle somewhere low in my belly. "Wind's coming from that direction."

I stand like a deer in headlights, muscles locked, a half-unfurled sheet clutched in my cramping fingers, my pulse hammering in my throat.

"What are you doing here?" My voice comes out raspy, surprise and exhaustion stripping away my usual armor.

"We're helping, Lorna," Leo says simply, the words hanging in the freezing air between us. No explanation, no apology for showing up uninvited at three in the morning—just those three confident words that hit me in the chest like a sledgehammer.

Hudson steps forward, frost crunching under his boots, his blue eyes electric in the beam of my light. A grin splits his face, inappropriately bright in this midnight disaster. "Weather alert came through on my phone. Farmers' warning network." He hefts the stack of frost blankets in his muscular arms. "Figured you'd need backup."

"I don't—" The reflexive denial springs to my lips, six years of stubborn independence making the words "need help" physically impossible to utter. My gaze sweeps across acres of vulnerable plants—my future, my children's future, crystallizing in real time. Pride and practicality wage brutal war in my chest. "The twins are asleep inside," I manage instead.

"We know," Levi says. His voice is soft, almost gentle, yet somehow slices through the howling wind. His dark eyes lock on mine with an intensity that makes something flutter low in my abdomen. "We brought everything we need. Just tell us where to start."

My heart slams against my ribs. Every instinct screams that accepting help means failure. It means being that woman who couldn't hack it alone. But another vicious gust of wind blasts across my face, bringing the scent of ice and dying plants, and I decide pride can go eff itself.

"The hybrid beds." I gesture toward the rightmost field, the words tumbling out. "Those are my experimental crosses. They're irreplaceable. If I lose them, I lose an entire year of work."

"Got it," Leo says, already striding away, boots crunching decisively on the frosty dirt. "Levi, help me spread the blankets. Hudson, set the heaters."

Leo's massive hands move with surprising precision, his powerful frame bending with unexpected grace over the tender shoots. The moonlight catches the intense concentration in his dark eyes, the careful way he tucks each blanket edge. Hudson is a blur of perpetual motion, somehow locating power outlets I'd forgotten existed, running cables with manic efficiency. And Levi—quiet, thoughtful Levi—weaves between them like a dancer, his methodical coverage of bed after bed revealing experience I never would have guessed at.

Minutes blur into an hour, the silence broken only by occasional murmured consultations. The rhythm of our breathing, the crunch of boots on frosty ground, the whisper of fabric being unfurled—it creates an intimate soundtrack that has my skin prickling with awareness. My body aches, muscles screaming, but the presence of three more sets of hands—strong, capable hands that I absolutely am not imagining elsewhere—transforms certain defeat into possible victory.

By 4:30 AM, every critical bed is covered. The knowledge floods me with such relief that for a moment, I fear my knees might buckle.

"The western field should be next," I say, straightening from securing a blanket edge. My back screams in protest, and I press a fist into my lower spine, trying to mask the grimace.

Leo catches the movement anyway. "When did you last take a break?" he asks, concern in his voice lodging somewhere behind my sternum.

I laugh. "Six years ago," I reply, already moving toward the next field.

A large, gloved hand catches me gently by the elbow, and the contact sends heat shooting up my arm despite all the layers between us. "Five minutes," Leo says. "Drink some water. Check on the twins. The blankets are holding and the heaters are working."

I start to protest, but the monitor at my hip chooses that moment to crackle with movement from the twins' room. Maternal instinct overrides everything else.

"Five minutes," I agree reluctantly. "There's water in the shed if you want it."

I don't wait for a response before heading back to the house, the beam of my headlamp bouncing ahead of me. Inside, I quickly check on the twins before splashing cold water on my face and grabbing fresh coffee and a handful of homemade granola bars.

When I return to the fields, I find all three men standing by the shed, talking in low voices that cut off as I approach. Something flashes in Leo's eyes when he sees the thermos and food in my arms—approval, maybe, or something hungrier.

"Are the twins okay?" Levi asks, accepting a granola bar with a grateful smile.

"Still asleep," I confirm, pouring coffee into the thermos cup and passing it to Leo first, purely because he's closest, I tell myself. Not because I've been watching his hands all night and wondering what they'd feel like on my skin.

His fingertips brush mine as he accepts the cup, and even through our gloves, the contact sends a jolt of warmth straight to my core. He holds my gaze a beat longer than necessary, then nods his thanks before taking a long drink.

Hudson grabs a granola bar, gesturing toward the covered fields. "So these dahlias, they're your main crop?" he asks, taking a gigantic bite. His eyes roll back in a way that makes my cheeks heat. "Holy shit, these are good."

"Yes, they're my main crop now," I answer, trying not to stare at his mouth. "I started specializing in unusual varieties and new hybrids a couple years ago."

"You developed them yourself?" Levi asks, interest clearly piqued.

I nod, suddenly self-conscious. "I have a couple dozen varieties that are exclusively mine."

"That's impressive," Levi says, and the unfiltered admiration in his voice makes something twist deep in my chest. Like he sees more than I meant to show. Like he likes it.

"It's just basic genetics," I deflect. "Nothing special."

"Nothing special about creating something entirely new that's never existed before?" Hudson raises an eyebrow, grinning around a mouthful of granola. "Sure, that's just an average Tuesday for most people."

Heat flares up the back of my neck. I never know how to hold a compliment without dropping it. My gaze falls, hands suddenly too clumsy as I twist the lid back onto the thermos. "We should get back to it. The western field still needs covering."

Leo drains his coffee and hands the cup back to me, his expression unreadable in the dim glow of our headlamps. "Lead the way."

We work for another hour, methodically covering the remaining beds. Dawn is just beginning to lighten the eastern sky when we secure the last blanket, the pale gray light revealing frost glittering across the entire landscape.

"We did it," I breathe, exhaustion momentarily forgotten as I survey our work.

"The heaters should keep the ambient temperature just high enough around," Hudson says, checking one of the units. "But you'll want to watch them through the morning. Forecast says the cold snap should break by noon."

I nod, and it hits me all at once. The kind of bone-deep exhaustion that settles in after hours of physical labor, on top of too little sleep and too much adrenaline. My muscles ache. My hands are shaking. And for the first time tonight, I let myself look at them. Really look.

Leo's eyes are already on me. Ice clings to the edge of his wool hat, his salt-and-pepper beard dusted with frost, but he doesn't look cold. He doesn't even look tired. His spine is still straight, jaw tight, eyes steady. All control. All restraint.

And of course my brain picks now, of all moments, to wonder how long he could hold that kind of focus in bed. How long he'd last. How long *I'd* last with him looking at me like that.

Levi stands just beside him, cheeks pink from effort, curls damp at his temples where his beanie has ridden up. He's too pretty for this hour. For this place. For me. And yet he offers me this quiet, crooked smile. Small, tired, and entirely too tender. Something low in my stomach folds in on itself.

And then there's Hudson. Stamping his feet. Rubbing his hands together like we're just getting started. Somehow, he still has a spark in his eyes. That electric kind of mischief that makes you forget you're exhausted. He catches me looking, and of course he winks. Quick, shameless, lethal. My breath stutters in my throat, and I look away too fast, cheeks hot, chest tight.

"I don't know how to thank you," I say, my voice scratchy from cold and sleeplessness. I'm speaking to all three of them, but my eyes settle just past Leo's left shoulder. Looking at any of them directly feels like stepping off a cliff I've spent years edging around. "The plants wouldn't have made it without you."

"Neighbors help neighbors," Leo says. His voice is even, matter-of-fact, like what they did tonight wasn't extraordinary.

I nod, trying not to read into it, and then I hear myself speak before I fully decide to. "The least I can do is feed you. After we've all had some rest. Maybe dinner tonight?"

The silence that follows is short but somehow loud. My stomach tightens with the weight of it.

"We'd like that," Levi says, his voice so gentle it almost doesn't register as dangerous. But it is. It sinks into the soft, unguarded parts of me I've worked hard to ignore.

We linger, all of us holding still for a moment too long. Like whatever passed between us out there hasn't fully let go. Like no one wants to be the first to step out of it. I push a loose strand of hair back under my hat, suddenly hyper-aware of the state I'm in. Mud-caked boots, half-zipped coat, hair a mess, cheeks wind-chapped and raw. There is nothing left of the put-together woman I pretend to be.

"I should check on the twins," I say, needing a way out. "They'll be up soon."

"We'll pack up the truck," Leo says with a short nod. "Leave the heaters running. We'll come get them later."

"Right. Yes. Thank you again." I take a step back, then stop myself. "Dinner at six. Nothing fancy."

"Six is perfect," Hudson says, voice dropping just enough to make my breath catch. "You sure you can handle all three of us?"

"Six is perfect," Hudson says, voice dropping just enough to make my breath catch. "You sure you can handle all three of us?"

My breath stumbles. Every nerve goes tight. I mean to toss something back—something clever, something that makes it seem like I have the upper hand—but what comes out is barely more than a whisper. "Guess we'll find out." I turn toward the house, heart pounding in places I didn't know had pulses. The mud clings to my boots, thick and unrelenting, like even the earth wants me to stay. My legs are shaky with adrenaline and desire, each step a deliberate act of retreat. I don't need to turn around to know they're still looking.

Inside, I shut the door behind me and lean against it like it's the only thing holding me upright. My body's humming, hands unsteady, throat thick with everything I didn't say out loud. I can still feel them out there—their presence clinging to my skin, the heat of their hands, the weight of what passed between us under floodlights and frost.

Somewhere in all that chaos, I invited them in.

And I don't know what that says about me. Maybe I'm braver than I thought. Or maybe I'm just exhausted. Not from the work or the cold, but from carrying all of this alone for so long.

I thump up the stairs and sink onto the edge of my bed, too tired to even remove my boots. I'll keep things friendly but professional at dinner. Express my gratitude appropriately. Maintain proper boundaries. That's the sensible approach.

So why is my last thought before sleep not about dinner or dahlias, but three very different, equally captivating men and what they might see if they weren't looking at me like a neighbor, but like something they want to touch. To spread open. To ruin.

The oven timer shrieks again, snapping me out of my half-focus on the salad. Six o'clock is closing in fast, and I'm nowhere near ready. Not the food. Not the house. And absolutely not myself.

"Daniel! Lorelai! Please pick up your blocks from the living room floor!" I call out, silencing the timer with a jab and pulling open the oven. A rush of heat hits my face, followed by the sight of the lasagna, golden and bubbling. One thing that hasn't fallen apart today.

"But *Mom*, we're building a fairy castle!" Lorelai's voice rises from the other room, already edging toward meltdown territory.

"The fairies can relocate to the toy box for now," I say, setting the hot dish on the counter and reaching for a towel. "Our guests will be here any minute."

"Are Mr. Leo and Mr. Levi and Mr. Hudson coming to help us build the castle?" Lorelai appears in the doorway, curls wild, face streaked with what looks like blue marker. She's a smaller, messier version of me with twice the confidence.

"Sweet pea, what's on your face?" I crouch down and dampen a towel to gently scrub at her cheek.

"War paint," she replies without hesitation. "Daniel said we need protection because three men are coming to our house, and in his book, that usually means a raiding party."

I bite back a laugh that bubbles up anyway. "Daniel's been reading too many Viking stories. Mr. Leo, Mr. Levi, and Mr. Hudson aren't raiders. They're neighbors. And they helped Mommy save her flowers when the frost came last night."

"So they're allies, not enemies." Daniel steps into view behind her, his arms folded and expression serious. It hits me in the chest how much he looks like my brother when he's thinking too hard.

"Definitely allies," I say, reaching out to smooth his hair. He ducks away, but not before I catch that flicker of affection he pretends not to feel. "Now both of you, please clean up the living room and wash your hands. Dinner's happening, ready or not."

As the twins scamper off, I check my reflection in the small mirror by the back door. I've changed three times before settling on a simple blue sweater that brings out my eyes and a pair of jeans that make my backside look like I actually have time to work out. My hair is contained in its usual messy bun, though I've taken slightly more care with it than usual.

"It's just a thank-you dinner," I remind my reflection sternly. "Not a date."

The doorbell rings exactly at six. The sound cuts through the noise of the house and sends a jolt through me that feels too much like anticipation. I press a hand to my chest, like that might calm the flutter behind my ribs, and move toward the door. But the twins beat me to it, feet thumping against the floor, their excitement loud and unfiltered, while mine stays quiet and tangled somewhere in the space between my lungs.

"Wait!" I call, but Daniel is already turning the knob, Lorelai peering eagerly around him.

The door swings open, and there they are. Leo, Levi, and Hudson, standing on my porch, their hands full. I don't even register what they're holding, because everything else hits first.

Leo's in a deep blue button-up that strains across his shoulders like it's barely holding on. Levi's wearing a soft gray sweater that makes my fingers twitch with the urge to touch it. And Hudson is in a faded henley, sleeves shoved to his elbows, arms flexing like they belong in some kind of calendar no mother of twins has any business thinking about.

Not that I'm noticing. Because I'm absolutely not.

"You're the plant rescuers!" Lorelai announces before anyone else can speak, pointing at each of them like she's assigning roles in a play. "Mommy said you saved the da... the da..."

"Dahlias," I say, stepping in behind the twins and placing a hand on each of their shoulders. "And yes. They absolutely did."

I glance up at the three of them and do my best to hold a smile steady on my face, hoping it hides the way my nerves are crawling just beneath the surface. "Please, come in."

Leo steps through the doorway first, ducking slightly to clear the frame. He holds out a bottle of wine in one hand and a small jar in the other. "We brought a few things. The wine's from a local vineyard. The honey's ours."

"You keep bees?" I take both, caught off guard in the best way. "I had no idea."

"Just started last summer," he says, stepping past me into the entryway. His shoulder brushes mine as he moves, solid and warm, and I feel it everywhere. "Had our first harvest in the fall."

Levi follows close behind, offering me a small, neatly wrapped package tied with twine. "Herb seeds," he says, voice soft. "From my garden. I noticed you mostly grow flowers, but thought you might want to mix in some basil. Maybe thyme."

My fingers close around the packet, and something shifts low in my chest. "That's really thoughtful," I say, meaning it. "I've been wanting to start an herb bed, but it keeps slipping down the list."

He gives a small smile that sends a flush creeping up my neck, and I drop my gaze, pretending to be entirely consumed by arranging the gifts on the entryway table.

Hudson comes in last, something wooden in his hands that looks freshly sanded. "Plant markers," he says, extending them with a kind of boyish enthusiasm that's hard not to smile at. "Made them this afternoon. Weatherproof finish and everything."

I take one, running my thumb over the smooth edge and the stark white surface, perfect for labeling. "These are gorgeous," I say, a little stunned. "I've been using cheap plastic ones that snap in two if you so much as look at them wrong."

Hudson shrugs, still watching me. "Just figured you'd want something that lasts."

My fingers tighten slightly around them, the wood growing warm against my palms. I don't trust myself to say anything. Not with the way he's looking at me. Not with the way that one sentence coils low in my belly and lingers there, heavier than it should. So I just nod, and set them carefully on the table.

Hudson's face breaks into a grin that softens every sharp edge, pulling a dimple into his right cheek that I absolutely refuse to find charming. "Told you she'd like them," he stage-whispers to Levi, who rolls his eyes with the kind of ease that says he's used to this.

"Can I see?" Daniel asks, already reaching for the plant markers. His normally serious face is lit with curiosity, brows raised in genuine wonder. "Did you make these with tools?"

"Sure did, buddy," Hudson says, crouching to meet him eye to eye. "I've got a whole workshop in the barn. Maybe you can come by sometime and I'll show you how it all works."

Daniel's eyes go wide. "Mom, can I?"

"We'll see," I say, softer than I intend, brushing a hand through his curls as I nod toward the dining room. "Dinner's ready if anyone wants to wash up. Bathroom's down the hall, first door on the left."

Lorelai takes it upon herself to give them a tour of the playroom, pointing out every glitter-covered creation like she's hosting a museum exhibit. I turn back to the kitchen, busying myself with final dinner prep, though my hands move on autopilot.

Because I can feel them.

Their presence shifts the air, presses against the walls. It's been just me and the twins for so long that having adults—*men*—in my house feels like someone's dialed the heat up without warning. Every room feels smaller. Warmer. Full of something I haven't let myself feel in a long time.

"Can I help with anything?" Levi appears in the kitchen doorway, sleeves pushed up to his elbows. His forearms are lean and corded, and the sight of them makes my mouth go dry before I can even pretend otherwise.

I force my gaze up to his face. Not safer. Not even a little.

"You could fill the water glasses," I manage, turning away and pointing to the cupboard like I haven't just forgotten how words work. "Plates are already on the table."

We settle into a quiet rhythm, moving around each other in the tight space. It should feel awkward. Instead, it feels... natural. Easy. Until his arm brushes mine as he reaches for the glasses, and that one small touch shoots straight through me. My grip on the salad bowl slips for half a second.

"Sorry," he murmurs, voice pitched just low enough that it skims along my spine. "Small space."

"It's fine," I reply, too fast, heat blooming up the back of my neck. "I'm just not used to having people in my kitchen."

He pauses, studying me. His eyes aren't just kind. They're attentive. They *see* me.

"It must be a lot," he says quietly. "Running a farm. Raising twins. Doing it all on your own."

The honesty in his voice knocks something loose in me. There's no pity in it. No judgment. Just simple truth.

"You adapt," I say, shrugging like that somehow covers it. "They're good kids."

"They are," Levi says, nodding. "But that doesn't make what you're doing any less remarkable."

Before I can come up with a response that doesn't sound like my heart just cracked open, Hudson strides into the kitchen.

"Something smells incredible in here," he says, leaning in close enough that I feel the warmth of him behind me. His voice is light, but his presence is anything but. "Tell me that's homemade."

"From scratch," I say, grateful for the interruption and acutely aware of how little space exists between us. "My grandmother's recipe."

"A woman after my own heart," Hudson declares, pressing a hand to his chest like he's been personally blessed. "Nothing better than home cooking."

I laugh before I can stop myself. "It's just lasagna. Nothing special."

"There it is again." He glances at Levi and then back to me, head shaking like he's discovered something both amusing and tragic. "Downplaying your talents. First the rare flowers, now this? What other secret skills are you hiding, Lorna MacLeod?"

He says my name like it's meant for quieter places, softer moments, and the sound of it curls deep in my belly.

I feel the smile tug at my mouth before I can stop it. "I'll never tell."

"Then I'll just have to keep showing up until you do," he says, and the words hang in the air between us, warmer than they have any right to be.

I hand him the salad bowl before I say something I can't take back. "Then you can start by being useful. This goes on the table."

Hudson dips into an exaggerated bow, eyes full of mischief. "Your wish is my command."

And the worst part is, some reckless part of me believes him. Every single word.

By the time we're all gathered at the table—the twins chattering from their booster seats, the three men somehow making my modest dining set feel laughably small—I've managed to pull myself back together. This is just a neighborly dinner. I can handle it.

And yet, as we eat, conversation flows easier than I'd expected. Leo asks thoughtful questions about my hybridization process, like plant genetics is something he genuinely wants to understand. Levi talks about the book he's writing, his voice soft and steady as he describes a collection of poems shaped by the Scottish landscape. And Hudson has the twins in stitches, spinning wild tales of woodworking disasters and turning every mishap into a performance.

It's nice.

No—it's more than nice.

For the first time in years, my dinner table feels full in a way that has nothing to do with food. It's a feeling. The kind of warmth that sinks into your chest and makes you want to believe in something again. And it has everything to do with the three men sitting around it.

"So how did you three end up sharing a house?" I hear myself ask as I scoop a second helping of lasagna onto Levi's plate. "It's an unusual arrangement."

A look passes between them—quick, quiet, but heavy. Something is exchanged that I can't quite read.

"It's a long story," Leo says eventually, his voice slower now, quieter. "The short version is, we've known each other a long time. When we all needed a fresh start, it made sense to pool our resources."

"Leo owned a ranch back in Australia where I worked," Hudson adds, twirling pasta with a little too much focus. "My mom, Ruby, and Levi lived nearby. When she got sick, things... changed."

A flicker crosses Hudson's face, gone in an instant. But I see it. The tension in his jaw. The tight pull of silence. And when I glance at Levi, that same shadow is there in his eyes, like grief still lives close to the surface.

"After she passed," Levi says softly, "none of us wanted to stay. The place didn't feel like home anymore. Leo had family here in Scotland. And the idea of somewhere completely new... it helped."

"So you ended up with the Morrison place," I say, filling in the rest. "That was what, three years ago?"

"Just over," Leo confirms with a nod. "Took about three months to make it livable. Old Angus Morrison wasn't exactly a handyman."

"Or a fan of soap and water," Hudson mutters, making a face. "Pretty sure some of those dust bunnies had names and voting records."

I laugh before I can stop myself. The sound slips out too easily, too warm. And when I look up, Leo's smiling. Not just politely, really smiling. The corners of his eyes crinkle, softening something usually held in check.

And that's when I realize I'm staring.

I drop my gaze and focus on Lorelai's plate, cutting her lasagna into smaller bites with hands that feel a little too aware of themselves.

"And what about you?" Levi asks gently.

"I bought the farm about six years ago," I say, taking a bite of garlic bread before continuing. "I grew up not far from here, actually, my family has an estate on Harris. But I was living in Edinburgh before... before the twins were born."

I won't mention the divorce. Won't bring that particular cloud into this unexpectedly pleasant evening.

But Daniel, with his characteristic directness, has other ideas. "Our dad doesn't like us very much," he announces matter-of-factly. "He lives in London with his new wife. We see him at Christmas and sometimes in summer."

A brief, awkward silence falls over the table. I fight the urge to slide under it.

"Well," Leo says after a moment, his deep voice gentle but firm, "his loss is our gain. Getting to have dinner with you three is the highlight of our week."

Lorelai beams at him. "Do you want to see my fairy castle after dinner? Daniel helped build it but I did all the decorating."

"Wouldn't miss it for the world," Leo tells her with a gravity that makes something twist painfully in my chest.

As dinner winds down and the conversation shifts to lighter ground—the weather, island gossip, spring planting schedules—I catch myself watching them when they aren't looking. The way they move around each other with instinctive ease. How one starts a sentence and another finishes it without pause. The teasing between Hudson and Levi, all sharp edges softened by years of shared history. The quiet way both of them seem to fall in line when Leo speaks, like it's not about control but trust.

There's something there. Something deeper than friendship, more intimate than blood. A rhythm, a pull, a knowing that doesn't quite name itself. And I don't understand it.

But God, I want to.

When Lorelai's head starts to droop over her half-eaten dessert, I glance at the clock and wince. It's well past bedtime. "I should get these two upstairs," I say, rising from my chair and reaching for the nearest plate.

"We'll help clean up," Levi offers before I can even ask.

"Absolutely not," I say, too quickly. "You've already done more than enough. I insist."

"At least let us stack the dishes," Hudson says, already collecting forks with a lopsided grin. "It's basic dinner guest etiquette."

Before I can protest again, Leo rises to his full height and begins clearing plates with quiet efficiency. The movement draws my eyes automatically. His presence shifts the entire room, makes it feel smaller somehow, warmer, more crowded in a way that has nothing to do with furniture.

"Go put the twins to bed," he says, calm and sure, like it's not a suggestion. "We've got this."

And just like that, the last bit of resistance drains out of me. I'm too tired to argue. Too tired to pretend it doesn't feel good, having someone else step in for once.

"Fifteen minutes, tops," I say, guiding two yawning children toward the stairs. "I'll be right back."

Daniel and Lorelai move through their bedtime routine with unusual speed, as if they can sense my mind is somewhere else. No resistance. No requests for one more story. Just sleepy compliance and the occasional question I answer with half a heart still lingering downstairs.

As I tuck them in and press kisses to their foreheads, Daniel catches my hand before I can stand.

"I like them," he says, solemn as ever. "They're not scary like I thought."

"I'm glad, sweetheart." I brush his hair back, lingering for just a moment. "They're very nice neighbors."

"Hudson said I could help him build a birdhouse," Lorelai

mumbles, her voice thick with sleep. "And Mr. Leo had horses. In Australia."

"Did he now?" I smile, even though they're both already drifting. "We'll talk about it tomorrow. Sleep tight, my loves."

I pull the door partway closed and make my way downstairs, steadying myself for the noise and inevitable mess waiting in the kitchen.

But there is no chaos.

Everything is clean. Dishes washed and drying in the rack. Counters wiped down. Leftovers portioned into containers and stacked neatly on the counter cooling.

The whole space hums with a kind of calm I'm not used to. Like someone stepped in and pressed pause on the chaos. Like someone saw the weight I carry every night and decided—just this once—I didn't have to carry it alone.

The three of them linger by the front door, jackets in hand, that quiet shift in energy that says they're about to leave but haven't quite let go of the evening yet.

"You didn't have to do all that," I say, gesturing toward the kitchen.

"We wanted to," Leo says, steady as ever.

"Thank you for dinner," Levi says. His voice is soft, but the way he looks at me when he says it sparks something low in my stomach. "Best meal we've had in months."

"Hey, I made that pot roast last week," Hudson says, pretending to be offended as he elbows his brother.

"Exactly," Levi replies without missing a beat, sidestepping Hudson's next jab with a grin.

I find myself smiling at their easy banter. "Well, thank you again for last night. For saving my dahlias. I truly don't know what I would have done without your help."

Leo studies me for a moment, his dark eyes intense in a way that makes my skin feel too tight. "The heaters are still in place. Forecast says it might get cold again tonight, though not as bad. We'll come back in the morning to collect them, if that's alright."

"Of course," I nod, desperately trying to ignore how close we're standing in the narrow entryway, how I'd only need to lean forward a few inches to press against that solid chest. "Whatever works for you."

Hudson glances at his watch. "We should get going if we want to feed the animals before it gets too late."

"Right, yes," I step back before I start rubbing myself on them like a cat. "Thank you again."

They file out one by one, each pausing briefly to say goodnight. Leo's hand brushes mine as he passes, the brief contact sending a jolt of electricity straight to my core. Levi's gentle smile has me grinning back like a teenager. And Hudson's parting wink nearly has me melting into a puddle on the floor.

And then they're gone, climbing into their shared truck, headlights sweeping across my porch as they back out of the driveway.

I close the door and lean against it, exhaling a breath I feel like I've been holding since they arrived. What in the world just happened? How had an emergency cold snap somehow morphed into the most enjoyable evening I've had in years?

And the worst part—the part I'm trying not to think too hard about —is that I'm already looking forward to tomorrow morning.

Already wondering what it'll feel like when they walk back through that door.

I push away from the door and head upstairs, trying to dismiss the thought. It's just neighborly gratitude, nothing more. I have the twins to think about, a farm to run, a life carefully constructed that has no room for... for what, exactly?

I brush my teeth and change into pajamas, my mind circling around the question without landing on an answer. As I slip between cool sheets, my last coherent thought is of three pairs of eyes all looking at me as if I'm something worth wanting.

And the dangerous, undeniable fact that I might be starting to want them back.

～

Lorna will be released November 22, 2025. Preorder here.

ACKNOWLEDGMENTS

To my husband—thank you for holding down the fort, picking up the slack, and working your butt off while I lock myself away for 12+ hour writing marathons. Your support, patience, and willingness to feed the kids (and sometimes me) makes this whole wild dream possible.

To my children—you'll probably never read these books (and that's absolutely for the best), but you fill my life with laughter, chaos, and light. On the hardest days, your joy is the thing that gets me through.

And to you—the reader holding this book in your hands or burning through it on your screen—thank you. For every late-night binge, every message, every time you've screamed into the void (or group chat) about these characters. You're the reason I get to do this. Your support turns stories into something bigger. Something real.

This wild, spicy, slightly feral ride wouldn't exist without you. I'm so damn grateful you're here.

ABOUT THE AUTHOR

Tucked away in the misty foothills of the Smoky Mountains with her husband, three kids, and a small army of furry overlords (four dogs and three cats who definitely think they're in charge), Daphne writes the kind of stories that make readers blush, gasp, and fall headfirst in love.

Known for her wickedly spicy romances and unapologetically vivid imagination, she's been spinning tales since she could first hold a pen. When she's not setting pages on fire with her latest book boyfriend, you'll find her curled up in her favorite reading nook, inhaling romance novels like they're dark chocolate.

Her mountain sanctuary is the perfect place to dream up deliciously scandalous stories—ones that flirt with the edge, melt Kindles, and occasionally break a heart or two along the way. Fair warning: her books are known to cause sleepless nights, spontaneous swooning, and a serious craving for more.

ALSO BY DAPHNE LEIGH

Charlie

Isla

Lorna (Preorder)

Knot My Boss

Wrong Number